GIBBON'S DECLINE AND FALL

A group of six women made a pact when they were students together in the heady sixties, vowing that each of them would find a place to stand where she could be woman as woman was meant to be, and thereafter she would never decline or fall from that place.

Fast forward to the year 2000: a ruthless politician is amassing a terrifying, fanatical power base; the suicide rate has gone through the roof . . . and the global birthrate has suddenly plummeted to near zero. Something evil is threatening the world. Of the six extraordinary women forming the Decline and Fall Club, five remain. The sixth, Sophy, disappeared three years before, her dazzling, unearthly beauty undiminished – and her early life still as mysterious as her apparent end. Her friends come to see that unlocking the secret to Sophy's disappearance will be the key to the survival of humanity.

With each new novel, Sheri Tepper's devoted following has grown as more and more readers discover this remarkable talent. Her richly imagined future worlds are filled with unforgettable characters, exotic backdrops and epic adventures. In *Gibbon's Decline and Fall* she outdoes herself, proving yet again why *Analog* dubs her 'one of the greats of literature'.

D0494686

Voyager

Sheri S. Tepper

GIBBON'S DECLINE AND FALL

HarperCollins*Publishers*

Voyager
An Imprint of HarperCollins*Publishers*
77–85 Fulham Palace Road,
Hammersmith, London W6 8JB

The *Voyager* World Wide Web site address is
http://www.harpercollins.co.uk/voyager

Published by *Voyager* 1996
1 3 5 7 9 8 6 4 2

First published in the USA by
Bantam Books 1996

Copyright © Sheri S. Tepper 1996

The Author asserts the moral right to
be identified as the author of this work

A catalogue record for this book
is available from the British Library

ISBN 0 00 224651 1

Printed and bound in Great Britain by
Caledonian International Book Manufacturing Ltd, Glasgow

". . . the most incredible stories are the best adapted to the genius of an enraged people. . . ."

Edward Gibbon

The History of the Decline and Fall of the Roman Empire

PROLOGUE

SUMMER 1959

THE AUNTS HAD CAUGHT CAROLYN, dragged her to the side of the boat, figuratively speaking, and were forcibly attempting to Crespinize her, while she, Carolyn, twisted on the hook in desperation.

"I don't think it's proper," she murmured politely, hiding panic, hoping the idea of propriety would make them pause. Fond hope. Hope betrayed.

"Albert is perfectly reliable," said Aunt Clotilde with a dreadful clatter of large, too-white teeth.

As, oh, indeed he was. Perfectly reliable. Perfectly self-satisfied. Perfectly capable of taking any ordinary weekend and turning it into the Worst Experience of One's Life. Carolyn, gritting her teeth, stared through the screens of the summer porch at the stretching blue of Long Island Sound and focused on the radio sounds in the background: "Mr. Sandman," being sung by who? Whom. Mr. Sandman. Send me a dream. Not Albert.

Aunt Atrena, who always spoke immediately after Aunt Clotilde, did so now in a tone that said, Pay Attention, Child. "Albert thought it would be a treat for you, before you start college. You know he would never do anything to embarrass you."

Aside from the embarrassment attendant upon being seen with him, that was probably true. And since she knew no one in Washington, D.C., chances are she could go down there for the weekend, take the tour through the FBI building (a signal honor, according to Albert, not allowed to Just

Anyone), see the Smithsonian, go to the opening of whatever show it was at the National Gallery, and be returned home unscathed.

"He will be so hurt if you don't go," said Aunt Livia, whose function it was to have the Last Word.

"Yes, Carolyn. He would be hurt," said Mama.

Which clinched it. What Mama meant was, if Carolyn didn't accept Albert's invitation, Mama would be hurt. The aunts would eat her alive. Albert and the aunts, including Albert's mama, Aunt Fan, had decided that Albert and Carolyn were to be a Crespin couple. Albert Crespin was Crespin through and through—a highly inbred member of the clan, Aunt Fan a kind of cousin to Albert's daddy and all that—unlike Carolyn, who was a Crespin only on her father's side, her father having inexplicably married outside his ilk, then unforgivably up and died before he could inculcate proper Crespin values into his only child. Though that wasn't supposed to matter, for Albert was Crespin enough for the two of them.

"Of course, Mama, Aunties, if you wish," Carolyn said, smiling sweetly. It was what one said as a last resort. It solved problems. It quieted tempers. It got Carolyn off the hook, at least temporarily, though she had a sick pain in her stomach that did not feel transitory.

Aunts Clotilde, Atrena, and Livia exchanged superior glances. There, the faces said. One has only to be Firm With The Child. Mama was looking into her lap, her lower lip quivering ever so slightly. She was frightened of the aunts; she was well and truly hooked and gaffed. Carolyn's father had left an annuity for his widow, an annuity that could be stretched to cover clothing and salary for Mama's maid and Carolyn's education and a few small charities, but it wouldn't stretch to such necessities as housing and heat and lights and taxes, so Mama and Carolyn either lived with the family or they didn't live. Unless Mama got married again.

Which, though Mama was quite young and lovely, she would never do. Clotilde, Atrena, and Livia believed that Mama's remarriage would be Unfaithful to Dear Roger's Memory. They'd won that one long ago.

And now that the matter of Albert and Carolyn was settled, they gathered up their needlework and went off to settle someone else's fate. Mama, with a grateful caress across Carolyn's shoulder, went in the other direction, toward the bathroom. She often spent hours in the tub, breathing moist perfumed vapors, safe in the only sanctum the aunts would not invade.

Carolyn was left alone on the summer porch, once shaded by huge old elms. She remembered summer-dusk games under the elms, herself leaning against a great tree, eyes hidden in her hands, slowly counting: twenty-nine . . . fifty-six . . . ninety-five . . . one hundred. Ready or not, here I come! Here I come seeking something that has no name, something hidden, something wonderful. Here I come, with no idea where it is but needing so . . . so much to find it. It was only her cousins, hiding out there, so why had she felt that she might find the other thing? Even now, when dusk came and she heard the voices of children playing, she remembered that feeling of mysterious anticipation. Marvel, just around the corner. Wonder, hidden in shadows, if she could only find it.

Everything had changed since then. All the elms were gone now. Once-shaded houses stood full in the glare of the August sun, as she herself now stood, no longer protected by leafy childhood, alone in the baking heat and burning light of Crespin conformity.

The Crespin men went into banking and law. Crespin women did not work outside the home except for certain charities, and they did not join many of those. If one joined groups, one might have to associate with persons one had not picked as acquaintances. One did, of course, practice one's religion devoutly, and one did entertain one's husband's business associates, but that was a different matter, akin to diplomacy. To prepare for that, one studied languages, one learned about opera and art, one even boned up on whatever esoterica a distinguished visitor was said to be interested in. In this Crespins were rather like royalty. Noblesse oblige, as a matter of course, but no damned familiarity allowed.

Crespin women, though not always pretty, were uniformly fashionable though not faddish, slender though not bony, aristocratic to a fault. They went to good Catholic prep schools, after which they might spend a year or so perfecting French or German on the Continent, under proper supervision, before attending college. At home they learned the Crespin vocabulary as they learned the catechism, and for the same reason. Salvation was dependent upon knowing What The Family Meant. There were patronizing words to remind inferiors of their proper place, there was inconsequential chitchat to keep strangers at a distance, there were courteous words for religious occasions and implacable phrases for inculcating Crespin-consciousness in the young.

Carolyn did not fit. She made friends with the maids, she discussed anything at all with people she met on the train, she argued with Father O'Brien about the catechism, and had so far remained stocky, untidy, ungraceful, willful, un-Crespinized.

"But, my dear child," Aunt Clotilde had said on a former occasion, "Crespin women do not Work Outside the Home. They certainly do not go into the professions."

"Crespin women do not go into anything but becoming interfering, arrogant old tyrants, so far as I can see."

Carolyn's mama, shocked: "Carolyn, apologize to your aunt at once!"

"Mother, I *am* sorry, but it's you and me I'm sorry for. You weren't born a Crespin, and I'm evidently a throwback or something. I don't want to be a

Crespin woman! I want to be a lawyer." Was it just that Father had been a lawyer? Or was it a longing for the real, the true, the eternal, rather than whatever the Crespins were?

Though she was fifteen at the time of that outburst, she had been Sent To Her Room. It was typical of Crespin culture that single women even in their twenties might be Sent To Their Rooms, and wives at any age likewise, though with a quiet word whispered into an ear. "My dear, you're over-wrought. My dear, go lie down for a bit." It did no good to rebel. The custom predated the Victorian age and had all the power of tradition. Women, when in public, were always groomed, poised, gracious, and socially adept, and Carolyn would conform or else. There were inevitabilities at work; in the end the aunts would have their way. They were the spinners of history, the passers on of tradition, those who trimmed and chopped away all spontaneity. Even the temporary freedom offered by college, the exposure to ordinary people, was part of the plan.

As for Albert, he was an American hero in the postlarval stage, a lawyer with the FBI. Albert was devout; he worked indefatigably with the Knights of Columbus. Albert had Served in Korea, albeit (strings had been pulled) in the office of the judge advocate. Until the time a few years back when Senator Joe McCarthy had gone down in flames, Albert had been one of the senator's more ardent supporters. Even now Albert saw himself as standing between America and all those who would sully her purity.

On the night of Carolyn's graduation from St. Mary's, Albert had taken her out to dinner and told her all about their plans, his and hers: They would be engaged when she graduated from college and married six months later, to allow time for the various prenuptial festivities that the aunts would arrange. It was too soon for a ring, but he presented her with an eighteen-karat charm bracelet, announcing in a patronizing tone that he would add pretty charms over the next four years. Carolyn supposed it was a kind of option plan. One charm bought him a Carolyn foot, another paid for a leg, another gained him the left tit. By the time they were married, she'd be all paid for, the last charm claiming the necessary part for the wedding night.

So, all right, she'd go to Washington and be shown where Albert worked. One thing the aunts were right about. She was safe with Albert. Albert had never provoked in her the tiniest throb of lust. His kisses were chaste, his embraces perfunctory, and she might as well be out with Father O'Brien. As a matter of fact, Father O'Brien, for all his years and his cassock, had more of a twinkle than Albert did.

Washington was very much as Carolyn had supposed it would be. Hot. Full of tourists. Not in the FBI building, of course, which Albert escorted her through in the manner of a high priest showing the ritual objects. How do you do, Mr. So-and-So? How do you do, Mr. So-and-So Else? Laboratories. Offices. Why in God's name would anyone look at this stuff? It was dull. Albert was dull.

"Carolyn, may I present my colleagues, Mike Winter . . ."

Yet another. She offered her gloved hand, made the polite smile at Mr. Winter, smooth and slim and rather weary looking for a person only a few years older than she, midtwenties, perhaps.

"And Hal Shepherd."

She turned to Mr. Shepherd, looked up into warm brown eyes, felt her smile broaden in response to the one on his face, felt her mind melt like ice cream, glow like summertime at the beach, like picnics and the Fourth of July. Hal . . . Mr. Shepherd. Older than the other one by at least a decade. He was like a teddy bear, like a sea wind, like a glass of fresh lemonade. His hand was warm and firm in her own.

"Carolyn. You bring light into otherwise dusky lives. I love your hat!"

And Carolyn, who'd been more than a little self-conscious about the hat, crowed inside like a baby rooster. This was a feeling she'd never had before, a kind of airy euphoria, a bubble of smile stuck in her middle.

"Mike and Hal and their wives will be joining us for dinner this evening," said Albert.

And the bubble grew shrunken and chill, whirled on itself, became a dust devil, a withdrawing wind. Wives. Well, of course wife. Of course he was married. He was in his thirties, like Albert. Of course, of course. Still, his smile stayed warm as they went down a wide corridor, as he put out an arm to save her being trampled by a group of purposeful, oblivious men who were headed in the opposite direction.

"Did you see who that was?" Albert whispered to Hal, ignoring Carolyn, forgetting Carolyn. His voice was awed, almost worshiping.

"Webster," said Mike in a toneless voice.

"L. S. Webster?" asked Hal, his eyes angry. "What's he doing here?"

"It has to be important," breathed Albert reverently. He stared avidly after the group moving down the hallway. Carolyn, every perception sharpened, took in every detail: Hal's face, Mike's face, Albert's face, following their eyes to the men moving away down the corridor. The man at the center of the group was only a shape, taller than the others, who, when he turned his head to speak, displayed a classically elegant profile set off by pale skin and black high-arched brows. A killingly handsome man.

Albert whispered, "Lord, what an honor, just to see him. . . ."

"Why's that, Albert?" asked Hal, one nostril lifted even as his eyes slid across Carolyn like a caress. "Why an honor?"

"Well, because. He's the founder of the American Alliance. The founder of the International Alliance. The richest man in the world!"

"Quite possibly," said Hal almost with distaste. He took Carolyn's arm, squeezing it gently. "Weren't you taking this young woman to lunch?"

"What? Oh. Carolyn. Yes. Sorry."

Hal and Mike went away, both of them frowning, though Albert didn't notice. Albert took Carolyn to lunch, and after too many moments of silence Carolyn reached for topics of conversation. "That man we saw, Webster? Who is he, exactly?"

Albert placed his finger across his lips to indicate he had heard her, then chewed at purposeful length, swallowed, and patted his lips with his napkin. "He's an international financier, Carolyn. An entrepreneur. In addition to the Alliances, he founded and supports the Institute of International Studies in London. He's enormously respected."

"Because he's so rich?"

He gave her an admonishing look. "Well, I'm sure there are some who respect him for that reason. I, however, respect his opinion, because he's right! He's also very powerful. He knows everyone, has access to everyone. If you want to see the pope, or the president of France or the king of Saudi Arabia, he can get you an appointment." A little laugh. "That is, if he wants to, of course."

Just to make conversation, Carolyn asked, "Does he have family?" It was a Crespin catechism question, always asked, about anyone.

"I haven't any idea," said Albert, rather startled. "I don't think he allows any public intrusion into his private life."

Including, it seemed, where he lived, what citizenship he claimed, where he'd been educated. Funny, Carolyn thought, that Albert could so obviously adore a man about whom he knew so little. Crespins were usually more discriminating than that, or pretended to be.

"What do you think he was doing at the FBI?" she wondered.

"He was with the director," said Albert in the rather haughty voice Crespin men adopted in speaking to wives and daughters who had ventured too close to the boundary of Men's Business. "Which, in and of itself, makes it improper for me to speculate."

"The director was in that group of men who walked by us?"

He nodded dismissively, with a shadow of a smile, as though to say, "There, aren't you a lucky girl to have seen him." She felt an ambiguity, as if in a dream, where one should know where one is but does not. The director of the FBI had been in the group, but at the time, Albert had commented only on Webster. Mike and Hal, too. How very odd.

That night Albert took them all to dinner in an expensive restaurant, where, so Carolyn thought, the menu had more flavor than the food. Mike's wife, Tricia, was sleek and dark and outspoken; Hal's wife, Barbara, was little and plump and quite witty. Carolyn tried to ignore the heat in her face every time she looked at Hal, and was able to admire the pictures Barbara passed around, two toddler boys, rotund little staggerers with Hal's eyes and Hal's curly, lovely-looking mouth.

Then they all went to see the new Hitchcock film with Cary Grant—all that chasing about on Mount Rushmore—and Albert took her back to her hotel room, kissed her chastely on the forehead, and bid her good night. She showered and braided her hair and climbed into bed. The night was quiet, the bed comfortable, but something kept nagging at her. Eventually she fell asleep, only to waken repeatedly, her heart pounding at a sense of imminent peril. She knew all about these night terrors, though she hadn't had them since she was a child, after her father had died. Then they had been provoked by loss and pain. What had provoked this one she couldn't imagine. All she could remember of the dream was a voice saying ominous and terrible words. It wasn't Albert's voice. It wasn't anyone she knew. Eventually, about dawn, she fell deeply asleep.

"Did you have a nice time?" Mama asked when she got back home.

She wanted to say, "I fell in love, Mama. With a married man who has two sons." She wanted to say, "I had this awful dream," or, "The funniest thing happened." A peculiar sense of caution stopped her from doing so.

"It was very nice," she said instead. "We had a pleasant supper with the Winters and the Shepherds, who are colleagues of Albert's." She didn't say "friends." The Winters and Shepherds were obviously friends of one another, but even though they had chatted politely through dinner, she did not feel they were Albert's friends, no matter what Albert believed. "We went to the movies, and of course I saw where Albert works."

"That must be impressive." An aunt, smiling, approving.

"Oh, yes, very impressive," she responded, trying not to sound negative.

"And next week it's off to school!" Mama, very jolly sounding, trying to make the best of it.

Carolyn couldn't help but feel sorrier for Mama than for herself. Once Carolyn was gone, Mama would be there all alone among the Crespins.

FALL 1959

The campus sprawled rosy brick over a hundred acres and buzzed with a thousand new students making their way through room assignments and registration. Extracurricular activities were posted on the bulletin boards in front of Old Main. Drama-club meeting on Saturday morning. Orchestra tryouts for non–music majors, also on Saturday morning. Women's-chorus tryouts, Tuesday and Wednesday evenings.

Carolyn had an unencumbered hour on Tuesday, so she decided to sit in on the chorus tryouts. She sang some, and if the standard wasn't too high, it might be fun to try out. She sat down next to a plainly dressed young woman with a strong, rather horsey face and offered her hand.

"Carolyn Crespin, from New York."

"I'm Agnes McGann. I'm from Louisiana."

An improbably perfect blond on the other side of Agnes leaned forward. "Hi, I'm Bettiann Bromlet, from Fort Worth."

She smiled, rather shyly. Carolyn, looking at the careful grooming and wealth of tumbled curls, wondered what she had to be shy about.

"Sopranos," called a woman in gray from the front of the room. "Please pick up a copy of the audition music from the table to your left. Contraltos, the table to your right, please. The accompanist's music is clipped to yours. This is for reading ability, ladies—we'll do you alphabetically. Be sure your name is on a sign-up card."

"I'll be near the front," said Bettiann. "Just for once I wish they'd do it backward. It makes me nervous, being first."

"Bound to be a few Adamses or Abrahams before you," Agnes McGann muttered.

But there weren't. Bettiann was called first. She handed the piano music to the person at the keyboard, went to the front of the dais, and sang competently. She read the music easily, and though her voice was small, it was true. Considering the shy smile, and the nervousness, Carolyn was surprised at the amount of personality she displayed, a bit too much pizzazz for Carolyn's taste. If Bettiann Bromlet was the general standard, Carolyn herself might decide to try out.

"Very nice," said the woman in gray. "Lily Charnes?"

"You've done that before," said Carolyn when Bettiann returned to her seat.

"Beauty contests," Bettiann murmured, flushing hotly. "My mom was all the time entering me in these pageants. Last time around I won a scholarship."

"Congratulations," said Carolyn.

The blond shook her head. "It's crazy that I won. I'm not that good-looking. It's all pretending. . . ."

Carolyn found this an interesting idea. She hadn't thought before that one could pretend to beauty, though of course it made sense. Certainly Bettiann's stage personality was not the same as that of the rather hesitant girl sitting beside her.

It was a while before they got to McGann. Carolyn asked her if she was nervous, but Agnes said no, not particularly. She'd had a good voice teacher at St. Monica's. They'd had a choir they were proud of and paid a good deal of attention to.

"Catholic school?" Carolyn asked. "Me, too."

"Really? I've been in boarding schools since I was six. My family was killed when a truck hit their car, and the settlement was put in trust for my education and keep. I've spent my life in Catholic school. Too long, Mother Elias says. She's the abbess at the Sisters of St. Clare near New Orleans, where I'm going to be a nun. I wanted to enter right away, but she wants me to get through college and take an M.B.A. first."

"An M.B.A.? For a nun?"

"They want to start an oyster farm, to make money for the abbey school, but there's no one in the order with business training—"

"Agnes McGann?" called the woman in gray.

Agnes had a voice better than Bettiann's, with a good deal more range. She, too, sang competently, though almost without emotion. Carolyn identified the style as churchy: angelic voices conveying as little human emotion as possible.

"Very nice," said the woman in gray. By this time Carolyn had it figured out. "Very nice" meant you were in. "Thank you very much" meant you were out. Hmm, "thank you" meant "maybe." When Agnes returned, the three of them went on sitting, curious about all the other putative singers.

"Faye Whittier," the woman called at last. The final one.

Faye was colored—tall, graceful, with her hair cut very short. Agnes had never seen hair worn like that, just a cap of it, natural. She thought colored people straightened their hair. The maids at St. Monica's had. The pianist tinkled through an introduction as Faye clasped her hands loosely in front of her, holding the music almost negligently. Either she knew this composition or she'd already memorized it.

The voice came like velvet, smooth throughout its register, organlike on a low note, whispering on a high one, easy, fluid, capable of infinite shading and power.

Carolyn decided she would skip trying out for chorus.

"Oh, God," whispered Bettiann. "If that's what they want! I'll never make it. I shouldn't even have tried. . . ."

Agnes shook her head, put her hand firmly atop Bettiann's hand and said, "No. You and I are fine for the chorus, but that girl will get all the solos."

When Faye had finished, "Oh, my, yes," said the woman in gray, conveying a fourth degree of judgment, one heretofore unexpressed.

Agnes, who was on the aisle, had a little fight with herself as Faye came from the dais. On the one hand, she was colored, and Agnes had no experience with colored people except for the maids and cooks at school. On the other hand, she was colored, and there'd been the recent Supreme Court decision on equal education. One should err, if one did err, on the side of friendliness—especially a nun should, or a person intending to become one. Besides, Faye was elegant looking.

Agnes offered her hand. "You have a beautiful voice," she said. "I'm very envious." Which was perfectly true, and she'd have to confess it, too.

"Don't be," Faye said with a flashing grin. "So far all it's done is get me in trouble."

Fifteen minutes later the four of them walked out together, down the sidewalk, turning at the same place toward the same dormitory, found they were all living in Harrigan Hall (Harridan Hall, said Faye, laughing) and were even in the same wing.

"Must be the new-girl wing," said Agnes. "Who's your roommate, Bettiann?"

"I haven't met her yet. Her name is Ophelia Weisman, and she's from New York."

"And yours?" Agnes turned to Faye.

"I thought they might put me with Jessamine Ortiz, because we already knew each other from school in San Francisco, but they didn't."

They met Ophelia, Bettiann's roommate, in the dorm lounge, a skinny gamine with dark tattered hair and enormous gray eyes behind huge glasses. Faye introduced them, first names only, to her friend Jessamine Ortiz, a slender Eurasian girl with a face so calm and shuttered it did not seem as lovely as it was. Jessamine was majoring in science and math, and so was Ophelia: Jessy had a landscaper father and a passion for biology; Ophy had a physician father and a passion for medicine. Both their fathers thought it was silly to waste college educations on girls.

"Dr. Dad thinks I should go to nursing school," Ophy announced, wrinkling her nose. "My mother was a nurse. She put Dad through med school, and then he divorced her and married a girl about my age. I do not like my father."

"Interesting," said Faye. "I think that must be a white thing. With some black people, it's the men who think they don't need an education." She turned to Jessamine. "All through high school we knew each other. You never said anything about your father's not wanting you to come to college."

Jessamine flushed. "My father is a really nice man, but he has this sort of traditional picture of women's place in the world. He says men are made to take care of women, that women are happier not knowing very much, because if they did, it might make them dissatisfied being wives and mothers."

Agnes silently agreed. Men should take care of women. They were stronger and larger and it was their proper role. And there was entirely too much fiddling about with women's proper roles. Still, women doctors were needed. So much more . . . modest to be treated by a woman physician.

Faye snorted, a sound that could have been outrage, or simple amusement.

"So how'd you get here?"

Jessy laughed, too, rather wryly. "My mother wasn't educated, but she's still dissatisfied being only wife and mother, so she started saving up for my education the day I was born. She had a father who felt the way my father does, and she always hated it. We never told my father. He thinks I won a scholarship."

"So who's your roommate?" Faye asked.

"She's from New York. Her name is . . . let's see, Crespin."

"I'm it," said Carolyn, offering a hand.

"And yours?" Faye asked Agnes.

"I haven't met her yet. I can't pronounce her name. It's spelled S-o-v-a-w-a-n-e-a a-T-e-s-u-a-w-a-n-e."

They puzzled over that for a moment, deciding it was probably Hawaiian. "Who's rooming with you, Faye?" Jessamine asked.

"They haven't assigned anyone," she replied, her eyes very watchful. "I been asking myself whether that's because I'm black or because I'm majoring in art."

"I doubt it's because you're an artist," Carolyn said matter-of-factly. "I suppose it could be because you're black. Or it could be they just haven't assigned anyone yet."

All of which made the subject of blackness all right to acknowledge, along with advanced education for women, which joined other subjects of conversation when Agnes invited them all into her room. They were still there, chattering away, when someone came to the open door and stood shyly looking in as their heads came up, one by one.

She was the most unusually beautiful creature they had ever seen, beautiful in a way they could neither dismiss nor envy, any more than they would dismiss or envy a glorious sunrise.

"Is one of you Agnes?" the beauty asked in an enchanting voice, low and rich, with a slight, indefinable accent. "Agnes McGann?"

Agnes raised her hand, gargled, could not get the words out.

The new arrival smiled. "I'm your roommate. SOvawah-NAYah ah'TAYsoo-ahWAHnay," she said. "Please, call me Sova."

Jessamine was invited to a fraternity party by a boy she'd met in biology class. He told her to bring her friends.

"It's a Halloween party, let's all go," Jessamine suggested to Aggie.

"I don't know," said Agnes doubtfully. "We weren't invited."

"They said bring friends. You're my friends. Ophy talked Bettiann into coming."

"Doesn't Bettiann like parties?"

"She's got this eating problem. She thinks she's fat."

"Bettiann?" Agnes laughed.

"Right, but don't laugh. Ophy says it isn't funny. It isn't logical, either. It's a psychological thingy that comes from trying to stay thin for all those contests her mother put her in. She feels guilty about eating. Sometimes she eats and then makes herself throw up. Or she starves herself. Anyhow, Ophy's read up on it, and she's made Bettiann into a project. Part of the therapy is to go places and act normal. Carolyn's coming. And I've asked Faye. Come on, Aggie, Sophy." They had tried calling her Sova, but it had inevitably become Sophy as all their names had transmogrified. The ABCs: Aggie-Betti-Cara. Plus Ophy-Sophy and Jessy-Faye.

Oh, very well, Agnes grumbled to herself. She hated parties, she always ended up by herself in a corner. Still, the others were going, so come evening she went with them. It was the first time all seven of them had gone anywhere together, but there was such a mob at the party, they didn't add appreciably to the crowd. There was beer. There was punch, which was made of brandy and several kinds of wine, had peaches in it, and didn't taste as lethal as it was. By eleven most of the people present were either unconscious, very drunk, or well on their way.

At which juncture two young men decided to escort Sophy home after the bash.

"No, thank you," she murmured soberly, though she'd had several cups of the lethal punch. "I will walk back with my friends."

But they wouldn't take no for an answer. One thing led to another, and a fight broke out. Agnes, who was always abstemious, pulled Sophy away from the fray, went in search of the others, gathered them up—even Carolyn, who was inclined to stay and see what happened—and the seven of them departed while the two combatants were still rolling around amid spilled punch and broken crockery. They were well down the block before the police car pulled up in front of the frat house, and soon thereafter they were all in Agnes and Sophy's room, drinking cocoa, eating popcorn, and laughing immoderately at nothing much.

"You certainly made a hit," said Faye to Sophy. "Cut quite a swath through the male population, you did."

"I don't like it," said Sophy. "It's really very disturbing." Her voice sounded more than merely disturbed; it quavered with outrage or shock. "I don't understand men."

"Do any of us understand men?" Jessamine asked in a faraway, cold voice. "I never have."

Carolyn glanced curiously at Jessamine and said, "It's not just men. Do any of us understand people? Including us? I don't understand me!"

That started them all off. Agnes, in a sober confessional mood, told them she had first decided to be a nun when Father Conley had told her she was fortunate to be plain and gawky because she would not therefore be an occasion of sin. Though calmly pale during the telling, she became flushed and agitated when the others told her she was not gawky, and this led to a discussion of female beauty, during which Bettiann told them about pretending to be beautiful, how it often worked just to pretend, and about judges who looked at little girls like so many pet puppies and tried to put their hands down her panties.

Faye erupted in outrage, saying the judges must all be Humbert Humberts, like in Nabokov's book *Lolita*, the one that had been banned, and Jessamine started to tell them something about herself but then broke off, very pale, and ran for the bathroom. Ophy told about her father's not wanting to pay for her education even though he could afford it, and how her mom had to go to court to make him do it, and Carolyn picked up the true confessions, tipsily telling them about Albert. Somehow she got off onto Hal's infectious grin and warm brown eyes. She couldn't put him out of her mind, she said, which wouldn't do, of course. Catholics did not get divorces or break up other people's homes. Neither did Crespins. In any case, she, Carolyn, was already promised to Albert. . . .

"Who promised you?" Faye asked, jeering. "I don't remember your saying you promised you."

Carolyn paused woozily, trying to remember who had promised her to Albert. "I don't know," she confessed with a pixilated giggle. "He's just . . . he's always been there. I don't want Albert, but I guess I think I will want Albert, because everyone always tells me I'll want Albert."

"You know what they're doing to you, don't you?" Faye asked, her voice slurred velvet, furry at the edges from the punch they'd all drunk. "They're cutting and pasting you, Car-o-line. They're taking everything that pleasures you and cutting it off. There's a thing they do to girls in Africa, cutting off they little clits so they can't ever get any pleasure there. It's a mutilation. Maybe yours dohn hurt so much right now, but it's the same thing. That's what they're doing to you. Mutilation."

The word was only a word, but it stayed with Carolyn like a mantra. She told herself later it was just that she was drunk, very un-Crespinly drunk, so drunk she hadn't even been offended by Faye's vulgar language, but it wasn't only that. It was true. The aunts were trying to mutilate her, and so was Albert. It was a revelation. Damn the aunts. Damn Albert.

The conversation went on to other things, and during all of it Sophy listened and listened, very much, Carolyn thought, like an anthropologist in a native encampment, her ears positively quivering.

"Where were you brought up?" Carolyn asked her during a lull in the conversation.

"Oh, here and there," Sophy said, flushing a little. "Nowhere in particular."

"Country or city?"

"Oh, country! Yes, very rural, my people. My upbringing was all very ordinary and dull, really. Farm life is very much the same from day to day. That's why I'm so excited about being here, learning all your stories."

"Our stories?" Carolyn laughed. "We don't even have stories."

"Oh, you do! You've been telling them tonight! I want to hear everything, all about you, all about women everywhere. . . ."

She gave a similar answer every time they asked about her. Sometimes she looked uncomfortable, sometimes she smiled, but she never said anything definite. Carolyn thought she was probably part European, part Native American, or even South American, basing that idea on the panpipes Sophy sometimes played—a very Andean instrument. Jessamine remarked that Sophy played the drum, too, which was Indian or maybe Asian. They asked Agnes, who, being Sophy's roommate, should know, but Agnes only shrugged. "She won't tell me. She meditates sometimes, usually early in the morning. She says she's invoking a guardian spirit, but that's all she'll say."

In anyone else it would have been infuriating. In anyone else it would have led to suspicion, or ill feeling. In Sophy it was part of her charm. Her drumming and piping were mysterious, her meditative exercises unfathomable, but they were part of Sophy, whom they loved, even though they did not understand her. They particularly did not understand why Sophy was constantly so troubled over men.

The defining incident happened in early November. Despite Faye's marvelous voice, she wanted a career in art, not music, and even so early in her studies she visualized things as artworks. This defining incident was remembered as a painting—perhaps of the Dutch or Flemish school, dramatically sidelit: *Interior with Figures*. The interior was the room that she and Sophy shared, full of the golden light of an autumn afternoon, amber sun-fingers reaching toward dark corners and along dusky walls. The figures were themselves: Carolyn crouched on the window seat, the slanting light making a ruddy aureole of her hair, the dorm cat sprawled bonelessly across her lap. Faye herself, wild hair bushing upward, walnut skin, eyes glittering like a jungle creature, catching glimpses of herself in the mirror as she stalked back and forth. Ophy, heaped on a corner of the bed like a disjointed marionette, wide mouth pulled into a jester's gape. And Agnes, sitting solemnly, straight-legged, against the door, staring at the trio before the mirror: Jessamine's sleek olive-brown presence at one side, Bettiann's tousled blondness at the other, and between them, staring into the mirror as into a crystal ball, Sophy.

She was like a rising star, lovely as the morning. Where had she come by that lovesome body, that perfect face? Doe-eyed Sophy. Night-haired Sophy. Sweet-lipped Sophy. Closemouthed Sophy.

Sophy at that particular moment with swollen eyes, an angry mouth, and burning cheeks. "What do I say to discourage him?" she cried into the mirror at their reflected presences. "Think of something."

Ophy threw up her hands. "Sophy, he's the best catch in the whole school! He's good-looking. He's rich! Have you seen that car of his? Besides, he didn't try to rape you! All he asked you to do was go on a date with him!"

Sophy's head went down, her eyes spilling, while Agnes sprang to her roommate's defense.

"What *he* wants isn't the point. Sophy doesn't want to go on a date. That's the point. She doesn't want to be asked to go. That's the point. She doesn't want to be begged, harassed, chivied, or wooed. She wants to be let alone."

"Then she should have gone to a religious college," opined Bettiann. "Or some girl's school."

"My . . . my scholarship was to this place!" cried Sophy, tested past endurance. "I didn't have a choice!"

There was a metallic quality to her voice, rather like a hammer striking an anvil to make first a clang, then a lingering reverberation that faded slowly into silence, an inhuman hardness coupled with an all-too-human desperation, as though two people . . . two creatures spoke at once. Faye stopped pacing; Ophy stopped grinning; Carolyn's stroking hand stilled. Even the lazy cat looked up, suddenly alert to a tension, a presence in the room that had not been there a moment ago. They all ceased breathing as they searched Sophy's tear-streaked face staring at them from the mirror, surprised to see only her face when that Gorgon's voice should have come from another, more terrible creature.

In later years Carolyn occasionally wakened from a sound sleep or turned from a present task, thinking she had heard the clang of that voice, like the door of a distant vault being closed, shutting something in, or out, a ringing adamant, weighty as fate itself. Yet, so she told herself, the sound was not unnatural. It had force, like the roaring of cataracts or the spume of a geyser, and it was earthly, not alien. So she felt when they heard that voice for the first time, when Sophy cried woe into the mirror:

"I don't want men to ask me out. I don't want them to think of me that way. I can feel their thoughts. It's like being raped inside their heads, little pieces of me ripped off and taken into them, used up. I want them not to think of me, not to discuss me, not to make bets with each other, can they get me to go out with them, can they kiss me, can they take me to bed!"

A silence came while the reverberations stilled. Then Bettiann said:

"It's only words and thoughts, Sophy. Words can't hurt you."

"Words can't hurt?" Sophy cried. "Why do you believe they can't? Words have hurt all of us! It's your mother's words that make you throw up your dinner almost every night, Bettiann. Words made you believe you're unattractive, Aggie! Words may make you marry a man you don't love, Carolyn! Words are as powerful as weapons, as useful as tools. They can injure like a flung stone, cut like a knife, batter like a club. They can open heaven or they can ruin and destroy!"

"Shh, now," Carolyn cried in sudden inexplicable terror, afraid to let silence settle upon that outcry, afraid to let it go on to another word, phrase, sentence. That voice, that particular voice of Sophy's, had to be stilled, quieted, put at rest, or it could destroy them. "You don't need to fight with us, Sophy. We're with you. Just explain what you mean."

Sophy wiped the tears angrily, using the back of her hand. "I . . . look at the lives of those who are greatly desired. I see pretty girls who burn hot, with sunny faces, their bodies like flame. They sing. They dance. They appear on the covers of magazines. I ask myself if it is merely coincidence that so many of them have such great troubles, so many die so young. It is as if they are eaten up alive, their souls nibbled away by all those who have fantasized about them, leered at them, used words and thoughts on them. In my people's stories maidens lean against the dragon's great scaled side under the shelter of a wing and learn secrets. In your stories maidens are chained to a stake for the dragon to burn or devour! The maiden may be mythical and the dragon invisible, but there is still truth in that. I don't want your dragons devouring me."

Agnes, lost, ventured, "Like . . . when someone takes a picture of a primitive person? They're stealing the soul?"

"Like that, perhaps," said Sophy, shaking her head in confusion. "If you cannot feel it as I do, then pretend for my sake that it's real. Pretend it's possible. I don't want them using me that way."

Carolyn nodded. "Then you want to be invisible."

"Exactly," Sophy whispered. "Oh, if I could be invisible."

Carolyn rose to her feet, hands on hips, jaw jutted. "Then we'll help you become so."

It took the others a few moments to catch up with her.

"She doesn't have to be beautiful," Carolyn said scornfully in the face of their doubt. "No law says she has to be beautiful."

And she gathered the five of them up into her hands like a deck of cards and dealt them out again: You go here, you go there, fetch this, fetch that, supervising Sophy's makeover without a moment's hesitation. Clothing first, baggy skirts and too-large tops, shapeless and of indeterminate colors, borrowed from Carolyn herself; a little liquid makeup on the lips and brows, fading them into the face; a little more on the lashes, making her eyes look bald. Faye saw to that. Hair pulled straight back into a knot, Bettiann's contribution. A touch of olive base, Jessamine's, to take the bloom from those cheeks. Ophy provided the glasses, frames only at first.

It was Agnes who suggested the book. "You need a heavy book," she said. "You can carry it up against your chest and walk sort of bent over. You'll look like a brain, armed with the shield and buckler of the female intelligentsia."

"I've got a thick book," said Jessamine. "I found it in the bottom of the cupboard in my room, with about fifty years' worth of dust on it. I'll get it."

She returned moments later bearing Edward Gibbon's *The Decline and Fall of the Roman Empire,* volume one. An old leather-bound library book, checked out years before by a feckless student, never returned. Sophy rose, took it into her arms, stooped slightly over it, and shuffled across the room. They all burst into laughter, even Sophy, though hers was a sound of honest joy floating on the sea of derision. What the rest of them took as a joke Sophy accepted as a reprieve.

In time her new self became familiar to them. With them, after a shower, her robe belted loosely around her, she was lovely as the dawn, but in public Sophy wore borrowed clothing, was camouflaged like a hermit crab, no longer the object of male fascination and desire.

It was a shared secret, one that made them more than merely friends. They became a club: the Decline and Fall Club. They swore an oath to one another. Even after they left school, they would stay close to one another. They would meet every year, and each of them would find a place to stand where she could be woman as woman was meant to be, and thereafter she would never decline or fall from that place.

1

SPRING: THE YEAR 2000

IN THE BARN WHERE CAROLYN Crespin Shepherd knelt, the muted grays
of hay and sheep blended indistinguishably in shadow. Outside, the field and
woods glistened in a day's-dessert of sunset, a sky like a split melon that oozed
bright juice over every greening twig and unfolding leaf. Out there was a fete,
a carnival, puddles from the departing thunderstorm throwing sun around
like confetti, but here were more serious matters, a murmuring woolliness
beneath the cobwebbed beams, the tidal smells of birthing.

Light and shadow. Brilliance and dark. Chiaroscuro.

The word popped out of nothing, a printed word, not an oral one,
not one Carolyn could remember using. Still, there it was, stored away in
her mental attic along with all the other pack-rat bits and pieces of mind-
furniture: old affections, old fears, old games. Hide-and-seek in the summer
dusk, shrubberies making monster-shadows amid polygons of lamplight from
windows, clarity and mystery, reality and possibility, *Ready or not, here I come!*
Well, now that the word had been dragged out, use could be made of it.

"Chiaroscuro," she said to the watchful young ewe who stood pressed
against the rough boards of the pen. "A good name for a black-and-white
lamb, Mama. First lamb of the new century and first lamb for you. We'll call
her Chiaro, for short."

The ewe's amber eyes remained fixed, the oblong pupils glaring. She
raised one forefoot and stamped, thrusting her body as far from Carolyn as

the pen would permit. Pressed between her mother and the timbers, the lamb protested weakly. The ewe only pressed the harder as it stamped again.

Carolyn drew a deep breath, caught suddenly between laughter and tears. The ewe was threatening her, warning her away. Sixty pounds or so of fangless, hornless sheep, incapable of any real defense, and still she stamped, still she protected, still those yellow eyes glared a primordial defiance. Behind her the lamb complained once more, a fretful baa while the mother stamped: Live or die, this lamb is mine!

It was so uncomplicated for sheep! "All right, Mama," Carolyn murmured. "That's all right. I'll look at your baby tomorrow."

The lamb had been licked dry, it had nursed, it had crouched to pee as female sheep and goats did and as rams and bucks did not. So much sufficed to tell Carolyn that all parts were female and functioning. No need to take this one up to the nursery box in the kitchen; no need for bottle feeding. Except for the shawl of white around the bony little shoulders, it was inky black. Chiaroscuro. A fancy name for a wee ewe-sheep.

Clutching at the top rail of the pen, Carolyn rose, pulling herself slowly upright, waiting for bones and muscles to accept the change of position. Not as easy to get up as it had once been, not as easy to get down. Things changed. Bodies changed. People changed. Thank God for sheep, who seemed always the same. Hal had taught her to love the timelessness of them, and lately she had lost the count of years in the slow movement of sheep grazing; in the incurious but watchful gaze of yellow eyes; in this annual ritual of birth, she and Hal making a fuss over the first lamb while the ewes stared and munched, muttering among themselves, "Lambs. Lambs. Me, too." They'd all have babies by the end of April, mostly twins: lambs to skip and race the pasture boundaries, black and gray, brown and white, playing lamb games. One could discover centuries in lamb games, so Hal said. One could discover aeons in the foolhardy and joyous, in life abundant and wasteful, running for the sake of life itself, no matter what fanged demons lurked beyond the fences.

There would be foolhardy life itself until there was no more grass, no more room for games. A year ago there had been scant room. This year there was none. All these lambs would have to go—to someone else, or to the slaughterer. There was no more pasture here.

She left the pen laggingly, conscious of pain in her right arm where she'd bruised it over the weekend shifting hay. At their ages neither she nor Hal should be shifting hay! Hal kept urging her to hire someone to live on the place, but she couldn't bring herself to do it. When Carlos's family had got too big for the little house and moved away, the resultant tranquillity had been wonderful. She had heard birds she'd never heard before, seen little animals she hadn't known lived there. Having anyone else around night and day seemed an intrusion on the quiet she treasured. Carlos came five days a week. That was enough.

She shut the gate firmly, double-checking the latch, assuring the protection of wood and wire between the vulnerable ewes and the wild dogs that roamed the river bottom, one-time partners in the primordial covenant, betrayed and abandoned to their own history, now become creatures contemptuous of man and all his works.

Hal had been brought up on a farm; he believed in the covenants. The wild covenant that destroys no habitat and hunts only to live, as the wolf or the puma hunts. The farmer covenant among mankind and those he houses and feeds. Out of millennial history, each owed to each, though the animals kept their accounts better than man did. Milk and meat and wool on the animal side, food and care and a life kinder than that of the wild on man's side. In return for a place by the fire and the leavings of the table, stalking cats owed surveillance of the granary, and horn-throated hounds paid their way with keen ears and keener noses, assuring that no traveler, of whatever intent, should approach unheralded.

As now, from up the hill, a sudden ruckus of dogs!

She could distinguish Fancy's yap, Fandango's bay, Hector's deep roar; an annunciation, fervid but without rancor; a canine alarm signifying someone they knew. Thank heaven it was friend or relation, for she was sick to death of the strangers who'd been haunting the doorstep lately: millenarians, trumpeters of Armageddon, Bible-thumpers by the pairs and half dozens, all determined to share their message.

Presumably tonight's visitor knew enough about the place either to wait for her or to come looking. She moved toward the barn door, stopping momentarily to fill her pocket with rolled grain. When she went out, a dark shape materialized against the fence across the lane. She fished in the grain pocket, held the rolled oats between the wires, felt them snuffled up by soft lips that went on nibbling after the oats were gone. Hermes. A wether. Orphaned at birth, hand reared, kept as a pet, both for his lovely fleece and for his peoplish habits.

She leaned over the fence and scratched his head between the horns, murmuring in her secret voice, sheep sheep—sheep sheep, peering across the shadowy form at the crouched blots near the watering tank. The rams: one pitchy black; one not so pitchy, the dark-coppery moorit; one light, the white one; and two intermediate shades that daylight would reveal as gray and a dark-faced tan. Five. All.

A voice from the top of the hill: "Mom? Are you down there?"

"Coming," she called, brushing her hands together and turning her back on the sheep. . . .

. . . the sheep, which became amorphous, like a cloud, like a rising pillar of mist, fading, tenuous, expiring on the air with a whisper of sound, like an echo of a door closing in some far-off place. Carolyn, unseeing, stopped suddenly, rubbing her brow fretfully, as though at some elusive but shocking thought, then shook her head and trudged up the hill toward her daughter.

Stace came toward her, huge glasses making an owl face in the last of the dusk, threw her arms around Carolyn, and squeezed. Carolyn carefully extricated herself, getting the sore arm out of reach.

"Lord, Mother, you look like a witch. Or a Norn, or something."

"I just washed my hair," Carolyn confessed, running a hand down the flowing gray tresses. "I didn't want to braid it while it was wet."

"And you were drying it in the barn?"

"There's a lamb. . . ." Her voice trailed off as she turned, peering back down the hill. Something. One of those elusive ideas that disappears before one can grasp it. A minnow thought, glinting, then gone.

"Now your hair smells like sheep," Stace said firmly, bringing Carolyn's attention back to the moment.

"It doesn't, really. It's my jeans." She looked ruefully at the sodden knees. "Let's go in. I'll change."

They went through the side door into the mudroom, where Carolyn shuffled off her sandals before leading the way past the kitchen and pantry into the small one-time maid's room she'd been using for a bedroom since Hal had attempted to scale the woodpile and broken his leg in the process. During the lengthy, complicated healing process he had slept restlessly, getting up and down several times in the night, tiptoeing ponderously, tripping over his feet or the crutches because he didn't want to waken her with the lights. She'd moved herself into the little room so he could get up and down all he liked without worrying about waking her. He had been sleeping better as a result, the healing was progressing, and she was looking forward to their reunion. The temporary room was merely utilitarian, though the bookshelves held a few of her favorite photographs: Stace as a baby, toddler, child, adolescent; Hal and his boys, her stepsons, at various times in their lives; her friends in the Decline and Fall Club, when they were young and when they weren't so young.

"Where's Dad?" Stace asked, seating herself in the wicker rocker.

Carolyn answered from the bathroom door. "Your uncle Tim picked him up and took him down to Albuquerque. He'll spend a night with his brother and have X rays in the morning. He'll be back tomorrow afternoon."

"How's his leg doing?"

"For a man of his age, as well as can be expected. Actually, he is better. He's almost quit being grouchy."

"Dad? I didn't know he was ever grouchy."

Carolyn went into the bathroom and shut the door. Hal's grouchiness was unusual. Carolyn could remember his being so only twice in almost forty years. The first time had been her senior year in college, Christmas of sixty-two, when he'd called her, told her he had to tell her something important, and she'd agreed to meet him for supper.

The first thing he told her was that his wife had died. She still squirmed with discomfort when she remembered how hard it had been not to seem pleased at that news. She'd bitten her tongue in the effort. "I'm sorry," she'd said at last, evoking a sympathetic image of Hal's wife, making herself mean it. She was sorry. She had liked Hal's wife. Envied, but liked.

It was he who had smiled, rather ruefully. "I loved her dearly, Carolyn. She wasn't sick, she wasn't weak, she had an aneurysm no one knew about, it burst and she died. Just like that. And I got angry and yelled, and grieved, and did all the things people do, and when I got over it and started thinking about female company again, I remembered you. . . ."

"How did you know where to find me?"

"Well, I asked Albert."

And that was when he'd become definitely grouchy, when he'd taken her hand firmly in his own, leaned across the table, and told her what vicious, unforgivable thing Albert had done. Yes, Hal had been grouchy, but no more so than Carolyn.

"Is he a total fool?" she had half screamed, making other diners look up and stare.

"Yes," Hal had said softly, making a shushing gesture. "And I'm so glad you decided not to marry Albert."

He could have been no gladder than she! She stripped off the dirty jeans and draped them across the laundry hamper, washed off the worst of the barn dirt, and wrapped herself in a soft, shabby old robe before returning to the bedroom to sit before the mirror. The robe was brown hopsacking, and her hair streamed across it in a gray mane, affirming Stace's opinion. She did look like a witch.

She reached for her comb. "What brought you out this way?"

Stace answered with an untypical silence, a diffident glance at her own reflection, as though to see whether her face was clean. Stace had inherited Hal's good looks and was always handsome so far as Carolyn was concerned, even when she was nose wriggling, lip twisting, eye slitting, as she was now. Stace flushed at Carolyn's scrutiny and turned away, running her fingers through her short bright hair, making it stand untidily on end.

"What?" Carolyn demanded, suddenly apprehensive.

Stace shuddered, drew in a breath, was suddenly awash with tears.

"Honey! Stace, love, what is it?"

"I think maybe Luce . . . maybe he's got somebody else, Mom."

"No! Not Luciano! I don't believe it!"

It wasn't believable. If ever a man was set upon fidelity, it was Luciano Gabaldon—whether fidelity to his science, to his family, or to Stace. He was an honorable man, and if ever a man was in love with anyone, it was Luce with Stace. "I don't believe it," Carolyn repeated.

"Mom, he's gotten so funny! We used to . . . used to work up a storm every so often, and he hasn't even made a move in weeks! Not weeks! And he won't talk about it. I hint about it, he just changes the subject. Honest to God, some days I just want to give up."

Carolyn couldn't stop her smile or the chuckle that came with it. "Oh, for heaven's sake, Stace, even though all the romance novels would like you to believe that men exist in a state of constant tumescence, you know that's not true. Maybe he's having a setback with his project at Los Alamos. Men are just as distractible as females are, and God knows we're distractible."

Stace sniffled, mopping at her face with the back of one hand. "Luce talks about the new containment project constantly. He goes around whistling. It's all he can think about! He's predicting unlimited energy from fusion within ten years!"

Carolyn remarked dryly, "That's what they said about fission! I hope he'll be satisfied with less, and in my humble opinion you've just answered your own question. He's preoccupied. Think of him as an artist, obsessed by a vision. He won't let up until he makes it real. Sex will just have to take a backseat! It does, sometimes. Don't worry about it."

Stace's eyes overflowed. "Do I want to be married to some lab rat who forgets I'm even around?"

She fled to the bathroom, drowning her sniffles in running water and muttered imprecations.

Frowning, Carolyn took up her comb, separated her hair into plaits, and began braiding, disturbed by this evidence of unusual irritation. Ordinarily Stace had Hal's sunny disposition. And Luce wasn't the kind of man to risk a relationship lightly. It had to be his work obsessing him. Lifework was like that; it did obsess. Hal's work with the Bureau had, until he'd retired; then country life had taken its place. Carolyn's love affair with the law had. Until suddenly it hadn't anymore.

Lips tight, she set the memory aside. After a time Stace returned, shiny-faced.

"I didn't come out here to talk about Luce and me," she said angrily as she plumped herself into the chair once more. "I didn't come to ask advice about my personal life. I don't want advice about it. I don't even want to think about it. What I really came for was to ask a favor."

"What do you need?"

"Actually, it's not for me."

"Who's it for?"

"Lolly Ashaler."

Carolyn frowned. The name was teasingly familiar. She'd heard it somewhere. Television. Morning news?

"The baby," Stace prodded. "In the Dumpster."

Oh, right. Now she remembered. "You mean the mother of the baby in the Dumpster."

"In a manner of speaking. You know my boss?"

"Dr. Belmont." The psychologist with whom Stace was serving her internship.

"Right. She does expert-witness stuff, profiles of criminal types, omniscience in action, all that kind of thing for the district attorney's office. . . ."

Carolyn felt a momentary gulp of the spirit, an enormous hesitation, as though for one split instant the world had stopped. She made herself say the name: "For Jake Jagger?"

"Right. El Taco Grande, himself. Rumor has it he's going to get into politics, maybe run for governor."

Darkness. A red glow. Carolyn had shut her eyes not to see. Would shut her ears not to hear, if she could. What was that sign Mediterranean people made, to avert the evil eye? That's what she needed. A way of recoiling, so as not to think about Jagger! Jagger, who had married Carolyn's friend, Helen. Jagger, who would end up killing Helen, as he may well have killed her sister Greta.

She took a deep, calming breath.

Stace was looking across the room, not noticing. "Anyhow, Jagger's office sent Dr. Belmont out to the prison to check out Lolly Ashaler, and she took me along as witness and to run the tape recorder."

Carolyn forced Jagger's wolf-grin image out of her mind and tried to concentrate on Lolly Ashaler. "I see."

Rather surprisingly, she did remember seeing: about a month ago on the evening news. It had been Channel umph. The one that touted its ability to be on the scene, and always was, ready at airtime with some talking head blurting breathless irrelevancies before a usually unidentifiable locale, indisputably there, wherever "there" was. The beginning of the Lolly Ashaler story had differed from the usual. Less persona, more cinema verité: movement, sound, an adequacy of chill light. A March afternoon left over from winter. Cops with their collars up, breaths steaming. A paved area backed by graffitismeared walls, the camera moving past a stained mattress and the decomposed corpse of a recliner, then on to a Dumpster gaping like an ogre's maw to spew a paper-wrapped bloody mess and the head of a dead newborn. The head was the only phony-looking thing in the picture: waxen and doll-like.

Uncharacteristically, the reporter had stayed out of it and let the pitiable speak for itself, but the TV station hadn't stayed on the journalistic high ground. All the reporters had plunged at once into avid melodrama, baying on the trail, issuing updates with glittering eyes in hushed and horrified tones as the police searched for the mother. The Mother. Then the mother who had abandoned. Then the mother who had killed. The father wasn't mentioned, an omission that Carolyn had noted at the time. All in all, a distasteful mess.

Carolyn frowned as she started another braid. "As I recall, the girl's so-called friends or neighbors ratted on her. Which put an end to the hoo-raw for the nonce. The circus sort of died down."

"Actually, it was back in the news last night."

"I must have missed it."

"You didn't miss much. That noxious blond reporter, Bonnie something, the one with the eyes? She put a panel together, what she called a cross section of the local public."

Carolyn made a face. "Did they talk about sending a message?"

"Oh, very definitely. They want to send a strong message."

"The media are into messages lately. Were they for public stoning? Or should she just wear a scarlet letter *M?*"

"They were talking about that woman a few years back. The one who drowned her kids. Poor Lolly."

"What is it you want me to do for poor Lolly?"

"Defend her," said Stace, looking at her feet.

Carolyn's face went blank. She felt it sag and close, like an old door with a loose top hinge. "The court will appoint an attorney for her, Stace."

"Her court-appointed attorney came up to us outside the jail to talk to Belmont, very buddy-buddy and insider-like. He thinks they ought to tank her tomorrow and set her clock for the year 3000. For God's sake, Mother, he was wearing an Army of God button."

Carolyn's lips pursed, and she clenched her teeth. A part of the American Alliance, the Army of God was a national religio-political coalition, nominally Christian, which had brought under its wing most of the factions who considered themselves traditional. Certainly an Army of God stalwart would be the worst possible defender for Lolly Ashaler. In the eyes of the Army, the girl was damned for half a dozen reasons already!

Carolyn muttered, "The girl, Lolly . . . she can ask for someone else."

Stace gestured angrily with her brush. "I know that. You know that. She's just turned fifteen, for God's sake. She's so dumb she doesn't know what's happening, much less what her rights are."

"I'm retired, Stace. Three years now." Since spending time with Hal had become more important than anything else. Or, as she occasionally accused herself, since daily confrontations with evil had become too much to bear. Which was it? Perhaps both.

"You're still a member of the bar. You're still licensed to practice."

"You must have a reason for asking me." She wound the finished braid into a coronet, tucking the ends between the coils.

"I don't want to prejudice you with my reasons. Just talk to her, all right? I told her . . . I told her you would."

Carolyn wanted to say no. Not. Not go up against cock-o'-the-walk Jagger, with his prancy feet and his rooster stance and his dead eyes. Jagger, who was married to her friend, Helen, and how was Helen managing to survive? Or was she? God help her. Carolyn ground her teeth audibly.

"Mom?"

"Stace, if Jagger is prosecuting, I'd be the worst person to defend her. I lost the Wilson case to Jagger. I blame myself for what happened to Greta Wilson." She blamed herself for believing in decency, for being blind to how far some people were willing to go to win. She blamed herself for leading Greta Wilson like a lamb to the slaughter.

"Her sister Helen didn't blame you, Mom. Her folks didn't blame you."

No, Helen hadn't blamed her. But, then, Helen had been married to Jagger long enough to know what he was like. If only she had told her sister Greta, or if she'd told Carolyn!

Reading the line of her mother's tightened jaw, Stace fell silent, and Carolyn turned back to her mirror, retrieving a handful of tortoiseshell hairpins in trembling fingers and anchoring her hair, one pin for each slow, calculated breath.

"Great-grandma's hairpins," said Stace, changing the subject, letting the matter cool. "When did you start using those?"

Carolyn paused, one hairpin halfway in. When had she? "I guess it was when I looked in the mirror and saw my grandmother's face." The non-Crespin grandma. The fondly remembered grandma.

"Well, still, Mom—tortoiseshell?" Her tone was a reproof.

Carolyn shook her head. "The turtle responsible for these pins is a long time dead. My not using the pins won't bring turtles back."

Stace replied doubtfully, "I suppose that's true. Like ivory piano keys. It doesn't bring back elephants to junk all pianos." She stood up, thrusting her hands into the shallow pockets of her jacket, thereby dislodging several envelopes that spilled to the floor as she scrambled to recover them. "I forgot. I stopped at your mailbox for your mail."

Carolyn frowned, holding out her hand. "Mail? On Sunday?"

"Mom, it's Monday."

"Is it?" Of course it was, if Stace said so. Lord, she was getting senile. What was it Faye used to call it? Halfheimer's Disease, or CRS—Can't Remember Shit. She was forgetting all kinds of things. People's names. Places she'd been.

"There's a letter from Louisiana, from Sister Agnes."

"Her RSVP, probably," murmured Carolyn, sorting out the envelopes and ripping the smallest one open with her nail file. The brief note bore no pious superscription and the fewest possible words.

Dear Carolyn, it seems ages since I've seen you all! Tell Ophy I am bringing oysters for all of us, especially for her, and for you. Love, Aggie. Enclosed with the invitation was a printed leaflet extolling the virtues of the contaminant-free and succulent oysters, ranch grown at the Abbey of St. Clare. Carolyn was a pig when it came to oysters. Ophy loved them, but there hadn't been any edible on the East Coast for several years and might not be ever again.

Stace asked curiously, "So Aggie is coming this year? She missed last year, didn't she?"

"She did. The abbess, Reverend Mother Elias, had died at age ninety something, and until a new one was elected, none of the sisters could get permission to do anything or go anywhere."

Stace leaned across her mother's shoulder to look at the framed photograph on the dressing table: the DFC, camping it up in costume, outside the kitchen door. "How long ago was this?"

"Your dad took that picture when I hosted the 1994 meeting. Six years ago."

"Why are you all dressed up like that?"

Carolyn laughed. "We'd just remodeled the kitchen, and Sophy insisted we should have a dedication. She said the kitchen was as close as people in our culture ever got to the sacred hearth, so we ought to dedicate it as holy ground."

Stace, still peering at the photo, said, "That explains the drums, rattles, and panpipes, I guess. Why feathers?"

Carolyn cocked her head, remembering Sophy's explanation. "Symbolic, I think. Birds build nests. Humans build homes."

"What did you do?"

"Actually, it was rather fun. We did some chanting in what Sophy said was her native tongue. We did some drumming, Sophy burned incense and sprinkled the room with attar of this and essence of that, and we planted some herbs in a special container on the kitchen windowsill. Sophy brought the soil and the pot and the seeds, all blessed, she said. I never asked by whom."

"Is that the little herb garden? The pretty green trough with the wavy glaze?"

"Rosemary, parsley, and thyme, in an emerald pot, yes. I don't know why they've outlived every other houseplant I've ever had, but they have.

Maybe they really were blessed. Anyhow, we ended the ceremony with a festive meal, and we all drank champagne."

"Why haven't I ever met the rest of them?" Stace asked plaintively. "I only know Aunt Bettiann."

"Times we met here, I think you were always off at camp or school or something."

"So tell me about the others."

Carolyn ran her fingers across the costumed images, then set a fingertip on the oval-faced, olive-skinned image at the left, tassels of red flicker feathers dangling over her ears. "This is Jessamine Iolantha Ortiz-Oneil. Her mother is Japanese, her father is Hispanic, she's a scientist married to a politician, a professional Irishman: all charm and no damn good. Patrick. They used to live in San Francisco. They moved to Utah in ninety-eight, when Bio-Tech went there, and she's still up to her neck in genetic research."

"This is the sculptor?" Stace asked, pointing to a sleek, dark-skinned woman with cornrowed and beaded hair decked with a long upright wing feather. "The one you say could have been an opera singer."

"Yes, that's Faye Whittier. She has a studio in the mountains outside Denver. She isn't doing her hair like that now. Last time I saw her, a few weeks ago, she was back to the way I first knew her, with a very short natural cut. She can wear it like that, she has a gorgeous head."

"Is she married?"

"Never. I guess you'd call Faye an evangelical lesbian. In my untutored opinion she's a very great artist. She's recently been commissioned to do a huge fountain for a new trade center in Europe, and she wants me to model for her. Don't laugh. She has in mind some kind of heavy-bottomed earth-mother figure, no doubt."

"I wouldn't laugh. I think you're very sculptural."

"Not a quality I would ever have claimed for myself! I'm worried about Faye. She didn't look well last time I saw her."

"And the skinny one beating the tom-tom? She looks like a lemur."

"She does, a little. It's the huge eyes behind the big glasses. Ophelia Weisman Gheist, M.D. We always called her Ophy. She married Simon Gheist, the journalist. They wanted children but were never able to have any. It's a pity, she'd be a great mom. She's still in New York City, trying to save lives in that battle zone she calls a hospital."

"And this gorgeous one with the panpipes is Sophy." The pictured face was serene beneath her finger, the dark hair smooth as silk. "Indian, wasn't she?"

Carolyn took the photograph into her hand, letting her eyes slide quickly across Sophy's face, managing to say, "I think 'Native American' would be the correct term, though even that would be a guess." She stroked the picture with a forefinger. "It's so hard to believe she's gone."

Stace stared at the pictured face. "She looks like an invention. No real person looks like that."

Carolyn snorted, amusement turning into agreement as she considered it. That great flow of silky dark hair, those huge, all-seeing dark eyes, that elegant bone structure, the utterly perfect skin with the roseate fires burning beneath it. She looked no older than thirty, but they'd all been in their fifties when this picture had been taken. Sophy might have been almost anything: a fairy-tale princess, a femme fatale, a demon succubus—she had the looks for it. Their friend, whatever she looked like.

"She was beautiful, but what I remember most is her absolutely hypnotic speaking voice. She used to tell us stories. We'd sit there, enthralled, loving her voice, no matter what she said."

"What kind of stories?"

"Some were . . . like folktales, from her people. There was one about girls going to the dragon for wisdom, how they went in groups and the dragon would always threaten to eat one as the price for enlightening the others because only when one is at risk is one truly awakened. And there were stories about women and the moon and the tides. And there was one about how sex got started. And then, later, when she began to travel, she'd bring stories to us about the women she'd met. Her stories weren't mere accounts; she was a spellbinder. Like it or not, one felt involved. Often we didn't like it because she dug up some really painful stuff. . . ."

Stace grimaced. "Like what?"

"She was interested in women's lives, how they lived, all around the world. So one story was about mothers forcing their little girls to undergo genital mutilation in Africa, and one was about mothers in India who fed unhulled rice to their girl babies so they'd choke to death, because the parents couldn't feed them."

"Real entertainment," said Stace, sounding sick.

Carolyn thought about that. "I don't think entertainment is what she was after. I picked up the notion she came from a matriarchal culture—some Native American peoples are—that wanted to understand the rest of the world, and she was looking for the key or the code word or whatever. She was always asking us to explain things to her."

"How did you explain all that?"

Carolyn frowned at her image in the mirror. "We couldn't explain it, so Sophy found her own explanation. Sophy said the tradition of women as property is still deeply ingrained and that many women assume they'll be used in some way without their consent. Since she roomed with Aggie, she'd picked up a lot of religious vocabulary, and she called it the Hail Mary Assumption."

Stace laughed shortly. "I'll bet Aggie loved that. You told me about making her over, into a frump. She doesn't look like a frump here."

"No," Carolyn said. "When she was with us, she didn't bother. We didn't threaten her; she didn't need to camouflage herself with us."

Stace continued the roll call. "And that's Aggie. She's the only one not wearing feathers."

"Aggie isn't liberated, Stace. She likes to think she is, sometimes, but she pretty much adheres to the party line. She felt it inappropriate to take part in our 'pagan' ceremony. She and Hal merely provided what she called 'respectful observation.' "

Aggie's strong-boned face stared at her, framed by the white of the short veil and collar, two lines making a worry track between her eyebrows. Agnes had always had worries. Carolyn smoothed the wrinkles with a forefinger. "When you meet her, remember it's Reverend Mother Agnes. She was elected abbess last year."

"And that's you, and Aunt Bettiann." "Aunt" was a courtesy title, one Bettiann had suggested when Stace was tiny. "Aunt Bettiann is gorgeous, too. I'm surprised she didn't become an actress or something."

Carolyn shook her head at the thought. "Bettiann actually thought of being a singer, but Ophy convinced her it wasn't a good idea. She told Bettiann she needed a career that didn't make her conscious of her appearance every moment."

"Why? She's lovely."

"I know, but we could never convince Bettiann of that. She was anorexic and bulimic. Ophy got quite exercised about it, because if anything, Bettiann was underweight. Ophy told her to find a job where her personal appearance was not an issue, where she didn't even have to look in the mirror, one where her abilities could be appreciated. Bettiann followed orders. She became a buyer for Neiman Marcus before she ended up married to William; then she talked him into funding a sizable foundation for her to run. She manages it very capably and does a lot of good."

"Did the anorexia stop?"

Carolyn frowned, unsure what to say. "I'm not really sure. She still gets a bit obsessive about food sometimes, but she's not haggard, the way she sometimes was when we were in our twenties."

Stace was still staring at the photo. "All the time I was in school, even grad school, I only met one or two people I thought I'd want to be around practically forever. But here you are, all seven . . . six of you, and your club's lasted how long? Close to forty years!" She curled deeply into the rocking chair, head against the pillowed back. "Was it like men, bonded by their war stories? Did you lead feminist protests? Did you march in freedom-of-choice rallies?"

Carolyn was genuinely amused. "You're too early by a decade, Stace! Racial discrimination was the issue in the sixties. Surprisingly—or maybe not, come to think of it—it was Faye who was focused on sexual discrimination. She tried to join the civil-rights movement, and she told us all she was allowed to do for black equality was make coffee, lick envelopes, and lick prick."

"Mom!"

Carolyn threw up her hands. "I'm quoting Faye, who enjoys what she calls lively vulgarity. The rest of us accepted sexual discrimination as the status quo we'd grown up with, the role our mothers had filled. I'd never heard phrases like 'sexual harassment' or 'date-rape,' for instance. In my day women stayed out of dangerous areas—including workplaces—and away from dangerous men. The idea that we had a right to go where we wanted without being attacked would have seemed nonsense to us. The idea of equal pay for equal work was futuristic, as was the abortion issue." She hid a shifty grin. "A single woman couldn't even get birth control at Planned Parenthood unless she already had at least one out-of-wedlock child or had a letter from a minister saying she was to be married within a week of the appointment."

Stace gave her a weighing glance. "Really? How did you find that out?"

"How do you think!"

"I can't believe it! You and Daddy?"

"Don't pretend you're shocked."

"Didn't you read books? Didn't you see the injustice?"

"Well, most of us probably read *The Feminine Mystique*, but that was later. Our consciences weren't really raised."

"So if you all weren't feminists, what held you together?"

"Probably my cousin Albert." She laughed shortly, this time without amusement.

"You never told me about any cousin Albert!"

"Albert Crespin. My intended. Or, I should say, he was what my family intended for me. He's a lawyer with the FBI. During Christmas vacation, 1959, my first year in college, he came over to the house. I was sitting on the sunporch, putting some snapshots into an album, pictures of us, the DFC. Albert leaned over my shoulder to see what I was doing. He made a sort of disapproving noise; then he put his finger on Faye's picture, on Jessamine's and Sophy's. Tap, tap, tap, very annoyed little taps. He cleared his throat— Albert was always clearing his throat—and said in his pontifical voice that I should be careful about the friends I made in college, that hooking up with the 'lesser races' was a mistake because that's where subversion bred."

"Mom! You're joking!"

"Not even slightly. I should have ignored him. Instead I blew my stack, told him off, told him my friends were black and yellow and red, homo and hetero, pagan, agnostic, and Christian, and then I added, totally gratuitously, that we were already dedicated to the decline and fall of society, as it was, so I was a subversive already, thank you very much."

"He must have loved that."

"He was extremely annoyed. I wouldn't apologize and I wouldn't recant. My aunts even got the family priest into the act, which just intensified my fury with the world in general. That was the end of my betrothal to Albert. I even gave him his damned bracelet back." She nodded slowly, remembering. "Things got pretty frosty at home. Mother eventually forgave me, but my aunts never did."

"So how did that unify the club?"

"Albert had no sense of humor, so he did his duty as he saw it and started an FBI file on the DFC! Of course, J. Edgar himself was antiblack, antiminority, and antiwoman, so Albert was just being one of the boys."

"How did you find out about it?"

"Your dad told me. After his first wife died, he asked Albert where I was, and Albert told him to stay away from me because I was a subversive! Hal tried to convince Albert he should destroy the file, but I'm pretty sure Albert wouldn't have done that. Wounded pride, if nothing else."

"My mother, the traitor."

"Yeah. Ain't I special!" She put the photograph back where it had been. "Feminist or not, it gave the seven of us something specific to be angry about, so we had to stick together, us against the world. We never really had an agenda except our fondness for each other. What we called holding our ground. Being together."

And they had been together until 1998. And they still were. All of them but Sophy, the sun toward which they had turned.

Carolyn put her comb away in a drawer, dusted the top of the dresser with a fold of her robe, frozen for a moment by her own image in the mirror. Where had this stout old lady come from? There, for a moment, she'd been twenty again.

"And you all resolved neither to Decline nor Fall," Stace prompted the story toward its close. "Do you still do show-and-tell at your meetings?"

"We still do, bragging on ourselves."

"Well, this year when you're doing show-and-tell, show them all the news accounts and tell them you're defending Lolly Ashaler."

Carolyn felt a chill, a premonitory horror that she resolutely denied. "You're really serious about this. I don't want to fail you, dear, but—"

"You're blaming yourself for something that wasn't your fault," Stace said firmly. "It wasn't. Dad says so, too."

She heaved a deep breath, giving up. "I won't promise to defend the girl, but I'll do what I can. I'll talk to her, I'll even make sure she gets a proper defender, but I won't take it on personally if it interferes with the meeting."

Stace nodded, opened her mouth to speak, but Carolyn beat her to it.

"I mean it. I won't do it if it interferes. Since Aggie missed the last meeting, I particularly want to see her."

She needed someone to turn to. Someone besides Hal to discuss this recent problem with. Hal was too close; it was like talking to herself. She needed someone else, someone level and sane who would look her in the eye and tell her she was imagining things. Someone, perhaps, with a pipeline to the Almighty. The fact that she would even think such a thing was the measure of Carolyn's distress. She had shut off that particular pipeline to the Almighty a lifetime ago.

Stace came over and gave her a hug, kissing her on the cheek, squeezing the sore arm again as she stared at her mother in the mirror, her own face pleading. "You'll see what I mean when you see her. You were talking about mutilation. Life has chopped on her a good bit. Just talk to her, Mom. Please."

Then she was gone, out and away, with the dogs bugling her departure as they had her arrival, leaving Carolyn with the picture before her, staring into the faces of her friends. Between the DFC and Hal, she hadn't been Crespinized. She hadn't declined and fallen—not too badly. She'd had, was having, a good life.

Despite her fear, maybe she owed something to someone who had declined and fallen through no fault of her own, if Stace's judgment was correct.

Hector whined urgently outside the kitchen door. Carolyn went to let him in, Fancy and Fandango at his heels. They followed her back to the bedroom, flopped themselves down onto and around the bedside rug while she went into the bathroom to pick up the clothing she'd left piled about. Jeans, shirt, underwear, and jacket into the wash. She'd put grain in the jacket pocket, which shouldn't go into the wash. She put a tissue on the vanity counter and turned out the pocket atop it. One or two oat flakes, half-caught in the seam. But she'd had a pocketful.

No. She'd fed Hermes.

Everything went away, like the light in the TV set when the power failed, dwindling to a dot, everything narrowing into a cone of awareness that ended in a buzzing nothing. She came to herself, head pressed between her hands on the chill tile of the countertop. She couldn't have fed Hermes because Hermes was dead. Gentle Hermes had been killed by dogs. Last month.

It must have been one of the rams she'd fed.

But the rams didn't come to the fence. Besides, all five of them had been there, by the watering trough. So who or what had put its soft lips to her palm?

She found herself crying, helplessly, stupidly. What a foolish thing to be making a fuss over! Silly! No harm done! She'd made a mistake, that's all. When she talked with Aggie, that's what Aggie would tell her, she'd simply made a mistake.

Though it wasn't a mistake. She knew it wasn't a mistake. The soft lips had been there, on her palm. The presence had been there, as it often was. The unquiet, the undying friend. The distant sound of panpipes that wakened her, the shadow that stood beside her bed at night in preternatural silence; the strange silhouette seen against a predawn window; the listener who often walked beside her in the pasture. The sound, as of an opening door, and then the sense of the someone coming through. The voice she heard when she was half-asleep. Carolyn, listen! Carolyn . . .

"Sophy," she whispered into her cupped hands. "Sophy, what do you want? Why are you doing this to me?"

2

NORTHEAST OF SANTA FE, UP the near side of the Sangre de Cristo Mountains, roads wind toward isolated dwellings set above the city, one here, one there, heavy adobe piled into sculptured buttresses and curving walls, rosy surfaces shadow-barred by beamed pergolas, sunny patios reaching under shaded portals and thence into the quiet cool of thick-walled, high-ceilinged rooms. Though the houses ape an ancient architecture that did without windows, here whole walls of glass flaunt an uninterrupted vista across the city, the canyons, the desert, south almost to Albuquerque. On that far horizon the Sandia Mountains stand behind their outliers in receding gradations of gray or blue or violet, paper cutouts against the lighter sky, vanishing into night when the lights of the city come on. Then the stars look down and the air is sweet with piñon smoke as centuries-old nut-bearing trees are burned for the momentary pleasure of those who, unlike the native peoples, never think of the food the trees produce.

One such place was the home of Jacob Jagger, district attorney and, like so many others in Santa Fe, not a native. Now almost fifty, he had been in New Mexico for a dozen years, scarcely time enough to rub off big-city attitudes, even had he wanted them mellowed and buffed, which he did not. Tonight he stood at the sliding glass panel of his living room, staring southward, though careless of the view, waiting impassively but impatiently, as he had waited for a number of years.

He heard a sound, the tiniest rustle, and turned to see his wife, Helen, standing in the doorway across the room from him, a pallid shadow in the dusk.

"What?" he said in a dead, toneless voice that had no hint of either pleasure or impatience.

"I wanted to be sure you have everything you want," she murmured.

"If I don't, I'll ask for it."

"I thought . . . maybe I'd just go on to bed."

"I think not. I might need something." He stepped into the room and stared toward her. She was only a dim column in the doorway, a pallid, unlit candle. "What are you wearing, Helen?"

"I'm presentable," she said with a hint of rebellion.

His voice hardened. "I didn't ask whether you're presentable, I asked what you're wearing."

She touched the light switch beside her. In the sudden glow she materialized, neatly dressed in southwestern skirt, silk blouse, fancy vest. She was, had been, a pretty woman. She also was, had been, of an independent nature. Even now she was wearing boots, which he disliked. Boots were masculine. Boots were impudent. He preferred that women look like what they were.

"Change the boots," he said. "Put on heels. Don't undress."

He did not watch to see if she obeyed. She had no real alternative. Putting her out of mind, he turned back to the porch and leaned outward, peering down at Hyde Park Road, which hugged the foot of the hill as it curved away to the west. An occasional car slipped along like a bead on a thread, only headlights betraying its presence. Nearer the town, Gonzales Road crossed Hyde Park, north and south. The car he was waiting for might come from that direction or from any direction, even from the north, down from the ski area. Though Jagger believed he had a close and secret relationship with Mr. Webster, his expected visitor, he had no idea where Mr. Webster lived or stayed or came from, any more than he was sure that his visitor would be Mr. Webster himself rather than some minion bearing Mr. Webster's instructions. A voice on the phone had said simply, "Mr. Webster would like you to be available tonight at eight, at your home." To which there was only one acceptable answer. No matter what plans he might have had, Jagger would have canceled them without a murmur. Anything for Mr. Webster's convenience.

Tonight it was evidently convenient for Mr. Webster to be late.

Jake was more than willing to wait. Late or not, this meeting might prove the culmination of the dream Jake had held since he'd been a child huddled in his tiny cold closet of a room, the door locked from the outside, shut away from the music and laughter out there, shut away from more mysterious sounds as well. Ma was different when she got with one of her friends. She changed. When she was alone with Jake, she didn't talk at all, but when she got with one of her friends, she never shut up. Jake often pressed his ear to the door, to hear what she was saying, but he could extract no sense from what she said, not from her words or the words of whatever man was with her.

At night he was locked in, because Ma's friends didn't want to be bothered with little Jake—Jake the mistake, Jakey the Rat.

Sometimes in the mornings one of Ma's friends would be sitting at the kitchen table eating eggs and bacon and sometimes pancakes. The friend got orange juice or melon or bananas. Jake got cold cereal. Once he had thought he could get away with a banana.

"Watch it, kid," said the friend. "You're messin' up my paper."

"Yeah, Jake, watch it," Ma laughed. "You be careful, now, Ratty."

He'd thought Jake the Rat was his name until he started to school and Ma told him his name would be Jake Jagger.

"Was that my dad's name?" he had asked her. "Jagger?"

Her lips twisted. The smoke from her cigarette made a curtain before her narrowed eyes. "What makes you think you had a dad, Ratty? You had a hit-an'-run, a pay and poke it, that's what you had." She laughed her bubble laugh, as if she were all full of something sticky, with slow bubbles rising up. Jake saw a TV show about Yellowstone once, and the mud pools reminded him of Ma's laughing: round, sticky bubbles slowly swelling and popping, each one a ha, a ha. "You better be careful, you better watch it."

Late at night, from behind his locked door, hearing the rhythmic rattle of her bedsprings, he would remind himself to watch it, to be careful to stay away from her friends, careful to stay away from her as much as he could. When he came home from being out on the street, when he opened the door just a crack, he could tell whether she was there or not by the smell. She had a wet, sticky smell that was more ominous than the musty, smoky funk of rooms she had merely occupied. It was a swampy smell. The bathroom smelled like her. The wastepaper basket in the bathroom sometimes smelled intimately of her, mysterious and hateful.

Jake had made himself a window in his tiny closet, using an old beer opener to scrape the mortar from between the bricks, removing the bricks, two layers of them, to create an irregular notched opening looking out on the alley. Once he had his window, he cut a piece of cardboard to seal it up and hid it behind a poster he cleverly mounted with tape. After that it was easier to be locked in. Even when he was only seven or eight, he kept the tiny space spotless and smelling only of Lysol and lemon oil that he swiped from the building janitor. His sheets, which he took down to the laundry room every Saturday morning, reeked of bleach. He stole the money for the laundry machines. At night, shutting out the sounds from his mother's room, he would lie on his back, his hands at his sides, the sheets drawn into a precise line beneath his chin, the air from outdoors sweeping over him and comforting him with its chill. The smell from outside was of exhaust fumes and hamburgers and garbage cans, but to Jake it was an otherness smell, a clean smell.

He could not always avoid her. When she was drunk, she became sly, hiding behind doors to catch him, grab him, set him on her lap. Then, the cigarette hanging from the corner of her lips, the smoke around her head like a cloud, she would ask him questions about his life, how was he doing at school, what did he think of her new friend. He learned to answer these questions as briefly as possible, to avoid the wrath that would inevitably come later if she went on drinking. She always started joking and ended up in a fury, and he learned to be far away when she reached the last stages.

Another window to the outside opened on the first day of school, when an eager young teacher told the class they could find out anything in the world if they paid attention and learned to read. To Jake it came as a revelation, the missing piece of the puzzle of his life! Here was the secret of existence he had known must be somewhere! All the mysteries of his existence would come clear, all the things he wondered about, if he would only learn to read. He did learn, quickly, passionately, with the ardor many boys reserve for sports. He read the backs of cereal boxes and the small print on packages. He read abandoned newspapers at the bus stop. And then, in a book checked out from the school library, he read the story of Johnny Appleseed. When he came to the last word, he turned back the pages and read it again. Casting aside as irrelevant all that stuff about apples, Jake knew immediately what the story meant. It was not actually about apples or trees at all, but about him. This man, this father man, went through the world dropping his seed wherever he went, making babies, raising a crop of sons. Like Jake. Or maybe including Jake.

When the teacher had a moment, Jake went to her desk, politely begging her attention.

"Yes, Jake?" She smiled encouragingly. Jake was a good student, an almost perfect student, but he treated her as though she were some kind of machine. Though he was never rude, he was never in the least friendly.

"In the Johnny Appleseed story. Did he . . . I mean, he could have put the seeds just anywhere, couldn't he?" Jake asked. "It didn't matter where he planted them. Just wherever he was, right?"

"That's right, Jake. He planted them as he was traveling, wherever he was, and the strongest trees lived, of course, to produce fruit that produced other trees. We call that natural selection." The teacher was young and eager.

Jake nodded, one short, definite nod, and returned to his seat. The story explained everything. His mother was just there at the time, convenient. She wasn't important. The father man, the mysterious wanderer, the stranger in disguise, had simply used her as a kind of flowerpot. The father man was the important one. Women, a lot of women, most women, maybe all women, were just conveniences.

He went on applying his reading skill to the daily paper, and to the newsmagazines he stole on Saturdays from the corner newsstand, and the books he continued to check out from the school library, returning them scrupulously on time so he could check out others. He read about cowboys and Indians and great hunters and adventurers, all men, and when he came across a female character, his eyes skimmed across that section, denying to his mind that any such person could exist in any context save that of convenience. He also read compulsively the stories of the rich, the famous, the powerful. He made a list of their names, a double column in a blank-paged little book that he swiped from a gift shop and carried with him always, and he read the list aloud to himself sometimes, like a litany or invocation. When someone on the list died or lost favor or proved capable of notorious error, he did not merely cross out the name but copied the shortened list anew on the following page. This list contained the names of Jake's candidates for his father.

Slowly over the years, as careless men died and foolish men fell from grace, the list grew shorter until, at last, only one name was left. This name appeared now and again in the *Wall Street Journal*, in the *Washington Post*, in the *London Times*, always in connection with powerful international interests. In a profile short on facts and long on aerial photographs of the enormous estates this man was said to own in half the countries of the world, *People* magazine called him the world's most powerful recluse. He was said to have a fleet of yachts and private planes and even his own railway car. He owned urban real estate all over the world, including a high-rise office building in Chicago, where Jake was. This man was said to keep an eye on his vast empire by wandering through it anonymously, which item of information fit Jake's suppositions exactly.

His name was L. S. Webster.

The more Jake read, the more convinced he became that Webster was his father. Birds of a feather, he told himself. Powerful men recognized one another, and sooner or later Webster would recognize Jagger if Jagger simply put himself in Webster's way. Since Webster's name was most frequently mentioned in association with the American Alliance, Jake grew up dedicating his time and money to the Alliance, helping it preserve the American Way of Life against attacks by inferior peoples, feminists, liberals, perverts, welfare cheats, lesbians, humanists, civil-rights activists, environmentalists, and anyone else who had no respect for Tradition.

Gradually, as Jake advanced from passing out pamphlets at rallies and soliciting money at airports to tasks of greater responsibility, as he went from small jobs accomplished in the public view to larger projects hidden from any view at all, he learned that the membership of the Alliance was wider and more inclusive than the world at large suspected. In addition to many rich and powerful men, certain governmental agencies were well represented among its members: the FBI, the CIA, the Pentagon. Jake met men from all these agencies; Jake recorded names; Jake was given a number of helpful hints and boosts along the way. He was supplied with money. He was given the names and numbers of contract men and mercenaries who could help his career by doing odd jobs from time to time.

Throughout all those decades of dedication, Jake saw Webster personally only once. It happened on October 31, 1985, when Jake was thirty-five years old. On that day he was accepted as a formal member of the Alliance. After weeks of feverish anticipation, during which he rehearsed over and over the casual remark he would make about his possible relationship to the great man, he had been ushered into a large office, high up in one of the most luxurious buildings in Chicago. Suffocating falls of ashen draperies covered the windows and muffled any outside noise. Bluish lamplight pooled on an ebon carpet thick as swamp ooze. From behind a desk carved like a catafalque, Webster rose, to beckon Jake forward with a single curve of a pale, expressive hand. Jagger, who had been cautioned to keep his mouth shut, had been amazed at his difficulty in moving at all, in simply keeping his balance.

What Webster said was: "Mr. Jagger, I am happy to welcome you to membership in the Alliance."

Thirteen words. Though it was far from the acknowledgment Jake had hoped for, Jake did not utter a word about fathers and sons—not then, not subsequently. Over the next few days Jake managed to convince himself that such a query would have been inappropriate, ignoring the fact that in that room, in Webster's presence, any query would have been impossible. There was something quite awful in Webster's manner, an aspect that stifled small talk. In that high, smothered room Jagger had not only seen but felt him, like a hot wave that started just behind his eyes and flooded throughout his mind, examining every thought and approving them all. Every insight: approved. Every ambition: approved. Every aspect of himself was accepted, as he was, as he intended to be.

A more fanciful man than Jagger might have made a story out of this, but despite all his reading, Jake had no imagination. He did not wonder about Webster's psyche or substance. He simply told himself that a man with Webster's wealth and power would be different from other men, and Jake revised his own expectations to accord with that difference. His rapid advancement in the organization and his acceptance by Webster himself was proof that a relationship between him and Webster existed. If Webster didn't want to talk about it or want others to know about it, fine. Jake could imagine some good reasons for keeping the matter private. He could wait.

Two years later he knew his patience had paid off when, as a doggedly faithful, unquestioning member of the Alliance, he was sent to Santa Fe with the suggestion that he marry well, beget children, and become well-known. With the help of people Jake had come to know well and pay well, he had done so, picking a wife on the basis of her fortune, wooing her relentlessly, charmingly, as he had learned to do with possible candidates for membership. He had wordlessly and methodically raped her on their wedding night and thereafter as needed until two pregnancies—the first had resulted in a girl— had been achieved. As soon as the children were old enough, he had packed them off to the Alliance headquarters, where children of members were educated. He was not fond of them. They were only pieces in the game, the boy an elusive stranger and the girl a receptacle for which some use might eventually be found. Just as his wife, Helen, was a piece in the game for which some other use might be found.

Below Jagger's aerie a car nosed its way onto Hyde Park from one of the tangle of little streets below Gonzales. It turned upward, the headlights painting twin cones of yellow across the juniper- and chamiza-flecked hill. Without meaning to, without knowing he was, Jagger held his breath. The car slowed as it neared the entry to the hilltop complex, slowed even more, hesitated, then turned in to begin the steeper climb toward the house.

Well. He lifted his chin, settling his collar, then smoothed his hair with both hands. It was good hair, graying but full, well cut, the forehead line echoing the line of his eyebrows, also gray and full. His face was heavy, but the heaviness was in the bone, in the prowlike thrust of the jaw, the impressive mass of the temples. Some might have judged the eyes too small for this face, too deeply set and veiled. No one would deny their concentrated alertness.

He watched a moment longer, making sure the car was coming to this house, then strode to the door and waited just inside. To open it in advance would seem too eager. To be slow answering it would be impolite. He let the steps approach, the doorbell ring, then counted one, two, three, four, five before thumbing the latch.

"Mr. Jagger," said an unfamiliar voice, coming from an unfamiliar person—a slight rumple-suited form wearing a creased, anonymous face behind thick-lensed glasses.

Ah, but Webster was there also, almost invisible in the dusk, looming over the shoulder of the little man.

"Mr. Keepe is one of our people," Webster said in his sonorous, hypnotic voice.

"Raymond Keepe." The smaller man nodded, bobbed, cocked his head, birdlike.

Jagger stood aside, half bowing them in. Keepe divested himself of a wrinkled topcoat. Webster wore none. Jagger hung up the coat and led the way down the hall into the spacious room beyond, where lamplight pooled on saltillo tile and leather chairs, on Navajo weavings and parchment-shaded lamps made from prize-winning Santa Clara pots.

"Very ethnic," Keepe said, smiling.

"It goes over well with the neighbors," said Jagger uncertainly.

"One must keep up with the neighbors," Webster murmured with slight amusement, as though responding to a witticism. He strode to the window and looked out over a hundred miles of desert and mountain, one hand briefly extended, as though to touch the fabric of the world. "You've done well, Jagger."

"I've followed orders, sir."

"Oh, we know." Webster turned, selected a chair, sat down comfortably, and gave Jake an approving look. "We've come to reward you for that."

Jagger flushed, paled, felt himself swaying, held his breath, and chose to say nothing.

Webster smiled.

"Mr. Webster is enjoying the fruits of success," said Keepe in an alert and cheerful voice. "Which he hopes to share with you. The Alliance has recently accepted several new applicants for membership."

"Ah," murmured Jagger. "Important people."

"Important entities," murmured Keepe.

"At least, so they believe," said Webster, a chuckle in his voice.

Jagger took a deep breath and dared. "May I ask . . . ?"

"The Vatican," said Keepe. "And its allies in Arabia, Iran, Iraq, as well as factions in certain other Muslim nations."

It was the last thing Jagger had expected. Though it was common knowledge in the Alliance that the pope's views on women accorded well with those of the ayatollahs, that matter was not usually spoken of publicly in the U.S.

"It was only a matter of time," Webster said, still with that air of amusement. "Better sooner than later."

Keepe said, "Better sooner, certainly, as we have only a few years left until final collapse."

"I thought twenty years or so," Jagger murmured, slightly confused.

Keepe shook his head. "So we had thought, but the destruction is moving faster than that. Our people say all the fish will be gone in five years; most of the birds in three to five more. The amphibians are already down to a few scattered species. Mammal species are half what they were fifty years ago, and the rate of extinction is increasing. Starvation deaths in Africa and Asia are up. The progun people are stronger than ever, and armament sales are being increased to fuel tribal wars on every continent. The final starvation, emigration, extermination cycle has already begun. Alliance must take control in the next ten years in order to be in a position to save our members."

"Some of our members," said Webster with a small smile. "It was never intended that we save them all."

Keepe accepted the correction. "Certainly, sir."

"Still," Jagger marveled. "The Vatican."

"The cardinals grew tired of hearing about women's issues." Keepe grinned. "Aren't we all most dreadfully tired of women's issues?" He sniggered, a tee-hee like a sneeze, as quickly over.

This seemed to stir some response in Webster, who looked up and asked idly, "Where's your wife, Jagger?"

"In her room, sir. Would you like to meet her?"

"Why would I want to meet her?" The voice was faintly chiding, as one might tease a much-loved child.

Jagger flushed at the warmth, at the acceptance it betokened, more than he had expected. "Only a customary phrase, sir."

That slightly amused smile once more. "Of course, Jake. Of course. I merely wanted to be sure we were not overheard."

"Tush," said Keepe. "It won't be long before we can forget such caution. Soon the return to our heritage, and after that the solution of many problems, including those of womankind."

Webster gestured impatiently. "This isn't why we're here."

"Of course, sir." Keepe leaned forward, becoming businesslike. "Mr. Jagger . . . May I call you Jake?"

Jake nodded, annoyed despite himself. What did it matter what this lackey called him?

"Jake, the Alliance timetable is being moved up. The American takeover will be in 2008 instead of 2012, as originally planned. We still plan a political coup. Obviously, candidates must be readied now. We'd like you to run for lieutenant governor this fall."

"Lieutenant . . ." Jake hid his disappointment. "Of course, if that will help."

Webster purred, "Inasmuch as something will almost certainly happen to the governor, we think it will help, yes."

Jake kept his face carefully blank. Governor. It wasn't what he'd hoped for, but it made sense.

Keepe sat back, hiking up his trouser creases with twitchy fingers. "Once you are governor, acting or de facto, we can consider the next step." He gazed expectantly into Jake's face.

"Next step?"

"The elections of 2004 and 2008. We'll need candidates for a number of offices. Including the presidency, of course."

"Of course," Jake managed to say above the thundering of his blood. Of course. The presidency.

Webster waved this subject away with the movement of one forefinger. "It's too soon to make any commitments about that. All you need to know right now is that Keepe is here to help you, Jagger. He'll take charge of your life for you. In fact, he already has." He laughed, an enormous joviality, as startling and unexpected a sound as an avalanche, amplified, larger than life. The room rocked delightedly with laughter while Webster warmed Jake with his smile.

Jake grinned back, showing his teeth. Here was what Jake wanted! To be like Webster! He did not say so. He merely grinned and nodded his understanding, his lips stretching, his head bouncing, all of themselves.

Webster fell silent, regarding Jagger approvingly once more. Jagger's mouth and head stopped moving, he dropped his eyes, as from a bright light. Averting his eyes was an instinctive reaction. Though he thought of it as a respectful gesture, it happened without his volition.

Keepe pursed his lips, nodded. "We're already in a very strong position in this country, of course. We've taken over all of the antigovernment militias, most of the religious groups who think of themselves as conservative, plus what's left of the KKK and the American Nazi party, but they're only pocket change. We now own the Republican party. Any moderates still hiding in there have been flushed out. We've been managing the press for over twenty years now, and the public is accustomed to our view of the world."

Jagger paid attention. "I didn't realize . . ."

"Oh, yes. People don't want to absorb new information. They like predictability. So as long as we don't surprise the public with the truth, we're free to move as we like. Very shortly we won't even have to be covert about it. And then, of course, people are sick of issues. Civil rights, human rights, women's rights—people are tired of all that. You understand?"

Jagger nodded, falling back on an all-purpose acknowledgment. "I'm flattered to be included in our plans."

Webster moved at that, lifting one aristocratic nostril. "Don't misinterpret this personal visit as an accolade. That would be premature." He took the chill from the words by leaning forward, opening his hand toward Jake as though inviting his attention. "I often make such trips, checking things, being sure there are no misunderstandings. A good rule is always to keep in touch oneself, to know things firsthand."

Jagger nodded obediently, hearing a father's voice in the words. This wasn't rejection; it was discipline. Jake was accustomed to discipline. He took a deep breath. "What do you want me to do?"

Webster gave him a glance of proprietary pride and said:

"I want you to be obedient, Jake."

Jake flushed at the emotion he was feeling, a great welling of warmth, a wonderful acceptance. He couldn't speak.

Keepe waited politely. When neither of the others said anything more, he leaned forward to tap Jake on the knee. "Our people have been over your past with a fine-tooth comb: your finances, relationships, everything back to your birth. There's nothing there—or I should say there's nothing there *now*—that could raise an eyebrow. The hospital records say your mother was a hardworking widow who died young. The Defense Department records say your father was an American hero who was killed in Korea. We've created a history for you, for anyone who goes looking."

Jake felt a moment of vertigo, almost of nausea. He had aspired to another fatherhood than the one they had just awarded him, but Keepe was going on, nodding to himself as though ticking off a list.

"I do my job well, Jake, and Mr. Webster expects us to work together. I'm sure you'll be easy to work with. I'll handle all the details: the campaign, the publicity, funneling the money in, everything. Right now I'd like to know if you have a current prosecution that would make a good media hook."

Jagger's eyes narrowed as he thumbed mentally through his caseload. "I don't think there's anything useful pending. It's the usual mix. Drunk drivers, garden-variety murderers, gang killings, a bank robbery, one teenager who stuck her baby in a Dumpster—"

Head cocked, Keepe held up a finger. "That might be interesting." He frowned, made a tiny chewing motion. "It has a kind of end-of-civilization ring to it, doesn't it? The fine, pure instincts of motherhood betrayed, a young mother corrupted by too much freedom. Was the baby dead?"

"Yes."

"Born alive?"

"I don't know," Jake said uncertainly. "I haven't looked at the autopsy report."

Keepe took a small booklet from his pocket and made a brief note in it. "If I decide to use it, the autopsy report will say it was born alive. In any case, I'll take care of that, you stay out of it. What is she?"

"She?"

"The mother? Racially?"

"Oh, I don't know. Mixed, I suppose."

"Welfare case?"

"I think so."

"That makes the prosecution easier. It doesn't matter that much what color she is. Who's defending?"

"Whoever the judge appointed. There are half a dozen lawyers in town who do most of that kind of thing. Heaven knows they can't make a living any other way."

"It doesn't matter. If we decide to use it, we'll make a national story out of it, panels and talk shows, the whole breakdown-of-the-family, end-of-civilization routine that's worked well for us in the past. In general, you can just be relaxed and charming. Don't speak off the cuff. Don't rant and rave. Be low-key and humorous." He handed Jagger an envelope. "Here are some general-purpose paragraphs to memorize; recite them every time you have a chance. Content isn't nearly as important as repetition. You can make people believe anything if you just say it often enough." Keepe nodded once more, to himself as much as to Jagger, a checkoff nod, as though a final point had been tallied.

Jagger took a deep breath, but Webster had something else to say. "One more thing, my boy . . ."

My boy!

"In the past you've taken very good care of yourself. You've 'fixed' things, from time to time." Webster paused, as though awaiting a response.

Jagger didn't speak, merely kept his face blank, slightly questioning, though his stomach clenched agonizingly. Had he overstepped? Had he done something wrong?

Webster whispered, "All of that may have been appropriate then. Your mother's death? Your foster father's untimely but no doubt profitable demise? And after putting you through law school, too. Your sister-in-law's 'suicide'? There were witnesses to that one, Jake. Guards at the jail."

"Were," murmured Keepe. "Aren't now."

"The accident that killed your wife's parents?"

Jake swallowed painfully. He'd needed the money. He couldn't just . . . Surely Webster knew that he'd had to . . .

Webster went on gently. "There was nothing in your past we couldn't cover, but we wouldn't want something to crop up in the future that we might have difficulty explaining. From now on do *only* what we tell you to do."

Unable to speak, Jagger nodded.

Webster went on. "You're politically clean. You don't have an unpaid parking ticket. Don't do anything to track in dirt. We have to keep that vision shiny."

From some hidden reservoir of rebellion, words bubbled up, words that Jagger couldn't stop: "But if he wants to use a specific case, you'll want me to win it. . . ."

The temperature in the room seemed to drop twenty degrees in an instant.

Webster said clearly, each word like a drumbeat, "Don't ever presume to tell me what I want, Jake. If we want you to win, you'll win. If it would make better publicity, gain you more sympathy to lose, you'll lose. The work of the Alliance is more important than winning or losing."

Keepe interjected, "The case is merely a hook to hang an image on. . . ."

And Webster again, "Win or lose will be our decision. Understand?"

"Yes, sir." The words were dragged out of his dry throat by pure will-power. He had never heard Webster use that tone before. He did not want him to use it again. Not to him.

When Webster raised his head, his face was calm and affectionate once more. "Don't talk about the millennium. Every member of the Alliance be-lieves that when the end of the world comes, he will survive. Every single one thinks there'll be a miracle to benefit him. We need to keep all of them thinking so, right up to the last." His mouth quirked strangely, as though this touched him in some particularly amusing way. "There will be a miracle, of course. My people—some of them—actually will survive. And we'll rule for a thousand years, Jake. You may depend upon that."

"Of course," said Jagger, dropping his eyes.

"Now we must go. I have other business tonight."

The words brought Jake up from his chair as though someone had pushed his button, again without volition. A tiny spark of rebellion in him insisted that Webster hadn't needed to use his power on Jake. He, Jake Jagger, was loyal. He would do whatever was needed without being compelled. But, then, Webster was compelling! Of course he was! It was part of his manner not to be turned on and off. Learn from it, Jake told himself as he dredged up another all-purpose phrase and managed by pure willpower to bend his tongue around it.

"I'm very grateful for the chance to be of service."

"Of course you are." Webster leaned forward and patted Jake on the shoulder. "I knew you would be. Keepe will see that I'm informed of your progress."

Standing in his graveled courtyard a few moments later, holding on to his physical composure with all his might, Jake raised his hand politely as he watched the car go off down the hill. His muscles wanted to let go, his skin was quivering, he had a sick looseness inside. It felt like nausea, fear, panic, imminent collapse, but it couldn't be any of those. It had to be overexcitement. The man himself had come there to meet with Jake. It was enough to awe anyone, but the proper attitude was respect, not this strange helplessness. Too much excitement. That's what it was.

Though he'd been . . . well, surprised when Webster had mentioned Jake's mother. Jake had been twelve when she'd died. He'd heard a thump just as he was leaving for school one morning. From the bathroom door he'd seen the red stain on the edge of the tub, seen her slipping below the water, a skein of blood making a wavering line of scarlet across her face, sticky bubbles coming from her mouth, breaking on the surface of the water, each with a ha, a ha-ha. Until they stopped.

While those bubbles rose and burst, one after the other, there had been plenty of time for Jake to open the drain and let the water out. By age twelve he'd been a large, strong boy. If he'd wanted to, he could even have pulled her out of the tub. Certainly, he could have called for help. He had done none of those things. He had simply stood there, quite calmly, deciding not to do anything at all. He remembered the steamy, swampy smell of the room, her smell, the smell of blood and smoke. He had wondered if the smell would still be there when he got home from school.

Eventually, when there were no more bubbles, he had picked up his lunch, packed by himself, and gone. That night, when he'd returned home, he'd let out the water and called the police. The smell was still there, but the presence wasn't. Even though he had been only twelve, he had known enough not to tell the police what she really was. There was a conventional way to handle such things, the way the TV showed people doing it, and he'd handled it conventionally, weeping convincingly, as though he'd cared. He'd said she was fine when he'd left. The police had been sympathetic.

Jake had known for some time he would find better opportunities elsewhere. A couple of years after her death, he did, through the efforts of a generous foster father, Ralph French. Daddy Ralph had tutored him and sent him to college and law school. Daddy Ralph had died suddenly from a fall when Jagger was in his early twenties. Daddy Ralph had left Jagger quite well-off. There had been other opportunities in subsequent years. And, of course, more recently there'd been the trust fund Helen had inherited when her sister Greta had died. And Helen's parents' money, which had also come to Helen. All of which had come to Jagger, because he'd needed it.

Webster knew about Greta, and about Helen's family, and Webster hadn't objected to any of it. But had he really known about Jake's mother and Daddy Ralph? Or had he only been guessing, putting Jake on the spot? Likely he'd been guessing. There'd been no witnesses at all. He couldn't have actually known.

Jake set the worry aside and concentrated on breathing as he marched around the drive, past the garages, onto the high terrace and out again, past the house and to the garages once more, swinging his arms, taking longer steps than necessary, mentally reviewing the event, rating himself on his performance. He graded himself after every court appearance, every professional or private confrontation, testing himself on a private scale that did not admit to loss, only to the extent of victory over those who opposed him. So he rated himself now, though there had been no opposition. He had done well. He really had done well. He could allow himself a little reward for achievement.

At the rear of one of the garages, just past the glossy length of the black Lexus, a heavy metal door led into a concrete-fronted bunker gouged into the soft sandstone of the hill. On the house plans this construction had been labeled as a storage area. The men who built it had laughingly called it the dungeon. Jagger called it his game room. Heads of deer and elk and bear speckled the walls. Antlers made a frieze along the ceiling. Tanned hides were stacked in one corner. A shelf held Jake's favorite books, the ones he'd acquired in childhood. Hunting stories. Fishing stories. Mountain men. Adventurers. Shoot-'em-ups. Jake had belonged to a gun club in Illinois, but he had never actually hunted until he had come to New Mexico. The tracking and killing and butchering of animals had been a revelation to him. He loved it. It was far better than sex, for Jake enjoyed sex only when he was very angry.

In the capacious closet along the inside wall was a huge freezer stuffed with meat from the hunt, butchered by himself on the heavy butcher-block table, now covered with plastic. Cutting up the carcasses was satisfying, but the idea of actually eating the meat was vaguely disgusting to him, so every year he gave it to the people who put on the Thanksgiving Day feast for the homeless. It was good publicity and cost him nothing. His cleavers and heavy knives, individually wrapped, lay atop the cover. On the front wall hung a corkboard panel, randomly covered with photographs and cards. The photographs were of Jagger beside the body of an elk, or a lop-tongued deer, or the furry bulk of a slaughtered bear, rifle proudly erect. Other pictures were of Jagger at the controls of his snowmobile or of his helicopter—the old one. He had no pictures of the new one, the one he'd just bought, ostensibly for hunting, but actually in anticipation of political campaigning. Among the photographs red cards stood out like a dozen bloodstains. They were lettered in Jake's hand with the names of opponents he had conquered. One of them had a judge's name on it. *Rombauer.* Rombauer was an old, pedophilic judge who hadn't known he was being photographed in the act until he had become wholly owned by Jake Jagger.

The room with its photographs and cards and mounted heads, the house itself and the woman who sat inside it so obediently, all these were Jagger's way of counting coup. Together they symbolized Jagger's status as a man. Though this room contained proof of many triumphs, none was as important as the one tonight. At most there would be six persons readied for the 2008 presidential election, and now it looked as though he would be one of them.

The triumph went onto a red card in firm black letters: *Jagger! Finalist!*

He wanted to crow, howl, dance, brag to someone, anyone, but he couldn't do that. His joy could have only himself as celebrant, only himself to chant his war song in this buried room, hearing his own words booming back from the walls as from the inside of a drum: Jagger, Finalist, Jagger, Finalist, Clever, Clever Jagger!

After a time even this euphoria palled. He wiped his moist lips on the back of his hand before dancing out, curvetting, though he didn't realize it, like a skittish show horse, all wide eyes and prancy feet. Back in the quiet house he walked firmly down the wide hallway toward his own room, glancing in passing at his wife's door. She was sitting inside, of course, trying to stay awake. If he waited a bit, he might catch her napping.

Inside the room Helen was sitting as he imagined her, hands folded in her lap, still dressed. She had heard the car arrive. Peering through the blind, she had seen the men get out of it, glowing like fire, like blood, and had, instinctively, without thought, crossed herself. It could have been those sunset rays of fuchsia light that ensanguine the mountains, the Sangre de Cristos. Still, when she saw the two visitors radiant in that bloody light, she had shuddered as at a vision of hell. She had felt eyes probing the walls and windows of the house as though seeking her out. She had moved back to escape those eyes, had gone to the dresser and dug out the familiar, now forbidden, rosary, clutching it as though it were a lifeline as she bent her head above the beads and removed herself in prayer from this place, this time, this company. She did not return from prayer until she heard the car leave once more.

It was all imagination, of course. Stress and abuse gradually destroying her mind. She knew that on one level, had even consented to it on one level. In her inmost soul she did not believe it and would never consent to it.

When the drone of the departing car dwindled away, she'd gone to the window again and seen her husband jittering about the courtyard like a crazy man. She'd seen him go into what she called his butcher shop, his game room, and remain there for a time. She didn't wonder what he was doing because she didn't want to know. When he returned to the drive, he was jumping like a goat, the way he did when he had done something dreadful and gotten away with it. He thought she didn't know how he did things. He thought she was too stupid to know how her sister Greta had died, how her parents had died. Let him go on believing so. If he thought she knew something about him, he was probably capable of killing her now instead of later.

She didn't mind the thought of his killing her, rather wished he had already done so, except for the deep, buried conviction that she had a duty yet to perform.

She heard him come into the house, heard his footsteps going past and a few moments later the sound of the shower, just the other side of the wall. She slipped out of her chair, out of the door, leaving it closed but unlatched, down the hall and into the kitchen. She desperately needed a cup of something warm. Quickly she boiled water in a saucepan, not risking the whistling kettle. Quickly she poured hot water into a small pot, added the tea bag, went back up the hall, and slipped into her room before the shower shut off.

The pot went into her bathroom, where she had cached a cup, a supply of sugar, a few cookies, some dried fruit, her bottle, filled by inches from the bar in the living room, her thievery hidden by watering the liquor. The bourbon-laced tea she drank gulpingly, almost burning her tongue in her eagerness, feeling the warmth, the sweetness, pour down her dry and aching throat into her knotted stomach. Tomorrow, after he'd gone, she'd remind herself she was a human being. He did not allow her to have money, but she found coins sometimes, in the couch, in the laundry. She had almost a dollar's worth hidden in the toe of one of her shoes. Tomorrow, after he'd gone, maybe she'd walk down to the call box at the road and call Carolyn, just to talk to a friend, just to let Carolyn know she was still alive. But now, for the children's sake, she must endure. For duty's sake, she must endure.

She said it as a litany, over and over. For Emily's sake, for Scott's sake, you must endure, Helen. Jake had told her that if she didn't obey him, the children would suffer. She hadn't believed him until Emily had broken her arm and the doctor had looked at Helen strangely, saying something about spiral breaks coming from twisting, twisting with great strength. Five-year-old Emily wouldn't say how it happened. She, too, was frightened. That was how Helen learned that Jake did not make threats. He simply informed people what he would do, and if they didn't obey him, he did it. The children, Emily in particular, were only pawns to him, pieces to be sacrificed to whatever horrid game he was playing.

When he came to her door at midnight, she had endured. She was sitting by the window quite calmly, hands folded in her lap.

"What a stupid cow you are," he said. "What a stupid cow, not enough sense to go to bed when you're tired." There was the tiniest shade of disappointment in his voice. She heard it if he did not. One time she had gone to bed before he told her she could. Did he think she couldn't remember? Even though he made up the rules as he went along, sometimes she knew very well what they were going to be.

3

IN NEW YORK CITY, APRIL was still winter. After sunset, as the temperature dropped toward freezing, the city shrieked in the icy air, strident and combative. Despite the QUIET, HOSPITAL ZONE signs near the emergency entrance of Manhattan South Receiving Infirmary, the bellicose clamor was, if anything, intensified. Voices threatened, security-car horns battered, sirens cut and slashed as ambulances howled themselves in and away. Though the building had been open for only a year, the stark facade was already verminous with graffiti, the hallways scuffed to gray, the enameled walls patinaed by pressing hands. People held on to the walls. They leaned their heads against the walls, seeking a shoulder where there were no shoulders.

Dr. Ophy Gheist had stopped noticing the dirt. When she'd arrived a year ago, she'd noticed the cleanliness almost with shock: the smell of fresh paint, the feel of slickly waxed floors. Now MSRI—which everyone, including herself, called Misery—was just another hospital like all other urban hospitals, a levee being washed out by the flood.

"Tell me again. What did he say?" she asked the man before her, concentrating on being patient. Doctors had to be patient these days, because patients weren't. So her husband, Simon, said.

The white-clad ambulance tech sighed, much put upon. "Before he pass out, he say he couldn't no more so he did himself."

"Couldn't what?"

"I should know what? Whattam I? Some kinna mind reader?"

She looked down at the bloody mess on the stretcher. The nameless, unconscious patient had shot off most of his shoulder in an attempt, presumably, to put a bullet through his heart.

"Whatever he couldn't do, it included killing himself," she commented.

"Yeah, well, tha's the truth. He didn't do that so good, either."

The ambulance door opened; gurneys came in, two or three of them. Someone was screaming, and she gritted her teeth as she made quick notes. Surgery would be complicated and time-consuming. More than one procedure, certainly. Rehabilitation would be problematical. The city would spend a million or so taxpayer dollars on this man's behalf, after which he would probably buy another gun and try it again. Next time in the head, she urged him silently. It's quicker and less messy, overall.

"What's the plan?" asked the AT.

She shook her head. "We'll get the bleeding stopped, we'll stabilize him, and then we'll send him on over to Ortho as soon as I can get him a slot."

The ambulance driver joined them, rubbing his neck, flapping his notebook with the other hand. "Benny Jenks. That's who he is. His wife showed up out there. She's with some cop, and the cop wants to talk to the doctor."

"Tell him I'll be there as soon as I can." She muttered orders to the green-suited Misery tech who was hovering at her elbow and watched Jenks's bloody form wheeled away before she turned toward the new gurneys, three girls, dark-skinned, dark-haired, no more than seventeen or eighteen. One was already dead, one barely breathing, the third was the screamer, howling mindlessly at the ceiling.

"Gunshot," muttered the tech in charge. "Both."

The barely breathing one couldn't wait; Ophy barked orders into the surgery com, getting a team together. No time to move this one anywhere but to the OR. "Was this a drive-by?"

"No. The guy was after them. She"—he pointed his chin toward the screaming one—"she says he yelled something about vessels."

Green-clad techs ran the gurney away while Ophy administered morphine to the screamer. The noise faded to a shriek, then to a catlike whine. The girl whispered, "Impure vessels, he said we were impure vessels. It was my uncle, and my cousins. . . ."

There was no exit wound. Ophy guessed the bullet was lodged in or behind the shattered collarbone. She sent the girl upstairs for X ray. She'd probably end up at Ortho, along with Jenks. When she turned around, an orderly was wheeling the dead girl away. There would be no autopsy. They'd stopped doing autopsies on gunshot victims three years ago. Why bother?

Ophy cast a quick look around for waiting bodies, saw none that weren't being tended to, took a deep breath, and went through the hissing doors into the waiting room. The air system was down again. The fans in the adjacent cafeteria weren't working. The place smelled of sweat and burned coffee, hot grease and dirty diapers. One bench, near the door, was completely occupied by bag ladies, a row of them, haunch to haunch. For some reason, lately they'd begun traveling in flocks, or coveys, or whatever one might call it. A bevy of bag ladies? A burden of bag ladies? No, no, of course: a schlep of bag ladies! A whole bench of schleppelas.

She grinned wearily to herself. She'd save that one for Simon. From across the room the bag ladies saw her watching them and beckoned to her. She waved, then raised a finger: A minute, the finger said. Give me a minute.

The ambulance driver was talking to a bald, stocky man with blood-hound jowls. That had to be the cop. The woman sitting next to them had a lot of stiff, colorless hair pushed up on top of her head and was crying mascara streaks. Ms. Jenks, most likely.

Ophy approached, breasting a wave of floral musk, civet gardenia. Jungle lust. Whatever the woman had soaked herself in did not help the overall aroma. The cop was fanning himself with a magazine, trying to find some clear air.

"Officer . . . ?"

"Phil Lovato, Dr. Gheist. Hey, you remember me!"

"Phil?"

He chuckled. "Been a while, hasn't it?"

She offered her hand, recognizing the chuckle if not the hangdog face or the shiny scalp.

"What're you doing down here?" She hadn't seen him in . . . what? Three years? Closer to five.

He shrugged, casting a sidelong look at the woman next to him, shaking his head just a little. Didn't want to talk with her there. Ophy obligingly moved away, and he lumbered after her. When they found an empty spot, she asked, "Aren't you still in Vice?"

He shrugged again, hands palm up. She remembered the gesture, one he'd used often when he'd brought prostitutes into the uptown infirmary, where Ophy would stitch up their knife wounds, set their broken bones. It was a "what can you say" gesture, a "that's life" gesture, one he used habitually. When he'd brought his wife to the hospital and she'd turned out to have a drug-resistant strain of TB, even when they'd finally lost her, he'd made that same gesture. An acknowledgment of the inscrutability of life. Go figure.

"So you're not in Vice anymore," she said.

"Yeah, well, when they legalized drugs, that cut prostitution way down. And with this AIDS thing, you know, jeez, there's hardly any working girls left. No more illegal drugs, no more girls, damn little vice left. Me, I decided being any kind of cop was better than no kind. What else I got to do, huh?

They got me back working nights." As though for the first time, he looked down at himself with an air of surprise, shaking his head. "Who'da thought it, right?"

He nodded toward the woman on the bench. "Anyhow, that there's Ms. Jenks. It was her husband tried to, you know . . ." He pointed a finger at his head and cocked his thumb.

The mascara-streaked woman saw his gesture. She shouted, "He didn't do that! Don't shoot your head, I said. Don't. I saw my uncle, he did that, his face was all gone. Not in the head, I told him!"

Ophy made a shushing gesture, then rubbed at the lines between her eyes as she and Phil rejoined the woman. "Your husband told you he was going to shoot himself?"

"Not when he did. Not then. Just sometimes, you know. He'd talk about it. Might as well, he'd say. You know." She mopped at her face with a sodden tissue, smearing the mascara streaks into dark blotches around her eyes, into the hollows of her cheeks, shadowing her face into a death's-head.

"How long has he talked about it?"

"Off and on. You know. Just off and on."

"You didn't think he meant it?"

"Oh, well, that's Ben. He's always been a talker, Ben. You know."

"Your husband said something to the ambulance tech. Said he couldn't anymore. Would you know what that was about?"

The woman flushed, a deep brickish red, like a bad case of sunburn. "It was just stuff at work. Gettin' there. Gettin' back. You know. Like it wasn't one thing. Every morning, every afternoon, the same thing, those bums, threatening to throw HIV-blood on you if you don't give them money. And women, like those over there, preaching at him . . ."

"Bag ladies?"

Her voice rose. "Preaching at him! Getting up on their boxes, grabbing people, men, goin' on like loonies! Or those other ones, the end-of-the-world ones. Ought to SLEEP them all! Ought to STOP them all. I mean that."

Ophy rubbed at her forehead again. Preaching bag ladies she hadn't heard about, but end-of-the-world ranters were commonplace. Even though there were fewer and fewer people coming downtown for the crazies to confront, there were still more and more crazies all the time.

Phil Lovato shrugged and struggled to his feet. Ophy beckoned him to one side again.

"Phil, there were three girls in there, seventeen maybe. One of them says her uncle shot them and yelled something about impure vessels. What's that about?"

He shook his head, jowls flapping. "Hey, Dr. Gheist, those are the guys with the beards, Pakistanis, I think, the crazy ones that call themselves the Sons of Allah. Their women go around all in black, you know, the faces covered all up, just a kind of peek hole to look out of."

"Why shoot these girls?"

"Because they were runnin' around uncovered. No veils, no robes, legs showin'. So the men, they think they got to cleanse the family. Purify it."

More girl bashing? Like two years ago when the Muslim fundamentalists had bombed girls' colleges all over the world, including Vassar and Wellesley! This wasn't Pakistan, for God's sake. This was the U.S. of A. Women had equal rights in the U.S. of A., or so she'd always assumed. "Shot because they didn't wear veils?"

"All it takes." He turned back to the straw-haired woman. "Ms. Jenks? You want a ride back home, or you going to stay here?"

Ophy said, "You might as well go home. Your husband won't be conscious for some time. And he may be at Orthopedic Center, up on Seventy-fifth, by the time he wakes up."

"That's all across town. Why'n't you keep him here?" Her voice rose to a mechanical whine, a vocal nail drawn down the chalkboard of her life. Ophy felt her eyes squinch shut, her senses recoil, her shoulders sag with weariness.

The cop pulled the woman to her feet. "You know why, Ms. Jenks. Infirmary's only for sortin' people out."

Ophy silently recited the litany Phil Lovato had begun: Receiving infirmaries for quartage: death certificate or emergency treatment at the infirmary; referral to specialized centers for continuing care; referral to rehab agencies for disabilities; referral to hospices for the dying. If Congress acted as seemed likely, there'd be a fifth alternative added for the autopaths who kept coming back and coming back. Autopaths used up over fifty percent of all doctor time, nursing time, hospital space. The taxpayers had revolted at spending half the nation's health resources on people who wouldn't be helped. So if they wouldn't quit smoking, drinking, drugging, getting into fights, the voters said to try what was working for the prisons. Put the autopaths in SLEEP pods until somebody came up with a solution.

There were no more public rehab programs. They were all private now. Substance Abusers Anon. People Abusers Anon. Society for the Developmentally Disabled. Society for the Perpetually Unaware and Only Dimly Cognizant. No more public spending on genetic problems that could have been prevented or avoided. No more dividing Siamese twins at public expense, taking care of crack babies at public expense, no more transplants for people over sixty-five. No more high-tech intervention for patients over eighty. Still a loophole there, though. The public still paid for failed suicides.

The bag ladies were still waiting, watching her expectantly. Ophy went

toward the mourners' bench, where they were hunched beneath their strati-
fied layers of clothing, holey sweaters over ragged T-shirts, draggle-hemmed
coats over the lot. "Is there something I can do for you ladies?"

"Dr. Gheist," said one, half smiling. "Ophelia Gheist."

"That's me."

"I'm Sarah Sourwood. Do you remember me?"

Ophy stared for a moment, brow furrowed in an attempt at recollection.
"I don't think . . ."

"Well, that's all right, dear. It was a long time ago. But you remember
Jen! You worked on her leg once, when she got hit by a cab."

She turned to the other woman, evading the question of recognition. "I
hope I did a good job."

"Very good. I brought my friends to see you."

"Have they also been hit by cabs?"

Laughter, surprisingly joyous. "No," whispered one. "We wanted to see
you. See what you looked like. In case one of us needs you, if we get hurt, in
the great battle."

"Now, what great battle is that?"

"The one that's coming. Your friend is leading it."

"My friend? Who?"

"Baba Yaga."

Automatically, she said, "I don't know anyone by that name. . . ." But
of course she'd heard the name. Sophy. Sophy had talked about Baba Yaga.
The crone. The hag. The healer. The grandmotherly personification of racial
wisdom.

Sarah didn't wait for comment. "Well, she says she knows you." Shrugs.
Winks.

Ophy didn't pursue the name question; a matter too complicated for a
busy day. "I've heard something about you ladies preaching on street corners.
What's that about?"

"Somebody has to," said one. "You have to give people warning before it
happens. You have to cast down the gauntlet and summon the beast onto
holy ground."

They all agreed with nods and murmurs. The rules said you had to give
warning. You had to declare war!

"Thank you for telling me." She half turned, as though to leave, but the
woman clutched at her arm.

"There's something else. We've brought her." The spokeswoman jabbed
her elbow toward the end of the bench, where a figure huddled. "She didn't
want to come, but we made her."

The woman looked up, eyes staring redly from circles of livid flesh.

She'd been beaten. The line of the cheekbone was dented, broken. Ophy drew breath, whispering, "Who?"

"Her pimp," said the bag lady without expression. "The beast made him do it. She hasn't been bringing in as much money as she used to now that the world is . . ." Her voice trailed off as she noticed Ophy wasn't listening.

Ophy was on her knees before the woman, looking at the injured eyes. One was half-obscured by a blood clot. Ophy got up, pulling the woman to her feet. "Come with me. We'll fix you up."

"You go with her," urged the spokeswoman. "You go with her, she'll take care of you."

Ophy called across the room to one of the aides, on his way from reception to the elevators. He brought a chair. Together they got the woman into it, and the aide wheeled her away toward the first trauma team with free time. Ophy lifted a hand in farewell and went after them, stopping in confusion halfway there, disturbed by some half thought, some illusive odor. Something about those old women, reminding her of something. Sarah Sourwood. Why did that ring a faint chime?

"Problem?" Stroking fingers caressed the back of her neck and drove the memory away.

She moved decorously away from the man who had walked up behind her, Dr. Smithson. Chief of Misery. Whose caresses were purely affectionate and bestowed on all ages, races, sexes, and species with equal largesse.

She stepped back and met his eyes, far above her own, noting the questioning lift of one eyebrow. "Actually, I was trying to identify a smell, I think."

"Smells like it always smells in here. Like a combination soup kitchen whorehouse. Reason I stopped you, Dr. Bir—Ophy-my-dear . . ."

"You started to say Dr. Birdbones. I've asked you not to do that, Smitty."

"I do try. But then I see you fluttering, and all my good resolutions go out the window. Mea culpa. Reason I stopped you, we've having a little meeting that you need to attend. Friday A.M., seven, the boardroom."

"About what?"

"Something mysterious the CDC wishes to consult us on."

"Ah. Mysterious? You mean you don't know?"

"I don't know. We'll all find out on Friday."

He gave her a comfortable squeeze, then went off looking for some other huggee. She checked the wall clock for the time, seven-seventeen, and walked toward her reflection in the glass door. She'd tried to break Smithson from calling her Dr. Birdbones, though she wasn't sure Ophy-my-dear was any improvement. He didn't need to remind her what she looked like. She knew she was all angles, all knobby elbows and long skinny feet and dark-circled eyes! Bedroom eyes. That's how Simon had described them. Used to describe them. Back when he had bothered to look at her.

"Hasn't he bothered to look recently?" the voice asked from behind her right shoulder.

Simon hadn't bothered to look recently because he hadn't been home in weeks. Now he was supposedly in Italy, and last week he'd been covering an economic summit in Germany, and before that he'd been in Paris at a European common-language conference, though so far as the French were concerned, common languages were too damned common.

Simon used to make it a point to get home every three or four weeks, no matter what. So? What was happening with him? And with whom else?

"Does that upset you?" the voice asked.

The thought shook her to her roots. Simon wouldn't do that. Jessamine's husband, Patrick, yes. Bettiann's husband, William, sure. Everyone knew Bill Carpenter fooled around. Bill was often in New York on business, and just last year Ophy had seen him coming out of a cozy little French restaurant with what looked like a high-priced lady, very snuggly during the quarter-block stroll it took to reach a cozy brownstone. She'd sat through a green light watching them, the traffic behind her piling up noisily. Did one tell one's dear friend, Bettiann?

"You decided not to tell her," the voice reminded her.

It would only hurt Bettiann, who still had her particular problem, after all these years. There had to be limits. If you told everything you knew or thought or suspected, you wouldn't stay friends long. Like back in ninety-seven, when they'd met in San Francisco and Jessamine's husband, Patrick, had made separate and well-thought-out seduction attempts on every member except Agnes. Evidently a nun was out of bounds, even for Patrick. Each of the others—except Sophy, for some reason—had thought herself singled out until a red-faced Jessamine had announced that Patrick had confessed to testing the loyalty of her friends.

"I don't know if he really did," she said ruefully, trying to laugh about it. "But if he did, well, Patrick likes to stir things up. I know I can trust all you guys."

Which would have been uncomfortable, but not fatal, if Carolyn hadn't remarked tartly:

"It isn't necessarily a matter of trust or loyalty, Jessy. It may simply be a matter of taste. I, for one, find Patrick personally repugnant."

"That annoyed Jessamine," Sophy said.

Carolyn's comment had annoyed Jessamine, certainly, and during the ensuing days, whenever Bettiann and Jessamine weren't around, the other five—four, really, since Sophy didn't discuss such things—had speculated whether Jessamine might have preferred any one of them to become emotionally involved with Patrick rather than pronounce him undesirable. Or whether, as Faye seemed to think, Jessy didn't really care what Patrick did, except he ought not to do it with the DFC.

"But you didn't blame Bettiann?" her friend asked.

No, Jessamine thought. They hadn't blamed Bettiann. Even Jessamine, if she'd known about it, probably wouldn't have blamed Bettiann. No matter how expensively groomed, dressed, and coiffured, no matter how rigorously exercised and massaged, Bettiann was still the girl they'd known in school, the swan who could not be convinced she was not an ugly duckling, the beauty queen who needed constant male attention to assure herself she was desirable while at the same time she avoided any intimacy that might test the proof.

"Dressed, I'm fine," she'd told Ophy long ago, when Bettiann was first married. "You know, clothes can make anyone look great. But even now that I'm married, I can't stand the thought of anyone seeing . . . you know." She'd wept. Ophy had held her, unable to comfort her. There was no logic to it, no rationality. It was a wound too deep for medicine to reach.

Patrick had reached it. But, then, according to Jessamine, Patrick was good at that. He could find an opponent's weakness and figure out a way to exploit it in the time it took him to shake hands. Patrick was a born politician; he was clever about people. Jessamine said he used people's weaknesses, playing them as if they were chessmen—pushing one here, jumping another there. What had he offered Bettiann? The promise of a cure, perhaps. "Why, Bettiann, have another drink, dear, I know how to get you over that. I've done it before. Just call me Dr. Pat."

No one had blamed Bettiann, with her particular problem, for falling for Patrick's particular line. No doubt stronger women had done so, perhaps even Jessamine herself. Of course, Bettiann's particular problem made it hard to blame William, either. It was an unhappiness, all the way around.

Lucky Faye, who had always preferred women; and lucky Agnes, who was married, supposedly, to heaven. Lucky Carolyn, whose marriage to Hal had been made in heaven. Sophy was out of it, of course, out of everything.

"You're out of everything," Ophy said aloud to her friend, hearing the words go away into untenanted space. She came to herself in a sudden panic, uncertain where she was, eyes darting around like trapped birds.

She was standing beside her car in Misery's basement garage.

She spun on her heel, searching the shadowed edges of the sloping ramps. She had been talking with Sophy. But she couldn't have. . . . But she *had* been! And when had she herself come down here into the garage? She was in street clothes, with her purse, though she didn't remember going to her office to change. Where else had she been? What else had she done? Who had been with her?

Frantically, she looked at her watch. Seven thirty-two. Only a quarter of an hour lost. It had been only a short lapse, a kind of daydream. Had she called Orthopedic to reserve a slot for the man upstairs? Yes. She remembered doing that. And she remembered sending the girl with the shattered collarbone there as well. Surely she couldn't have done that without any thought at all?

Leave it, she told herself. Just leave it. This wasn't the first time it had happened. She probably had been talking to herself, pretending Sophy was still alive, pretending she could still be there to listen, to help. Any other suggestion was ludicrous. She was not haunted. She was not possessed. Tomorrow she'd arrange for a psychiatric on Jenks, and while she was at it, perhaps she'd better get one for herself. Doctors couldn't diagnose their own problems.

4

A CHILL SPRING MORNING IN *New York, with the bag ladies gathering, one from here, two from there, lines and files of them, making their way along the avenue, there dispersing into the invisibility the city grants, two here, three there, down a little alley, into a recessed entrance, a hobble of hags, a dilapidation of old dames, an assembly of anility, hanging around.*

One cluster, then another: click of heels on morning pavement, little hammers gently tapping; a soft laugh.

Emily. Jennie. Have you met our guide?

The one being introduced has tender eyes, a gently curved mouth, hair and body hidden under shapeless garments, like the rest of them, anonymous, and yet, oh, the power that flows from her. So much. So sweet. Like wine, or a marvelous drug that has not yet been discovered. One like themselves, to all outward appearances, yet the inward self shows to anyone who looks.

Well met, a murmur. Well come, and bless you.

She is with them only briefly, before moving on elsewhere, leaving one woman whispering to another: Oh, Sarah, aren't we lucky, having a guide? Somehow I thought she'd be wearing armor. Like St. Joan, don't you know?

I imagine she wears what she chooses. Something she chooses carefully. Her own garb, always, for her own reasons. Not because of fashion.

Laughter again, wry and accepting, as sets of heels go off tap-tapping.

Where is it? The place?

Just down the street. There on the corner, where the red carpet is, and the awning. We're early. We won't all go in at once.

Why did we pick this one?

It was on TV, on the E channel. They do a show on the latest in fashions. We voted on this one as the worst.

I'm glad it's not far. These shoes! And this girdle! Are they really necessary?

Some asperity: We're the mission leaders, and we'll seem more in character wearing them. We're supposed to be respectable small-town buyers.

A ladylike snort: I had a shower at the shelter to smell in character. How do you like my dress?

Salvation Army?

St. Vincent de Paul. But I thought not bad.

Not bad at all. And the others?

All of them got cleaned up for the occasion. Edna shoplifted panty hose for her bunch. Rose's group went to the beauty college, for a makeover. They're waiting, see, in the alley there. And by the crosswalk. And in the coffee shop. And coming down the street on the other side.

Aren't we elegant! So many! Must be thirty of us.

Oh, there are lots more of us than that, hundreds and thousands and tens and hundreds of thousands for the final array. . . .

I've been wanting to ask . . .

So? Ask!

Will we die, then?

A long pause in which thoughts simmer, almost invisible, like heat waves rising from pavement.

I don't know. She has never said. But, then, what else do we have to do with our lives? Ah?

So many of us.

So many, yes. But this little affair won't take many. This is only a divertissement!

They wait. Soon the guide returns. They hear her voice whispering to them, an intimate sound, like the shush of their own blood.

These are the words to remember: Even a great storm starts with a few drops, a spatter, a wet spot touching an age of dust, a mutter of thunder breaking a conspiracy of silence. So, hearing this thunder, the world pricks up its ears; smelling this rain, the world widens its nostrils and scents a change in the wind.

Already the first drops are falling. Already the thunder growls on the horizon. But we do not want them to forecast the storm—not yet. We want them to be preoccupied with other ideas, with amusements, with jests. We are here today to divert their attention from what's coming.

So near the end, and they still don't know what's coming?

They still don't. No. So let us amuse them, let them look at us, let them laugh at us old ladies and what we do, let them mock us and point fingers and sneer; let them write columns about us for a little while longer, while the clouds gather.

The voice falls silent. The women swirl and regroup, pass and repass, murmuring to one another:

There's the place. There's a guard out front. Do you have the invitations?

Here they are. Harriet got them. She joined the cleaning crew at the print shop. She got enough for all of us.

Who's the man talking to the guard?

That's Rene Raoul. The designer himself. New Yorker *magazine did a special on him. They call him the crown prince of fashion.*

Rene Raoul, née Robert Weiss, lets himself back through the bronze doors of Chez Raoul, recently identified by the cognoscenti as New York's most exciting new fashion house. His eyes sweep the foyer, all *très chic*, and the showroom, recently redone in ebony and magenta. His stable of models is already assembled in the dressing room with the handlers. The girlies are having their little egos massaged, their little hysterias calmed, their bony little bodies stroked, their foxy little faces made up. Though it will be almost an hour before the show starts, there are already a few buyers scattered around the room, yawning over the coffee and croissants he has furnished. One of them is Liz Porter, the fashion editor of *Fatale*. He stops to drop a kiss on her wrinkled cheek.

"Dear Liz," he murmurs.

"Dear Bobby," she murmurs in return with a wink. Not that she lets on. Bobby has been Rene Raoul for almost five years now, and his accent is good enough to fool most people. "How's Hank?"

"Hank, my dear, is in Barcelona, if you can believe that."

"Chasing olive-skinned young bullfighters, no doubt."

"He swears he's true to me," this with a pout. "Though I'd imagine you're right. How's Esmee?"

"Her usual temperamental self. Quieter than usual lately, to tell the truth. She thinks she's getting old, but aren't we all? What do we have on the agenda today?"

He simpers in self-mockery. "Liz, sometimes I'm too naughty! This time I'm almost ashamed of myself. Boredom, I think. I'm showing some absolutely ridiculous outfits today. It's amazing what one can get women to wear!"

She gives him a warning look. "Not all women, love."

"Well, no, of course, not all. Some women are just too smart for their own good." He twinkles at her. "Still, most women aren't like you, love. There's one model back there who's been putting her little fingies down her froat for a whole week, just so she'll fit into the evening dress she's showing. It's ridiculous even in size four. Any bigger than that, one would look like Dumbo's mama. Now, who in hell's that?"

He is looking at the curtained arch where two elderly women are presenting their invitations. Liz glances at them without interest. "Buyers for small-town department stores, I should think. Someplace like Unfortunate Falls, Montana."

He giggles. "I've got to get back. If I don't watch the babies, they'll sneak diet Cokes, and then they'll have to pee right when they should be changing."

The room settles into virtual somnolence while the audience assembles. The coffee urns in the foyer do a steady business. The caterer's people restock the trays of croissants, get out more butter, more marmalade. More old women arrive, some quite well groomed, a few who look, so Liz thinks, as though they'd slept in an alley. The room becomes crowded.

Music finally, then gentle applause, and Raoul himself at the lectern, wearing horn-rims and a charming smile, still the wunderkind, the young man who had taken Seventh Avenue by storm.

"Ladies and gentlemen: Refer to your lists, please. The first garments in our ready-to-wear line are our Avenues of the World selections, based on ethnic themes. First, from Morocco . . ."

Liz looks and makes notes, now and then glancing around at the other watchers. The old women, those who look like small-town buyers, aren't taking notes. They are interested, no doubt about that. They seemed fixated on the models, but they aren't taking notes. Not on the chiffon harem trousers with the studded leather short shorts beneath; not on the knit tank tops with the armholes cut deep to show the sequin bra; not on the minikimono with the gold-chain obi. Liz looks at her own list in surprise. All she's done herself is say no, no, no. She can't get a column out of that!

But, my God, no woman on the runway weighs more than ninety-five pounds dripping wet! Size four, size six, they look like children dressed up in Grandma's old Halloween costumes. Breastless. Androgynous. Sylphs. Not human women. Ordinarily, they can look marvelous wrapped in an old tablecloth, but even they look ridiculous in these clothes.

She rubs her forehead fretfully. Thinking about it calmly, she has to admit the collection isn't any worse than last year's, and last year she'd found things to comment on and approve of. Or even the year before! But this year . . . this year she can find nothing to . . . nothing to think of wearing. All she can think about is what Bobby said about the models "putting their little fingies down their froats." The words evoke a faint nausea, which she seems unable to shake.

So what has changed? Not Raoul née Bobby. It has to be Liz herself. God, is she getting old? Esmee says Esmee is, but Liz? Liz the immortal?

There are murmurs. Rene looks up from his lectern, eyebrows raised, finding the audience restive. Doggedly, he goes back to the script: "And from Norway we have . . ."

Out comes the model, hair bleached white with sprayed-on black stripes, cut in a ragged shag barely an inch long, stick-thin body dressed in a bulky orange-, white-, and black-figured Scandinavian sweater cut off at the level of her crotch, and beneath it, so far as Liz can see, a narrow ruffle of black chenille disclosing a gold-lamé string-bikini bottom, the costume set off by thigh-high shiny gold plastic boots with three-inch heels.

"Ah, fer crisake," says an old voice in a tone of outrage.

Raoul looks up again.

"Ladies," one of the old women yells above the noise. "All right, ladies!" Her voice is mocking, edged.

Women rise and began milling around. Shopping bags rustle. A solid phalanx of old dames is suddenly on the runway, moving purposefully toward the dressing room. Raoul stutters to a breathless silence. The lectern goes over with a crash. The microphone screams with feedback sound. Without even thinking about it, Liz steps up onto her chair, then onto the runway, following the crowd, where the story is.

The dressing room stinks of turpentine and is full of the sound of liquid sloshing. Women are emptying cans and bottles all over the racks and the loose clothes lying about, over the boots and shoes standing ready. One of the old ladies opens the back door, onto the alley.

"Out," she says, and the other old women begin herding the models before them like sheep, like geese, seeming not to hear the treble honks and baas, the magpie curses. Then they are all outside in the alley, including Liz, while behind them the dressing room whooshes into flames and a high-heeled boot goes through the back window in a cataract of tinkling glass.

Liz tries to get away, get to a phone, but the women won't let her go. She is trapped behind a solid phalanx of large, heavy bodies, most of them, Liz notices for the first time, wearing sneakers and planted like trees, roots way down, not moving an inch.

The fire bursts upward, taking the roof. The old women break their phalanx. The models dart off in all directions, full of shrill complaint. Liz, suddenly released, runs for the street, for the phone, for the fire alarm as the last sneakered woman slips out of the alley and disappears onto the streets.

Liz finds Bobby-Raoul in the smoke-filled space outside the front door, screaming obscenities amid a small crowd of those who had been inside. No one missing. So far as Liz can tell, no one is injured, no one burned.

Raoul turns to her, grabs for her, tears of impotent rage on his face, and they stand on the sidewalk, clinging together while the store burns and Raoul yells and red engines howl themselves to a halt, and finally some official with a fireman's hat says it's definitely arson, as though they hadn't known that all along!

What does the sign on the sidewalk mean? the fireman asks.

That's when Liz first notices it, spray painted on the concrete:

STRENGTH AND HONOR ARE HER CLOTHING!

"What does that mean?" the designer screams in her ear.

"I think . . . I think it's from the Bible," she says. "Proverbs. Something like that. . . ."

Meantime, far down the streets, a soft shuffle of feet on the sidewalk, sneakers and anklets, shopping carts retrieved from alleys, old hats sheltering old eyes, pushing off into the city as sirens go screaming by, one going this way, one that, a pair here and there, just bag ladies, out for the day, bothering no one.

What's next? one asks another.

The Scalawag shoe place. Tomorrow.

Will she be with us again?

She's always with us. She always has been. We just forgot.

William Carpenter arrived on the thirtieth floor of the Carpenter building, slightly mellowed by the two drinks he'd allowed himself while lunching with his tax man at the club, but not so detached that he didn't notice something not quite right with the office staff. Carpenter and Mason Advertising had something untoward going on.

"Afternoon, Mr. Carpenter," said the receptionist, quickly glancing at the phone, as though commanding it to ring, which it promptly did. She answered it with an expression very much like relief. So. She'd wanted not to meet his eyes, not to talk to him, not to take part in their usual thirty-second flirtation, wanted him to get on by, out of her vicinity. Storm warning. Interesting.

Down the deeply carpeted hall, on the way toward his own sanctum, he saw doors shut that normally stood open and heard behind them an irritated buzz, like bees getting ready to swarm. Outside his office, however, Maybelle Corson was much herself, as she gave him her meager smile and a handful of messages: Bettiann had called, his lawyer had called. Nothing about the buzz, so it wasn't something Maybelle knew about.

Nonetheless, the buzz was there. Even inside his office, as he returned calls and scribbled notes to himself, he could feel the tension. Carpenter and Mason Advertising occupied the twenty-fifth through the thirtieth floors, and William had always been able to tell the temper of the office just by listening to the hum that came through the walls, the echoes in the ducts. This afternoon there was something frantic going on.

"Maybelle?" he said, pressing a key.

"Yes, Mr. Carpenter?"

"Come in, will you?"

She slid through the door like an eel, smooth as silk, her dark-colored, high-necked, long-sleeved dress with its neat collar and cuffs like something out of the forties or fifties.

"What did Bettiann want?"

"Just to know whether you'd be home for dinner."

"Call her and tell her yes. Now, what's going on out there?"

She shook her head slowly, not to dislodge a hair of that tightly moussed coiffure. "I'm not sure, sir. There seems to be a good deal of whispering behind closed doors. It started this morning, shortly after we opened."

"Find out."

"Yes, sir." She oozed out once more, nose twitching busily, already on the trail. Maybelle Corson had her sources. A clerk here, a secretary there, a junior staff member somewhere else. She cultivated them, maternally. She got them little promotions or little raises or better desks, nearer windows. She handled little matters, like sexual harassment, without making a court case of it. Then, when Maybelle needed to know what was really going on with this account executive or that layout department, they told all.

He dug into the messages. General Motors's sports vehicle, El Tigre, wasn't selling well, the ad manager wondered if it might be the new ad campaign. Ditto the ad manager for Forever Young, a new line of skin products. Hell. William hadn't liked either campaign; they'd felt wrong, somehow—too pushy, too sexy—but that's what his people had come up with, and that's what the clients had bought. He didn't second-guess his people unless he had to, and he never second-guessed clients.

His buzzer. "Yes?"

"Mr. Carpenter?"

"Come in, Maybelle."

She oozed in once more. "Everyone's chattering about riots, Mr. Carpenter. Evidently it started with a New York fashion house being burned yesterday, and then several Scalawag shoe outlets were burned this morning, and the TV says it's being blamed on the advertising—"

"What!"

She came closer to the desk, lowering her voice almost to a whisper. "Scalawag stores in Chicago, New York, Boston, Miami, and Washington,

D.C., have been burned. Just the stores, no injury to people. There may be others, as well, but those are the ones we've heard about. Mobs of women invaded them and trashed them, sir. They left signs taking off on the campaign slogan: 'Scalawags, the Walk of a Woman.' "

He stared for a moment in disbelief. "Signs?"

"Well, graffiti. Saying various things, sir. 'The walk of a woman, away,' was one. And, 'The walk of an angry woman.' "

"What the hell does that mean?"

"I don't know. Nobody knows."

"Get Vitorici in here. And Liz Johnson. And ask Webber to handle my Spinsoft appointment."

She scurried out, not so smoothly this time, lines between her eyes. "Leave the door open," he called. "Send them in as soon as they get here."

Which was only moments. Vitorici arrived almost at once, as though he'd been launched from a cannon. He looked worried, tie awry, his usually polished surfaces abraded. His assistant, Liz Johnson, slipped through the door only moments later, her egglike cheeks smudged, hairdo perforated by pencils, mouth screwed up.

"All right," said William. "Let's have it."

They looked at each other, her eyebrows raised, his squirming like caterpillars, she shrugging, he lip chewing, both shifting uncomfortably. Vitorici elected himself spokesman.

"I've been trying to get better information, Bill. The whole thing is rather sketchy at the moment. At first we thought it was like the college bombings, or like the women being shot on street corners, but in this case the perpetrators *were* women. We've thought of lesbian protests, maybe, or a buyers' strike, or some kind of consumers' demonstration. Perhaps we've totally misread the buster generation."

"Are you saying this is an age-related thing?"

Vitorici looked around, got no help from Liz Johnson. "Well, the . . . the perpetrators are all . . . elderly. And the campaign was aimed at the teen-to-twentyish woman, which means any woman wanting to look that age. Women agile enough to manage the shoes, I mean. . . ."

"He means four-inch heels aren't for everyone. Or platform soles," said Liz in a crisp, no-nonsense voice. "You may recall I advised against that 'Walk of a Woman' approach. The visuals, that whole fashion-show sequence with the extreme clothes and makeup. I also complained about the quasi-rock bump-and-grind music."

"Bump and grind?" Vitorici yelled. "Do you know how much we paid for the right to use that song? It won an Oscar!"

"It won an Oscar as a romantic ballad, but then the production people had it rearranged as stripper music," she snarled. "And the director had the models twitching their bottoms like belly dancers. I also objected to his using anorexic models with no breasts or hips who look as though they've just been released from a gulag."

"Enough," William muttered. The two shut up, he red in the face, she very pale. "Has anyone claimed responsibility? Has anyone issued a statement?"

Liz answered. "No one was arrested. They all got away. It was very well planned, just like the thing in New York yesterday. Noon news broadcasts said the fire departments in the various cities had received a communiqué, but they didn't quote it."

William let out his breath explosively, unaware he'd been holding it. "We'd better talk to Scalawag. Who's their sales manager? Mierson?"

"You'd better talk to more than Scalawag," said Liz grimly. "If this is happening to them, I'd worry about Seal-sleek Swimwear—and the Lovelace lingerie account, and the new Forever Young skin-care line—"

"Why them?"

"In my opinion the ad campaigns are equally insulting, for one."

"You worked on all of them," Vitorici yelled.

"I got outvoted on all of them," she hollered with equal vehemence. "The female viewpoint was not considered germane."

"One thing at a time," snarled William. "Set a meeting with the Scalawag people first. And as soon as the rioters, trashers, whatever, are identified, send someone to talk with them. I want to know who put them up to this."

"Who put them up to it?" asked Liz, eyebrows raised.

"Who put them up to it," he asserted. "We could chase our tails all over the place looking for motivations that aren't there, when the whole thing may have been planned by the competition."

"Euro-boot is hiring rioters to lower Scalawag's market share?" Her question trembled on the verge of laughter.

"Do it, Liz." His voice was threatening, not a voice he usually used with his people.

"Of course, Mr. Carpenter," she said coldly. "Immediately."

Damn. Now he'd offended her, and if it turned out she'd been right . . . damn.

As they left, Maybelle was hovering at the door. She'd obviously listened to it all.

"Yes, Maybelle?"

"It's not my place to comment, Mr. Carpenter, but I don't think it's a conspiracy—"

"Not your place," he snarled. "You're right, Maybelle."

"Yes, sir." She went out, silently fuming. So let him find out for himself. Up until a month ago Lilian, Maybelle's youngest daughter, went to the mall every chance she got, after school, on weekends, hanging out, spending what money she had on clothes and shoes. Not Scalawag, of course. Cheap imitations of Scalawag was the best she could do, prancing around with her bottom swinging. Then she stopped going. When Maybelle asked why, she said it was boring. She said none of her friends were going anymore. She said she was through spending all her money on stuff.

"Stuff?" Maybelle had asked, openmouthed.

"Mother. I only did it because everybody else did. We're all through. We're saving for cars, for college, for something useful." She'd looked up patiently, smiling kindly on old Mom, as though their roles had been reversed, leaving Maybelle at a loss.

"Where did you get this approach to life?"

"I don't know." Lilian had shrugged. "It just makes sense."

Four daughters, and this was the first time one of them had ever left Maybelle speechless.

Let William Carpenter find out for himself. Let him figure out what the hell was going on!

Arrangement on a desk. A Steuben bud vase holding a spray of green orchids. A gold-and-onyx-mounted desk calendar at current date, April 9, 2000. Two boxes of stationery: one informal, with flowers—Bettiann Carpenter—one printed in businesslike dark gray on pale taupe—Mrs. William Carpenter, Eleven Foxtail Lane, Dallas, Texas. A complicated phone with a built-in directory. Two pairs of glasses; one bifocal, one for reading. An old, cheap address book, the cover scuffed, the corners worn, open at the D's, *Decline and Fall Club.* A silver-framed signed photograph of a grinning redhead in cap and gown: Love to Aunt Betty, I made it, Stace. Another of a beautiful though sulky-faced youth: To Mom from Junior—the word "Junior" underlined and in quotes—Who would have been just as angry and dissatisfied and depressed if he'd been named anything else—as William frequently pointed out.

The desk had been crafted of solid black walnut to fit the alcove where it stood. The carpet had been special-ordered from Afghanistan. The pieces of furniture that had not been custom-made were collector's items. The fabric in the drapes was pure silk, loomed in Italy. The convex mirror above the credenza in the hall was eighteenth century, ornate yet dignified, reflecting a fish-eye image of the paneled, book-lined room, the desk and its occupant, Bettiann Carpenter née Bromlet, fifty-some odd but looking at least fifteen years younger. And damned well better, considering what it cost William to keep her svelte and well maintained. Good thing William had inherited all that oil money. Even on his salary he might not be able to afford her otherwise.

She stared across the room at the dwarf in the mirror, ignoring the distorted body and face to peer at the flawlessly arranged hair. Apricot Ice, the hairdresser had said. Carrot Puree, it looked like. William would have a fit, if he noticed at all. Sighing, she turned back to the desk.

Five unsealed envelopes lay in a fan on the polished wood before her. The sixth sheet of notepaper was beneath her hand:

Dearest Sophy . . .

Dearest Sophy, the Decline and Fall Club will meet in July this year, almost forty years of meetings—except for 1998, the year you went away. That year we didn't want to talk about your doing it, and we couldn't imagine talking about anything else, so we didn't hold the meeting at all. It was my year, but I just couldn't. None of us could.

Dear Sophy, I'm working very hard at do-gooding, but it's only so I won't feel so guilty. Every day I make myself eat, the way I promised you. I think of you all the time. Dearest Sophy, wish you were here.

She drew a heavy line through the last few words. She didn't wish Sophy were there. Sophy was there, so near as made no difference. Sophy wouldn't go away. Sometimes Bettiann would be sitting at the phone, talking to someone, a pencil in her hands, and when she hung up and looked down at the pad, there'd be words there, things Sophy might have said or written. Or when she woke up, there'd be lines on the pad on her bedside table, Sophy's thoughts, often argumentative, sometimes contradictory. Sophy was still giving her what for! After all these years.

Bettiann gathered up the sealed envelopes and tapped them into a neat pile. Invitations to the other five to dinner in Santa Fe, Bettiann's annual treat because Bettiann had money. Or William did. Pity Mom had drunk herself to death long before the denouement, after all those years of telling Bettiann what beauty pageants were for. Mom had always said they were a respectable way for girls to offer themselves, a respectable place to show the wares to possible producers or sponsors or husbands. Looky but no touchy, of course, not until after the modeling contract or the movie contract or the wedding ceremony.

Well, it had worked. William had seen her first in a beauty pageant. He'd been a judge. He'd presented her with the college scholarship, and he'd looked her up after she'd graduated. He'd had this kind of Pygmalion idea about himself, or this Galatea idea about her, one. And even though she'd known William had money, she'd thought she was marrying for love. She'd thought love would make it okay. She'd thought William could make a miracle. It wasn't until later she knew she wasn't, it hadn't, he couldn't. She flushed. No one could, not even damned Patrick and his promises. . . .

If Sophy hadn't gone, they'd be meeting in Vermont this year. She'd asked for the year 2000, back at the beginning, when they were girls. She'd wanted the millennium, but she hadn't stuck around to claim it. With Sophy gone they'd celebrate the millennium in Santa Fe, with Carolyn as host.

"Host" to rhyme with "ghost." Sometimes Bettiann would be so aware of the ghost that she'd actually look up, expecting her to appear. William even teased her about it.

"Who're you expecting, babe? You got a lover?"

"Why, William," Bettiann always said. "What a thing to ask!" William knew she didn't have a lover. William knew that's the last thing she'd ever have, or want. Even the idea of a lover made her sick to her stomach. She'd tried it once . . . well, twice. It hadn't worked either time.

Abruptly, she remembered Faye's voice, from long ago.

"Tell us something you really hate, Bettiann!" It was when they were in school, that night they'd all gotten squiffed at the party.

"I hate having people touch me," Bettiann had said, the words coming up like lava, superheated and uncontrolled.

Which wasn't enough, by itself. She had to tell them all of it; how her mom, who was an unmarried mom back when being an unmarried mom definitely wasn't okay, had entered Bettiann in a beautiful-baby contest when she was two, and how they had won fifty dollars.

"That was all it took," Bettiann had told them. "Fifty dollars was all it took to get her going!"

The first win hadn't quite paid for Bettiann's costumes. Second time out, when Bettiann was three, they won five hundred. By the time Bettiann was five, they were winning a thousand, two thousand, living on what she won, taking buses back and forth across the country, living in cheap motel rooms, meeting the other moms, going up against the same kids, time and again.

Polished Mary Janes and bobby socks. Petticoats and hair ribbons. Blond hair in ringlets. Mascara on the lashes over those blue, blue eyes. Cute sayings for the judges. *Half a sandwich is enough, Bettiann, you don't want to look pudgy.* Little songs and tap routines—military tap during the war. Tidi-rump dum dum, tidi-rump dum dum, tidi-rump dum dum dum didi didi dum, dressed in the toy-soldier outfit, the little wooden gun and the round rouge circles on her cheeks. *Sparkle, honey, sparkle. Don't eat so much, baby, you'll get fat!* White satin skirt and halter top with a stand-up collar. The collar had a treble clef and music notes sewn on in black braid. Little Miss Music, that one was. *No french fries, Bettiann. Just say to yourself, I'm not really hungry.* Green satin shorts and midriff tuxedo jacket with gold lapels and a gold-sequin bow tie. The shorts were too tight, and Mom said, *See, I told you, you eat too much. You can't get fat, baby. You've got to give the judges what they want.*

Funny that she couldn't remember the actual contests, only the tiny costumes, the worn little shoes, cracked black through the gold or silver paint, packed in tissue paper in boxes under Mom's bed where she'd found them after Mom had died. The costumes got more expensive the older she got. And the tap shoes. And the pain in her stomach that never seemed to go away. The doctors said it was nothing. After a while Mom quit taking her to doctors and just gave her Tums, but her stomach went on hurting and there wasn't any end to the contests, one pageant after another, one sparkle after another.

"Didn't you go to school?" Faye had asked. "How did you learn to read?"

She couldn't remember learning, all she could remember was doing it. She read everything. It all went in there, inside, all smooched up together, no reason or order at all, no sense of history or sequence, just everything. She couldn't add two and two, until one of the women they were traveling with took her in hand and taught her, all one summer, mile after mile. Bananas are three pounds for a dollar, how much change for two pounds from a buck? Sardines are eleven cents a can, how much for seven cans? Peanut butter is fifty-five a big jar, how much for four jars? And that's what they lived on mostly: sardines and peanut-butter-and-banana sandwiches made with day-old bread.

"The law caught up with us when I was eleven," Bettiann had told Ophy one night after lights out, lying in the companionable dark of their shared room. "I had to go to school, or the welfare would take me away. . . ."

So she went to school, feeling like a moron until suddenly all that reading fell into place. She knew more than most of them and knew how to get around adults more than any of them. Teachers weren't as tough as judges. They, too, responded to sparkle. School wasn't bad, except Mom started to drink. Not that she hadn't before, but not so much.

And that set the pattern for the future. Fall and winter and spring, school and Mom's drinking, and being on welfare. Not eating was easy on welfare. By the time Mom bought beer, there wasn't money left over for much else. Summertime and holidays they went on the road, with Mom more or less sober. And Bettiann, winning and winning and winning. She had that sparkle, that shine, even though Mom had to tell Bettiann how to flirt with the judges. Men liked that, Mom said. They liked little girls to flirt.

Bettiann hated it. Hated flirting, getting close. Even the MC's arm around her made her stomach crawl because there wasn't any Barbie-doll body under her clothes. On the outside she could pretend, but on the inside was only this wobbly ugliness, hidden under the costumes. The worst was when she was sixteen, the judge was young and good-looking, and the prize was five thousand, which they needed, and she tried to flirt with him, really tried. But when he caught her by the dressing room and grabbed her, held her, put his mouth on hers, it made her sick. She cried, and then threw up, and couldn't even go on with the contest.

"You have to stay with me, Mom," she'd cried. "You've got to stay with me. He caught me alone, back there, you've got to stay by me!"

"It's sort of a game with men," her mother had tried to tell her, angry and puzzled both at once. "He wasn't going to hurt you."

The word stuck in her head. Was it all just a game? Was that what she was doing, just playing a game? She decided to ask a man they all called Uncle Frank, Max Frank, a pageant organizer who went from state to state, setting up the contests. They all knew him. He knew them. He drank a little too much, but he was safe. After rehearsals were over one night, she waited until he'd had a couple of drinks in the bar; then she went in and sat down with him and asked him if the pageants were a game. She figured, if it was a game, maybe there were rules she should know. Maybe there was an easier way to do it!

"A game?" he repeated, the smoke from his cigarette making a veil between them, his voice slurred from the liquor. "Why, sure, I suppose. Kids like you, sixteen, seventeen, you bring us your yum-yum and we bank it just like money. You work for prizes—which don't cost us anything, the sponsors put those up—and when you get a little used up, we cut you out to make room for the new ones coming along with their yum-yum all shined up. So long as the yum-yum keeps coming, we win. I guess if you got a winner, you got a game."

"Somebody has to lose, though. Don't they?"

"Well, most of the girls lose, honey. You know that. You can only have one Miss Wisconsin Sausage."

That broke him up, but Bettiann didn't think it was funny. Right after that was when she began to obsess over everything. The costume. The makeup. The hair. The lights. If the costume was right and the makeup was right and the lights were right, she could pass long enough to get through the bathing-suit parade, which was the worst part, even though it was a total lie. Inside the suit, the lights, the makeup, her real self was there, hidden behind the sparkle of pretend. She was getting older, losing the yum-yum, the flab was there, the reality was there, and she was scared to death somebody would see it!

That's what she'd confessed to Ophy and only Ophy, there in the dark of their shared room at college, when telling secrets seemed safe. She couldn't bear to think about having sex, having some man look at her. . . .

"But you're beautiful, Bettiann. . . ."

"No. Not under the clothes."

"But I've seen you. You've got a great body. Not like me, all bones."

"No. You're not listening. You know what it's like? It's like I'm a kind of a jug with a flower in it. Everybody looks at the flower, so none of them see the jug. The jug is ugly, it's heavy and cracked, but so long as I hold that flower out there, nobody looks at the jug, right? That's the sparkle, you know. Men see that, the flower, and the rest of me is there, too, but so long as I keep them looking at the sparkle, they don't see it. . . ."

The last pageant was the summer she was seventeen, with a four-year scholarship as first prize, that or fifty thousand dollars. When she'd picked the scholarship instead of the cash, Mom had screamed at her for two solid weeks and had then gone seriously back into the bottle.

Bettiann wept to Ophy. "Mom says I'm only going to get married and have babies, I don't need an education, but suppose I don't! I'll be too old for the pageants soon. I can't go on doing contests. I hate it! I shouldn't give her my whole life, should I?"

"No," said Ophy in her firmest, most professional-sounding voice. "You shouldn't give her your whole life, Bettiann. You didn't make her start drinking. You're not responsible for that."

Basking in the sun of Ophy's acceptance, Bettiann had warmed to an almost self-approving glow. "It's all right. I'm here now. I don't have to do the bathing-suit parade ever again."

Which hadn't been quite true. She still did the parade, though now she wore couture clothes. She'd fooled Bill the same way she'd fooled the judges. She held the sparkle out there, and that's all he saw. Instead of the ramp-strut it was the bedroom-tango, with the filmy negligee and the teasing smile, and then, pray God, the lights out so she could quit worrying about what was under the expensive silk. But William, damn him, always wanted to do it with the lights on, and that made her freeze up, because even now, even after all these years, even with the makeup and the hairdo and the exercise class and the clothes, it was still the same body lurking under the fabric.

Who could compete? Who wanted to try anymore? If there could just be some honorable retirement! Some way to get out of it all. Sophy had told them that: "You need a way to stop! You need to become Baba Yagas and get out of it all."

Like all Sophy's advice, past tense. Past and gone. Sophy's car had been found in a lonely place, near a convenient bridge over a very deep lake. On the car seat was a letter from Bettiann. The state police had called her wanting to know how, and when, and why.

Who knew? They'd all asked why, except Aggie. Bettiann had wept and Faye had raged, and Jessamine and Ophy had wanted to hire detectives, and Carolyn had kept after the missing-persons people for at least a year. But not Aggie. Bettiann had assumed Aggie had reacted that way because of the mortal-sin thing Catholics had about suicide, but later she thought Aggie might know something the rest of them didn't. Aggie had been weird ever since the 1997 meeting in San Francisco.

"Maybe Sophy was tired of who she was," Faye had said. "Tired of being female."

"Aren't we all," Bettiann cried to her reflection in the hall mirror. "God, aren't we all!"

"Aren't we all what?" her husband asked, suddenly appearing in the mirror, a crescent-William bending inquisitively around her distorted image. He had come in silently, earlier than expected, letting himself in instead of ringing for Bemis.

"Sophy," she said, surprised into truth. "Sophy was tired of being female. So Faye said."

He came across the room to her, the easy stride, the impeccable suit, the dark hair becomingly grayed at the temples, success incarnate, all well groomed and charming except for a slightly troubled look. What could William possibly have to be troubled over? He hugged her, his hi-there-female-person hug, the one he used for her, and the cook, and his secretary, Maybelle. All of whom were women of a certain age who did their jobs very well.

"You said, 'Aren't we all?' " He gave her his full face, oh so handsome still, cleft-chinned, clear-eyed, sexy. Like those old movies of Cary Grant. Time was, after a few drinks, that look had set her aflame, all right. Get a few martinis down and a dark room, and it was like the Fourth of July.

"Aren't we all what?" he demanded.

She grunted, surprising herself at the unlovely sound. "Aren't we all tired of the trappings: Aerobics classes. Hair salon. Shopping. Whole days traipsing back and forth in high-heeled shoes. Fittings."

He stepped back, brows drawn together. "You'd rather not shop, maybe? You don't enjoy it?" Something edgy there.

"Enjoy it?" She laughed her melodious laugh, the one she'd worked on. (*Lower the pitch, Bettiann. Women must never sound shrill!*) "Shopping for women is like sports for men, William. Something to do when we have nothing important to do. It's a pastime. When I was in my twenties, I think I did enjoy it. Seeing the new styles. But now . . . I've seen them all. It's second time or third time around. Skirts up, skirts down. Lots of fabric, skimpy fabric. Bright colors, dull colors. And recently the clothes have been . . . ludicrous. Ridiculous. Like a dirty joke somebody's playing on women. Certainly not something I could wear to look nice for the next charity luncheon. Sometimes I wish . . ."

Now he had deep furrows between his brows. He pulled over a chair, sat down beside her.

"What do you wish?" he asked, seeming really to care.

"Wish I could let myself relax, like Carolyn."

"That's the old one," he said with faint disapproval. "The dumpy one."

"She's no older than I am. But she doesn't dye her hair, and she doesn't go to exercise class three times a week. She doesn't wear ridiculous clothes just because they're fashionable, or three-inch heels. She . . ."

His eyes narrowed. "You've always worn them. Even your bedroom slippers."

Suddenly, unaccountably, she was furious. "For God's sake, William! Women my age wear them, yes! And fashion models wear them! And if we wear them all the time, the tendons in our legs shrink so we can't put our heels down anymore. It's part of the whole . . . thing!"

He dropped her hand and sat back, face serious. "You're saying high heels and extreme fashions are a sign of an affluent . . . ah, decadent society?"

"No. I don't know what I'm saying, but that's not it."

"But you'd rather not be fashionable?" He was being patient, really wanting to know.

She shrugged uncomfortably. A wife didn't keep a husband by making him be patient, for God's sake. "I didn't mean to make a federal case of it. What I *really* meant was . . . Well, it would be nice to live in a world where women didn't expect to be uncomfortable just because they're female."

He looked at her, stared at her as though seeing her for the first time. She tried to read his face. What was he thinking? That it was her job to be fashionable? That he had her for that reason?

He wasn't looking at the sparkle!

What was he looking at?

5

THE PHONE RANG IN CAROLYN'S bedroom, early in the morning. She picked it up to hear an operator asking if she would take a collect call from Mrs. Shy-oh.

Mrs. Chaillot. It was what Helen Jagger called herself, an ironic code.

"I'll take it, operator." She heard a buzzing sound, someone swallowing painfully. "Is that you, Helen?"

"Yes." Laughter, a little hysterical, on the edge of control. "Who else but the madwoman."

"What's happened?"

"Not much. Just a frantic desire to hear a human voice. I've been thinking about Greta's little boys, and I got so sad. . . ."

"Helen. Your sister's out of it. Be thankful she's at peace."

"It's the children! She had to be out of her mind to leave them like that. What if I'm driven out of my mind, Carolyn? What if I think I can't stand it anymore. . . ?"

"I told you I'd pick you up anytime, day or night. I told you I'd bring you here to take you anywhere you wanted to go. You don't have to stay there."

"It's the children."

"I can put you in touch with a network, Helen. They hide mothers and children. We can arrange to have the kids picked up, you picked up, both at the same time."

"Oh, I've dreamed about that, Carolyn, but it wouldn't do any good. They're in special schools! Scott's attending the American Institute. Jake says it's for kids who need to be kept quite safe from any improper influences. He means me, of course. I don't know where the place is, or where Emily is. Even if I could find them, Jake would find us. He'd kill them. He's told me so."

Carolyn heaved a deep breath, silently beating her head against a symbolic wall. She'd been through all this before.

"He still won't let you answer the phone? He still checks the phone bill? He still doesn't let you have any money?"

"He won't let me use the phone, no. I'm calling from a public phone half a mile down the road. He calls home now and then, just to be sure I don't answer. The only money I find is what he leaves in his pockets, and even then I have to be careful because it might be bait. I found the money I used to call you under the cushion of his desk chair. I think he moved us out here just so every call would be long-distance! He figures I'm too proud to call you collect, as though I had any pride left. . . ."

"At least let me bring you some money. And a phone card. The bills will come here, he won't even know."

Long silence, then a sob. "All right. There's a stone lantern down at the entrance road, it has an arched opening on each side. Put some money in there, in the corner, where it doesn't show. Quarters, Carolyn, please. So I can at least get the operator. Bring me a bottle, too."

"Helen! You're not drinking?"

"Maybe one or two drinks a week. When things get . . . impossible."

"I'll do it tomorrow. Has he hurt you?"

Helen's voice took on a note of quavering pride. "He doesn't hit me. I know the rules. That's how I triumph, knowing the rules well enough not to get hit."

"He'll end up killing you."

The ghost of a chuckle. "I'm not afraid of dying, Carolyn. Like they say about seasickness: It's only the hope of dying that's keeping me alive."

The phone went dead. The line buzzed vacantly in Carolyn's ear, like a call to forever, waiting to go through. Sighing, she hung up the receiver, hauled herself off the bed, and stalked down the hall to the big bedroom. Hal was sitting against piled pillows, peering at a book.

"Hi," she breathed, crawling in beside him.

"Hi, yourself. To what do I owe the honor?"

"I'm miserable."

"Something on the phone? I heard a distant alarum, a clangor, a tocsin. . . ."

"Helen Jagger."

"Poor soul," he said solemnly, meaning it, gathering her up into his strong old arms and kissing her ear. "What has that bastard Jagger done now?"

"Nothing more than usual. You know, when I first met Helen and Greta, they were as independent and strong as any women I'd ever known. Jagger went after Helen like a terrier after a rat, but why she married him, I'll never know. And now Greta's dead and Helen's just limp, all the starch battered out of her. He doesn't even need to hit her, he just threatens to hurt the kids and she caves in. He's got them in some cult school, someplace like that compound in Waco. The American Institute?"

"An Alliance school? It probably would be like the Branch Davidians in terms of access, but it's bound to be one hell of a lot bigger."

"She doesn't even have family to turn to, and I can't help thinking part of it's my fault, Greta's death and all."

He hugged her again, saying chidingly, "It was a divorce case, Carolyn, plain and simple. We lawyers don't ordinarily walk into a courtroom expecting to confront Mr. Hyde."

"I should have been paying more attention."

"You couldn't have known in advance that Jagger was like that." Hal removed his glasses, laid them on the bedside table, and rubbed the bridge of his nose between his fingers. "There aren't many lawyers who will create evidence out of whole cloth in order to win. Even I didn't imagine he'd do that, and I had more reason to suspect him than you did." He extricated his arm from around her, restored his glasses, and swung his legs out of the bed. "Pity I'm not still with the Bureau. Maybe I could get him bumped off."

Carolyn plumped her pillow and settled herself. "Is that the proper word usage? Isn't it something about terminated with extreme prejudice?"

"That's more CIA, I think. Oh, hell, I was just an analyst. I was never into that stuff. I probably couldn't touch Jagger anyhow. Rumor is, Jagger is connected at the top. He's said to be a protégé of Webster's."

"Webster?" The name was familiar, but she couldn't place it.

He stood up and stretched, wincing when the muscles in his leg and back protested. "You saw him one time, love. Remember? First time we met. You in that adorable hat! When Albert was showing you through the Bureau, Webster was with the director."

"Oh, of course! The Alliance founder and head honcho."

"That's him. A man who's lately very cozy with the Vatican, according to Mike Winter. Also very cozy with several Arab states, serving as liaison among all of them."

"Liaison for what?"

"The Vatican wants the help of Islam in carrying out its agenda."

She sat up, glaring at him. "What agenda? When did this happen?"

"Has been happening. For years, sweetness."

She threw up her hands, her voice rising: "Stop calling me sweetness and explain what you're saying!"

He leaned against the bedpost, assuming a professorial expression. "The imams and the pope made common cause some years ago and have been supporting each other at population conferences and at status-of-women conferences ever since. Back in ninety-five, for instance, the pope and the Arab states moved together to prevent women's groups from attending a women's-rights conference in China. They didn't succeed, but they came close, and they've had better luck since. The Vatican has been acting with the Arab states to defeat population-control measures at the UN for ten years or more. And it was the Vatican acting with the Islamic states that defeated the UN women's educational effort in ninety-eight, the so-called women's-empowerment crusade. The imams don't want women empowered. It was Islamic terrorists who bombed the dormitories at Vassar and Wellesley, and the same men had previously blown up girls' schools in Pakistan and Egypt. They were brought into the country by a certain religious order—guess which one? *Capisce?*"

"Where did this come from?"

"I told you, Mike Winter. He tells me things."

"You don't tell me, evidently!"

"I thought you knew. Bits and pieces have been in the papers all through the nineties."

She knew that. She could remember the bits and pieces, but not this . . . this planned subversion. She shook her head, angry at herself. "I guess I didn't . . . connect it."

"Well, Mike found out about the connection to the Vassar-Wellesley bombings a few days ago. He got it from the Israelis, because our own intelligence people have been told to keep their nose out. Which doesn't surprise me."

"You're saying the FBI is on . . . on Webster's side."

"Well"—he made an equivocal gesture—"*comme ci, comme ça.* One of the difficulties of being the good guys is that even open societies have to have secret police, and secret police turn toward repression as a compass points north."

"And Jagger's one of the bad guys."

"He's an Alliance man." He leaned forward, stretching, rubbing at his injured leg, which itched. "Which raises the interesting question, are you considering our daughter's crazy request?"

She got up, annoyed, not at Hal's asking but at the subject itself. "Her asking me to defend the Dumpster mama? I've been diddling around, not saying yes or no. Stace finally called and jogged me. I'm going to see the accused today. Want to go with me?"

"Prisons do not greatly enliven my day."

"You could keep me company on the drive; you could read some more of whatever you're reading. . . ."

"I was rereading. Sophy's first book of *Women's Stories*."

"What got you onto that?"

"My talk with Mike. In the light of that conversation, Sophy's books have acquired a certain . . . ah, prophetic resonance. All these antiwoman factions getting together would have been her worst nightmare. I was wondering how she saw so much of that kind of thing thirty-five years ago? Did she go looking for it?"

Carolyn walked to the window, forehead furrowed, wishing this conversation were about something else. "Of course she went looking for it; it was what she wanted to know about."

"But, still, a woman, alone . . ."

"We used to say that. 'Sophy, you shouldn't go there, not alone!' I'd have been scared to death to go some of the places she went, but she'd just smile and set off without a qualm. Of course, she had one thing the rest of us lacked, and that was an almost supernatural facility for languages. She picked them up in days. She could take on local color, too, wherever she was, so as not to seem a stranger. If it meant wearing head-to-toe black wrappers, she'd do it."

"She sure had a nose for tragedy."

"It was more a nose for . . . "

"For what?"

"I'm trying to remember. She told me once she was looking for the basic imbalance. Something that was wrong, not natural."

"That's what I always thought about her."

"Sophy? That she was unbalanced?"

"No. That she wasn't . . . natural. You know, as a man, there's a kind of . . . oh, recognition signal you get from women, and I mean all women, even those who aren't interested in you in a sexual way. Maybe just a lifted eyebrow or a smile or a word said a certain way, whether they're eight or eighty. It's not a come-on. It's a sort of categorization, a mental filing. You know what I mean?"

"I suppose."

"Well, Sophy never filed me as a male. She accepted me, just as she did you, but for all she cared, we were both the same sex."

"How funny," she murmured, trying to adjust her image of Sophy to include what Hal had just said.

"Definitely odd," he emphasized, reaching for his cane. "Carolyn, dear love, if you will scramble me some eggs for breakfast, with some of that Jack cheese and some green chiles, please, I'll keep you company today."

"If your leg's well enough."

"The leg notwithstanding. That's part of the covenant—faithfulness, like a good dog." He grinned at her. "Me and old Hector."

"Both so well trained. Such good dogs." She gave him a hug, then rubbed his back and shoulders while he made appreciative noises. "Do come, Hal. I feel all sort of adrift. I don't really want to do this, but I'm afraid I'm getting sucked in. I hate it, I really do. I hated it quite badly enough before Helen called, and now I really hate it."

"What happened to Greta Wilson wasn't your fault," he said again.

"Dear old Halcyon, I know it wasn't, not really. But, damn, inside me somewhere it feels like it."

By ten o'clock they were well south of Santa Fe on the way to the New Detention Building, built three years before to replace the old prison. When Carolyn found a place to park that was shaded by the building, she asked, "Want to come inside?"

"I've seen it, thank you." He picked up his book and settled himself, winking at her. For an ex-law-enforcement type, he was protective of his perceptions, sometimes almost squeamish. Hal said you could see enough dirt without looking, so why go looking? She left him with a wave, forced her lagging footsteps to become a brisk walk as she went through to reception, then lost all her purposeful momentum outside the steel gate, where the guard behind the counter poked at a computer and peered nearsightedly at her HoloID.

"Lawyer?"

She nodded.

"You're not the lawyer I've got here."

"An attorney was appointed to handle her case. Ms. Ashaler has asked to see me. She has the right to an attorney of her own choosing."

The guard sneered, started to say something, then caught himself as another guard came into the space behind the counter.

"All carry-ins on the counter, please," he muttered.

She hoisted her briefcase onto the counter, opened it, let him look through her purse. No guns. No knives. No nail files that could be used as weapons. "Room G," he growled at her.

The gate opened with appropriately ominous noises. She thought people who designed prisons must have manuals specifying suitable noises: echoey, metallic resonance; deadened thump of footsteps. The corridor she walked along was a case in point: a threatening, blind people-pipe, with anonymous metal doors opening at either side. On her left, centered in a newly painted stretch of wall, stood a wire glass double door, high and wide, the thick glass only slightly obscuring the view into the room beyond, where cells had once been stacked three high around an open light well. The sign on the door now said VAULTS—AUTHORIZED PERSONNEL ONLY.

Behind her someone cleared his throat.

"Ms. Crespin? Carolyn?"

She turned to confront a familiar face, a guard she'd frequently encountered in her lawyering days. "Josh! What are you doing here?"

"Transferred out here from the old jail. You wanna see the cold storage?"

She looked around herself, almost furtively. "Would it get you in trouble?"

"Nah. Kinfolk come here all the time. Another year or two, they'll be taking kids through here on field trips from school. Only reason they have guards is they're worried about the crazies, turning off the pods, you know."

She did know. There had been a lot of wild talk from the civil libertarians who had protested that deactivation and hibernation came within the meaning of cruel and unusual punishment. The facts seemed to indicate otherwise. There was no prison rape of those sentenced to being STOPPED— that is, deactivated—or those sentenced to being SLEPT—hibernated. There was no cruelty from guards or other inmates. There was no education in more efficient criminality. There was no brutalizing. There were no escapes. Prisoners did get older, of course. Joints stiffened and skin wrinkled, hair receded and turned gray, just as though the sleeper had been up and about. Chronic health conditions didn't change. It was not a reprieve; one lost the same chunk of one's life one would have lost in prison, but when the sentence was over, one was at least mentally and psychologically undamaged . . . well, unchanged. Older but no wiser, shrieked the libertarians. Older, but otherwise no worse off, said the courts. Plus, the psychologists murmured, testosterone levels would drop as sleepers aged, making them less likely to be troublesome in the future.

Josh held the door open for her, and after another quick look around, she went through into an area that felt momentarily familiar. It couldn't be familiar. She'd never been in this room. She had, however, seen pictures. She'd seen documentaries. She wasn't surprised by the ranked tanks, or pods, hundreds of them, aisles and decks of them. She found herself counting, estimating. The room was between two and three hundred feet long, separated horizontally into three decks by heavy expanded metal flooring. On each deck the pods were stacked three high, with three aisles separating two double stacks and two single stacks against the sidewalls. Five or six thousand pods, give or take, each pod occupying about a tenth of the cubic feet a jail prisoner would have needed. Each pod was labeled with the name and age of the inhabitant, the crime of which he'd been convicted, the date of release. Each held a steadily glowing green light and a digital clock, counting down the years, months, days. They'd been tanking people for how long? The research had been secret; it had been going on for years but was announced only in ninety-seven. The government made the manufacture of hardware a top priority that same year, with federal loans for conversion of the prison systems. The defense industry switched from tanks and planes to pods, saying thankful prayers under its breath, and a new federal law allowed people sentenced to more than two years under the old penalties to be SLEPT instead of imprisoned. A little less than two years, they'd been tanking people. So many of them, in such a short time!

She was surprised by the sound and the smell. It was damp in the room. She stepped closer to the right-hand rank, peering through a faceplate at the sleeper within. Young. God, so young. Sallow skin. Eyes closed, lashes fringing the cheekbones. Mouth relaxed, calm. *Violent crimes against children*, said the label. Twenty-five years. Release date, FAT, February 25, 2025.

"FAT?" she asked.

"For approved treatment. If there is one. By then."

"A treatment for what?"

"For whatever made him choke those two little girls and then rape them."

"And if there isn't a treatment?"

"He stays here until there is a treatment or the green light goes off, whichever comes first."

"The light goes out if they die?"

"Right. This don't keep them young, it just keeps them going."

She wandered down the line of pods. Fully half bore the letters. FAT. Why hadn't she known about FAT? Or had she? Known about it and forgotten it, purposefully.

She turned back, on the other side of the aisle. These cubicles were shorter, just big enough for a person reclining in a rocking frame. Monitors were fastened to head, belly, arms. A tube snaked from a gauge and disappeared into the mouth. From the neck down the body was concealed beneath a light rigid covering, but one could see the tubes that ran from beneath it. Eyes stared straight ahead, but not a muscle moved.

"These pods are for the ones who are STOPPED?"

"The manual calls it 'penitential deactivation.' The pods are a little bigger, because they're still being fed. They shit. That's what the smell is. The sprays go on twice a day to wash 'em down."

She noticed it for the first time, a slightly feculent stench under the resinous cover-up. "Can they see us?" Carolyn whispered, feeling goose bumps popping out on her arms, switching briefcase from hand to hand to rub them vigorously. The place was horrid; nightmarish, but hideously personal; intimately awful. "The ones who're STOPPED, can they see us?"

"The ones facing us can. They can see, hear, taste—or could if anybody fed them anything except through that tube. They just sit there, STOPPED. Nobody's got the antidote but the Department of Prisons, and they don't come up with the dose till the sentence is up."

"How in hell did anyone ever come up with something like this!" she snarled, knowing full well how.

He took it as genuine curiosity. "It was accidental. Some guy out in California was makin' designer drugs, you know, and he made a mistake, put a atom in the wrong place or something. Some people took the drug, and they turned off. Like Parkinson's disease, only worse. Some doctor used L-dopa on 'em, they woke up. Only trouble, the cure didn't last. They all ended up turned off again. So when some government scientists found the cure in ninety-seven, the government took all the rights to the drug and the cure. It's a hell of a lot cheaper than keeping them in cells, and you don't get no riots, no rapes, no guys gettin' a shank in the ribs on their way to dinner."

"Why both? Both the tanks and this?"

"Oh, this is short-term. Anything from thirty days up to a year. SLEEP? That don't rehabilitate anybody, nobody claims it does, but STOP? Now, that might do some rehabilitation. I tell you the truth, it'd sure as hell rehabilitate me!"

She turned away from him, fighting panic. "Josh, do they come out sane?"

"I've only seen a few," he admitted. "They seemed all right. Course, they were short-termers. Not more'n a year."

"So we don't know about the long-termers."

"STOP's only for short-termers. And the long-termers won't be my worry. All the SLEEP ones for ten years or more, they get moved to that row over there against the wall." He pointed to an area beside an open overhead door, with a forklift parked beyond it. "Whenever there's a truckload, I haul 'em down to those tunnels near Carlsbad. The ones they dug for nuclear waste."

"The Waste Impoundment Pilot Program? WIPP?"

"WIPP, yeah. Only they never got around to puttin' waste in much of it. So we use 'em for people storage instead. Lotta space down there; might as well use it for something."

She shook her head, depressed.

He said, "Hey. Don't look so down. If they're guilty, it's better, honestly. The young ones, they don't get raped. They don't get beat on. And I don't have to do any beating. It's better for both of us."

"They don't feel anything," she cried, surprising herself. "Not anything!"

He shrugged. "What would they feel? People who do stuff like that?" He ran his hand across the label she had read. Violence against children. "This guy was only happy when he was rapin' some six-year-old baby he'd just strangled. You want him to go on feelin' that? Maybe better he's not feelin'."

She felt the walls closing in, felt a swirling, unfocused anger, stopped short, took a deep breath. "You're right, Josh."

He let her out the door. "You know those old fairy stories about ogres, Carolyn? There's lots of true stuff in old stories like that. Ogres are true. That's one there, in that box. Looks like a nice kid, but it's really an ogre. Born that way."

She almost stopped, stunned at his words, reaching for a mental association that wouldn't come.

He patted her clumsily on the shoulder. "You always wanted people better than they are. You always did. Always surprised you when they turned out bad."

He patted her once more, then wandered back into the room, humming under his breath. She mechanically turned the other direction, searching for the door marked G, finding it only a few steps farther on. She paused outside the door, almost leaning on it. Ogres. Like Jagger. And that room, with all the pods in it. When she'd entered the room, she'd had a weird sort of déjà vu, as though she'd seen it before, and she knew she hadn't.

She shook her head, bringing herself out of paralysis. The thought of Jagger did it, like a snake hypnotizing a bird. Maybe he counted on that. The freezing power of absolute dread and frustrated fury. She goaded herself, making herself move.

Beyond the door was a mere closet, little or no improvement on the hallway, a plastic-covered cell of some indeterminate shade between cream and taupe, with a bolted-down table and light plastic chairs, unsuitable for use as ad hoc weapons and probably chosen for that reason. The only variation in texture came from outside the streaked window where a metal grill broke the slanting sun into rough diamonds across the table and floor.

Carolyn put her briefcase on the table, took out a package of chewing gum, a legal pad, and a fiber-tipped pen. Her small purse went into the

briefcase, which she locked and set on the table. The voice-activated microphone built into the case would record whatever went on. The pad and pen
were for show. At one time she'd brought cigarettes, but this place, like all
others, had become no-smoking territory. Now she offered gum. It was a way
of making contact, of breaking through the inevitable suspicion. Not that it
always helped. Sometimes nothing helped.

The door opened and a stumbling figure was propelled into the room.
Carolyn caught only a glimpse of the wardress's thrusting arm and scowling
face before the door swung shut once more. The girl stayed where she was,
swaying, head hanging, arms protectively wrapped across her chest, hands
clamped in her armpits.

"Lolly Ashaler?" Carolyn asked.

The girl snuffled but did not reply.

Carolyn rose, went around the table, pulled out the other chair, and
took hold of the girl's upper arm. The skin quivered beneath her hand, like
that of a whipped dog. Sheep got like that when they'd been chased by dogs,
slashed at by teeth. They stood and quivered, waiting to die.

Carolyn stopped gripping, patted instead, little pushes that guided the
girl toward the chair and into it. She seemed not so much reluctant as inert.
Patted at, she moved. Patted on, she sat, her dull eyes fixed on the tabletop.

Carolyn sat opposite her and waited. The girl slumped, making no effort
to meet her eyes, the slime-green jail-issue shirt rumpling shapelessly around
her, the not-quite-matching trousers sagging around her ankles.

"Lolly?"

No response.

"I'm here to help you, Lolly. I can't do it unless you talk to me."

The words came all at once, a single spurt, like vomit. " 'Fyou wanna
he'p me, lemme the fuck alone."

Carolyn spidered one hand atop her head, fingering her scalp, fighting
the urge to snarl, to curse, to get up and leave without another word. Her jaw
had been set ever since she'd entered the building. Now she felt the familiar
pain in her ears from the rope-hard muscles. She'd fought it every step getting
here, her scalp tensing and pulling like rawhide drying. Now her head was a
drumhead, throbbing with every word the girl spoke. Damn it, she had left all
this! She had stopped dealing with all this! For the love of heaven, what was
she doing here?

She heard her own teeth grinding and stopped, appalled. Anger was a
defense. There was nothing here in this room, at this moment, to defend
against. There were ways to relax, ways to control panic and rage. It could be
done. If one really wanted to do it.

"Sorry," she breathed, concentrating on the flow of air: one slow breath
in, one slow breath out. Another one, in and out, and another yet while

deciding what to say. "I'm sorry, Lolly. I can't make them leave you alone. I can try to get you out of here if you talk to me. Or I can go away. I'm only here because my daughter asked me to come."

The girl's eyes flicked toward her. "She the one with the doctor?"

"That's right. She talked to you, and you told the guard you wanted to see me. That's why I'm here."

Silence. Then: "Her. The redheaded one."

Carolyn breathed. "Yes. The redheaded one."

"She knows."

Carolyn let out the last of the breath and folded her hands on the legal pad, careful not to clench them. "What is it she knows, Lolly?"

"She knows what I was tryinna say. That doctor don't know shit. Din' even let me talk!"

"Tell me. Maybe I don't know shit, either, but I'll listen."

Carolyn waited, watching. The girl shook her head, so strongly that her lips flapped with the motion, a comic look, chimpanzee lips. Her nose was a mere lump, reddened at the end. Ms. Potato Head, Carolyn thought. Nothing strong, nothing angular, not the nose, not the jaw, not the brow. A wholly forgettable face surrounded by an uncombed mess of pale-brown hair. The girl's skin was her best feature, pale, thick, and flawless, though unnaturally yellow. It could be genetic, but perhaps she had jaundice. Perhaps she had hepatitis. Carolyn took up the pen, wrote "jaundice?," looked up once more. The girl's eyes were fixed on the pen, suddenly narrowed. It bothered her to have things written about her.

"Tell me," Carolyn urged again, putting the pen down.

The girl's head came up. She looked through Carolyn, speaking to the wall. "I dowanit wrote down."

"All right. I won't write it down."

"The Fourtha July."

"What about it?"

"When they did it. To me. It was the Fourtha July, and they all had firecrackers and they was puttin' 'em in cans and throwin' 'em in windows and stuff. And I wen' out and said, hey don't throw that stuff in here."

"They were doing it? They who?"

"Those boys. And one of 'em says come on, Lolly, we got some beer."

"They knew your name?"

"Sure. They live there, where I live. I know 'em."

"Can you tell me their names?"

"Henry B., he's sort of my cousin. And the one he calls Crank. And Crank's brother."

"Three boys?"

"No." She frowned in the effort at recollection. "More than that. Som-

mathem Messicans was there. Geel-bert, he was there. And Hay-soos. All
those Messicans, they live down the block."

"Mexicans?"

"Don' speak English yet, you know."

"How old are these boys?"

"Geelbert, he's ony a kid. Haysoos, he's maybe nineteen or twenny, I
guess. Him an Henry B. Crank's as old as me."

"How old are you?"

"Fifteen. Las' month."

"So you were fourteen when you went with the boys. Where did you
go?"

"I said where we goin', and they said they got beer hid. An I said you
sure hid it far enough, and they said it was hid inna alley. So we got to kinda
the alley place, behind some stores. And first they said they had beer, and
then they said they din' have no beer, they had this firecracker they was gonna
put up me and light it on fire so it'd go off, and Hay-soos says sure they do,
they all got firecrackers like that."

A long silence. Carolyn breathed and breathed, searching the face opposite her own. Nothing. Only a leak of tears, a slow seep, unconsidered, perhaps
unfelt.

"What happened?"

"Henry B., he got me on that old mattress and they was all over me, and
they was shoving things in me, and Hay-soos, he was yellin', and one of 'em
put his hand over my face, and I couldn' breathe. . . ."

Carolyn reached for the pen, remembered, put it back down, stared out
through dirty glass and metal grill toward the sky, lost in sun-dazzle, not
looking at the girl. She couldn't look at the girl.

"They raped you? All of them?"

"I dunno. Maybe. I couldn' hardly breathe, and ever'thin' went kind of
red, and Hay-soos kep' yellin'."

Carolyn tapped the pad thoughtfully, a slow thrum of fingers. Silence
was the usual concomitant of rape. Silence, secrecy, the knife at the throat,
the threat, don't yell or I'll kill you. Perhaps gang rapes were different, particularly if the participants were not afraid of discovery. "What was he yelling?"

"He was goin', 'Lookit me, I'm doin' it.' Or maybe that was Crank. I
dunno."

"So he was raping you?"

"I dunno which one. Maybe it was all of 'em. But one of 'em was
yellin'."

"Then what?"

"I dunno what! Ever'thing was red an' black an' it hurt. They wen' away, an' it got dark. An' I was there, an' it was dark, and there was this thing hurtin' me, an' I pulled it out."

"What was it?"

"A bottle. Some old wino's empy bottle, all bloody. Blood all over my—" She stopped, searching for a word nicer than the word she'd been about to use.

"On your body," Carolyn said firmly. "Between your legs."

A sniffle of agreement. "I felt around for my panties, and I found 'em, but they was ripped all up, so I threw 'em away. An' I went home."

"Did you tell anyone what happened?"

"Tell who? My mom wasn't there. An' her boyfriend, he wasn't there. An' I went over to my grandma's house, but she was gone to the hospital. An' when I got back, Henry B., he was there, and he went like mean, and he said if I told, he'd kill me, or Hay-soos, he'd kill me, and he put his face right in my face an' his hands on my neck. . . ."

"So. You decided not to tell anyone."

"Henry B., he goes mean like a snake. He kills folks. He does drive-bys, you know, for kicks. He says he gonna kill me, he prob'ly will. He says forget it, so I do. It didn' hurt too long. But I didn' get my period, you know, an' I thought it was because I was bleedin' so much when they did it. . . ."

"When did you find out you were pregnant?"

"I started to get all, you know, throwin' up all the time. There's a woman lives downstairs, she said I was pregnant."

"You didn't know until she told you? What about your mother? Didn't she know something was wrong?"

"Yeah, well. She don' notice much."

"So you didn't know, and your mother didn't know, but the woman who lives downstairs told you you were pregnant."

"And then I stopped throwin' up, so I thought maybe it was all okay, an' I forgot about it. But then I got the pains, an' all this water came out, an' I took the paper towels to wipe me, an' I went back there, to the alley where they did it to me."

Carolyn looked at the girl, puzzled. Why there?

"The mattress was there. Nobody was there, an' it was a place I could lie down an' I didn' wan' anybody hearin' me yell. Because if they heard me, maybe they'd take me, an' maybe I'd say something, an' then Henry B., he'd find out. An' the pain just came and came and came, an' after a while the stuff came out of me. An' then more stuff came out. An' I just wrapped it all in the paper an' put it in the Dumpster. An' I put a wad of the paper in my pants, because I just kept bleedin' and bleedin', after all that time not . . ."

Carolyn raised her eyes. "Did you know it was a baby, Lolly?"

"It was all bloody mess. A blobby thing. Not like a real baby."

"What do you mean, not like a real baby?"

"Not . . . you know. Like a baby. Pampers an' little shoes. All that."

Carolyn took another breath. Slowly. "You didn't expect a baby just born to have Pampers on, did you?"

"I'm not stupid," she snarled. "But they'd be there, wouldn' they? If somebody has a real baby, they have the stuff, don' they? You can't have a real baby without the stuff for it. How's it gonna grow up without the stuff?"

Carolyn found her hand atop her head again, stroking, massaging, amazed at the pertinency of this. If someone planned a baby, they had the stuff. "Who told you that, Lolly? Your mom?"

A snort in reply.

"Your grandmother, maybe?"

"She died!" It was an accusation.

"I'm sorry. Did she tell you that before she died?"

No answer. A sullen silence, all the words used up, all the anger spent. Well, she had told what she had to tell. Later one would have to ask if she'd had sex before. Later one would have to ask if she knew about birth control. Later one would have to know why she really went with the boys, what had been in her mind. Loneliness, perhaps. Desire to be liked. Flattered to be asked. It didn't matter right now.

"Lolly, listen to me. This is important."

A sullen look.

"Don't talk to anyone about what happened. Don't talk to the police about it, or the people here at the jail. Don't talk to the lawyer the court appointed. Don't talk to anyone except me about it. No matter what they say, you just tell them talk to Carolyn Crespin, she's my lawyer. No matter what they promise you. Understand?"

"You gonna get me out?"

"I'll do what I can. If you don't talk to anyone but me."

Another sullen look, but no disagreement. Carolyn pushed the packet of gum across the table, opened the briefcase, restored her pad and pencils, flicking off the recorder in the process, took out her purse, and put the strap across her shoulder. "What will you say to them?"

"Talk to my lawyer, Carolyn Crespin."

"That's right. And don't talk to any of the other women in here, either. They may be snitches. If someone else says he's your lawyer, tell him no, he's not. Ms. Crespin's your lawyer. Don't let them get a word out of you but that. I'll see you soon."

The wardress was slouched against the wall outside, smoking a forbidden cigarette and regarding Carolyn with complacent contempt. "Report me," the look said. "See what happens to your client then."

Carolyn took no notice. This wasn't the place, and the woman was only doing her job as she saw it, which was first to survive and second not to get injured too much in the process. And there were good guards like Josh, people old enough to have outworn their ideals without compromising their ethics, ones who had reached a credible detente between using and withholding force. She'd met good cops and good district attorneys, though too many were like Jake Jagger, courting power far more passionately than they courted justice.

Who would it be in the Ashaler case? Surely not Jagger himself. Not unless he thought he could get some media exposure out of it. Which he could if he played into the fears, hates, and resentments of the voting public. Jagger didn't give a shit for justice, but he was in love with publicity. Still, for a case like this it would probably be Assistant DA Emmet Swinter.

Speak of the devil. A minor demon, at least. Emmet Swinter himself, standing at the reception desk and leaning toward another man in intimate converse. The other man caught sight of her, turned from the counter, and came at her with his head thrust forward, like an attacking animal. His eyebrows squirmed like tortured caterpillars over bloodshot eyes, and she remembered his name: Vince Harmston. Stace's mentioning the Army of God should have told her who he was.

"You're Carolyn Crespin." It wasn't a question.

She nodded, breathing in very slowly, concentrating on the breathing.

"What the hell you think you're doing interfering with my client." It wasn't a question. He bristled with antagonism and self-righteous fervor.

Carolyn made herself take a deep breath before she replied, made her voice stay low and level though she wanted to scream at him. "She didn't hire you, Mr. Harmston. You were appointed to defend her, but she's chosen to have me represent her instead. She has that privilege."

He turned an angry red. "You shouldn't tangle with me, counselor. I can keep pickets outside your house twenty-four hours a day. Tell all your neighbors what kinda person you are!"

Her eyebrows went up in actual surprise. "What kind of person am I?"

"We both know the answer to that question," he sneered. "Emmet says your relative there in Washington told him all about you, you . . . subversive!" He turned to stamp away from her, charging the computer-operated door with such vehemence he almost collided with it.

Carolyn fought off the momentary blankness, the responsive fury his words had caused. So Albert Crespin, damned Cousin Albert, was still at it! She turned and stared pointedly at the guard, who looked quickly away, feigning interest in his paperwork. Emmet Swinter had disappeared. Both men showing up here at the same time probably wasn't coincidence. She'd bet anything the guard had been told to let the DA's office know if anybody showed an interest in Lolly Ashaler.

Which didn't explain Swinter's being in touch with Cousin Albert. Or vice versa. Did the DA's office intend to make a circus out of this case? She shook her head at herself, full of old, familiar emotions: fire in the belly, acid in the throat, heat across the head, muscles tight, adrenals pumping, rage running through her veins instead of blood. The knot in her chest that frightened her, that shut off her breath and seemed ready to stop her heart.

Now, now, here she was, jumping the gun, as Hal would have said. She wasn't even sure the DA's office had definitely decided to prosecute Lolly Ashaler. What had their tame psychologist told them?

She went out into the sun once more, spotted the car with Hal's bulky silhouette in the front seat, head down, either dozing or still occupied with Sophy's stories. Hal was seventy-three, and for the last two or three years he'd been in the habit of these little catnaps. Still, aside from the broken leg, he was hearty and hale. Maybe he'd have some idea, some strategy, some good sense where Carolyn herself could find, at the moment, only pity and dismay, added to that kernel of terror that was associated, somehow, with that room full of pods. She, normally among the most skeptical of women, had actually perceived it as an omen.

6

LATE AFTERNOON IN SALT LAKE City. The California Memorial Labs basked whitely in the glow of a cloudless sky. Inside, on the second floor, Jessamine Iolantha Ortiz-Oneil, M.S., Ph.D. fished a key from her pocket and unlocked one side of a large double door. The sound of the latch was almost inaudible, but by the time she pushed the door open, the apes were boiling through the far wall into the inside cages, gibbering, howling, ha-ha-hoo-hoo.

She signed a greeting. "Good afternoon, children." She closed and locked the door behind her before walking between the two large community cages toward the windowed west wall, where enclosed gangways overhead gave access to the huge tree-filled compounds in which the apes spent most of their time. As she approached the tall window at the end of the aisle, dozens of pairs of eyes watched her eagerly, quieting abruptly when she stopped to stare out into the sun-dazzle, pretending she didn't notice them. To her left were the refrigerator, the food cupboards, the sinks and counters, all gleaming in stainless steel. Every ape in the room was familiar with this routine.

"Ach-a-a-a-a," said Don Juan from his place in the pygmy-chimp cage. His tone said clearly, "Don't mess around."

She turned and signed to them. "Fruit," she said. "You want some?"

A cacophony of acquiescence, bonobos on one side going hoo-hah, sia-mangs on the other howling and leaping. There were bananas, apples, and oranges in the cooler along with a huge sack of Mexican mangoes. Jessamine spilled a selection into a basket and carried it back past the cages, offering treats to all and sundry. Priapus and Don Juan, the two largest males, were not at all shy. They not only accepted the fruit she gave them but grabbed for the basket as well.

"Grabby," she chided them in signs, mimicking their toothy grimaces. "You guys act like monkeys, huh?"

Priapus cocked his head at her, a habit of his, as though he were deciding what to say in reply. He gripped his mango tightly in one foot to free his hands, placed his right thumb under his chin and drew it forward, tickled his ribs, stroked his penis. "Not monkey, Priapus." He did the ribs again, then gestured toward the opposite cage. "Monkey there."

Jessamine made the monkey sign, pointed at Priapus, laughed, and Priapus laughed with her, pointing back at her, lips pulled back to make a fangy grin. You're a monkey. All the apes in this compound had been raised on sign language, a small vocabulary stringently taught and uniformly required from all handlers in lieu of speech. One-to-one sign teaching had never gone very far, but there had turned out to be an interesting synergy when a whole group was raised from infancy on signs. They even signed to one another, though not anything past the babble stage. Their interests seemed to be restricted to food and petting, and perhaps intragroup status, though they had no signs for that. Two words in a string was about it, except for Priapus, who occasionally surprised her.

Don Juan concentrated on his banana, pretending she didn't exist. If she turned her back, he'd reach through the bars like lightning and grab her hair or shoulder. He'd never bitten her, but he liked to make her think he would. Sometimes he looked at her from the back of the cage, tapping his lip with finger and thumb, the sign for delicious. Val and Pinto thought it was funny. Jessamine wasn't so sure. He hadn't done it lately, so maybe he didn't consider her tasty anymore.

The siamangs were in a way noisier and more active, but at the same time more orderly and polite. They each waited a turn, then retreated to their special perches, couples affectionately huddled, singles in small groups. Bottom, one of the older youngsters, stayed at the front of the cage, sticking his arm through and begging for more. Jessamine tickled him, and he leaped away across the cage floor, giggling to himself, a dry sound, like the rubbing of leaves together. The siamangs were monogamous, so they didn't need the constant sexual social negotiations and reinforcements that took up so much of the bonobos' time. Bonobos, the so-called pygmy chimps, shared sex in total promiscuity, using it to reinforce social bonding. Oridinary chimps had sexual attitudes more comparable to human ones: alpha males mated with whomever they wished while trying to keep other males from getting any at all; females and subordinate males sneaked around; every tribe member bounced uneasily between biology and social position.

Lily, one of the new mothers among the bonobos, sat in the corner against the bars with her infant, and when Jessamine offered her a mango, she reached through the bars to take Jessamine's hand instead, peering up at her with a look of pain, or perhaps longing.

"What is it, sweetheart?"

Pulling her hand between the bars, laying it on the infant, pressing it to her own lips. Lily. And that look again. Which might mean help me, see me, talk to me.

"I see you," Jessamine signed, her first and second fingers moving outward from her eyes. "I see you, Lily. I see Lily's baby." A rocking motion for baby.

And the hand again, pulling her hand through the bars to touch the baby. Then the right hand coming out, circling, coming back. And the eyes again, looking out, through the bars, at the bars as though to say, Take me with you.

What was it? Lily knew how to sign, though she wasn't as good at it as some of the others. Still, she knew the signs for food and drink and warmth and feeling sick and baby and a dozen other things. "What, Lily?"

Only the eyes and that circling hand, as though she said, Oh, take me with you, I am weary of this place. As though someone were trapped in there. Inexplicably, Sophy's face was there, superimposed over the chimpanzee features, Sophy's eyes over those other eyes.

Time stopped. Breathing stopped. Her eyes blinked shut and stayed that way, shutting it out. She shuddered, forced herself to look. Nothing. Not Sophy caged. Not Sophy behind bars. Just Lily and the baby. Jessamine turned away. This had happened before, and it was ridiculous. Nonetheless she waited for the usual concomitant. It came, a sound barely heard, as though a door had shut somewhere. A metal door, she thought. A clang, only so soft that she didn't know if she'd really heard it or imagined it. Stupid. She was doing this to herself, fantasizing all kinds of things. How silly. How ridiculous. She needed more sleep and less aggravation.

Lily called to her, but she didn't turn back. Instead she left the empty basket at the cross aisle that led behind the chimp cages to the lab and let herself through the locked metal grill.

Inside she saw her co-worker, Val Iwasaki, bent over his computer terminal like a concert pianist concentrating on fingering. He had beautiful hands and an interesting face, a mixed face, rather like her own, and a solid, muscular body hunched over the console where he was working on primate-canid genetic comparisons, their current project, one that had occupied them for the last couple of years.

He turned to wave hello. "How were the meetings?"

"Dull. A waste of time." She glanced at her watch. "From nine to three, six totally wasted hours. Even the lunch was lousy."

"Did you run the blockade getting here?"

"What blockade?"

"The mob in the mall. I ran into them when I came back from lunch, marching and chanting."

"I didn't come that way. What was going on?"

"One of the Army of God bunches was chasing women out of the mall, using switches on the ones with bare legs, telling them to go home and take care of their kids. God's Faithful, I think they called themselves."

"You're kidding! Where were the police?"

"Watching from a distance in case some militant female tried to fight back."

"At least they're not shooting the women, like in New York," said Jessamine, looking ruefully at her own bare legs. "Or blowing up colleges."

"Probably not," Val replied with a quick sideways grin.

"By the way, Val. Have you noticed anything strange about Lily lately?"

"Not Lily particularly. They've all been a little weird. You know all that touching and stroking and screwing that goes on constantly among the bonobos, all that keeping peace and negotiating relationships? Well, lately they haven't, or not so much. And Don Juan's been moody."

"More than usual?"

"A lot more. A lot of strange masturbatory behavior. I see him sitting in the corner, facing the corner, examining himself."

"Is he in pain? You think . . . what? Some disease?"

"I don't know. I asked Pinto to sedate him next week, so we can get a blood sample and run some tests." He leaned back, stretching. "I picked up a couple of short matches this morning. Bonobo-wolf. Outside the CoTAM list." The CoTAM list included genetic material *Common To All Mammals*, the base blueprint, as it were, for mammalian construction. DNA matches outside that list were particularly interesting in that they sometimes spelled out characteristics of specific species.

"Don't hope too much," Jessamine said distractedly. She stretched, running her hands across the glossy cap of her hair, smoothing it, twisting her shoulders to settle her twitchy arms. "They can be disappointing. I found a wonderful siamang-wolf match the spring of ninety-seven, before you joined us. We had a guy doing some consulting with us, and between consults he was working on a canid project he and some colleagues had dreamed up back in ninety-three, ninety-four."

"Dogs?" He looked up. "What was that?"

"The theory behind it was that dogs have been bred for special characteristics for so long that it should be possible to find the genes for specific characteristics. Like, what's the DNA for loyalty? Or where's the shepherding gene? As I recall, they derived basic canid genomes from both wolves and cur dogs. Then they matched specific breeds against those bases to find the variations.

"My people, meantime, had been working on a problem of siamang reproductive failure—which we solved, by the way—and in the process we'd transliterated a lot of siamang DNA. I thought since the canid project claimed to be having some luck translating genetic sequences into actual behavioral traits, I'd see if any of their wolf sequences matched siamang ones. It wouldn't be any Rosetta stone, but at least it might give us a clue as to what some of the siamang DNA actually does.

"So we ran the wolf sequence against our key siamang; then we eliminated the CoTAM and concentrated on what was left over. Theoretically, the leftovers should have been DNA that wolves and siamangs shared, but that some other mammals didn't. Bingo. We came up with a long DNA sequence shared by siamangs and wolves but not by all other mammals. It was like I'd gone to look for a needle in a haystack and had sat down on it! The whole cross-species project was new then. I was so excited." So excited she'd burbled all about it at the DFC meeting, waving her discovery at them, thoroughly confusing them all. She smiled reminiscently.

"What significance did the sequence have? What did it control?" Val prodded.

She came back to herself. "That's what we wanted to know. I talked to the man doing the dog studies; he said the matching sequence was part of the nose-brain research they'd done trying to find the genetic difference between sight hounds and scent hounds—greyhounds and bloodhounds. He thought maybe my siamang-wolf DNA had to do with the development of the accessory olfactory bulb—"

"Pardon me?"

"It's a little structure in animal brains. It's connected to another little organ in the nose, the vomeronasal organ, which is what they detect pheromones with. Anyhow, I thought whoop-de-do, siamangs and wolves have this same gene, does the gene do the same thing in both? Does it control the same behavior? And does this same gene also exist in pygmy chimps? So I ran the sequence against what we had at that time on the bonobos."

"And?"

"Lo and behold, the program came up with two fairly long partial matches, and when we looked more closely, they turned out to be the two ends of the long siamang-wolf sequence."

"Wait a minute." He turned from his console, brow furrowed. "You had a siamang sequence that matched a wolf sequence. Call that ABC—"

"No. Call the siamang-wolf sequence A-BBBB-C and call the chimp sequence A-XXXX-C. The A's and the C's are identical in all three animals. The siamangs and wolves have BBBB's, which made genetic sense, but the chimps' XXXX's were a long string of repeated base pairs, over and over and over."

"What base pairs?"

"CCG's, over and over and over."

"Strings of CCG's are junk. Meaningless."

"Right. That's what we thought, which was all very interesting. The A-BBBB-C sequence had something to do with smell, and here our chimps had the two ends of the sequence, but the middle was degraded or lost. Smell and reproductive behavior are very strongly connected in a lot of species. . . ."

"You thought you had a clue to chimp sexual behavior!"

"Other way around, actually. I thought it might be a clue as to why wolves and siamangs mate for life while bonobos are totally promiscuous. I assumed, for purposes of experiment, that it did have something to do with smell, maybe the development of an organ that would bind to a unique pheromone. A specific he-wolf, for example, might imprint on the smell of a specific she-wolf, and after that no other mate would smell right. Just like goslings imprint on the first moving thing they see after they hatch.

"So I did some baseline tests on smell acuity on a couple of the chimps; then I built a cut-and-paste RNA sequence to unzip the X's and insert the B's, and I attached it to the viral carrier we were using then—"

"It still wouldn't affect an adult," he objected. "You'd have to insert it in a fertilized egg."

"I planned to do that, but since some tissues can be affected even in an adult, and since I had the stuff, I decided to try it. I sprayed the stuff into the nostrils of a couple of the chimps to see if the sequence would incorporate in their nasal cells and modify sensitivity to smell or change their sexual behavior. . . ."

"What happened?"

"They showed no increase or decrease in detecting odors, they didn't sniff each other any more or less than formerly, and the fornication rate remained constant." She seated herself before her own terminal and stared at the blank screen.

"Can chimps fornicate?" he asked, straightfaced.

"Can they ever!"

Both of them laughed, Jessamine shaking her head ruefully. It had been so disappointing! For all the progress they'd made in transliterating the genetic code into its sequence of bases, large-scale translation of real meanings was still elusive. DNA was not a blueprint for an organism; it was a set of instructions for growing one in a constantly changing environment, and the environment was an essential part of the instructions.

Val's brow creased. "So then you went on to try it in an embryo? Right?"

Jessamine caught her breath. Even after three years she felt her mind recoil, the gates clang down, not to be reminded. Her older daughter Carlotta, dead. Her new little granddaughter, dead. She swallowed, took a breath, and made herself answer.

"It was ninety-seven, Val. The quake happened. The lab was destroyed. The computers, my records, everything. The apes were all right, they were at an inland facility, one of the breeding farms set up to maintain the species when they went extinct in the wild. I never tried my sequence on an embryo because all the records were gone. I'd have had to start from scratch again, and I didn't have the heart."

Val, hearing the strain in Jessamine's voice, made an apologetic grimace.

Jessamine went on. "Also, they made the viral carriers illegal that next year. You were in Japan, so you missed all the wonderful details. A whole tribe of the Army of God descended on Washington to say the quake was a sign, that Christ was coming back to raise the dead, and he wouldn't know which creatures to raise if there was human genetic material mixed into other creatures."

"You're kidding."

"No. Some of us tried to tell the legislators we shared most of our DNA with mice and ninety-nine percent of it with chimps, that there was only one percent difference between us and apes and only one hundredth of one percent between individual people, but the legislators got thoroughly confused, or maybe they just decided not to fight it. Some of them are probably millenarians, too."

"Like the guys in the mall this morning. One of them leaned in my window and told me ten more years. That's all we've got before the world ends. I thanked him for his advice and got out of there. They could be right about the end of the world. We've lost half the species in the world just this century."

And half the remaining species lived on in a kind of twilight world. It was a frightening thought, one she preferred not to dwell on. She sat at her own console and began sorting through the papers stacked to one side. Before her the do-now pile grew taller as she added stuff that should have been done yesterday. Behind her Val tapped and muttered.

"Another day, another sequence," he said.

"Umm." She stared over her screen to the window.

Val turned off the workstation, stood up, and pulled a jacket pocket inside out, dumping the contents onto the desktop, coins rattling. "Thank God it's Friday. I badly need a couple of days off."

"I guess. I don't think a day off will help me much."

"You and Patrick ought to do something fun this weekend, go someplace exciting."

"We haven't done that lately. In fact, I've done very little with Patrick lately. He's getting hateful."

Val cocked his head, brow furrowed. "Jessy?"

"He is," she said defensively. "The last few weeks he's become absolutely awful."

"He needs a job. Most people do!"

"He does indeed, but what Patrick actually says he needs is a son."

Val was at her shoulder. "A what?"

"He listens to the news, sixty-year-old women being dosed with hormones in order to be pregnant. He tells me it could be done."

Val turned toward her with a horrified expression. "Maybe it could be done, but, my God, Jess. Does he know what you'd have to go through?"

"He doesn't want to hear about it. He says I care more for my job than I do for him." Being honest, she had to admit it might be true. She said tonelessly, "I don't know what to do. The idea disgusts me, Val. This poor old planet is so overcrowded already, why in hell do we need fiftyish-sixtyish women having more babies?"

"You'll do what's right for you," he asserted, striding back to his desk, where he extricated his car control from the rat pile, discarded half the remainder into the wastebasket, and restocked his pockets with the rest. "You're not responsible for Pat's unhappiness. You didn't cause the earthquake."

Jess shook her head apologetically. "You're right. But he's after me all the time, and sometimes I just don't want to go home."

He looked at her, a long, weighing look, and she flushed.

"I wasn't implying—"

"I know what you weren't implying," he said softly. "But the invitation is still open. Anytime you do imply."

"I'm your boss, sort of. I'm your senior, in more ways than one. I'd be arrested for harassment," she giggled, her eyes full.

"I'll sign a waiver," he said seriously. "Anytime."

"Thanks, Val. You make me feel . . . better." Girlish, was what she meant. He was at least ten years younger than she was. And attractive. Pleasant company but no . . . no bugles blowing. No bugles blowing even in fantasy for a long time, which was a little odd. Shouldn't sex drive taper off as one aged? Why had it just stopped, all at once?

Val looked pointedly at the clock. "Are we quitting, or what?"

"We're quitting. That is, you're quitting. I've got to get this stuff sorted out."

He raised a hand in farewell and was gone, out the grilled door, past the cages. Jessamine heard his voice raised in hello, good-bye to the apes. Then silence. Through the west window, across from her workstation, she saw some of the apes returning to the compound, losing themselves among the rapidly greening trees, Priapus moving purposefully after one of the younger females.

He reminded her of Patrick. Could she do what Patrick wanted? Take some other woman's ovum, let Patrick fertilize it, then she, herself, incubate it for him? Would that satisfy him? Probably not. What he really wanted was a younger, more biddable wife with whom he could procreate and prove himself a male.

At the far side of the cage Don Juan stood silhouetted against the foliage at the end of the cage, standing erect, his arm around Lily. She was leaning on him in a way Jessamine had never seen a bonobo stand before. Almost as the siamang mates sometimes stood. If she didn't know chimpanzees better, she'd almost believe they were in love.

From her studio in the hills southeast of Denver, Faye Whittier looked across the shoulder of the girl she was embracing to see the sickle moon, newly whetted, mowing a field of early stars. The moon and the girl had certain things in common, both curvaceous and inconstant and given to cloudy moods and inattentive loveliness.

"I'm tired," said the girl. "I'm hungry, too."

"Just stand here a minute," Faye urged. "I'm getting the feel of your body. We're getting a good start."

The girl glanced sideways at the clay maquette on the table. "It looks all lumpy to me."

"They always look lumpy at the beginning. Later on they smooth out. Like you, all smoothed out."

She shut her eyes and ran a sculptor's hand along the girl's glistening flank, holding this shape close while thinking of quite another shape, holding this substance while evoking another substance, summoning into this reality another reality, another identity, another time, letting the summoning permeate and brew, infusing herself with memory.

The girl moved impatiently.

"Shhh," said Faye.

The girl relaxed, sighing. Faye let the longing well up, let it engulf her, lift her, make her weightless. She floated, in intimate contact with her other self, the self discovered in childhood when she had stood in the darkened bathroom, naked before the full-length mirror, seeing someone else in the shadowy glass who was not herself. Then she had run questioning fingers over her own shoulders, her flat bronze chest, down her hips and thighs and between her legs, seeing that other do likewise, that other smiling, accepting what Faye felt, what Faye wanted. This was the mirror feeling, the feeling of absolute acceptance and peace.

When she was older and her breasts came, the longing had become more urgent. The tenderness around the thrusting nipples, the soft furriness of her crotch, brought with them an ache deeper than these surface complexities could explain. What she felt hurt her, though it wasn't a pain. With a pain one could say it hurts here, or there, but this was pervasive, something like grief, but grief over what? Over something that was missing! Some essential substance she'd had, once, maybe in some former life, a completion that cried to her out of time, begging her to return.

This was fanciful, and she knew it, but sometimes the ache was so intense it made her want to cry, and sometimes it went on for days.

"You in some mood," Mama had said more than once. "What's the matter with you?"

What had been the matter with her? Where had the sadness come from? Why this sense of loss when she'd never lost anything? Nobody she knew was sick. Nobody she knew had died except Daddy, long ago, when she was two, and she didn't even remember him.

"Child, what you grieving for?"

That's what Faye wanted to know. What she was grieving for had no name. And "grieving" was the wrong word. It was more than that—a wanting, an urging . . .

It wasn't boys. The boys had flocked around her fifteen-year-old sister, Edith, she like a shining pheasant with her bronze skin and tight black feathery cap, bird-walking flirtatiously, head first to one side then the other, eyeing the boys. They had flocked around thirteen-year-old Jill-ellen, she a little gangly yet, but with a doe-eyed sweetness about her, a smell like honey and flowers, an inviting glance. The lanky boys, the young cock birds, they'd followed after, they'd stood around, not too near, tossing admiration to Edith and Jill, like flowers cast before divas. And she, Faye, right in the middle at fourteen, her new breasts straining against her shirtfront, dizzy dreams waking her in the nighttime, was not at all interested. The male sex wasn't what bothered her.

"That Bill Harrison, he's a nice boy," this from Mama, who had offered to make Faye a dress, a special dress for the special dance. "He asked you to go. Why not tell him you'll go, Faye? We'll pick out the material and we'll make you look so pretty!"

Mama would have done for Faye, of course, just as she did for Jill and Edith. She'd have helped Faye with her hair, straightening and curling, and she'd have counseled good manners and not letting boys get too familiar, all the stuff Faye had heard over and over and knew by heart, all that carefulness and pride masking the underlying excitement that would lead, inexorably, to babies and grandbabies.

Faye didn't want it. Her rejection was not passive but active. She rejected the boys' inviting words and their adolescent shifts of voice, rejected their strutting and prancing, finding them ludicrous and strange, like alien creatures, not human at all, not like the self in the mirror. Not like the shadow self waiting somewhere, somewhere behind veils to come to her.

Mama couldn't understand it. Faye couldn't understand it, either. And then, like a thirsty desert traveler who happens upon an oasis, she found art. Her first trip to a museum brought her face-to-face with some of what had been missing, with the image of the beloved. She saw it in marble and bronze and paint, all around her, the images that were like the mirror self. Those images were all she needed, until she met Sophy.

Sophy. Who had made everything completely clear. One look from Sophy, Sophy's hand held in her own for a brief moment, and Faye had known what she'd been waiting for. What she sometimes, as now, pretended she held: Sophy herself.

The pretense never really worked. This sweet body, however sweet, was not Sophy's. The person tenanting this flesh was not the right inhabitant. The voice was not the right voice, the touch was not the right touch. This was a fraud and a delusion, and she should not use this girl so!

She dropped her arms and stepped away. The girl, released, turned toward the worktable and regarded her clay image from beneath drowsy lids.

"When it's finished, will you put my name on it?"

Faye blinked, ran her fingers across her close-cropped hair, and restrained a shiver. "Why, sure."

"So's my boyfriend can see it. You won't tell him about . . . you know."

"About my making love to you, Petra? I'd say that's private."

"Just so's I could get my expression right. A nepisode."

An episode, yes. And Petra's expression had been absolutely right. Blinded. Lost in eroticism. Totally unaware of the world and all its fragile wonder. Exactly what Faye had wanted for this particular figure. Though she had to admit that artistic intuition had been adulterated by curiosity. The episode had not been only to get Petra's facial expression right. Faye had also wondered if she herself was still capable of feeling anything, if that body, that lovely, nubile body, could stir her. In her mind and heart she was faithful to one and only one love, but from time to time over the years her body had longed for the feel of real flesh. Or had done so in the past. How long past? She couldn't even remember!

Stroking Petra's sleek body, she had felt no lust. Seeing those beautifully rounded haunches rotating slowly, that perfect skin glossy with excitement, she'd felt none. Nothing. She had not felt it, as she had not really felt anything in some time. She presumed it was because of what the doctors had told her. She had not asked specifically about libido. When one is talking about life, lust seems relatively unimportant.

Petra said, "You'll put my name on it, and the title. Springtime. That's what I want."

Faye nodded soberly. Springtime was one way of putting it. There were more accurate titles: burgeoning life, heedless reproduction, the luxuriant wastage that went with mindless fecundity. Petra would not understand those meanings.

"I wish Narcisso could see it," she murmured. "It looks sexy."

Give the girl a gold star. "Narcisso would like it?"

"Yeah. Maybe he better not, though. I don't want him to know about . . . you know. Because when you did that, it wasn't really me. I'm not that way about girls."

Faye sighed dismissively. "Well, girl, I know that. I know you just want to get married and have lots and lots of babies." Petra was one of eight. Narcisso had half a dozen brothers. Whether they could support them or not, they would have a brood. What else?

Abruptly, the girl's face clouded, tears swam in her eyes.

"Petra? What's the matter?"

"Nothing. Let me alone."

"People don't get all red-eyed over nothing. What is it?"

The face confronting her hardened, lost its adolescent naïveté, became a woman's face, angry and uncompromising.

"I said nothing. It's my business. It's private. Let me alone." She looked at the studio clock. "Cisso, he'll be here for me soon."

Faye gritted her teeth and turned back to the window. Damn. Now the face was all wrong. Well, let it be. Faye could remember the emotion, and often it was easier to work from the emotion, letting the model go. Sometimes the vision was clearer without the banality that personified it.

"You go ahead and get dressed; we'll say that's enough for today." She went to the sink for damp cloths to shroud the maquette. On the way back she stopped, caught afresh by a different angle of view, the lines of the work, the surge and inevitability of it. Good. Oh, it was good. That upreaching arm, clutching toward heaven, trying to grasp all sensation, all at once. That spread-legged, arched-back, abandoned form carried aloft on the great wave. Even the beginnings of the face were good, that openmouthed, half-lidded gaze, turned inward, seeing nothing.

Petra redid her eyes and slipped into her panties and the knit dress in which she'd arrived. She looked more naked as she dressed herself than when she'd been unclothed, writhing like a stripper, smoothing the dress over her bust and hips, slipping into her high-heeled sandals. As a last ritual she leaned back to stick out her tongue at the life-size bronze that was hidden behind the screen.

"When you want me next?" she asked, posed, one hip provocatively outthrust.

"I'll call you," Faye answered, trying not to sound peevish. The bronze had not merited the disrespect.

The girl shrugged and sashayed out, bottom swinging, banging the door behind her. It took real effort to bang the studio door, but Petra managed it every time. Faye opened the door quietly, went out onto the little landing, and stood looking down the winding wooden steps to the graveled driveway where the red car stood, orange and yellow flames painted on the hood and along the sides, clearly visible even in this evening light. "Scorcher," it said on the doors. Beside the driver's door stood a youth who matched the car, completely true to type: the hair, the studded jacket, the studied slouch, the smoke pouring from his nostrils. He looked up at her from hooded eyes, his lips bent into a masterful sneer, flipping the cigarette away in a shower of sparks. Gravel spat from the spinning wheels as Scorcher went away, the engine noise fading and returning, fading and returning as it traversed the switchbacks among the pines.

Faye went down and found the smoldering cigarette near a pile of tinder-dry needles, angrily stubbing it out and burying it under a stone. This wasn't the first time he'd damned near started a fire. Perhaps Petra should find a new job! Or a new boyfriend.

The last of the car noise was gone when she returned to the studio. As though startled by the silence, the lights brightened, the sensor that controlled them responding to the decrease in daylight. Faye turned them off before drawing a plastic bag over the shrouded maquette. Tomorrow she'd finish the face and start on the fruit of those fecund loins, the flood of children. The maquette was due in August. She wouldn't get the go-ahead on the full project until the model was approved.

Anxiety came in a wave, making her shudder. They had to approve it. She needed the money. With all these medical bills mounting up and up . . . Oh, she needed the money, but that wasn't all she needed. Added to the formless longing of childhood was a mature longing of her own. She wanted to be great! Not for notoriety or fame, but only to do something, even if it was only one thing, that was fine. The goal was within reach, she knew it, she could feel it, but she needed time and she might not have enough time. She'd never been in love with anyone but Sophy. She'd never had any hobbies or demands except music and her art. She'd given up all commitments, all relationships—or they'd given her up. Mother and sisters still believed she'd chosen what she was, still believed she could choose otherwise. Faye had even considered giving up the DFC, except they were all she had now, and she needed them.

Despite the pressure, she was too tired to do anything more tonight. She was out of power. She needed a recharge, a few hours of nothing-ing, a night to read a little, something well loved and easy. A night to listen to music and recover her sense of herself. She would walk across the porch to the kitchen and take the bottle of chilled wine out of the refrigerator. She would sit in her sunset window, quietly, purposefully not thinking about the doctors, turning off the phone so Herr Straub could not call her to argue, yet again, that she should resign the commission. Herr Straub was persistent as a tick and as wounding as a stampede. After each of his assaults, her confidence sank another notch. She didn't need Herr Straub to question her ability; she could do that herself.

As she turned to go, she was stopped by the presence in the corner. Petra must have moved the screen, for the bronze stood in silhouette against the north window, the line of the shoulder, the outheld hand, the head, ever so slightly cocked, as though listening to something.

"Shall I bring you some wine, love?" she asked, her voice breaking slightly. "We could have a little wine, a little music."

Her hand went to the light switch, only to stop there, frozen, for there was a sound in the room, a murmur as though a distant door had opened and let through a hint of some faraway clamor. It could have been the wind, murmuring in the air ducts, but it wasn't. Slightly, very slightly, the figure in the corner turned its head, regarded her thoughtfully, then moved, twisted, became smoke, became fog, became nothing.

Faye cried out, in surprise as much as fear, thrusting herself against the door. "Sophy!"

There was nothing there. There could have been nothing there. She turned the lights up full; then tentatively, step by step, she went to the edge of the screen and peered around it. There, totally hidden from the room, the statue of a nude Sophy stood, dusty and unchanged.

It had been a trick of the light.

She knew it hadn't been a trick of the light. She sat down, losing herself, not thinking at all. There she sat, waiting, just waiting, for something terrible or wonderful to happen. She couldn't even make herself worry over which it might be.

1

IN THE GROUND-FLOOR CHAPEL at the Abbey of St. Clare, Reverend
Mother Agnes McGann knelt alone before the altar. Behind the altar stood a
triptych, the center panel painted with the risen Christ. To the left was a cool
Creation, a leafy wilderness in which God Almighty was assisted in his labors
by a swarm of officious angels. To the right was the Last Judgment, the same
angels thrusting the damned off the cliffs of eternity. The painter's name was
writ large upon the center panel. Faye had looked him up for Aggie, somebody
Andrews, died in the early 1900s. Definitely second-rate, if that, said Faye.
Agnes, eyes drawn irresistibly to the right-hand panel, where she searched for
her own face among the damned, comforted herself with Faye's last judgment
on the artist.

Around her the abbey buzzed quietly, a hive almost at rest. Upstairs the
sisters were getting themselves ready for bed with much attendant rustling
and water noises: Toilets flushing, basins draining, showers running. Careful
footsteps. Doors closing gently. Even the decorous rustle of ankle-length cot-
ton nightgowns, assumed if not heard from this distance. There would be no
talk until tomorrow after mass. Though the order was not enclosed, though it
included among its members many women who had at one time been quite
worldly, silence was still observed from evensong until breakfast, the vow of
obedience was still enjoined, the vow of chastity was considered paramount.

Until recently Reverend Mother Agnes had thought she had managed obedience and poverty quite well, though she acknowledged that the true fulfillment of celibacy had eluded her. Sophy, whose hand she had never held beyond a momentary greeting, whose cheek she had never pressed except to bid hello or farewell, had often haunted her dreams in intimate, erotic detail. To delay if not to eliminate this nightly occurrence, Reverend Mother Agnes McGann had formed the habit of coming each evening to ask God's protection against her subconscious. The dreams were no doubt a test of her character and spirituality, for though she had lusted for Sophy, she had always been chaste, always loved Sophy celibately despite her passion. Which didn't accrue to Agnes's credit, of course, since that was the only way Sophy allowed herself to be loved.

Faye loved Sophy, too, of course. Faye always had. There was no point in Agnes's being jealous over that. Faye had been just as frustrated in that love as Agnes had been. As Aggie was! Her feelings should have changed after what she had seen in San Francisco, but they hadn't. No matter her mental confusion, her love for Sophy remained intransigent.

"If one witnesses an act that might be sinful, Father Girard?" She knew the answer, but she needed it confirmed.

"Might be sinful?"

Was it a sin? Had it been frightening, as Agnes had thought at the time? Frightening and weird and perhaps diabolical? Or had Agnes herself been hallucinating and the act harmless? "Maybe meant as a joke, but perhaps with serious implications, Father." Anguished attempts at explanation would only confuse the issue. She knew what Father would say.

He said it, throwing in a kindly chuckle as lagniappe. "Aren't you being overscrupulous? All these *maybes* and *perhapses?* God can decide what a sin is, Reverend Mother. Leave it to Him. Meantime, why don't you pray for the soul of the person involved and any who may have been sinned against? That way you'll cover all the bases."

She had already prayed for Sophy, assuming Sophy needed praying for, though she'd felt guilty doing even that. Who was she to say Sophy needed her prayers? Perhaps Sophy had done what she had to prevent a greater sin. But, then, there'd been all the rest of it, the part she'd never told anyone because she didn't know whether to believe it herself. If she told Father Girard, he would think she was a few crayfish short of a gumbo, he really would. There was probably a simple explanation, if Sophy were still here to make an explanation.

Sophy wasn't still here. Not the Sophy of college days, not the Sophy of 1997, not any of the myriad Sophys in between. She who should have been changeless had transformed herself again and again. Two years after graduation she was already a different person.

Agnes had been finishing up her M.B.A. that year, ready to enter St. Clare's that fall. Ophy had been in med school in New York, Carolyn in law school near Washington, where she could be near Hal. Faye had spent the two years since graduation studying art in Europe. Jessamine had taken a job in a lab in San Francisco and was pursuing graduate studies part-time. Bettiann had a job as assistant fashion buyer at Neiman Marcus.

And Sophy, their hostess for the meeting, had been living in a commune near Mystic, Connecticut. The other DFC members stayed in a cheap motel nearby, and they met daily to wander the shore, the woods, the sailing museum. Either they'd held the meeting early that year, or it had been a cold summer, for Aggie remembered dappled sunlight off the waters and a chill breeze through the leaves. They'd been poor, all but Carolyn and Ophy, who treated the others to a couple of meals in restaurants. Otherwise they had all chipped in for hamburger and pasta and rice, filing stuff they could prepare at Sophy's shack-cum-slum-cum-group home and share with the women there and with their children—all of them singularly lifeless and hangdog, Agnes had thought.

"What is this?" Agnes had demanded. "What're these women doing here? What're they here for?"

"Survival," Sophy had confessed almost fretfully, as though expecting them to criticize. "They've all been battered, Aggie. By fathers or husbands or boyfriends, mostly. They've all got scars. I've sort of rounded them up. It's my share of the covenant, not to decline and fall, you know. Caring for them. Helping them. Trying to give them a place to stand, so they won't decline and fall, either." She said it pleadingly, as though begging for help.

That, from Sophy, had been an uncomfortable revelation. Though Agnes, along with the rest of the DFC, had sworn not to decline and fall, she'd thought that oath less important than her religious vows, but here was Sophy doing more with her DFC promise than Aggie had yet done with all her hope of holiness. What made it more annoying was that Sophy had never seemed interested in human service. Quite the opposite, in fact.

Agnes had felt almost envious. No thought then that Sophy might have been doing it for some other, alien purpose. No thought that Sophy might be something other than what she appeared to be. Not then. Then Sophy could do no wrong.

"Is this going to be what you do with your life?" Agnes had asked.

But Sophy had shaken her head, saying ruefully, "I don't want to do it at all, Aggie. I get involved out of pity, but intellectually, I know it does little or no good, bit by bit this way."

"It's good for your soul. . . ."

"That's terrible," Sophy had cried, actually sounding angry. "To value other people's pain for such a reason! I hear such a lot of soul petting and sentimentality over these women and their children, but I hear very little willingness to do anything about causes!"

"But, Sophy, what would you have us do—"

"I don't have an answer," she had cried, still angry, still resentful. "I shelter one, there are six hundred more who need shelter. Somewhere there has to be an answer!"

Sophy's anger should have been a clue. Agnes should have paid more attention. Anger was a sin. Anger could make people unbalanced. Aggie hadn't done anything about Sophy's anger, though she had considered setting up a fund to help Sophy's women when she'd made the final disposition of her trust before entering St. Clare's. The priest she had talked to about it wasn't sympathetic, however. Helping women leave their husbands was not in accordance with doctrine. Helping women take children away from their fathers wasn't theologically sound, either. Besides, women often incited violence by being disobedient or sassy, the priest said, and fathers had the right to chastise their wives and children. If occasionally men were too rough, prayer was the answer, not separation. The Church provided marriage counseling. Let these women take advantage of it!

Aggie had to agree, of course. Separating married couples was not an appropriate act, not for a nun or for anyone. She loved Sophy, yes, but if it came to a choice between Sophy and the Church, there could be no choice. Sophy was only a mortal love, after all, but the Church was her life, for eternity.

During the next seven years Ophy graduated and went overseas to do research on cultural differences in obstetrical care. Jessamine married Patrick O'Neil, had two baby girls less than a year apart, finished her Ph.D. in an esoteric field of molecular genetics, and received a promotion in her biotech company. Bettiann, despite her doubts and reservations, was swept off her feet by Bill Carpenter and, after several miscarriages, had a baby boy. Carolyn and Hal moved to New Mexico and had a baby girl, and Faye—who by that time was receiving praise for her work plus some sizable commissions—had come out as a professed and militant lesbian. And Agnes herself had remained at St. Clare's to take her solemn vows, which could have separated her from the DFC forever.

Should have, she told herself now. Should have. Mother Elias had wanted to be kind, however, and had insisted that Aggie take a little vacation each year to visit her old friends. So Aggie had gone on seeing Sophy, loving Sophy. Risking herself.

Sophy had hosted the 1972 meeting in a cottage on the shores of Lake Champlain. Carolyn had inherited the place from her great-aunt on her mother's side and had offered Sophy a fifty-year lease for a dollar a year, to be paid at the DFC meetings. When 1979 rolled around, however, they couldn't meet at the cottage, for Sophy had once more filled her home with battered women she was trying to make independent.

Instead, they had stayed at an inn in Middlebury, where, during their traditional show-and-tell, they had toasted Ophy's marriage to Simon Gheist and had heard a new set of stories about the women Sophy had taken in.

"Don't you ever try to . . . reunite these couples?" Agnes had asked, deeply troubled by all this. Though she still held to chapter and verse on the Church's teachings about marriage, her work in the parish with real women made it more difficult. "Do you ever help them work out their differences?"

Sophy had regarded Aggie thoughtfully. "I don't think they have differences, Aggie. The women I've taken in have done everything humanly possible to please their husbands."

"If that is true, why are their husbands angry at them?"

"Beating women excites some men. They like it. They aren't mad at their wives, though they usually pretend to be angry over something, to give them an excuse for the first blow. They enjoy hitting, Aggie. For some men it's like skydiving, or hang gliding. It fires them up. They go on a testosterone high! That dark, skinny woman you met—Sarah—she's just recovering from a skull fracture her husband gave her because, so he said, she overcooked the beans. He raped her while she was lying on the kitchen floor unconscious, bleeding from the head."

Though Aggie had shuddered at this, she had told herself life was, after all, intended as a time of trial. "But if she had paid attention to what she was doing, if she'd tried harder to please him—"

"He'd have hit her for something else. What is it, Aggie? Surely you can't think being raped while beaten unconscious was Sarah's fault?"

Aggie did think it was women's fault—if not proximately, then through original sin. All the daughters of Eve shared the same guilt, the guilt of disobedience. Only one woman in history had been perfectly obedient. The sacrament of marriage united people for life because there was grace enough within it to solve any problem. God never asked anything of people they weren't capable of doing. She'd learned that as a child!

"What happened to the man?" Carolyn had asked Sophy.

"He got seven years. He'll be out in three or less."

"And what is she going to do?"

"I'm trying to get her to go far away from here and take some kind of work. Something to keep herself and her child."

Bettiann had cried, "But, Sophy, she married him! She owes it to him to—"

"To nothing!" Faye had erupted. "Let's not talk about this, Bettiann. The rest of us will gang up on you and Aggie, and you'll get your feelings hurt."

Bettiann hadn't been convinced. The only times William had ever hit her, she had damned well deserved it. "They're married," she had insisted stubbornly. "When you get married, it's for better or worse, and somehow they should be able to work it out."

"I've seen how it works out," Ophy had snarled. "It works out with the woman being brought into the emergency room, and sometimes it's too late, and I can't save her life. Sometimes it's the kids who're brought in, and I can't save them, either. I used to keep score, but the numbers got so depressing, I stopped counting. God knows how many women and little girls I've signed death certificates for in the last ten years."

Sophy had nodded, thoughtful as always. "I sometimes wonder if these women are married to men at all. Maybe they are married to the enemy. Or to his minions."

Whenever Sophy spoke of the enemy, her voice acquired a mysterious, almost metallic, clangor, the dissonant tolling of alarms, a harsh and bitter sound, almost alien. Hearing this strange timbre, Aggie had changed the subject: "I saw your recent infanticide story in the *New Yorker*." On the horrors of infanticide, at least, she could agree with Sophy. "Ophy sent it to me."

Sophy had said distantly, "I got quite a bit of mail about that piece. It's strange. The situations I write about are almost always widely reported in the newspapers and on television, yet people don't seem to react strongly until I redo the truth as fiction! I thought perhaps if I put the stories into a book . . ."

They had gone on to talk of other, less disturbing things. Sophy's first book had come out soon afterward, a slender volume called simply *Women's Stories*. It included many of the stories she had told them about her Asian travels: of Burmese village girls sold to the brothels of Thailand, of Indian brides burned to death by dowry-greedy grooms, of women's schools burned in Bangladesh, of Muslim "honor killings" of girls who were victims of rape. The book contained a list of shelters and women's movements to which contributions could be made. Each member of the DFC had contributed to at least one of them, though Aggie and Bettiann had chosen agencies that worked predominately with children.

Despite their differing viewpoints, Aggie had always envied Sophy her certainty. Though Sophy had struggled to understand, she had never seemed to doubt her own actions. Whatever she had done, she had done surely, as though guided by some invisible beacon. Throughout Aggie's years as a nun, whenever presented with difficult choices, she has asked herself what Sophy would do if Sophy were Agnes. Since Sophy hadn't been Catholic or even

Christian, since she and Aggie hadn't agreed at all about women's roles in life, it was an odd question to ask, but Aggie had asked it nonetheless. She had used her image of Sophy as a mariner uses a compass. She had kept her direction, had worked hard, had set aside almost all distractions. She had done well, so she was told by others.

So why was everything so solemn? Why was there so little joy?

She had asked Sophy that question one time when the two of them were alone. Desperately, she had asked it. "Shouldn't there be joy, Sophy?"

"We should each have a place," Sophy had told her—her hands on Agnes's shoulders, her eyes fixed on Agnes's eyes. "A lofty and rejoiceful place, Aggie, on which our hearts can dance. Perhaps the abbey isn't it."

"But I longed to be a nun," Agnes had cried. "I believe in the Church and her teachings. How can you say that?"

Sophy had seemed as mystified as Aggie. "I don't know, Aggie. Except that it seems true."

Came a whisper of sound, bringing Agnes back to the present, a soft shush, like the opening of a door. She raised her head and saw movement, someone walking from pillar to pillar in the side aisle. A graceful, flowing motion with the feeling of beauty behind it. The idea of loveliness. Someone young, dressed in the wide-coifed habit the order had not worn for decades.

She turned her head resolutely away. She would pay no attention. It had been a shadow shifting. Too many times lately had she imagined shapes, always moving away, away from the altar, or away from the chapel, or away from the chapter house. Whichever way Agnes was going, the shadow went the other way.

It was hallucination. She was working too hard, not sleeping well, and seeing things was the result. The flowing shapes made her acknowledge her failure at forgetting Sophy, as she had promised herself and her confessor she would do. Her eyes drifted upward to the Last Judgment once more, she imagining herself among that mob of females, stripped naked, mouth open in a howl of despair, being driven off the edge of the earth into the void while the angels regarded the plunging forms with satisfaction. Most of the damned were female. The painting was full of women falling, screaming, trying to cover their nakedness. Many paintings of the Last Judgment seemed to populate hell with naked females. Was it the artists or the Church that took such prurient pleasure in sending women to hell? Like old Father Conley, back at St. Monica's, doing one of his little chastity lectures, talking about modesty, all euphemisms and avid looks. Beautiful women would burn in hell, he said. Beautiful women were occasions of sin. Saying it, his tongue came out, like a frog's tongue, licking his lips, savoring the notion of women in hell, finding the idea delicious.

True sacraments could flow through bad priests. That was doctrine.

Father Conley had the mystical quality of maleness, which Christ had shared. That quality made him acceptable as a conduit for grace. Though he had been uncharitable and maybe even sexually obsessed, the grace that flowed through him was still pure, and pure grace, flowing from God, was enough. Amazing grace—which would be enough for Agnes, too, if instead of wallowing in might-have-beens about Sophy she concentrated on becoming more obedient. Obedience, as Father Girard had pointed out, would not be as spiritually rewarding if it were easy.

One became obedient by refusing to remember, her confessor said. By rejecting all memory of Sophy. By denying any pleasure in those memories. By refusing to hearken to anything that brought her to mind, including these recent visions, these sounds. Well, by God, Aggie would do it. She would shut down her memories, relentlessly. She would succeed eventually. Resolution was her middle name. She would tell Father Girard everything, she would receive absolution, and she'd forget Sophy. And since she couldn't do that if she went on meeting with the DFC, she would give up the DFC.

The chapel door opened. Again she saw movement from the corner of her eye. This time it was real. Sister Honore Philip, coming to kneel just behind her. Aggie raised her head.

"Reverend Mother. Are you all right?"

There weren't many in the convent who would risk breaking silence to be sure the abbess was all right. Not many who knew when the rules had to be bent a little.

"I'm all right," she said, rising, holding out her hand. "I didn't mean to cause you concern."

They dipped together before the altar, went together up the silent aisle. The abbess was still thinking about love, and repentance, and becoming pure. Sister Honore Philip, who was responsible for the hospitality offered by the abbey, was considering the ironed bed linens that would be needed for the archbishop, who, though extremely unwelcome, was soon to come visiting again.

"There's this woman I know," said Charley Carpenter, brother of Bettiann's husband, William, from the deep chair near the fire.

"There's this woman right here you know," said the nymph from the bed. She wore black stockings, a lacy corset-cum-garter belt, and nothing else at all.

"Yeah, well, this woman, she's married to my brother Bill. She's a little younger than him, maybe six, seven years, and she still looks sharp, you know. Groomed. She thinks I'm too old for you, babe."

"Maybe she thinks I'm too young for you," the nymph pouted.

"Women that age, they get jealous. You know. No matter what they do, they don't look young anymore. What I think is, they oughta all be retired."

He chuckled, a deep, liquid sound. "Pensioned off. By God, that's an idea. We oughta pension them off! Starting with ole Bettiann."

The nymph rolled into a more provocative position, watching the effect in the mirror as she raised her leg slightly. The image turned her on. She moistened her lower lip. "Charley . . ."

"She belongs to this club."

"Charley. Facrisake. Come awwwn." She drew out the word, a teasing sound, like the meow of a Siamese cat.

"You all hot to trot, babe? You all juicy and ready?"

"Charrrleeee."

"Want me to do you? That it? Want me to do you good?" He bent toward the table, opening the drawer.

"I want you, Charley. Not that thing."

He held up the dildo, tipping it this way and that. "Not a bad substitute, babe. Not bad at all. Let's give it a try."

She sat up angrily. "Damn it, Charley. I don't need to get all dressed up for that thing. What the hell? Last six weeks all you want to do is stick that thing in me, watch me come. Last I heard, sex was a team sport. I'm not doing exhibition games. Shit!"

He fell back into the chair, shutting the drawer with a thrust that rocked the table. "Do it yourself, kiddo. That's the way you want it."

"Are you sick?" she demanded. "This is spooky, Charley. This isn't right. You afraid I've got some disease? You know damn well I don't. What's goin' on here?"

"I'm fifty-two, babe. You need some young stud—"

"I'm not interested in studs. Studs aren't safe. They swear they'll be careful, they'll be faithful, and it's all a lot of shit. If that's all I wanted, that's easy, screw around a little, be dead before you're thirty. My best girlfriend in school, she's dyin'. My cousin, she's got the HIV. That's easy. I don't want that, but I didn't figure on some old guy with good sense givin' out after just a couple months."

She swayed into the bathroom, slamming the door behind her. Charley stared into the fire. He should be very upset by this. Angry, maybe. Annoyed, at least. The best he could summon was a very, very slight discomfort, as though the room were a little stuffy. He needed to take a walk. Take a hike, she'd say. Well, maybe that was true. He liked being with her, liked the glances they got, the stares. He liked her looks, no question about that. He didn't dislike doing her, either, if that's what she wanted, but it didn't turn him on. Not right now.

He'd had a spell like this once or twice before. Sort of as if his power had been turned off at the main. Once with his first wife, once with his second. Both times he'd found himself a new woman, and that had fixed things. This time, though . . . he didn't really feel like looking.

Funny thing was, he'd told Bill, and Bill had said he felt pretty much the same way.

"It's the TV," he said. "I've got the same problem. The urologist says he's seen a lot of it lately. Too much porn, you know. After a while you get so used to it, nothing works anymore. All that heaving and heavy breathing, all those naked girls. You get immunized."

Charley thought what he probably needed was a vacation from women. Do without for a while; then it was all the nicer.

"Hell of a thing," Charley said aloud. "One hell of a thing."

"What is?" she demanded from the door behind him.

"Life," he replied with a grin. "Hey, babe. Where'd you like to go for dinner?"

CAROLYN HAD A DREAM.

She had gone to the prison, to the big room where the pods were. Someone was taking her through the room—not Josh, but someone else—and that person was walking behind her.

She was terrified by the footsteps of the person behind her. She tried to turn, or to look through the faceplates on either side, but her hands were manacled behind her, and the person behind her prevented her looking by twitching the end of the chain.

In her dream Carolyn went on walking, turning, down this aisle and another. Halfway down the last aisle, the one next to the wall, one of the pods stood open.

"That one," said the voice from behind her. "That one is yours."

Carolyn called Jessamine.

"You sound awful," said Jessamine.

"Nightmares last night," Carolyn confessed with a shaky laugh. "You know, usually you can't remember dreams? I can't forget this one." She described it briefly, shakily.

"Carolyn! That's awful! You called me for an exorcism or something?"

"No, Jessy. I called you because I've got this case." She went on to explain all about Lolly Ashaler. "It's spelled A-s-h-a-l-e-r, but pronounced 'Ashler.' No idea where it comes from. Not a local name. I haven't any idea how to defend her. I've racked my brain. Hal and I have discussed it. . . ."

"How is Hal?"

"His leg's almost healed. He'll be walking without the crutches or canes before long."

"That's better news than your new acquaintance, Lolly. She does not sound charming."

"She sounds like what she is," sighed Carolyn. "One of your apes would make a better appearance, Jessy."

"Well, I've seen apes act like that."

"Act like what?"

"Give birth and just walk away. I've got some tapes, as a matter of fact."

"Why do they do it?"

"Mostly the ones who do it were reared in isolation from other chimps. You know some of these animal nuts, some people with more money than sense—they see a baby chimp so they buy the baby chimp, and they raise it as they would a human baby. That's fine until the chimp weighs around eighty or a hundred pounds and is stronger than any human, plus being full of sexual urges. Then suddenly it isn't fun anymore."

"I've seen studies about that," Carolyn mused. "Jessy, any ideas are welcome."

"If I have any, I'll let you know."

Carolyn called Ophy.

"Your client's incompetent," opined the doctor.

"To stand trial?"

"I wasn't speaking in a legal sense. I meant she's reproductively incompetent. I see it quite a bit here in New York, kids thirteen or fourteen getting themselves pregnant, and no more idea what to do with a baby than what to do with themselves. No school, no training, nada, zero, zip."

Long silence at the other end of the phone.

"Carolyn?"

"I'm here, Ophy. I just got the glimmer of an idea."

She called Faye, who was not sympathetic.

"Hey, girlfriend, don't tell me your troubles. I think heterosexuality sucks in all its aspects, so I can't help you with the outcomes."

"I'm not asking for help. I'm casting around for ideas."

"If I come up with any, I'll let you know. Right now I'm too busy to think."

"What are you working on, Faye?"

"This damned fountain commission. Or this damned commission for this fountain. Something or other is damned about it. Parts of it are sheer genius, and parts of it are driving me crazy. Right now I'm cutting up babies."

"I won't ask," said Carolyn, faintly amused.

"So don't. Love you," said Faye, hanging up the phone and returning to her task. She was cutting up babies and children, clay models of them, at any rate. She had more than a dozen little bodies on the table before her, chubby hands and feet, plump little legs, baby mouths and baby faces, African, Asian, European. The leather-dry figures slid neatly through the fine blade of her scroll saw, and as neatly out again, halved, quartered, three-quartered, divided into the parts that would emerge above and within the great wave that poured from the loins of Fecundity.

Faye laid the baby segments on the worktable, flat sides down, looked up at a shift in the light, and stopped frozen as the bronze figure in the corner moved! She was immobile for only a moment before she caught her breath and laughed weakly at herself. This time it was only the light sifting through the branches of the pine that shaded the studio. The wind blew, the shadows moved. The figure itself was as it had been when she'd moved the screen this morning, motionless beneath a crown of fake laurel and a dusty velvet drapery, props left over from a work Faye had done last year. Someone, perhaps the cleaning woman or Petra, had carefully curved the leaves to fit the shape of Sophy's face; someone had artfully folded the fabric that flowed from shoulder to floor.

The figure hadn't been, wasn't intended to be, covered. Moved by sudden impulse, Faye wiped her hands down her thighs and jerked the drapery loose in a great billowing cloud of clay dust that descended over the bronze figure in slow motion, as detritus sinks slowly into the sea, bit by bit, making a smooth, uniform layer. The sculpture took no notice but merely stood, as Sophy had often stood, watchful, waiting for things to be explained. As though she could not herself judge any issue until she knew what the rest of them thought about it, making them think exhaustively about things they didn't want to think about at all.

Faye fetched a wet cloth from the sink. She mopped the smooth limbs, sloshing water on herself, on the floor, as the clay melted into a thin slip, a matte finish that had to be polished away with another cloth. When she stood back, the remembered Sophy had returned, just as Faye had first resurrected her in one fevered, sleepless span of days, a life-size form, brought into being with no maquette, no studies, not even any sketches. When she'd finished with the figure, she'd fallen onto the studio couch and slept for forty-eight hours. God knows what she'd thought she'd been doing.

Even the sleep of exhaustion had brought no sense of release, only a feeling of futility at the fragility of the clay—what had Ophy used to call it?

Dried mud in extremis? Mere clay hadn't been enough. She'd hired two men to help her get it into the van. She'd carted it down to Santa Fe and stayed at the farm with Carolyn while the Shidoni Foundry had cast it in bronze. Then she'd brought it home to do the patina herself, hours and hours spent caressing that well-remembered body with fire and acid, highlight and shadow. After she'd done everything she was able to do, she had cried on the bronze shoulder, for it still hadn't been enough. This was Pygmalion in reverse. She could not bring love to life. She could only memorialize a love already gone.

The figure had stood in the middle of the studio for months, being cried over, talked to, then worked around. When Faye had needed the floor space, Sophy had been shifted to the corner, behind the model's screen. Now she stood in the open once more, right hand held out as though sagging under some great weight. Mortality, perhaps. Something Faye was very aware of just now, though she hadn't purposely modeled the arm in that way, hadn't even noticed how it sagged until after the figure had been cast.

Stroking the clay into shape was a kind of necrophilia, Faye supposed, as close as she had ever come to physical contact with Sophy. Sophy, who had never wanted to be touched.

"But you model for me nude," Faye had challenged her. "Don't you worry about my thoughts?"

"When your hands are in the clay, Faye, you don't think," Sophy had announced.

Which was true. Which had always been true, though Faye hadn't known it until then.

"What do I do with you now?" Faye whispered, bracing herself for the usual emotional cocktail: grief, anger, terror—so emulsified as to be gulped down together, all or none.

It came. And it departed, leaving no answer behind. There had never been an answer, and Faye couldn't take time to search for one now. The consortium had to be placated, cosseted, sold!

They wanted, so they had told her over a sumptuous dinner in Paris, an extravagant sculpture to center their new trade plaza; something with European references, with historic ties; something that expressed growth and bounteousness after a time of harshness. Faye had listened to all this with understanding nods, holding her wine consumption to a few cautious sips and keeping her brash irreverence under wraps. God knows, the last half century had been harsh enough. The aftermath of war, the Cold War, the collapse of Communism, and the return of tribal barbarity here and there and everywhere. How did one symbolize or personify European rebirth in such a context?

There were some on the committee who doubted it could be done and who were forthright enough to have said so during their initial dinner. There was one who was *certain* it could not be done, certainly not by Faye, though he had waited until after the dinner to come to her privately and tell her so. Herr Straub had advised Faye she was a compromise candidate, not the consortium's first choice. Herr Straub had also said there had never been a great woman sculptor; Faye's things were pretty, certainly, but not great. Besides, Herr Straub had said, the artistic tradition of her own people was quite foreign to the European tradition.

Thus having insulted her womanhood, her artistry, her culture, and her race, he had departed in the self-congratulatory mood of one who had done his duty, however painful, leaving Faye in a mood of grim, though rather frightened, defiance. In that same mood she'd gone hunting for inspiration, gypsying her way across Europe, footsore in Barcelona, weary in Berlin, grudging the fruitless hours spent staring at public monuments, looking for something a woman of color—or any woman—might say to a man like Herr Straub. Uncharacteristically, she had come to doubt herself, to think perhaps Herr Straub was right. Perhaps no woman of any race could capably design a monument to mercantile avarice.

Then, on the very day she was to fly home from Florence, she'd wandered into the Uffizi and come upon the Botticelli *Primavera*, a painting she hadn't seen since student days and hadn't really looked at even then. Though huge and famous, it wasn't done in a style she admired. The figures were lumpy, the allusions—so she assumed—outdated, and she'd forgotten anything she'd ever known about it. What was it? And why?

In answer to her unspoken question, the voice of an English-speaking docent echoed across the gallery, "We see in the *Primavera* various personifications of fruitfulness. . . ."

"Fruitfulness." The word evoked Sophy's house in Vermont, a breakfast-time argument over an article found in the morning paper. A fourteen-year-old girl, allegedly pregnant by rape, had been imprisoned by her parents in order to prevent her seeking an abortion, which she had threatened to do, and had then died during a late miscarriage. The charges were manslaughter, the jury said guilty, but the judge suspended the sentence, saying the parents had acted out of good motives, in the girl's best interest.

"I don't believe it," muttered Faye, slamming down a juice glass with such force she broke it and cut herself.

"Now, Faye," Aggie had said, taking the battered hand in her own, stanching the blood with a paper napkin. "Even though the abuse was a terrible thing, surely you can understand her parents' feelings."

"Aggie!" Carolyn had cried furiously. "For heaven's sake, don't give us the party line. Not from you! Don't tell me if you're raped, accept it as God's will. Don't!"

"But that's true," Aggie had cried.

Sophy had shaken her head. "So you always told me, Aggie. You were impregnated by rape? It's God's will. Accept it. This is your tenth baby, and you're dying? Accept it. You're thirteen years old? Accept it. Your daddy got you pregnant? Accept it. Twenty Serbian soldiers gang-raped you? Accept it. Why is fruitfulness always supposed to be God's will?"

Ophy had laughed, agreeing. "It's what you called the Hail Mary Assumption, Soph! We assume a woman is only a vessel, and once that sperm's in there, it's holy!"

Faye was looking at the *Primavera*, but she saw Sophy's face. While the docent herded his muttering, sore-footed charges away toward some other great work, Faye analyzed the painting in the light of that remembered argument: There was the pregnant victim stumbling in from the right, Cloris, a nymph, looking fearfully over her shoulder at the pursuing rapist, puff-cheeked Zephyr. Cloris was suffering from mythological morning sickness, vomiting up flowers, and was obviously sick and miserable, but there, just to her left, was her metamorphosis: Flora, a smiling goddess with flowing hair, dressed in a flowery gown. See, said the artist: The assaulted, cowering victim becomes fruitful, and with that fruitfulness comes apotheosis: Violence is transmuted into virtue; rape is rationalized; forcible impregnation is deified, just as the fathers of the Church have long insisted. The painting was not only about fruitfulness; it was also about transformation.

Back then, in Sophy's kitchen, Faye herself had attempted to end the argument. "Let's not spend the whole meeting arguing. Women get the short end a lot of times, and I'm tired of talking about it. It's just the way things are!"

It was Sophy who had answered. "You're wrong, Faye. Things are changing."

"I've noticed no improvement."

"No, I mean, all these things that happen to women, they're getting worse!"

"Well, I wouldn't say—"

"Truly. They are! I've been making it my business to find out! The incidence of abuse of women, all kinds, bride burning, rape, mutilation, battering, killing—the rate has increased steadily for the last several decades. Do you think that's natural?"

Faye laughed. "As natural as daylight. Population increases, more women to abuse, therefore more abuse. Why? You think something is causing it?"

"I wasn't referring to increasing numbers, but to increasing rates," Sophy said. "I do think something, or someone, is causing it."

Sophy had been so serious, so positive, like Red Riding Hood saying, What big teeth you have, Grandma. They'd all laughed, even Carolyn.

Faye didn't laugh as she stared at Botticelli's masterpiece. The fountain was suddenly there in her mind, a concept based on the Botticelli painting, but transformed. In the sculpture the raping wind would be invisible, its presence indicated only by an invisible force that thrust up a huge wave, the tidal wave of humanity. Taking the place of both Cloris and Flora would be the new incarnation of Fecundity, mindlessly erotic, flower crowned, borne aloft on the wave and spewing innumerable infants from her loins to dive and dabble down the flowing curve. The curve itself would have meaning, the smooth, ascending curve of human numbers. In the Botticelli work there were five other classical figures; Venus Genetrix at the center, the three Graces left of center, and a rather lackadaisical Mercury at the far left. In Faye's version these, too, would have their metamorphosis, though she had not considered them then.

Now, almost a year later, the model was gradually fulfilling her initial inspiration. She had finished the figure of Fecundity, and the great wave into which she was placing the children's bodies. The effect was good—massive, but flowing. When she had the children arranged to her satisfaction, she leaned back, stretching and yawning, rotating her head to relieve sore neck muscles.

She stopped, aghast.

From the corner Sophy, crowned in laurel, draped in velvet, regarded her from hooded, secret eyes.

Faye felt her fingers pressed tight against her mouth, muffling a sound she didn't want to make. She'd thrown the dust-laden props onto the floor. She'd washed Sophy and left her clean. See, there were the muddy puddles, the edges drying in gray craquelure. She'd left the garland and the fabric on the floor. She hadn't touched them. She hadn't done it. She couldn't have done it! But there had been no one else. No one else at all.

That night Faye dreamed she was walking through a cavern. How she had come there, why she was there, she had no idea. The cavern was dimly lit with flaring torches that reflected fragments of light from statuary stacked all around her, piles and lines of them, sometimes heaped three or four high. The torchlight reflected from bronze and stone, marking an eyelid here, the line of a cheek there, the curve of a breast, a hip, a thigh.

"They don't speak," said an oily, unctuous voice in a tone of enormous satisfaction.

The voice wakened her, shuddering. For a moment she remembered it all. A few moments later all she could remember was the words: "They don't speak."

Vince Harmston met District Attorney Jacob Jagger and his assistant Emmet Swinter, as though by chance, at the Monday lunch buffet of the Northern New Mexico Club, an organization that billed itself as something like Rotary or the Optimists, but was actually one of several hundred similar clubs that served as recruitment arms for the Alliance.

The three men carried their filled plates to the far end of one of the long tables, remote from the dais. They rose for the invocation, given that day by the bishop—a guest invited to address the group briefly after lunch on the topic of intercultural relations, a topic in which even the speaker had very little interest. Despite the public setting, the three men wished to discuss a private agenda: the prosecution of Lolly Ashaler.

Harmston told them briefly and blasphemously of his meeting with Carolyn Crespin.

"So the guard was right, and you won't be representing the baby killer," said Swinter around a mouthful of stringy beef.

"That's what he said, Emmet," remarked Jagger in the dead, toneless voice he used when he was more than merely angry.

Swinter fell silent, paling.

"This Crespin woman," Jagger said. "Don't we know her from some-where?" He could not for the moment remember how he knew her. He made no effort to remember female names.

Harmston cast a glance at Swinter, who replied with an anxious look in his boss's direction. "I know about her. There was a guy with the same name called me a few years back. Name was Al Crespin, with the FBI. He was her cousin, he said, keeping track of her because she belongs to some subversive group, something left over from the sixties. . . ."

Jagger sat up, leaned forward, eyes fixed.

Vince murmured, "Trouble is, that's forty years ago. Lots of kids went a little off back then."

"You didn't tell me about this, Emmet," Jagger said, still in that dead, cold voice.

Swinter shook his head apologetically. "It was before you were with the office, Mr. Jagger. This guy said Carolyn Crespin was part of this group of militants, terrorists, women scattered all over the country, set on overthrow-ing the government."

"What else?" Jagger asked eagerly.

"Reason she was still running around loose is she was married to some

FBI guy. And her cousin said the husband always protected her, tried to get her file destroyed. . . ."

Harmston was puzzled. "She's never done anything political. Hasn't even practiced in the last few years, sort of retired. She has a place up toward Chimayo."

Jake had it. He remembered. "She came up against me in a child-custody case." Of course! The Crespin woman had represented Helen's sister, Greta Wilson. Jagger had represented Wilson himself, and he had squashed Greta Wilson and Carolyn Crespin like bugs underfoot. He smiled. "We don't need to worry about her. I beat her so badly last time, she'll never forget it. It's not every day a lawyer loses a case so badly that the client commits suicide."

Emmet concentrated on his plate. It had been whispered at the time that Greta Wilson might have had some help committing suicide. She had this huge trust fund that went to her sister if she died, and the sister was married to Jagger. Greta Wilson wasn't the first person to hang herself in the county jail, and usually it was because somebody looked the other way while somebody else helped the hanging along. Not that Emmet intended to say anything to Jagger about that.

Vince shrugged. "Well, you've got the little whore dead on. She killed her baby. No question about what happened. . . ." He fell silent as Jagger turned toward him.

"The question may be raised how she got pregnant."

Harmston said, "What the hell difference does that make? These stupid little shits screw like jackrabbits. So they get pregnant!"

Jagger merely stared at him, leaving it to Swinter to reply.

"He means this Crespin woman may find some plausible line of defense, that's all. Like if the kid was raped—"

"Dr. Belmont didn't say anything about rape! There's nothing on the tape."

Jagger said very softly, "Vince, there's nothing on the tape at all except the questions Dr. Belmont was instructed to ask."

Emmet lowered his voice almost to a whisper. "Belmont's a good girl. She does what she's supposed to do, and she wasn't supposed to ask about rape." He leaned back in his chair, cast a roving glance around him, making certain they were not overheard. "Mr. Jagger preferred to keep rape or incest out of it, but then we'd figured on your handling the defense."

Jagger purred, "I doubt it's necessary, but, still, this FBI informant might come up with something useful. Always nice to discredit the opposition." The words were casual, but the tone was clear. Emmet was to take care of it, soonest. Without waiting for a reply, Jagger rose and moved across the room to speak to Judge Roger Rombauer, leaving the two men behind him to exhale—long, relieved breaths.

"Jake is in a mood, isn't he?" muttered Harmston.

"You don't call him Jake to his face," remarked Swinter in a snide tone. "Better not call him Jake to anybody."

"Sorry. I meant Mr. Jagger. What's he so up about this trial, anyhow? It's not much."

Swinter murmured, "You know what Mr. Jagger stands for, Emmet! He's not a member of the Alliance just because it's good for business—he's a real American. He's willing to stand up against the people that want to ruin our country, and you know who they are, Vince. He's not afraid to say a lesbian's really a pussy-suckin' dyke. You know what I'm sayin? Mr. Jagger told me, he said, this little bitch baby killer, she's a symbol of everything that's wrong with our country. I mean, when women forget their duty and their place, that's the end, right? Mr. Jagger wants to send a message."

Harmston nodded thoughtfully. "Crespin's from New York, originally. Lots of Jews in New York."

"Nah," said Swinter, his brow furrowed. "She's not a Jew. She's Catholic. Or used to be. So we'll see what we can find."

He shook his head, slightly annoyed. With an attractive female witness or opposing lawyer, Jake had a way of letting his eyes travel up her legs and under her clothes. By the time he was through looking up her skirt, the whole jury would think she was selling it on the street. Unfortunately, however, the Carolyn Crespin he had seen out at the jail was stout, sixtyish, and looked like somebody's grandma. Not a prime target.

He turned in his chair, casting a glance at the dais. "Here comes Mr. Jagger, and there's our speaker, ready to tell us all about brotherly love."

9

OPHY SAT IN HER OFFICE at Misery, holding a coffee cup in one hand as the other busily sorted bits of paper into piles. Patient notes. When in hell was she going to get time to record this stuff? She couldn't concentrate, anyhow. Simon had called last night. Hi, darling, how you doing? Great, great, gotta run. Got a story brewing in the Balkan Protectorates.

"Simon," she'd pleaded, hating the whine in her voice. "When are you coming home?"

Silence at the other end of the line. God, why didn't he just tell her, whatever it was? "I need you," she murmured. "I really do."

Throat clearing.

"Tell me," she demanded. "Simon, for God's sake, tell me!"

"Ah," he said. "Damn. Ophy, I'll be home next week. Let's talk about it then."

Talk about what then? Had he met someone else? Was he in trouble? What the hell?

It did no good to speculate. Speculation only made the matter seem worse. Weighing down the paper scraps with a couple of books, she slipped out of her suit jacket and into the long lab coat she habitually wore at Misery. Get this meeting out of the way, get her notes recorded, and she'd be caught up by noon. It was Friday. Starting tomorrow, she would have four days off. And Simon, damn him, was playing world traveler!

Was he covering bag-lady terrorism, wherever he was? Were old ladies making bonfires of cosmetics and stockings and sexy underwear? *Time* magazine called it the revolt of the unwashed against the overdecorated. How about the Family Values Shock Troops with their switches and whips, driving women off the streets? Or the Sons of Adam, who were still picking off unveiled girls on street corners? Were they wherever Simon was, as well? How about the cultists? Three more bunches of bodies found this week, a total of over five thousand bodies since the first of the year, burned, shot, poisoned, hanged—lots of them children. The mad leading the mad, the blind leading the blind. Was Simon covering all that?

The conference room was on the second floor, off a back corridor and facing the light well at the center of the building, a quiet location. The dozen or so people already in the room were as quiet. Most of them were working on their first or second cups of coffee, needing more before they'd even be awake. The chief sat to one side, well-shaven morning face rosy with aftershave, but no more alert than the rest of them.

Ophy came in, mumbling "Good morning" to the others, some of whom grunted in reply. She fetched herself a cup of coffee and joined them at the table, two seats down from the chief. She had her nose sunk in her coffee when the door opened and strangers came in.

"Here they are," muttered the chief, nodding toward the man and woman who stood murmuring to one another in the doorway. "Lotte," he called. "Come on in."

The couple advanced, he putting his briefcase on the table before turning back to close the door. With some effort Ophy brought her mind back to the table as the chief made introductions:

"Lotte Epstein. Joe Snider. Dr. Ophy Gheist, chief of quartage here at MSRI; Jean Morrison, Southside and MSRI ob-gyn; Genevieve Simmons, Citywide Internal Medicine; her associate, Roger Falls. Ben Morrell, Surgical Services . . ." And so on and so on.

"If you all have coffee, I'll turn this meeting over to Dr. Epstein. Lotte and I are old friends; we met in school; she's been with the Centers for Disease Control as long as I've been in medicine. . . ."

His voice trailed off and he sat down, gesturing vaguely at the plump little woman to his right. She was a grandmotherly type, all rosy-cheeked, with soft white hair. Her expression wasn't grandmotherly, however, unless it was Red Riding Hood's grandma. She looked urgently apprehensive. Ophy sat up straighter and paid attention.

"We can't enforce a silence order, but we're asking that you not discuss this meeting with anyone, not even with one another outside this room. This is one of several such meetings we've had and will be having. We're looking for data. . . ."

"What?" demanded Genevieve Simmons, thrusting out her jaw. "Data about what?"

"Give her time, Genevieve." The chief cleared his throat. "Let Lotte tell it."

Lotte cleared her throat. "All right. Back in early 1998 we began to receive reports from health departments that cult deaths, suicides, and suicide attempts were all increasing. The suicide rates had been rising for years among teenagers, but in ninety-eight they began climbing the age ladder. The cult deaths covered all age groups. We also saw a doubling in the number of sexual assaults, though they stayed in the usual age group, midteens to midthirties. The opinion among psych people was that people were joining cults out of fear, were killing themselves out of fear, that even the sexual assaults had some basis in stress." She cleared her throat. "Kind of an 'I'm going to die anyway, why not get it over with?' or maybe, 'I'm going to catch AIDS eventually, why not get it over with?' It made as much sense as any other theory.

"Six months ago, however, though the cult deaths were still at an all-time high and the suicide rate was still climbing, rapes had fallen almost to nothing. The psych people still thought the cause was the fear of violence. As you all know, however, random public violence began to abate in ninety-eight, in the wake of drug legalization and increased home officing. The fewer people out in public, the less public violence. Polls show that the public believes hibernation and deactivation vaults have removed the worst offenders from circulation. In other words, rightly or wrongly, the public perceives a reduction in violence. Naive common sense dictates that when a fear is eliminated, or at least ameliorated, conditions arising from that fear should also be ameliorated."

"You're saying they weren't?" Dr. Simmons again.

"From the beginning we were troubled by the fact that many of the suicides were people who didn't fit the theory, people who were at very low risk of either dying by violence or contracting sexual diseases. Amish men and women, for example, who had had little or no sexual contact prior to marriage, who were married while young to equally young virgin spouses, who do not and have never used drugs."

"Fear doesn't have to be realistic to cause problems," blurted Dr. Swales. "And why in hell isn't somebody here from Psychiatric?"

"We met with the people at Central Psych first," said Joe Snider. "Days ago. They said the same thing you did. Fear needn't be grounded in fact to cause problems. So they looked at our data—which include about nine times as many men as women, by the way—and they postulated the suicide attempts as a response to the loss of male status through enforcement of sexual-equality laws, as a response to lowered self-esteem, or maybe as a response to unemployment, societal disintegration, or overcrowding. They quoted animal studies at us. They pooh-poohed the whole thing."

"Meantime," Lotte Epstein interrupted, "the number of reported suicides continued to rise. We can assume people who get into cults or try suicide are seriously depressed, and we know depression does not exist in a vacuum, so we began looking for some corollary effects."

"Like what?" Morrell asked impatiently.

She looked in his direction, responding patiently. "Is there increased demand for mental-health services? Is there increased absenteeism in industry? Increased sales of antidepressant drugs? Anything and everything that might give us a handle on this."

"Divorce," said Ophy, aware of a sharp discomfort. "You'd expect the divorce rate to go up. If not divorce, then couples ah . . . maybe . . . living apart. Things like that." She shook her head gently, trying to dislodge whatever it was that scraped inside her skull.

Snider nodded, made a note. "Anything else?"

Jean Morrison asked, "Since you've got attempts included in your data, someone must have asked the survivors why they did it."

Lotte shrugged. "Of course. They give us as many answers as there are victims. Fear, sex, stress, money, pressure, worry."

"What about the birth rate?" Ophy asked. "If more and more people are depressed, wouldn't you expect the birth rate to go down?"

"We've seen no significant change through 1998, which is the last year we have complete data for. We actually have more recent data on the suicide rate than on birth rates. Birth and death statistics are handled differently in every state, and there is no uniform system that will give us up-to-date compilations. We seem to be about two years behind on the routine stuff. Perhaps Dr. Morrison has a handle on that?"

Jean shrugged. "We're going through one of those little seasonal slumps right now. I haven't noticed any big changes."

Ophy poured herself a glass of water from the pitcher before her, moistened her dry mouth, then turned to Lotte Epstein. "What do you want from us? Confirmation that this is happening?"

"We know it's happening. We don't know whether we're seeing the iceberg itself or only the tip. We want to alert the medical establishment, but we want to do it quietly, so we don't have a panic. There could still be some simple explanation."

Ophy shook her head. "It's bizarre. Could it have anything to do with the other bizarre things that are happening? The bag-lady riots?"

"They might both be manifestations of some underlying cause, I suppose," said Lotte. "Maybe overcrowding."

"But overcrowding couldn't be the only cause," interrupted Snider. "We tested that hypothesis, of course, but some of the earliest cases came from sparsely populated areas. Wyoming. Montana. Nevada."

Lotte held up her hand, silencing the babble that erupted. "We've had this same conversation a dozen times with a dozen different groups. We don't expect you to come up with a solution. We may be panicking over a statistical blip! All we're asking is that you be alert, that you take meticulous histories on any attempted suicides. That you get as much information as you can on successful suicides and cult-related deaths. We've worked out a questionnaire, and we'll leave copies; get as many cases filled out as you can, quickly, please. Of course, if any one of you has a flash of insight, that would be most welcome, too. These cards have both my office and home numbers if you think of something brilliant."

She wound up the meeting in businesslike fashion, saying to the room at large, "I think Dr. Gheist may have a point about other bizarre behavior. Ask about that, as well. Get information about environmental factors, also. We have nothing at this point to indicate this is anything but chance, but we should exclude no possibility. In return for your cooperation, we'll let you in on anything we come up with."

A general mumble. Ophy fastened her gaze on the opposite wall and let the speculation continue around her. There was something tapping at the back of her mind, tiny finger taps on a closed gate. Something. She knew something, but she couldn't remember. Maybe when Simon came home. He was always good to talk with when she was puzzled. Maybe when . . . maybe if.

Ophy was in the shower that night when she remembered what it was that had been bothering her: One of Sophy's books had included a story about a battered wife in the U.S., and she had half remembered it during the meeting. Why had that come to mind? What did it have to do with this morning's discussion? Sophy's stories were almost entirely about women and children, but according to Lotte, it wasn't mostly women who were dying. It was mostly men.

She stared at the shower curtain, water running down her face. Tomorrow. Tomorrow she'd call Lotte Epstein.

No, damn it. Tonight.

Dripping wet, she went into the bedroom, burrowed in her purse for Lotte's card, found it, punched in the number. It rang a dozen times before it was picked up.

"Lotte? This is Ophy Gheist, we met this morning at the meeting?

Right. Listen, can you get data on battered women and child abuse? Can you find out if the rates have changed any over the past couple of years?"

"You expect them to have risen?" Lotte asked. "They've been rising steadily for the past thirty years."

"Oh."

"That is, through 1997. We don't have complete ninety-eight or ninety-nine yet."

"So they could have gone down in ninety-eight and ninety-nine?"

"Down! Down?"

Ophy laughed uncomfortably. "I don't know, Lotte. Just look at what you've got, even if it's partial data, will you?"

"You must have some idea what you're looking for. Or why you're looking for it."

"Oh, I have an idea. But it's so strange, I don't want to talk about it until I know for sure."

The place was a hospital ward, obviously. Ophy couldn't remember how she got there, but there she was, walking down the aisle between the rows of beds, rows that stretched so far away she couldn't see the end of them. All of the patients were asleep. At the foot of each bed was a rack for the record, and she lifted a record as she went by, one here, one there, realizing as she read them that it was a women's ward. These patients all had the same illness.

"What is this?" she asked the nurse who was following her, pointing at the diagnosis scrawled on the record. "I can't read this. Not on any of them."

"I can't tell you," whispered the nurse. "I'm not allowed to tell you. You'll have to ask the doctor."

"But I am a doctor," Ophy said. "I am a doctor. . . ."

"No." The nurse shook her head. "I mean a real doctor."

"Forgive me, Father, for I have sinned." Mother Agnes knelt in the confessional, eyes downcast, determined this time to tell the whole story, get it all out. "Father, I have been troubled by. . . ." She stopped, blinked, cleared her throat.

"By impure thoughts," Father Girard finished for her. "Predictable, Mother Agnes. Your sins are at least predictable."

"No, Father." She frowned, annoyed. She hadn't confessed to erotic dreams for weeks. Strange. She hadn't had them, or at least didn't remember any. Well! What a blessing. God had answered her prayers! She almost chuckled but was returned to herself by the sound of Father Girard clearing his throat. "No, Father, it's something else. It's this . . . vision I've had, am having."

"A vision?" His voice sharpened, tightened, and Aggie's lips turned up in wry amusement. Sins of the flesh didn't bother the old man a bit, but just a hint of visions and he'd be calling the archdiocese for instructions. God forbid a nun should have visions! "What vision?"

"One I had a couple of years ago, Father, plus something that's going on now. I keep seeing . . . seeing this young nun. She's dressed in the old habit, the one our order used to wear. She's always in motion, going somewhere. I see her out of the corner of my eye. Whenever I see her, I think she is Sophy."

Long silence. Then that terribly gentle voice that betrayed patience under duress: "I thought we had agreed, Reverend Mother, that you were to forget Sophy."

"We did agree, Father. I have tried."

"Is there some constraint? Willful lack of obedience, perhaps? Or is it something you haven't told me? Something you should have told me?"

"Something I'm trying to tell you now, Father."

"Then tell me, and we'll decide once and for all."

"This vision I've been having . . . it isn't the first time I've had a vision associated with Sophy."

"Go on."

How could she go on? How put it into simple words? She swallowed deeply and tried: "It was in 1997, Father. I was visiting friends in San Francisco. I entered a room and saw Sophy. . . . There was an effulgence. I thought she was an angel. There were wings, and she was surrounded by this dazzling light. Everything was confused, as though the light was broken by a prism, a shattering glory, so vivid . . ." Her voice trailed off. The image never left her mind: Sophy poised in glory, her lips curved in a smile.

Another long silence. "What did your friend do or say?"

"She looked into my face and put her finger to her lips."

"And now you're saying you remember this image frequently?"

"Yes."

"And this memory prevents your spiritual growth, or, let us say, your spiritual peace?"

How could she say yes? How could she say no? The words came out in an anguished howl. "But I don't know, Father! It seems to be connected to this other vision, this continuing one. . . ." She gasped, horrified at the sound of her own voice.

A long silence. "Over the years I have come to know you rather well, Reverend Mother. I have never found you to be an imaginative person. For that reason, if no other, I would think it unlikely you merely imagined what you saw. On the other hand, you should accept that what you saw may have been something as simple as sun-dazzle reflected from a windshield in the street."

"A harmless mistake," she whispered. Had she been worrying herself sick over a simple optical illusion?

"It could be that. Considering your distress, however, I would be remiss not to consider something more sinister. Your friend, you have said, was not Catholic, was not even Christian, yet you always regarded her as a good person. Your thinking of an angel is evidence of this regard. I, however, considering the long-term effect this friendship has had on you—the guilt and pain you feel and have felt—must consider that what you saw may have been the very antithesis of angelic."

She had thought of this herself. She had rejected the idea, but she had thought of it. "You think she may have been . . . satanic? That what I saw was diabolical? But it was beautiful, Father!"

"Evil can be very beautiful, Reverend Mother. How otherwise would it seduce so many? And how many times have you confessed that you found your friend seductive? Is she not the source of much of your guilt?"

He waited, as though for a response, but she couldn't make one. "You've told me everything?" he prodded.

"I think so, Father."

"We've talked about obedience before. You have trouble with that, Reverend Mother. Those nuns who become leaders in their orders do tend to be strong-willed, which means they do have troubles of this kind. You must set this memory aside. You must forget Sophy. You must make it a test of your obedience to do so. When you find yourself remembering it, do not turn it over in your mind, questioning and worrying. You have confessed it. You have turned it over to God. You do not need to trouble yourself over what it was or why it was, because God knows the truth of the matter. So put it out of your mind as you would put away any other temptation from Satan himself."

"Sophy never acted seductive, Father."

"That, too, may have been part of her glamour." He sighed, letting her hear the sigh. "You're being evasive. You must set these equivocations aside, Reverend Mother. Accept that you were mistaken, that the matter is of no further concern to you. It's time to make a choice as to where your soul lies. You must affirm the totality of your commitment."

She drew a breath, so deep that it hurt. "Yes, Father."

"Also, Reverend Mother . . . use the meeting with the archbishop as a test of your obedience."

Her breath caught in her throat. So the archbishop had already told Father Girard what he was there for. "Yes, Father."

". . . in the name of the Father, and of the Son, and of the Holy Spirit."

"Amen."

She came out of the confessional behind the row of massive pillars and iron grills that walled off this portion of the cavernous nave. The chapel in the abbey proper was cozier, more hospitable, than this great stone barn. She felt adrift and not at all cleansed. She felt wrung out, beaten, battered. Was she guilty of seeing what she'd wanted to see? Had she turned a bit of sun-dazzle into a revelation? Or had Sophy really . . . really been . . . something other than what they had all thought?

She went through the heavy door into the long glassed-in cloister that extended from church to abbey, used as a promenade for exercise in rainy weather, opening on the east into the sisters' cemetery and on the west into the abbey garden. Death on the one hand, life on the other, with a sheltered prayerful journey between. The symbolism was not accidental. It had been arranged long ago that the sun would set over the garden and rise over the grave. Not this life, but the next. The last and best excuse for pain and suffering, explaining everything, insusceptible to proof.

Beyond the cemetery were the poultry houses, and beyond them the silver sheen of the shellfish ponds with the pump houses and the packing-house nearby. Oysters from the Abbey of St. Clare were featured on the menus of half the restaurants in New Orleans and more than a few in Boston and New York. Not to mention their own kitchen, which had served oysters last night to Father Girard and to the archbishop. That's probably when Father had learned what the visit was about.

She glanced at her watch; ten minutes left before her appointment, but the archbishop was no doubt stamping his feet and chewing at the bit, annoyed at her even though she wasn't late. She could have been there, waiting, but she'd figured she'd need all the help she could get, physical and spiritual. Being in a state of grace had seemed a good idea, but she felt worse, not better! Gritting her teeth, she headed for the parlor. No point in making the man more restive than he already was.

He was waiting, as she had known he would be, a dour man with blue jowls and mistrusting eyes. He gave her barely enough time to sit down with a murmured pleasantry before launching his obviously prepared speech:

"After long and prayerful consideration, Reverend Mother, I must tell you of my concern that the work the sisters are doing in the shellfish farm is not appropriate for nuns." His voice was as smoothly melting as butter, his lips as gently curved as a plaster saint's.

She sat like one graven in stone, denying she had heard what he had said.

"Pardon me, Your Excellency, but I don't understand."

"As you know, several years ago the Holy Father directed us to assess the work of the various religious and lay groups in each archdiocese in terms of spirituality. To have a convent that is totally self-supporting, almost profit making, casts in an awkward light the vow of poverty taken by the members of your order."

She drew in a deep breath. "Forgive me, I still don't understand. The sisters get nothing from the proceeds aside from a modest diet, much-mended habits, and a Spartan level of heat in winter. Our efforts have been directed toward the support of the church and the school. Everything we earn goes into one or the other, Your Excellency."

"I'm not accusing you of making improper use of the funds, Reverend Mother. I am saying there are higher duties even than a school. A school that is, by the way, educating women far above their special position in life."

Far above their what? What special position? The girls would have to work. How were they to live unless they worked? They had to eat! They had to clothe themselves! Even if they were lucky enough to marry a "good provider," they would have to work at some time during their lives if only to provide medical care or education for their children! She felt herself swaying, losing her resolution. She had promised to obey!

"They need to be able to support themselves, Your Excellency."

"Consider the lilies of the field," he purred. "God will provide, will he not?" He put on his counseling face, an expression of grave though kindly concern. "Don't you think your efforts have been too successful? You are able to support the church and school from your fisheries. Thus the parents of the children in the school are required to pay very little tuition. The parishioners provide very little support for the church."

"They are not well-to-do people, Your Excellency. Many of them could not possibly afford tuition, and the best efforts of the entire congregation could not possibly support the church. It's a monstrous edifice." In Aggie's opinion it should have been razed a century ago instead of being rebuilt bit by bit through a century's effort by the Abbey of St. Clare.

He stared at the ceiling, fingers pointed together, thumbs rotating. "For the sake of their souls, they should be making a greater effort."

"You wish us to stop the fisheries project for the sake of their souls? We are to tell them this?"

He looked only momentarily startled, like a man who has suddenly put a foot in a hole. "No . . . not precisely. We simply feel the management of such a very large business by an order of nuns undermines the special role of women in the Church. It was Adam, after all, who was directed by God to bring forth food by the sweat of his brow. And it was Eve who was told to obey. I remind you of that, Reverend Mother. You, too, are expected to obey.

You took a vow of obedience. The young women currently occupied in the fisheries might be better, more spiritually, occupied elsewhere."

Father Girard had already reminded her of the vow of obedience, she reminded herself. The vow had not been to obey the archbishop, particularly—but set that aside. She gritted her teeth, kept her voice calm: "Each sister is fully involved in our life of prayer whether she teaches in the school or harvests oysters from the ponds."

"Having sisters doing physical labor is not appropriate."

"Several of the disciples were fishermen."

"They were men."

She swallowed deeply, trying desperately for control. "Since we are highly mechanized, the work done at the ponds is somewhat less laborious than the work done in the laundry, which is traditionally women's work. Scrubbing floors, also women's work, is even more laborious, as is the annual digging up of the flower and vegetable beds."

"The laundry and gardens are more housewifely, more acceptable." He said it as if by rote, without emotion, a programmed response like a computer voice. He didn't care what argument she made. He had an answer for each. It didn't matter that the answers were illogical and self-serving. He was not interested in discourse.

She said with horrible conviction, "You have someone else in mind to run the business?"

He shifted, raising one nostril. "A committee of the local chapter of Catholics for the Faith has agreed to take it over."

"A committee. Made up of whom?"

He raised and rotated his chin, as though his collar were too tight. "Mother Agnes, is that really relevant?"

"Completely relevant, Your Excellency. At Mother Elias's request, before entering the abbey I took an M.B.A. in order to be capable of setting up and running this business, which she and her council had researched and determined upon. I have since trained others to take my place. I learned during the course of taking my degree that we would need biologists and biotechnicians, and some of the sisters were dispatched to acquire education in those fields. We have one Ph.D. chemist. Does your committee have these human resources?"

He said angrily, "I have not inquired—"

"These are not jobs that can be performed by unqualified people. There are serious public-health implications to the sale of shellfish. We work without salary, and we work full-time. I don't know where you will find other well-qualified people who will work full-time without significant paychecks. The Catholics for the Faith have not taken a vow of poverty as we have."

"That's a matter—"

"Also, since your committee is undoubtedly made up entirely of men, we would not be able to allow them in our enclosure."

"That can be handled. We can, for example, subdivide your property, build a wall across it. They have, after all, offered to share the profits of the farms fifty-fifty with the archdiocese."

She could not keep silent. "Fifty for the archdiocese. Fifty for Catholics for the Faith, whose main claim to fame, I seem to recall, is their opposition to an increasing role for women in the Church?"

Now he was angry, his eyes narrowed, his lips twisted. "The pope spoke once and for all on that subject in 1994, Mother Agnes. No female priests! Jesus picked men as his disciples."

It was true. It was the one final argument that the men in the Church always fell back on. Jesus had picked men. Carolyn said no, not only men. Sophy said no, not only men; she'd researched it, and there had been women in the early Church, lots of them. Jesus had picked Jews, too. Jesus had picked married men, but the archbishop didn't mention that. She took a shuddering breath. "Your Excellency, fifty percent of nothing is nothing. By the time you pay full salaries, and allow for a learning period, there'll be very little profit even if an unqualified local committee could do the work, which I don't believe it can." That ought to reach him, if money was the motive.

"When we build the wall," he said stubbornly, his jaw tight.

So it wasn't just the money. What was it? "The land the fisheries occupy was a gift to our order and the donor specified that it reverts to other legatees if we do not occupy it in its entirety. I know there are heirs who would pursue the matter."

He turned a fiery glance upon her. Agnes set her mind upon obedience and tried to find a way out of this tangle. Whatever this matter had to do with, it wasn't spirituality. She mustn't let herself get furious with him. She mustn't let herself! She could hold on to herself if she just understood what was going on.

She summoned up a conciliatory tone, struggling to keep her voice calm and level and patient, oh, God, patient.

"I'm sure you would agree that it would not be good for our laity to hear we are in a wrangle over who has the best qualifications to run a business which was begun here and has always been here. Our ability to manage is proved, and the results support the church. We would not want to deprive the church by turning this resource over to someone who does not have proved ability. Perhaps if Your Excellency would explain it to me . . ."

He stared out the window, his thumbs spinning around one another like little rotors, his face still set with anger. "It is not a plan I can discuss in detail. The Holy Father simply feels that at this millennial time it is appropriate for the Church to make a special effort to renew the faith of its people."

"I haven't heard about this special effort. Please tell me what you can about it."

He lifted one nostril again. "The Holy Father feels we have moved, in some cases, rather far from our spiritual foundation. We have been involved, not only in this country, in disputes that discredit our universality. The New Catechism, providing as it does that Islam is included in God's plan of salvation, has given us a ground for further discussions with members of that persuasion, working toward a universality of faith for all mankind. You mentioned the increasing role of women in the Church. There is some feeling among both Christian and Islamic teachers that women's roles are already quite demanding, and perhaps that they should return to their more traditional and very special place in God's plan. . . ."

What was going on here? She gritted her teeth and said expressionlessly, "Let us look at the accounts. Perhaps we can find some way to help."

He smiled, a smile that had nothing conciliatory in it. "Let us hope you can do it willingly and with a generous heart, Reverend Mother." She heard it as a threat.

When he had gone, she went to the cloister, half stumbling, to lean against one of the stone pillars as she peered out blindly. So much for being in a state of grace. It was not proof against pain such as this. His words had been more than a threat to a business. They had come to her like a threat to a child, her child, her creation. The fisheries were profitable because of the labors she and the sisters had put into them, and every dime was allocated to their daily work.

"What better way to fight the unifying message of holy wisdom than to sow inequality between men and women!" said a voice from behind her in a clear conversational tone.

She spun around, looked into the garden, saw the flick of a white veil disappearing around the corner of the church. Who had spoken? No point in lying to herself. It was Sophy. Father had told her to forget or be damned. How could she forget? Sophy wouldn't let her forget!

She had resolved never to tell the DFC what she'd seen at the meeting in San Francisco. She had decided to go to this one last meeting, only this one, and keep her mouth shut during it except to say good-bye. Whatever Sophy had done or meant to do, Sophy was now gone. If Agnes herself left, there would be no one to speak of it, ever.

Now, in an instant, her decision was overthrown. She pressed her fingers into her temples, trying to find the source of that bone-deep ache, trying to assuage it. No good. She went out of the cloister into the garden, found a sun-warmed bench, and collapsed onto it, not even bothering to straighten her skirts, weary as though the bench were an Everest she had achieved after long and arduous effort. Well, she had climbed and climbed and climbed. All her life she'd turned toward the steepest slopes with a ready heart. Now Father wanted to take away the memory of Sophy, and the archbishop wanted to take away all her achievement. No question about it. They would make her decline and fall.

The DFC had argued for years over what a "decline and fall" might be, but surely this would qualify under anyone's definition. Faye thought Carolyn's marriage was a fall, and Bettiann thought the same about Faye's being a lesbian, and Jessamine shook her head at Bettiann's living on her husband's income, and Ophy thought Jessamine marrying someone she didn't really love was a fall, which Jessamine denied, then admitted, then denied again. And Agnes thought Ophy sometimes did things as a doctor that were a fall, and, of course, so far as Carolyn was concerned, Aggie's being a nun was a skydive from thirty thousand feet with no parachute.

And Sophy? Sophy had listened to all this attack and defense openmouthed, but only briefly. When the argument had threatened to become personal and acrimonious—a rare thing among the seven of them—she had cried out:

"Stop it! We can't decide for one another what a fall is. Each woman can only decide for herself. Ever since men destroyed Elder Sister's medicine bag, conscience is all women have."

"Oh, wonderful! You've got a new story for us," Aggie had cried, grateful for the interruption. Some of Sophy's stories were delightful, and some of them were painful, but either would be better than this wrangle they were in. "On a scale of one to ten, how many hankies will we need?"

Sophy pursed her lips. "This story isn't sad exactly."

"Good," Aggie said, echoed by the others with rueful laughter, all equally glad of the respite.

"This all happened long and long ago, at the beginning of the world," said Sophy. "Nothing sensible lived then but the Mother of all, which is wisdom. Time came Mother was lonesome, so she let her womanly blood flow into the ashes of her fire, and she mixed this with clay, and from this she molded seven daughters and baked them in the life-fire.

"When they were baked, Mother named them and admired them and taught them to converse and dance and sing, and she gave them freedom to think and speak, in order that she might learn from them and with them, for one mind, she told them, is only one mind, no matter how wise, and it benefits from the thoughts of others.

"And when they were well grown, she told them to make a live world by taking their womanly blood and mixing it with ooze from the swamp or at the edges of the sea, and building it into creatures and trees and plants, many kinds, large and small, but to make each kind slowly, changing it as was needful, and

not to make more of their own kind until they understood well how the world worked.

" 'Each thing you make influences each other thing,' she said. 'First you must learn how things work together, or you may destroy your heritage before you know what it is.'

"So the earth daughters lived for a long time without any other people, building many different creatures and seeing how they fit together and how they changed over time, learning how the earth worked.

"Then one day the oldest sister said, 'To spread the life plan among each kind of creature, we have given it sex, so that each young one born is different from all others who have come before, changing throughout the ages, and of these changes are lives and histories made, so that in time each thing that can be, will be. Such is the purpose of Wisdom; therefore, we, too, should have young in which our own lifeplans are mixed and changed. Shall we do as the wolf does with her mate, or the doe deer with their king, or shall we be like the lizard that lives on the rocks and needs no male at all? Shall we be as the spider, who eats her mate to have done with him? Or the tree that mates in the wind? Shall we have males or not?'

"And after talking it over and looking at all the males, they decided it would be pleasurable to have males who were handsome as the stags and bucks who trumpeted upon the mountaintops.

"But a younger sister said, 'If we have males hanging around all the time, they will get in the way and become quarrelsome. They will be as the stags are, always crashing their heads together.'

"So the oldest sister thought a long time, and finally she said, 'We could make males some other way.'

" 'But they are so handsome,' cried the sisters. 'Look at them, Elder Sister, at their heads so proud, at their haunches so strong. Look at them! Aren't they handsome?'

"Elder Sister looked at them, and they were very handsome. She said, 'It is true, they are proud and virile. But the stags crash their heads together because each one wants all the females to bear his young. Even when the females do not want them, the males chase them and harass them, to control them. If we make handsome, troublesome males like this, they will want to control us, and that will lead to evil. As you know from watching the creatures we have made, when sex is alive in the world, creatures think and smell and see only the sex part. So if we have males, we will put their sex and ours in a medicine bag, and we will let it out only when we want children. That way we can have young from time to time but still be peaceable.'

"And another sister asked, 'But what will they do with their time? We raise the food and build the houses. What is there for them to do?'

"So Elder Sister said, 'Males can explore the world and all its wonderful places. Males can hunt and fish and tell stories of great wonders. Males can paint their faces and make costumes out of fur and feathers, and in time they may grow wise and seek other of Mother's children who live among the stars.'

"And all the sisters thought this was a good idea, so they let their womanly blood flow into the ashes of the hearth fire and gathered up the mud they made and mixed it with the ooze from the swamp and so created men and baked the fire of life into them. But before the men were quite baked, the women put every man's sex into a medicine bag, and also that part of themselves that would respond to the men, so they would not be troubled with it. And so the men came to life. They hunted and fished and painted their faces. They told stories around the fire. They captured animals and tamed them. And they helped the women when they had heavy things to lift, but they were not so very different from the women, and life was comfortable.

"Until the time came when the women wanted children, so they decided to open the medicine bag and let sex out. When they did this, all the men began to crash their heads together and sing songs of themselves and prance around the cook fire. And the women admired them and took them, and they made love, making children. But very soon things were not at all peaceful, as men began to fight with one another, and to leave one woman to chase and harass another, and to beat women who did not do as they said, and the women themselves lusted after other men. 'This is not good,' said Elder Sister. 'We are not seeing one another clearly, we are seeing only the sex part.' So the women shut up sex in the medicine bag once more, saying, 'We must not let this bag be opened except rarely.'

"But one man, the man who had lain with the eldest sister, saw what she did with the medicine bag, and he went to his brothers to tell them what had happened. He found his brothers in their house, all mourning the loss of their sex, for it had made their lives exciting and dangerous. 'I know where it is,' he said. 'If you will all come with me to hold her down'—for Elder Sister was very strong—'we will take the medicine bag away.'

"And this is what they did. They came in the night, while Elder Sister was sleeping, and they held her down while the one man found the medicine bag, and they tied her so she could not stop them when they ran away. They could not open the medicine bag, so they took their knives and cut it into tiny pieces, to let their sex out. And the pieces of the medicine bag stuck to every man's sex, and the little pieces are there today, wrapped around the tips of men's penises, a sign of their pride and their shame, for it is the sign of rape and force, and some men even cut it away, so as not to be reminded that they took sex by force and against women's will.

"Of course, the women's sex came out of the bag as well, and since that time men have strutted their sex all the time and have fought and crashed their heads together, and women have lusted after improper males, and men and women have not seen one another clearly, so that men have laid hands on women to force them to do what women would not do."

"End of story?" Carolyn had asked, enthralled.

"No," Sophy had replied, staring into the distance as though mesmerized. "I have to give it a new ending because of all the new stories I've learned. I think that Elder Sister was very angry, and she started making a new medicine bag right away, and every time there is a rape, she weaves a little. Every time a man beats or kills a woman, she weaves a little. Every time men lock a woman up, or veil her face, or beget children on her out of pride in their manhood but without regard for the children's future lives, Elder Sister weaves a little, and in the fullness of time the bag will be rewoven and sex controlled once more. Then we will see one another clearly and we will have peace again."

"I'm so glad we have that to look forward to," snapped Ophy, thinking of herself and Simon. "Honestly, Sophy, you don't want women to have any fun."

Sophy's face had changed, as though she'd forgotten them for the moment and was only now coming to herself again. "Well, that's what I was saying. That's the reason decline and fall has to be up to our consciences. We have such different ideas about what women are. For instance, in your religion your priests say woman brought sin into the world when she bit into the apple, but my people would say man brought sin into the world when God asked who did it and Adam blamed Eve. Which is the greater sin? Intellectual curiosity? Or betrayal? Scientific experimentation? Or disloyalty?"

This sent them into laughter, and the original argument was forgotten. Or at least mislaid. Such different ideas among the seven of them. To Agnes the weirdness at the 1997 meeting, followed by Sophy's suicide, had been the ultimate fall. How had Sophy squared that with her conscience? Had Sophy even had a conscience? Or had she been something else, something that didn't need a conscience?

Something that had stopped being . . . no. There was the nagging seed of doubt. There was the burrowing chigger, the itching place that demanded scratching. Deny it as she would, reject it as she had tried to do, Agnes wasn't convinced that Sophy had stopped being. Perhaps Father Girard had touched the reality of the situation when he had said that Sophy might have been . . . demonic. She could have been. She could still be. Out there somewhere, in here somewhere, in Aggie's very soul there could be this canker festering, this worm gnawing. There was something Sophy wanted from Agnes, perhaps something evil, and Agnes was terribly afraid of what it might turn out to be.

10

CAROLYN MET STACE AT CASA Sena for lunch midweek. The warm-weather tourists were not yet packing the town, so they didn't have to wait to get a corner table away from the main flow of diners and waitpersons.

"Though," said Stace, "if it's waitpersons, it really ought to be dineper-sons also, oughtn't it?"

"Or diners and dinettes," said Carolyn, taking a thoughtful sip of her margarita. She didn't usually drink at noon but today needed something to blunt the edges. "Maybe diners, dinesses, and dinettes, including the kids."

"That isn't something that's ever bothered you, is it?" Stace laughed at her.

"Words? Not really. Mankind is a good word." She set down her glass with a thump. "Or humankind. I'm afraid we've spent a lot of feminist energy on meaningless symbols rather than essential functions. All through the seventies and eighties we should have been pushing for a truly bicameral government: a men's Senate and a women's Senate, a men's House of Repre-sentatives and a women's House, with each sex electing a president in alter-nate terms." She lifted her glass again, toasting her daughter. "Instead of gingriching issues affecting primarily women and children, like pregnancy, childbirth, abortion, welfare, childhood education, and the like, men would leave them to women to decide. Men could then pay full attention to issues of preeminent concern to men, like restructuring professional baseball."

Stace blinked. "What's the matter?"

"Why do you ask?"

"I know you've got a militant side, Mom, but you don't generally go on like this."

"Oh. That. Well, for one thing, I've been having crazy dreams. Unpleasant, I guess you'd say. And for the other, you know very well what's the matter. Lolly Ashaler is the matter."

Stace flushed. "I should have figured that."

Carolyn dipped a finger into her water glass and drew a wet circle on the tabletop. "Here's a cipher, a blank, a female virtually without personality, a girl who at age fourteen was gang-raped, impregnated, and subsequently threatened with death. Her grandmother, who died around the same time, was her only emotional support. Her sole sexual education has been by TV, hampered by inadequate vocabulary to understand much of it. Her sole child-care experience has been what she herself received as a child, which was nil. She is functionally illiterate. She gave birth unattended in an alley, was revolted by the mess, wrapped it in a roll of paper towel, and stuffed it in a Dumpster. She knew, at some level, that this was 'sort of' a baby, but she was not prepared to mother it. She said she didn't have the 'stuff,' and she was correct on several semantic levels: In fact, she did not have the emotional, spiritual, experiential, or material stuff. Though she couldn't articulate it, she was a living refutation of the Hail Mary Assumption."

"The what?"

"I'll tell you all about it when we get our strategy set. Let's just say she was stating the first law of human parenthood according to Crespin: It's not what your reproductive organs do that counts, it's what your mind intends before that moment. Lolly intended nothing at all, she had nothing to intend with. Now she's in jail, and we have one of the most dangerous men in the state howling for her blood for murdering her child." She wiped out the circle with a swipe of her hand.

Stace kept her eyes focused on the menu. "One of the most dangerous men? Mom?"

"That's what your father calls him. And it says in the morning paper he's going for murder one, the death penalty."

Stace's jaw dropped. "But she's a juvenile! We don't execute juveniles in this state."

"We've tried juveniles for murder one before. And I'll bet Jagger figures he can get the law interpreted in a way that will allow execution."

Stace was stunned. "He's saying it was premeditated?"

"That's what murder one means. Did Belmont hear you tell Lolly about me?"

"No. Dr. Belmont left the room first, while I was still packing up the tape recorder and labeling the tapes. No one heard me tell Lolly about you except Lolly herself."

"Don't mention me to Belmont. Don't mention our relationship." She sighed. "Normally, my first act would be to get Lolly out on bail, but I don't think I will."

Stace looked up alertly. "Why?"

"She's been threatened. Also, I can defend her best if she remains pretty much as she is now. If I let her out, some do-gooder may take her in and clean her up. The more respectable she looks and sounds, the less likely I'll be able to get her off."

Someone came to take their order. Stace mumbled, Carolyn pointed distractedly, and the person went away.

"God, Mother! Murder one. I can't believe it."

"Have you seen what the papers are making of this case? Jagger is riding this thing for a good deal more than it's worth. Lolly's evidently going to be used as a human sacrifice."

Stace shook her head, her face white. Abstractedly, she buttered a bit of bread and bit into it.

Carolyn smiled bleakly. Her voice dropped to a murmur. "Have you heard of the American Alliance, Stace?"

"Some sort of ultraconservative think tank, isn't it? Dad mentions it occasionally."

"Back in their Washington days your dad and Mike Winter were analysts responsible for keeping track of the ultraright, even though the Bureau was far more worried about commies and blacks and revolutionaries than it was about fascists. Mike is a good bit younger than your dad; he's still with the Bureau, and he keeps in touch."

"I don't get the connection to this case, Mom."

"Possibly none. But Jake Jagger is an Alliance protégé."

Stace stopped chewing. "Is he really?"

Carolyn smiled bleakly. "Would I kid you, kid? After that run-in I had with Jagger some years back when the walls came crashing down on my head, your dad told Mike about it, and Mike told Hal to watch out for me because I was tangling with a powerhouse. According to Mike, Jagger has a lot—and I mean a *lot*—of Alliance money behind him."

"What's he doing here? I mean, this state is hardly a power base!"

"You yourself told me he came out to get into politics. Arkansas doesn't have a lot of power, either, but it was a good political stepping stone to the presidency. I'm telling you this so you'll be discreet. Do not go shooting your mouth off about this case among your friends."

"I still don't get what all that has to do with this trial."

"Exactly my question. Politics and right-wing organizations should have absolutely nothing to do with this trial. This is a stupid little case! There are Dumpster babies found every year, all over the country, in New York and Kansas and Hawaii and California and Georgia and everywhere else. Infanticide and infant neglect exist in inverse ratio to the accessibility of abortion services. We know that. So why should there have been an article about this particular New Mexico baby in the *Wall Street Journal* this morning? Even given the *Journal*'s rightist bias, there's no way they'd have covered the story in the normal course of events. Someone is plugging this particular Dumpster case, talking it up, publicizing it, speculating on the first-degree murder charge as a 'trendsetter' toward the 'reestablishment of morality'—I'm quoting."

"I guess I missed it. All I read was the comics."

"Oh, this is comical enough. The only reason for the coverage is to identify Jagger with a particular cause, and that cause is to redefine women's role in life and then to punish them if they don't perform it. The fact that it's a national publication, not a local one, argues that he may have been picked for something at the national level."

"He'll really want to win, then."

She nodded grimly. "Win or lose, he'll really want to be seen as a true believer, fighting the forces of evil. Lolly's so pathetic she doesn't stack up like much of an opponent, so Jagger needs to build her up some. Or he can add some bigger devil to fry along with her. Like me, for instance. If he makes the connection between you and me, he might come after you."

Stace gripped her hands in her lap. "Come on. You're exaggerating."

Carolyn flushed. Why was she doing her best to scare Stace just because she herself was scared? She took a deep breath. "Maybe I am. Maybe I'm just having a bad case of the jitters. Time will tell."

The server arrived with their food. They bent to their plates, glad of the interruption. Carolyn chewed and became calmer, like a ruminant, she told herself. Chewing convinces one the world is all right. Still . . .

She asked, "What did your psychologist come up with in her report to the DA's office?"

Stace rearranged silverware. "She wrote it up as a common guilt reaction. She said Lolly was afraid to tell her mother she was pregnant, so the 'murder' was a cover-up for the crime."

"I doubt her mother was ever around long enough or sober enough for Lolly to tell. And what was the crime? Getting raped."

"Dr. Belmont didn't know about the rape. Lolly only answered . . . sort of answered Dr. Belmont's questions. I picked up on some things Belmont didn't seem to hear. Belmont didn't mention rape in her report."

Privately, Carolyn thought that Dr. Belmont had probably done whatever she had been directed to do by Jagger's office, no more and no less. Dr.

Belmont did a lot of business for the DA's office. Neither her selection nor that of Vince Harmston as defense attorney had been coincidental. Judge Rombauer had appointed them both, and it was a known fact that Jagger had never lost a case before Judge Rombauer.

When she had almost finished her lunch, Carolyn set down her fork and leaned on her elbows, speaking softly. "I've asked the DFC to help me with this. Jessamine and Ophy are going to testify. Bettiann has offered some funding help. I need a couple of researchers and some investigative work when time comes for jury selection. Bettiann's offered to help pay for it."

"I didn't realize it would be quite so . . . nasty."

"It's going to be damned hard work and very unpleasant! Jagger is never content merely to win. He likes to leave blood on the ground."

When they had paid their bill and reached the sidewalk, Carolyn commented, "I really think it'll be better to leave Lolly Ashaler in jail. She's safer there. There she can get bathed and fed and decently clothed. That's more than I can guarantee outside."

"Once the media knows you're defending her . . ."

"If this case is being publicized, they could come after me like coyotes after a rabbit, yes. I'll worry about that when the time comes."

They hugged briefly, then turned away in opposite directions, Stace to return to her work, Carolyn toward the parking garage. Since thinking about Jagger had already ruined her day, she might as well sink the rest of it in a visit to Lolly.

She drove south on sun-spangled pavement, watching dust devils chasing one another across the dry soil between the shrubby growths. There were those who said these deserts had been grasslands once, overgrazed by cows into their present state of desiccation. After the rains, in July and August, the desert would bloom with fragile green and sturdy gold, evanescent grass and almost immortal rabbit brush. However dead and lifeless things looked, the magical rain always made them bloom.

There had been no magical rain to make Lolly bloom. When Carolyn got to the interview room, after stopping to have a few words with Josh, Lolly was already there, slumping in the chair as though she had not moved since the time before, as dead and as arid as the desert.

"How are you feeling?" Carolyn asked.

A shrug. A sideways glance.

"I wanted to talk about whether we should try to get you out, Lolly."

"Try to? They said I can. Get out."

"They? Who?"

"Those womens in there. They say I can have bail."

"You can have bail if you have five thousand dollars, Lolly. Do you have that?"

Long silence. "They said like a hunnert, maybe."

"The judge set your bail at fifty thousand. That means you have to have five thousand to pay a bondsman."

"You goin' to pay it?"

"Me?" She fought down rueful laughter. Laughter would be a mistake.

"You. Ainchu my lawyer?"

"Lawyers don't pay bail, Lolly. Besides, if you get out, you may be hurt. Even killed. The boys who raped you know you're going to testify. They know they could be arrested."

The girl looked up, no longer quiescent, scenting danger. "They rather get ridda me. They don' like the tanks."

"The hibernation tanks?"

"They hate the STOP tanks worse. Like bein' dead but awake at the same time."

"So you're better off here, aren't you?"

"Yeah." It was said almost with relief, as though some nagging worry had been in an instant identified and dispelled.

"How's the food?" Carolyn asked.

"Pretty good. We had mash potato las' night. We had turkey-burgers. They was pretty good." Her voice came awake, almost cheerful. "They's a woman here, she works in the kitchen, she gives me extra stuff 'f I do her, you know."

Carolyn did know. The distaste showed in her face.

"Hcy. I gotta livc, you know! You got no right tellin' me——"

"I wasn't telling you. I was just thinking if the district attorney's office finds out you've been doing a little sideline prostitution, it's going to make it harder for me to keep you out of the tanks."

"Me?" The astonishment was real and unalloyed. "Me! They don' tank girls!"

"Yes. They do. Not many, but they do. Women who kill children they do. Juries don't like putting women to death, or putting them in prison for life, but they don't mind putting them in the tanks. It's quicker and more certain than the death penalty, Lolly." The same effect, without all the controversy.

Sullen once more. Thoughtful, though, the brows drawn in. There was a brain struggling for light under that mop of hair. IQ about eighty, maybe. Maybe born that way, but more likely stifled from whatever it might have been with a more challenging rearing.

"There's a beauty shop in the jail, isn't there, Lolly?"

"Yeah. Place we can wash our hair, do it up. Gotta pay, though, for the stuff."

"Get a haircut, if you can. I'll pay for it."

Suspicion, the sullen expression, back. "Why I gotta cut it?"

"You don't have to. I thought you might like to."

"Don' like to."

She's fifteen, Carolyn reminded herself. Outside, she's an amoral little hooker. Inside, she's fifteen.

"There are some questions I need to ask."

"Awright. You can ask." A little defiance there.

"Before the boys raped you on the Fourth of July, had you ever had sex, Lolly?"

"Yeah. A few times."

"Who with?"

"I dunno names. Guy, he offer me money if I do 'im. Tha's all."

"Oral sex?"

"Wha'?"

"With your mouth?"

"Yeah."

"Not the other way?"

"No. Well, maybe. A few times."

"Because you wanted to?"

"Nah! Why'd I wan' to? It's jus', if he ask me nice an' I say no, then he beat on me and do it anyhow, so I get hurt two places. If I say yes, then at leas' I don' get hit."

Carolyn swallowed deeply. "Did you ever use birth control, rubbers, anything like that?"

"One guy, he had rubbers. He says maybe I got AIDS."

"Do you know about birth control?"

"Know it's a rich people's thing. They tryin' a wipe us out."

"Who told you that?"

"People. They come around, they say birth control's tryin' a wipe us out."

"Who's 'us,' Lolly? Who do you mean?"

"Us. Us black people."

"But you're not black. You're white—like we say here, Anglo."

Lolly looked confused. "The people that come aroun', they was black."

"The ones who told you not to use birth control."

"They was black. They tol' me birth control is genocide." She said the word almost proudly. "Genocide. They tryin' wipe us out, an' we got to follow the Leader an' keep our women pure an' populate the world."

"They were Black Muslims?"

"They said they was Army of God people. Because it's a new thousan' years, time for us holy people to rise up."

The hair rose on the back of Carolyn's neck. She swallowed painfully. "But if you're not black . . ."

"Us poor people gonna rise up, too. They got no right to keep us from havin' babies. They owe us, they gotta feed us an' all the babies, an' the more babies we got, the stronger we get."

"But you didn't want to have a baby."

"I didn' have the stuff. . . ."

Carolyn sighed, sat back. "Just for a minute, Lolly, think about it. If people are sick, we try to get rid of the sickness. If people are poor, we try to get rid of the poverty. Is that bad?"

"Gettin' ridda me, that's bad."

"Not getting rid of you. Stopping you from being poor."

"How you gonna do that 'less you get ridda me?"

Good question. How could one ever stop Lolly from being poor? Carolyn tried to find an answer as she put her papers away, coming up with nothing at all. "I brought you some candy. It's all right. I showed it to the guard outside. You can take it."

She did take it, a quick snatch, like an animal, afraid some other animal would get it first. She did not say thank you. On her way out Carolyn stopped across the hall, at the double doors leading into the tank room. Halfway down the aisle between the racks a slender Hispanic woman knelt in prayer, one hand resting on the tank just above her, the other, wound in a rosary, striking at her breast, once, twice, three times. She looked familiar. Carolyn stared, surprised to recognize a former housekeeper, Emilia Gonzales.

"Emilia?" She opened the door and slipped into the vast room. "Emilia?"

The head turned, the blind eyes gradually became aware. "Ms. Shepherd? Carolyn?"

"What are you doing here?"

"Teofilo. He's here." She gestured.

Carolyn joined her beside the tank. Inside the glass the handsome face slept, serenely unaware. She remembered an olive-skinned boy with eyes like stars and a beautiful smile, playing with the dogs in the driveway while his mother did the cleaning. Emilia had worked for Hal and Carolyn for almost five years and was one of the few people who ever called her Ms. Shepherd.

"Your boy? He was just a baby last time I saw him."

"He grew up," Emilia said.

The clock marked the years until end of sentence. Twenty-nine years, ten months, eleven days. Illegal firearm sales. Assault on a police officer. Flight to avoid prosecution.

"I will be old when he gets out. Too old." Tears leaked from her eyes, finding accustomed runnels down cheeks long eroded by tears.

"Emilia, I'm so sorry. I didn't know."

"I went to your office. They said you retired."

"They should have called me at home."

"I looked. Your name isn't in the book."

As it wasn't. Damn it, Jerry should have called. He knew how close she'd always felt to Emilia!

"Was there an appeal, Emilia?"

"The lawyer, he said it wouldn't work."

"What happened?"

"He find this gun when we cleaning out my brother's house, after my brother die. It belong to my brother, Geraldo, so Teo took it to sell it to a man. The man was a policeman, he grab Teo, Teo got scared, he push him and run away."

"I'll see what I can do. Who was your lawyer?"

"His name is Harmston. He didn't do nothing for us. Teo's brothers, they want to do something, you know, something crazy. Get him out somehow. I say no, no, is enough we got one boy lost."

Carolyn hugged her, patted her. Damn. This boy didn't belong here! Harmston. That lazy, stupid bastard.

"Emilia, I've got a case right now, but I swear, as soon as I'm through, I'll do something about this. I promise!"

"God bless you if you do, oh, yes." Released, Emilia knelt once more, her hand going to her breast as before. She was visiting this tank as she would a grave. For all intents and purposes, her son Teo was dead.

Josh was watching from the end of the aisle nearest the door, shaking his head sadly.

"She's got a kid in there."

"Yes," Carolyn said. "I know him. He doesn't belong in here, Josh."

"I know him and his brothers. Nice kid. He don't belong in there, that's for sure. Come over here." He led the way down a side aisle. "Look there."

He pointed out three tanks, all together. Behind the faceplates children's faces looked out at her—beardless, slender, not more than thirteen or fourteen years old. Cisneros, Diego, Ravenna. For a moment she was astray, in a dream. She had been here before, seen this before. . . .

"Kids," said Josh. "Babies. I know for a fact these three guys wasn't the ones who robbed that store, but old God Almighty Rombauer, he likes somebody in the tank, never mind is it the right one. Some days I get to thinkin', if I knew for sure which was which, I could empty out a lot of those tanks and pop me somebody in that belongs here. Not like it used to be, guards and gates and all. Only live people we've got here are the ones waiting trail. Nobody'd ever know."

"You could do that?" She stared at him, intrigued by the idea. "Just untank somebody?"

He put on a conspiratorial face, whispering, "Not hard. I've seen 'em do it. You just poke a few buttons, wait awhile, help the guy out, then you sterilize the case and set the buttons for the next one. The stuff you shoot 'em with before you put 'em in the tank, it's right there in the storeroom. There's nothing to it."

"Poor Teo. You're right about there being some bad people, Josh. And there's some that aren't bad who get called bad."

"You tellin' me? Lots of people in here don't belong here. These three kids? They're here because Rombauer didn't want them where they could talk about what happened to 'em in judge's chambers. You know what I mean."

Her jaw dropped. She, like everyone else who frequented the courthouse, had heard rumors. "Rombauer . . . he abused them?"

"He told 'em to come to a little party in his office and he'd shorten their sentences."

"How do you know?"

"Cisneros's sister. She comes to see 'em every week or so. Her brother told her, she told me. Course, we all know about old Bugger-Boy Rombauer. He's been that way forever."

"Oh, I wish I could prove that."

"Jagger can prove it, that's why his cases go so good. This guy of his, Dale Martin, ex-cop, ex–Green Beret, ex–a lot of things. Does a little spyin', you know. Maybe breaks a arm here or there. He drinks too much sometimes, talks a little too much. He says the DA planted a camera and got some pictures."

"Martin," she mused. "And he works for Jagger?"

"Now, that's a guy belongs in here. I oughta switch 'em."

"Somebody would find out," she said musingly.

"Nah. You put somebody else in the tank, but you set the buttons like it was for the first guy, set the humidity control a little high so the faceplate fogs up. Then they'd never know."

"Until the sentence ran out," she laughed without humor.

"I s'pose." He grinned widely, amused at the thought, then walked with her toward the barred door, jingling his keys. "Except the way they change sentences around, they might not even know then!"

"You mean sentences get changed once they're in here?"

"Oh, sure. You got a guy doing ten in New Mexico, you get papers from Montana saying he's supposed to be doing fifteen up there, you just punch in fifteen more and send Montana a FUD form—that's a federal uniform depository form. End of the year you got more out-of-state guys in your tank than you have in-state guys being tanked somewhere else, you get paid for the difference. Why bother shipping the pods around? Hell, all that room we got down at WIPP, might as well make some money on it."

Outside, the dust devils still chased one another across the desert, much ado about little. The April sun still shone, but the light seemed gray, like February seen through a dirty window. The drive home seemed endless and purposeless, except that Hal was waiting. When she drove in, smoke from the barbecue grill drifted toward her through the budding trees. So he was up and about.

"Where you been? I was getting worried about you!" He put down his cane to pull her into a great two-armed hug, like a hungry bear. She melted against him and they stood there, solidly planted, not wanting to break apart.

He did, however, pushing her out at arm's length. "You got a call."

"Who?"

"Helen. She said to tell you she heard Jake talking on the phone. She said Jake must be prosecuting a case against a client of yours, because he mentioned your name. She says she's afraid he's up to his old tricks."

"Did she know who he was talking to?"

"Some guy named Martin. He works for Jagger. She's going to call you in the morning, she says."

"Second time I've heard that name in the last hour or so." She told him what Josh had said. "Helen didn't say anything else?"

"That was all. Just the sound of the click and the buzz of the line. She was in a hurry, whispering."

Carolyn clenched her fists, her jaw, felt every muscle tense. Well, of course Jagger was up to his old tricks! Witnesses would lie, evidence would be created out of whole cloth. He'd arrange it all!

"Do it," she snarled into the air. "Do it, Jagger. I'm not going to get trapped in a cell so somebody can fake my suicide. If anybody dies this time, it's going to be you."

"Hey, sweetheart." Hal pulled her into his arms once again, half laughing, tears at the corners of his eyes. "Hey, there, love. It's me! Remember me?"

She laughed at herself helplessly, without humor. Lord. She was like that ewe-sheep. Stamping her foot and glaring when she hadn't a fang in her mouth or a horn on her head. All this threat and fury when chances were neither she nor Hal could do a damn thing about it. Unless they got some help from somewhere.

Night in Nuevo Los Angeles, and the bag ladies are at it again. "Listen!" is the command they're painting along the concrete bottom and sides of the Los

Angeles River. There, in scarlet spray paint highlighted in yellow, each letter fifteen feet high, the message is written: "Listen!" "Pay Attention." "Think."

Night in Denver and the Family Values Shock Troops are at it again, working the mall outside the movie house, rushing out at groups of girls, lashing at their legs with whips while the girls scream and scatter like chickens threatened by a fox. "Go home," the men bellow. "Go home where you belong!"

"I belong here just as much as you do!" one tall girl shouts back. "This is a free country!"

"For men it is," comes the response from three or four, moving in on her, trapping her. "For men it is."

When the other girls have gone and the men have dispersed, the argumentative one is still there, prone, blood from her head skeining the tiles. Though the whips had not looked that dangerous, the handles had been weighted with lead. The witnesses creep out, by ones and twos, to pick up the fallen one and carry her away. Later they will call for an ambulance, but they will not go to the police. This isn't the first time, and they have already learned not to go to the police.

Night in Chicago, New Orleans, Charlestown, Detroit. Night in Omaha, Cheyenne, Missoula, Seattle. Everywhere groups of old ladies here and there, doing incomprehensible things and moving on: groups of men doing equally incomprehensible things, which often leave the wounded or dead scattered behind them.

"Count the dead," the bag ladies paint on the sides of buildings, on the sidewalks, down the streets. "Lemmings or men, death is the answer."

"Go home," shout the men, brandishing their whips. "Go home to your father or husband, where you belong."

Night in Pakistan. Night in Bangladesh. Night in Egypt, Greece, Cyprus, Sicily. Night in London, Rome, Barcelona.

Snag-toothed hags, wrinkled dames, draggle-hemmed women moving down alleys, painting words in a hundred languages. "Girl babies are buried beneath the mango tree. Their blood is in the mangoes." "Ashes of brides blow on the wind. Do you dare inhale?" "For every man who goes hungry, five women starve. Their blood is in your rice." "Watch out for women ghosts; they are all around you."

Stout men, strong men, red-faced and round-bellied; lean men, wiry men, olive-skinned and flat-stomached, whaling away with their whips at any female found on the streets, turning weighted handles on the few who don't take the hint.

So far the two groups have not encountered one another face-to-face. Like antiphonal choruses in a Greek drama, they speak at one another across the waiting stage of the world, readying for the drama to come.

11

ON FRIDAY, AFTER STOPPING FOR a few groceries, Jessamine turned into her driveway and hit the code pattern on the security pad, hoping to find the garage empty and Patrick gone. He often went drinking with the half a dozen other expatriates who were his closest friends, sharing gloom and enmity among themselves and getting it out of their systems. No such luck. His car was in the garage.

In the kitchen half-melted ice filled a bowl beside the sink; a bottle of Scotch stood half-empty beside a cutting board that held a knife and shreds of lemon peel.

"Hi," she called in a carefully neutral voice. "I'm home."

"And how's the little working wife?" he asked from the door. The glass held at his mouth was almost empty. He'd been lying down; his sandy hair stuck out in all directions. "Here she is to break my tedium. Maybe she can fix the TV, it's on the blink."

"It was fine this morning. I watched the news."

"The movie channels are all messed up. I can't tell a boob from a bottom."

"Tragic for you."

"Boring. So. Amuse me. What exciting tales of the office and labs does she have to relate?"

"Not much, Pat. Sorry. One dull meeting, otherwise same old cross-match project."

"Ah, yes. Same old, same old. Same old Jessy. Same old Pat. Aren't you a little tired of that?" The rhyme came out unintended, surprising him, and he giggled, the sound that identified an intermediate stage of drunkenness. Past the early cozy, sexy stage, but not yet nasty. Into that little-boy stage, ain't we devils, hyuck, hyuck. If he went on, he'd get nasty, then weepy, then he'd be sick, and finally he'd fall asleep. Jessamine had it down to a mantra: sexy, funny, nasty—weepy, sicky, out.

She dropped into a kitchen chair. "Well, Pat, I'm not tired to the point of desperation yet. Are you?"

"Yeah," he said, dropping all pretense, setting the glass on the table, pulling out a chair for himself, spearing her with a jabbed index finger, all at once blearily businesslike. "I'm tired of it, Jess. I want something for me. I want you to go back to California with me. I want you to have a baby for me. I want a son."

She took one long, shuddering breath, then another. Well, well, well. So he'd been waiting for her, getting his demands all marshaled.

"I've thought about it," she said, forcing herself to be calmly reasonable. "And I don't want to be part of the senescent fertility movement, Pat. I think it's obscene."

He raised an eyebrow, his lips sneered. "What happened to love, honor, and obey, Jess?"

"I never said 'obey,' Pat. And I've always honored you."

"You call this honor!" His gesture included the house, the state of affairs, everything.

She shut her eyes wearily. "I didn't cause the earthquake, Pat. When Bio-Tech moved here, you chose to come with me. And you chose to turn down all the jobs you were offered once we got here." None of them had been world shaking, true, but some of them had been interesting, and any of them might have led to something better.

"Well, now I choose something else. And if you won't do what I want for a change, then t'hell with you, I want a divorce."

She recoiled from that anger as from a snake, her skin prickling, her mind seeking cover, a moment's dizzy cowering before she rejected such evasion. He had only said what she herself had thought recently, what she'd said to Val, what she'd almost hoped Patrick would say, so she wouldn't have to.

Her reply surprised even her with its tone of weary composure. "Then let's have a divorce. Whenever you like."

His eyes opened wide, as though he'd been struck, hit from some totally unexpected quarter. "J-j-just like that?"

"What do you want me to say, Pat? We've had two children, Peg and Carlotta. That's the number we agreed on. I'm not going to be dosed with hormones to bring one more child into a world that's already dying from excess people. But that's only my point of view. Yours is yours. You want to get back into politics, and you've said yourself that you have the wrong religion to have a political future here in Utah. I presume you will have a future if you move back to California."

"I've been ap-approached by the Alliance. They wan' me for a candidate, yeah," he snarled, trying to be dignified and succeeding only in sounding drunkenly spiteful.

Another deep breath. "The Alliance. They've always claimed to be nonpartisan. Are they sponsoring candidates these days?"

"Now they are. An' they have an inner— interesting platform." He stared at her blearily, the drink dissolving his normally well-defined features, turning him sodden. "And maybe you're right, I need somebody a little younger. . . ."

"All right, Pat. If you say so."

"You don't even sound like you care!"

She laughed, truly amused. "I'm up on the social and mating habits of primates, Pat, so they don't surprise me much. Any more than Bettiann's baby boy looking a lot like you surprised me much. If you really want a son, adopt him. I understand William would let him go cheap."

He said furiously, "Goddamn. You didn' say a word, and you knew all along!"

Had he really thought she hadn't? She wasn't stupid, or blind. Bettiann had had miscarriages, one after the other. William had a low sperm count, so she said. And then, suddenly, February 4, 1970, nine months after their first meeting in San Francisco, a fine red-haired baby boy. So let it alone. She shouldn't have mentioned it.

Pat wouldn't leave it alone. "You didn't say anything! You never even acted upset!"

"Pat, if you want the honest-to-God truth, I had mixed emotions. I was a tiny bit angry for me. I was a tiny bit glad for Bettiann, because she wanted so badly to give William a son. And I was a tiny bit curious as to how you managed it, considering Bettiann's problem with intimacy. What did you do? Get her drunk? Convince her you could cure her? Or did you do it with your clothes on?"

The anger leaked away, leaving his face vacant and rather foolish. "All right," he mumbled. "So you knew. So all right."

Abruptly, he heaved himself up and ran for the bathroom off the front hall. She heard him vomiting noisily, heard water running. He'd gone right through nasty to sick without stopping at the weepy stage, where he usually complained about his mother's having preferred Pat's sister to him. Thank God for small favors. She laughed, cried a little, shook her head at herself, unable to decide whether this was tragedy or farce.

Whatever it was, finish it. Don't let it die a lingering, painful death. Put an end to it. When he didn't return to the kitchen, she went looking for him, finding him supine on his bed, arm over his eyes.

"Do you feel like talking?"

He *arummed* at her, gave what passed for a nod.

"We've got some money in the bank. You should take half that. The insurance money for the California house went into this house, and even though this house is too big for me, I'd rather not move just now, so if you don't mind, I'll refinance it to make up the difference."

Again that nod.

"The jewelry you've given me, Peg should have that."

"All right." He fumbled for her hand, fettering her wrist. She let him hold it, passively.

"Pat, can I ask you something?"

"Yeah."

"Three years ago, the last time the club met in San Francisco. Before . . . you know. Despite the fact that we're all past the usual age of seduction, you went after my friends, all but Aggie. . . ."

"I don't do nuns," he laughed beneath his arm. "I went to parochial school! What do you think I am, Jessy?"

She knew very well what he was. He was Don Juan or Priapus, with better posture and less hair. "Bettiann I can understand. You'd found the key to her needs a long time before, but you went after the others. Why?"

"Shit, I don't know. You always seemed so tight, the bunch of you. Tighter with them than with me. I figured maybe light a firecracker under it. . . ."

"Just for fun? Like when you were a kid at Halloween, blowing up mailboxes?"

"Sure. Why else?"

"Did it matter to you that the DFC mattered to me?"

"I told you, that's why. . . ."

He couldn't realize what he'd just said. Surely he couldn't have meant it just the way he'd said it? "What did Sophy say when you went after her?"

A stillness at that. A rigidity. "I didn't get too far with her."

"Meaning you did with others?"

"Meaning . . . ah, hell, I was drunker than I shoulda been. I was seeing things."

"What things?"

"Dragons," he said, laughing at himself, moving uneasily at the memory. "I opened the door to her room. I heard the shower going. I started to go toward the bathroom door, and there was this dragon. Or maybe it was a dinosaur."

"You're joking!"

"Hell, Jessy. It wouldn't be the first time I was drunk enough to see things. Pink elephants, blue snakes. When I looked again, it wasn't there, but it shook me up some. I still remember it, eyes, scales, something strange. Just the liquor, but it stopped me. I didn't bother your friend Sophy."

"But you did some of the others?"

"That's for me to know. Give you something to think about."

She didn't need to think about it. Aggie and Faye were lesbians, even though Aggie didn't admit it. Ophy and Carolyn were happily, faithfully married. That left only Bettiann, whose weakness Patrick hadn't been above using for his own amusement.

He interrupted her thoughts. "You've asked your question. Now I'll ask mine."

"All right."

"You never were really committed to me, were you, Jessy?"

"As a husband?" she asked, surprised.

"As a person. You never really gave yourself to me."

His choice of words was unfortunate. Anger, thus far withheld, was just under the surface. "How do you mean, Pat?"

"Well, you know. You always had other things in your life besides me. Work. Friends that were more yours than mine."

"Didn't you always have work? And friends I didn't even know? And love affairs, as well, which is something I never had?"

"It's different for men." He said it scornfully. "I've pretended to buy that equality stuff for years, but it's bullshit, Jess. The Alliance people, they have the right scope on—"

Her anger erupted. "Do they really! So we go back to men doing what they want and women also doing what men want, right? You've never heard the story of David. Maybe it's time I told you about David."

"David? Who the hell is David?"

"Was, Pat. Who the hell *was* David. I was sixteen when I met him. He was a college boy; he roomed with our neighbor's son; our neighbor introduced him to me. He was extremely handsome, dark eyes, a slender, muscular build, a very sexy body, and intense, rather scary eyes. He bought me an ice-cream soda. He bought me flowers. He flirted with me, all just in the neighborhood, visiting his roommate's family. Being around him was like being on a roller coaster, all that intensity, focused on me. It was exciting.

"After a few weeks he asked me to go out with him, on a real date. Of course, at that age, in the fifties, I had to ask Mother, and Mother wanted to meet him. So he came to the house and Mother looked him over. When he left, she took me into her bedroom. She shut the door, pulled the shades, sat beside me on her bed, almost whispering. 'Get away from him,' she said. . . ."

"Get away from him?"

"Just listen, Pat. She said, 'Get away from him. I watched him watching you, Jessamine. He's a slaver. Get away from him, do it gently, if you can, but quickly, quick as you can, get away. He eats you with his eyes.'

"I didn't want to send him away, but she frightened me and I had never once disobeyed her. We had a loyalty, Mother and I. We were the only women in the family—we two stood together against the world of father and brothers and uncles and boy cousins. Mother was quiet, and my father told her when she could breathe, and my brothers ate her up with their needs and wants, and I was the only person she had to share with, to be a woman with.

"So I did what she asked. I told David that my mother thought I was too young. It was already too late. He wouldn't let go. He went on calling me, visiting next door, meeting me on the way to or from school. Back then, in the fifties, there were no laws against stalking, and he stalked me, day after day. He told me I was not to do anything, not to go anywhere, not to be with anyone unless he gave permission. He said he controlled me, that he owned me."

"Jessy. . . ."

"I cried at him, no, no, I wouldn't be anyone's property, not like that, but he wouldn't listen. Everywhere I went, he was there. Everyone I saw, he was watching. And one day, on my way home from school, he jumped out of the bushes along the road and dragged me behind them, into a sort of thicket. I thought to myself no, no, this can't be happening, it can't, but he tore my clothes, he held me down, he pushed himself into me, red in the face, panting, eyes bulging out, banging me, biting my breasts, choking me. . . .

"And when he was finished he put a gun against my breast and told me I belonged to him and would never belong to anyone else. He had made me his own, he said, and now he was going to kill me so no one else could ever touch me.

"All I remember happening next is I went crazy. I bucked and screamed and somehow the gun went off." She unbuttoned her blouse, pulled her bra down to show him the livid track, like the track of a whip.

"You said . . . you got that in an accident, a car accident. . . ."

"The bullet went across me, into his neck, his jaw. I felt the gush of blood all over me, it was hot. I pushed him off me and watched him while he died, still reaching for me—stood there, watching, glad he was dying, hating him, hating his wanting me.

"After David I was damned careful about 'giving' myself, Patrick! I saw my mother give herself to my dad. The only part of herself she kept separate was the part that was there for me when I got home all soaked in blood, the part that cried and held on to me at night when I had nightmares, the part that waited for my period with me, praying with me that he hadn't made me pregnant. That, and the part that went on putting money away for my education, the part that whispered to me when we were alone, 'Get an education, daughter. Be your own person. Don't do what I did, what that man would have had you do. Don't fall into this trap.' "

"You kept it from me! You never told me this, not any of it." His voice held no sympathy, only outrage.

"What would you have done if I had?"

"I wouldn't have married you, for one thing," he shouted. "I thought you were a virgin."

There was silence. He heard his own words and flushed, eyes darting, perhaps wondering where they had come from. Had he even meant them?

He had meant them. Perhaps *in vino veritas*, but still, at some level, he had chosen to be unforgivable. She rose and went to the door.

He tried offense: "I suppose your club knew," he shouted at her back. "Your precious club."

She answered him without turning. "Yes. They knew." She had been almost forty before she'd found the courage to tell them, and she'd never told Bettiann, because she was afraid Bettiann would tell Patrick. Perhaps even then she'd foreseen Pat's reaction. She shut the door on his raging voice.

In the bedroom she'd moved into months ago, when Patrick's penchant for daytime napping, late-night wanderings, and endless porn on TV had begun to interfere with her sleep, she shut the door and slumped onto the bed, feeling a slow leak of tears. It felt like postpartum depression. This feeling had that same looseness, that enormous emptiness. Anger would be better than this vacancy. Times like this were a lot easier if one could be angry.

Anger had been her succor when the David thing had happened. Anger had enabled her to tell the story to the DFC, eventually, and she hadn't been the only angry one. Faye had been furious:

"Pity the bastard is dead. He should have been castrated."

Castrating rapists was one of Faye's more militant causes, and it wasn't the first time one of her causes had set them off.

Aggie, as usual, had argued merciful incarceration: "All the feminist material I read defines rape as a crime of violence. And even eunuchs can be violent and cruel."

Ophy had been wiping Jessamine's tearstained face, and she had turned, the towel in her outthrust hand flapping like a battle flag. "That's only the feminist party line, Aggie. Eunuchs can be cruel, sure. No regime ever had any trouble recruiting torturers, or creating them out of anybody, even kids. People can be taught not to be cruel, however, but you can't teach a sexual predator not to be predatory. There's more than one cause of rape."

Aggie had said in her kindly, nunny way, "Is that a fact, Ophy? Or is it just your opinion?"

"Oh, for heaven's sake, Aggie, it's not opinion. You want to see testosterone go over the top? Just test a football or basketball team right after a hard-fought winning game. And don't be surprised if after the game some of the team members force any girl they can catch. Or run a hormonal assay on a guy who's been beating his wife for half an hour or so. Testosterone through the roof! Testosterone rises with violence, especially victorious violence.

"Then there's serotonin, which governs self-esteem. Primates with low serotonin are at the bottom of the pecking order. They have all that reproductive system pushing at them, they have no position to lose, and the pressure builds until they explode, risking everything on the next throw of the biological dice. Grab the nearest female and drag her behind a bush. Is it low serotonin or high testosterone? How much of it is under control?

"Then there's the rape or rape killing by a man who hates women, sociopathic violence: pure hate, the sex used only for humiliation. Then there's the man who acts out his fantasies and believes the woman really wants him: pure nutcase. Then there's the guy who uses violence to work himself up to sex, then kills the woman not because he hates her, but simply because she's a witness who might cause him some trouble. And, of course, when I was in med school, standard wisdom was that women, including little girls of six or seven, caused rape by being seductive."

"But that's silly," Sophy responded. "That's ridiculous."

Ophy stared at Aggie, daring her to disagree. "It's what this country believed a few years ago. It's what much of the Muslim world believes right now. Rape isn't men's fault. Men want to have sex, and what men want, men should have, so any woman who provokes male urges by showing her face or hair, or who is defenseless for any reason, or who just happens to be in the vicinity, why, she obviously asked for it. If she hadn't wanted sex, she would have stayed home, behind high walls, protected by her menfolk. Since she didn't, she has obviously dishonored her family and may, therefore, be raped and then killed with impunity."

"That's sick," said Faye.

"To us it's sick, but much of the male world believes it, nonetheless. All around the Mediterranean you'll find cultures that believe men can't control themselves and shouldn't have to try. And damn it, Aggie, a lot of the ones that aren't Muslim are Catholic."

Jessamine wiped at her cheeks. "Ophy's right. God, I've read everything that's been written about it. Testosterone's part of it. Serotonin's part of it.

Hate is part of it, and mental illness and even religious attitudes. Should we castrate to lower testosterone? Should we treat with Prozac to increase self-esteem? Or should we lock up all deviates and conduct a religious war to wipe out the paternalistic religions that lay the blame on the women?"

Sophy had shocked them all:

"But it isn't only men," she'd cried. "I know those feelings. I feel them, too."

They had glanced at one another uncertainly.

"No, I do feel them," she said. "This push inside. This hunger. Sometimes this anger. I think and I think, but still I feel it. I have felt it driving me."

Faye shook her head, smiling. "You're just horny, honey. We all are, from time to time."

Aggie shook her head. "You mustn't dwell on the feelings, Sophy. You must set them aside—"

Sophy threw up her hands. "Oh, Agnes! Set them aside! Your poetry, your songs, your drama, your dance, your books, all your arts speak incessantly of the struggle between your minds and your bodies! Set them aside? Men want to possess women, but their wanting often comes to frustration and indignity, so they regret their wanting, some of them come to hate their wanting. We women want to possess men, but our wanting often brings pain and loss, so some of us come to hate our wanting as well. Even the men and women who are lucky, who enjoy one another and have affection for one another, even those whose passion and wisdom are in the same pocket, watch their children with anxiety and their grandchildren with despair, for they, too, will be at war with themselves."

Jessamine laughed. "Among my bonobos everyone wants everyone all the time, and everyone has everyone all the time, and no one cares. Pity we're more like regular chimps, where the alpha male gets his pick and everyone else sneaks around."

Sophy cried, "Yes. It is a pity. We live like the torrent duck, buffeted this way and that, all our lives spent battling the flow only to stay where we are. If we could choose, is that what we would want? Only to stay where we are?" Her voice rose, almost to a scream. "How do we fight it? How do we grow to become wise persons with all this aching and pushing going on?"

Ophy went to her, hugged her, calmed her. "Shhh, Soph. Here we are after a couple million years of natural selection has produced a race that overpopulates and makes war and dominates and rapes, and you want to know about wisdom! Natural selection doesn't select for wisdom!"

Faye found her voice and remarked, somewhat tartly, "Sophy, my mom used to say you get wise when you get old, when your body slows down and gives your mind some room. Maybe that's the best we can hope for."

The conversation had stayed with Jessamine. She shook her head at the memory. When she'd married Patrick, she'd thought he was the best she could hope for. After David, being around a man, almost any man, had alarmed her, but Patrick had set off no alarms. The Pat she'd known before they were married might occasionally strike with words, but never with his fists. He could woo with words, he could make love elegantly, and he had not seemed possessive. He had offered a safe haven. If he had been ill, she would have cared deeply. If he had died, she would have grieved honestly. She could relax around Pat. If it hadn't been love, it had been close to it.

But now, now Jessamine wanted to slow down and give her mind some room. She wanted to become what Sophy called a Baba Yaga: an old hen, crouching on the top rail of the fence and clucking warnings to the chicks. If the rooster would just come up there and hunker down and stop crowing, they could talk about life and share the last of their time together.

But no; he still had his cock-a-doodle, and he would not trade it for this satisfying androgyny of experience. If the hen will not submit—or, perhaps, regardless of whether she will or not—the rooster will go down among the pullets and begin again.

The hell with it! Estrogen replacement and plastic surgery be damned. One could not pretend to pullethood forever.

So Pat. So be it, Pat. Farewell Pat.

Her tears had dried. They were the last she would shed for him.

Helen called Carolyn on Friday, about noon.

"I had a revelation," she said, her voice conveying an icy control that Carolyn found ominous.

Carolyn asked, "What kind, Helen?"

"The kind that tells me Jake will do whatever he wants to whether I obey him or not. After we were married, he told me I would do what he said or something would happen to my family. I did what he said, but Mom and Dad died anyhow. He killed them. Just the way he did Greta."

Carolyn was aghast. "My God, Helen. Your parents? You know that for a fact?"

"You mean, can I prove it? No. Of course not, but I know it's true. He married me for my trust fund, Carolyn, the one my grandfather left. Then I got Greta's share of the trust when she died. Then I inherited from Mom and Dad when they died. Jake took everything I had, and I've had to take everything he wanted to dish out. I'm not doing it any longer. I've got to do something, Carolyn. I've got to do something to get back at him. Tell me something I can do."

"Let me pick you up—"

"No, Carolyn, you're not listening! Tell me something I can do to confound and disrupt this man!"

Carolyn shivered, partly for Helen, partly at the thin edge of fanatical intensity in that voice. After a long pause she said, "Does he have a safe, there at the house?"

"A safe? I don't think so."

"Does he have any place where he keeps things, private things?"

"His so-called game room."

"Somewhere he's supposedly got some pictures of Judge Rombauer sexually involved with some Hispanic kids. They'd have been taken fairly recently, within the last year or so. If we had those pictures, Hal and I, we might be able to spike his guns."

"He keeps the game room locked."

"Combination lock? Keypad, maybe?"

"I think a keypad, yes."

"Well, maybe he's written the combination down somewhere. People do things like that. Or he's used a date or address or phone number he remembers. Something like that."

"I'll look. Oh, Carolyn, it'll give me something to do!"

The phone went dead. Carolyn threw herself onto the bed, arm over her eyes, trying not to weep. It did no good; the tears leaked. She sat up, wiped her eyes, then froze. She'd heard a sound. . . .

Far off, something opening. Resonance coming through the opening, alien sound, the hush of immensity.

"Sophy," Carolyn said clearly, "if that's you, if that really is you listening to me, watching me, I beg of you, I plead with you, please help Helen. The way you used to help people. She needs you. She really does."

She listened, but there was no answer. She lay back, her eyes shut. After a long, brooding moment something shut, and the world was only itself again.

Hal spoke from the door. "Who was on the phone?"

"Helen."

She felt the springs sag as he sat beside her and took her hand.

"Ah. From the look of you, I thought so." He stroked her arm and dried her cheeks with a corner of the pillowcase, then stood and pulled her up after him. "Enough of this brooding. Come along, dear one. Let's you and me go fix some tea."

It was Hal's medicine for all ills. Hot tea, amber or green, with honey in it. "To remind us of sweetness," he always said when sad times came along. "We need to remind ourselves of sweetness."

Would there be any sweetness for Helen?

◆ ◆ ◆

Ophy was late for her appointment with a security car she'd summoned to the front entrance of Misery.

"Sorry I'm late," she muttered, shaking his hand, giving him her destination.

The driver nodded. "Emil Fustig, ma'am. This destination a friend of yours?" He pulled the security car out into the avenue and began one-handedly changing lanes with great verve.

She held on, knowing this dodging about in traffic for what it was—an attempt to avoid trackers, followers, people who might be up to no good. Security drivers assumed that every rider was a target for terrorists. It was part of their code.

"No. It's a woman I've met only once, the wife of a patient. I need to see her for some research I'm doing."

"You don't know her place, then. Well, it's not too bad a block she lives on. It's a C zone. Not that it means much. It's been quieter lately, you notice? Not so many bombings. They haven't bombed any girls' dorms for most of a year."

"I read the other day that the violence rate is way down."

"That's what the tourist bureau says, sure. Don't know whether to believe it or not."

She put her head back, wobbling her jaw to loosen it from clenching her teeth, which she'd been doing all morning. "It's not just the tourist bureau. We've noticed it at the hospital during the last few weeks. There's less random violence. Except for the Sons of Whoever, shooting women. I had two more victims this morning; it's why I was late."

He stared at her in the rearview mirror, asking in an interested voice, "And what about these old dames preaching? What's that?"

She shook her head at him. "You got me. They say there's a war coming, but, then, so do the men with the whips."

He swung wide around a corner and pointed ahead. "Guys who'll rape a little girl and then call her a tramp. That's the place, with the green awning. You just sit tight until I've looked it over, okay?"

She sat. What was the point in hiring security and a bullet-proof car if you didn't follow the rules? Her driver checked the street in both directions, including the entrance to the nearest alley, before he parked, locked the car behind him, walked over to the door, and looked the lobby over for anyone lurking. He returned to unlock the car and fetch her, walking her quickly into the lobby and over to the screen. She punched in the Jenks woman's apartment number and stood ready, smiling nicely, trying to look unthreatening.

"Yeah? Who?" The image was snowy, streaked, barely decipherable.

"Ms. Jenks? I'm Dr. Gheist, from the hospital. I called. Remember? Can I come up and ask a couple of questions about your husband?"

"Who's that?" she asked suspiciously, peering over Ophy's shoulder.

"He's a security driver. He'll just bring me to your door. He won't come in."

Self-service elevators were no longer programmed to make interim stops. They went only from lobby to requested floor, or vice versa, and fire stairs had to be accessed by code from the computer downstairs, which was supposed to open the door automatically in case of fire. When they arrived on fifteen, Ophy stayed in the elevator while the guard looked around, then went with him to the apartment door. She knocked. Ms. Jenks let her in. He stayed in the corridor, leaning against the wall, hands hanging at his sides.

"Somma them," the woman muttered, shutting the door hastily behind Ophy. "Somma them're worse than the ones they protect you from, you know? What is this, now? What do you need? I told those people at Ortho ever'thing there was to tell." She led the way through the minuscule hall into a small living room, crowded with unmatched furniture, the walls speckled with small unframed pictures, florals and landscapes and nudes.

Ophy tore her eyes away from a strawberry-pink nude petting an unlikely violet cat. "I'm sorry to bother you, Ms. Jenks. We think your husband may have had a kind of . . . depression. It seems to be going around, sort of . . . ah, like an allergy or the flu. We just wanted to know if you noticed anything about him? Or felt it yourself?"

The straw-haired woman subsided, anger draining away. "Like a allergy, huh? I be damn. What're we allergic to?"

"That's what we're trying to find out. So you're feeling depressed as well?"

"Well, sure, hell, he tried to kill himself, didn' he? That's sort of depressin', wouldn' you say?"

Ophy went down the questionaire Lotte had provided. "Had he changed his eating habits? Sleeping habits? Sexual habits?"

Ms. Jenks shook her head, no, no, and then, at the last question, less certainly.

"Maybe?"

The woman shrugged. "He didn't care about it that much. When he just quit, I thought he was prob'ly, you know, just tired of it."

"May I sit down?"

"Sure, sure, sorry, sit. You want a beer or somethin'?"

"Thanks. No. Just these three or four questions, and I'll get out of your hair. Now, you say he quit? Did you . . . ah, get upset about that? Maybe say something that would have upset him?"

"Me, what would I say? Thank you, God? Hell, he was no good at it ever. He did sex like he did those paint-by-numbers pictures he's always workin' at.

Dab, dab, dab. Poke, poke, poke. If I ever got to come at all, it'uz just blooey. No . . . no rhythm to it, you gnome sain?"

Ophy concentrated. Gnome sain. Ah. *Do you know what I'm saying.* "Yes, I know what you're saying. You didn't miss the sex. You just missed his wanting it."

"Right. Not much, though."

Ophy made a note. Now for her own question, the one she really wanted answered. "Was he ever a violent man, Ms. Jenks?"

"Vilent? You mean, dyever hit me?"

"Um. Did he ever? Even years ago? When you were both younger."

"Hell. He ever do that, I'da broke his head for him, gnome sain?"

One little bit of corroboration denied. Damn. She rapidly filled in the rest of the form, said thank you, rejoined her guard, and returned to the corridor.

"Didn't take long," the driver said, falling in beside her, punching for the elevator.

"Just needed a few bits of information about her husband. He tried to kill himself."

"Lot of that goin' around."

"Really?"

"Five guys I know either did it or tried. Not the ones you'da thought, either. I mean, you know some a these big guys, always showing off their quads, you know—he makes it okay and some kinda nerdy guy, he can't handle it, he offs hisself."

"Handle what?"

"Oh, you know. How life goes. How it don't." He laughed. "Me, I think it's about time we had a rest from it."

Ophy returned to Misery and picked up her car. She and Simon had an apartment in a quad-block uptown, and on the way there she thought about Mr. Jenks, and about Simon, who had not come home, who had not called. If he did call, could she get away with asking him if he'd been depressed lately? Even though Ophy was a physician, she was not, as Simon had pointed out more than once, his physician.

"Let us have a little mystery," he had murmured in her ear. "Let us leave a little distance between us. Let us not know, always, what the other is thinking."

A disturbance in the street brought her from her reverie. She stepped hard on the brake, coming up inches behind the bumper of the car in front of her, which had stopped just short of ranks of men robed in black with pointy black headdresses, faces bare, like a dark-clad Ku Klux Klan. Each man bore a whip or cudgel of some sort; at least one of them carried a scythe. At the center of the squad a line of drums made a relentless pom, pom, pom. The men were chanting some doggerel or other.

Ophy locked the door and cracked the window to hear the words:

"We are here a thousand strong; women, go home where you belong!"

And a long pause, some men looking around themselves, trying to keep their lines even, then again, with the drums going bom, bom, bom, the ragged chant:

"No matter what their age or race is, women must not show their faces!"

Ophy fought down the impulse to giggle and closed the window tight, checking to be sure the doors were locked. The car next to her was a police car. The officer at the wheel was watching her reaction, grinning at her expression of distaste.

A short-skirted girl came out of a corner drugstore, head down, and started for the street, not watching where she was going. She collided with one of the marchers, fell back, and put her hand to her head as though dazed. The man she had bumped made a halfhearted gesture with his whip, then did a quick Elmer Fudd two-step getting back into position as the last of the procession crossed the intersection and went off down the street. A marcher two rows over saw this exchange, shook his head angrily, and flicked his whip at the girl, butt first, catching her on the forehead. She stood there stupidly, blood streaming down her face as the police car squealed its wheels and took off after the marchers.

The whole episode had a kind of cartoon idiocy to it. The words had been stupid, but the tone had been threatening; the drumbeat had been inexorable, but many of the marchers had seemed tentative about the whole thing. The one guy's action had been almost comic. He'd been more worried about staying in step than anything else. Ophy pulled into a parking space and went back to the young woman, who was by now leaning against the wall, sobbing. Two men, one old, one young, approached hesitantly from inside the corner store.

"What in the hell?" breathed the elder. "What do they think they're doing!"

Ophy pressed a clean tissue over the wound.

"Why did he do that?" the wounded woman cried. "I didn't do anything to him! I think he's crazy!"

"Honey, you and me both," said the older man. "All my years in this town, I've never seen so many crazies!"

"Is she going to be all right?" the younger man asked.

"I'm going to drop her off at the hospital, okay? I'm a doctor. That cut needs a couple of stitches."

"Are they going to arrest them? Those men?" asked the younger man. "God, they ought to arrest them."

Moved by some obscure impulse, Ophy asked, "You never felt the urge to join one of those marches?"

"Lord, no! Some people I know, they have, but me? Not on your life. Listen, I'll follow you to the hospital. I can bring her home. She just lives upstairs."

"Thanks, Rog," sobbed the girl. "Will somebody tell my mom?"

The older man offered to do so. Ophy said to the younger, "If you have transportation, why don't you take her over to MSRI?"

The younger man put his arm around the girl's shoulder and led her away to his car, murmuring soothingly at her.

"You have any idea why they did that?" the older man demanded. "Any idea at all?"

"You got me. I haven't any idea."

And she hadn't. The whole episode had seemed ritualized, even to the cop keeping watch from the sidelines. Perhaps the Elmer Fudd guy had been a trainee terrorist? A neophyte Nazi? And the other was the old professional warrior who knew when to knock heads? She was still puzzling over it when she reached the quad-block Simon had insisted they move into a few years earlier, when the violence had been at its height.

Their quad was typical: a four-square-block area with the two cross streets walled off at the outer ends and topped with razor wire; all the outside building entrances walled up and the outside windows grilled to the roofline, where a tangle of electrified fencing overhung the street and crosshatched the roofs to prevent the unlikely possibility of wall climbers or people dropped by helicopters.

Quad-blocks were closed fortresses; the most dangerous part of living in one was the short walk from the car to the security gate. Ophy parked, got her HoloID out of her purse, pinned it to her shoulder, went through the security gate on her parking level, exchanging greetings with the yawning guard, who let her into the elevator. At street level she entered the lock and put her hand on the identity plate that opened the final gate.

Once through that, she was home, among people she recognized as neighbors, all of them wearing photo IDs. Any strange face had better be labeled by a visitor's badge with a great big number on it. Anonymity, so the quad-block charter went, was the nursemaid of crime; no anonymity was allowed.

She walked the half block to her building lobby, where she found a woman from her floor waiting for the building elevator. They rode up together, buddy system, each keeping an eye on the other until they had their door unlocked. Ophy stood for a moment agape. The dead bolt on her door was unlocked.

"It's okay," she called, waving at her neighbor and taking a deep breath. So Simon was home. Finally.

He was sitting in the living room, the blinds drawn, a wine bottle beside him on the table, something soft and unobtrusive tinkling in the background. Harps, flutes, tom-toms. Jessamine had noticed more and more of that kind of music lately. Loose and windy music, without pattern or melody. A mere wandering of sound, an evocation of space and tranquillity.

"Simon."

"Hello, love." He turned his narrow, foxish face toward her, brow furrowed, one slender arm raised to greet her.

"I didn't know you'd be here."

"I am here. Decided the time had come. Face the music."

Getting to him was like swimming. The atmosphere was thick with his mood, whatever it was. Apprehension? Anxiety? She sat down on the table, leaned forward to take his hand, which gripped hers hard, as a drowning man might grip a floating log. "Simon! What is it?"

"I don't know, Doctor, love. Something wrong, somewhere."

"Are you hurt? Are you ill?"

"I don't know."

"What do you know?"

"I know I love you as much as ever, but something is wrong with me and I don't know what."

His voice was so weighted with sadness, it made her want to cry, but surprisingly she felt relief, a weight fallen away, some heavy load of apprehension dropping to leave a less horrible mystery in its place.

"Oh, shit, Simon, so that's it. But it's not just you. You're not alone! It's an epidemic!"

He sat up, regarding her beneath glowering brows, slightly angry, this dramatic scene, so well set, so long rehearsed, slipped suddenly into the banal. "What are you talking about?"

"You're depressed, right? You think you should be full of joie de vivre and the Old Nick, but you're not. Maybe you've even considered suicide. I said it's going around. Lots of people have it. Men. Women. We had a meeting about it. Oh"—she clapped hand over mouth—"I keep slipping! I'm not supposed to talk about it!"

"A secret epidemic?" His brows went up, a tilted glance under a forelock of curly hair. "Come on, Ophy. . . ."

"It is! The medical establishment is afraid there'll be panic. Besides, we don't know what it is. A bug. A virus. An allergy." She laughed. "Just this afternoon I slipped and told someone. I told her it was an allergy."

"What am I allergic to?" he demanded. "Life? Women? Or you in particular?"

She shook her head, moved to hold him, was pushed gently away. "Simon, I love you. Damn, don't let this—don't let this get in the way of our loving each other, understanding each other. I just *said* it was an allergy, making it up; I don't know what it really is. Nobody does."

"Who did you meet with?" Now he was the journalist, getting the story.

"You can't write about this, Simon. You mustn't."

"Why not? I've been in the dumps for months. Think of all the poor bastards out there who're going crazy. Isn't it better if they know?"

"Know what! We don't know anything, except that it's happening. The suicide rate's up. Cult-related deaths are up. Rapes are down, but assaults on women are up, or were a few months ago. Probably still are with these guys marching around. . . ." She described her encounter on the way home.

"The KKK?" His jaw dropped.

"I said dressed like the KKK. Only in black."

"Who were these people you met with?" he repeated.

"People from CDC."

"Is it everybody? Just older people? What?"

"You're not old! And it's not any particular age. It's people. They kill themselves, or try to. More men than women. No certain reason. They just do."

"A disease? Maybe a sexually transmitted disease?"

"Not according to the CDC people. People like the Amish have it. People who've never been sexually exposed."

"And women. What about women? What about you!"

She recoiled. What about her? She didn't know. She shook her head helplessly. "I don't think I'm depressed. Any more than usual, that is. Things can be pretty depressing at Misery."

"There should be riots!" he said almost angrily.

"Depressed people don't riot, Simon! It's too much effort! And it's been kept quiet, so the people who aren't affected don't know about it!"

"There've been those old-woman riots."

"Well, yes, but that's . . . philosophical. I was talking to the chief about it the other day. It's a kind of old-women's wisdom cult. They're very matter-of-fact about it."

"You must know more than you've told me!"

"Simon, I honestly don't!" She rose, began to pace. "It's a mystery. We don't know how far-reaching it is, we don't know what the cause is, we don't know what the ramifications are, we don't know."

"How long has it been going on?"

She frowned, trying to recollect. "About two years. Since ninety-eight. I mean, that's not certain, but that's when the first cases came to CDC attention. They could have been . . . infected long before that, of course. AIDS was already quite widespread by the time people figured out what it was."

"What do the survivors say?"

"I don't know. They give reasons. Stress. Fear. Being tired. According to the CDC woman, most of them have no physical problems to speak of. That was true of the case I investigated today. . . ."

"Tell me."

"This little guy lost interest in life, in sex, his wife maybe nagged at him, he decided to kill himself, but he botched it."

"How many is it affecting?"

She cast her mind back to the meeting, the lines on the charts. "We have no way of knowing the total. The suicide rate is up almost a hundred fifty percent in two years."

He leaned back. She took a deep breath, went to sit beside him, insinuating herself under his arm, hugging him. He felt good to her. He felt lean and tough and totally right. She sighed, leaning her head against his chest. "You feel good."

His arm tightened about her. "So do you." His voice was husky. She looked up to see tears gathering below his eyes.

"Simon. Whatever you worry about, don't worry about that, this, us. Don't. We'll start you on Prozac or something. Something's bound to work. Get you on an even keel, anyhow." She stopped abruptly, making a mental note. Could this be a withdrawal reaction to some widely used drug? Like an antidepressant? Had Simon used anything?

He didn't notice the hesitation. "I never really planned on an even keel, Ophy. Even keels are for dolts. I always preferred a blaze of passion. But what do I do now? What's recommended?"

"We get you to a doctor—not me, don't worry. Someone better than me. And we hold on to each other."

"And I'll write the story," he muttered, wry-faced. "God, I'll win the Pulitzer. How the world got so damned depressing, everybody died of it!"

12

IT WAS LATE MONDAY AFTERNOON when Bettiann received the call about Charley. William wasn't at his office; Maybelle didn't know where he was. Both she and Bettiann tried his cellular phone without result. Finally Bettiann left a message with Bemis and another taped to the banister where he couldn't miss it if he came home: *"Your brother Charley at Methodist Hospital, car accident, don't know how bad. I'll be there. Betts."*

Three hours later she was still there and still didn't know how bad. The state trooper who came to sit opposite her didn't know, either.

"Would you mind a few questions?"

She shook her head.

"You're his . . . ?"

"His sister-in-law. I couldn't locate my husband. I left a message for him and came on down. Just to be here, in case . . ."

"Would you know if your brother-in-law drank very heavily, Mrs. Carpenter?"

"Sometimes." She shrugged uncomfortably. "I've never known him to drink and drive, though. Charley was always good about that. He'd always call a taxi or get someone to drive him if he'd been drinking a lot."

"Would you know if he'd been depressed lately?"

She gestured, palms up. "He wouldn't tell me. He might tell Bill. We only saw one another at the club, on social occasions, or at holiday time. . . ."

Bill chose that moment to arrive, breathless, white in the face, and the trooper switched his attention away from Bettiann.

No, said Bill, Charley wasn't depressed. No, he didn't drink and drive, not ordinarily.

When the trooper left them, Bill turned on her, muttering, "Why didn't you call me!"

"Bill, I did! Your secretary didn't know where you were. I left a message with her."

"I had my cellular."

"She tried your phone, Bill. So did I. You didn't answer."

He flushed, started to say something, then stopped. He'd been up to something. He had that certain expression around his eyes. So he'd been with some woman. Probably. Possibly. The expression was a little strange. More puzzled than guilty. If not a woman, then who?

"Why did he ask those questions?" Bill demanded of the air. "He was hurt in an accident, wasn't he?"

"He drove into a bridge abutment," Bettiann told him. "I overheard them talking out at the nurses' desk. They have a witness who saw him do it."

"So he lost control of the car. . . ."

"You're not listening, Bill. He didn't lose control of the car. He *drove* into a bridge abutment."

"*Intentionally?*"

"That's why they're asking those questions. They think he tried to commit suicide."

"Charley?" His voice was outraged, but only momentarily. He sat down, burying his face in his hands. "God. Charley."

She sat beside him, putting her arms around him. There weren't many times when one could comfort William Carpenter. He was a man who despised gifts; who cared only for what he bought and owned. Sympathy wasn't something he could buy, so he didn't often get it, or accept it. As now, shaking her off, wiping his face, sitting up. "What are they doing for him?"

"Trying to stop the internal bleeding. Trying to keep his heart going. There's a lot of alcohol in his system. He's got broken bones. Ribs. Arm. Leg. Maybe skull, they're not sure yet, they can't x-ray until they can stabilize him."

"How long have you been here?"

She peered at the jeweled watch on her wrist, blinked and peered again. Her contacts were hurting. She hadn't brought her glasses. She never wore them except when she was alone. "I got the call around four. I really did try to get you, William. . . ."

"I was at the doctor's."

"What?"

He got that peculiar look again, then said, "Indigestion. Nothing. It's almost eight. You go on home."

"I'll stay with you."

"You don't need to. You're tired. You look tired. Go on home. Get some rest."

Run on back to the pasture, Bettiann. Master will round you up later, give you some grain, maybe a pat on the head. She blinked back tears and took a deep breath.

"I would like to stay with you, Bill. I'd prefer it."

"Go home," he said, not looking at her.

She went. When she got to the car, she blinked out the contacts and flooded her eyes with drops, feeling the scratchiness ease, the drops slide down her cheeks like tears. She had a pair of glasses in the glove compartment for emergencies. If Carolyn were here, she'd ask why Betts was wearing contacts at all. Because Bill preferred it. Why did she sing soprano in the Episcopal choir? Because Bill's associates went there. Why was she head of the country-club charity committee? Why was she doing and being what she was doing and being? Because this is what Bill had bought and paid for.

Why was she being not herself? Sophy would ask that. Who are you, Bettiann? Lately she'd been obsessed by that question. She even dreamed about it. In the dream she was walking down a long, long hallway, and on either side of her there were mirrors. Every time she passed a mirror, she saw a different person. All of them were female, all of them might be she, though she didn't recognize herself. Some were pretty and some were plain, and in the dream she kept asking, "Who are you, Bettiann?"

If she still didn't know who she was, did it make any difference? After all these years, why was she dreaming about it? Why was she asking the question?

Because you're tired, she told herself. Because you haven't eaten anything today, and you know better. Because Bill was being funny about this Charley business. As though, maybe, he knew why Charley had done it. As though he knew something he wasn't telling her. Something she wasn't important enough to be informed about.

Friday night, not long after falling asleep, Carolyn woke into an utter silence, suddenly alerted by a touch on her shoulder, a delicate tapping, a whisper in her ear. It was only after she'd swung her legs out of bed and sat there for a moment, staring into darkness, that she heard the low rumble from the hall. Hector. His growl muffled but continuous.

Fancy and Fandango were standing, muzzles pointing down the hall toward the kitchen, their teeth showing. If all three dogs were away from the bed, who had wakened her?

Carolyn put the question aside, slipped into her robe, and got the gun Hal had given her, taught her to use, and insisted she keep at hand. She thought briefly of waking him, then decided not. He still wasn't that steady on his legs. Only when that notion was discarded did she tell the dogs, "Go."

They went, silently, old Hector moving like a young dog, with no trace of his usual arthritic gait. Marvelous what a little adrenaline could do.

They were poised outside the kitchen door. Carolyn reached across them to press the latch, and three dog bodies thrust it open with a cacophony of barking, growling, snarling. Their quarry was brought to the floor before Carolyn got the lights on, one dog hanging on to each arm and Hector standing over him, neck hair raised, teeth bared, a hideous growl rumbling in his chest.

He was young and spotty and greasy-haired.

"Gettum off me!" he screamed at her. "Gettum off me!"

"Hold still," she told him. "If you're still, they won't bite you. If you yell or try to get up, Hector will take your throat out."

Hal had insisted that Hector be professionally trained. Neither Fancy nor Fandango had been, but since they seemed to be following Hector's lead, she left them to it.

Hal was at the door, very pale, leaning on his cane. "What in hell . . ."

"Prowler," she said, feeling her muscles twitch, her jaw rigid.

Hal reached for the phone. She sat on the kitchen stool while he called the sheriff, gun at the ready until they arrived, her eyes never leaving the lanky delinquent on the floor as she murmured encouragement to the dogs. What was this creature doing out here in the country? How did he get here?

"On their way," murmured Hal. "Give me that gun, Carolyn, you're holding it all wrong."

"Sorry." She passed him the weapon and offered him the stool, but he preferred one of the chairs at the table.

"Hector," said Hal. "Come."

Reluctantly, Hector came, still muttering in his throat. Fancy and Fandango followed his lead, sitting at Hal's feet, ears up, noses pointed at their prey.

To Carolyn, the wait seemed endless, though it was actually only about ten minutes. The dogs heard the car before she did. She went to the kitchen door and opened it, giving herself a view of the driveway. When the car drew up in a shower of gravel, she stood where they could see her. She didn't intend to offer some reason to be shot, either accidentally or accidentally on purpose. Now, why had she thought that? Talk about paranoid!

"In here," she called, standing out of the way.

The two men eased by her, and she closed the door behind them.

"Fredo," said Hal, greeting one of the men by name: Fredo Gonzales, a longtime local resident, with family sprinkled over three counties. "Hal Shepherd," he said, offering his hand to the other man, who took it somewhat reluctantly. "My wife, Carolyn," said Hal.

The other deputy didn't look at her. He didn't look at the prowler, either, though the prowler was looking at him with more than passing interest. Did the two know one another? Carolyn looked pointedly at the deputy's name tag: Al Whitfield.

"You recognize him?" Fredo asked Hal.

"Never seen him before, to my knowledge," Hal replied. "Have you, Carolyn?"

She shook her head, cleared her throat. "No, I haven't."

Fredo Gonzales went through the boy's pockets and came up with a wallet and a crumpled bit of paper. "He's got a map all drawn out."

Carolyn took it from him, spread it on the table where Hal could see it. It was a map to their place, labeled in handwriting. With a sudden frisson Carolyn recognized the handwriting. She'd seen it before. Those cramped little letters. Where?

"Before you take that," she said, "I'd like to make a copy of it."

"That's evidence, ma'am, we can't—" started Whitfield.

"You got a copier?" Gonzales interjected, ignoring him.

"Just down the hall."

Leaving Hal to supervise in the kitchen, she led the way to Hal's study. The room was slightly dusty, and it smelled unused. Since the accident he'd used the desk in the big bedroom. The copier clicked on readily, however, and Carolyn set it for two copies, picking up the first one and presenting it to the deputy.

"Write your name on the copy for me," she asked him.

"I'm taking the original," he said, puzzled.

"I know. I just want to identify the copy, in case anybody asks. Write your name and date it for me."

He gave her a blank stare but did so, after which she returned the original to him, ignoring the additional copy in the bin. With him looking on she put the signed and dated copy into an envelope and stuck it between two books on a shelf. "In case the evidence clerk loses that one," she said.

This time he understood. He grinned, "It's been knowed to happen. You still a lawyer?"

"Sometimes. Mostly retired."

"Wish I was! Retired, that is." He tucked the map into his pocket.

"Was there a car or motorbike or anything out on the road?" Carolyn asked.

"We didn't see any. One car out in front here."

"That's mine. Hal's is in the garage. How did this kid get out here?"

Fredo shrugged. "Hitchhiking, maybe." He led the way back to the kitchen.

"This here's Don Bent," the other deputy said when they returned to the kitchen. "That's what his driver's license says. Been here awhile—it's a New Mexico license. Lives in Mesilla." He looked past Carolyn, speaking as though by rote. "You figure he got away with anything?"

"I imagine the dogs caught him before he had a chance," said Hal.

"I just come lookin' for work," said the greasy-haired youth. "That's all."

"At eleven o'clock at night? In the dark? And you broke the lock on the door?" Fredo Gonzales was incredulous.

"Wasn't me broke it. Was already broke."

Carolyn shook her head. "No. It wasn't broken at ten o'clock when I locked it before I went to bed."

"Dogs always sleep in here?" asked Whitfield, all too casually.

Hal's head came up, and he stared at the deputy.

"These dogs do," Carolyn said, feigning indifference. "Other dogs sleep other places. Then there's the hired men. And parts of this building are covered by alarms."

She turned to see Hal's eyebrows raised, his lips twisting slightly. Much of what she had just said was invention. Invention now, she conceded, but not for long.

They hauled the young man out and away. The sheriff's car threw gravel against the patio wall as it departed, rocketing off down the drive with more speed than sense.

"You didn't like the guy with Fredo?" Hal asked softly. "Didn't trust him?"

"Did you?"

"Not really. He was a little too interested in our arrangements, wasn't he? Did you get the impression he knew the prisoner?"

"He couldn't have been less curious about him. That might mean something, in my humble opinion."

"So? What was he doing here? Is this what Helen warned you about?"

She pondered the question. "I think not. Josh—the guard out at the prison—says Jagger has a dirty-work guy, an ex–Green Beret, ex–one thing and another. Guy named Martin. Somebody like that'd be too slick to get caught like this."

She braced the kitchen door with a high-backed chair; then she and Hal made the rounds of the house, checking the other locks and leaving all inside doors open for the convenience of the nervous dogs, who were exploring every corner and closet. They ended up in the study, where she took the unsigned copy from the bin, scribbled the date and Fredo's name on it, then switched it for the one he had signed. The signed one came out of its envelope and went into her wallet. The one she had just faked went back between the books.

"Bait?" asked Hal, eyebrows raised.

"Well, if Fredo mentions I've got a signed copy of the map, somebody might come looking for it."

"You recognize the hand?"

"I think I do, yes. I'd guess Swinter."

"Now, how in hell would you recognize his writing?"

"It was a lawyers' meeting, Hal, years ago. Swinter had a new toy, one of those conference screens you can write on, then it duplicates whatever's on the screen in letter-size copies. He was passing his scribbles out to all and sundry. . . ."

"You're sure?"

"Not entirely, no. Not until I pull the old file. It's down at Jerry's office." Jerry was her former partner.

"What do you think the greasy kid was up to?"

"God knows. Murder? Theft? Exploration? I don't think he sort of dropped in accidentally. He came here intentionally."

"But not sent by Jagger?"

Carolyn considered the matter. "No. This was a dumb stunt. I'll stick with my first guess. Emmet Swinter. Or . . . Vince Harmston might have been dumb enough to do it."

"Emmet Swinter's about as bright as your average roping calf."

Which was true; the man's natural sense had been warped by a lifetime of evasion. Carolyn shook her head, telling herself to watch it. Her own could be warped, too, by too much generalized suspicion. Easy. Careful.

"I wish we knew," Hal murmured. "When can you lay your hands on the handwriting samples?"

"Tomorrow. If Mary hasn't cleaned out the files, I know right where they are."

First thing in the morning, however, they would see about improving security measures for the farm. Speaking of which, the prowler certainly hadn't walked the twenty-five miles from town. Which might mean someone had brought him. . . .

Someone who was not in custody and might come back. She didn't mention the thought to Hal.

◆ ◆ ◆

At Jake Jagger's house the phone rang very early in the morning. Jake snapped awake and reached for it.

"Young guy just got brought in," said a familiar voice very softly. "Broke into somebody's house. Somebody named Shepherd. Sheriff's office brought him in. Gottim down here, and he says call Swinter. Tried. Can't get him."

Alertness. "I understand."

"Don't suppose you look forward to havin' him up for arraignment on Monday."

Anger, coldly controlled. "Since I'm very busy, that would probably be accurate."

"What I figured." The line went dead.

From the doorway Helen's voice asked, "Is something the matter?"

He turned and regarded her in silence. She quailed visibly, slowly backing away.

He said in a measured voice, without a trace of emotion, "I should have thought you would have learned by now not to ask questions about my business. I should have thought whatever else you are incapable of understanding, you would understand that."

"I do understand. It's just . . . so late. I thought it might be about the children."

He sighed, a much-put-upon but patient man. "The children are no longer your concern."

"I'm their mother, Jake. . . ."

He merely stared at her. "Why, so you are," he said at last. "How thoughtful of you to remind me."

"I worry about them," she cried.

He shook his head at her. "I've told you your worry is misplaced. Scott is no longer your concern; he is at the Alliance Redoubt, attending the Institute. He's doing well. Emily is no longer your concern; she is at the training center. She has recently been promoted into a select class, and from now on she will have no problems. You may rely on that, Helen. The girls in her group have no problems at all."

She stifled the complaint rising in her throat, swallowed the sob, made herself ask calmly, "Jake, why? What have I ever done that you treat me like this?"

It was a moment before he answered, almost surprised, "I do it because . . . you women . . . my mother . . ." He turned and spat, his face working, something writhing in his belly, escaped from his iron control. Awed, she witnessed his struggle, quailing again when he turned in her direction once more.

He spoke slowly, almost gently. "You ask why? That's what I wanted to know. How could someone like me have something like that for a mother?"

He turned away, lips twisting. "I'm a logical man. I don't just ask questions; I find answers. I read books. I learned about women, about all that filth in your minds, and your stinking bodies. All that blood and ooze, like a swamp!" The last few words spewed out, followed by a little cloud of expelled saliva.

She shrank back, away from him.

He wiped his lips. "Do you have any idea what men could be if women didn't drag us down? If we didn't have you hanging on us and weakening us? The Alliance is learning how to deal with women, Helen. The Alliance has had people studying the matter for decades, people from all over the world. We have found the best way. When we take over, oh, the world will be a very different place!"

He was still staring in her direction, but he didn't see her. He was seeing something else, hypnotized in some vision of a future she could not conceive. He turned his back and walked away from her, as though he had forgotten she was there.

She slipped out, closing the door behind her.

He came to himself in his bathroom, staring at his own image, eyes wide and wondering. The woman had forgotten who he was. Whose son and protégé he was! He should go in there and show her who he was, what he was. He should do it to her, just to prove who and what he was. Cry, struggle though she would, stupid and weak and rotten . . .

But . . . then . . . it was a lot of trouble for nothing. He disliked the feel, the smell. He preferred to relieve his occasional impulses in the shower, where all was clean, clean water, clean soap, everything washed away, leaving nothing. There were more important things to think about just now. He should save his energy, husband it. He would take care of her in some other way.

He went back into his room and lay down on his bed, pulling the covers up, straightening them precisely, a fraction of an inch below his chin, putting his hands at his sides, closing his eyes. Now that his son's future was determined, now that the girl had been chosen, he could not think of any reason to keep Helen.

And he certainly didn't need that stupid bastard Swinter. He'd told the man to find out about the Crespin woman through channels, from the FBI, not to send some damned stupid kid out to reconnoiter when nobody needed go near the place! He, Jagger, had already taken care of that. What an idiotic thing for Swinter to do! If he was dumb enough to have done that, what other stupidity might he have committed? If Webster found out about this . . .

If Webster found out about this, Jagger might not be one of the finalists. In fact, he'd be lucky to be a survivor.

Despite what Webster had said, Swinter would have to be taken care of! It would have to be an accident. Like his mother. Like his foster father. Like

Helen's parents. Or maybe suicide, like Helen's sister, Greta. But he'd have to make sure there were no witnesses at all, so Webster wouldn't know.

There in the comfortable drowsiness, on the boundary of sleep, he forgot that there had been no witnesses before, but, still, Webster seemed to have known.

Outside Jagger's room Helen stood for a long moment silent and motionless, her face white and sticky, terror and grief in equal measure. Dear God, how do you allow such monsters to exist? Dear God, help me put this horror to rest!

She did not return to her room. Instead she went down the long hall and across the living room to the room Jagger used, though infrequently, as a study. He preferred his office downtown for work, or his game room for relaxation, but he used this desk occasionally to make calls, and he kept some papers here. She opened the drawers in his desk quietly, one by one, also the pull-out writing surfaces, then turned over the blotter to look at the bottom. She found nothing written on any of them. The middle drawer had a few envelopes, some stamps. The file drawer was almost empty, only a few household papers and insurance policies. A folder with the plans of the house, copiously annotated. In the bottom drawer she found a book with blank pages, its cover worn and scuffed, Jake's name printed in a childish hand inside the front cover. The pages bore carefully printed lists of names. Men's names. She recognized some of them as onetime giants in politics or commerce, since fallen into death or disrepute. The first lists were quite long, extending over more than one page. Further on, the lists became shorter, and then shorter yet. The further she went, the more mature the handwriting became. The last page with writing on it bore one name only: L. S. Webster. The date below was October 31, 1985. After that, only blank pages.

Jake would have been thirty-five in eighty-five. Ten thirty-one eighty-five. It was the last entry in the book and the only dated one. As though that date had been a culmination. He had said something to her once about Webster. Something about the first time he'd met Webster. He'd been over thirty when that had happened.

Maybe it didn't mean a thing. And then again, maybe it did. She stood in the hallway once more, listening. Nothing. He was asleep.

She got the rubber gloves from under the kitchen sink, then slipped out of the house, walking around the edges of the driveway so her feet would crunch no gravel, slipping silently into the garage. There was a flashlight on the shelf, one Jake kept there. It served to light the door to his game room, and there was a keypad, just as Carolyn had thought there might be.

Ten. Thirty-one. Eighty-five. Nothing. She reversed the order and did it again. Fifty-eight, thirteen, ought one. Nothing. She started to turn away, then tried once more, doing it English style. Day, month, and year. Thirty-one, ten, eighty-five. The light above the door blinked, and the door itself slid open.

She went in, using the flashlight, the smell hitting her in the face, a deep, musty smell. Eyes watched her from the darkness. She almost dropped the flashlight before remembering the heads, the mounted heads. She'd seen them when he'd brought them from the taxidermists. She knew about the big freezer. The butcher table. The sink. Everything clean and neat. One thing you could say for Jake, he was fanatically clean. He was always taking showers and changing his shirt, always spraying disinfectant. He never left anything out of place. He washed his hands three times an hour. He always lined things up, always put things away. No loose ends for Jake.

A file cabinet stood in one corner, not even locked. She pulled the drawer open gently, ran the light along the folders inside, then the next drawer. People's names. Tape recordings in some of them, pictures in some of them. Rombauer was in the third drawer. A videotape, and pictures, black-and-white, glossies; Rombauer, naked under his shirttails, legs bare except for black socks and shoes. The boys were entirely nude. Dared she take all the pictures? There were dozens. No. If Jake looked, he'd see they were missing. Take the tape and some of the pictures. Put another tape deck from one of the other folders in the Rombauer folder, pick a dusty folder, a yellowed one, one he wouldn't be looking at. That way, if he just looked casually, he wouldn't know anything was missing.

She found such a file at the back of the second drawer. It bore the name of a man dead for five years, and it contained a videotape. The label was loose at one edge. She pulled it off and replaced it with the one from the Rombauer tape. Excellent, she whispered to herself, feeling a little surge of vengeful joy where she had felt only fear for as long as she could remember. Thirteen years. That's how long. Married to Jake Jagger for thirteen years. Lucky thirteen. Emily was twelve. Scott was ten and a half.

The relabeled tape went into the Rombauer folder. The Rombauer tape went into the deep pocket of her robe. Then the pictures:

Carolyn had said Hispanic boys, so she went through them carefully, focusing on faces instead of on what they were doing. There were lots of Hispanic boys, but in some shots Rombauer was younger looking, in others he was wrinkled and gray-haired. Those were the most recent ones; those were the ones she took, noticing that someone had penciled names on the backs of the photos. The participants were identified. Jake had written their names, tying up loose ends.

There were envelopes and stamps in the house. She'd do that tomorrow. They didn't have a rural mailbox; Jake picked up their mail in town; but the neighbors half a mile down the road had a rural box, just across the road from the phone box she sometimes used. One could slip a letter in there. Or one could even wait beside that mailbox tomorrow morning and hand the post-man the envelope.

One way or another. She slipped out of the room, closed the door softly behind her, saw the light go out. She had left no fingerprints. She even remembered to leave the flashlight where she'd found it.

When he went to work tomorrow, she would finish the job.

On Saturday, Agnes and Sister Honore Philip went over the books, preparing for the archbishop's return.

"I don't know what to do," Mother Agnes confessed. "We have to find a way to give him what he wants." She went to the window, clutching her hands together to prevent her wringing them.

"Yesterday I thought you'd calmed down," murmured Sister Honore.

"I had, a little. Then last night I had this terrible dream about him . . . the archbishop," she confessed. "In the dream he's already built the wall across our enclosure, this long, high stone wall, and the wall is full of these tiny, tiny cells, and he's put one of us in each of them, and he's leading me down the wall toward the last tiny little cell, and that one's mine!"

Sister Honore was shocked at the words, but more so at the tone of voice. "Reverend Mother!"

Aggie shuddered. "Oh, I know I sound hysterical. In the dream I was so scared that I woke up with my heart pounding, so frightened I couldn't re-member who I was. I sat there for the longest time, trying to find myself, and then I heard Sister Mary John coughing and I woke up. I'm being too proud! I know it. I should be able to relinquish more easily, but his idea of taking over the oyster farm makes no sense! The archdiocese won't make a dime out of the fisheries, not if they pay qualified people! And if they hire unqualified people, they won't have any business inside of a year."

Sister Honore Philip looked up from her columns of figures, her sensible face giving nothing away, but her eyes all too knowing. "Maybe the money is the least of it."

Aggie turned toward her, eyebrows lifted. "You think he has some other reason?"

"Is it impossible that he wants us to feel more humble?" asked Sister Honore, her eyes down. "I've noticed that some of our . . . advisers feel that women become . . . hard when they succeed at anything but motherhood, or cooking. Breeding or feeding, as Sister Oleg says. I'm sure that's the main reason for the ban on birth control. Women are kept humble by children. And by the poor. How can we achieve sainthood without the poor?"

Aggie bit her lip and summoned patience. Sister Honore rarely lectured her, but when she did . . . !

This morning Sister Honore went on with her sermon: "There is money we can spare. The girls' scholarship fund."

Agnes spoke to the window glass. "That would be terribly hard to give up. Some of our girls are bright. They need to be able to go to college. They need the same chance I had. When I was in university, several of the DFC were there on scholarship. Faye. And Sophy, and Bettiann."

"Your club is having its meeting sometime soon, isn't it? Will you be going?" The tone was faintly accusative.

Aggie equivocated. "This time. I didn't go last year because of the election, and we didn't meet in 1998, when one of our members . . . when Sophy . . ."

Sister Honore closed the book unobtrusively, leaning forward. Mother Agnes was not often this open to conversation, but she needed to be talked to. Father Girard had spoken to Sister Honore, suggesting that Reverend Mother needed talking to. "You used to speak of her often, Reverend Mother. What was she like?"

Agnes stared blindly, eyes focused on some inward vision. "She was the most mysteriously beautiful person I've ever known, but when we were together, she seemed the most simple and . . . present."

"Hmmm," Sister encouraged.

"She used to tease me. I don't respond to teasing well, I get flustered, but she could do it, so I didn't mind. When we went to the San Francisco meeting in 1997, the two of us were together on the plane from Denver. I asked her what she'd been doing. She told me she'd been meditating in the desert, that she'd been exploring the caverns of despair to see what the enemy planned for us. She said one couldn't ask for help until the need had been defined, but now that she knew what the enemy planned, she thought she could define it."

"What did she mean by that?"

"I thought she was teasing. But she said . . ."

What had she said?

"She said the stories her grandma and aunts used to tell her were women stories, tales of wise women, warrior women, healing women, ruling women. She said when she came among us and heard our stories, all the women were weak or silly or unfortunate. Little Red Riding Hood. Snow White. Sleeping Beauty. Without the rescuing male, they were eaten up; without him they slept forever. In our stories women had no strength or passion of their own. In our stories woman's fire does not burn, her joy is uncelebrated, all her knowledge is put to nothing. She said she was looking for the center of women's being. . . .

"And I interrupted her," said Mother Agnes to Sister Honore. "I was always interrupting Sophy, very sure of myself, wanting to set her straight. I said the center of women's being is God." She made a face and then stared at her folded hands.

"What did Sophy say?" asked Sister Honore.

"She asked me whose God. I told her there was only one. And she said I was mistaken, that we like to think we all worship the same God, but we don't. She said the God I'd been taught about wasn't right for women.

"I said she was confusing God with what men say about him, but she said I was the one who was confused. She quoted what she called the first law of the supernatural: No God can be bigger than the gate that lets people into the presence. If the only way to that God is through a narrow little gate with picky little gatekeepers, then that God is no bigger than that gate nor wiser than the keepers. If a woman wants to approach divinity, she should not go through a narrow gate built by men. Women should find their own way."

This conversation confirmed Sister Honore's worst suspicions. No wonder Father Girard wanted Reverend Mother to forget about Sophy! "What did you say to that?"

Reverend Mother Agnes shook her head slowly. "I told her I thought we Catholic women had opened ways for ourselves. And she said no, we had only bloodied our heads on gates that were long ago locked against us. She told me I was like a little mare in harness, believing I was being allowed to run, but soon I would feel the bit in my mouth and the weight of the wagon."

Sister Honore nodded, her lips compressed. "Well, of course she was right about that. The saving of souls is a heavy wagon to haul. We do it because we believe in it, because we love God."

Agnes was too intent to notice the contentious tone. "Sophy said she sought the center of women's being, the place where the spirit of women is at home. She said she saw that place as the summit of a mountain; from that summit any movement in any direction would be a decline and a fall. She said when she found it, she would build a shrine there. When she found it, she said, perhaps I would even help her. . . ."

"Ah," breathed Sister Honore. "I see." She did see. It was heretical. No doubt at all about that.

"I didn't see," Reverend Mother Agnes whispered, tears on her face. "I didn't see how far she was straying. I couldn't think of an answer. I changed the subject. Then in San Francisco something happened, and it was too late to say anything. Even then, perhaps, I could have helped her, but I didn't. . . .

"And after that I never saw her again. And Father Girard says I must forget her, deny her, consider that she may not have been my friend, that she may have been sent by the devil. . . ."

Sister Honore sat back, ready to do battle. "Don't you think that's probably true, Reverend Mother? She certainly has troubled you greatly. Wouldn't you be better off doing as Father suggests?"

Aggie shook her head sadly. "Well, Sophy's first law of the supernatural certainly doesn't fit our faith. If she was wrong about that, she may have been very wrong about a lot of things."

"*If* she was wrong?"

Reverend Mother turned, suddenly aware that she was actually trying to undermine the faith of one of her community. Not only being disobedient herself but fulminating disobedience in others. All because of Sophy. Because of what she had been, or still was.

Sister Honore frowned, longing to go on with this line of conversation, but Reverend Mother was already distressed, and it wouldn't be thoughtful to pursue the matter. "Back to the weight of our wagon, Reverend Mother," she said cheerfully. "You were saying it will be hard to give up the girls' scholarship fund."

"It will be very hard," said Reverend Mother, chill with realization. "Perhaps it is meant to be hard. Perhaps there are some things so precious that one can only be tested when one is asked to give them up."

Saturday evening, after Hal had gone off to bed, Carolyn stretched out in the little bedroom with the phone beside her, called Ophy, and talked with her for almost an hour about Lolly Ashaler. She followed that call with a similar one to Jessamine.

"You're serious?" Jessamine asked. "You're really serious? You're going to defend her by attacking the Hail Mary Assumption?"

"Can you come up with some better way?" Carolyn asked irritably. "She's completely unprepossessing, Jess. Totally unsympathetic. She has sensations but no ideas, she has speech but no vocabulary, she has wants but no aspirations. She's a mess, but if you can think of something better, tell me!"

"Well, no."

"Can you get the stuff I need?"

"Yes. I think I can. Some of it. I don't know where you'll get the news tapes. . . ."

"Simon was with Ophy when I called her. He's getting them for me. He has all kinds of media contacts. Movies. TV. Maybe Patrick could locate—"

"Patrick's leaving, Carolyn. We've called it quits. He's going back to California. The Alliance wants him to run for office."

"The Alliance!" Shock made her wordless. All she could come up with was, "Jessy. I'm sorry." It sounded insincere. Damn it, it was insincere.

"You're not sorry he's leaving, Carolyn. Neither am I. The fact that he's associating himself with the Alliance means I couldn't go on living with him. Patrick's changed a lot in the last few years. He used to claim to be proud of me, but that was when he could stand on his political pinnacle and look down on my work. Since it's been supporting us, he hasn't liked it much. I think right now he's seeing me as a horrible example of feminism gone wrong."

"You're honestly not hurting?"

"Honestly not. He's such a . . . Do you know, he told me he tried to seduce the whole DFC just to see if he could blow us up, like putting a firecracker in a mailbox? If he hadn't had d.t.'s and been seeing dragons. . . ."

"Seeing dragons?"

"In Sophy's room. He was drunk, Carolyn." She laughed. "I guess it's funny, in a sort of sick way. Patrick always gets drunk when he's bored, and when we were having our meeting, he was bored out of his skull. I had a dream about his being drunk the other night. A funny one. Patrick was drunk, and he got all the male apes drunk and then let them out. They locked me in a little cage, all of us females locked into these little tiny cages, and—"

Carolyn interrupted firmly. "Jessy, I don't think that's funny in the least, and I'd just as soon not hear about it."

"All right. I won't tell you." Long silence. Then, "Let's have the list of things you need."

Carolyn read it. "And you'll come to the meeting prepared to testify?"

"If you can get the case scheduled for then and get a judge to accept my testimony, Carolyn."

"Ophy said the same. And it won't be easy. I have no doubt the DA will have his crony on the bench."

Carolyn thanked her and hung up, looking up to see Hal leaning on his cane in the doorway, very pale, the daily paper dangling from one hand.

"What?" she asked.

"I thought I'd do the crossword before I fell asleep, so I took the paper back to the room with me. I hadn't really looked at it this morning." He was deeply distressed; his face showed it.

"Hal! What?"

"The kid. The one who broke in here last night. Don Bent. He's dead."

She stared at him. "That's in the paper?"

"Hanged himself in his cell."

"He did not!"

"That's what it says."

"I don't care what it says." She felt herself shaking. "My lord, Hal. That's what they said about Greta Wilson! Helen's sister."

He sat on the side of her bed and picked up the phone. "I'm going to call Mike Winter."

There was a lengthy wait before Mike came to the phone. Hal held it away from his ear so Carolyn could hear.

"Hal! What's the occasion?"

Hal talked about Carolyn's case, concluding with the prowler who had ended up dead.

"Do you have proof that—"

"Of course not, Mike! Would I be calling you if I could make a case here? The fact that the boy who broke in here last night was dead this morning raises our hackles and gives me the feeling this is bigger than local, that's all."

Long silence at the other end, a receding murmur as though someone might be carrying a phone into a quieter corner. "How can I help, Hal?"

"We don't expect the cavalry to come riding over the hill. Carolyn wants to win this case, of course, but she's reconciled herself to losing, which is almost a foregone conclusion with Judge Rombauer on the bench. Rombauer's dirty, everyone knows it, but nobody does anything about it, and we don't expect you to fix him. Carolyn figures if she can't win, she can appeal."

"If she appeals, however, she's up against Jagger again, and we've come to suspect he has a tendency to solve problems by people committing suicide or falling accidentally dead."

Mike hummed and hemmed. "I think you can figure whatever Jagger is doing, Webster may be pulling the strings."

Hal thought about it for a long moment. "It would help to know for certain, Mike. If we're going to protect ourselves, it'd be nice to know who we're protecting ourselves from. Jagger? Albert? Webster himself? And if the latter, why?"

Long pause, then Mike murmured, "I've got some information I'll put together for you. In the meantime, if you get hold of anything on the judge that can be used to help Carolyn, I'd be pleased to bring pressure to bear, right up old Albert's nose."

"Albert is still there, then."

"In high favor, my friend. Old Albert is right up there among the mucky-mucks."

"Damn him."

"Thou sayest." And the disconnect.

"Not much help," remarked Hal to Carolyn as he hung up the phone. "I get the feeling Jagger doesn't blow his nose without Webster's knowing, but it's hard for me to see how this case has anything to do with Webster."

"Maybe it's like the ecologists say," Carolyn murmured. "Everything's connected to everything else."

"Possibly." He nodded, thinking it over. "You look depressed, sweetness."

"I am. I'm . . . fearful. Everything I see and hear seems to be an omen. I've been having ominous dreams. So have some of my friends, if you can believe that! If I didn't know better, I'd think the millenarians are right. Everything's coming apart."

"Not that bad," he said, hugging her. "It can't be that bad."

Stacey Shepherd perched on the couch in Luce's living room, sipping the cup of coffee Luce had delivered along with sweet words and a lingering stroke across her shoulder. So, fine. He always did that. Always insisted on cleaning up the mess in his own kitchen, letting her have her coffee while he did so. As he was doing now, whistling, because he was happy she was there, so he said. Claiming his territory, Stace used to say. Male bird in bright plumage, singing on his own cattail, letting all the other birds know where was where and what was what, cleaning up his own kitchen because he wanted her to know he was fully capable of sharing household duties after they were married.

If they ever did get married!

She got up restlessly, running her hands along Luce's bookcases. He'd built them himself, clear pine, personally selecting each board, joining them beautifully; then he'd crammed them with tattered backs and torn covers, science texts and his old science-fiction collection, lots of them signed first editions, books shoved in any old where, Feinman jostling Heinlein, Asimov cheek by jowl with Hawking. Sometimes he read stories to her. Sometimes they made sense. Stace was no great shakes on science, never had been. It had always seemed cold to her. Not that Luce was . . . had been cold. Until recently.

"Hey, gorgeous," he called. "Did I leave my coffee cup in there?"

"I'll bring it," she told him, rising to do so. "You sure you don't want any more?"

"Oh, maybe half a cup." Humming now. Full of music, this man was. Full of crap. Besides, Luce liked measurable things. He wanted things quantified. "Luce, you never . . . ," she would say. "How many times don't I?" That was his kind of question. "How many times don't I . . . ."

She passed him the cup across the counter, then perched on one of the kitchen stools. "Luce?"

"Yes, ma'am. You want another cup?"

"I want to talk."

"So talk. You're the psychologist, so tell me about these old ladies, why they're burning the shoe stores and stuff."

"That's not what I want to talk about. I want to . . . to ask why. You know, we haven't made love lately."

He looked up, suddenly alert, hands quiet, eyes searching her face. "Not for a while, no."

"Why is that?" She took a sip of coffee to soothe a suddenly dry throat.

He looked puzzled. "You haven't given me the signal," he said at last. "Not lately. I figured you were preoccupied."

"The signal?"

"You know, the go-ahead. The flag. The starting gun. The bell for round one."

"I didn't know I ever . . . gave a signal."

"Sure you do," he said, shaking his head. "I think. It's the way you . . . look, I guess. Or smell. Hell, I don't know. Something that sets me off."

"And lately I haven't done it?"

"Not lately. I figured it was the new job. They can be pretty demanding—new bosses, new projects. I know. I've had enough of them."

She was staring into the coffee, as though into a crystal ball. "Luce, I thought you were the one who gave the signal."

"Me? I always tried not to. You know, being considerate. Dad told me that when I was fourteen: He said it was better than the Scout motto. Not 'Be prepared,' but 'Be considerate.' " He dried his hands on a paper towel, threw it into the trash, and took her hand to lead her back into the living room. "Hey, it's nothing about us. I mean, Stace, I'm in love with you. Like forever. Whatever's bothering you—me, us—it doesn't even touch how I feel about you."

He drew her down on the couch and cuddled her, his arms tight around her, and she waited for the signal, from him, from herself, searching memory, searching sensation. Something. Sound. Smell. Feeling. Something. They were warm and cozy and pleasant and loving, but the other thing, whatever it was, didn't happen, even though they were both thinking about it.

About it. But finding it hard even to remember. Stace could remember what they'd done, what they'd said, but the actual feeling . . .

He was fondling her breasts, stroking them. "Your bra's all stretched," he said. "It's loose."

"It's a new one," she said, sitting up, adjusting the straps.

"Take off your shirt," he said.

She peeled it off, let him kiss her shoulder, run his hands down her back. She loved his hands. They stroked easily under the straps of the bra. Easily.

"It's the same size I always buy," she whispered.

"You're . . . smaller," he said.

She went into his bedroom, took off the bra, looked at herself in his mirror. She didn't usually look at herself undressed—no real reason to—but she *was* smaller. She was almost flat-chested. Just breasy enough so people would know she was a girl. Like a twelve-year-old, maybe. Or a ballerina.

He came in behind her, took her in his arms.

"I'm shrinking," she whispered. "The incredible shrinking boob! What shall I do?"

"Darling, I don't know," he said.

Faye had finished the figure of Fecundity, had paid Petra off and bade her farewell, only to have her call a few weeks later asking if she could bring Narcisso, her boyfriend, by to see the statue.

"The maquette," Faye corrected. "If you want to, Pet. Not for long, though. I've got a lot of work laid on this week."

She was deeply immersed in the transformation of Mercury and the three Graces, but when Petra and Cisso arrived, Faye propped the door open and went out onto the balcony so Petra could show off alone.

"That's you, huh?" The boy's voice was soft, much softer than Faye had expected. "Nice. Lookit all the little kids. We used to go swimmin' like that, me'n my brothers, skinny-dippin'."

Faye turned slightly, so she could observe them without seeming to watch. Was this the same young man she had seen before? It was the same car, no question of that. There couldn't be more than one. But the young man himself seemed different. Her sculptor's eye saw a change in his stance and the way he held his head. Softness. His shoulders were softer, sloped and relaxed instead of raised and stiff, the difference between ballet and flamenco. There was something almost demure in the stance.

"Y'think I look, you know, sexy?" Petra asked him.

"You? Oh, sure. Sure you do. Real sexy. But it's okay. The face isn't that much you, you know. You worried about your Dad seein' it, he'd never know it was you."

They came out. "I need to talk to her for a minute," said Petra. "You go on. I'll be right there."

As he went down the stairs, the girl stood, hunched a bit, warming herself. She looked frozen, as though she'd been out in the chill of the night. The heat was on in the studio, and Faye drew her back inside.

"All right, Pet child. What's eating on you?"

The girl looked up, her face strained with woe and doubt. "Narcisso," she whispered. "He don't . . . he's not takin' me to bed anymore."

And a very good thing, too, Faye told herself. "Good for him," she said.

"It's not good," the girl cried in anguish. " 'Cause I don't know why!"

"Maybe he got smart. Maybe he doesn't want you pregnant."

She shook her head. "He use to say he want me to have his baby. Even when I don't want to, he hits me and says I should be a woman and have his baby."

"Hits you?"

"Yeah, you know. Not too bad. Just enough to show me, like he says, who's boss. But he don't hit me now, and he don't take me to bed."

"Maybe he thinks you should be married first."

The girl looked up, her expression changing. "You think?"

"If he's in love with you. Yes."

"That never stop him before. Maybe he's got AIDS," the girl whispered. "That's what I think."

Which could be true. "Have you asked him?"

She shook her head miserably. "We don't talk about that stuff."

Of course not. Do it ceaselessly, sequentially, serially, even promiscuously; hear it discussed ad lib, ad nauseam on every channel; but do not speak of it applying to oneself. Taboo. Taboo.

"What can I do?"

"Ask him." She examined the girl's face. "Do you still want him? Maybe if he doesn't ever make love to you, do you want him anyhow?"

"He got me all mixed up. He won't take me to bed, but he takes me to the store, and he never use to. He don't hit me no more, but he's nicer than he use to be. We have more fun, you know? An' I can't figure it out."

Faye could understand her disbelief; what she couldn't understand was the change in Narcisso.

"Why don't you just enjoy it, Petra? Can't you do that?"

"I guess." She didn't look at all convinced as she went down the steps with her eyes fixed on her feet. The boy came to meet her, putting his hand affectionately on her shoulder as he helped her into the car.

The graveled road was faceted with sun as the car turned and went away, not too fast. An enigma. Something totally unexpected.

And nothing she could figure out at the moment! One of the many things she had no time for! She stalked purposefully into the studio, put the covers over the maquette, and returned to her work. Botticelli's Mercury was to be transformed into a composite Noah-Dionysus-St. Francis, savior of wild animals, surrounded by the animals themselves, ones that had gone extinct in Europe. Wild boar. Forest bison. Elk. A bear—not a teddy type, but one with wildness implicit, nose down, teeth showing, paw scooping up a flapping fish.

She hadn't decided on a replacement for the central figure of Venus Genetrix yet, but she would replace the three Graces with three avatars of nature, exemplars of what Carolyn called the covenant: shepherdess, gardener, dryad.

"You'd know about that," she said to Sophy, who stood naked in the corner. The wreath and drapery had been put away, in a locked cabinet. Now

Sophy simply stood there, reaching out, her arm sagging under the huge, invisible weight it held. Looking at her own hands, Faye said, "You'd know about forests and animals and birds and all that."

"*They are the teachers,*" Sophy replied. "*When the first women studied what the world was like, they learned from birds and animals. When I was in the desert, I learned from them, too. . . .*"

Faye looked up from the clay. She couldn't remember Sophy ever talking about the desert. The form stood there unmoving, and yet she had heard Sophy's voice, very clearly, talking about the desert!

Had the statue spoken to her? Had she remembered Sophy speaking, or had she remembered someone quoting something Sophy had said?

Probably a bit of all three. Memory of Sophy, memory of someone speaking of Sophy, and the sculpture itself speaking, the bronze talking to its creator.

13

SIMON WAS AT THE DESK in the study when Ophy got home from Misery late Friday afternoon, the surface before him littered with untidy piles of paper scraps, different colors and sizes, all scratched over in Simon's spiky hand.

"What are you doing?" Ophy asked, dropping her bag and coat onto a chair near the door. "It looks like you've been here all day."

"Sorting notes for a story," he said. "I realized this morning that I've already got a lot of stuff on this plague of yours. I've been covering it without knowing it. If my editor won't assign me, I'll do it freelance. Look at this." He picked up one pile. "These are notes I took in France. *Elle* magazine. You know?"

She nodded. "Fashions, isn't it? Like *Vogue*?"

"Sort of a glamour mag. I met one of the editors at a cocktail party. He was crying a blue streak over business. Subscriptions were off, down by twenty, twenty-five percent. He couldn't figure it out.

"At the time it meant very little, though I made notes of what he said. You know me: I always make notes. So after our talk last night, I got to thinking about the old women's riots here, you know, and today I started digging about. *Gentlemen's Quarterly*. *Womenswear Daily*. *Vogue*. I got a snarky idea, so I included Victoria's Secret, Frederick's. I made some phone calls. Doing a feature piece, sez I. How's business? Now, if business was good, they'd have crowed about it. Instead they say this, they say that, they ask why do I want to know."

"Why those particular magazines?"

"Depression is an ego problem, isn't it? Fashion is ego related."

She dropped into the chair across from him. "You're trying to verify the depression epidemic?"

"I thought of the different kinds of ego stuff. Cars, maybe. For women it's clothing, and maybe that ties into what these old biddies are doing. Cosmetics, maybe? My theory is, if there's an epidemic of fear or depression, the first things to nose-dive will be stuff like clothes and cars."

"How can you quantify this? You didn't get any numbers from these people you talked to."

"Thus speaks the scientific mind. No, love, no numbers. Just a lot of uncomfortable silences."

"How would we get some real data? The people from CDC, they're dying for something real, Simon. Are you planning on writing something now?"

"Of course not now. I don't have a story yet. I have a dozen or so phone calls that produced only negative information. 'Fashion Biggies Touchy About Sales' is not a story. No, I'm just digging. I thought maybe you'd join me for a night on the town."

"Where? What's up your sleeve?"

"Well, the car dealerships are closed at night, so I thought Frederick's, maybe." He grinned and ran his fingers through already untidy hair. "We could look around, maybe have supper out."

"Wandering around at night? How safe is it?"

"The town seems pretty quiet to me. Early in the evening should be okay. We'll pick up a security team if you like."

"I guess we should. No point taking chances, even though the town does seem quiet. Things have simmered down lately."

Quiet or not, Ophy dressed down. Solid low-heeled shoes, dark trousers, loose sweater under a looser coat. No jewelry. No scent. Her HoloID in a zippered inside pocket. The face that looked back at her from the mirror looked anemic and hollow-cheeked.

Simon didn't seem to notice. "Very good," he said approvingly. "You look like one of us journalists—no-nonsense and all that."

"I look like a waif."

"No. You look determined in a waiflike way."

"I'm not sure what we're doing this for."

"For your people from CDC. For my newspaper. For the two of us, because we want to know."

That much was true. She did want to know. Besides, Simon had offered to help her and Carolyn with the defense of that pathetic girl in Santa Fe, so it was only fair that she keep him company tonight.

They called for a two-man security car from the gate of the quad-block, waiting patiently after it arrived for the gatekeeper to phone-check it. When the car had been double-checked, they went through the gate. Ophy recognized the man riding shotgun as her driver from the previous day.

"Hey," he said through the grill to the backseat. "You're the doctor, right? You ever find out about that allergy?"

"Not much," she admitted. "Emil, wasn't it? Emil Fustig? Any more of your friends coming down with it?"

"Coming down," he laughed. "That's the truth. Only I guess it's more a case of not getting it up in the first place." He laughed again. "No offense. You bein' a doctor, I don't guess you mind jokes like that."

She frowned, not getting it. She started to ask him, but Simon spoke first.

"You're not bothered by this whatever it is?"

"Oh, hell, I was never into all that stuff," the man said. "Some guys, they gotta work out, they gotta drive a fast car, they gotta chase women like tomorrow was the last day of sex season. I mean, some guys do what they want, you know? They don't believe nobody."

Throughout all this the driver had kept his mouth shut, his eyes on the street. Now he asked, "Where you want to start?"

"Would there be a Frederick's open?" said Simon.

"Only one the old ladies didn't burn down yet. Down the street from The Naked Truth," said Ophy's acquaintance. "That's on the corner."

The driver made a quick left, then a right. Ahead of them a bevy of pink and purple neon nudes cavorted up the face of a building, disappearing at the fifth floor into an incandescent nova: THE NAKED TRUTH, flashing forty times a minute. The driver took them past, then double-parked in front of Frederick's.

Ophy stopped outside the brightly lit window, scanning the array of crotchless panties, garter belts, and bustiers as she might any collection of artifacts. They carried no emotional load. She did not, as she might have at one time, imagine how she would look in that flimsy babydoll, whether that lacy see-through might be seductive. Instead her eyes went through the display to the counter inside, where a middle-aged woman confronted a large, vehement man. The shotgun moved protectively in front of them as they went in.

"Look," the man was saying. "I know business is terrible. It keeps getting worse, too, but that don't mean I can stop collecting the rent. You got it, give it to me. You don't got it, I'll give you notice of eviction. All neat and nice and according to the law." He turned, seeing them come in, and appealed to them. "Ain't that right? Rent is rent, right? It's like death and taxes."

"Is business really bad?" asked Simon, all sympathy.

The woman mopped angrily at the tears still wetting her face. "We got word this week they're closing most of the stores the old ladies didn't burn down. I've got twenty years with them. They offered me a mail-order job in California. California! What do I do with my folks? What do I do with my apartment? I'm trying to tell him it doesn't do any good to ask me, I don't have it to pay him. So let him evict."

"No customers at all?" Ophy asked.

"Oh, sure. The regulars. I got women buy their stuff here every few weeks, a pair of panties, a bra, maybe a slip. Fancy stockings, maybe, for dress-up. Same stuff they always buy, like it's a habit, you know. I got a few guys, transsexes, cross-dressers, you know—they still come in to get all dolled up. Even that's a lot less than it used to be."

"It's the same all up and down the street," offered the rent collector. "There for a while my boss figured it was a conspiracy. Like the old-lady riots, maybe all the women was doing a rent strike. . . ."

"All up and down the street," Simon mused as they went back outside. "Let's see who's open."

They pushed the buzzer outside a porno shop, were scanned, then admitted to find it empty except for one plump and smooth-faced clerk, the phone propped at his ear, the broom he should have been using propped against the wall. He murmured and hung up at their approach.

"Binness? Lousy. That was my boss onna phone, he says it's so lousy, he's not even comin' in from Lon Guyland. He says why'n I take up smokin, so's mebbe I c'n fry the inventory. Ha."

Ophy ran her fingers along one stack of boxed tapes, drawing them away dust laden. "Been a while since anybody changed stock," she commented.

"What'ud I change it for?" the youth asked, almost belligerently. "Guy makes our movies, he's on vacation or somethin'. Nobody's got nothin' new."

"Is this still anecdotal?" asked Simon as they went out into the chilly air. "Does it seem to you consequential that the producer of porn movies has not delivered for some time? Does it seem to you likely that he has not been able to get any actors qualified to . . . ah . . ."

"Act?" suggested Ophy. "You think the actors are all too depressed to take off their clothes? This thing is . . . universal?"

"Way I hear it, that's pretty much so," said the shotgun from behind them. "A month ago I'd hear guys griping about it. Now? It's like nobody cares."

"Come on," Simon said eagerly, dragging her by the hand. "Let's stop in The Naked Truth for a drink."

"Not my kind of place," muttered Ophy.

"Just for a minute, Doctor. Summon up your professional detachment."

The shotgun stayed with them as they went inside, seating himself at a table about three feet from the one Simon and Ophy took, toward the back, away from the runway, where the girls pranced, gyrated, slunk, or crawled. The Naked Truth made a big thing out of costumes: colorful, fantastic, and expensive costumes that set off the flesh while allowing no single sequin to obstruct a clear view of breast, buttock, or pubic hair dyed emerald, sapphire, or ruby red. High-feathered collars jiggled by, like the tails of peacocks. Long trains swished the runway, beginning just below the neat little bottoms. Jeweled corselets, leggings, and gloves set off the sexual parts. Many of the women wore masks, also feathered or jeweled. Those who did not looked bored.

"The place is damned near empty," said Simon, leaning back to talk to the shotgun. "Isn't it usually pretty full by this time of night?"

"Last time I was here, yeah. That was a while ago, though."

The waitress, when she showed up, looked as bored as the girls on the runway.

"Kind of dead tonight," Simon commented.

"Every night!" said the waitress. "This is my last one here. I can't make it without tips."

"What are you going to do?" asked Ophy.

"Hostess in a seafood place. Even with no fish left but fake shrimp, fake crab, soybean fish cakes, they're still busy. This place is dying on its pudendums, and that's no joke."

The place seemed already dead. They left their drinks almost untouched and went outside.

"Enough anecdote?" Simon asked when they reached the sidewalk again. "You want to go on?"

She shook her head, baffled, stunned. So fast. A few weeks ago she hadn't even heard of this. And here it was, everywhere, all at once. As though it had started slow, built up gradually, then, wham, critical mass in a matter of days!

"There aren't any prostitutes," she said, staring along empty curbs at the passing traffic. "I heard the numbers were down, but there aren't any!"

"Forget the working girls," he said, putting his arm around her. "Hey, Ophy. Let's have dinner."

She nodded. The shotgun accepted an invitation to join them. The driver said he'd stay with the car if they'd bring him something. They found a Chinese restaurant half a block down and across, a busy Chinese restaurant that showed no signs of disruption or failing business.

"Food isn't included," Ophy said, watching a scurrying waiter carry a heavily laden tray past their table. "This place doesn't indicate any loss of appetite."

"Guys I know still want to eat," agreed the shotgun. "They still like a beer, still like to watch baseball, not football so much, women still seem to be doing what they usually do. Kids are going to school like usual. It's not like the end of the world."

"Look at the women," whispered Simon. "Ophy. Look."

She looked, seeing nothing strange. The women were laughing, talking, shushing children, handling chopsticks. . . .

"What?"

"No makeup."

She looked again. He was wrong. There was some makeup, but it was the habitual kind. Her own kind. A swipe with the base, another swipe with the lipstick, forget the eyes unless you're going out. Of all the women in the place, only half a dozen had done their eyes. She said as much.

"Hold the fort." Simon slid out of the booth and went to one of the eye-women, crouched down beside her, and showed his credentials, smiling.

"What's he doing?" asked the shotgun.

"Telling her he's doing a story about women and makeup, or something like that. Telling her she's one of the best-looking women in the room, does she always do a full makcup job. Something that'll make her feel good, make her talkative."

"Right." The shotgun accepted delivery of spring rolls, dipped one into hot mustard, and bit into it, reflectively. "He's good at that, isn't hc? I try that, she'd have me arrested. Look at her, smilin' at him."

Simon moved on to another woman, and then another. When he returned to the table, he looked grimly pleased.

"All the gals who did their eyes do it every day. They're models, receptionists, front people. It's as much habit with them as the swipe wipe is with the others. Another thing, look at the shoes."

She looked. She couldn't find heels anywhere, just flats and low pumps. "And they're not depressed?"

"Do they look depressed to you?"

"Not much."

"It isn't depression we're after, Ophy. It's something else."

"Sex," said the shotgun around a mouthful of shrimp and pork, his voice slightly surprised. "I thought the two of you had it figured when we went to Frederick's. It's sex."

"What about sex?" Simon asked.

"It isn't people are depressed, so they don't have sex. It's people don't feel sexy, so some of 'em get depressed. You got it backward."

"Some of them get depressed?" Ophy asked. "Because . . ."

"Oh, some guy because that's all he really liked doing. Or because his wife wants a kid, or because . . . You know, any old because. Mostly men. Doin' sex is all some men have to brag about, you know. Got no brains, got no ambition, got no skills, but they can fuck like a bunny. Or used to could. And some of 'em, they think God is punishin' 'em, so they get together in some prayer group or other, whippin' themselves, endin' up killin' themselves or maybe blamin' women, so they go out bopping dames, end up killin' some. Like the guys in the black hoods; that's their problem."

Ophy breathed slowly in and out, knowing what he said was true but still unwilling to buy it. So simple. Too simple. "I had one case, his wife said he wasn't that upset. . . ."

"How'd she know?" he asked reasonably. "You take some little shrimpy guy can hardly keep it up half a minute, inside himself, maybe he's King Kong."

"What's your name again?" Simon asked the shotgun.

"Name's Emil Fustig. My friends call me Fusty."

"You're not depressed?"

"Hell, no. There was always too much screwin' around. Even when you didn't do it, you said you did. You know, you've got to pretend, otherwise you'd start doubting your manhood, right? If we didn't have sex and football, what would we talk about?"

"Well, what have you been talking about lately?"

"Sort of interestin'. Driver I know, Max Benevidez—always usta talk about his last lay or his last bar fight or how he'd rather die of AIDS than do without—he's been talkin' about how he used to play trumpet. He thinks it might be fun to start a little mariachi group. Joe Zanger—last winter he was told off for sex-harrassing the dispatchers—he's been doin' crossword puzzles. Won himself a hundred dollars last week in a crossword contest. Funny, I'da swore he didn't know more than fifty words total. Me, I don't notice much different. Not much interested in football anymore. You noticed how the game's gone downhill? But I always was a reader. Now instead of the beer and the game, I'll stretch out with a book."

"You married, Fusty?"

"Me? Sure. Me 'n' Francis been married twenty-six years. She's a real good old girl. Always did like her a lot."

"Children?"

"Two of 'em. Boy and girl. Good kids. Francy's got her mind set on grandkids, too. That's the only thing worries me."

"Worries . . ."

"I been scared to ask. What if the young ones don't care about sex anymore, either?"

Later that night Ophy and Simon lay close, side by side, skin against skin. He felt wonderful, Ophy thought. All the warm, wiry length of him, bony toes, like hers, mostly hairless except the line down his belly. Quite wonderful. Like a baby. You always wanted to stroke babies, their skin was so nice and soft. Warm and sleek and familial. She felt like an otter, curled up in a burrow, joyous with life.

"I've been going crazy," said Simon, his lips close to her ear. "I used to stay away from you purposely, did you realize that? I'd extend a trip, from a week to ten days, from ten days to two weeks, teasing myself with the thought of you here. I'd put it off, like a kid saving candy. I'd look at women in bars, teasing myself with them, thinking they were just an echo of you. I'd wait until I was on fire to come home to you.

"The last time, that's what I was doing. I thought if I stayed away long enough, old habit would come to the rescue. It didn't work. I wanted you. I loved you. But the fire was out. No—banked. Warm, not hot." He laughed, and the tears spilled. "I couldn't make myself horny!"

"I never knew that," she said, amazed. She hadn't. She'd looked forward to his return, she'd learned to count on those skyrocket reunions, but she'd never known he'd planned them, stored them up. How long had it been? Six months, almost. Half a year!

"Tomorrow," Simon laughed, dabbing at his face. "Tomorrow I'm going to talk to car dealerships."

"We should talk to pedophiles," murmured Ophy. "Prisoners."

"They're all tanked. I can't talk to them."

"Maybe some awaiting trial? Some they haven't tanked yet."

"What am I looking for?"

"Sexual attraction is genetic. Hetero, homo, pedo, whatever. This thing that's happening, is it happening to them, too? Gays? Or only to heteros? Is it happening to pedophiles? Do they still want to molest children?"

"Rapists?" he asked.

"Yeah. Do they still want to?"

"Pornographers don't, according to that guy. . . ."

She shook her head, nuzzling into his neck, mumbling, "I knew this was it, Simon. Sort of subconsciously, I knew it all the time. I told Dr. Lotte to look at the child-abuse rates, at wife battering. I'll bet you anything they're down."

"If sex is down, violence is down, you mean?"

"For anybody over puberty. We should look at playgrounds, kids' games. G. I. Joe and Barbie."

"What about Barbie?"

"She's been immortal, and I hate her. Talk about role models! Barbie the bulimic! Barbie the anorexic. Bettiann wanted to be like Barbie—damn near starved herself to death trying."

"Maybe Barbie's no longer immortal. Maybe somebody just brought her down in flames."

"St. Barbie, burned at the stake." She yawned around a giggle.

He held her closer. It wasn't an unfamiliar feeling. It was the feeling they had always had after they made love, this quiet closeness, this warm tenderness. No sadness in it at all. No regret.

"What if Fusty's worry is true?"

"I don't know, Simon. Honest to God, I don't know. Hormonal therapy, I suppose, for anyone wanting a child."

"Testes kept alive in tanks? Ovaries ditto? Artificial wombs?"

"It probably wouldn't come to that. We don't really know. . . ."

She was right. Nobody really knew. Not yet.

14

MONDAY MORNING EARLY, OPHY CALLED the chief's office and said she was on her way to see him. He was on the phone when she got there, talking to Lotte Epstein, or, rather, grunting replies to questions or information coming from the other end. He hung up with a frown.

"She says they've got a new directive from the White House. Federal marshals are being sent to every media outlet: papers, TV, radio. No one is to even hint that there's anything going around. The President has declared a secret national emergency, if that makes sense. She says to tell you domestic violence is down. She says way down. What's that about?"

Ophy laughed, a high-pitched, almost hysterical, giggle. "It's sex, chief."

"Sex what?"

"Sex. It isn't depression. Or it isn't depression as a cause. It's sex as a cause. Loss of interest in same. Which results in depression in some cases, which results in suicide in some cases. Or did."

"What the hell?"

"Just listen." She sat down opposite him and gave him a terse account of Simon's investigation. "So when the shotgun says sex, we both realize, right, it's sex. I mean, I feel like the stupidest ass in the world! God, I should have seen it. Wouldn't you think somebody would have? Only excuse I can offer is most of us who were looking for reasons aren't all that young anymore, and people don't always talk about their own sexuality, you know? Not truthfully, at least."

"But, Ophy, what could've happened? What does it mean?"

"I'm not a prophet. How should I know?"

"You say sex? What about you and Simon?"

"What about us? We're not immune. What about you?"

"Since Joy died, I haven't . . . I guess I hadn't noticed. . . ."

"See, that's what I mean! You hadn't noticed! Simon said it's like your nose—if it doesn't itch, you don't know it's there." She giggled again, almost hysterically. "I had kind of a notion, right after the meeting we had here, way before Simon and I started looking. I called Lotte, asked her to check rates of domestic violence. . . ."

"So what does it mean, domestic violence is down?"

"Testosterone, chief. Sex and dominance, lust and violence, all arising from the same hormonal stew! If sex is down, logically dominance and violence should also be down. I don't know about serotonin. Nobody's looked, but I'm betting it's up. Rape went up for a while: Men were feeling insecure and they blamed women; but now people should be feeling pretty good about themselves. If I'm right, assaults and murders will be down, gang wars over turf will be down. People should have lost interest in violent team sports— soccer, football, hockey. Simon thinks maybe not baseball, maybe not tennis or golf or skiing, though I'm not so sure. We'll have to wait and see. And the bottom's going to fall out of the birth rate."

"When?"

"Nine months from right now. From this last few weeks, as a matter of fact. This effect has been building slowly for a long time, years, two or three at least. Just recently it reached the total saturation point."

"What am I going to tell the staff! I mean, what am I allowed to tell the staff?"

She left him there, staring at the wall, and went to her own office to call Jessamine. As far as she was concerned, the no-talk order didn't include family, and the DFC was family. It was two hours earlier in Utah, so she got Jess out of bed.

"Jess? It's Ophy. You awake? You want me to hang up, call you back in an hour?"

"Ophy? Ophy! What's wrong?"

"Do I only call you when something's wrong? Right! I only call you when something's wrong. Listen, Jess, the weirdest thing . . ." She explained briefly, concisely.

"I be swoggled," muttered Jessamine when Ophy's voice trailed off. "What in hell?"

"That's what my boss wants to know. That's what the CDC people want to know. Where has this come from?"

"Out of Africa," muttered Jessamine. "Like AIDS? Of course, there've been rumors of biological warfare, maybe something Saddam used a decade ago, during the war, or something the Serbs got from the Russians. I wouldn't put it past them."

"You think it's a disease?"

"If it cuts off all sexual desire, it'd be a self-limiting disease. Can't get far that way. Explains a lot, though."

"Like?"

"Like what's the matter with Patrick. He's left me, or is in the process of leaving—I'm not sure which since he keeps coming back to get things. Maybe he's just confused. Don't say you're sorry to hear he's going."

"All right," Ophy answered soberly. "If you're not sorry, I'm not sorry."

Jessamine laughed, not amused. "Are you scared? You sound a little scared."

"Damn it, Jessy. Of course I'm scared, in a sort of relaxed way. I keep stoking myself into a panic, then in five minutes I'm all relaxed again. Whatever it is, maybe it short-circuits the adrenals or something. When I look around, most people are sort of going along, not bothered very much."

"There used to be a researcher here at the labs talked about this happening."

"This? This what?"

"This—no more human beings. He believed in Gaia. He said we'd go too far, populate too much, destroy too much, and the planet would strike back at us."

"Is he still around?"

"He moved to Australia, oh, a year or so ago. He was serious, though. He really meant it." She took a deep breath. "Are you going to call the others? Carolyn? Aggie?"

"Carolyn, probably. Are you going to help her with the trial, Jess?"

"Our meeting's scheduled concurrent with the trial. I told her I'd take some extra time, just to be available. Are you?"

"I'm planning on it. If you haven't read her account of her interview with the girl, the rape scene, read it. In the light of this whole business, it's very revealing."

Ophy called Carolyn, got no answer, tried the other number she had for Carolyn, and this time the phone was picked up.

"Have you heard about the epidemic?" she asked.

"What epidemic, Ophy?"

"The libido-loss epidemic. There is one." She explained, words tumbling over one another.

"So that's what's going on," said Carolyn, thinking of Stace and Luce. "I couldn't figure out . . ." She'd have to call Stace right away.

"Do you suppose some biological-warfare experiment got loose or something?" Ophy wondered.

"God knows," said Carolyn. "Maybe Sophy's story was real and Elder Sister decided it was time to put sex back in the medicine bag." She laughed rackingly.

After a painful silence Ophy said, "All her stories were real, Carolyn. That's why they hurt so much. What happened to her? I ask myself a hundred times a week, what happened to her?"

"Oh, God, Ophy. So do I."

A thousand miles away Ophy took a sobbing breath. "Carolyn, do you ever have the feeling she's back?"

Long silence; then, "Do you?"

"All the time. She's suddenly there, just behind me. I talk to her over my shoulder. Time goes away. Then I wake up, ten minutes, half an hour later, and I'm somewhere else, doing something else."

Carolyn made a sound, halfway between a moan and a chuckle. "With me it's when I go down to feed the sheep. I feel this body bumping me, very softly. Or I feel soft lips nibbling the palm of my hand. Nothing's there, but something was. Or, at night, I have the feeling there's someone in the room. . . ."

"Do you suppose . . . the others?" Ophy sniffled and gulped. Why was she crying?

"I'll ask Faye. You ask Jessamine."

Faye was touchy on the subject. "All right, all right, Carolyn. Don't push! Yes, damn it! I did a full-size sculpture of Sophy right after she disappeared—that is, after we knew she'd disappeared. Kind of a frenzy I went through, trying to sublimate grief, I guess. I had it cast, and now it's here, in the studio. Lately it's been up to tricks. Vanishing. Talking to me. Dressing itself up when I'm not looking."

"Is it a nude statue?" Carolyn asked after a thoughtful pause. "Remember how she always used to insist that you not make her recognizable. And remember that whole thing about being lusted after. Sophy wouldn't have liked being a nude, not if it looked like her."

Silence at the other end, then, "Damn. You're right. Of course she wouldn't."

"Something else, Faye. . . ." Carolyn told her about the libido epidemic.

"So that's it," muttered Faye. "Good lord, Carolyn!"

"You knew something was wrong, Faye? You've lost interest in girls?"

"Carolyn, I don't need you dissin' my private life, but, yes, I suppose I have lost the impulse, sort of, but that's not what I was thinking. I was thinking about this little girl model I've been using. Curvy little thing, juicy as a bunch of grapes. She has a real macho boyfriend, handsome little Lahtino—you know how they look when they're young, all that whippy muscle, all that fire and sizzle before they go to guts and guzzle the way they do. Well, lately she's been crying on my shoulder he doesn't take her to bed anymore. Doesn't knock her around, either, which is probably more surprising. I couldn't figure what happened to him, but this sure explains it. My lord, girl. What in the name of heaven is going on?"

"Jessamine thinks it may be Gaia. My first thought was Sophy's story about Elder Sister, remember?"

"Oh, I sure do. You think maybe that's it? After all these generations she finished the medicine bag and bottled us up?"

"What'll this do to Bettiann?"

"You think she'll put on mourning for her dead clit?"

"Faye!"

"Well, hey, sister. You want me to go all reverent or something? You know damn well sex was mostly torture for Bettiann. Bettiann won't mind. Wish I could say that much for William."

"You're right. Bettiann won't mind nearly as much as William. I don't want to tell Aggie at all, but she'll probably know about it by the time we all get together. The government can't keep the lid on forever."

"This'll be a meeting to end all meetings!"

Finally, resolved not to mention the epidemic, Carolyn called Bettiann. Did she ever feel Sophy was, somehow, still with them?

"Oh, Carolyn . . . yes," said Bettiann with a low laugh, almost of relief. "She's here in this house most of the time. Like in the next room. Or just coming up the walk. I write things down without knowing what I'm doing, and when I read it, it sounds like her. Not her words, but her ideas in my words, you know."

"Have you kept it?"

"Kept? You mean the writing?"

"Have you kept it, them?"

"Yes, I have. I've kept them all."

"Bring them, with you, Bettiann. Bring them to the meeting. For show-and-tell."

The final score, when Ophy and Carolyn talked again, was that five of them had seen or heard or experienced Sophy.

"Maybe all six," said Ophy. "We haven't asked Agnes."

"She's been so touchy."

"She's thinking of resigning. I've heard it in her voice."

"Has she declined and fallen?"

"She doesn't think so. Maybe she thinks the rest of us have. Did you tell Faye about the epidemic?"

"Yes. I didn't tell Bettiann, though."

"Why?"

"Because William's in advertising. If she slipped and let William know, the whole world would know. It's going to get out, you know. They can't keep a lid on this. Still, I'd just as soon the leak didn't get traced back to me."

And, at last, Carolyn phoned Stace. Stace hadn't said a word about Luce since that long-ago Monday. At least now she could know that she wasn't alone. And Luce was used to keeping secrets.

Stace seethed and steamed and muttered, all rather halfheartedly.

"Talk to me," Carolyn demanded. "Are you angry? Are you scared?"

Long silence. "Mom, I've lost a couple of bra sizes. Luce is also smaller in the . . . reproductive department. I've stopped menstruating; either that or my period's like six months late."

"Maybe you're pregnant?"

"I thought I was for a while, but no, Mom, I'm not pregnant." She sighed deeply. "I've asked around, my friends, people my age or younger. None of the women are menstruating anymore. Some of them have been to doctors for tests, some haven't. Some thought they were pregnant, some didn't. There's this one friend of mine, had boobs like the front of a truck. Forty double-D, hanging out there like headlights. All of a sudden she's almost flat. She's delighted. She said her chest always overbalanced her, made her look top-heavy, she was always spilling food on it. Ill wind and all that, huh?"

She hung up. Carolyn lay back on the bed, the phone still in her hand. Strangeness on strangeness. Libido epidemics and Sophy still around and Elder Sister's medicine bag, and Gaia, and, according to the millenarians, the world was coming to an end. But if that was so, why was this stupid trial still progressing, point to point, join the dots, as though it made any kind of picture? What would Jagger do when he found out what she knew?

Hal appeared in the doorway. "What's going on? All these whispered conversations?"

She told him.

"My God." He fell into a chair, mouth open.

"Yeah. I wonder if He had something to do with it."

Hal had talked for years about putting an electronically controlled gate at the entrance to the farm, just to avoid the hassle of people who turned into the driveway and came all the way down to the house before realizing they were in the wrong place. He had never got to it, but the men he had talked to on Saturday had promised to do the installation on Monday when they came to wire the house against intruders. Just because one pimply youth was dead, it didn't mean there weren't more where he had come from.

There were a dozen No Trespassing signs in the barn Hal had never got around to putting up, partly because Carolyn had thought posting the place would only draw attention to it. Now, however, it seemed attention was to be drawn, willy-nilly, so Hal sent Carlos out with a handful of signs to be posted every hundred feet along the front fence.

"You have a little trouble?" Carlos asked.

"Carlos, we had a lot of trouble. Friday night the dogs caught a burglar in the kitchen."

Carlos turned to Carolyn. "You been doin' somethin notty?"

She shook her head at him. "What makes you ask that?"

"I hear things. Down at the bar, this kid askin' questions. Spotty-face kid."

"Could be him, Carlos. What did he want to know?"

"Oh, all about you, you live alone or not, who comes see you, who the family is, you know. Real nosy. You remember Emilia? Teofilo's mama, she use to work for you?"

"I remember her." Oh, God. She'd forgotten about Emilia.

"Teofilo's brothers, they tell the spotty-face kid he shut his mouth or they shut it."

Carolyn cringed mentally. Emilia must have told her sons that Carolyn had promised to do something about Teo. She bit her cheek, making a mental note. Carlos interrupted her line of thought.

"You got that little house out there, one I use to lib in before so many kids."

"Right." Carlos and his wife had lived in the old bunkhouse until the third child had come along. There were now seven children, a fact that Carolyn tried not to let color her opinion of Carlos, who was otherwise both sensible and hardworking. In Carlos's opinion men had been created to make babies, women to bear them, and what happened to them afterward was God's problem.

He shrugged a question. "What you say my brothers lib in the house for a while? They sabe on rent, you got somebody here at night."

"Which brothers?" Hal asked, eyebrows raised.

He laughed. "Not Cippio, not Jaime. They get drunk too much. I think maybe Fidel and Arturo."

As far as she knew, Fidel and Arturo, though recent arrivals, were reliable and reasonably sober. She looked at Hal, who nodded his okay.

"Good idea," she said. "But no parties."

He nodded. "No parties. Arturo, he has this big dog, his name is Leonegro. Bery black, this dog. Bery smart, too."

Carolyn nodded. If she kept her dogs in the house, it made sense to have another one around outside, particularly at night. "Carlos, tell them not to talk about where they're staying, okay? If somebody comes here, let it be a surprise."

He grinned at her and went off with Hal.

At ten she drove into Santa Fe to her former law office. Mary, the office manager, located in about thirty seconds flat the notes Carolyn remembered. The notes were as Carolyn remembered them. Swinter had got off on immortalizing his scribbles, passing out copies by the ream. She took the map from her wallet, spread it on the table, and placed the Swinter copies beside it. The map had obviously been traced from the property survey that was available in the county clerk's office. The words "road," "farm," "house," and "barn" were written on the tracing, the *o*'s with tight little anal-retentive loops, the *d* and *b*, the *h* and *f*, all with a single vertical upstroke, an idiosyncratic rendering of the *r*'s. The letters were written exactly as Swinter wrote them. If Swinter had not drawn the map, he had at least labeled it.

She took the copies to Jerry's office and asked him if he had a minute.

"Anytime for you, Carolyn! What's going on?"

She told him, laying out the pages.

Jerry took off his glasses and polished them on his tie. "Why on earth would Emmet Swinter send somebody to prowl your house?"

"I'm defending the mother of the baby in the Dumpster, Jer. I think the DA's office was counting on Harmston doing the job."

Jerry blinked slowly, thinking out the implications of that. "How'd you get involved?"

"Someone asked me to."

He rubbed his hands over his head. "You sure picked one hell of a case to bring you out of retirement. What do you want me to do with this?"

"I want you to know about it. I'm putting these two pieces of paper in your custody. This one is the copy I made last night, in the presence of a deputy sheriff, of an original found in the pocket of a man who broke into my house. The original was retained by the deputy as evidence. The deputy signed this copy and dated it at my request; there's his signature. This other paper contains samples of Swinter's writing. I believe both were written by the same hand, and I suggest that be verified by a graphanalyst."

"And then?"

"Then you hang on to them. Just in case something happens to me."

He got up, moved around in an agitated fashion. "In case something happens to you? Carolyn! For God's sake, you're talking about respectable members of the bar. . . ." He collapsed back into his chair, shaking his head.

She leaned across the desk and put her hand on his, making him look directly at her. "I'm not talking about respectable members of the bar. I'm talking about Jake Jagger. The kid that broke into my house supposedly hanged himself in his cell. Would a kid do that over a minor break-in?"

He sat back, mouth slightly open, removing his glasses, going through the polishing ritual, taking a moment before he could say, "People do strange things."

"Remember the Greta Wilson case, Jer? Back before Jagger was DA? Greta was an abused wife. She filed for divorce because her husband was beating on her *and* the kids. Her husband hired Jagger. Jagger was married to Greta's sister Helen, mind you, but that didn't stop him. Jagger brought in perjured evidence, said she was a satanist, got her locked up. Next morning there she was, hanged in her cell. I know damn well she wouldn't have done it."

He said again, "People do strange—"

She pounded on his desk, snarling at him, "She was a devout Catholic, Jer! She knew I was going to get her out. Jagger knew it, too. I know she was murdered. I know the kid that broke into my house was murdered."

He got up again, making fussy motions with his hands, pushing the idea away, with all its implications. "But it makes no sense! Why would anyone want to prowl your house?"

"All Hal and I can come up with is they're looking for something to discredit me somehow." Carolyn cleared her throat. She didn't want to talk about Albert. "At one time or another I've gone on record as a feminist. I've supported abortion rights. I'd call myself a conservative fiscally, but on most women's issues, like equal pay and the need for child care, I'm a liberal, which is a dirty word to the Alliance, and therefore to Jake Jagger."

He nodded soberly. "I still think you're being paranoid, Carolyn."

She left the papers in his hands, nonetheless.

Monday afternoon Jagger got a call from Keepe.

"Mr. Webster is getting some disturbing information from our foreign allies. There seems to be some kind of epidemic going on."

"So?" said Jagger, wondering what the hell that had to do with him.

"He's asked me to speak personally to a number of our people to see if they have heard anything."

"Anything about what, Keepe? About an epidemic? You mean like the hantavirus we have out here?"

"My sources aren't sure. It seems to be a psychological epidemic. The CDC is asking about assaults, rapes, suicides . . ."

Jagger took a deep breath and held it. What was this? "I'm sure you know the Alliance authorizes squads of dedicated men to . . . ah . . ."

"To enforce purity among women, yes. Sons of Allah, and the Black Brigade, and some other offshoots of the Army of God. But evidently whatever the CDC is looking at doesn't involve any of our people."

Jagger grew testy. "Can you be a little more specific, Keepe? You're not giving me the picture."

"This is not to be repeated, Jagger. Our Iranian friends are concerned that some disease may have been let loose, maybe during the Gulf War. They're having trouble getting men out for their political demonstrations; they seem to be afflicted with . . . well, it's a kind of lassitude! Also, Public Health people in Washington have been trying to identify some kind of contagion. They've been asking questions about depression and suicides."

"I haven't heard anything like that."

"Ask around."

"How shall I reach you?"

"We'll be in touch." The line went dead.

Jagger hung up the phone and stood staring at it, deep in thought. Keepe had sounded furious, reining it in, but barely. Naturally, the flap would have started with the Iranians, or with Libya, or Iraq, or Morocco. The religious groups were the weak links in the Alliance. You couldn't count on men who preferred martyrdom to survival. If one of the theocratic countries flared up, it could threaten the Alliance as a whole!

In Jagger's opinion it was rumor, one in an endless series. Ever since the Gulf War people had claimed that sicknesses were caused by Iraqi weapons, or by U.S. countermeasures that had gone wrong. AIDS could take ten years to manifest itself, however, so it wasn't impossible that something from the Gulf War was just coming to the surface. Still, it was damned unlikely! Both Iraq and the Pentagon were members of the Alliance. If either of them had used some kind of disease as a weapon, the Alliance would know about it!

Jake made a short list of people to call, including some of the militias in Utah and Montana, where there'd been nerve-gas testing decades back. Maybe they'd come up with something.

In the wee hours of Tuesday morning Carolyn heard Sophy saying very clearly, "Carolyn. Wake up."

Carolyn sat up suddenly, all at once aware of the darkness around her, the breathing of the dogs on the floor, the light curtains moving almost imperceptibly in the light of a late moon. It hadn't been a dream that had wakened her; it had been a definite voice saying sensible words. She held her breath, struggling to hear. She couldn't hear anything, but still she knew there was someone moving outside her window. And there'd been someone in the house.

She eased herself over the edge of the bed and sat there, pajama clad, reaching for the drawer pull in the bedside table, feeling for the flat chill of the automatic at the back of it. Hector sensed her motion and groaned, turning over, half opening one eye. She could see the reflected light, a tiny mirror, blinking moonlight at her. "Shhh," she said.

His eyes opened wide; his head came up, ears up, listening as she was listening. When she got to her feet and moved toward the door, he moved with her, silent, stepping over Fancy and Fandango as though they were inanimate lumps in the path. They didn't move, were not aware.

Her door was shut. She eased it open, laying her hand on Hector's shoulder. He stayed with her as she moved silently through the kitchen, as she tested the outside door, still tightly locked. They went the other way, back down the hall past the bedroom, toward the open door of Hal's study.

They were in the study doorway when all hell broke loose outside: a bay like the Hound of the Baskervilles; growling, yelling, a receding pother of animal and man. Carolyn stumbled toward the door but arrived on the scene of battle too late to see the conflict. Carlos's brothers, bare-chested, holding up their trousers, sprinted toward the sound that came from outside the new gate: a revving engine, spinning wheels. They were too late. The car sped off when they were only halfway down the drive. When they returned, Leonegro was beside them, carrying a sizable piece of denim, which he shook like a rat, growling.

She said, "What a good dog!" Leonegro had to be part mastiff. One of those Italian mastiffs that end up weighing close to two hundred pounds. He wasn't any taller than a Great Dane, but he was much heavier, with a head like a trip hammer and a loose, heavily furred skin that looked designed for battle.

"Where did you get him?" she asked Fidel, forcing her voice to remain at a sensible level.

"My father in Mesico, he gib him to me. He was onny so big, *como un' chivito.*"

"He got bigger."

"He is bery espensib to feed," said Fidel, with a sideways look at her.

She swallowed deeply. "If you'll get that piece of cloth away from him, I'll buy him some dog food. Unless he'd rather have half a dozen live goats."

"Dog food is good."

The huge dog looked up at her and grinned a dog grin, tongue flopping out to clean his muzzle. Dog food would be fine, the grin said. In ten- or twenty-pound lots. Fidel managed to get the cloth away from him and gave it to Carolyn. It had blood on it, not a lot. If the prowler hadn't been maimed, he'd at least been punctured.

She gathered her robe around her, feeling the weight of the handgun in the pocket, as she went back into the study.

Hal, from the hallway, asked, "Is this going to be a daily thing?" He took the stained fragment from her, looking at it closely, turning it, sniffing it. "I think we'll send this to Mike. Be nice to have something to do a DNA match on, just in case."

"Whatever," she said, depressed. The envelope between the books was still there. She drew it out and opened it, knowing before the flap came up that it was empty. Even Leonegro had missed the incoming, though he'd been in time to pursue the outgoing.

"Fredo talked," she said.

"Maybe he just mentioned it to his partner."

"Then his partner talked."

"Lots of law-enforcement types belong to the Alliance, Carolyn."

She dropped into the old leather chair and shuddered, unable to stop. This had been no bungling teenager. Some very skillful person had been in here, and how had he managed that?

Hal was asking himself the same question. Two minutes' search turned up a small round hole cut in the glass of one window, near the window latch. "Two days later we'd have had the place wired. Even now, if I hadn't been looking, I'd never have seen it."

She sighed. "If I hadn't been looking, I wouldn't have known the envelope was empty. I wouldn't have been looking if something hadn't wakened me."

"What?"

"Sophy, who has quit playing sheep and is now playing guard dog!"

He raised his eyebrows. "A protective phantom? Good for her! You realize it could have been months before we knew anyone had been here."

"Well, no. I'd have checked the envelope sooner than that."

"Come on back to the big bed. You don't want to be alone."

She didn't want to be alone. She went with him, snuggled up against him, heard the dog's claws rattle across the brick floor on their way to the rug, where they turned around and around before settling. Hal's breathing became calm and steady. She lay there, warm and presumably safe, yet unable either to rest or to sleep. Shadowy prowlers edged along her consciousness, making sudden sorties that startled her awake. At six she gave up, eased herself out of the bed, and followed the dogs to the kitchen.

Carlos came in as she was fixing coffee, handed her the daily paper, and said, "You got peoples out there in the road."

"What kind of people?"

"With signs. Much yelling when I climb over the new gate." He sounded slightly hurt as he said, "You din gib me a key."

"You weren't here when they gave me the keys, Carlos. There's one hanging by the kitchen door with your name on it. Put the dogs in the pen, will you, on your way out?"

She fetched binoculars from her bedroom and took a look at the people by the gate. There were about a dozen, wearing flimsy, windblown tabards that identified the Army of God. The signs they carried, obviously prepared for some other contingency, didn't make much sense in their present context. Evidently the demonstration had been hastily assembled. And why?

Hal came in, yawning. While having coffee and breakfast and reading the paper, they looked out at dark clouds, driven by high winds, and counted the cars that passed, only five in the next two hours. People with jobs were already at work, and the neighbors didn't need to use this stretch of road at all. There were a dozen ways to reach the highway without passing this place, and she was sure the grapevine had suggested to everyone that they do precisely that.

Hal remarked, "We could clear them out of there. The new harassment law's specific about that."

"I know. But why waste our time? What would be the point? You always told me the Army of God is made up of rank-and-file zealots, interchangeable mob-components, spitters, and stone throwers."

"Even mob-components can be dangerous. It's good the alarm guys will be here to finish wiring the house this afternoon."

The men showed up about eleven, just as the picketers were departing. With no audience, with rain squalls passing through every few minutes and grit-laden winds gusting up to forty and fifty miles per hour, the Army of God had had enough.

The security men worked through the afternoon. As he was leaving that evening, the foreman commented to Carolyn, "I hate to tell you, or maybe you know. Your phone is bugged."

"My phone!"

"The one in that office there, and all the extensions. It's got a real good little gadget hooked up where the line comes into the house. You want me to remove it?"

He seemed sympathetic about it, but only slightly curious. For him it was all routine, she supposed. In his world people spied on people all the time. Carolyn shook her head slowly. "No. Leave it. I'd rather find out who did it, and I can do that best by leaving it in place."

"You're sure?"

"I believe so. That's not the line I use much, anyhow. Would you check the other phone for me?"

"I only saw one line—"

"I know. The other one was the original house phone fifty years ago, before they put in the new cables. It comes into the back of the house from across the river."

He checked the phone in the room Carolyn was using and declared it clean, then sold her a little gadget that would tell her if anyone fooled with it. When he left, she sat staring at the needle on the dial, musing for a long time. How long ago had the house phones been bugged? During the visit that Leonegro had almost put an end to? Or before that? When the spotty-faced kid had broken in? He could have installed the gadget, then decided to try a break-in. Possibly. What had she said over that phone during the last few days? Not much. There'd been the call from Jessamine. She'd said what? Libido epidemic, something. Would the mysterious phone bugger be interested in the fact she knew there was such a thing? She'd talked about Sophy's still being around. And she'd had a call from an old friend in Chicago who'd wanted information on the Santa Fe Opera. Did the bugger care about that? And they'd called Mike Winter, at the FBI! Where had Hal called from?

Her throat loosened after a moment. Hal had made the call from her bedroom phone. And why hadn't she herself thought of being bugged? Out of desire not to appear paranoid, perhaps. She'd been aware of danger, but too self-consciously diffident to take strong action!

No more, she promised herself, blood hammering painfully in her temples. No more.

Stace told Luce about the epidemic when he got home from work Tuesday night.

After a long silence he licked his lips. "How long has it been going on?"

"Mom said maybe for two or three years. But only recently everywhere. Like that curve, you know, the one that starts out shallow and all of a sudden goes through the top of the graph."

"An asymptote," he murmured. "Once you're halfway, you're as good as there." He shook his head in disbelief.

She said, "Somebody'd better be figuring out what's happened before it's too late to make babies anymore."

He laughed, a hacking gasp, without humor. "It's like hard science fiction." He gestured upward, at his tightly packed bookshelves. "You got a problem? Somebody better figure it out, maybe build a machine to solve it. You got a situation? Somebody'll invent something to handle it. That's the plot of a thousand stories. Like the Manhattan Project, back during World War Two. Or NASA, putting a man on the moon."

"Luce. . . ."

"You know, Stace. I'm part of a generation of kids, boys mostly, that was raised to believe there's no problem we can't solve; that somebody—some elite—will always come up with something. Population's outgrowing food supply? Someone will think of something. Got an epidemic? Someone will find a way to cure it. We don't need to change *people* so long as *somebody* can come up with a technical fix!"

Her lips twisted, almost a sneer. "Of course you mean someone *else*?"

"Oh, yeah, sure. It's got to be somebody else, some elite. The people who create the problem won't solve it. Maybe they could, but they won't. Miners and manufacturers and lumbermen believe destroying the earth is acceptable because it means jobs. Every mommy and daddy thinks it's other people who are overpopulating the world, not their third and fourth and fifth kids. Half the world's species are extinct; the rest soon will be. Not their worry. Someone else has to solve things."

"But, my God, Luce. It does have to be somebody else. I can't solve problems like that. We can't."

"I know," he whispered. "I knew in my gut it was something like this! I knew! All of us, we've got ourselves into a mess, so we're expecting somebody else to get us out. But what if it's like AIDS? What if they can't?"

So far, at least, they couldn't. Luce was quite right. Around the world a thousand labs went on the equivalent of a wartime footing, around-the-clock shifts doing genetic analysis, attempting to determine what had happened to mankind. Tight-lipped people everywhere were asking the same questions. Pathologists were doing exhaustive studies of every dead body they could lay hands on, looking for difference. There were some obvious changes. Women's breasts had shrunk, leaving only gentle curves to indicate femininity. External genitalia, both male and female, were much smaller. Women's hips and thighs had become less fleshy. Though neither ovaries nor testes showed any signs of atrophy, neither were they making reproductive cells, and erectile tissue no longer functioned. Men previously bald were now growing hair. If there were brain changes, they were too small to be easily detected in persons living or dead. Was it a virus? A retrovirus? Was it a genetic change? A spontaneous mutation? In response to what? Had individuals changed hormonally, biologically, chemically? To find genetic changes, current men would have to be compared to their former selves, but full genetic inventories did not exist for their former selves. There were, however, lots of men and a few women in tanks. Some of them were biopsied, then wakened, then assayed again a few weeks later, but answers could not be expected to come quickly. With all those allelic variations, one's genome might be quite eccentric and still be within the range of normalcy. Even with computers, comparing total genomes could take one hell of a long time and then yield only equivocal results.

Hormone replacement was tried, without success. Recipients had serious, life-threatening allergic reactions to testosterone or estrogen. Whoever, whatever, was playing with humanity was at least one move ahead.

While the laboratory staffs sweated and cursed, most of the world's people either didn't know or pretended not to. Those who suspected were tiptoeing through their days, hoping they were wrong. Some, the less noticing among humankind, those for whom sex had always been a sometime thing, thought they might be suffering from a touch of flu or a lack of sleep, a little indigestion, a fit of depression, each believing himself alone in that regard. Some, for whom sex had been a duty, felt relieved that the duty was no longer expected. One stand-up comic skated perilously close to mentioning it on nationwide TV, only to be shackled and led off by federal marshals, off camera.

The ignorance wasn't total. Certain groups seemed to know something! Bag ladies knew something! The armies of marching men knew something! What they knew and what they intended were obscure, however, and seemed to bear little relationship to day-to-day life. It was almost as though those two groups were moved by something outside the everyday world, by some alien or spiritual force that was playing checkers across the earth, immune to the malaise felt by the rest of mankind.

The rest of mankind, for whom the machinery of life ground on. Consumers went on consuming, though the pattern of their consumption was changing. Even without the depredations of the bag ladies, extreme fashions were not moving. Uncomfortable apparel or shoes were not selling. Auto showrooms suffered from a glut of expensive cars. More books were being read as many TV shows lost their audiences, particularly the trashy talk shows, the sexy soaps and sitcoms, and the late-night porns. The 900-number sex-talk lines were as dead as the spotted owl, the sea turtle, the elephant, the rhino, the gorilla . . .

Individual sports equipment was in big demand; team competitive sports were sagging. The baseball season was in full swing, but stadiums were uncrowded and TV coverage went largely unwatched. Advertising was in chaos. Barbie and G.I. Joe had suffered a fatal decline; teddy bears, building blocks, roller blades, and bicycles went on as ever.

Simon's boss, after a behind-closed-doors conference with Simon, sent him on an around-the-world jaunt to investigate how far the plague had spread: from where, starting when. Nothing could be printed yet, but much could be learned that would be printed later.

Simon's nose led him almost immediately to one symptom of change: the divorce rate had skyrocketed. Couples were splitting by the hundreds of thousands. They were dispassionately, casually, going their separate ways without rancor. Men who had beaten their wives regularly, constantly, who had threatened them with death if they tried to escape, now yawned as they watched them go. In India arranged marriages had simply ceased, as had the burning of brides. In the Sudan parents were not having their daughters' external genitalia cut off, as had been the tradition for centuries.

Among some religious groups all these changes, those that were known and those that were suspected, were cause for grave concern. For millennia religious power and prestige had been built on a foundation of sexual proscription. Now the sudden absence of sex came like the surgeon's knife, abbreviating both doctrine and doctrinaire. What were sin fighters to do without the favorite sin? Without traditional lusts, what good were traditional values? There were secret meetings, covert assemblies, men working deep into the night as they sought to confound whatever devil had been so presumptuous as to purify humanity without first asking permission from its moral advisers.

In India a Hindu prophet claimed that in the future all men would be reborn as something other than humans because men had been too destructive of other life and now must learn to respect other forms by living in other shapes. Since all humans were to be reincarnated in other forms, human babies were no longer needed. The Hindu prophet was assaulted by a Muslim prophet, who claimed that the Hindus had caused whatever was going on. The Muslim prophet was counterattacked by a Buddhist, and everyone retired bloody from the field of battle with injuries more symbolic than fatal. Accounts of this brouhaha were heavily censored before publication.

June moved toward its end. The Vatican, with much pious misdirection, canceled planned visits of His Holiness to various parts of the world and announced instead a conference of all bishops for early autumn, the first in many years. The cardinals, still conservative but now neuter to a man, were at a loss. Everywhere the Church was preoccupied, even in Louisiana, where the archbishop was too busy worrying about survival to think about the oyster farms. The question of support for the Church's secret project was not renewed.

The date for the trial of Lolly Ashaler was only days away. According to the quickie phone-in TV polls, long a staple of the twitchy titillations that had taken the place of the evening news, the vast majority of persons felt Lolly Ashaler should be found guilty and executed. Carolyn, hearing this nonsense, wondered whether people had been paid to call in anti-Lolly responses or whether the station had been paid to announce a totally false result. According to the media, feeling was running high against Lolly, but Carolyn hadn't noticed any such run of opinion. The rumored hostility and anger was only reported, not apparent.

One aspect of the coverage, however, Carolyn found deeply disturbing. According to some editorial pages and some talk shows, Lolly had killed not just a baby but "the future of mankind." The Santa Fe paper editorialized that "the current desperation of humanity" had been Lolly's fault, she had committed "the final sin," had added "the spiritual last straw" to the sin burden of mankind. While "the current desperation" was undefined, Sodom and Gomorrah were mentioned in passing, along with the Flood. Carolyn saw a coordinated effort in all this, no doubt on Jagger's behalf. Seemingly, even if the world died tomorrow, Jagger intended to stand with one foot atop the corpse declaring himself victorious.

"The world situation was the girl's fault?" asked Ophy when Carolyn called her—on the bedroom phone—to discuss testimony and strategy. "Where do they get that idea?"

"The morning paper printed it, but I imagine Jagger or one of his minions came up with the idea: Lolly has so offended God by killing her child that God is punishing the entire human race by withholding babies. This time it won't be by flood, or by fire. It'll just be extinction. Which, if you're an environmentalist, must seem like divine retribution. Maybe the Gaia hypothesis has some truth to it."

Carolyn rubbed at her forehead, staring at the papers on her desk, which would be exhibit something or other in the upcoming trial. She was so tired she couldn't think.

"I suppose the guilt can be wiped away by blood sacrifice," Ophy growled.

"That may be the reasoning behind Jagger's going for murder one with the possibility of the death penalty. He wants to prove she intended all along to kill the baby. She's to be the scapegoat: If we spill the blood of this bad, bad woman, God will relent."

"You sound weary, Carolyn."

"Lately I feel that I'm living in a badly written, badly directed foreign movie that's running on late-night TV in black-and-white with lots of static and inadequate subtitles. It's extremely difficult to follow, just like this trial."

"What is he pushing it for?"

"I don't know. Before this libido plague came up, I thought I knew what Jagger was up to: pure ambition. Now I can't figure the guy. If he knows what's going on—and even with the news blackout he *has* to know what's going on!—why does he want public office? I can't imagine any sane person wanting public office right now. Being in charge of anything would be hell."

Ophy laughed. "Didn't we read something in college about preferring to rule in hell rather than serve in heaven? And then, too, I keep thinking about

Sophy's story where Elder Sister was supposed to be weaving a new medicine bag. . . ."

Silence at the other end.

"Carolyn?"

"I'm here. If one weren't modern and scientific and skeptical, one could certainly believe somebody was fixing us."

The following morning Carolyn was finally overrun by the media. The TV stations couldn't get their trucks past the new electric gate, but they came trudging down the driveway, nonetheless, cameras and recorders at the ready. The assault turned into a rout when Hector, Fancy, and Fandango came boiling out of the house in full cry, to be joined by Leonegro. The resultant reportorial scatter bore some resemblance, Carolyn thought, to a flock of startled leghorn hens, taking off in all directions.

"Down at the road, they ask for somebody. What I say?" asked Carlos when he arrived for work.

Carolyn had spent several sleepless nights thinking her way through this question. "Say Ms. Crespin will send a statement to the gate in a few minutes."

"Ms. Crespin?"

"My lawyer name, Carlos. Here on the farm I'm Mrs. or Ms. Shepherd, but when I'm a lawyer, I'm Ms. Crespin."

"You don't have to say anything, you know," Hal commented.

"I know. But if I don't at least make a statement, I'll come across as hiding something. Better get it over with."

She went into the office and took a few moments to write out a statement: Lolly Ashaler felt she would be more comfortable with a female attorney; the American system presumes innocence until proof of guilt; Ms. Crespin presumed her client was, indeed, innocent. She ran a dozen copies of it and sent Carlos to distribute them to the newsmen.

The statement, reduced to a fifteen-second bite, was on the evening news, followed by an oleaginous Jagger, who said it was rumored that some feminist organization had hired Ms. Crespin to defend the baby killer. Everyone knew that's what feminists were interested in. Ms. Crespin, so he said, was from a big eastern liberal Catholic family, but it was rumored she'd repudiated the faith in which she'd been reared. She'd belonged to a reportedly subversive group, too, he'd been told. Of course, that's when she was younger, and it might not mean anything.

There was also an interview with Emmet Swinter, who said he knew for a fact that Ms. Crespin had been picketed by the Army of God for her unholy secular-humanist views. Which explained the reason for that.

"Wow," Stace commented when Carolyn phoned her. "Now you're a

backsliding Catholic, a feminist, a liberal, *and* a subversive who's been picketed by the righteous."

"It's no more than I expected," Carolyn replied dully. It was no more
than she'd expected, but it still hurt, in the way a sudden blow hurts, as much
from surprise as from trauma. "Actually, the tone is somewhat milder than I
feared. Someone must have told Jagger to tone it down. By the way, the office
phone is bugged, so when you need me, call me on the one in my bedroom."

"Bugged? When? Had you talked to Ophy and Jessamine before you
knew?"

"Yes."

"So now Jagger could know what you plan for the case!"

"I never discussed the case on the bugged phone."

"But if Jagger knows who's going to be testifying . . ."

"He'd know anyhow. Jagger is entitled to my list of witnesses just as I'm
entitled to his."

"This is a mess. I'm sorry I ever asked you."

"Actually, Stace, I'm not thrilled about it, either. Jagger scares the hell
out of me."

"Of course he scares you. He gets people killed!"

"Well, I'm not about to kill myself or let someone sneak in and do it to
me. I've even felt, during my more optimistic moments, that if we could have
been assigned to some other judge than Rombauer, we would have had a
chance of winning the case."

"But not with him."

"No. Not very likely. We can appeal, however, and that's what I'm
counting on."

She hung up the bedroom phone, then went purposefully into Hal's
study, where she made herself comfortable before making a prearranged call
to Ophy on the bugged phone. They chatted briefly and inconsequentially
about the upcoming meeting.

When this had gone on long enough, Carolyn took a deep breath, enun-
ciated very clearly, and said, "I'm fairly sure Lolly's mother was an alcoholic
even when she was carrying Lolly."

"You're thinking of fetal alcohol syndrome," said Ophy, also speaking
very clearly.

"It's a possibility."

"Oh, it's a very good possibility. FAS victims are very much like Lolly.
One of the characteristics of the disease is that victims are unable to see the
consequences of their actions. They don't reason from cause to effect."

"Is that scientifically established?"

"Very much so. The disease has been known for about fifteen years. It's not dissimilar to fetal crack addiction. Certain centers in the brain are destroyed."

"But if she'd had some other environment—"

"It wouldn't have mattered. FAS victims raised in fine, supportive environments do very little better than others. They simply don't understand cause and effect."

"Hell, Ophy, rats understand cause and effect!"

"Rats have to, in order to survive. What I'm saying is, FAS victims don't, and they can't survive unless someone takes care of them. They don't know if they go out without clothing, they'll freeze. They don't know if they don't eat, they'll die. They don't understand that if they set fire to the house, they can burn up. They can be trained to do some things, just as you'd train a dog—or a rat—to do them, but they are not human persons. Not by our definition, Carolyn."

"Well, you don't convict nonhumans of murder."

"Not since the Middle Ages," said Ophy. "I think it's an excellent defense."

Carolyn thanked her and hung up, then sat smiling grimly at the bugged phone. There, Jagger. Chew on that.

Jake Jagger had a late, quiet meeting with Martin, his chief snoop, driver, pilot, and occasional assassin. Jagger's office windows looked down on a street almost bare of traffic, a few late diners strolling back to their hotels past closed shops.

"I need to ask," the snoop said a little stiffly. "You not satisfied with the way I been doin' the work?"

Jake's head came up. "Why would you ask that?"

"There was this kid arrested out there. I already had the bug on her phone line. I told you—"

"I did not send anyone," Jake snarled. "If someone else went out there, they did it on their own."

"Well, I'm just saying I don't need backup. I tell you I did something, I did it." The snoop simmered briefly, then referred to his notes. "The bug I put outside on the phone line's working okay. This doctor from New York told this scientist from Utah that there's some kind of a beedolus something. The woman in Utah called your subject and told her about it."

Jagger shook his head impatiently. "Never mind that, Martin. Skip across everything that doesn't pertain to the trial. I need only trial information right now."

Martin shifted to the next page. "She, the lawyer, she's going to say the girl is crazy."

"Insane?" asked Jake Jagger.

"She's got some kind of alcohol something. Her ma was a drunk. Here, I'll play the section."

He did so, and Jagger smiled his thin, predatory smile. "Fetal alcohol syndrome. Fortunately, I've had the girl's mother drying out down in Albuquerque, just in case we need her. Another few days, she'll say whatever we need her to say. What else will the doctor testify to?"

"That's about all for her, but this other dame, the one from Utah, she's a what they call it, geneticist. She's on the witness list, but the lawyer hasn't talked to her yet. When she does, we'll find out what she's planning on."

Jagger nodded slowly. "Well, stay on it. Let me know the minute they talk. We need to find out where she's coming from."

The snoop shuffled his tapes together and whacked them into an even stack.

"Two things I need you to do," said Jagger. "Since these witnesses are coming to the Crespin woman's house, the phone bug you put in won't pick up their conversations. See if you can bug the house itself, the places they'll be talking, at least."

"It'll mean drugging that damn dog! Damn near took my butt off when I went to get that paper! Easier to shoot him."

"If you shoot him, she'll know you've been there."

The man of all work sighed. "I ordered some special gimmicks that'll do the job, and they're coming in FedEx on Friday. Friday night the women'll all be talking up a storm with each other, probably stay up late, be really sleepy. Everybody'll be asleep, except the dog. I'll tranquilize the dog and get the bugs in then. Kitchen, dining room, living room, I guess. That's where they'll mostly hang out."

"I thought they had the place wired since you were there."

Martin sniggered. "I know the system. It's not much. I've got through tighter ones than that."

Jagger nodded slowly, thinking. "You know, Martin, if anyone was responsible for that kid going out there, it was probably Swinter. He's getting to be an embarrassment, doing stupid things like that. I think Mr. Swinter should have some kind of accident that would stop his doing such things."

The snoop raised his eyebrows, just enough to indicate he'd heard Jagger speak. That was enough. Jagger handed him a thick stack of bills and then walked beside him as he went into the outer office and from there into the hallway that led to the street, making sure he left the building. He did not want Martin running into Keepe, who was due to arrive shortly.

When he did so, Jagger offered his hand and a drink.

Keepe ignored the hand but accepted a light Scotch.

"I didn't think I'd be seeing you again so soon," said Jagger.

"You left a message about that matter Mr. Webster is interested in. He feels it's extremely important."

The words carried an implicit threat. What Jagger knew had better be urgent. Jagger, annoyed at Keepe's tone, rose from his desk and walked to the open window, breathing deeply. "I spoke with some militia people in Utah and Montana. They're convinced somebody has been testing some kind of nerve gas on them."

Keepe narrowed his eyes. "Nerve gas? Why did they call you?"

Jake turned angrily. "For crisake, Keepe! You told me to ask around, remember? I remembered there had been some nerve-gas episodes in that area way back, after World War Two. Army testing that got out of hand or something, so I asked them if there's any current trouble."

Keepe ruminated on this, his eyes watchful. "Who did you talk with? The United Aryans? Howard's American Patriots bunch in Montana? Or that militia of Mason's? What you call it?"

"Vigilance Force. I spoke with Ralph Howard, but he says he's talking for Mason and for Rilliet, too."

"Rilliet?"

"He's prime elder of the Reinstituted Congregation of the Saints. When I started with the Alliance, they were on my contact list, kind of an offshoot bunch. He's got most of those polygamists hiding out back in the mountains allied with him. Idaho, Montana, Utah, that bunch. The United Aryans are talking about a coup, and they've got the Saints interested, and Mason's militia's providing the armament."

Keepe spoke through his teeth. "The Alliance needs many things, Jagger, but at this moment we don't need oddball little armed cults with delusions of grandeur attempting highly unrealistic local coups. Even though the NRA is one of our best supporters, armed conflict just now is not needed. The Alliance takeover is already planned and moving. All the Aryans and polygamists and militiamen need to do is be patient. Once we're in power, they can lynch all the blacks and rape all the lesbians and kill all the government men they like."

For a moment Jagger was silent, startled by Keepe's words. Such acts were implicit in what the movement stood for, but they were usually referred to as "cleansings," or "purifications." It wasn't Alliance policy to be as specific as Keepe had just been.

Jake cleared his throat. "He was talking about threats to his manhood, which could mean anything."

"I suggest you calm him down."

Jake forgot his own rule and pushed. "You think something did get loose? Maybe something from the Gulf War?"

"We don't *know*, Jake. Obviously, if we *knew*, we wouldn't need all this chitchat!"

Again that strangeness of tone. That remote . . . displeasure.

Jake pressed again. "Is there something else, Keepe? Something wrong?"

The other man was coldly angry. "Don't be an idiot, Jake. Of course something's wrong. When Mr. Webster is annoyed, so are the people who work for him, and Mr. Webster is extremely annoyed at all this. The Alliance has agents planted in most Washington bureaus, including the Centers for Disease Control, but our people can't get a handle on this! It's said to be some kind of suicide epidemic, but in times of stress people often commit suicide—it's nothing new. Suicide cults at the turn of a millennium or century aren't new, either. Why should the CDC be involved? Why should the Alliance suddenly be full of people blaming each other? Iran thinks Iraq did it. Did what? we ask. Put something in their water, they say. What is the something? What does it do? They don't say. Libya thinks the Israelis did it. Did what? Polluted their soil, maybe. The Orthodox think the Reform Jews did it. The Reformed think the Orthodox did it. The Mormons! You've only talked to the offshoot groups, you should hear the elders on the subject!"

"What's going on?"

"I think it almost has to be a purposeful campaign of misinformation, designed to disrupt the Alliance. Rumormongering. Webster agrees. He says his opponents would like nothing better than to throw the Alliance off course by manufacturing some crisis. . . ."

"Opponents? I wasn't aware we had any organized resistance. You can't mean those old ladies. . . ."

Keepe gnawed at his lip, nibbling. "Mr. Webster said his opponents. He didn't specify who the opponents are, and whatever Mr. Webster sees fit to keep to himself, I do not intrude upon. I merely stand ready to change ground as needed. Flexibility, that's the key. At present we'll continue as planned."

"We're going on with the case? With the trial?"

"As of today, as of this hour, we are proceeding with the trial. The media people are in our pocket. The talk shows are full of us; the editorials have been written, many of them have already been printed. The TV movie has already been produced except for the sequences dealing with the trial itself. *The Sin of Gomorrah* will appear on two consecutive nights on NBC the week the trial ends. The minute the trial opens, we'll move into the national debate. Law versus lawlessness. Morality versus immorality. Womenfolk being properly protected at home by armed male family members, versus letting them out onto the streets to be victimized, turned into prostitutes and baby killers . . ." His voice faded, and he frowned.

"You sound doubtful," said Jake, surprised. The man actually sounded unsure of himself.

Keepe said fretfully, "It's the campaign we planned, and there's nothing wrong with it."

Jake glared at him. "Then what? What the hell's going on?"

Keepe glared back. "It's a perfectly sound campaign but it's not working. People aren't responding to it. I've got a boiler shop working full-time calling in to the talk shows, but there hasn't been but a handful of genuine calls. I've got a mailing house generating letters to the editor, but nothing's coming from the public! We've announced the results of polls that should have people screaming for blood, but nobody out there seems to give a damn!"

Jake bit down angry words. "Is my campaign in jeopardy?"

Keepe teetered on his toes, up down, up down. "Not necessarily. I haven't gotten where I am by hanging on to a losing strategy just because it's worked before. At any point we can switch to a nonspecific campaign that stays well away from any controversy at all. If we have to, we'll base your campaign on name recognition alone, on your smiling face, and on feel-good commercials."

"You mean throw the trial away?"

"It's too early to decide."

It was Jagger's turn to frown. "Either way, you don't want me to talk about the end of the world? I thought that's why we were getting into office, because of what's coming."

Keepe straightened his papers, frowning. "What's coming is reality. Politics has nothing to do with reality!"

"And ten years from now?"

Keepe grimaced. "Ten years from now the world will be dying. All the little signs that people have been arguing about for decades will suddenly become huge and unmistakable. Remember the Japanese nerve-gas bunch that went belly up a few years back? We have a hundred other groups like that. At a signal from Webster they'll all put their plans into motion. They don't expect to survive, but they do expect to rule in the next life, so they come in handy as suicide assassins. We figure on a billion deaths from them alone."

"But *we* will survive! Keepe and Jagger, you and me, we will!"

"Thee and me and a million or so others on the A list, and we'll stay on the A list just so long as we do what's required and *avoid all disturbances*! Webster told you that. Don't do anything except what we tell you. Leave it to us!"

He stood and buttoned his rumpled suit coat, all the time making little jaw motions, chewing the cud of their conversation. "I'll tell Webster about the people you've talked to."

Jagger rose. "I'll do what I can to calm them down."

When the outer door closed behind Keepe, Jagger stood thoughtfully for a long time, thinking about "disturbances." The situation with the Aryans wasn't the only one that might turn into a disturbance. Besides that and Swinter, there was at least one other item of unfinished business.

He locked his office behind him, went down to the mail room, and borrowed a couple rolls of strapping tape. Then he got into his car and drove to the market, getting there just before closing. He bought a few staples, taking them off the shelves almost at random, plus several boxes of garbage sacks. When he got home, he opened the door into his game room, turned on the lights, went in briefly, then came out and left the door wide open. She was in the kitchen, fixing supper.

"There are groceries in the car," he told her. "See that they're put away. I want the plastic sacks and the tape in my trophy room, for packing meat." He did not see her look of astonishment as he went down the hall toward his own room.

She was completely baffled. Jake had never let her go into his trophy room. Never, in all the years they'd lived there. And why stuff for packing meat now? It wasn't hunting season. She didn't ask; she merely obeyed. At the car she sorted out the boxes of garbage bags and the tape. The garage door stood ajar, light pouring out, and with sudden clarity she saw it as a hinged jaw waiting to swallow her.

The curtain at the window twitched. He was watching her. Her mouth was suddenly dry with an absolute certainty of danger. She took the other groceries and carried them into the house, setting them on the kitchen counter.

"I'll put the other things away in a moment," she said, turning from him and going down the hall toward her bedroom, her bathroom. Her bathroom was the one place he would not follow her. The one taboo place, to him. She shut the door firmly behind her, locked it, opened the bathroom window, and went through it onto the low junipers planted below. They cushioned any sound she might have made.

She couldn't go across the driveway. He would look there. She couldn't go down the hill toward populated areas. He would look there, too. Purposefully, quickly, without taking time for thought, she darted down the driveway to the road, up the road for a hundred yards or so, and then away from it onto the slope of the hill among the low junipers and crouching piñons. She began to climb upward, toward the mountains.

Jake waited in the hallway. He opened the front door and peered out to be sure the steel trophy-room door stood wide open, light pouring out. He had put a card on the bulletin board, her name in red, in letters large enough to see from the door. He counted on it drawing her into the room if she should hesitate for any reason. He stepped outside and looked at her bathroom window, curtained, lighted.

He could wait. He was patient. He went back into the house and sat in the living room with a book, alert to her return down the hall. It was almost half an hour before he began to suspect she might be gone.

Helen managed to get over a mile into the hills before stepping on a stone that twisted beneath her foot, throwing her to the ground. It was full dark, with a crescent moon hanging low in the west, giving just enough light to make out the blackness of junipers and piñons, not enough to show the footing.

She looked back the way she had come, seeing the lights of houses here and there, thinking of Jake's helicopter, which she had never seen but had always visualized as a vehicle in Jake's image, with eyes that could see through walls and weapons that could kill. He would come soon. He would follow her. He would chase her into the hills and kill her there. Someone would find her bones, in a year or ten or a hundred. Well, let them. She had done what Carolyn had asked. That much, at least, she had been capable of.

She went on climbing, limping, pain in her ankle jabbing at her relentlessly. Higher on these slopes, the piñon forest gave way to ponderosa pines, and under the shelter of those trees, one could hide like a little animal, crouched against some trunk, invisible from the air.

She heard a sound and ignored it. It was far away; it was meaningless. Still, it was persistent, like the buzz of an insect trapped behind glass. Unfamiliar. Strange.

She stopped, stood up tall, looked around herself. It was still there, a kind of humming. She got onto her hands and knees and crawled to the nearest juniper, squirming in beneath it to crouch there, her head on her raised knees, making herself a stone, a blot, a shadowed nothing. The humming went on and on, seeming to grow no nearer, and after a time she looked up, puzzled. It wasn't the thwack, thwack, thwack of a helicopter. It was a different sound altogether.

She peered out at the night, up the hill, down the hill, across the valley. There was a light across the valley, and it was moving. Helicopters, at least the ones she had seen on TV, had glaring lights, like searchlights. This was an amber glow, a bubble of firelight on the hills, low, next to the ground, where no bubble of light should be.

The amber bubble moved slowly, making no threat. Up a hill and down again, disappearing into the valley. Appearing again at the crest and dipping once more, finally achieving the slope on which she sat huddled beneath the tree.

Whatever it was, it hummed its way purposefully toward her, gradually becoming visible. A school bus. An old, beat-up yellow school bus, rumbling along as though it were on a road. Which it wasn't!

The bus came up the long slope toward her, swerving around chamiza and piñons, passing her to swing around in a gentle arc and pull up beside the juniper where she hid. The door opened. An old voice, quite kindly, said, "You need a ride, lady?"

She was having a dream. Either that, or she'd lost her mind. In either case it was silly to hide. He obviously knew where she was. She crawled from beneath the tree, rose to her feet, flinching as weight came on the twisted ankle.

"Here," he said. "I help you." He came down the step, a very old man, wrinkled and brown, wearing a soft shirt and baggy trousers and boots that were worn into shapelessness.

She felt herself slipping into hysteria. "Who?" she giggled. "Who are you? Why are you here?"

"My name is Padre Josephus," he said, patting her shoulder, taking her arm. "I hear from a friend of yours maybe you need some help."

At the prison, in the visiting room, Lolly began the visit by shouting at Carolyn. "She knock me down, an' I get all cut up."

"She who?" asked Carolyn, completely lost.

"That woman in the kitchen. I ask her does she wan' me to do, you know, an' it's like she goes nuts an' breaks this whole tray full of bottles, an' she knock me down, an' I get all cut up on the glass."

"I'm sorry. Is it healing?"

The girl extended her bandaged hand. "Yeah. They put in four stitches, though. She went nuts. She says somebody stole her nature from her. Some *bruja*. Some witch. Was it some witch stole it?"

"I don't believe so, Lolly. It's just something that's happening." Something that was happening so universally that the secrecy about it was ripping at the seams. "Don't worry about it right now. The trial's next week. This weekend I'll be bringing two women to see you. One of them's a doctor. She'll want to talk to you, examine you. I've arranged for her to use the infirmary here. They're going to be witnesses for you."

"Is my mama gone be a witness?"

"Why do you ask?" Carolyn said softly, stopping herself from casting a surreptitious look at the light fixture above her. She was ninety percent sure there was a microphone there. Maybe even a camera.

"My aunty came. Mama tell my aunty, she gone be a witness. They put her in the hospital, so she can't get drunk before then."

Bingo, thought Carolyn. They'd picked up on the fetal alcohol defense. Good. "Well, if she wants to be a witness, we'll certainly use her, Lolly. It's good that she's drying out. Maybe she can quit drinking. Wouldn't that be nice?"

Wouldn't that be nice! She sounded like a kindergarten teacher. She sounded like an idiot. Well, the more idiotic, the better. She left Lolly, patting her on the shoulder.

From the hallway she spotted Josh through the window in the vault-room door. He was showing something off to a visitor. Carolyn waited until he was alone, then slipped in through the double doors. "Josh, I need a favor."

"Anything I can do."

"This girl I'm defending. It's important I get her looking halfway decent for the trial. I don't want her to look like a hooker, and something hookerish is what she's going to want to wear."

"They don't never learn, do they?"

"No, they don't. If I bring some clothes, can you be sure they're the ones she has on for the trial?"

"I can try. Couple of those women guards back there, I'd say they're bein' paid off."

"If it takes money, I'll pay."

"That legal?"

"It's not suborning a witness, Josh. Greasing the skids a little, maybe."

"Won't promise, Ms. Crespin, but I'll see what I can do. Hey, didja hear what happened at the courthouse?"

"What's that, Josh?"

"Lately, the whole calendar's been messed up, people droppin' cases, cancelin' appearances, cases bein' settled out of court, whatever. Anyhow, Judge Loretta Frieze, she's the chief judge, she's been reschedulin' stuff, movin' it up, reassignin' the cases. So she had this big fight with Rombauer."

"You're kidding!"

"Judge Frieze told him he better watch it because he's gettin' too many cases reversed on appeal."

"You're kidding," said Carolyn again, slack-jawed.

"He said he'd be more careful. The way my friend tells it, he looked like he'd been kicked by a horse when he left there."

Carolyn went outside, trying to figure out how she felt about all this.

She'd been depending on Judge Rombauer being just what Rombauer always was. If he actually tried to appear impartial, she might have a hard time on appeal. Damn. Double damn. Another of life's little uncertainties working itself out.

On the other hand, if Rombauer started being careful, she might have a chance of winning the case on her own, first time around.

It should have been a comforting thought, but it wasn't.

15

ON FRIDAY MORNING THE WAITING room outside Judge Rombauer's courtroom was overfull of people, fifty of them at least, the panel from which the jury would be chosen in the case of the people of the State of New Mexico versus one murdering fiend or one helpless rape victim, depending upon whose side one was on. To hear the media tell it, the world was on Jagger's side.

United against the world, the DFC had agreed to support Lolly's defense. Ophy and Jessamine were to be expert witnesses; Faye had been chief preparer of exhibits; Bettiann had supplied funds; and Agnes had been asked to serve as chief liaison with heaven, praying for a miracle.

"If you think you've got any credit up there, Aggie," Carolyn had said. "I don't think I do."

Aggie had swallowed the retort that came to mind and accepted the role. She'd seen children like Lolly in the parish. Though she didn't generally sympathize with the type, she agreed with Carolyn that they were incapable of "deciding" to do anything.

Josh had kept his word about the clothing. Lolly was neatly dressed in jeans and a loose shirt. Carolyn made a mental note to send Josh a gift of some kind. He was a true friend.

The clerk, referring to his notification list, began calling names at nine in the morning. The first twenty people rose and shambled into the courtroom, their manner so uniformly decorous and blank-faced that they might have been cloned, none of them showing the slightest expression of interest: men, women, black, brown, and pale, including one turbaned Sikh, associated with the Sikh community in neighboring Rio Arriba County.

Carolyn spoke to the panel about scientific evidence. Could they weigh scientific evidence if it was clearly explained? One man, a scientist who had worked for years at Los Alamos, said yes—somewhat forcefully. Others believed they could also, if it was clearly explained. One man said he could understand it perfectly well, but a lot of science was just wrong, like evolution, for example.

Ordinarily, Jagger would have gathered that particular juror to his heart, but if fetal alcohol syndrome was to be offered as a defense, he wanted people on the jury who would understand the scientific evidence he intended to bring to the contrary. He marked down to be excused, therefore, not only the creationist, but also a woman who saw no reason to understand science because she believed people just made it up. "Like pi," she babbled. "They say it's three point one four, when anyone can see it would be so much easier if it was just three."

Carolyn, pretending not to notice Jagger's uncharacteristic queries, laid down a false trail by asking about drugs. Did the jurors believe drugs could make people do strange things? Most of them believed so. One gentleman believed it was purely a matter of character. No one, he said, could make him do anything he didn't want to. Carolyn marked him down to be excused. She asked about birth control and abortion: Did anyone have strong feelings about these issues? Each panel member denied having feelings, one man and one woman with such vehemence that Carolyn put question marks by their names.

No one expected that the jury would be selected in one day. Both sides anticipated finishing the selection on Monday and beginning the trial on Tuesday, the twenty-seventh. They were not in a hurry.

Some of Bettiann's support was being used to pay an investigator who would be available until the trial was over. This past week he'd been looking into the lives and histories of members of the jury panel, and Carolyn, glancing down the list he had prepared, found a number of items she considered helpful. By four in the afternoon, to everyone's surprise, there were fourteen jurors, evenly split as to sex. Jagger had excused the unscientific, of whom there were several, and the Sikh. Jake knew nothing about Sikhs but distrusted them on principle.

Carolyn, turning from her notes, intercepted a glance between the two jurors who had been so definite about contraception. It was a very self-satisfied, self-important little look, like one canary-fed cat to another. Seeing Carolyn's glance, both of them put on poker faces, which raised the hair on the nape of her neck. She had a couple of peremptories left, and her mouth opened to use them, only to close it again. If they had lied, if she could prove they had lied, there might be grounds for a mistrial, if she needed grounds. If she needed a mistrial. She looked down at her notebook, where her fingers were busy underlining the two names. Hitchens. Bonney.

The judge was waiting. "Ms. Crespin?"

"I am satisfied with the jurors," she said. Aside from that glance she'd intercepted, she was fairly well satisfied.

"I am satisfied," said Jagger with a straight face. He was extremely satisfied. With this jury and Rombauer, he couldn't go wrong. Rombauer was always good for some fine oratory, and he could weave a set of instructions that hog-tied a jury to only one possible verdict. Nonetheless, Jake preferred that the trial look good. The people on this jury were capable of weighing facts, and Jagger had lots of facts to give them. If that didn't do it, he had Gloria Hitchens and Alf Bonney on the jury, two of Harmston's prolife warriors who would accept no excuse for baby murder and would hold out for conviction until January if necessary. He wouldn't need to sweat it. Gloria and Alf would take anything he gave them and make a noose out of it. So to speak.

The fourteen were impaneled and sworn, twelve jurors and two alternates, though the members wouldn't know which were which until the testimony was in. By ten after four on Friday afternoon, the task was finished, far earlier than any of them had expected. But, then, Carolyn mused, who would have expected a district attorney to have listened to opposing counsel's phone calls? Or a defense attorney who knew damned well she'd been bugged and had misdirected the prosecution.

"We had planned jury selection to continue on Monday," the judge intoned, tapping his folded glasses against his long, pale hand. Rombauer was a gray man with turtle eyes, bony though not thin, an ominous presence inside his dark robes, like a hangman doubling in justice, cunning old Fury himself. His voice was insinuating and sometimes querulous, as when he said: "The prosecution was expected to begin on Tuesday. Will there be any difficulty in moving it up to Monday, Mr. Jagger?"

"I shouldn't think so, Your Honor."

"Very well. We will begin hearing this case on Monday morning, nine A.M." He warned the selected jurors somewhat severely not to discuss the trial, then let them go.

Almost a year since Lolly was raped, thought Carolyn, keeping her face carefully blank as she tried to ignore the TV camera aimed at her. Jagger started to leave, then stopped to speak to an unkempt little man who turned his head and glanced at Carolyn, his face both arrogant and avid, one that slid across her flesh like an edge of paper, razor thin, making her touch her cheek, feeling for blood, as though he had thrown a knife rather than a look. Outside in the corridor the investigator was waiting for her. She drew him into a corner and gave him the two names she had underlined.

"I don't know what it is with these two. Just the way they looked at each other. It's probably too late, but I think there's something there I ought to know about."

He promised to get on it right away, though he probably wouldn't have anything until the first of the week.

Behind her in the courtroom, Jagger and Keepe continued their conversation.

"I don't know what you mean," said Jagger, aggrieved.

"Mr. Webster sent me particularly to remind you," said the other with stony insistence. "He told me to catch you this afternoon and remind you, you're not to fix anything this time. Nobody is supposed to die or get injured, nobody is supposed to suddenly refuse to testify, nothing is to happen that is in any way . . . notable."

Jagger snarled. "Damn it, if it's worth playing, it's worth winning."

Keepe lowered his brows, almost scowled. "Jake, you're not getting it. You're not listening. Winning may not be the most important thing this time. At the moment we're planning for you to win, but you shouldn't have any plans at all except to do what we want you to do."

He turned on his heel and left, not looking back, thereby missing the expression on Jagger's face. Helen would have been able to interpret that expression. If Webster had been there, face-to-face, telling Jake what to do, Jake would have done it without question, but Jake's sense of his own relationship to Webster effectively prevented his obeying messengers and flunkies. Keepe, so Jake told himself, was a flunky, and his use of the word "we" was an insult to Mr. Webster.

Besides, Jake was already committed. He'd already given Martin his instructions. The Crespin woman's house would be bugged tonight. Swinter had probably already been disposed of. It was even possible that Helen had been found and eliminated. Damn her! He could have sworn she was too well trained to bolt like that, and he knew she was too stupid to get away with it! How had she escaped? Somebody had to have helped her! If Martin hadn't found her yet, she might be trying to reach the children. Well, let her try. She'd never find the Alliance Redoubt in a million years. Jake himself knew only that it was somewhere up near the Canadian border.

From the nearby parking garage Carolyn maneuvered her way to the street. Ophy had arrived that morning, Faye was driving down from Denver, Jessamine from Salt Lake, and the others would be flying into Santa Fe during the afternoon. Stace had been invited to dinner, and she'd volunteered to come out early and help the cleaning woman get the rooms ready. Aggie, Faye, and Bettiann would get the single bedrooms; Ophy and Jessamine would share the big room that Hal had been using; and Hal would move into the little room with Carolyn, bad leg or no bad leg.

Carolyn stopped at the take-out place she used now and then, whenever the weight of a day made cookery seem impossible. Hal had offered to fix their supper, but being on his feet for very long was still painful for him. Besides, she'd ordered stuff that would keep and could be rewarmed if anyone arrived late.

She spread the provisions across the backseat and got behind the wheel once more. Though she'd resolved not to think about the case, it kept at her, nagging at her. Perhaps it was the fact that Aggie and Bettiann would arrive today. Of all the DFC they were the ones who would be least convinced of Lolly's innocence, the ones most likely to approve the blind action of the law. Not justice. No one expected justice anymore. What was justice for a Lolly? What did one do to her? And why? Why punish an abysmally ignorant walking womb who could do nothing but get pregnant? Not read with understanding, not write intelligibly, not do a job well enough to be paid for it. Not sew, not cook, not clean a house, not plant a garden. Not do any practical thing, but only screw or be screwed, as event or lust dictated, and then bear when nature demanded. Would punishment change her? What did one do with a girl who had nothing to give a child because she'd been given nothing as a child, a victim herself, a wasted life, pitiable and sorrowful, but without a single redeeming trait? She was like a mangy cur, mangled in traffic, lying there suffering, guilty of being only what it was, but with a salvation too problematical and too damned expensive for even a passing Samaritan to contemplate. The merciful thing was to pick the pathetic thing up, take it to the vet, and ask him to put it down. Except one couldn't do that with people.

Aggie would say, of course, that there was no such thing as a wasted life, that every life had meaning. So try to put that idea into motion. Try to do for her! Suppose someone adopted Lolly now and gave her fifteen years of the most tender and exquisite care, would that undo the damage done in the first fifteen years? Would that give her life meaning? If it did, where was the treasury that would furnish the people and resources to make recompense for every other wasted life? It reminded her of one of Hal's favorite lectures:

"There are no demonstration projects, love. Any do-gooder can save one life or a dozen by spending x dollars, but that doesn't demonstrate anything unless you've got x dollars multiplied by the total number of lives that need saving. Stopping poverty one victim at a time is like mowing a lawn one blade at a time. The problem grows faster than the cure can be applied, and the only people who profit are the agencies who claim to be cutting grass while they're actually applying fertilizer."

If Carolyn managed to keep Lolly out of the tanks, was Lolly any better off? Was it more ethical to keep her out or put her in? She pounded on the wheel with both hands. This was exactly the kind of endless rumination she used to go through before she retired, worrying away the miles between office and home because she'd known the day had been spent turning over the caseload, like compost, while it went on rotting. She drew in a shuddering breath, turned on the car radio, and concentrated on her driving. Ready or not, there were people depending on her.

She stopped at the mailbox to pick up the mail, leaving the gates open for the expected guests. She was just opening the door when a dusty car nosed its way through the gate and came trundling down the drive—Jessamine, at the end of a day-long trip from Salt Lake. Ophy erupted from the kitchen door to welcome them both. There were hugs all round. Exclamations. How nice the farm looks. Here we are. Same as always. They carried the suitcases and the take-out supper inside, setting things anywhere while Carolyn made a quick clink of ice in glasses, gin and tonic, fresh limes. Stace emerged from the back of the house to be introduced. Hal stuck his head into the kitchen to be hugged; then he shooed them out onto the patio while he tinkered with the food she'd brought home.

"You look good!" said Jessamine. "Oh, you both look good!"

"We look like us," said Ophy, waving her glasses, grinning from ear to ear. "Can't do much about that."

"So what's happening?" cried Jessamine. "When does Aggie get here?"

"Everyone gets here tonight," said Carolyn. "Aggie's been fetched from New Orleans in William's private plane, and she and Bettiann are landing in Santa Fe. They've got a rental car. They're bringing oysters."

"Lovely to be so rich!" said Ophy, buttering a tortilla chip with guacamole. "Nice for Aggie, too. I told Carolyn I think Aggie's leaving us. This'll probably be the last time we see her."

"I've been thinking that for a while," said Jessamine. "She's been a good scout, hasn't she? She's tried with us heathen. She's getting older now, she needs her certainties."

"She's no older than the rest of us," said Carolyn firmly, almost angrily. "We'd all like some certainties."

"The rest of us had other things to hang on to," Jessamine admonished. "You and I had family, Carolyn. All three of us had careers. Faye had her talent. Bettiann had her family, and her foundation. Aggie only had her religion."

"It's all she wanted," said Jessamine.

"I'm not so sure about that," mused Carolyn. "Her religion has provided every bit as much a career as any of us have had, and I've always thought Aggie settled for renunciation as a definite second choice."

"The first one being?" asked Ophy.

"Oh, well, it wouldn't be fair to speculate." Though Carolyn did and had, for some time. Aggie was or had been in love with Sophy. From a distance, of course. From a vast, uncrossable distance. As they all were.

"So!" Ophy drained the last bit, crunched ice, got up to get herself a refill. "What's the agenda?"

Carolyn made wet circles with her glass. "We've got two days, just for us. The trial doesn't start until Monday. I'm hoping we can get through it in two days, let it go to the jury maybe Tuesday afternoon, or at the latest Wednesday morning, so you guys don't get held up here forever."

"Are we the only two you're using?" Ophy asked.

"As expert witnesses, yes, but everyone's involved. Faye made some exhibits for me. Bettiann paid for the investigator."

"And Aggie?"

"Chief cheerleader and implorer of divine help. She has let me know that she doesn't approve of Lolly one bit. Neither she nor Bettiann think what Lolly did is at all excusable, but they don't think locking her up is going to help matters any. Or, needless to say, executing her."

Ophy frowned. "Bettiann and Aggie have always opted for tradition, as I recall. We haven't changed much, have we, Carolyn? You and Faye were always the radicals. Jess and I were the polite ones, middle-of-the-roaders. We're all pretty much where we were when we started out, but no matter where we're coming from, we're still all working together."

"I wasn't always radical," Carolyn objected.

"And I wasn't always polite," said Jessamine.

"That's not the way I remember it," Ophy insisted. "Whenever I think about us, I see Carolyn or Faye throwing down the gauntlet, Aggie and Bettiann being offended, and me and you, Jess, trying to make peace. Well, let this time be no exception. At least we'll end up in a cooperative blaze of glory."

"A blaze of glory, or an utter decline and fall," said Carolyn, the words slipping out unintended.

The other two fell silent for a moment, considering failure.

"We'll have tried," said Jessamine in a firm voice.

"We will." Carolyn reached out to hug them both.

"I'll need to see your client," said Ophy. "Examine her."

Carolyn nodded. "I set that up for Sunday morning. Did Simon get the films together for us?"

"They're gorgeous," murmured Ophy. "He got old news tapes from Boston, when they were integrating the schools—wonderful stuff that was simply swimming in matching faces, just what you ordered. A friend of Simon's is a top-flight computer graphicist, and he did the comparison overlays."

"Looks like we're set," said Carolyn. "Remember the phones in Hal's study and here in the kitchen are bugged. I've unplugged the extensions in the bedrooms. If it's just business or travel arrangements, go ahead and use the ones in the study or kitchen, but if you want to make a private call, use the phone in my room. . . ."

"What's that all about, Carolyn?" Ophy begged. "Why you?"

"I don't know, Ophy. I think Jagger just has to win, regardless. Don't let me forget to tell the others when they get here. There's a car coming. Must be Faye!"

Faye arrived. Bettiann and Aggie arrived, along with the icy keg of oysters. Faye and Jessamine carried in the maquette from Faye's van and put it on the end of the dining-room table where they could walk around it and admire it from all sides. The back of the fountain was a roughly curved stretch of rugged rock—shoreline rock on the right, mountain rock on the left, where animals laired or prowled, most of them extinct in the wild: bear and boar and deer and wolf, rabbit and owl. The male figure standing before them was long-bearded, patriarchal, a fox in the curve of his arm, an eagle on his shoulder.

"He looks like Hal," cried Carolyn, hugging the real Hal.

"I had a picture of the two of you," said Faye gently. "One we took the last time we were here. Of course, in the picture your hair and beard were shorter, Hal. I lengthened both. I didn't think you'd mind my using you."

"I rather like the Noah role," Hal rumbled. "Quite a monument. How big is this thing going to be?"

"The figures are to be monumental, one and a quarter life-size, and there'll be a surrounding shallow pool. The whole thing will stand in a semicircular recess at the edge of the plaza, and the water will actually spill out of the pool at the back, into a water stair that leads down to a smaller plaza on another street below. From below you'll see just the rugged back side surmounted by the soaring figure of Fecundity. In this maquette I've shaped the big wave out of clay, but in the fountain itself there'll be a curved, wave-shaped surface of thick, watery glass, with pumps forcing water up along it to make the wave shape. . . ."

"That sounds very complicated," said Hal in an interested tone.

"I have a hydraulics firm helping me. They did a mock-up with real pumps to get the right shape—it's really quite realistic. When the water's moving, you won't see the support inside the wave at all. The figures will actually seem to be supported by the water. The pools below will be real water, of course, with real fish swimming in them and the children partly submerged, as they're shown here."

The three female figures were as yet only rough shapes, indications of what was intended: a crouching shepherdess with sheep, a kneeling dryad, a gardener holding a sheaf of grain. Faye wanted to use Carolyn for the shepherdess, Ophy for the nymph, and, to Aggie's surprise, Aggie as the gardener. Faye had brought costumes to dress them up in during the meeting so she could take photographs and make sketches.

"What goes there in the middle, in front?" Bettiann wondered, pointing at the vacant promontory.

"The center figure in Botticelli's painting is Venus Genetrix," Faye answered. "Venus in her role as fertility deity."

"You'll be using something else?"

"Definitely something else, though as yet I'm not sure what."

Hal was invited to join them for supper, which they dawdled over. "Tell me about the case," Aggie demanded over coffee, determined not to think about this being the last time.

Carolyn wrinkled her forehead. "Do we want to talk about the case tonight?"

"Sure," said Jessamine. "We're going to be talking about it sooner or later."

"Okay," Carolyn said resignedly. "This is how we think it will go. Jagger has Lolly's mother on the witness list and also one of her grade-school teachers—"

Ophy interrupted. "Dr. George Fulling is on the prosecution witness list also. He's an expert on developmental anomalies."

"Right," said Carolyn. "The prosecution will use Fulling to refute Lolly's having fetal alcohol syndrome. Ophy and I laid a red herring over our bugged phone."

"Why did you do that?" Aggie asked, puzzled.

Carolyn said, "Because we wanted people on the jury who could weigh scientific evidence, and normally Jagger would get rid of anyone with good sense. He likes them credulous, the dumber the better.

"So he's put this doctor and Lolly's mother and one of her grade-school teachers on his witness list to refute our claim that Lolly is a fetal alcohol child (which claim, need I say, we are not going to make), and we can use these same people to establish the abuse Lolly suffered at home. We've also got records of hospital admissions starting when Lolly was about nine, which show bruises and spinal fractures, plus one episode of sexually transmitted disease when she was ten. We want to give the jury the picture: why she dropped out of school, why she is the way she is. . . ."

Jessamine nodded. "All the prosecution cares about is showing that Lolly isn't retarded. If she's not retarded, then she's supposed to be totally responsible for whatever happens to her."

Carolyn said, "We're going to counter this by attacking the Hail Mary Assumption."

"You're what?" asked Aggie, dangerously quiet.

Jessamine and Ophy had been waiting for this. They shifted uncomfortably.

Carolyn said, "Just listen, Aggie:

"Media coverage of this case has used a lot of phrases like 'Corrupted motherhood,' and 'Breakdown of civilization.' Jagger's case must begin with the assumption that all women are equipped with a strong, overriding maternal instinct; that all babies arouse this maternal instinct; and that any woman who does not respond maternally is a rotten person who must be guilty as sin; what Sophy called the Hail Mary Assumption."

Aggie shook her head slowly, saying, "I think you'll find that most members of the jury are likely to make that same assumption. And while I won't say 'Guilty as sin,' I still don't think of her as an innocent."

Carolyn took a deep breath. "Well, Aggie, we all know that. But if any of the jurors have open minds, we've got a lot of material which should at least throw that assumption into question."

Hal smiled rather grimly, leaned back, put his fingers together. "You're not going to call it the Hail Mary Assumption in court, presumably."

"Of course not," Carolyn agreed.

They fell silent, several of them covertly examining Aggie's face, which was very white and withdrawn.

"Time for dessert?" asked Stace when the resultant pause had stretched too long into silence.

Hal struggled out of his deep chair. "While you ladies have your dessert, it's time for us outsiders to do the dishes." He and Stace went off down the hall, leaving the six of them to relax over more coffee, brandy, and a sinful chocolate torte that Faye had brought with her. They spent an hour or two trading stories of the "what I've been doing" variety, including Aggie's story of the archbishop, and all of them tried to stay away from anything controversial.

"I hope we didn't upset you with the Hail Mary bit," Carolyn said later when she encountered Aggie in the hall. "I know how you feel about these things, party line and all that."

"It's a . . . bad time for me just now," Aggie murmured. "Please don't be angry with me, Carolyn. The archbishop's request has made me question things I've taken for granted for years. In a way, I can see your side of this. I see similar things in the parish all the time, men ignoring the children they father, and the Church taking very little account of it. Let some single father leave his kids with sitters all day because he has to work, or even with a mistress or second wife who doesn't give a hoot for the kids, that's okay, but let a single mother hire a nanny so she can work to support them, that isn't okay, she's unfit, and they take the kids away.

"I see the fundamental unfairness of that. The sexism of it. I've always seen the sexism of it, just as you do. You solved the problem by giving up your religion. I will not give up my religion, so I may simply have to accept sexism. We sisters have done it for hundreds of years. Perhaps they have been more welcome in heaven than the feminists today. God moves, as we have always been taught, in mysterious ways."

She went down the hall with a still and shuttered face, leaving Carolyn to stare after her, positive that Aggie was indeed going to leave them. Well, if it had been their last time, it had been a well-shared time. Carolyn comforted herself with that thought as she crawled into bed beside Hal, being careful not to wake him.

"Nice girls," murmured Hal, too drowsy to be PC.

"Wonderful friends," she corrected. "It was good to be with them. We had a good time."

It was the last good time for a long time.

The news broke Saturday. Despite Carolyn's best efforts at occupying the smaller half of the bed, Hal had not slept well, and when Carolyn got up, he announced his intention of staying right where he was for an hour or so. Carolyn patted him on the shoulder, pulled the light covers up around him, and left him there while she started the coffee and walked out to the road to get the paper. She was accompanied by a strangely lethargic Leonegro, who ambled beside her with his head down, as though he'd lost something along the way. She unfolded the paper as she strolled back, only to be stopped short by the size of the headline that took up half the front page.

Her first thought was how sensible it had been to let the news out on a weekend. People would have a day or so to get used to the idea before the workaday world started over again on Monday. Her second thought was that one or two days wouldn't be anywhere near enough for anyone to get used to the idea.

When she got back to the house, Aggie was waiting outside, her white-bordered short veil whipping in a light breeze.

"I turned on the TV in the kitchen," she said. "Carolyn, they're saying—"

Carolyn handed her the morning paper. "I know."

The others were assembled, gathered around the little TV Carolyn kept in the kitchen, Bettiann full of exclamations and horrors, the rest of them suspiciously unresponsive.

"You knew!" challenged Aggie, catching a conspiratorial glance between Ophy and Jessamine. "Ophy, you knew!"

"Ophy merely thought something of the kind might be happening," Carolyn soothed diplomatically. "You know, in his work Simon picks up rumors from all over the world."

"But you didn't say anything to me." Aggie was angry, her skin ashen. "Why didn't you tell me? You should have told me."

"It was only a rumor," said Ophy firmly.

"But what is it? What's happening?"

"No one knows," said Jessamine, looking up from the paper, one obviously hastily composed in the middle of the night, banner headlines and all. "It says right here, Aggie. No one knows. Some indication of a genetic change, that's all. Happening to everyone at once could mean it's a virus. . . ."

"A disease!" Aggie cried.

"Well, many viruses cause disease, yes, but they don't have to. Some viruses change the organism. This may be one that makes some kind of hormonal change. That'd be my guess."

"That thing you told us about a few years ago, Jessamine," Aggie demanded. "You talked about a universal carrier. . . ."

Jessamine frowned. "The viral carrier?"

"Didn't you tell me you're not allowed to use it anymore?"

"There are several viral carriers, and we can't use the primate carrier anymore. Not since ninety-seven."

"Because it was dangerous! What if somebody did use it! Maybe someone—"

Jessamine shook her, though gently. "Aggie. It's possible. But unlikely. Besides, the virus by itself is harmless. What we used it for was to carry pieces of genetic information into living cells, to change the cells by changing the genetic code inside them. There are still some permitted usages, like using it to cure genetic diseases like cystic fibrosis."

"You brought something to show-and-tell, in San Francisco in ninety-seven. What was that?"

"I brought a vial containing a solution of viral carrier in which I'd incorporated a stretch of genetic information. It was a siamang-wolf match. I thought it had to do with detection of pheromones, with the sense of smell. . . ."

"You said it had something to do with reproductive behavior."

"I said I *thought* it might, yes. Because both siamangs and wolves are monogamous. But when I tried it on the bonobos, it had no effect, Aggie."

"You tried to . . . infect the chimpanzees with it, right?"

"I don't like the word 'infect.' We tried it on the nasal mucosa of a couple of chimps to see if their smell acuity or reproductive behavior would change. It didn't."

Aggie was silent, still very pale. "Oh, God," she whispered. "Oh, God."

Carolyn poured a cup of coffee and held it to Aggie's lips. "Hey, Aggie. Come on."

"This is why," said Bettiann in a dull voice, looking up from the paper. "It's why William's been like that. It's why Charley tried to kill himself."

"Who?" asked Ophy, suddenly alert. "Who?"

Bettiann babbled. Agnes stared into the coffee cup as though mesmerized, mumbling something about the Vatican must have known, that's why they'd called the conference.

The phone rang: Stace.

The phone rang again: Simon calling Ophy from Paris.

And yet again: Patrick calling Jessamine from Nuevo Los Angeles.

"No, Patrick," she said. "I didn't know. . . . No, I didn't want to get pregnant because I didn't want to carry some other woman's child just to massage your ego. It had nothing to do with this. . . . Patrick, why are you yelling at me! I didn't do it."

"Yes, you did," said Aggie.

Jessamine turned on her angrily. "Aggie. For God's sake!"

Aggie's face was gray and hard as stone. "Not for God's sake. No. You did it, Jessamine. Out of pride. Out of hubris! Thinking you know more than God. . . ."

"Patrick, give me your number. I'll call you back, maybe tonight." She turned back from the phone. "Aggie, what's with you?"

"I've been trying to tell you, you did it. In 1997. You brought it to show-and-tell. It was a little vial with a black seal at the top. I can see it, see you holding it. I can still hear your voice. Genetic material, you said. Viral carrier, you said. . . ."

"And I told you, it wasn't what I thought it was—"

"It *was* what you thought it was when you brought it. But when you left the meeting, it was water."

"What are you . . . !"

"Sophy took it."

Sudden silence.

Aggie sobbed dryly. "I saw her. Everyone was getting coffee. She took it from the table where you'd set it. She emptied it into a little bottle. She filled the vial from the water pitcher. She put the top back on. She looked up and saw me watching. She smiled at me and put her finger to her lips. . . ."

"Aggie! And you didn't tell me," Jessamine cried.

"I *couldn't* tell you! She was so bright, with this light around her. I saw . . . like, wings, scales, strangeness! I got dizzy; I thought there was something awesome there; I could see the gleam of eyes, something like . . . rainbows. She was shining. And when it was over, I thought, oh, I'd been hysterical and it was only some kind of joke. Or she knew something we didn't and she was protecting us from ourselves, protecting you from yourself, Jessamine. . . ."

"And now you think she . . . she what? Used it to infect humans? What humans? Us? You think she infected us with the stuff?"

"There was a literacy conference in Rio the fall of ninety-seven," said Aggie. "I attended it. Last year Faye was all over Europe and around the Mediterranean, researching her commission. Two years ago you and Hal went to Hawaii, Carolyn, to visit your boys. Bettiann, you and William took a Pacific cruise in January of ninety-eight, didn't you?"

"Australia," said Bettiann. "And New Zealand."

"I went to China," said Ophy. "A medical meeting. And you went somewhere, Jess."

"India," said Jessamine. "A human genome conference. My boss was supposed to go, but his wife was ill. . . ."

"Maybe it wouldn't have mattered," murmured Agnes. "Maybe by then your boss carried it, too. Maybe it spread by itself."

"You're saying Sophy infected—"

"You don't like the word 'infected,' " Agnes interjected in a shrill, unnatural voice.

"You think Sophy put the stuff in our coffee?" Jessamine cried.

Bettiann screeched something; everyone began babbling.

Carolyn yelled at the top of her voice, "All of you, shut up. Hush. Now, sit down here, quietly. All of you. Aggie, tell us calmly, precisely, quietly!"

Aggie rubbed her eyes with the heels of her hands. "In 1997. We met in San Francisco, at Jessamine's house. For show-and-tell we all had one thing or another. I remember *all* of it, I've *thought* about it over and over. God, I haven't been able to think about anything else! Jessamine, you brought this vial of stuff from your laboratory. You talked about pheromones, about maybe having found the genetic basis for monogamy, and Faye laughed and said not for her, thanks, and somebody made a joke. I remember it all. Every word!

"We left our show-and-tell things on the table when we went into the kitchen for coffee, all but Sophy. She never drank coffee. I came back to the living room first, and she had the vial in her hand—she was emptying it into a little bottle, like a pill bottle. Then she picked up the pitcher on the table and poured water into the vial, and put her hand over the top of it—I thought putting the top back on—and then she set the vial back where it had been. There was this confusion around her, light, aureoles, feathers, sparkling, I said her name, Sophy, and she looked up smiling and put her finger on her lips. . . ." Aggie showed them, putting her own finger upright against her lips, the universal sign of silence.

"What did you think she was doing?" Carolyn challenged.

"At the time? I thought . . . there was something awesome there, with her. Something . . . not human. At the time I thought maybe something angelic. Or I told myself that. Father Girard thinks it could have been something diabolical. Later I told myself she was . . . telling Jessamine . . . not to interfere with nature. Later I convinced myself she'd been making . . . a gesture. An . . . admonition. Later I thought . . . she felt it would be better if such things weren't done, and she was telling Jessamine so."

"And you more or less agreed with that?"

Aggie wept. "The whole thing was so strange! The feeling of it, the light. There was something else in the room, something besides Sophy. And she wanted me not to say anything. So I couldn't tell you, and if I did, you'd think I was crazy. I didn't even confess it then, for fear Father Girard would think I was crazy. And if I wasn't crazy, then that meant Sophy was . . . was possessed? Or something. And then later I told myself yes, if Sophy was telling us not to interfere, I did more or less agree. You know my feelings about those things. I've always felt we trifle too much with things we should let alone! And then later, after Sophy was lost, gone, the only reason I could think of for her to kill herself was if . . . if she had been possessed by something evil and done something with that stuff, or maybe even if she'd thought it was harmless, then found out it hadn't been harmless at all. . . . Maybe she had done something . . . something she couldn't live with. But by then it was too late."

Jessamine cried, "So you believe that when I took the vial back to the lab, all it had in it was water?"

Aggie cried, "I thought you'd notice the seal was broken. I knew it was sealed, and I thought you'd notice, or that Sophy would tell you, or . . . or something."

"God," whispered Ophy, awed. "Lord. Jessamine . . ."

Jessamine shouted, "Damn it, the vial *was* still sealed when I got it back to the lab." She frowned angrily. "Ophy, honest to God, it was still sealed." It had been! She remembered slitting the seal with a knife.

Carolyn sat stone-faced while they murmured around her. Mysteries. Why? How? The how was a tiny mystery compared to the other. So the vial had been sealed. Either Sophy had pretended to do something with the contents, leaving the vial sealed, or she'd actually done something with the contents, somehow resealing the vial. Or she'd palmed the vial and substituted a like one. "What did you use to seal it with, Jessamine?"

"It's a common material," breathed Jessamine. "A liquid polymer. You dip stuff into it, and it dries into a hard plastic coating. We use it in the lab to make seals airtight, to cover metal parts, to make them nonreactive. It's used in workshops, labs, factories. Even hobby shops. You can buy it lots of places."

Carolyn asked, "When there was no effect, didn't you test the contents of the vial? To see if it was still . . . what you thought it was?"

"I would have, yes. Of course. But before I had a chance, Patrick and I went on vacation, and while we were gone, the Big One came and the labs were destroyed. All my records. All . . . everything. Not the animals, they were at the breeding farm, but everything else, gone. . . ."

"Why?" demanded Ophy. "Damn it, why!"

"Why what?" asked Faye. "You mean, why did Sophy do it? She did it to be like Elder Sister. To make us peaceable." And she broke into raucous laughter. "Oh, boy, will we be peaceable."

"Hush," said Carolyn, steel in her voice. "All of you."

Silence gathered.

"I'd like to suggest that we all be very, very careful. It's important that we don't talk about this, that we make no allegations to anyone about anything, that we offer no opinions on this matter."

Silence.

Then Faye: "You're speaking as a lawyer."

"I'm speaking as a lawyer. You may think you know something Aggie, but you could be wrong. Saying what you think you know, however, could get Jessamine sued. Or hurt. Or even killed."

Aggie cried, "But we have a duty. . . ."

Carolyn shook her by the shoulder. "Aggie, I'm thinking of you, too. You're in as much danger as Jessamine is—you, your church, the abbey. If Jessamine is in any way culpable—and we're not at all certain she is—so are you. Some people would say *you* had a duty to stop Sophy. Or to tell Jessamine what you'd seen, right then, at the time. But at this late date blabbing out our uncertainties to all and sundry is not a duty, it's simply foolhardy. Particularly inasmuch as we're not sure *anything* happened."

Ophy whispered, "But she's right. We do have a duty—"

"Oh, yes," Carolyn agreed with a firm nod. "We have a moral duty to find out what happened. A moral duty and a human responsibility to find out what actually happened."

"How can we find out?" cried Agnes. "Sophy's dead!"

Faye turned a searching gaze on Carolyn, and she upon Ophy. Jessamine gathered Bettiann with her eyes, then all of them turned their eyes on Aggie in a combined stare that had almost the force of hands laid upon her.

She shifted nervously under the stares. "What?"

"We don't think she's dead," said Faye. "We don't think she's dead at all."

And then silence again, a silence that gathered depth from their having said it, together, five of them; a silence that throbbed and hummed like a seashell held to the ear, the shush of the great sea within every self.

Aggie whispered, "What do you mean?"

Faye said, "We mean we see her, Aggie. Or hear her. Or feel her around. We mean she pervades our space. Or inhabits our beings. Or something."

"The nun," said Aggie, hushed. "I keep seeing this young nun. She's beautiful. She's like Sophy. The blessed dead don't come haunting. And that means Father Girard was right. She was a . . . a something evil. A devil. Devils can be lovely, you know. Tempting. . . ."

"I don't believe that!" Jessamine said. "I do not believe Sophy was capable of evil. I do believe you've seen her, Aggie, because the rest of us have experienced similar things. You see a young nun. Ophy talks to someone over her shoulder. Carolyn gets visited by dead sheep. Faye has a statue that dresses itself up. Bettiann writes things she doesn't know she's writing, verses, things that sound like Sophy. One of my research animals acts as though she's, ah . . . possessed. So when you come right down to it, we don't think Sophy's dead. Or if she's dead, we don't think she's gone. But I will not accept that she's evil!"

"Then what is she? Where is she?" Aggie stood up and looked around herself, almost hysterically. "Here?"

"Shush," said Carolyn. "Aggie, don't have a hissy. Whatever it is, it's benign."

"Benign! You say that as though you knew! You don't know! You could look Satan in the face and call him benign, Carolyn Crespin! If she's done this—"

"If she's done this, she's done it for a reason. If she's still here, she's here for a reason. For God's sake, Aggie! You *knew* Sophy. How could you even consider that she would do something wicked? Would she ever have hurt anyone? Did she ever hurt anyone? Sit. Calm down."

They sat. Except for Aggie, they calmed, though the room seemed to reverberate with tension like the last echo of an enormous gong, a wavering pressure, a pounding of the pulse in the ears. Aggie felt herself withdrawing from them, utterly convinced now that Sophy, their friend Sophy, had not merely been a stranger, but had also been alien. Inimical. And the DFC had helped her do whatever it was she had done.

"What're we going to do?" Bettiann asked, almost a whine.

"Find her," said Carolyn. "We're going to have to find her. Or at least find who she was."

"Ghostbuster," giggled Bettiann. "Not exactly a big ambition of mine." Tears spilled down her cheeks. "This is all . . . crazy."

"Admittedly," Carolyn agreed. "Nonetheless."

Faye demanded, "How? How do we do it?"

Carolyn spoke slowly, thinking it out as she went:

"We start by remembering everything we can that she ever said about her people, places she'd been, things she'd done. We find some of those women she lived with in Vermont, and we ask them if she ever said anything about her people. The last few years, ninety-five, ninety-six, she told us she'd traveled around a lot. . . ."

"A funny thing," laughed Jessamine, almost hysterically. "Patrick said there was a dragon in her room."

"A what?"

"He admitted he was drunk. That time in ninety-seven, when he made the move on all of you . . . all but you, Aggie. He said he didn't get very far with Sophy because when he went to her room, the shower was on and there was a dragon in her room."

Aggie felt her mouth twisting. "I'm not surprised. Not now."

Silence. Faye laughed jeeringly. "A few weeks ago, I saw her vanish. I was leaving the studio, and I turned and spoke to her, only I thought it was her statue. And she turned her head and looked at me; then she vanished, like smoke. And there was this sound, like something far away, opening or closing."

"What are you saying?" demanded Carolyn. "That she's not . . . not human? That she's what? Supernatural? Or are you with Aggie? You think she was satanic?"

"She was Native American," said Ophy angrily. "She was. I knew her. As for Patrick, he was drunk. Faye, you were hallucinating, and, Aggie, you're playing sour grapes! I can buy a presence, some sort of subconscious evocation—I've felt that myself—but I don't buy physical manifestations and I don't buy evil. Let's be logical about this. The university had to have some kind of address or location for her when she applied there. Some record of her scholarship."

"Tracing someone's background can take time," Bettiann said. "It can take ages."

"It can't take ages, and we'll all have to take the time," Carolyn remarked. "All of us. Now. We've got today and tomorrow. . . ."

"Jessy and I have to see your client tomorrow," said Ophy.

"Right. Well, some of us have two days." Carolyn heaved a deep breath. "Starting with the university is a good idea. Unfortunately, it's a weekend."

"I'm an honored alum," breathed Bettiann. "I can get access. And you don't need me Monday."

"Why, Bettiann!" Faye grinned wolfishly. "An honored alum?"

"The Carpenter Foundation endowed a big scholarship fund." She flushed. "I can get to the president, I know him. He'll have somebody open up for us."

"We should start now." Aggie pushed her veil over her shoulders, straightened her cuffs, and stared wildly at nothing. "We can't wait. If the rest of you are busy, I'll get started now."

Faye was standing just behind Aggie, pouring coffee, and she nodded significantly to Carolyn over Aggie's shoulder, saying, "I'll go with you, Aggie. Carolyn doesn't need me."

"The three of us," said Bettiann very calmly, reaching forward to clasp Aggie's hand. "We'll take care of it."

"Sophy must have given them a home address," Faye remarked. "She had to have gone to high school somewhere. Then, when we've done what we can at the university, we'll see if we can find any of the women who lived with Sophy."

Bettiann rose. "Aggie and I came in William's plane. It's still at the Santa Fe airport. William didn't need it for anything, so it's just sitting there. I know where the pilot's staying." She got up and went to find an unbugged phone.

Aggie rose, not quite steadily, murmured something about wanting to be alone for a few moments, and went down the hall, toward the room she'd been using.

Faye, looking after her, shook her head slowly. "Can you believe this? That Aggie didn't tell us!"

Carolyn said, "Something's been bothering her. We all knew that."

"But why would Sophy—"

"None of us ever knew why Sophy would do anything," cried Jessamine. "When we were with her, we thought we did. But we never really knew. We never even knew who she was."

"She said she had an enemy," Carolyn mused. "Long ago she told me that. One of the reasons she didn't tell us who she was, where she was from— she had an enemy. I didn't think she meant it literally, not at the time, but it may have been literally true. There are cultures in which families have blood feuds that go on for generations."

Faye rubbed her forehead. "She told me once there was something important she had to do with her life."

Ophy laughed without humor. "Was this it?"

"This what?" Carolyn demanded. "Aggie may completely have misinterpreted what she saw, or she may indeed have been hallucinating. We don't know that Sophy did anything."

"Even if she did take the DNA stuff, she could have put it in an incinerator," offered Jessamine. "Besides, to make a real change, the stuff would be used on embryos, not fully developed organisms."

Carolyn held out her hands, patting the air, calming them. "There's no point in arguing with ourselves. Any way we turn, we're too short on facts to argue anything. We think Sophy may be . . . present. But we're not sure. We think she may have done something, but we're not sure. We—or at least Aggie—is afraid she may have been diabolical. We need to know the truth about any or all of these things, and honest to God, dear ones, we should be very wary of hypothesizing beyond what we do know."

She turned to Faye, saying seriously, "Keep an eye on them. Keep them from falling apart, Faye."

"That's why I'm going, girlfriends. You try to keep Aggie here, she'll go all to little bitty pieces like a windshield when you hit it with a baseball bat. You notice she didn't take off the habit this time? Always before she'd take off the habit, borrow some clothes, and dress like us, at least when we were alone. Not this time. She's on the edge right now. Been that way, probably, ever since San Francisco."

"There's that. But, also, warn Bettiann not to blurt anything out the way she does sometimes." Carolyn sighed. She felt the walls closing in. Maybe the judge would get sick and the trial could be postponed. Maybe there'd be worse riots, a general insurrection! Maybe they'd declare martial law, and everything would just stop for a while!

"Just get it done, Carolyn," said Faye, watching her keenly. "Don't sweat it. Don't get into a state. You've got the trial all planned, it'll only be a few days, we can handle this. Just focus on what you've got to do and get it done."

"Yeah," said Carolyn with a shudder. "You're right. I shouldn't be vacillating like this. It's all planned, and it isn't a complicated case. It shouldn't take more than two or three days, even if Jagger does . . . something rotten. Call me on the other number, every night. Remember not to use this phone."

"I'll take care of it."

After they were gone, while Jessamine and Ophy were back in the big bedroom planning their testimony, Carolyn and Hal wordlessly straightened up the kitchen, coming upon the pile of mail Carolyn had brought in last night and not even looked at.

"What's this?" asked Hal. "Brown envelope. No return."

"No idea," she said. "Open it."

He fetched a knife and slit the tape-sealed envelope, spilling the contents onto the table. "My God. It's Rombauer. Sans robes, need I mention."

She looked, then looked away disgustedly. "Helen sent this," she said. "Helen found where Jagger kept the pictures."

"Who are the kids?"

Carolyn knew the faces. "They're in the tanks, Hal. At the jail. I saw them there. I thought at the time, they're such children! And Josh said they didn't belong there. Cisneros. Diego. Ravenna. Wrongly accused and wrongly sentenced, according to Josh."

"Rombauer sentenced them?"

"Wouldn't you? Kids that are SLEPT can't testify against you. I wonder how many kids he's buggered and then put to sleep over the last few years! What do I do with these?"

He nodded once or twice to himself, figuring it out. "Leave them with me, Carolyn. Decrepit though I am, I may still be able to get something moving."

Early Saturday afternoon Jagger's home phone rang: Martin, the snoop, in a state of high excitement. "You gotta hear these tapes, Mr. Jagger. You gotta hear them right now."

Jagger had slept late and prepared himself a large, lazy breakfast with fruit and sausage and fresh farm eggs. He had eaten it in lordly solitude, enjoying the silence, wishing he had achieved it years earlier, teased only slightly by an itchy concern over Helen's whereabouts. He had not seen the paper or heard the news, and it took Martin some little time to explain to him what had happened.

"Get over here," said Jagger. He went to the television and spent the intervening time switching from channel to channel.

"What kind of epidemic did they say?" Jagger demanded again when Martin arrived.

"A beedolus epidemic."

"What the hell?"

Martin quickly assembled his materials. "Here's the morning paper; I figured you might not have it. I'll play the first tape for you." The snoop fiddled with his player, making squawking noises. Then Jessamine's voice came into the room.

"*Have you heard about the epidemic?*"

"*What epidemic, Jess?*"

"*The libido-loss epidemic. There is one. Ophy says so.*"

"*So that's what's going on. I've been hearing things. . . .*"

"*Do you suppose some biological-warfare experiment got loose or something?*"

"*God knows! Why haven't we heard about it?*"

The snoop pushed a button and the voices stopped.

"Ophy is the one from New York?" asked Jagger.

"Yeah. The doctor."

"What does she mean, biological-warfare experiment?"

The snoop shrugged. "Some people are saying the Iranians, or the Libyans. Blowin' up the World Trade Center and those women's colleges back east, they didn't get the Muslim terrorists much respect, so they're doing this instead. This beedolus epidemic."

"Libido loss, Martin. It means sexuality."

"A sex epidemic? Like AIDS?"

Jagger was coldly angry, mostly at himself. "When was this taped?"

Martin referred to his list. The first tape had been days ago, it turned out.

Jagger snarled, "Why am I just now hearing about this?"

Martin was aggrieved. "I started to last time, but you told me you only wanted stuff about the trial."

Jagger fumed. "What else do you have?"

"I got the bugs in late last night, and here's the first stuff from this morning." Martin played it, then again, then certain parts of it several times more, Jessamine asking who could have started this, Aggie's voice saying, "You did," Carolyn's voice cautioning silence.

"It's important, right?" Martin asked.

"I'd say so, yes," Jagger muttered, concentrating on the words coming from the speaker, mouthing them, memorizing them.

"What do you want me to do?"

"I don't know, Martin. I'm going to have to think about it." Jake opened his mouth to ask about another matter, then bit his tongue. Better he not know about Swinter. Or about Helen.

Martin, dismissed, went back to his spinning recorders. Jagger hadn't even asked about the disposals, and that was funny. Jagger usually wanted to know. Maybe it was better he hadn't asked, since Martin had had no luck finding Jagger's wife. She'd disappeared, as if she'd dropped off the earth, and that was crazy. Where could she go? She didn't have any money. She didn't have any friends. Church, was what Jake thought. She'd gone to some church for sanctuary and was hiding out so nobody could find her. Martin had had a guy do that in Mexico once. So he'd bombed the church, and that took care of that.

Even if he couldn't find the woman, somebody was bound to find Swinter. Maybe today, maybe next week. The longer the better, was Martin's view.

Jagger, left alone in his aerie, thought first of calling Webster or Keepe, then thought again. The women were talking about the epidemic, the thing that had Webster off balance! One woman was accusing the others of actually having done this. Was that true? Did it matter if it was true or not? If he told

Webster, he'd have to tell Webster how he knew. And Webster had said don't fix anything. He mused over this, growing increasingly uncomfortable as he did so, almost as though someone were watching him. If he drew Webster's attention to this matter, the matter of the bugging would have to come up. On the other hand, if he didn't tell Webster about it, Webster might find out. In which case . . .

He spent half an hour considering the matter before he decided he had to pass on the news and picked up the phone. He had spoken to the Utah bunch and the militia, so he could call Keepe with that information, mentioning casually what had been overhead at the Crespin house. And if Keepe made any kind of fuss, he'd deny that bugging someone's house was equivalent to fixing something.

Keepe, somewhat to his relief, was not available through the Alliance number, which was the only one Jagger had. Away for the long weekend, said a minion.

Jagger left a message, then went out to get the papers, including the New York papers, putting the bug on Carolyn's house temporarily out of his mind. He had for so long controlled his own destiny that he did not for a moment consider that some other person might have also planted listening devices. It did not cross his mind that he himself might have been overheard.

16

When Aggie, Faye, and Bettiann arrived at their alma mater late Saturday afternoon, there seemed to be no one around. The university still sprawled its mellow brick across green acres under mossy oaks and maples a century older than the structures they sheltered, but humans were few and scattered.

"He said he'd have someone meet us at the admin office," said Bettiann.

The old administration building was locked. The student center was open but empty, except for a few people in the kitchens.

"Didn't I hear about a new admin building?" Aggie remarked.

"Of course," Bettiann snarled to herself. "Of course there is. Over where Harridan Hall was."

"I wish you wouldn't call it that," said Bettiann. "The poor woman's name was Lou Anna Harrigan."

"Everybody called it that then," said Faye without apology. "It probably went unisex; they mostly did."

Outside the new administration building, a car was parked. As they approached, an angular woman with an air of brisk efficiency got out of the driver's seat and came toward them.

"Mrs. Carpenter?"

Bettiann stepped forward. "Yes. I'm Bettiann Carpenter, from the Carpenter Foundation. I spoke to Fred Willard."

The woman glanced at her watch, lips compressed. "I'm Rose Jensen, the office manager. I've got the keys right here. Come on in."

Bettiann introduced Faye and Aggie as they trudged up the stairs. The heavy door was unlocked to let them through, then locked again behind them. Bettiann was saying they had just flown in her husband's private plane; she'd been thinking for years about making a gift to memorialize her old friend; her husband often said, invest in education, that's where our future lies.

By the time they reached the offices, Ms. Jensen had warmed up considerably. "You really want to talk to the people in the development office when you decide on the terms of your gift," she said, "but I can access the alum files to find the information about your friend. . . ."

They went through a large outer office into a smaller one, and through it into one smaller yet. "This is a separate system, not connected to anything else, so it's not vulnerable to hackers who want to make their records look better than they were. All the alum files are in this computer," she said over her shoulder. "At least almost all. We're back to 1892, thus far, and I told the dean just the other day we'll be back to the founding fathers by the end of the year."

"Eighteen fifty-two?" cried Bettiann. "Well, congratulations."

"It was really fifty-three before they took any students," Ms. Jensen said. "Now. What was your friend's name?"

"It's an odd name. Sovawanea aTesuawane." Bettiann spelled it. "She was in the class of sixty-three, as we all were. We called her Sophy."

Screens lighted, scurrying lights made beeping noises. The class of sixty-three appeared in alphabetical order. The cursor hunted up Sovawanea aTesuawane and went digging for another file, while Bettiann babbled indefatigably on:

"When Sophy died, we all thought of a memorial, of course, but we were too upset, too bereaved to think straight. We decided to wait until we could consider it calmly. Well, we've just held a meeting, and we've decided to see if we can't set up a scholarship fund for girls from her community—"

"But we couldn't remember exactly where she was from," said Faye, getting into the act.

"We seem to be having somewhat the same difficulty," said Ms. Jensen in a tone of annoyance. "We've added some new software to this system, but only Friday I was *assured* they had the bugs out of these files. Look at that! Unknown. Not found. Silly. It says right there she was a recipient of a Susan R. Lagrange scholarship. She didn't get that sitting in the middle of a mud flat. They must have had an address for her."

More tapping, digging, glancing at watch and muttering. Aggie rubbed her fingers under the tight white band that bound her forehead. Normally the band shaped the wimple, served as the anchor for the short veil, and was otherwise ignored. All the way out on the flight, however, she had felt as if it were squeezing her brain, tighter than it should be. Ever since Sunday morning the habit had felt unfamiliar to her, though she'd worn it now for over twenty years, and before this one, another one that was even heavier.

"Do you miss the old habits?" asked the woman at the keyboard with a sideways glance. "Two of my aunts are nuns, and they say they miss the old long habits with the big wimples. So beautiful they used to look back in the fifties and sixties. Like angels."

"I do miss the longer skirts sometimes," said Aggie. "There was a certain gravity to all that weight of fabric. A kind of gracefulness." A kind of peacefulness, too. A sense of stability. Like an anchor.

"I always thought so, too." She cast a quick smile in Aggie's direction, then said, "Ah. There it was all the time. Sovawanea aTesuawane. Piedras Lagartonas, New Mexico. Only it says care of someone, someone, here it is. Chendi Qowat. Postmaster. Isn't that an odd name? It must be Indian."

Bettiann was already writing it down. "Do you have any other information on her at all? If she received a scholarship, surely . . ."

"Well, her transcript is here, of course. Language major, wasn't she? Gracious! French, Spanish, special studies in Asian and African languages . . . a very good student, too. The scholarship information wouldn't be here. All that would be over at the Lagrange Foundation office: her application for a scholarship, and supporting letters from her teachers or community people. Since she's deceased, I'm sure there'll be no problem getting access to it. They're very sensible people over there, not long on formality. Though you won't be able to see them until Monday, of course. Everyone will have gone home by now." She glanced at her watch again. "As must I! We have a family date for a birthday party!"

They were out, going back down the long hall, Ms. Jensen saying good night to the janitor, good night to the security guard at the door, good night to them. "Sister, Ms. Carpenter, ma'am, so nice to have met you."

And gone, with a little kindly wave, trip-trip down the sidewalk, off to feed the family, the dog, the cat, off for the birthday party. Past her trotting figure the sun sank onto the treetops, barring the campus with long shadows.

"I know some people with the Lagrange Foundation," said Bettiann. "I've attended workshops with some of the trustees. The founder inherited a lot of money. She decided to use it to educate minority students, ghetto kids, recent immigrants, that kind of thing."

"What will they have in the way of documents?" Agnes sounded exhausted. Her eyelids were swollen, as though she'd been weeping.

"Just what she said. There'll be a letter of application. No doubt some supporting letters from people who knew her. If the foundation kept them, which they may not have done. It was a long time ago."

"Monday," said Faye. "That's a pain, when we don't even know if they've kept the information."

Bettiann said, "No, that's what I was saying. I know the president of the Lagrange board of trustees. His name is Matt Rushton. I'll call him now."

"An imposition," murmured Aggie.

"Of course it is, Ag. But it's important. You know how important." She laughed, a breathless little sound, both deprecatory and amused. "Money has its privileges, Aggie. Faye has her talent, you have your faith, what've I got? Might as well use it, whatever."

By the time they met in the hotel dining room for supper, Bettiann had already made her call.

"They've kept everything," she said. "Unfortunately, the stuff before the midseventies isn't computerized. It's in document boxes in the basement, and if we want it before next week, we'll have to find it ourselves, because there's no one working this week at all. One of the young women who works there will come down in about an hour and let us in."

"Good work," said Faye with a sidelong glance at Aggie.

Aggie seemed not to have heard. Aggie seemed lost in some private vision.

"What is it, Aggie?" Faye whispered.

"Lost," said Aggie. "And mistaken. All those years."

Faye reacted to closed and dusty spaces—attics, basements, storerooms—as some people reacted to graveyards—with a superstitious edginess amounting almost to aversion. Beth, the young woman who let them into the small, dimly lit room in the basement of the Lagrange Foundation building, seemed to feel only annoyance.

"This is a mess," she said frankly. "It should all be cleaned up, but I've only worked here for three months. The executive secretary, Mr. Johnson, he left at noon Friday on his vacation, and the person I replaced moved to Memphis, so I can only tell you what they told me. There's corporate business, and there's grant information. They should be in separate boxes; the year is on the outside of the box. Inside the boxes things are supposed to be alphabetical. Some scholarships are processed months before they're used, you know. So if this friend of yours started at the university in fifty-nine, then the papers may be in fifty-eight. Okay?

"Since you know Mr. Rushton personally, he says it's okay to leave you the keys. When you're finished, please put stuff back where you found it and lock the door to this room behind you. Call this number from a phone up-stairs, and a security man will come to let you out and reset the alarm and walk you to your car. Leave the keys with him. I'll get them from the security office on Monday." She handed them the keys and a card and was gone.

"Well," breathed Bettiann, suddenly wordless. The small room was air-less, the only light from a wire-encased bulb above their heads. The walls were bare gray concrete; the shelves were metal, spray painted the darkest possible green, like funereal cypresses.

Faye shuddered. "Let's find it." She started down the aisle formed by two rows of boxes. "These are all nineties."

"Eighties," said Aggie from a dry throat. The boxes sagged onto one another, their edges softening, becoming shapeless. "Seventies."

"Sixties here," Faye murmured. "Sixty-five, sixty-four. Here's sixty-three."

Bettiann had come along the wall, on the other side of the pile. "Fifties here," she said. "At least four . . . no, five boxes for fifty-eight and fifty-nine."

There was a long table by the door. They unstacked the boxes to get at the fifty-nines, lifted them to the tabletop, then stared at one another help-lessly. The tape sealing the cartons was heavy, untearable.

"What would you all do without me?" said Faye, fishing in her pocket for her all-purpose knife-cum-screwdriver-cum-can opener. She slit the taped boxes neatly down the middle and at each end. Each of them took a box and fumbled with it, turning it so the folders inside faced front.

"This is invoices," murmured Aggie. "Paid bills, month by month."

"Same here," said Bettiann. "This one's grant-related correspondence." She lifted out a handful of folders. "*T*'s. Maybe they put her in the *T*'s. Tabor. Terres. Thomas. Thompson. Talley. Tully. Trujillo. Turner. Tyson."

"Alphabetical?" Faye remarked.

"Maybe they were originally. They've been shuffled." She piled the ones she had looked at on the table and took out the *S*'s, finding among them two *T*'s and a *W*. "Let's alphabetize."

They set the invoice boxes on the floor and made piles of folders down the long table, *AB*'s, *MNO*'s, *WXYZ*'s. No Tesuawane. No aTesuawane.

They alphabetized within piles and refiled them in the boxes. "What other name?" asked Aggie. "If not under her name, then under whose?"

"Qowat," said Faye. "The postmaster. Chendi Qowat."

Bettiann turned back to the *Q*'s. "No Qowat," she said.

"Piedras Lagartonas," said Faye.

"Here it is," said Aggie, busy with another folder. "Piedras Lagartonas." They moved closer together, as though to conserve warmth, laying the folder on the table before them. Inside, only two sheets, yellowed at the edges. One a printed application form, laboriously completed in ink by some-one at the Piedras Lagartonas Public Schools. The second a form letter from the Lagrange Foundation. ". . . regret we have committed all our funds for the upcoming year . . . keep the application for your students on file. . . ."

"But the university files said she got it," Aggie cried.

"This could be about someone else," mused Faye. "Let's try fifty-eight."

There was nothing at all in fifty-eight, or in sixty or sixty-one. Or in sixty-two.

"She was never here," Aggie laughed dryly, without humor. Was this like everything else about Sophy? A lie?

"I don't think that's it." Bettiann was examining the tape on one of the boxes. "You know, this layer of tape is sticky and not at all yellowed. Some of these boxes have been resealed very recently. The ones from fifty-nine. Some-body's been into them, just within the last few days. Someone in a hurry. Someone who wanted to go home or out on a date and who found the things they wanted, then just shoved everything back in any old which way."

"Things they wanted?" Aggie asked.

"To answer a phone query, maybe," said Faye. "Bettiann isn't the only person with clout. There are others. They call, they say, get all information out of your files on this person."

"Why?" Aggie asked. "Who besides us is interested in Sophy?"

"Well, that's really the question, isn't it? Someone is. Some flunky gets sent down here to pull the file. That person takes the files . . . where?"

"Upstairs," said Bettiann. "To the copying room if they're supposed to make copies. To the boss's desk if he or she wants to look at them first. Or in a file basket somewhere if they're to be brought back down here."

"We have the keys," said Faye, jingling them. "Let's look."

They looked. To the left of the entry hall was a large boardroom with rest rooms and a kitchen behind it. To the right, behind a small waiting room and receptionist's area, were two offices with names on the door, Executive Secretary, Deputy Secretary. Past the offices was a file room, and behind it, across the back of the building, the secretarial area, four desks sharing one large many-windowed room with a door onto a small sunny garden. The desks were clean, neatened up for the holiday, with very few papers showing. The papers pertaining to Sophy were in a wire basket on one of the desks, originals in one folder, copies in the other, with a note. "Mr. Johnson, these are the files you wanted."

"Can we make copies of this stuff?" asked Faye.

Bettiann led them back into the file room, where the copier stood against the wall. "No log," she said. "No lock. Evidently they don't worry about people using the machine. Which makes it nice for us." She stocked the feed tray with experienced hands, pushed all the right buttons, handed the copies to Faye, and put the originals back in the folder: an application, letters of support, a high-school transcript.

"You seem to know your way around," said Faye.

"I have a foundation of my own," Bettiann retorted. "I work there sometimes. At the Carpenter Foundation we couldn't have got away with this. We keep a copy log. And a fax log. And a postage log."

Agnes took the folder and went back into the clerical room. "We'll leave these where we found them."

"Johnson's name is on the director's office door. Somebody asked him for this information," said Faye. "Why? Who?"

"As you pointed out, we have the keys," said Bettiann. "Let's see if he made notes."

The office door wasn't locked. The space inside was carpeted and paneled; it held a leather chair, a mahogany desk. Several small yellow notepads lay at the front of the unlocked shallow top drawer. Agnes leafed through them, coming upon the note almost at once:

"Here," she said, putting it before them.

The firm black lettering said simply, *aTesuawane, writer? Books? Other writings? Lagrange 1959–63. biographical info, known associates for agent Crespin, FBI.* And a phone number.

"Books?" whispered Aggie. "Writings?"

"Remember Carolyn telling us the FBI had a dossier on us?" said Faye with a jeering laugh. "Crespin FBI is Carolyn's cousin Albert. Maybe we're all under investigation."

Bettiann asked, "Do you suppose the local library will be open?"

"Not today," said Agnes. "What do you want, Sophy's books?"

"Of course. I'd like to know what the FBI wants with her writing. I can't remember anything in them that would interest the FBI. They were simple stories of actual things that happened to women and girls, plus some folktales and some essays. Of course, I've got the stuff I've been writing without knowing why. It's in my suitcase. Carolyn asked me to bring it for show-and-tell."

In the suite Bettiann had arranged for, they took the brown manila envelope containing what Bettiann called her "spirit writing" and dumped it onto the table.

"All Sophy's stories were about women," said Aggie.

"These aren't anything like that," said Bettiann.

"There's a lot of paper here," Faye commented. "How long you been doing this, girl?"

"Too long. A couple of years, I guess."

They leafed, stopping to read bits, sometimes silently, sometimes to one another. Suddenly Agnes said in a voice that was almost amused, "Listen to this!

> "Sister lizard dancing, back foot, front foot,
> sun hot rock sitter, rising on her toes,
> warming on the rock-top, skipping from the rock's-root,
> left foot, right foot, so she goes,
> watching for the wing-swoop, talon-snatch and beak-scoop,
> sequin scaled and glittering, what is it that she knows?"

"I remember that one." Bettiann shook her head. "I was on the phone with this man who wanted a donation to his church, and he wouldn't stop talking, and I doodled and doodled, and when he finally hung up, that's what was on the paper. Later on I saw a nature program on PBS and they showed a lizard doing that, lifting its feet so they wouldn't burn on the hot rocks."

Aggie said firmly, "You didn't write this, Bettiann."

"I wasn't conscious of having written it, no. Sophy wrote it."

"It doesn't sound terribly Sophy-like, either. She didn't do jingly stuff like that."

"She did, too. She wrote songs for us all the time. You just wouldn't sing them."

Faye moved between them. "Come on, Aggie! Don't get in an uproar over Bettiann's subconscious. We're looking for clues, so let's look for clues."

"I deny lizards in my subconscious," Bettiann said firmly. "And I can't rhyme cat and mouse."

"I'm still wondering why the FBI would be interested in an almost forty-year-old dossier," snapped Faye.

"We don't know that it's all that old," Bettiann replied. "All we know is that's when Carolyn's cousin started it. Maybe he's been adding to it right along."

"We don't even know he's still alive. And adding what?" Agnes cried, turning to them. "For heaven's sake, what could he have added? We're all boringly blameless!"

Bettiann replied, "Rumors. Myths. Conjecture. Remember when we met with Carolyn last time and Hal was talking to us about the old FBI paying informers for information? How the informer makes his living that way, so if he doesn't have anything real, he makes something up."

"Right. Maybe he's got the Sisters of St. Clare down as a terrorist organization." Faye stretched, snarling. "So far we've got nothing except the name of a place. Sophy's letter of application to the foundation is three paragraphs.

The three people who wrote in support could be anybody. Her high-school transcript is unremarkable; most of us had better ones. She sent a couple of essays along with the application; they're no more subversive than her books were."

"Still, we'll want to talk with the people who wrote letters in support."

"Tess somebody. Flo somebody. All in Piedras Lagartonas, New Mexico. No point going back with this little bit. Let's finish what we have to do here in the area. Let's find some of the women Sophy used to take in."

"From Mystic?" asked Agnes.

"I don't even remember any names from there," said Bettiann.

"From Vermont, then," said Faye.

"Jessamine will know." Bettiann yawned widely. "She used to send outgrown clothes for the children. Lord, it's almost midnight. Let's call."

Carolyn, Jessamine, and Ophy were assembled in Carolyn's bedroom, waiting for Faye's call, which came at about ten o'clock. Faye sounded appropriately weary as she recited the facts they had elicited thus far: Piedras Lagartonas, the names on the support documents, Agent Crespin of the FBI, and Sophy's writings. They were going to Vermont first thing in the morning. Did the western contingent remember the names of any of Sophy's abused women?

Jessamine ran to get her address book, returning momentarily to prop the phone on one shoulder and leaf through the entries. "Names, yes, but no addresses. I used to send packages of clothes my girls had outgrown, but I always sent them in care of Sophy. Here are the women I used to send things to: Laura Glascock, Betty Hotchkiss, Sarah Sourwood. You remember Sarah. She made that marvelous chowder."

Ophy sat up, staring at Jessamine. Sarah. Sarah Sourwood. It was Sarah Sourwood who had been sitting in the waiting room at MSRI with her friends, the bag ladies. It had to be coincidence. It couldn't be the same woman.

Jessy went on. "Here's one—Rebecca Rainford. She was Sophy's lieutenant, her assistant. I can't imagine it will be easy finding any of them."

"Probably not," Faye replied. "Though I'm amazed at how capable Bettiann manages to be." She gave them the phone number at Middlebury Mansionhouse, where they'd be staying, and Jessamine wrote it down.

They had put off having dessert until after Faye's call, and now they went back to the kitchen and got out the brownies they'd made during the afternoon, topping each with a mound of vanilla ice cream. Brownies with ice cream, cocoa with marshmallows, popcorn in gallon lots—ritual foods of the DFC, reminiscent of dormitory gatherings in a time when their dormitories had been all female and pigging out was the limit of their depravity.

"Middlebury," mused Carolyn around a mouthful. "That takes me back. Remember when we stayed there?" She got up to fetch a pad and pencil and jotted down quick notes between bites. Piedras Lagartonas wasn't a name she recognized. "Hal? Piedras Lagartonas. Mean anything?" When he shook his head, she reached for her Spanish dictionary. *Piedras* was "stones," of course, but *lagartonas*?

"Lizards," she said. "Lizards, female. It also means 'sly minxes.' We'd say 'foxy.' The stones of the sly ones, clever ones, something like that. Hell, I've never heard of it!" She reached for the state atlas, with its series of maps of every road in the state.

"I don't much like the turn this is taking, this FBI involvement," said Jessamine.

"I see Albert Crespin's filthy little mind in that," said Hal. "Are you finding it, Carolyn?"

Carolyn shut the atlas with an irritated shake of her head. There was no Piedras Lagartonas.

Ophy asked, "What is he—are they—up to?"

Hal laughed without humor. "If you mean the FBI, they're looking for terrorists! They're after Ophelia Gheist and Carolyn Crespin and Jessamine Ortiz-Oneil. As soon as this sex thing happened, I'm sure the whole Bureau went crazy, burrowing off in all directions, digging into old files like a bunch of rabid gophers. I haven't the slightest doubt that Albert lied to me about erasing the DFC file."

"I don't think I'd like Albert," Jessamine grated between clenched teeth.

"I never liked him, either," said Hal as he left them and headed down the hall toward his den.

Carolyn sighed. "I was young and stupid then. Teasing him like that was just dumb. Like smarting off at your mother, telling her you're going to try drugs, or move in with your boyfriend."

"What you told him was true, in a way," said Ophy.

Jessamine tapped her fingers on the table, a drumroll. "We wanted fewer nasty old men saying they were controlling us for our own good."

"I wouldn't have put it that way," Ophy said chidingly. "But, yes."

Carolyn agreed. "Of course we did. Of course we do! But Albert was FBI, and he was *Albert*. He was rigid, self-satisfied, totally sure that his view was the correct one. If Albert were growing up today, he'd join a militia because he'd be positive that he knows what's right for America! I knew what he was like. I just wasn't paying enough attention to that, or to what was going on in the world."

"A lot of antiwar stuff in the sixties," Ophy mused. "Protests. Sit-ins. Students occupying administration buildings or turning into terrorists over-night. Even some unlikely women robbing banks, driving getaway cars, like that one who turned herself in a few years back. Given the context, I can see why he believed you."

"Simon is going to love this," Ophy said with a lopsided grin. "His wife, the subversive. I'll never live it down."

"Faye said they couldn't find anything informative in the scraps Bettiann's been writing," Jessamine fretted. "I wonder if Sophy's books had anything in them. . . ."

"I have them," Carolyn said. "We can look."

Hal was in the study, immersed in another road atlas. Carolyn leaned across him to fetch Sophy's three slim volumes from the corner they had occupied for years.

"Nothing in there," he grunted. "I've looked."

"Well, Jess wants to look again." She went back to the kitchen and passed the books around. "One for each of us. We can take them as bedtime reading tonight."

They leafed through the books between spoonfuls, without much energy. Ophy gathered up the empty plates, put them in the sink, then picked up book one.

"I'll take it to bed with me."

Hal returned to report no progress on finding Piedras Lagartonas.

Carolyn yawned. "Let's not lose sleep over it. Despite all this furor, the trial has to be put out of the way first."

Jessy and Ophy trailed off to bed, leaving Carolyn and Hal alone.

"I wish Albert's mother had believed in abortion," growled Hal.

"Aunty Fan? She loved Albert dearly. According to Aunty Fan, Albert could do no wrong. I'm so thankful you saved me from Albert." She laughed quaveringly. "Sometimes I scare myself, thinking what might have been, instead of what was. If I hadn't met Faye, or Ophy . . ."

"It's been a good life." He tilted her head down and kissed her on the lips, a soft, lingering, lovely kiss. Not passion. Something better, more lasting, than passion—the complete understanding they had always had, from the beginning. A mated pair, they were. Like geese. Hal had always said so.

"How's your leg?" she asked, caressing it with her fingertips. "Able to get you back to the bedroom?"

"Always able to do that." He rose, leaning on her slightly. She turned off the lights behind them.

Sunday morning Jagger went into town for a meeting with Raymond Keepe. Keepe had asked for the meeting, at Webster's direction.

"I tried to call you yesterday," said Jagger. "But you were away."

"I was away, yes," said Keepe through his teeth. "Mr. Webster summoned me back! The place was like an anthill. Now that we know what's going on, all the weirdness makes sense. Have you heard about the lab in Washington that's been doing hormonal assays? Testosterone levels in men are only one fourth what they were six months ago."

"All men?" asked Jagger tonelessly.

"I haven't heard that anyone is immune." Keepe scowled, drew his lips back in a grimace. "According to Mr. Webster, all our allies are in a tailspin. They're threatening World War Three. Iran and Libya have pulled out of the Alliance. They're blaming the Great Satan for infecting the Islamic world with this disease. They've proclaimed a jihad against all unbelievers, and they've started stoning women in the streets, sort of indiscriminately, for supposedly having spread the disease. The U.S. military has been put on full alert.

"Japan accused China of putting birth control in the water supplies to control its population, thereby affecting the fish that are eaten by Japanese. The commentator said there were rumors of nuclear threats having been made. Three countries not known to have atomic weapons are claiming to have them. The President's going to appear on TV this afternoon—"

"So what?"

"So Webster has put the Alliance plan on hold. For now. Until this sorts itself out, any move might be in the wrong direction. All active political campaigns are off for now. We're going into a holding pattern."

Jagger heard this as he might have heard the clamorous echo of a tomb door slamming shut with him inside. It was all he could do to keep from screaming in frustration. "Until when?"

"Until somebody finds out what caused this. The U.S. has evidently had every available laboratory working on it for some time. This is what all that CDC nonsense was about, of course. Other nations are no doubt doing the same. Webster says the cause will no doubt be found very shortly, and someone will figure out how to fix it."

"Like we fixed AIDS," said Jagger in a heavy voice.

"It's nothing like AIDS."

"You don't know what it's like! Nobody knows."

Except, he thought, a group of women near this very city, who had said on Sunday that one or more of their members had started this thing.

He asked, "What if I could tell Mr. Webster who caused it?"

Keepe looked up alertly. "Foreigners? What? Iranians? Chinese?"

"Americans."

Keepe smiled thinly. "Oh, come on, Jake."

"Women."

"Women? Some kind of psychological castration? Chop it off you—yes, they're good at that. But something like this? Women haven't the brains for something like this. They don't think that way."

"Most women don't, right, but there's always a freak." His eyes were fixed on something distant. "Anyhow, suppose it was people I could name? Would that make a good campaign issue? Would that move me up in the estimation of the Alliance?"

Keepe thought about it. "If you could prove someone specific was responsible, male or female, and if you could get them to cough up the cure or antidote or whatever, I suppose you might come off as a hero."

"The public likes heroes."

"Oh, yes. You could probably be elected President on the strength of finding out who caused it. But, personally, I find it very far-fetched, and in my opinion, so will the Alliance."

"But if I could do it?"

Keepe shrugged. "It couldn't be a kind of Joe McCarthy bluff with your waving a piece of paper and saying you have the names. You'd have to have more than that. You'd have to have the cure."

Jagger got up angrily, thrust his face at the other man. "Quit patronizing me, damn it. If I named real people, if I could prove they did it, then even if they didn't have the cure, knowing how they did it will tell us where to look for the cure!"

Keepe pushed his chair back, shook his head slowly, his brow furrowed. "You're serious."

"Keepe, if you knew me at all, you'd know I'm rarely anything but serious!"

Keepe stared at him, forehead creased. "Listen, Jake. . . ." He licked his lips, looked around himself, as though fearful of being overheard. "Listen, if you're going to get involved in something like that, you should talk to Webster right now. He doesn't like people going off on their own, and he finds out everything that happens. I don't know how he keeps up on things the way he does, but he's . . . omniscient in some ways."

Jagger tapped his fingers on his desk, fascinated despite himself. "Omniscient?"

Keepe laughed, a hollow sound. "Anything Webster cares about, he's right on top of, even when you think he's somewhere else. Like he was . . . twins or triplets or something."

Jake guffawed. "In two or three places at once?"

"Don't laugh, Jake. It's not a joke. I swear to . . . Well, just take my word for it!"

"So he's got a double," said Jake dismissively. "Or several doubles. It wouldn't be the first time. Celebrities do that."

Keepe breathed deeply, not quite a sigh, more a gasp. "Whatever, Jake. If you're going to do something, tell Webster. He doesn't take kindly to people trying to go around him."

"It was just a brainstorm," Jagger said, staring out the window. "An idea. I'll have to think about it." He, like Keepe, found it hard to believe that women were bright enough to do something like this. He would have said women weren't smart enough or efficient enough, but, then, their taped conversation hadn't sounded so much like a plot as it had a mistake. Women could make mistakes, no doubt about that. And it didn't really matter whether it had been done accidentally or purposefully. One of the women had done a stupid thing, and another one of them had done something worse and then disappeared, and they had all covered it up. They were all responsible.

The man who brought them to account would be a hero. Especially if it led to a cure.

"What are you going to do?" asked Keepe.

"I don't know. Even if the Alliance plans are on hold, I still have a trial to finish. And, as I said, it was just a brainstorm. Something that clicked. I'll think it through. If there's anything in it, I'll do what you suggest."

Keepe was accustomed to reading faces, and he found Jagger's features easy to decipher. Jake didn't intend to consult Webster, and this fact placed Keepe in an awkward position. Whatever Jake did, the Alliance would find out, at once or eventually. And when they did, Webster would find out also that Keepe had known about it.

As soon as he could, he got to a phone and dialed the emergency number he had been given. It yielded a voice that gave him another number, and that one another yet. At last he got someone who asked a few brief questions; then came a series of clicks and tones that ended when Webster's familiar voice came on the line.

"What?"

The single word rocked Keepe on his feet, stunned him, left him shaking as he told his story, making it as brief as possible. Something about Webster's voice was different!

"You think he knows of women who really did have something to do with it?" Webster asked.

The vocal difference had to do with . . . with timbre. As though in all previous conversations Webster's voice had been somehow muffled and now it was not. Something in the phone line, perhaps? Or the place Webster was speaking from? To make this cutting resonance, this agonizing sound.

"Keepe! I asked a question!"

Keepe moved the receiver well away from his ear and moistened his dry mouth. "I have no way of judging that, Mr. Webster. The one thing I'm sure of is that Jagger thinks so, though how he would have become aware of it, I have no idea."

He heard something that might have been a chuckle, it, too coming through the phone with that unmuffled clarity, like the slash of a rapier. Keepe shut his eyes and squeezed them tight. He had been injured by that laugh. He knew he had. Cut, somehow. Somewhere. He waited for the pain that would come, had to come as the voice went on:

"Oh, I have a very good idea, Keepe. Jake is a creature of habit, but, then, most creatures are, have you noticed that? Break a dog to the whip, and he cringes when you speak. Give a dog running room—I like to give my dogs running room—and he jumps gates. Perhaps Jagger has jumped one gate too many. You did tell him that winning the case wasn't the most important thing? You did give him the hint . . . ?"

"The hint, sir?" Keepe croaked. He swallowed deeply and tried again. "Hint?"

"That I want men willing to lose if I tell them to." The words came out of the phone into his head and manifested themselves as wheels of fire, hot and dangerous. Behind his eyes they spun, sparkling.

Keepe had to swallow again before he could answer. What was the matter with him! "Oh, yes, sir. More than a hint, sir."

Webster laughed again, and Keepe almost dropped the phone as he jerked it farther away from his ear. Oh, to stop that sound. If only he could . . . could stop that sound.

Webster said: "Jake evidently didn't take the hint. Poor Jake. He wants to win so badly. He's probably bugged the home or office of opposing counsel, female, which probably means the women Jake is talking about are friends or acquaintances of hers. Very interesting. Certainly more of a lead than I've had from any other source. Thank you, Keepe. I have a record of all Mr. Jagger's recent visitors and conversations. Stay where you can be reached."

Stay where you can be reached. Each of those six words came with that razor clarity, that fiery power, cutting him through, cauterizing the cuts, leaving him afraid to move. If he moved, he'd fall into pieces, into shreds. He had to heal first, had to let his cells regenerate; otherwise, he would fall on the floor in strands, like noodles. The image was clear in his mind.

Still, his mouth moved, Keepe surprised that it was possible to move any discrete part of himself without detaching it. "Of course, Mr. Webster."

He dropped the phone onto the floor in his attempt to hang it up. He couldn't pick it up, he was shaking too much, his muscles kept going into spasms. He nudged the phone into the cradle with his foot, leaving it on the floor. Oh, my, he said to himself, as to a child. Oh, my, my.

Keepe had had a wife once. He did not often think of her, but he remembered her now. Elaine. She had told him it was a mistake to work for

Webster. She had told him she couldn't stay with him if he worked for Webster. He had laughed when she went away. He had called her a stupid bitch. He had understood even then that Mr. Webster was an extremely powerful and dangerous man with motives and strategies that were outside Keepe's experience, but Keepe had been sure he could work for Webster without getting involved in whatever it was Webster was doing. Elaine had said it wouldn't work, but Keepe had said he could do his work and get paid for it, that Webster didn't own Keepe, he only hired him.

"Give me credit for some sense," Keepe had told her. "I stand at a professional distance, on my own separate ground as an independent person."

"You're building a house upon sand. You're a fool, Raymond."

"How dare you!"

"I dare. Just now, I must."

Later he learned she was pregnant. Later he learned she had had a child, but those were the last words she had said to him. When he had returned home that evening, she was gone and he never heard from her again. Now that professional distance he had bragged of was gone as well. Now his separate ground was gone. Elaine had been right. It had been sand; it had melted away; he had felt it go from beneath his feet. There was no distance at all between himself and Webster; there was no independence. He and Webster were of one substance—Webster's substance. They were of one purpose— Webster's purpose. That intent lapped around his feet like a flow of lava, its heat charring his flesh. His feet were going to burn off, and when they did, he would fall into the stream of Webster's self. This was not metaphor. He saw the red glow of that self, smelled the brimstone reek of it, felt the pain of burning. There was no way he could stay alive, not even by letting his feet be burned off. Inside himself a trapped creature screamed and ran to and fro.

Now, now, he assured himself, squeezing his eyes shut, swallowing deeply, moving abruptly as to break the mental webs that bound him suddenly to this place. Now, now, this would not do; it was time to call a halt, time to reassert individuality, time to redefine the relationship. Perhaps it was even time to resign from this job. . . .

Some separate part of his mind said all these things in solemn words, which he heard quite clearly, words that echoed slightly in the fiery and vacant vaults where he found himself, like someone calling a lost child in a place too huge to search. He heard the words, he understood the words, but they had no connection to reality. His body paid no attention to the words. The only reality was where he was.

His hip joints burned away until he leaned against the wall. He felt his backside sliding down the wall, his knees burning, bending, deeper and deeper until they could bend no more, at which point he fell forward, folding in upon himself, curling, crouching, until he was tight against the floor, huddled in the smallest possible compass over and around the silent phone, as though he and the phone were one organism, as though it were the umbilicus that bound him to the source of all his life. No matter what the words in his head said, he was doing what Webster had commanded. He was staying where he could be reached. Forever, if need be.

17

BY MIDMORNING SUNDAY, BETTIANN was sitting in the living room of the suite at the Middlebury Mansionhouse, surrounded by the phone books of the close-by communities, looking up names, variations on names, persons possibly related to names: Hotchkiss, Sourwood, Rainford, Glascock.

Faye, returning from a short walk to get the cobwebs out of her head, asked, "What are you doing? Where'd you get the phone books?"

"Hotel manager got them from a friend of his at the phone company." She smiled and pushed half of the books in Faye's direction. "I told them we're looking for an heiress."

"You told a fib?"

"Umm. Better than saying we were looking for ex-victims. I think I've found one, by the way."

And she had. L. Glascock—not Laura, but her brother Lenny, who said Laura lived near a neighboring town, and gave them directions: big house, no phone, set back from the road, look for dogs, cows.

"Cows everywhere," Faye objected. "Dogs everywhere."

"We'll find it," said Bettiann. "It's a place to start."

They waited until Aggie came out of the bedroom, eyes swollen again. She'd been crying more or less since they'd arrived: silent weeping, the worst kind.

"Aggie . . ." Tentatively.

"I'm all right," she said angrily.

Obviously she wasn't. She was no better when they went hunting Glascocks through the high summer day, puffed clouds hanging in the west, white clapboard houses backing explosions of day lilies and blue candles of delphinium, fields of swaying clover, dandelion verges, silos and barns soberly anchoring the country lanes like weights at the corners of a picnic tablecloth. The Glascock place, found at last behind a gnarled orchard, was weedy, peeling, sagging, gray, and well used, but comfortable and welcoming nonetheless.

"Laura? She's inside." A grease-stained and overalled teenager, only briefly distracted, went back to his enigmatic absorption with the innards of a tractor.

Laura was a little younger than they, but more worn, more lined, and more contented, so Faye thought, taking in the calm face and relaxed figure with an artist's evaluating eye.

"Of course I remember Sophy," she said, voice rising like a cork on a wavelet, bobbing and lilting. "Come sit on the porch! How could I forget Sophy? Where is she? How is she?"

"Lost," said Bettiann as they sat down, she on a rocking chair, Aggie and Faye on a rickety bench. "Disappeared. We're trying to find her. Talking with anyone who might have known her, anyone who might have talked to her."

A sudden watchfulness, a look almost of suspicion. "What do you mean, disappeared?"

"We haven't seen her in a couple of years," said Faye carefully.

Laura laughed. "Well, that's no big thing. She's been busy, that's all. You read the papers, don't you?"

"The papers?" asked Bettiann.

"All those old ladies—didn't you think of Sophy right away, when you read about that?"

"Old ladies . . ."

"Burning those fashion places, those shoe shops. Remember how she worried about you?" This to Bettiann.

"Me?" Her voice squeaked.

"You. You're Bettiann Bromlet, aren't you? Bettiann Carpenter? Are you still trying to starve yourself into a Barbie doll? The ideal woman of the marketplace? One who is less than the sum of her clothing?"

"Why did she tell you about me?" Bettiann asked, more than a little annoyed.

"Oh, tush, we needn't pretend. She told us about all of you. She said you, Bettiann, couldn't live in your own body because it wasn't the image you'd been given. She used you as an example when she talked to us about becoming our own icons. Oh, she'd get in a rage, Sophy would. She said we had to reclaim ourselves, relearn to be miraculous and marvelous. . . ."

Bettiann was shocked into silence, but Faye shook her head slowly, trying to reconcile this with the Sophy she thought she had known.

"I never heard Sophy say that. I never thought of her as particularly . . . interventionist."

"Tssh," Laura hissed. "Of course she was. She said she'd spent her life finding the ground on which to fight the final battle."

"I don't understand."

Laura hitched her chair forward until she was almost touching them, fixing them with her eyes. "Didn't she tell you? There is a great battle brewing. Some perceive it as between God and the devil, light and darkness fighting it out, with earth as the spoils. Just like two rams on the hill, going at each other with their great curly horns. That's the so-called Christian idea of it, a very much all-male thing, women and children irrelevant except as prizes of battle, wouldn't you know. The battle that's coming isn't between a good male force and an evil male force. It's more basic than that. It's between balance and dominion."

Aggie murmured, "Sophy rejected Christian concepts, did she?"

"She rejected the idea that battles are fought only between male forces with woman as the ground they fight on. Sophy said she had found the enemy, that he was powerful and dreadful, that he trampled on the graves of girl children and threw brides into his furnace, that wherever women were reviled, he was there, whispering into the ears of their persecutors. She said he had as his aim the extirpation of all burgeoning, all blessing, all that is female in nature. . . ."

"The world wouldn't last long with no women," said Bettiann.

"*His* world would. Sophy claimed we couldn't let the battle be fought on those terms. She said the enemy mustn't be allowed to call all the shots. She said we have to oppose him." She compressed her lips, eyebrows raised, like one awaiting response to a password.

They looked at one another helplessly, still without understanding.

Laura shook her head, baffled. "You don't understand, do you? Didn't you know what she was doing, all those years? Didn't you talk to any of us, the ones she saved? The ones she set into motion and sent around the world?" She looked from face to face, seeing only incomprehension. "No. I can see you didn't. You were like family, right? And she was little sister? Children should be seen and not heard? So you didn't listen."

"We listened," cried Bettiann, not at all sure that they had.

"Not well enough, it seems. Well, better late than never. You've come to the right place to find people who know Sophy well. There are many of them around here, half a dozen of us within twenty minutes of one another."

"All doing well?" Aggie asked. "All . . . happy?"

Laughter. "Happy? Sometimes. But, then, happy is a sometime thing.

When Younger Sister broke the happiness jug, bits of it scattered everywhere, so Sophy always told us. She said not to worry about happy, just get on the way because we'll find bits of happy everywhere we go."

"I never heard about the happiness jug," breathed Faye.

"Oh, we heard all her stories. She set a lot of us on the way."

Aggie again. "What way is that?"

That lilting voice, with a touch of Irish in it, suddenly chanting: " 'Onto *the winding way, past the wicket gates left cunningly ajar, the ones with the barkers outside, urging you to come in for security, love, fame, love, riches, love. Past the lanes leading to the pastures of stupid cow, the kennels of bitch; past the paved roads leading to pedestals and plinths where virgin saints and mothers-of-many stand; past the doors opening on nurseries for pretty babies, or to harems, guarded by eunuchs of despair.' "

"Narrow the road and strait the gate," said Aggie, as from a great distance.

" *'Many the paths and no gates, ever,'* " Laura contradicted her. " *'Many paths to allow for meandering, for as the water flows, so will we, but no gates, for every gate has a toll collector. Go through none, and none can close behind you to trap you in a place you don't belong. Track by your star; but keep an eye on your feet, for stones are set in the road to make you stumble.'* That's what Sophy said." Abruptly she folded her hands in front of her and began to sing lustily:

> " *'Men show us their roads across the land,*
> *which they have built straight and wide,*
> *where their tollgates stand on every hand*
> *controlling the countryside;*
> *And the gates, they say, are the only way,*
> *for women to save their souls,*
> *and when we ask why, the gatekeepers cry*
> *that we've got to pay their tolls*
> *to keep us demure, to keep us pure,*
> *to keep us at duty's call,*
> *for we never can be as good as a man*
> *since we were the cause of his fall. . . .' "*

Bettiann cried, "Sophy wrote that for show-and-tell, years and years ago. It was a song—Faye set it to music as a trio. Faye and I sang it, but Aggie wouldn't—"

"It wasn't respectful," said Aggie in a distant voice. "It was . . . is heretical."

Laura laughed, agreeing. "Sophy isn't respectful, no."

Faye shook herself, like a dog coming out of the water. "What we need," she said, rather more vehemently than necessary, "is to know if any of you ever heard Sophy talk about a place she might be going or wanting to visit? Her home place or somewhere she'd been that she'd like to return to? We really, desperately need to find her."

Laura shook her head at them, but she said she would call the others. Let them sit out in the orchard shade and drink iced tea for a time while she did so. Minutes later they were ensconced on sun-faded chairs beside an old cider press while above them infant apples shone, sun-polished jade cabochons among the boughs.

"They won't know anything," said Aggie.

"They may," said Bettiann. "Don't give up, Aggie."

"She isn't giving up," said Faye, staring fixedly at Aggie. "She doesn't want Sophy found."

"No," Agnes cried explosively, thrusting out her hands as though to push them away. "I don't! All my life I've fought and fought for my vows, fought for my celibacy, fought for my poverty! Fought to believe it was important! Poverty, chastity, obedience. I thought obedience would be easy—all those years of Catholic boarding schools, I'd learned to be obedient. Poverty was nothing. When you want nothing much, what is poverty? But celibacy . . . oh, I knew that would be hard, hard. You don't know, you pretty women, you easy women, you women who bring the partners like bees, humming around you. . . . You don't know what it's like, the longings, the wondering, the curiosity! You don't know the pictures the mind makes in the night so you wake from dreams with your body trembling, echoing, thrashing so it won't stop but goes on and on. . . . And now . . . now everybody! Everybody chaste, everyone pure, without effort, without trying, and all my sacrifice is meaningless! Meaningless!"

Faye startled, stared for a moment wide-eyed, then laughed like a dog bark. "Hey, Aggie. I'll bet you're not half as pissed as the pope."

Aggie recoiled as though she'd been slapped.

Bettiann snapped her teeth at Faye, put her arms around Aggie. "Aggie, please. Faye's just . . . you know Faye. We don't mean to hurt you. We would never hurt you. We love you."

Agnes muttered, "It's not your fault, Bettiann. It's Sophy's influence on her, on all of us. All those years. I thought it was Carolyn who was undermining, Carolyn who was the skeptic, but it was Sophy all the time. Sophy who was working us and working us, getting us to the point where she could use us, like a weapon, to do this devilish thing!"

Faye said quietly, "Maybe God decided to make it easier on us. Maybe it's a miracle."

"A miracle brought about by whom? St. Sophy?" She laughed, the giggle turning into uncontrollable shaking. "Oh, Bettiann, all those years rooming with her in school, she there in the next bed, breathing soft in the night, it was so hard not to reach out to her, so hard not to touch her. Now I must fight against her with all my being, when I loved her so. . . ." The words hung in the air like the stench of vomit, sour with regret.

The feeling behind the words was discomforting, almost repellent. They had little time to be troubled by it, however, for the women began arriving—some familiar faces, some not, some with their children, some with one another, with their own answers to Faye's unspoken question.

"She was a saint," they said. "She was our warrior angel. She gave us a place to stand. . . ."

Aggie drew in a slow breath, as though it hurt her, and gritted her teeth. Bettiann took her hand and patted it.

One of the women stood, her hands clasped loosely in front of her, and said: "I am Ellen, and I will tell you the words of Sophy, as heard by us of the First Dispersal:

"Sophy said: 'When I had traveled around the world, having seen in all nations what it was I had come to see, I was much troubled in my spirit at the power of the enemy who moves among us, so I went into the desert to seek the source of women's being, for in that source is our strength.

" 'I went to a mesa, high above the desert, where the stone is full of the shapes of little things that swam long and long ago in shallow seas. I went to a house deserted these thousand years. Roofless and doorless it was, with an age-old hearth on which to light my fires. Sweet smoke blessed me by night. Kind wind blessed me by day.

" 'All around me lay the evidence of time. Before me lay all the works of man, the nations and peoples of the earth; above me the hawk circled at the zenith, the stars moved, and around me walked the creatures of the world. I saw no person except the man who came to bring me food and water; a wrinkled man who lived in an old yellow bus, a man I had known forever. His name was Qowat, Josephus, keeper and protector, shaman and seer. He came every week in his soft brown shoes, his feet mumbling over the stones, scuffling the sand.

" 'I was there long days and long nights, seeking Her in meditation. At last She came to me at midday, sunlight crowned, rainbow clad, out of a prismed cloud. She asked me what I sought. I told her I sought help for the women of this world. She bent above me, touching me with her hands, and said that help must be defined before it can be given. She wrapped me in her cloud and left me there, telling me to think well.

" 'Though I had spent years among the women of the world, see-ing their sorrow, I could not define what help it was they needed. Long I stood wrapped in Her cloud, pondering: What help could do good without harm? What help would be wise and just? What help would benefit women without punishing men, for are they not our brothers and our sons? At sun-set I was still there, watching the red clouds burn the last of the day into ashes.

" 'It was then the stranger man came striding across the mesa as though it were a road, himself shining like a lantern in the dusk, his own heat lighting his way. I saw that he wandered to and fro on the earth, and up and down in it; his wandering had brought him to me. He stopped near me, tall and dark and shiningly beautiful, and I thought of the stags on the mountaintop, lifting their muzzles in the dawn. He sensed me, though he could not see me in Her cloud, and he held out his hands, summoning me. He whispered he would give me everything I saw if I would let him make love to me. His eyes were little fires like the smallest borehole of a volcano, the red-rimmed orifice of flame, leading to hotness upon hotness, to the core of burning where flesh vanishes and is transformed into pure heat, pure ecstasy. Inside me, I burned with wanting him. Everything born of human woman, never released, never let go, wound like a spring. I tried to say no, and the words choked me. I could only stand there, thinking no, I would not, while he stood and grinned fiercely, burning me, but burn me as he would, he could not touch me unless I willed it so.

" 'I knew he was the enemy I had been seeking.'

"And we asked her, 'What was he like, the enemy?' "

"She said, 'He came to me as a man, tall and ageless as mountains, with eyes that see into the doubting places of the heart and a mouth that gives kisses like wounds. He came to me as the possessor, the holder, the restrainer. His are the words of dominion which are spoken from the loins, saying not *Thou mayest* but *Thou must*. He is the seizer who destroys all life but his own. He is the self-worshiper who makes gods in his own likeness. It seemed to me I had known of him forever, and though he was of your people, not of mine, I knew he was my enemy as well as yours.

" 'Deep into the night he sought me, turning his head this way and that, scenting me as a hound scents. At last he went away. I could feel his skin against my own long after he was gone, as though he had left a hot web around me that went on burning. Thus, I said to myself, is woman made ashes by wanting. Thus, I said, is woman tempted from her own being into destruction.

" 'But though I still felt his heat, I could feel also the rock beneath my feet. This rock was the floor of an ancient sea that had burgeoned with life, and it was not he who made it. I looked out upon the peopled nations of the world, and it was not he who created them. Around me moved feather and fur, the snick of teeth and the dart of talon, and it was not he who taught them their skill. Life in all its diversity was from Her, and I stood upon life and he had not moved me from that place.

" 'All night I watched, and at dawn She returned, out of the rose cloud, wrapped in mist. Veiled and hidden though She was, I knew Her voice. She stopped beside me, She took my face in Her hands and asked me if I had decided what help was needed. I had not. She said, "To know what help is needed against your enemy, don't you need to know what the enemy plans for womankind?" Then She went away again, Her feet leaving strange tracks in the sand, like a great bird.'

"And we asked where Sophy went then.

"And she said, 'I sought the answer to Her question. I traveled far, hard roads into the lair of the enemy, to see what he planned for womankind, and I found his plans made manifest in that place. I went from there to meet my sisters beside the sea, and there She came to me for the third time out of a sunlit wave upon the sea and I told Her what help was needed. And now the beast has been summoned onto holy ground, the battle is joined, and I have come to send you forth.' "

Bettiann said, "She was talking about San Francisco."

The woman nodded, smiling. "Yes. She was content when she came from meeting with you. Strength had come upon her, and she gave of it. She laid her hands on us and we felt the light flowing into us. She named us the First Dispersal, and having named us, she sent us out, into the world."

"How many of you?" asked Faye.

"Oh, hundreds by then. Maybe thousands. Some like Sarah Sourwood, to go among the old dames of the cities who would carry the war into the marketplace, for all wars must be fought there, sooner or later. And some of us to set up places of refuge, as Sophy herself had done for us. Do you remember Rebecca Rainford? She was one of the first to set up a place of refuge. Some of us went to the brides in India, and the girls being cut, and the mothers told to kill their baby daughters. Some went among women who were alone, teaching them to join together, for there is hope in two women, help in three women, strength in four, joy in five, power in six, and against seven, no gate may stand. Some even went among men to tell them of the battle that was coming, to explain that it is not male god against male devil, nor is it female against male; it has nothing to do with gender but with dominion."

"And you all made it?" Faye asked. "You all survived?"

Nods, smiles. "Survived? Well, some lived, some died, but all kept a place to stand. Once you stop trying to go through the gates, it seems so much simpler. Find your sun-warmed stone, she used to say to us, find it high in the sun, dance there, build your house there, then reach down to pull others up!"

"She was from Piedras Lagartonas," Bettiann said. "Do you know where that is?"

"I know what it means," said Laura. "Lizard stone, the stone of the clever mothers. She said it was named for her, too. 'Piedras Lagartonas' is also 'Petra Sophia.' The stone of wisdom, the home of the wise crones, the Baba Yagas."

"But where is it?"

The woman shrugged, murmured with the others. "South," they all agreed. "She said it was hot." "She came north from there to Albuquerque." "It wasn't in Mexico. . . ." "No. I remember! South of the Spring of Contention."

"Is that a place? Or a condition?"

They didn't know. Faye went back to the car and took out a folded sheet of paper, bringing it back to Laura. "Does this mean anything to you?"

"What is it?" Bettiann asked.

"That thing you wrote about the lizard," Faye replied.

Laura passed it around, and they nodded, smiling. They had heard Sophy talk about the dancing lizard. "It has to keep dancing, or it burns up," one of them said. "It is one of the metaphors of divinity, that one must keep moving or the fire of creation will go out. Change is what it's about. The constant movement and ferment of change and evolution."

When they'd said it all, they went away again, without fuss, with great affection for one another, arms reaching, hands patting, heads bent together, words whispered or spoken, the whole like a dance, circles within circles, the music unheard but the rhythm of it plain.

"Thank you," Faye said to Laura when they were alone once more. "If there is anything I can ever do for you, any of you, please call upon me." In her mind she was creating a statue of the Goddess, a womanly figure, very Laura-like, holding out her hand to pull others up.

Then back again, to the hotel suite in Middlebury, where Agnes shut herself in her room. Through the closed door they could hear her voice murmuring, praying.

"What's going to happen to her?" Bettiann asked. "What is she doing in there?"

"She was grieving over Sophy," Faye said. "Now she's grieving over herself. She didn't say a word when the women were talking, but I was watching her face. She didn't believe them, or she didn't believe what they were told."

"Did we get anything we can use?" Bettiann rubbed her forehead where lately the lines had refused to be smoothed away.

Faye responded musingly, slowly, thinking it over. "The Goddess. And the old man who brought her food. The striding man who offered her the world if he could make love to her, whom these women identify, I think, as a . . . the devil, and whom Agnes identifies as . . . something else. She, Sophy, went into his lair. What does that mean?"

"I don't know," said Bettiann fretfully. "Another thing was, she laid hands on these women. That's what . . . religious leaders do, isn't it?"

"You're asking the wrong person, Bets."

"She never . . . laid her hands on us."

Faye sighed. "These women were her students, her followers. Her disciples, if you will. We were her friends. Maybe she felt it would be presumptuous with us, that we wouldn't appreciate it. Or maybe she knew us too well. Or maybe . . ." She did not finish the thought. Maybe Sophy had wanted them to find the way for themselves. Or knew that some of them wouldn't.

Bettiann was still fretting. "We can't go looking for a goddess or a devil. The old man was human, though. What did she say his name was?"

"She said Qowat. Qowat, Josephus, something. Chendi Qowat is the name on the application Sophy made to the foundation. He could be still alive. Why not? We think Sophy is. Come on. Let's call Santa Fe and tell the others what we've found out so far."

They had just finished the call when Aggie came from her room, wiping her eyes. "I'm ready to go back to Carolyn's. Everything they said today made it clear we had no idea who Sophy was. Or what she was. We're not going to learn anything more here."

Bettiann shook her head. "We'll go, Aggie, but not until morning. We're tired out, and for a few hours we're going to rest. We're going to walk down to Frog Hollow and buy something funny for Carolyn and Ophy and Jessamine. We're going to have dinner out and quietly drink some wine. Then if you can't sleep, I'll give you one of my sleeping pills, and tomorrow we'll go west again."

It was not the Bettiann whom Aggie was accustomed to, but she did not argue.

In a different place an old yellow school bus drove down the rainy streets of a middle-size city where evening lamplight shone at windows and streetlights made misty spheres of radiance above rain-licked pavement. The bus passed a small boy dressed in a yellow raincoat and hat, sailing boats in the gutter. The boy waved, and the old man who was driving the bus waved back. The bus passed a dignified dog trotting purposefully about its business and taking no notice of bus or driver. It passed a man and woman walking close together, head and shoulders concealed by an umbrella. The driver turned a corner and pulled to the curb in front of an ordinary house: white clapboard, green shutters, trimmed evergreens in the front yard, a covered porch at the front and side. The porch light was on, as though someone was expected.

He turned and nudged his only passenger, who was drowsing.

"Where are we?" Helen asked.

"Where you'll be safe," said the old man, getting to his feet. "This is Rebecca's house. You'll be all right here."

"For how long?" she cried. "Until he finds me?"

"Perhaps he won't find you."

"My children," she said, something between a whimper and a prayer.

"Everything is changing," he said, putting his hand on her head. "Everything is in flux, moving like a stream over rocks, full of eddies and wavelets. Whatever happens will happen soon. It will not be long until you can be together." He pressed his cheek against hers. "Or it will not be long before being together won't seem important. Go in. This is a refuge. They have been told you are coming. They are expecting you."

The bus door wheezed open. She stepped down onto the sidewalk, hearing the door shush closed behind her. She was halfway to the house when the house door opened, spilling indoor light onto the rain-wet walk to make a golden river. Behind her the bus hummed itself away. She did not turn to see it go, for her eyes were fixed on the woman who came to meet her and take her by the hand. She looked to be about sixty. Her face was tranquil.

Children were playing inside. Their laughter came clearly into the night, along with the voices of women. There was the smell of cooking.

"I'm Rebecca Rainford," said the woman. "Welcome."

Carolyn took Ophy and Jessamine to the jail to examine Lolly, returning well before noon on Sunday.

"How'd it go?" Hal asked when they returned.

Carolyn shrugged. "Lolly was very much herself. Ophy did a thorough physical; Jessamine took her through a couple of nonverbal tests."

"Enough to get an idea of the level she functions at," murmured Jessy. "Carolyn hadn't misled us. She's just as described. Lily the chimp probably has better sense, but then, Lily's mother raised her carefully."

It was the only notable happening in a day otherwise spent in edgy sloth, nothing accomplished, though everything was worried over. The evening was marked only by Bettiann's call telling them what the eastern contingent had come up with and saying they would return sometime on Monday. After a quiet supper everyone retired but Carolyn. She sat up late, obsessively going over everything that might go wrong, noting down everything that Jagger could use against her and every wrong step she might make. She included in this lengthy list the possibility that Josh might not be able to continue overseeing Lolly's clothing.

The wisdom of her foresight was clear the moment she saw Lolly in the courtroom on Monday morning, hair teased into a mane, eyes made up, lipstick a smear, and a scarlet dress so tight it looked painted on. Carolyn grabbed her, steered her out into the bailiff's anteroom, and from there, with a female guard, to the women's room, where Lolly was, over feeble protestations, stripped to her underwear, washed, brushed, combed, and redressed in a set of clothing that Carolyn had brought with her just on the off chance.

"I looked good before," she wailed.

"You looked like a hooker," said Carolyn firmly. "Juries put girls who look like hookers in the tanks. Who dressed you up like that?"

"My mama. She said somebody give her the clothes. . . ."

Carolyn could imagine who had given her the clothes. When they went back into the courtroom, the girl was neatly dressed in clean jeans, low-heeled shoes, and a knit polo shirt. Though elsewhere this might have been too informal for court, in Santa Fe it was sufficient. Her hair, though somewhat the worse for the quart of mousse that had been gooped onto it, was reasonably neat.

"Now, what're you going to do?" Carolyn asked when she was seated.

Lolly made a sullen face.

"Look, kid. If you want to get tanked, fine. I won't waste my time. If you don't want to get tanked, then cooperate." Carolyn had chosen not to mention the death penalty, on the theory that it would only send Lolly into a complete funk if she understood it at all.

She mumbled. "I'm s'posed to sit still, and not chew gum, and not make faces, and not, like . . . say anything, no matter what nobody says. But I can tell you things in a whisper if I need to."

"Right, Lolly. It's going to be long, and it's going to be boring. Just do the best you can."

Carolyn seated herself, feeling the surge of people behind her. The courtroom was like a tidal pool, with people pouring in and out, shifting groups of them, whispering and exclaiming. They were discussing the news, the epidemic, the change. *My wife thinks this. My husband told me that. My mother said. Judge so-and-so thinks. Did you read this? Well, I think what will happen is.*

Carolyn eavesdropped unabashedly. They were not talking about Lolly, or the case. So what were they all doing here?

The question was answered when the bailiff entered, looking at his watch. Some of the visitors aped the action, then drifted out and away, followed by others. The ebb and surge had been courthouse workers, clerks and secretaries now gone to their own offices and courtrooms, leaving only about ten people behind. So much for the great interest in this case the media had claimed! Carolyn felt a certain weary annoyance about that.

The bailiff called order. Judge Rombauer came in amid a rustle and confusion of getting up and sitting down. The case was called. The jury filed in, some members of it smiling and nodding at people in the courtroom. Were they neighbors? Relatives? Carolyn shook her head slowly. What attendance there was had come to watch the jury more than they had the trial.

The attorneys went through their ritual minuet, declaring their presence and preparedness. Carolyn thought, absurdly, that the whole thing should be set to music. Drums for the bailiff, fanfare for the judge, solemn horns for the jury.

And then the trombone, proclaiming an oily importance: Jagger, who began the prosecution case by calling, in sequence, police officers John Martinez and Ben Lujan, who testified to being tipped about the baby's body, subsequently finding the body, and transporting it to the pathologist. Pictures taken by the police photographer were entered into evidence.

Carolyn elicited information about the mattress, which wasn't shown in the police photographs, and the fact that it was bitterly cold at the time.

Jagger called the pathologist, who testified to the identification of the baby as Lolly Ashaler's baby, through DNA testing. The cause of death of the slightly premature male newborn weighing five pounds eight ounces was exposure, he said. Extreme cold.

Jagger asked, "The child was born alive?"

Very brief pause. The witness looked at the ceiling. "It was, yes. It took at least one breath—there was air in the lungs." When his eyes came back down, he glanced at Carolyn and flushed.

Well, well, she thought without surprise. First suborned witness of this trial. The baby hadn't been alive. Or hadn't lived to take a breath.

Carolyn rose and approached the witness, noting the clenched jaw. The bastard was afraid she'd catch him out in his lie, and she wasn't even going to ask him about that.

"Doctor, when you saw the body, how was it presented to you?"

The jaw relaxed a little. "I don't understand what you mean."

"Was the body clean, washed?"

"Of course not. It was as found, with the umbilical cord intact, still attached to the placenta, wrapped up in paper toweling."

"Placenta, cord, and body, all sort of wrapped up together?"

"That's right."

"To the layman, a bloody mess?"

"I suppose." He sneered his disregard for laymen, an expression that changed to surprise when she said simply:

"Thank you, Doctor. That's all."

Dr. Belmont testified that Lolly was mentally normal and suffered from no psychiatric disease. Carolyn asked her how many times she had seen Lolly and was told one time only.

An elementary schoolteacher, Maria Gallegos, testified that she had taught Lolly Ashaler in fifth grade. Lolly had been a slow student, but not in any sense retarded. Jagger grinned at Carolyn when he strutted back to his chair.

"Mrs. Gallegos, do you remember Lolly well?" Carolyn asked.

"Fairly well."

"Even though it was years ago that you taught her?"

"Yes. I remember some of them. She's one I remember."

"What made you remember Lolly?"

"Objection, Your Honor. What causes any given memory is irrelevant."

"The prosecutor wishes us to believe in this witness's memory, Your Honor. I think we have the right to question it."

"The witness may answer." Rombauer frowned and made a tally on a sheet of paper. The paper was roughly divided into two columns, one headed with a *J* for Jagger, the other with a *D* for the defense. The tally went into the defense column.

The teacher said, "She was always hungry. I don't think she was given food at home, not at all. I used to bring a sandwich in my purse for her. Toward the end of that year she moved in with her grandmother, and she put on a little weight and looked better."

"Did Lolly ever come to school injured?"

"Sometimes, yes."

"What kinds of injuries?"

"The kind that made me refer her to the school nurse, who referred her to the hospital and a social worker."

"What do you think caused the injuries?"

Jagger stood. "Objection, Your Honor. This calls for a conclusion by the witness."

Carolyn said, "The witness is an experienced teacher. She sees children all the time. She has enough experience to draw conclusions of this kind."

Rombauer said in a bored voice, "Sustained." He made a tally in the *J* column.

The teacher looked daggers at Jagger, which he pretended not to see.

The woman had something she wanted to say. Carolyn gave her an opening. "Was she a good student?"

The witness's reply came too quickly for Jagger to stop her. "No, because someone was beating on her. Probably her mother's boyfriend, that's usually who it is about that age."

Jagger was getting to his feet.

Carolyn asked, "About that age?"

"Puberty. When they start to look like women—"

"Your Honor," thundered Jagger.

"The jury will disregard the last questions and answers," said Judge
Rombauer, giving Carolyn a dirty look.

"Thank you," said Carolyn to the witness.

Jagger was on his feet. "Mrs. Gallegos, did Lolly ever tell you she was
abused by someone?"

"No. Not directly."

"Did she tell you that's why she went to live with her grandmother?"

"Not directly, no."

"So that's merely your interpretation, right?"

"On the evidence I saw," said the woman stubbornly, thrusting her chin
forward. "That child was hurt, and she was hungry. Then she lived with her
grandma and she wasn't hurt or hungry anymore."

Jagger shrugged, letting it go. He had established that Lolly was normal;
that's all that really mattered. He called Lolly's mother to the stand, Maxine
Ashaler.

Maxine said she never drank when she was pregnant with Lolly, only
years later, when Lolly was in school. Lolly was healthy, she said. The public-
health nurse used to come see Lolly every month or so, and Lolly was healthy.

"Your witness," said Jagger with a grin, not bothering to hide his triumph.

"Ms. Ashaler, how old are you?"

"Twenny-nine."

"So you had Lolly when you were fourteen?"

"Yeah. 'Bout then."

"How did your mother feel about that?"

"She wannet me to, you know, not have the baby. She said I couldn't
take care of it. Because I'm, you know, a little slow. But some people, they
help me have it. They give me baby clothes and stuff."

"What people?"

"People. They said I had a right."

"They gave you baby clothes? What else did they give you? Money to
support you and Lolly?"

"No. Jus' the clothes. Not new ones."

"Did they take you to the hospital for checkups? Did they buy you
groceries?"

"No, I said awready. Jus' the clothes." The woman looked fretfully at
Jagger, who was paying no attention. Judge Rombauer seemed to be asleep.
"They wasn't even new clothes."

"So it was your mother who supported you and who took care of Lolly when she was a baby."

"Yeah. Well. She said we should get married, him and me, so we did, but he went off. So me 'n' Lolly, we lived with Mom."

"Ms. Ashaler, you do drink a lot now, don't you?" Carolyn asked.

"Well, not right now. I got dried out."

"Up until Mr. Jagger put you into the hospital, you did drink."

"Well, yeah."

"Why?"

"Why what?"

"Why do you drink?"

"Whattahell kinda question's that?"

"I'll try to make it clearer. Do you drink because it makes you feel better?"

" 'Sthere some other reason?"

"You drink because it makes you feel better. When you don't drink, you feel bad pretty much all the time. Is that right?"

"I guess."

"You moved into an apartment of your own?"

"Yeah. Later on."

"When Lolly was ten or eleven years old, did your boyfriend live with you?"

"Yeah."

"And you and he used to drink together, right?"

"Sometimes. Sure."

"Did he abuse Lolly?"

"All he did was he hugged her some, put her on his lap, like."

"Hugged her so she couldn't move, and put her on his lap with his penis sticking into her, isn't that right?"

"How'd I know? He said he never did that."

"When he was drunk, he used to hit her?"

"When he's drunk, he hits on ever'body. Not just her."

"So Lolly went back to your mother's place."

"Yeah."

"But then your mother got sick and died."

"Yeah."

"No further questions," said Carolyn.

After lunch Jagger called Dr. George Fulling, who went over his qualifications and experience at length, went on for some time about fetal alcohol syndrome, and then testified that Lolly Ashaler did not have it.

"Hospital records indicate she was a normal infant. Emergency-room records of several childhood injuries show no sign that she was anything but normal. Looking at her now, I can say that her eyes appear normal, her nose appears normal, she displays none of the facial characteristics of an FAS person."

"In your opinion, does she have any genetic problem?"

"Not in my opinion."

"Thank you, Doctor."

Carolyn frowned at her notes, as though dismayed. Jagger grinned, then hid the grin behind his hand. Carolyn rose. "Dr. Fulling, you mentioned that Lolly Ashaler was treated for several childhood injuries. Can you tell us what those were?"

"Why, let me think. She broke her wrist on the school playground, a spiral break, not too serious. And a broken rib, from a fall. And there were contusions once."

"You don't work with abused children, do you, Doctor?"

"No. I don't."

"So you probably wouldn't know whether the injuries in the record were consistent with injuries observed among abused children?"

"I'm sorry. I simply wouldn't know."

"Do you recall from the records a treatment for a venereal disease when Lolly was ten?"

The doctor frowned, said with distaste, "Yes. I do."

Carolyn frowned. "Dr. Fulling, you said Lolly was normal. Is there a range of normalcy?"

He looked surprised. "There is wide variation, yes."

Jagger rose. "Your Honor, what bearing does this—"

Carolyn interrupted. "This witness testified that my client is normal, Your Honor. I am merely trying to ascertain the meaning of 'normalcy' as used by this witness."

Judge Rombauer frowned, as though remembering something unpleasant, then mumbled, "Overruled, Mr. Jagger. The witness may answer." He made a tally.

Carolyn, looking up in surprise, realized that Rombauer was keeping score! He'd been told off by Judge Frieze, so he'd decided to overrule Jagger every now and then. What was he doing, flipping a coin? Or just alternating yes's and no's?

She went on bemusedly, "Let me see if I understand you. In most respects normal people are genetically much alike, but they can vary considerably in the details."

The doctor nodded. "There are many variations among people who are considered normal."

Jagger rose. "Your Honor . . ."

Rombauer nodded. "Move along please, counselor."

Carolyn smiled. "So two people can both be normal, and still be quite unlike each other?"

"I said that."

"That's all, Your Honor. Thank you, Dr. Fulling."

Carolyn had important questions for only one of the afternoon witnesses, the last one, the neighbor who had told Lolly she was pregnant.

"Mrs. Maquina, when you told Lolly she was pregnant, was she surprised?"

"I dohn know. Maybe."

"It's important, Mrs. Maquina. Do you think Lolly knew she was pregnant?"

The woman stared into the middle distance, face working, saying at last: "I dohn guess so, no. She never seem to know much. Never seem very much anything, you know? Never happy. Never cryin'. Awways just sort of . . . nothing."

"Thank you, Mrs. Maquina."

The prosecution was finished. Rombauer recessed the trial for the day. Carolyn went home to find that Ophy and Jessamine had fixed dinner and the eastern contingent, newly arrived, was setting the table.

"I may have found a clue to Sophy's whereabouts," Hal told them when they were seated around the table. "That is, based on what you told Carolyn on the phone last night."

"How?" breathed Bettiann.

"Where?" demanded Faye, more to the point.

"Well," said Hal around a mouthful of chicken casserole, "I started with a bunch of dead ends. The foundation correspondence mentions the Lizard Rock or Piedras Lagartonas schools, but the state education office has no record of there ever being a school at such a place; the postal service says it never had a post office by that name. You got the name of a postmaster, but the federal postal service has never heard of Chendi Qowat.

"The women in Vermont, however, remembered Sophy saying the place was south, near Mexico. I've got a friend who was with the post office in Deming when he was younger. We used to go fishing together and then lie about what we caught, so I called him, told him we were trying to find this Lizard Rock place, and he broke out laughing. Said there hadn't been such a place for thirty or forty years.

"So I asked him where it had been when it was a place, and he told me when he was a young man, he used to drop off mail for Lizard Rock at a roadside box in Cloverdale, to be picked up by someone else. He says once in a while there was an old man waiting for him, driving an old school bus."

"Old school bus?" asked Faye. "Sophy said the man who brought her food in the desert lived in a . . . what? Old yellow bus . . ."

"So you told us. Anyhow, the route man said the old guy told him he was from Piedras Lagartonas, which was a little south of the Spring of Contention—"

"Which is what one of Sophy's women said," Faye interjected.

"There's no such place," said Agnes flatly.

Hal picked up a map book from beside her and handed it to her. "I wouldn't have thought so, either," he said. "But I spent a little time with a magnifying glass, going over the latest edition of Shearer's *Roads of New Mexico*, the 1998 edition. Here on page one twenty-four, just below the gray-blue area labeled Coronado National Forest. Blue letters, very small."

"My lord," said Agnes reverently. "That's what it says. Spring of Contention. But there are no roads anywhere near it."

"Which is probably why nobody knows where it is," offered Faye.

Hal said, "I looked up that section in some of the previous editions of that atlas, going back to the eighties, and they also show the Spring of Contention. It's probably a spring to which the water rights have been contested. Some of these water cases can go on practically forever. Whatever it is, it's been there awhile."

"The distance cross-country from the nearest improved road is about ten miles," said Carolyn, unfolding another map. "Here on this topo map it looks like one could pick a route that avoids the steeper hills. There are a lot of dirt roads down there, and there may be others that aren't on the map, as well. We'll find our way."

"But where, exactly?" Agnes asked. "Where is this?"

Eyes still fixed on the map, Carolyn said, "It's in the far southwest corner of the state, a thirty-by-fifty-mile chunk of Hidalgo County that sticks down into Mexico. I've never been there."

Hal stretched, got up to get a glass of water, saying over his shouder, "Hunters go there looking for javelina. Cloverdale and Antelope Wells used to be on maps of the area; they're not even shown on most maps now. There is a border crossing called the Antelope Wells crossing, south of where the town used to be, but that's across the continental divide from what you're looking for."

"How do we get there?"

Carolyn turned to the front of the book, where the whole state was shown on a single page, and traced out the route. "We borrow a Land Rover from some friends of mine. We drive south to Las Cruces, here, then west to Deming, then west some more until road one forty-six cuts off to the south. Let's see, then we go south to the town of Hachita, set in the Hachita Valley alongside the . . . Little Hatchet Mountains—sort of a bilingual landscape.

Then where? Here we take a more-or-less road, number nine, west again, about thirty miles to this town called Animas. From there we head south on another more-or-less road, number three thirty-eight, which, hmmm . . . pretty soon becomes a less-and-less road. We'll definitely need a cross-country vehicle."

"And?" prompted Faye.

"And," Carolyn said, "we'll hunt for whatever Piedras Lagartonas is or was, if anything."

"And what do we expect to find?" demanded Jessamine. "A ghost town? A cemetery? Sophy's grave?"

"I haven't any idea," said Carolyn. "But I think we have to go down there and—"

The ringing of her bedroom phone, from down the hall, interrupted her, and she got up to answer it.

"Carolyn?" came the voice. "This is Mike Winter."

"Mike! Do you want Hal?"

"I have a message for Hal. Tell him I called in some IOUs, plus I'll be sending you that stuff he asked for. Okay?"

"He's right here, Mike—"

"No time, dear. Just tell him." And he was gone.

They were talking about something else when she returned to the kitchen; she didn't mention the call. Only when she and Hal were alone together later that night, in bed with the door closed, did she tell him what Mike had said.

"Called in some IOUs?" she said doubtfully.

He shrugged. "Those pictures Helen sent you? The information on Rombauer had to be investigated by the locals, but they'd have paid no attention to me, or to you. Jagger would be able to prevent that."

"So what has Mike done?"

"We'll have to wait and see. Something. Though it's getting rather late to be helpful."

"He mentioned stuff you asked for?"

"I asked him to send whatever he knew about the Alliance and this guy Webster."

When the court reconvened on Tuesday morning, defense's first witness was Ophy Gheist, M.D.

Carolyn asked, "Dr. Gheist, do you have experience in obstetrics?"

"I do. My specialty was gynecology and obstetrics up until ten years ago, when I switched to emergency medicine."

"Was your experience confined to the United States?"

"No. I did postdoctoral research in primate reproduction as well as the childbirth practices of native peoples in Africa, South America, and New Guinea. I also studied obstetrical and gynecological health systems in countries medically more advanced than the United States."

"There are countries more advanced?"

"Several, yes."

"How do you characterize an advanced system?"

"If we take low maternal and neonatal mortality and morbidity rates as the indicator, we'd say an advanced system is one that identifies all women at risk of pregnancy, regardless of age or economic condition, and provides that entire population with preventive health care, which must include contraception, particularly contraceptive implants for sexually active women who aren't responsible: the very young, those who have certain disabilities, and those who are substance abusers. This early intervention prevents the conception of babies who would be drug addicted, who would have fetal alcohol syndrome, or who would be infected with HIV, all of whom are now born in great numbers in this country."

One of the jurors frowned slightly, as though at a sudden thought.

Ophy noticed the interest and spoke directly to that juror: "Also, in advanced systems there is routine provision of pre- and postnatal care, childbirth education, parenting education, and monitoring of the infant for several years following birth. Needless to say, there is also provision of food for children, so none of them go hungry. Holland and the Scandinavian countries have systems like this. They have almost no teen pregnancies or drug-addicted babies, and no hungry children."

"How does this differ from a system that is not advanced?"

"Some systems are primitive and some are barbaric. Primitive systems exist where people don't know any better or don't have the resources to provide care. Infant and maternal mortality are high. Barbaric systems are interested only in babies; they don't care if the woman is dying or drug addicted or alcoholic or if she's twelve years old or retarded or has AIDS. They will not make it easy for her to prevent a pregnancy or to abort one. For an example we can look at Communist Romania. The regime wanted babies, they insisted that every woman have at least five, they forbade contraception and forced women to have children they couldn't provide for. Many of the chidren were abandoned. When the Communist government was overthrown, state nurseries were packed with hundreds of thousands of abandoned children, many of them sick, many of them congenitally disabled. You can see the same thing in Latin America, where contraception is forbidden by the Church and hundreds of thousands of children are simply abandoned on the streets." Her voice tightened. "There are killer squads in those countries, armed men who go out at night and shoot kids. I've talked with some of them. They feel they are public-health workers, eliminating a menace, just as they'd shoot rats."

The jury stirred uneasily. Carolyn let the discomfort build for a moment before asking, "How would you characterize the system in the United States?"

"At the present time, under the current administration, we actually have two systems in this country—an advanced one for well-to-do and well-educated people, and a barbaric one rather like Communist Romania for the poor."

"Into which category would the defendant fall?"

"She's poor and uneducated."

"And what does our barbaric system provide people like her?"

"Little or nothing. The current government doesn't routinely provide sex education or abortion or contraception or parenting education. Public-health programs aimed at the poor have been cut. Feeding programs for poor women and children have been cut. Frequently, women don't even get to the hospital to have the baby."

"Why is that?"

"If a woman is an addict, if she's very young, if she's mentally retarded, if she's sick, if she's ignorant about pregnancy and childbirth, if she's scared, if she had no one to help her, if she doesn't know she's pregnant or denies that fact, she might not get to the hospital. Sometimes denial is so great that the whole episode is unreal, including the infant itself."

"You're saying the woman doesn't realize she's pregnant?"

"It's a matter of learning. Among all animals, including humans, getting pregnant is purely biological. Impregnation, pregnancy, and birth are all mechanical, instinctive, totally programmed. We like to pretend that we can control it, that a woman can control it. The truth is, she alone cannot. If a girl is not to become prematurely pregnant, her family or society has to protect her. Girls living in areas where there is no protection have no defense. They are at the mercy of sexual predators and a million years of evolution. Not getting pregnant takes a lot of thought and planning and care and attention and goodwill. Getting pregnant doesn't take any thought at all, it just happens."

"What about the 'just say no' approach?"

"I think you can visualize what happens when a girl weighing a hundred ten says no to two or three male predators weighing a total of five hundred pounds. Or if she says no to her mother's boyfriend. Or if she says no to her incestuous father or brother. Or if she says no to someone who's drunk or high. Or if she says no to her own boyfriend, the guy she stays with because he protects her against ten other guys, or maybe simply because she has no one else."

"So she gets pregnant. Then she has the baby."

"Then she has the baby. If the child is going to live, it has to be cared for. Girls learn how to provide care by watching mothers. If they don't learn how, their own babies die."

"You have seen this happen?"

"I've seen births where the infant was simply ignored, or disposed of, and I've seen babies die of neglect."

"But that's rare?"

"No! It isn't rare. We like to pretend it's an aberration, but it isn't. There are lots of Dumpster babies every year in this country, and for every Dumpster baby that's discovered, there are probably twenty that no one ever knows about. And on top of that, every doctor or public-health nurse knows of infants who die later, or end up in foster care or institutions simply because the mother doesn't care about them or know how to care for them."

"But isn't motherhood instinctive?"

"It's instinctive among animals who have young in bunches, like alligators, pigs, dogs, fish. It's instinctive among animals who don't live very long, like mice, rabbits, spiders. It's instinctive among animals with precocial young, like an antelope or a chicken. It isn't instinctive for animals who live a long time and have helpless babies, one at a time. If an infant needs care for years, you have to learn how to provide it. Some primate females pick it up fairly quickly; others don't learn it until they've had several pregnancies; most important, some aren't interested in learning it or can't learn it. It's like music: Some people are born with perfect pitch, others can be taught to sing a little, and some are born tone deaf. It's not their fault—they just can't hear music. Not every person with ears can be a good musician; not every person with a throat can be a good singer; not every woman with a uterus can become a good mother."

The courtroom rustled; there were whispers; Judge Rombauer looked up with the expression of someone waking from a doze.

Carolyn asked quickly, "Dr. Gheist, are you familiar with Lolly Ashaler's history?"

"I am, yes. I've seen her medical records. I've examined her medically and I've taken a case history and talked with her at length."

"Had she learned to be a mother?"

"She hadn't even learned to be a person."

Someone in the courtroom giggled. There were murmurs in several voices. Rombauer tapped his gavel. Jagger, who had also been distracted, rose with his teeth clenched. "Your Honor, I object to this continuing—"

"Do move it along, counselor," said the judge with an apologetic look at Jagger.

Carolyn waited for the room to quiet. "Does Lolly Ashaler fit the pattern of a woman who doesn't know enough to mother a child?"

Ophy nodded slowly. "She's totally ignorant of mothering. She was not mothered as a child. Her own mother acquiesced in her sexual abuse; her mother's boyfriend gave her a venereal disease; the pregnancy was caused by a gang rape—"

Jagger again. "Your Honor! This hasn't been established."

Carolyn: "Your Honor, we will establish the rape. In the meantime the witness is a physician. She has talked with the defendant; she has examined the defendant."

"Hearsay, Your Honor!"

Judge Rombauer stared over the tops of his glasses.

Carolyn took a deep breath. "May we point out that Mr. Jagger called Dr. Belmont as a witness, and all Dr. Belmont knew about the defendant is what the defendant told her during one interview. A case history taken by a professional is not usually regarded as hearsay."

Rombauer was flipping a mental coin again, she could tell. He had his pencil ready to make his little tick mark.

"The witness may answer."

Jagger subsided, jaw set.

"Doctor? You were saying?"

"I was saying this girl was neglected, abused, finally gang-raped and abused further. She shows scarring around the vagina that's consistent with the forcible insertion of sharp-edged objects. She had no experience of care or nurturing. She wouldn't have known what to do with a baby, even if it had been cleaned up, wrapped in a blanket, and put in her arms. Much less did she know what to do when she was all alone in a cold alley, on a rotten mattress, half-frozen, and not thinking at all."

"Dr. Gheist, did she murder the baby?"

"In my opinion she couldn't even think in those terms. She didn't have the vocabulary to tell herself what was happening. She was in great pain, this bloody mess of tissue came out of her, she wrapped it up and put it where one puts such things. She didn't think the word 'baby,' and she didn't think the word 'kill.' If you take a kid who's never seen a car and put him behind the wheel with the car running and the brake off and tell him to drive, it will be senseless to accuse the kid of vehicular homicide when he kills someone. It is just that senseless to hold young women responsible for babies they are totally unprepared for."

"Thank you, Doctor."

Jagger rose, his jaw set.

"Doctor, you say this girl was all alone, half-frozen. Why?"

"Because there was no one with her and the weather was cold."

"Wasn't she alone so no one would see what she did? Didn't she go there because it was a good place to get rid of the baby?"

"She didn't know what was going on."

His lip curled. "Come now, Doctor. We have sex freely discussed on television, all day and all night. We have the most esoteric details concerning reproduction fully covered on talk shows. What do you mean, she didn't know what was going on?"

Ophy turned pink. Her lips thinned. "I know of no obstetrician who has ever recommended that a woman get her childbirth information from Oprah, Mr. Jagger. Expectant mothers attend childbirth classes for weeks in order to learn what goes on during labor. They see films; they are instructed and drilled; and they practice. They even have labor coaches to help them. If they could pick it up from talk shows, none of that would be necessary."

"Dr. Gheist . . ."

"I'm not finished. Lolly Ashaler had none of that. She was told she was pregnant, but nobody told her about labor. She was in pain. She was afraid because she'd been threatened. She went back to the same place she'd been raped and had the baby there because she wanted to hide. She literally didn't know what was happening."

"Was that rational, to go into a cold alley and give birth on a rotten mattress?"

"Of course it wasn't rational, she wasn't rational. When a creature is sick and in pain and scared, it is instinctive to crawl away and hide, which is what she did."

"And you have seen mothers leave their newborns and just walk away?" His tone accused her of lying.

"I have, yes."

"Where?"

"During times of civil war in Africa, and I've also seen it in documentary films."

"What a pity we do not have them here," he said, his voice heavy with sarcasm.

"I think the court will have an opportunity to see them," Ophy said angrily.

Jagger turned, standing where he was, and stared at Carolyn. She caught his gaze full, the dead depth of his eyes regarding her incuriously, as though she had ceased to matter, as though in that instant he had disposed of her.

"Ms. Crespin?" asked the judge.

"No further questions, Your Honor." Her throat was dry. She barely got the words out. He's only a man, she told herself. Only a man.

Rombauer glanced at his watch, mumbled something about having an appointment and recessing early for lunch, to reconvene at two. Carolyn told Ophy and Jessamine she'd meet them out front, then went out into the hall on her way to the rest room. She needed a private moment. She felt as if she'd been running a marathon.

She was stopped by a hand on her shoulder. Jerry.

"What are you doing over here?" she asked.

"Came to see you, Carolyn. Come on over here." He led her around a corner in the hallway, out of sight of the people milling around outside the courtroom. "I heard it on the car radio, so I thought I'd better tell you."

"What? I've got people waiting, Jerry—"

"Emmet Swinter. They found his body just before noon. Southeast of town somewhere, out in the desert, off a side road."

The urge to pee vanished. She swallowed. "Murder?"

"The report said a car accident. He'd been dead for days. Open bottles in the car. Possibly alcohol related. I knew old Emmet fairly well. I never thought he had a drinking problem."

"First the kid who broke into my house, who had a map in his pocket. Now Emmet Swinter, who labeled the map for him." She felt her face grow tight. "It wasn't an accident, Jerry. You'll say I'm being paranoid. Damn it, I know it wasn't an accident."

"Who, Carolyn?"

"Jagger." She almost whispered the name.

"Surely he wouldn't . . ."

"Himself? Maybe not, but he's got people who would. According to my sources he's got a guy named Martin who does his dirty work. Disposals included."

He regarded her soberly, took off his glasses, polished them on his tie, put them back, rubbed his head. All the usual Jerry gestures. "Be careful," he murmured. "Damn it, Carolyn. Be careful."

How does one be careful? she asked herself on the way to lunch. Be careful of what, whom? Be careful when? One might as well try to be careful of falling asteroids, or earthquakes. She moved automatically, ordered food without thought. When they had been served, she pushed her food around, unable to eat it.

"What's the matter?" asked Jessamine. "Don't you like the way it's going? I thought Ophy was great. She had every person in that courtroom thinking."

"Ophy was great, but I hate long breaks in testimony," Carolyn muttered. "You just get rolling and then everything stops."

She could not see her own face, which was tight, pale, and apprehensive.

"It's all right," said Jessamine. "We'll get up steam again." She shared a worried look with Ophy. Both of them watched Carolyn, but Carolyn was focused somewhere else.

When court reconvened, Carolyn called Jessamine to the stand. "Will you tell the jury your professional qualifications?"

"I have a Ph.D. in molecular genetics. My recent work has focused upon the genetic components of behavior."

"Can you explain what that means?"

"We inherit some behavior, some we learn. We inherit breathing, for instance, but we have to learn to blow a trumpet. When we're born, we already know how to cry or laugh or giggle, but we have to learn words. We're born knowing how to eat, but we have to learn table manners. We inherit sexuality, we have to learn parenting."

"Can you tell us how these matters are studied—parenting, for example?"

"Studying primates tells us a great deal about humans. . . ."

Jagger was on his feet. "Objection, Your Honor. What monkeys do is what monkeys do. Is counsel suggesting that the defendant is a monkey?"

"Your Honor, if we may proceed, the connection will be clear."

Rombauer opened his mouth, closed it, checked his tally sheet, and said fretfully, "I will allow it for the moment, counselor."

"Before you talk about primate research, Dr. Ortiz, perhaps it would help to clarify the connection and similarities between primates and people."

"I have some charts that will show you the genetic similarities. Humans and primates are genetically alike in many respects."

The charts were admitted in evidence and put on easels where the jury could see them. Faye had outdone herself; she had taken the information provided by Jessamine and made it seem simple and understandable. The charts showed overlaps in genetic material, similarities in behaviors, diet, life span, child rearing.

"We share ninety-nine percent of our DNA with chimps. Even with siamangs we share a very high percentage, ninety-five to ninety-seven percent. Both animals are very closely related to us; chimps are the closest. We have the same blood types. We are different from chimps by only one percent. That one percent accounts for our hip and leg structure, which allows upright striding, and for our throat, tongue, and brain structure, which allows us to create and learn complex language. Other differences are actually rather minor. Most important in this case: Chimp babies and human babies are very much alike when they're born; they can suckle, make noises, wave their hands and feet; they have to learn almost everything else. Whatever apes have to learn when they're born, we have to learn when we're born."

"So we can look at the chimp for clues to our own behavior."

"Exactly. Our behavior and our development. If we take a female baby chimpanzee and raise it in isolation, where it gets no affection and has no opportunity to see others, it never learns how to relate to others. If we then put it with others of its kind, it will mate and give birth, but almost certainly it will not parent. We learn from this that mating and birth are instinctive, but parenting is not."

"So a primate raised in isolation cannot be a good mother."

"That's true. The degree of neglect may vary, but there is always neglect. It is true of apes, it is true of people. And it's not only true of parenting, it's true of other behaviors. I have a film that will illustrate some of the similarities."

Carolyn took the tape from her table. "Your Honor, we would like this film entered as defense exhibit B."

Jagger rose. "We have not seen this film, Your Honor. We have no way of knowing what it represents."

Carolyn said, "Though the film was ordered some time ago, it arrived only recently. It is a documentary, drawn from news clips and nature films."

Jagger said, "We have only defense counsel's word for that!"

"Approach," Rombauer ordered. When they were close before him, he said, almost in a whine, "Counselor, if this tape illustrates the point your witness just made, why is a film necessary?"

"Your Honor, the prosecution is alleging first-degree murder with a possible penalty of death. They have shown pictures of the dead infant. My client deserves the best possible defense, including evidence that may offset the prosecution's use of pictorial evidence. We have no pictures of the defendant being raped or in childbirth. We do have pictures of similar situations, however, and they are the next best thing."

Rombauer chewed his lip, obviously thinking. Would this or wouldn't it lead to reversal on appeal? Silently, Carolyn blessed Judge Frieze. At least the old man was having to think about it. Jake obviously didn't like that fact. He was fuming.

Rombauer said, "I will allow the tape to be run. I have your word, counselor, that there is nothing on this tape but what you have described."

"Yes, Your Honor."

The tape was put into the courtroom visual system, appearing on a large screen beside the witness chair.

Jessamine gave a running commentary. "We'll start with a couple of sequences that illustrate the similarities in instinctive behavior. This first section was taken several decades ago, before chimps went extinct in the wild. This is a small troop of wild chimpanzees. To the right of the picture you will see a leopard. When the leopard gets closer, watch the faces and behavior of the chimpanzees."

The leopard was noticed. Chimp eyes opened wide. Chimp lips drew back in a fanged grimace. Panic there. Fear. Anger. The apes screamed defiance, showing their teeth, their noses wrinkled, arms drawn back, some holding sticks as weapons, a bouncing, screaming display, apes advancing and retreating, hit and run, panic, anger.

Jessamine said, "The next sequence shows this same group being approached by a stranger, a chimpanzee who is not a member of this troop."

The expressions were similar to the first time, panic and fear and anger. The larger males ran toward the stranger, struck him, retreated, while the females and young screamed from safe vantage points. The intruder stood his ground only briefly, then retreated.

"Please note these individuals," said Jessamine as images of single chimps were removed from the context and placed one by one in a line across the top of the screen. Females. Males. Fear. Anger. Attack. Arms raised to throw missiles. Lips pulled back, noses wrinkled. "Remember those six faces. We'll be coming back to them.

"This next film was taken in Boston decades ago, when the Boston schools were integrated and black children were bused into Southy, a white neighborhood. Please observe the faces in the crowd."

Policemen holding back crowds. Buses carrying black children. White people massed behind the police showing panic, rage, and fear; lips drawn back to show teeth, arms raised to hit or throw. The film centered on one particular view while the head and shoulders of a middle-aged woman were circled; then other views were held while other persons, male and female, were circled. Six heads and torsos were removed from the context and lined up on the screen under those of the previously selected apes. The expressions and stance were similar, and when the human figures were rotated slightly, then moved up and superimposed on the apes, it could be seen that, allowing for the difference in anatomy, they were virtually identical.

"These Bostonians were civilized people," said Jessamine. "They had language, literacy, and religion, but when their familiar world was threatened, they forgot language, literacy, and religion and responded instinctively in the same way a chimpanzee would. We might find the same facial expressions, the same physical reaction, among people anywhere in the world. Chimps raiding a food store look much like looters raiding a TV store. Apes killing one of their own do it furtively, just as people would. Apes killing a stranger are like lynchers—hooting, yelling, urging one another on. I have thousands of feet of tape showing similar faces: in Guatemala, where a mob attacked a woman they believed to be a kidnapper; in Serbia during the Balkan wars; in Somalia and Rwanda during tribal conflicts; in Armenia, Algeria, and Ireland during religious conflicts; here in the U.S. outside abortion clinics. They are the purely animal expressions one sees in any mob.

"The next sequence covers reproduction." The film went on. Clips of chimps mating, chimps giving birth, mothers licking the babies clean, cuddling them while other females watched, babies being passed around for all the females to hold. "Notice the young female to the left," said Jessamine. "Sitting next to the mother with the newborn. Notice her face, notice how she smells the baby and touches it. Notice how closely she follows the mother, watching the baby all the time. In a few days she will start borrowing the baby, carrying it around as she practices caring for it. She will watch and practice like this for months, until the baby is able to move on its own; then she will start borrowing another baby. This is how apes learn to parent. They can't do it unless they've learned to do it.

"This next sequence is of a female who was raised in isolation, giving birth."

They saw the birth, the expression on the face. Fear. Anger. Panic, as the feeble infant was pushed away, buried under straw, trod upon, ignored.

"Chimp infants are helpless for the first four weeks of life," said Jessamine. "Mothers have to carry them at least that long, until they can cling. If an infant isn't carried and nursed, it dies."

The courtroom was quiet, every eye fixed on the screen.

"The last sequence on this film is human. It was taken during the Bosnian conflict of ninety-three–ninety-four. A woman photographer was part of a team documenting atrocities committed during that conflict; she'd been caught away from her team when an attack occurred, and she took refuge in a barn occupied by a half-dozen refugees. The woman at the back of the picture had been repeatedly raped by Serbs, impregnated, had escaped, had been hiding, and this film shows her giving birth."

The film, in badly lit black-and-white, observed a haggard woman lying on the straw, hands frantically pulling, feet braced, face contorted. Then a sudden relaxation. For a time the woman lay as though stunned. There was another quaver, and she lay for a time again. Then she sat up, pushed herself away from the bloody mess in the straw, and pulled clean straw down to cover it. The straw moved. The woman looked away from it, her face twisted. She staggered to her feet, stepped over the straw without looking at it, and went away. The film ended.

Carolyn waited while murmurs in the courtroom subsided. "Do you see a parallel, Dr. Ortiz, between the film you have shown us and the case before this court?"

"I can cite many studies which establish that parenting is a largely learned activity. I know from talking with the defendant that she never learned anything about parenting. Though we have used chimps as examples, men and women are also primates, and their instinctive behavior is similar. I have seen women reject newborn infants when hurt or helpless. I know that the defendant had no help at all and she was impregnated through forcible, painful rape. She was an extremely poor risk as a parent."

"Did she commit murder, Dr. Ortiz?"

"If there was a murder, the murder was done by the society that allows young men to grow up as rapists, the society that allowed this girl to stay ignorant, that offered her no help before she became pregnant, and that offered her no help once she was."

"I have no further questions," said Carolyn.

Jagger was already on his feet. "Dr. Ortiz," he said, voice bearing down on the "doctor," sneering the title, making it doubtful. "You are telling this court that this defendant is not responsible for killing her child?"

"She never thought of it as her child, any more than that Bosnian woman did. She didn't think at all."

"She gave birth to it!"

"Her *body* gave birth to it. Our bodies do a lot of things we don't want or intend them to. We catch the flu, but that doesn't make us experts on infectious diseases. We break out in hives, but that doesn't make us allergists. When a girl gets raped, why do we believe that being pregnant makes her an expert on childbirth and parenting? It's ridiculous."

"She was a mother! She had to take care of it!"

His voice was outraged, almost trembling. Carolyn looked up, curiously. Here was the Hail Mary Assumption in spades. What would Jessamine do with it?

"No," Jessamine said at last. "That rule was made by men. Men have no experience of childbirth or pregnancy; few of them have experienced rape, but they believe their seed is somehow so important that women must not only submit to it but also honor and serve it impeccably. Men make laws saying so. Notwithstanding, the law can't make a woman accept a pregnancy she hasn't wanted and agreed to. She may choose to accept it, of her own will, but merely being impregnated doesn't make a mother. It never has."

She took a breath; then, moved by some obscure impulse, she blurted, "As for fathering, raping a woman sure doesn't make a father."

His eyes blazed at her. "You're aware that courts have repeatedly held the rights even of biological fathers who were unaware of the pregnancy."

Jessamine met his eyes calmly, refusing to be browbeaten. "In 1999, however, the Supreme Court let stand a state law that says no man can ever assert parental rights to a child unless he was legally married to the mother of the child at the time of the conception and at the time of the birth. Human parenting is done by intention. Without that intention human parenthood doesn't happen. Cells don't make a parent. Being there does."

Jagger was ashen, almost immobilized by fury.

"Counselor?" asked the judge, eyebrows raised. "Mr. Jagger?"

For a moment he merely stood. "No further questions," he grated, almost unintelligibly.

"Ms. Crespin?" said the judge.

There were a dozen questions Carolyn wanted to ask, but not here, not now. Why was Jagger in a rage? It was more than anger at her for having tricked him. More than annoyance. Something primal, some age-old grievance he had with the world.

"No further questions of this witness, Your Honor. I call Gilbert Devaca."

Lolly reached up and clutched her sleeve, whispering urgently, "What you doin' with him? You don't want to talk to him!"

Carolyn leaned down. "Lolly, take it easy. He'll be a good witness for you—just hush. I'll take care of you."

Gilbert Devaca was sworn, a stocky boy in his midteens, who gave an address just down the block from the Ashaler apartment.

"Mr. Devaca, on the Fourth of July last year, 1999, did you and a group of boys take Lolly Ashaler over to the area behind El Camino machine shops?"

"Yeah. We was just foolin' aroun'."

"When you got there, was Lolly Ashaler raped?"

"Well, yeah, I suppose. Crank, he had her. An' Henry B., he stuck a bottle in her."

"You didn't do either of those things?"

"No."

"Did she object? Did she fight?"

"She was yelling and there was blood all over."

"Why was Lolly raped?"

"She was . . . it was kind of a test, like."

"A test."

"Henry B. said Crank couldn't do it no more, and Crank said Henry B. couldn't, so they got Lolly over there to show they could. Me 'n' the others, we was just there."

"No further questions, Your Honor," said Carolyn.

Jagger declined to ask any questions at all. He sat in his chair, ruminous with anger, staring at two members of the jury, his face clearing as they nodded to him very slightly—so slightly, no one should have noticed.

Carolyn, however, had seen it. Taking a deep breath, she rested her case, saying, "Before summation, Your Honor, may I have a brief recess?"

"Court will reconvene in fifteen minutes."

Carolyn slipped down the aisle and out into the corridor. Where in hell was her investigator? He'd said he'd be here! She looked around for a phone. He had a beeper, if she just had time to . . .

Then she saw him, coming up the stairs. He caught sight of her and nodded.

"What?" she whispered when he came closer.

He handed her several photostats. "They've been arrested two or three times each, in Albuquerque and elsewhere. Clinic blockading. Those are copies of the indictments. They haven't even lived in Santa Fe County long enough to be called for jury duty. They moved in after they were selected. Somebody played games."

"Bless you," she said.

A few moments later the bailiff called for order. Carolyn stood. "Before summation, Your Honor, may I approach?"

Judge Rombauer beckoned to her and to Jagger. Carolyn leaned on the desk, passing over the copies.

"What is this?" the judge asked.

"I have been made aware," Carolyn replied, "that these two jurors lied during jury selection. I specifically asked the panel if they held strong opinions about birth control and abortion. I am now informed that these two people, who answered negatively, have both been arrested for such activities in Albuquerque. These are copies of the indictments."

"I can't see that it makes any difference," grated Jagger, his voice no angrier than his eyes.

Carolyn murmured, "To the contrary. We would assume such persons were prejudiced against the defendant. In any case, they lied. They're guilty of perjury. Also, I have been informed that these people are residents of Bernalillo County. They never should have been called for this jury panel."

"We'd have to check that," snarled Jagger.

"You're asking for a mistrial," said the judge, almost hopefully.

"The alternates haven't been named yet," Carolyn said. "It would be possible to take these two out. It would leave us with no alternates, but on the other hand, deliberations are unlikely to be lengthy and alternates are unlikely to be needed. . . ."

"I'll take it under advisement," said Rombauer, his eyes moving down the copies, from one to the next. "Ah, um, since it's already four-thirty, I think we'll leave summation until morning. That'll give me time to consider this."

Carefully not looking in Jagger's direction, Carolyn gathered up Ophy and Jessamine and departed.

"Jagger was mad," whispered Jessamine.

"He looked like a stroke about to happen," Ophy agreed.

"I know," Carolyn murmured, glad she had parked some distance from the courthouse that morning. At least her car hadn't been sitting right there, inviting someone to put a bomb in it.

When they arrived at the farm, they found the kitchen busy, with Faye, Bettiann, and Agnes much in charge.

"How'd it go?" Hal whispered into Carolyn's hair when she went to the bedroom to change.

"Like yesterday, the courtroom all but empty. If it had just been some other judge. Any other judge. Oh, Hal, I don't know what Jessamine said that did it, but Jagger got so angry at her testimony, he's almost boiling. . . ."

"He's dangerous, Carolyn."

"You don't know how dangerous." She told him about Swinter. "When we came out of the courthouse, I actually worried about whether there might be a bomb in my car!"

"Tomorrow somebody should drive you and pick you up."

"That may get us through tomorrow. What do we do afterward? If we win, he'll come after us. If we lose, he'll come after us. He won't forget this." She wiped at her eyes, which had overflowed. "Hal, I've been feeling this sense of . . . menace, I guess. I'd thought it was the trial, but it wasn't. Isn't. I thought it was Jagger, but it's more than that. I can't shake it!"

"My fault," he murmured. "I brought up Webster's connection."

"Is it Webster that's bothering me? I really don't know for sure. All I know is, I keep wanting to look over my shoulder. I keep feeling like I'm being watched." She shuddered.

"You need to get away from here," he said. "We both do. As soon as this case is over, we'll take a vacation."

Jessamine and Ophy offered to drop Carolyn off at the courthouse Wednesday morning, and then to go elsewhere within range of Carolyn's beeper. Protective paranoia, as Ophy defined it, which was preferable to passive paranoia. Accordingly, the three of them rose early. While Jessamine made coffee and Ophy toasted muffins, Carolyn found a stick and went down the drive to pick up the paper. Her state of mind was measured by the length of the stick she carried to fish the paper out of the box, in case there was a bomb inside. The paper fluttered to the ground, and she turned it over with the stick before picking it up. She didn't look at it until they were at the table. Even then she almost missed the item, not a large one, at the bottom of the front page.

"They got him," she blurted.

"What?" Jessamine asked.

"Rombauer. They've arrested him!"

Almost whispering, she read it aloud. Deactivation vaults had been opened at the behest of the attorney general's office. Three juveniles, restored to movement and sense, testified they had been molested by the judge in return for promised lighter sentences. The setting on their vaults had been life, though the sentence had actually been only two years.

"What will they do?" Ophy asked. "About the trial?"

"I haven't a clue." Carolyn picked up her cup, feeling her hand shake. "One thing I do know. Rombauer won't be on the bench."

"What do we do?"

Carolyn stared at the clock, almost without seeing it. "There's no one at the courthouse this early, so we can't call. Probably the best thing to do is go on into town as planned. We'll find out when we get there."

She went to wake Hal, who had his head buried under the pillow, resolutely unconscious. She had to tell him three times before he opened his eyes.

"So it came off." He grinned sleepily, the grin of an old wolf who hadn't forgotten anything he'd ever known about wolfing. "Your friend Josh is quite a guy."

"You had him in on it?"

"I had the pictures, but they weren't enough by themselves. So I found Josh, and he gave me a statement, and I faxed the statement to Mike, along with the pictures, and Mike said he'd push the AG's office to release the three kids and get statements from them. A local reporter got the copies of the pictures from, need I say, an anonymous source, and if it went the way we planned, he and the photographer were waiting when they untanked the kids. My bet is the kids told their story, and why not? They'll probably sell their life histories to make a TV movie."

"Lord, we may actually have a chance with this case! Jagger will be apoplectic!"

He yawned, almost chuckling. "A better chance than I thought you had yesterday."

She shook her head, trying to get whirling thoughts to settle. "Jessy and Ophy are driving me to town. Chances are the trial will be delayed. If it is, we can't afford to waste the day. As soon as it's a reasonable hour, would you call the McCrackens and ask if I can borrow their Land Rover? They offered last time we dog-sat for them while they were in Jamaica. Maybe there'll be time for the DFC to go hunting Lizard Rock."

He pushed himself up against the head of the bed, frowning thoughtfully. "You don't want me to go along?"

"Hal, I can't imagine a seven- or eight-hour drive plus several miles' walk would do a thing for your leg! Besides, someone needs to be here, and . . ." Her voice trailed off. And, she'd been going to say, she had a feeling this was DFC business—among them, only among them.

"I don't like the idea of your going off alone," he said firmly.

"I won't be alone. There's six of us. And here we're sitting ducks. At least on the road we'll be a moving target."

She hurried through dressing, chivvying Jessamine and Ophy into the car and giving them her beeper. "Stay within range. I'll call as soon as I know something." She was in the courtroom by a quarter to nine. The door to the judge's chamber was open, and Judge Loretta Frieze stood in the doorway, talking with the clerk. Seeing Carolyn, she nodded and raised her hand, summoning.

"When Mr. Jagger arrives, I'll have an announcement," she said. "Meantime, I can't see leaving the accused in jail. She's . . . subject to . . . well, she's simply been there far too long." She glared at Carolyn, who had never raised the subject of bail.

"I didn't ask for bail, because she'd been threatened," Carolyn explained. "There was no one to help her on the outside. She was safer where she was."

"Given the current situation, she should be quite safe, don't you think? May I release her in your custody?"

Carolyn fought down an urge to scream. It was the worst possible time for such an arrangement. Judge Frieze had obviously made inquiries into Lolly's welfare, however, and any such gesture should be received generously. She nodded, trying to sound accepting as she said, "Of course, Judge Frieze. She can stay out at the farm." All the beds were taken, but there was a comfortable couch in the study. Probably as comfortable as any other place Lolly had ever slept. But then she couldn't saddle Hal with Lolly while the rest of them went off on this wild-goose chase. They'd have to take Lolly with them.

Carolyn brought up the matter of the perjured jurors. The judge said something brief and unexpectedly obscene, then moved back to her discussion with the clerk. They were obviously trying to rearrange the court calendar, as there was much flicking of pages and penciling of notes.

The double doors at the rear of the courtroom banged open, and Jagger, his anger preceding him like a hot wind, burst into the room with a couple of flunkies in tow. He snarled at Carolyn, grinned viciously in the judge's direction, and threw himself into a chair as though he wanted to destroy it. Judge Frieze gave him an admonishing look and beckoned him to join her and Carolyn.

"I've reviewed the court reporter's transcript. I don't see anything obviously leading to mistrial, though closer reading may bring something to light. Neither of you is precluded from moving for a mistrial."

Jagger merely glared.

Carolyn shook her head. "Not if that jury matter is taken care of."

The judge nodded. "There's no way to proceed with the case today, however. No one's available. In five minutes I'm due to hear another case, but it should be over by the end of the week, and we could continue this case on Monday. There's only summation, right?"

They agreed on Monday. The bailiff went to inform the jurors. Jagger left, glaring straight ahead, not sparing Carolyn a glance. Carolyn called her pager, and Ophy said they'd be back within minutes. They had a few minutes' wait before a guard brought Lolly in, clad as she had been on the previous day, her face blank. The clerk made note of Judge Frieze's order concerning her, and Ophy took her in tow while Carolyn stopped to call Hal and see if he'd arranged for the car. It was in the drive, he said. Fully gassed and ready to go. He'd even started putting together the camp stuff.

Jagger, raging, received a phone call from Martin.

"Checked it out, like you said. I took a look from the hill across the road. They had a big cross-country kind of vehicle in the drive, and the man was packing stuff. I came back here to the office and ran all the tapes. The Crespin woman just got back to her place a few minutes ago. The other women are all there, including the girl. They're mostly moving around outside, so I can't hear what they're saying, but they're going somewhere."

"A cross-country vehicle would indicate someplace remote?"

"That's how I'd see it."

"All of them?"

"They're all packing up. Hunting the one that disappeared, maybe?"

"I want to follow them, Martin. Can you arrange that?" If the women went somewhere remote, he should be able to overtake them, follow them until they found the missing one, then pick them off one at a time, like shooting deer, overpower the last one or two, and get the real information. He'd do it alone, no witnesses. When he got the information, Webster would give him a gold star. He felt the accolades, like champagne in his blood.

Martin said, "I can follow them in my car, put a transmitter on their car when they stop along the way somewhere. Women always do."

"A transmitter I can follow from the helicopter?"

"Sure. I'll send somebody to the airport with the receiver, have them put it in your chopper."

"Thank you, Martin. As usual, you're very helpful."

"That's all right, Mr. Jagger. Always happy to be of service."

Jagger hung up, pleased with the information. If that bitch lawyer and her bitch feminist friends thought she was going to prevail over him, they had another think coming. Webster didn't need to know the details. He would take care of the details himself, very quietly, no one the wiser!

Martin, in his office, hung up the phone and turned to the men seated across from him. "He wants to go after them."

Raymond Keepe waited for Webster to speak. Ever since he had met Webster this morning, he had waited for Webster to speak, to move, to gesture, to indicate what was to be done.

Webster spoke. "I see. Will his machine hold three or four?"

"No, sir. It's a two-seater."

Another wait, then the calculated question: "Can we get a machine large enough for three or four? With you as pilot?"

Martin bit down his feelings about this suggestion. He did not want to go anywhere with Keepe or Keepe's boss. Still, he managed to get the words out: "I've got a friend who's got one, if it's not out on charter. But if you want me to pilot, I'll have to get hold of a man quick to follow those women and put a transmitter on their car—"

"Do so. Shall we meet you at the airport?"

Martin asked, "You two *and* Mr. Jagger?"

Webster said, "No, Martin. You and Jagger and Keepe. I may or may not join you. But you don't need to advise Mr. Jagger you're going with him. We'll let it come as a surprise."

Martin went with them to the door. When he came back to the desk, he opened a bottom drawer and rummaged around for a half-empty bottle before he picked up the phone. He normally didn't drink on the job. He supposed he was on a job, though it was no longer Jagger's job. With Jagger he'd always known right where he was, known exactly what Jagger wanted, known exactly how to satisfy him. With this new man . . .

With this new man he felt as he had once in California when an earthquake had happened. Everything moving, and no way of knowing when it was going to stop or whether he'd be alive when it did. It wasn't Keepe so much as it was this Webster guy he worked for. Keepe . . . he was just some kind of shadow. All he'd done was sort of sit there and quiver. But Webster! When he spoke to you, it was like being a hooked fish. You could feel the barbs in there, hanging on. Then, after he left, it was as if the hook were still there and the line still attached. You could feel the pulling. As if he could reel you in anytime he wanted to.

Martin laughed at himself mockingly. Too much late-night stuff on TV. He took a long pull at the bottle and let it settle warmingly. Way too many horror movies on late-night TV.

The DFC was ready to go by eleven. The Land Rover had been serviced and all its fluids topped up, so said Hal. The spare had been checked, and all the parts to the jack were present and accounted for. Agnes, after a few cross words with Faye, had been convinced to change into blue jeans and shirt, and Bettiann had been nagged into sensible shoes.

They settled themselves inside the blocky vehicle, at first tentatively, shifting about, then with those small dispositions of belongings that mark temporary human territories. Carolyn's maps and thermos and sack of apples;

Ophy's medical journals. Behind them, Agnes had her knitting and Bettiann her camera, while Faye spread her sketchbook and colored pencils in the backseat next to Jessamine's field glasses and bird book. Sleeping bags and personal things were in the roof carrier; coats went into the cargo space behind the backseat, with Lolly nesting among them, cushioned among pillows and blankets.

They were ready to leave when a FedEx truck came down the drive in a cloud of dust to deliver a packet addressed to Carolyn. The return address was innocuous. Winter Mercantile, Baltimore, Maryland. Mike Winter lived in Baltimore.

Carolyn signed for the packet and shoved it under the maps beside her, leaving the car window open to let in the morning air. Hal leaned in and kissed her. "Stay in touch," he said.

"I will," she promised, starting the car.

"We don't know if there's anything where we're going," said Agnes, almost angrily.

Carolyn responded. "That's right, Aggie. We don't. We're playing hide-and-seek, just the way we did when we were kids, out in the dusk with the night coming, everything dark, ominous shadows all around, rather scary, as I remember. You've told us we've been hiding our eyes, refusing to see. Well, now they're open and all the counting is over. Ready or not, here we come."

Agnes pinched her lips and subsided. Before they left Vermont, she had called the abbey, explaining that there was an emergency and asking Sister Honore Philip to take care of things in the interim. Conscience told her she should go back, leave this investigation to others. Conscience told her it was her investigation as much as theirs. Conscience told her she had made this quagmire for herself, and anything she did might be wrong. Truth was, conscience was no damned help. She was merely going along, letting the others take her where they would. She did not believe they would find Sophy, but if they did, she was sure Sophy would prove to be something terrible. All those years of religious education, all the times she had read how demons had tempted the saints, how the devil had tempted witches into his service, and she had never realized that she herself was being tempted by a demon. She had not felt important enough to be singled out for temptation. When she became Reverend Mother, she should have realized that she was important enough. And Sophy had probably known she would be abbess, known it years ago. Foreseen it. Devils could foresee things.

Beside her, Bettiann was wondering, as she had every now and then since the previous Sunday, whether William would want to stay married—assuming this current condition of mankind went on, as it seemed likely it would. William had phoned Bettiann last night, but during their conversation they'd been careful to say nothing to one another. Of course, William had never said very much to her. He talked to her about as much as he talked to the Mercedes, or to the cook he'd hired away from the Morrisons. He talked more with the chauffeur than he did with her. Guy talk. Would he ever talk to her? If so, what would he say?

In the backseat Jessamine was trying unsuccessfully to think of nothing. Ever since Saturday morning she'd been unable to get the 1997 DFC meeting out of her mind. She kept going over and over it, all the details, all the things they'd done. She couldn't believe what Agnes had said about Sophy and the vial. The seal had been intact when she'd taken it back to the lab. Stupid and ridiculous of her to have taken it home to show the others, yes, she'd admit that. She could just as well have taken a dummy vial, but she'd been so excited about the stuff itself! A genetic key to behavior. A way to understand people better! Why hadn't she just described the stuff? God knows! But the seal had been intact. Intact. She'd broken the seal when she'd used the carrier to spray the bonobos.

Agnes could be right. The human race was certainly acting as though they'd been infected with something. Human lifestyles were changing remarkably. Daily motivations were changing. And there was that sign Lily had made, again and again, that circling sign. We! That's what the sign was. We! Not we bonobos. We, you and me, Jessamine. Jessamine and Lily . . . we females. We women! What about we women? Sophy was a woman. Sophy cared about women. Jessamine shut her eyes and shook her head slowly, side to side. Stop thinking. Thinking didn't help!

Beside Jessamine, Faye was sketching the line of Ophy's head and shoulder, wanting that particular line for the dryad in the fountain. The whole concept was coming together. She knew now it would be great! If the consortium honored their contract. If she could solve the problem of the central figure. If she had time to finish it.

Staring through the windshield, Ophy was thinking of Simon, wishing he were there with her. Only that. Nothing else.

Beside her, Carolyn, who had firmly resolved to stop thinking of anything unpleasant, found herself thinking of nothing else. Aggie had become a stranger who regarded them all with suspicion. As though they'd been contaminated . . . by Sophy, probably. The feeling of menace was still with her, also: an itch at the back of her neck, a pricking of her scalp, a formless troubling in some corner of her mind, a ghost that wouldn't rest and wouldn't identify itself. What was she afraid of? Being killed by Jagger or by his minion? Surely he wouldn't try that unless she was alone, certainly not when there were seven of them. What else? Maybe she was afraid they'd find Sophy and learn that Aggie was right and Sophy had done something . . . weird. Was something . . . weird. But Sophy wouldn't have done anything evil. She just wouldn't have.

Was she worried about Hal? Leaving him alone this way? That was ridiculous. He wouldn't be alone. Stace and Luce had promised to look in on him tonight, and again tomorrow. Or was she responding to some more global troubling? Something bigger than, worse than, more terrible than . . .

She made a wordless exclamation, and Ophy looked at her curiously.

"What?"

"Nothing, Oph. Goose walking on my grave, that's all." She gritted her teeth. When she got back, she'd arrange for an exorcism! Until then . . . "Begone," she muttered silently to the dark lurker inside her head. "Get away. Avaunt thee." She pictured the lurker fleeing, departing, then concentrated on driving, creating a litany out of the dashboard indicators: oil pressure, mileage, temperature, rpm's, reading them over to herself, subvocalizing, then starting over to read them again.

Behind the backseat, curled into a nest of pillows, Lolly thought about going somewhere. She couldn't remember going anywhere ever before. Nobody was hitting her. Nobody was wanting her to do sex. Nobody was wanting anything from her. Here she was, like an egg. The thought came fuzzily, then settled. She'd made one once, in school, for Mrs. Gallegos. She'd made it out of construction paper and crayons. A nest made of scruffled-up pieces of brown paper with a blue egg in it. Waiting for some bird to come sit on her, hatch her into something.

It was an interesting thought. The first she could remember ever having.

18

As Jagger drove across the tarmac toward his little chopper, he saw Martin waiting beside it. Jagger frowned, felt the frown collapse into a grimace, then attempted a smile, achieving only a weak and effortful result. Martin wasn't alone.

Should he go on? Or go back? He couldn't go back. They'd seen him. Keepe and Webster both.

He parked the car, making himself look pleased and surprised at their presence.

"This is wonderful," he said, managing a grin. "Are you here to meet me, or are you headed somewhere?"

There was a pause before Keepe answered, as though suddenly energized. "Both. Mr. Webster feels you may need help."

"Help? Well," he allowed himself to look abashed. "I suppose it's possible. I didn't want to bother anybody, though, not until I know whether there's anything to this . . . this rumor."

Martin shifted uncomfortably.

Webster spoke smoothly, calmly, as though they were discussing the weather. "More than a rumor, wouldn't you say? Your colleague here, your . . . associate says these women may know something . . . everything about what's happened."

"It's remotely possible," agreed Jagger, concentrating on keeping his voice even and agreeable. "That's why I was going to follow them."

"Follow them where?"

"Wherever they're going. They're looking for the missing one, Sophy, the one who's supposed to know what happened. I thought it might be useful to find her. . . ."

"It's a place called Piedras Lagartonas," Martin said stiffly.

"Piedras what?" Jagger asked.

Martin replied, "That's what I picked up before they left. The Crespin woman said it was down in the southwest corner of the state. If it's there, it's not on any of my maps. They left about half an hour ago."

"And how were you going to follow them?" Webster asked.

Jagger swallowed, attempted a boyish smile. "Martin . . . was going to put some kind of beeper on their car. When they stopped for gas. With a receiver in my bird."

"I sent someone else to do it," said Martin. "And the receiver's in that red chopper over there."

"You're . . . going yourselves," said Jagger. There was a lump in his chest. Webster was watching him unblinkingly, and under the force of that gaze the hard lump in his chest swelled and throbbed, pressing on his heart, shutting off his breath.

"Is there some reason we shouldn't?" Webster asked mildly.

"No. No sir. Not if you want to. I was just trying to save you trouble."

"Oh, I shan't trouble. I'll leave the trouble to you and Martin, and to Keepe. I'm sure the three of you can manage such a very simple thing. Particularly as I have . . . other things to attend to just now."

"I see," murmured Jagger, who did not see.

Webster smiled at him quite terribly before turning that searchlight smile on the others as well. "You'll follow the women until they find this Sophy. If they find her, you'll let me know. If they don't find her, you'll let me know and I'll decide what to do about that. There's no hurry to take off, is there, Martin?"

The man shook his head, swallowed, struggled to get enough saliva in his mouth that he could speak. "No, sir. We'll go a lot faster than they can."

"Then we have time."

Webster's face remained fixed in its dreadful smile as he took Jagger by the arm. Jagger staggered beside him, suddenly aware of pain. Heat radiated upward from the arm Webster held, up and across Jake's shoulders and chest, a burning sensation, an incapacitating agony, a horrid intimacy that moved toward his belly and groin, an inward violation, like being impaled on a fiery spear.

Webster said, "Sit here, on this bench. Let's have a little talk."

Martin and Keepe remained where they were, turned slightly away, as though not wishing to observe whatever was taking place. Martin did this sensibly, as a man accustomed to not seeing too much, or hearing too much. Keepe did it involuntarily but with a horrible conviction that he had already seen and heard too much. His mind had not been his own since that terrible phone call. He seemed incapable of independent thought except at some remote, deep level that was unconnected to his body. His body wasn't his own. He wanted to walk away from this place, and he couldn't make his body do it. Instead, it twitched and jerked as though someone were pulling his strings. Unable to do anything of his own volition, he stood beside Martin, staring across the airport at the distant mountains, trying desperately to be unaware.

Behind them, across the tarmac, Webster and Jake were seated side by side.

"Now," Webster said to Jake. "Tell me all about these women."

Jake's mouth opened and words came out, without plan, without thought. Jagger found himself telling about the aborted trial, quoting swatches of testimony, describing Carolyn as he had encountered her before, saying things he did not know he knew, making conclusions he did not know he had made.

"Excellent," said Webster. "Very good, Jagger. What a very good candidate you would have made. . . ."

The words cut through to the self inside. "Would," he gasped. "Would have made?"

Webster patted him on the shoulder. "Would have made. Not now. You were disobedient, Jagger. Emmet Swinter wasn't supposed to die, Jagger. You were supposed to do exactly, precisely as you were told."

"But . . . but . . . Father . . ." The words came out in a quavering bleat, like a sheep, a goat, *Baa . . . baa . . . Faaather.*

Laughter boomed like thunder, cracking the sky. Across the field Keepe reached out and clung to Martin's arm, held on to him, his eyes fixed firmly on the ground, not to see, not to look. A tearing sound came from behind them and ran between them, a real rip in the fabric of the earth, a tear that propagated itself across the tarmac, endlessly opening. It widened gapingly, a tongue of shadow licked out, and the rift closed with a noise like a gulp.

Martin removed Keepe's hand from his arm and stared blindly at the mountains. He wasn't here, he told himself. He was somewhere else.

Webster whispered, "Surely you don't mean that word, Jagger. I, Jagger. I? Look at you. Did you really think I would beget a son like you?"

There was a mirror in the air between Jagger and Webster, a consolidation of space, a shining surface in which Jake saw himself, naked, potbellied, and pig-eyed, dribbling urine, dripping saliva, shivering, his hands twitching, stinking of fluids, no better than a woman. . . .

"What," Jagger gulped, the words coming up like knives in his throat. "Who. Who are you?"

"Oh, my boy," Webster whispered to him from out of a radiant smoke. "You should have asked that question a long time ago."

The drive southwest took the DFC straight through Santa Fe, down the highway to Albuquerque, then south toward Las Cruces, between the Black Mountains and the Jornada del Muerto.

"Journey of death?" asked Agnes. "Not a good omen."

"Not an omen at all," said Carolyn crisply. "It's historic comment, Aggie, not fortune-telling. When the Spaniards came through, they found no water and a lot of hostile warriors. A lot of the invaders died out there."

"As we may," said Aggie.

"Now, Aggie." She made herself smile. "Come on! Nobody is going to bother us."

"You don't know that. Someone . . . something could."

"Aggie?" Bettiann leaned toward her, putting her hand on the other woman's arm. "Please. We're going to be all right."

"Sorry." Agnes shuddered. "I'm scared, and not just for my life."

"Well, we're all scared," said Jessamine from behind her.

"You didn't see what *I* did. In San Francisco."

"No. I didn't. But I don't think it was diabolical. I don't believe Sophy was a devil. Nonetheless, we're all equally apprehensive about what we're trying to do, so let's try to keep up our spirits."

"If I'm guilty—" Aggie started to say.

"You don't have any monopoly on guilt," Ophy interrupted. "Maybe we're all guilty, we don't know. We don't know where we're going, or what we'll find, if and when we get there."

"We don't have to go," said Carolyn over her shoulder. "We can go back home, forget it."

"No," Aggie grated. "No, we can't do that."

There was silence for a time.

"Where are we going to sleep?" Bettiann asked, her nose slightly wrinkled. "It doesn't sound as though we'll find accommodations where we're going."

Carolyn responded, "If we get near Cloverdale, which probably isn't there anymore, we'll sleep on the ground. There are seven sleeping bags in the roof carrier. Ours and the ones Hal borrowed from the neighbors. There are three five-gallon water cans up there and my camp kit as well. I haven't used it in a while, but I remember how to light the stove."

"Food?" asked Ophy.

"We'll stock up in Deming. With all the retirees moving down there, it's become quite a good-size town."

"If one of my friends did this, I'd tell them it was a dumb idea. Six . . . seven women going off alone like this?" Bettiann sighed plaintively.

"What are you afraid of, Bets? Rape?" Faye laughed, making a hiccupy, burroish sound, ee-yaw, ee-yaw.

"Not funny," Bettiann replied.

"Not really, no," Faye agreed.

They fell silent again, all of them convinced they were doing a ridiculously dangerous thing, going off into nothingness like this. Carolyn read their minds. "I ask again, anyone want to go back?"

Silence. After a long time Faye said, "We can't. We swore an oath not to decline and fall. Not making this journey would be a fall. Whatever we can do, we must do."

Murmurs from all the others: agreement—some strong, some weak, but agreement.

And Lolly's voice, "Who you lookin' for?"

Faye said, "An old friend of ours. Sovawanea aTesuawane."

"That's a funny name. Sounds like the people my grandma used to know when she lived in the south in Terrenos Perdidos."

Carolyn pulled the car to the side of the road and turned slowly around, speaking into the silence. "Terrenos Perdidos, Lolly?"

"That's what she called it. The place she lived when she was little."

"It means 'lost lands.' Did she live there with people?"

"She tole me about 'em. They wasn't people, not ezackly. They had names like that one you said. Okeah was one. And Setwon. And Toulenae. Those was my grandma's sisters."

"Your grandma was Spanish, Hispanic?"

"She could talk it, but she said her sisters was something else."

"Where was this place? Do you know?"

"Down south, she said."

"And what did she call the people?"

Lolly shrugged. "She never called 'em anything. No, she did, I just remembered. She said they'd been there a long time, longer than us, so they was the real first Americans. Then she'd laugh."

"Right," said Carolyn. The others sat in stunned silence while she pulled the car back onto the road, which dropped off before them to allow the view of a hundred miles of open desert. At the edge of vision, beyond Las Cruces, was El Paso and then Mexico. That way lay a populated, traveled road. The way they were going, there'd be no one at all. Jackrabbits. Kangaroo rats. Javelina. And Terrenos Perdidos? Where in heaven's name had that come from?

"You know," said Ophy, "one thing that bothered me about Sophy, she never got to know any really nice men."

"Sophy deserved someone nice," Carolyn agreed. "She should have met someone like Hal."

"Or Simon," Ophy offered.

"Or William," said Bettiann.

No one said anything.

"Like William," she insisted. "We . . . when sex wasn't all mixed up in it, we had wonderful times. He wanted me for sex, you know, but then . . . it got in the way. We could have been really good friends if it hadn't been for sex!"

"I never thought of William in that light," said Ophy a bit sarcastically.

"Well, you should. You get past all that ad-man talk, William is a very unselfish, very honorable kind of man. But he's got . . . appetites, just like most people, and they screw things up. . . ."

"Did," amended Faye. "Did screw things up."

"For most people." Bettiann sighed. "I wonder if it's too late. For William and me."

They stopped in Albuquerque for gas, all getting out to stretch their legs. Carolyn stayed close to the car, circling it, happening upon a man who seemed to be peering at her axle.

"Thought you had a oil leak there," he said, wiping his hands on a grease-stained rag. "Musta been somebody else."

He moved away. Carolyn looked where he had looked, seeing nothing. When she raised her head, he was gone, into the garage, perhaps. She looked back at the car, worried. Why had he thought she might have an oil leak?

She forgot about it on the drive to Deming. They were already weary when they found a grocery and bought fruit, bread, lunch meat, cans of soup, fruit drink, and cola. When these provisions had been stowed, Carolyn stood beside the car, searching the sky, the surrounding streets, the people moving about.

"What is it?" whispered Faye.

"Nothing. I don't know," she replied. "Just this feeling. I've had it all day."

When they left, their eyes were drawn to the three jagged peaks that serrated the southern horizon. Las Tres Hermanas. Three sisters.

"Fates, weren't they?" asked Ophy.

Carolyn said, "Horribles seem to come in threes. Norns. Gorgons. But then, I was convinced that Sophy sounded like a Gorgon sometimes."

"How does a Gorgon sound?" Ophy asked.

"Fatal," Carolyn replied. "Inexorable."

Aggie laughed. It was a witchlike cackle, and they all pretended not to notice. An hour later they turned south once more, on a road that arrowed into the south, changing direction only once in the twenty miles to Hachita. The sun was halfway down the western sky. While Carolyn bought gas, they used the station rest room, wiping dusty faces with dampened paper towels, then got back into the car for the thirty-mile trip to Animas, the graveled surface churning beneath them, pebbles hitting the underside of the fenders in a constant rattle, long stretches of washboarding rattling their teeth as well.

"There's a campground in Animas," Carolyn told them. "Or we can still make it to Cloverdale before dark."

"Cloverdale," said Faye in a weary voice.

Weary or not, there was no dissent. They had only one day. They had to do it all in the time they had, so they went on through the sleepy cluster of buildings that was Animas, then turned south, past the bare baked rodeo arena, its skeletal stands tilted to one side. A bit farther on they saw the squat bulk of Tank Mountain on their right. On either side the world sloped up, four or five miles east to the low, undulating line of the continental divide, closer on the right to the arroyo-riven slopes of the Peloncillo Mountains, bald and hot under the westering sun. Lolly slept in her nest like one drugged, lost in dreams.

"How far?" asked Bettiann with an exhausted twist of her shoulders.

Carolyn shrugged. "Another half hour. Maybe a little more. This road is lousy."

It went from lousy to worse, changing from gravel to dirt; Carolyn slowed and went into four-wheel drive. The mountains both to left and right became higher. On the right, sets of ruts wound off among the canyons, disappearing, appearing again. They swung to the right at a place the road divided, the left-hand route marked by a faded sign, Private Road. A couple of miles farther on, the road turned abruptly westward. Carolyn announced the odometer reading, went two miles more, then edged off the road and stopped, leaning on the wheel in exhaustion.

"The best way to get where we're going, the one with the fewest arroyos or mountains in it, is to leave the road now and drive south, cross-country, about four miles, then three or four miles west. That should bring us just south of the Cloverdale mountain, the one you can see ahead, a little to our left, with a lower peak between us and it. If we can't go in the car, then we'll have to walk. This isn't rugged country, according to the topo, but I told Hal if we aren't back by Friday, he's to report us lost."

This announcement left them momentarily wordless.

Agnes climbed from the car and stood looking around herself. The sun was still above the peaks to the west, a scarlet bonfire, flushing the lands with bloodied light. "We spend the night here?"

The others joined her, turning slowly, their vision ending only at the crooked horizon, nothing moving, not a bird, not a beast, not even the whir of a grasshopper. Despite this vacancy, Carolyn still had the oppressive sense of being watched. She told herself it was foolishness. There'd been no one on the road but themselves. No one but Hal knew where they were going. Still, she jittered from foot to foot, watching the others as they stared indecisively, nervously.

"I'd be inclined to get off the road," Carolyn remarked finally. "Drive south about a mile, down into a draw, if we can find one." She frowned, wondering why she wanted to be hidden.

Ophy said, "I agree it would be better to be off the road. Sometimes hunters shoot from cars. This is pig-hunting country, and I don't like being in the line of fire."

Carolyn's face cleared, and she climbed back behind the wheel. Of course, that was the reason. To get out of the line of fire.

They drove slowly south among cactus and many-branched cholla, brilliant with bloom, the ground dipping and tilting around them. Carolyn watched their progress in the rearview mirror, stopping when the road vanished. Though they were not conscious of having descended, they were below road level when she stopped.

They had descended into a shallow bowl into which the western hill reached a long, rounded ridge, an eastward-pointing finger. Carolyn drove around the end of the finger and west along its almost vertical wall, feeling a stone scrape harshly against the axle. She parked in the shadow of a sprawling clump of mesquite that overhung the east-west wall. With the car tight against the wall, they were invisible from the road. Invisible from the air, too, unless someone flew very low from the south.

The others got out, moved around, stretched, wandered off to find privacy beyond a clump of mesquite or a pillar of eroded earth at the edge of the draw. The silence was less perfect there, broken with insect sounds, buzz chirp, rattle, buzz chirp.

"I'd be happier if we hadn't left tracks," Carolyn said to Ophy.

"That's easy to fix. Help me get the canvas cover off the roof carrier."

Carolyn untied tapes and tossed the canvas to Ophy, receiving a square metal gadget in return.

"This was by the rock we went over. Did it fall off the car?"

The gadget was new and shiny, so it had obviously come with them. When Carolyn leaned down to look under the car, the thing in her hand stuck fast to the fender. "Magnetic," she said.

Ophy stared at her, saying nothing. Carolyn put her finger to her lips, wrenched the gadget loose, and went with Ophy as she followed their tracks northward. When they arrived at the road, Carolyn said, "How's your arm?"

"My arm's not great, but I do jog most days." She took the gadget and set off eastward on the road, vanishing over a slight rise. Long, slow minutes went by. Shadows lengthened into darkness. Eventually, Ophy came over the rise again, empty-handed. When she reached Carolyn, she stopped, leaning over, panting. "It's at least a mile down the road, by a rock, like maybe it got scraped off. What was it?"

"Another bug," Carolyn answered. "Some kind of transmitter."

"Who?" breathed Ophy. "When?"

"I don't know. Cousin Albert's buddies? Jagger? Whoever Jagger works for? As to when, I honestly don't know, Ophy. Not before we got the car. Not while it was in the driveway. Maybe when we stopped in Albuquerque." She frowned, remembering the man who'd thought she had an oil leak. God! How long was she going to go on being blind? She had to do better than this!

They turned and walked back to the car, dragging the canvas behind them to wipe out their tracks. The wind cooperated, blowing sand in ripples to cover their trail. Ophy did not speak until they were almost up with the group; then she asked, "What do you think we're going to find tomorrow?"

Carolyn laughed, almost choking. "Oh, God, Ophy, I don't know. This whole thing is unreal. I don't believe it for a moment. What are we doing here?"

"Trying to find an old friend. Or find out what happened to her. Though it may turn out we're just camping out."

"Hal taught me to like camping out, long ago. . . ."

Her voice trailed off. Ophy wasn't listening. She was thinking about something else.

"Carolyn . . . have you taken a good look at Faye since she's been here?"

"She doesn't look good, does she?"

"If I had to guess, I'd say cancer."

"I haven't wanted to ask."

"I'll see if I can find out. Doctor's privilege." She kicked moodily at a rock. "What's next?"

"Light the camp stove, heat some food. Make nice level places for the sleeping bags while there's still a little light. Scoop out a hollow where your hip or bottom goes. It's hard to find the rock that's burrowing into your backside when it's pitch-dark."

"I'll get them started." And she was off to find Faye and delegate her to help round up the others.

There was little or no conversation while they focused on bedtime chores, smoothing flat places in the sandy soil, spreading their sleeping bags.

None of them did more than pick at the food, and even Lolly was less voracious than usual. She fell asleep as soon as she had eaten, leaving the others sitting around the stove, sipping tea. Carolyn was busy with her maps, planning tomorrow's journey. As she shifted the pile, she came upon the morning's FedEx packet, forgotten at the bottom of the stack. She ripped it open, took out the photocopies within, began to go through them.

"Girls," she said softly. "Ladies. You should hear this."

They gathered, edging toward Carolyn where she bent above the letter, reading by the light of the stove.

"It's a letter from Mike Winter, an old FBI friend of Hal's. Hal asked him to tell us what he could:

" 'Dear Hal and Carolyn,

" 'Your local bad guy, Jagger, is a protégé of the so-called American Alliance, an arm of the International Alliance. For the last few decades the Alliances have been grooming candidates for political office or moving them into government bureaus here and abroad, wherever they can exert the most influence. Opinion here is that Jagger is or was being groomed as a possible U.S. presidential candidate.

" 'The Alliance has always avowed patriotism in public and kept its real agenda quiet. This changed during the Gulf War, when female American soldiers suddenly appeared on Saudi soil. Nobody said boo to the U.S. so long as Kuwait was endangered and the missiles were incoming, at least not officially, but Arab clerics made no secret of being incensed at seeing females driving trucks, running around bare-faced within spitting distance of the holiest sites of Islam. Subsequently, according to our sources, a number of high-ranking imams held some ultrasecret multistate meetings at which it was decided their sacred way of life could be preserved only by putting women back in their place, once and for all, or words to that effect.

" 'There was a complication. The conspirators felt putting Muslim women back in the tenth century wouldn't be a final solution so long as other women in other countries were still moving around in public, getting themselves educated, running businesses, and so forth. Information moves across borders too easily these days, and if they wanted their own women suppressed, it would be necessary, ultimately, for all women in the world to live by the same rules. They turned to their good friend in the Vatican to help them out—they've supported him on population and abortion issues, now's time for him to support them on the status-of-women issues—and very shortly both the Muslim states and the Vatican joined the Alliance, which has covertly opposed women's rights for years. (See enclosed, 1943–1998, etc.)

" 'We should have seen this coming, but the intelligence communities of the Western nations had been so focused on Communism and middle-eastern terrorism, they didn't put this antiwoman agenda together until ninety-eight, *when the Muslim fundamentalists began bombing women's colleges both here and abroad. Almost immediately we traced this activity back to the Alliance. Almost ten thousand young women died in those bombings, over a thousand of them in the U.S.*

" 'The Alliance repudiates any form of population control on two grounds: The first is unspoken and has to do with the absolute right of males to pass on their genes as often as possible. The second one is stated publicly: The Alliance claims population control is unnecessary because millennial wars, famines, and epidemics are going to wipe out ninety percent of all people within the next ten or twenty years. If natural disasters don't accomplish this, the Alliance is prepared to help it along. That Japanese cult that started the nerve-gas business back in ninety-five was a member of the Alliance; and we've traced shipments of nerve-gas chemicals and biological materials to Alliance headquarters, a place they call the Redoubt.

" 'Learning even this superficial information has cost several agents their lives, none of them FBI because we've been told to keep our hands off. With the help of some friends in the IRS, we have been able to trace some Alliance income sources. Though most support comes from Mideast oil, I've been more professionally interested in support from inside the U.S. I've enclosed information that may surprise you. Or maybe not.

" 'Last item: No one has any information on Webster. We didn't know anything about his father and we don't know anything about him. Except for the difference in age, they could both be the same man. This one is said to have succeeded his father as head of the Alliance about forty years ago.

" 'Destroy this after reading.

" 'Mike.' "

Carolyn passed out the papers that had come with the letter. They moved from hand to hand, quietly rustling. Agnes muttered brokenly.

"What?" murmured Fay.

"This sheet traces the flow of money from a certain archdiocese in the U.S.," she said in a tight voice.

"Was that why your archbishop wanted to cut off the money for your school?" asked Carolyn. "So he could support this?"

"I don't know," Aggie said, pushing the pages away. "The Church does want us to return to our more . . . traditional roles."

Ophy looked at her curiously, wondering at her tone. "How do you feel about that?"

"Perhaps . . . perhaps it's time we did," Aggie said.

"You don't mean that," whispered Faye.

"I'm not sure. Perhaps I do. Perhaps I've been misled, about a lot of things. . . ."

Ophy shook her head as she leafed through the papers on her lap.

"There's a Hasidic group here that's supporting the Alliance. They're pouring money from the diamond trade into Alliance coffers. Their headquarters is just down the street from Misery. I've treated some of the women."

Jessamine murmured, "And I seem to have been working for other supporters of theirs. The NRA supports them, too. And the so-called prolife people. Shit."

Bettiann asked, "What does he mean, the FBI has been told to keep their hands off?"

Carolyn said, "The one and only time I ever saw Webster was at the FBI. Albert took me there when I was about eighteen. Webster was with the FBI director, which would lead me to assume the top FBI people may be members of the Alliance."

They did not have many questions. The pages were numerous. The ones that might have been hard to understand had been notated in a precise hand with arrows and parenthetical explanations.

"Shall we burn them as Mike requested?" asked Carolyn.

"Yes," said Faye. "Quickly. This is all disgusting."

She crumpled the papers, lit a spill from the stove, and set them alight, pushing the unburned portions into the flame. A thin smoke rose into the last of the sunset, drifting, dissipating. A small wind stirred the few tiny scraps of paper that had only partially burned. They sat looking at the ashes, stunned, seeing there all their lives and purposes, reduced to ashes. If the Alliance succeeded, there would be no women doctors, sculptors, scientists. There would be no women lawyers or philanthropists or managers of fisheries. Though Aggie was pretending that might be a good thing, that's all it was. Pretense.

Darkness swallowed up sight. Each of them went to her own sleeping place and lay there, staring at the stars popping out in the darkening sky, listening to cricket noises. Then Carolyn sat up, aware of another sound. To the north a chopper passed and returned, passed and returned. They all heard it, whop, whop, whop, nearing, then fading; low, then high, like a circling mosquito.

It began to come toward them. To the north Carolyn saw a light from the sky.

"Quickly," she cried. "Gather up your stuff and get into the car. All of it. Hurry!"

They variously rolled or leaped from sleeping bags, gathered up bags and clothing, ran or hobbled toward the Land Rover. Ophy ran back to get something. Carolyn seized up the stove by its handle. The sounds of the chopper were coming closer as they struggled into or behind the car, against the clay wall.

"Roll down the outside windows," Carolyn instructed. "So they won't reflect light. Put the sleeping bags out to cover the sides of the car. Ophy, put your sleeping bag over the windshield and top."

She herself reached through the open window and turned the rearview mirror down, away from the sky.

The whop whop whop came closer, louder.

"Lolly," whispered Jessamine. "She's still out there!"

She started to get out, but Carolyn grabbed her arm. "Leave her. She's all rolled up. If she doesn't wake . . ."

Then the chopper was above them, its searchlight probing the desert, peering behind yuccas and into arroyos, setting skeletal chollas into glaring relief. The light slipped through the mesquite above them without stopping. It crossed the place they had sat to have their supper, slipping through the ashes of Mike's document, scattered gray on a soil almost as gray. It slipped across Lolly's huddled form in its olive-drab bedroll, and went on south without stopping, a dark dragonfly shape against the stars, supported on its narrow beam of light. When it had gone some distance, it turned west.

Worldlessly, Ophy put her sleeping bag along the wall of the arroyo in the shadow, then lay down once more. Without comment the others followed suit.

"Sophy said she had an enemy," said Carolyn into the silence. "She spent her life trying to save women, and she said she had an enemy. She must have known about the Alliance."

No one offered comment. The helicopter noise diminished, the night filled with cricket noises once more, and eventually, uneasily, they slept.

In Calcutta, Paris, Durban, Adelaide; in Beijing, Osaka, St. Petersburg, Stockholm; in Buenos Aires, Lima, Mexico City, Rangoon; in cities all around the world, as evening came, old women assembled under cover of the dusk. Up out of the clamorous hollows of subways, down from the attics of abandoned warehouses, out of doorways, out of alleys, out of the back doors of neat houses in the suburbs, out of all-night do-it-yourself laundries, out of shelters and slum warrens, from behind Dumpsters, and out of shacks they came, drifting together like tattered leaves blown by an autumn wind, swirling, casually turning, joining in larger drifts that went spiraling down streets and alleys to join others already there.

"Did you hear the beast baying?" they asked one another. "Just as the sun went down, did you hear it?"

In the same cities, as dark fell, men came out of bars onto the sidewalks, muttering among themselves, small clots of them swaggering off in one direction or another to meet another little clot, also swaggering along. Trucks with rifle racks and NRA bumper stickers pulled over to the sides of the streets and men got out. Police cars ghosted to a stop under overpasses, in dark alleys, and officers got out to join other men on the street corners. When the marchers with their robes and whips and drums came along, men were already there, lined up along the sidewalks, watching, ready to join the procession.

"The summons," they told one another eagerly. "It's the summons. . . ."

When dark came, there were no young women on the street. Not one. Not a twentyish waitress just getting off. Not a thirtyish clerk who'd worked late taking inventory. Not a female officer, all of whom had called in sick or decided to catch up on paperwork or gotten tied up somewhere on a case. There were not even any rebellious teens, with their ratty hair and short skirts. The men had been summoned (so they thought, assumed, had been told) to go hunting, but there was no one on the streets for them to hunt. They were there to strike a counterblow for . . . for something or other. To let them know they couldn't get away with it anymore.

But there was no them on the streets at all.

A far-off mutter, a whisper, like wind in the grass. A lifted nostril, a raised upper lip, a stag scenting the wind, a bull nosing the air.

"Women down there," said one to another, pointing with his chin, jutting his jaw in the direction of downtown. "I can smell 'em."

"Women down there," said another. "He can tell."

So the lines turned as men began to walk, without rhythm at first, then gradually to march in time with the pom, pom, pom of the drums.

Somewhere in the direction of their march, the old women waited.

The DFC did not sleep long. Carolyn woke suddenly to the sound of a cat purring, a kettle boiling, a purling noise off somewhere in the darkness. She rolled out of the sleeping bag and stood for a moment in the chill air, naked-legged, turning to find a direction. The sound was coming from the west, she thought. Perhaps a little south of west.

She shook Faye awake, then Ophy, then the others, telling them to get dressed, gather their stuff together, just in case they had to take off in a hurry. The noise came nearer, and then sound became visible, a glow, a halo, a ball of pale-yellow light rolling toward them in the night. When it came nearer, they saw it was a bus, a vehicle faded to the pale organic yellow of late-fall aspen leaves, a fleeting gold aging to gray. When it stopped beside them, they could make out the words "Lizard Rock Public Schools" in peeling letters below the windows.

The door opened. A very old man came down the steps. He smoked a pipe redolent of woods and mosses and resins, aromatic, exotic, an odor evocative of forests, perhaps even of jungles. The assemblage of bus, man, and smoke was so unexpected that Carolyn felt herself deactivated, able only to stand staring at the vehicle and its driver while her mind sought for the difference between dream and reality and her hand furtively scratched her leg where something had bitten her during her brief sleep. None of the others was more capable than she. All of them stared as she did, as silently and as astonished.

It was Lolly who walked barefooted across the chill sand to stand spraddled before the old man, rubbing her belly with unselfconscious vigor. "Hi!" she said.

"Hi," he replied.

"Did you know my grandma? Her name was Immaculata Corazon."

"I knew her when she was a little girl."

"Her sisters lived down here. Their names are Okeah, and Setwon, and Toulenae."

"That is true."

"They do live here! They really do!"

He nodded. Lolly turned and came toward Carolyn. "Did you hear him? He says my grandma's sisters still live here!"

"I heard him," said Carolyn.

The old man raised his voice a little. "Was a helicopter looking for you, a little after sundown?"

No one commented on that. Faye zipped up her trousers and stepped into her boots before approaching the old man. "Where is she?"

"She?"

"Sovawanea aTesuawane. You wouldn't be here unless you knew we were here. You wouldn't know we were here unless somebody was expecting us. She's the only one who would be."

"Ah." He tapped his head reflectively. "You are clever."

"No," she said. "I just lack time for politeness or preliminary. She isn't dead, is she?"

He shrugged. "What is death, after all?" His English was unaccented, pure, without hint of origin.

Jessamine said, " 'There'll be more to birth than being born, and less to death than dying.' Sophy wrote that to me, after my child and grandchild were killed. 'So long as earth bears golden corn, and hears the wild wings flying.' "

"Yes," the old man said again. "While there are yet growing things and the flights of birds wrapping the world, there is continuance. Are you ready to go?"

"The person, people, in the helicopter," said Carolyn. "Do you know who they were?"

"They are only servants. A man named Keepe. A man named Martin. One man called Jagger."

"Servants?"

"Of a creature who was not born, ever."

"That's a riddle."

"Perhaps, but he smells to me like an unborn one. A crawler out of time."

"That sounds just lovely," snarled Faye. "And you've come for us?"

"Surely. When you're ready to go. Put your things in the bus. I will bring you back to your car later."

Carolyn locked the Land Rover and followed the others onto the straw-yellow vehicle, which was rather better inside than out. It had half a dozen worn but comfortable seats toward the front, a cargo area behind them, and then a partitioned space that looked lived in. Several sacks of scratch grain and pig chow were piled by the side door.

The bus belied its outward appearance by starting smoothly, almost soundlessly, and moving effortlessly southwestward across the desert, its headlights disclosing little rutty roads that ran north and south and southwest, the wheels sometimes traveling along them for a short distance, never for more than a few hundred yards, then swerving off onto desert once more, turning to miss clumps of twisted gray mesquite, disturbing no leaf. Carolyn, who was nearest the back, leaned out the open window to feel the spin of tiny dust devils. In the dim light of the taillights, she could see no wheel tracks left upon the sand.

Faye was riding with her head tipped onto the seat back, eyes shut, face very lean and drawn. Skull-like, thought Carolyn, putting the image away from her in revulsion. Maybe Ophy had found out what was wrong. Agnes had not said a word since rising and seemed disinclined to do so now. She had her rosary in her hands and two hectic patches of color stained her cheeks. Ophy and Jessamine sat together, talking about something technical, as though they were on a tour. Bettiann was nearest Carolyn, her face quiet and empty, hands folded in her lap. Lolly had curled up on a seat, head pillowed on her arms, and was asleep again, like some small animal. She seemed able to sleep at any time, in any place. All she needed was a bushy tail to cover her eyes.

West and north of them the mountains rose abruptly—not high, a thousand feet perhaps—as they went south and still farther south, then west-ward around a curved toe of the mountains, crossing other dim rutty roads that wound away to water tanks and windmills, coming at last to a place where the land sloped gently down toward the west. The old man shifted gears smoothly, and they proceeded more slowly, winding among large stones.

Though it was night, they moved in the bubble of amber light that brightened the farther they went.

Carolyn rose and went to the front of the bus, dropping her pack and herself into the empty seat nearest the driver. "What is your name?" she asked.

"I am Chendi Qowat. Also called Padre Josephus."

"Both postmaster and priest?"

He shook his head, laughing. "No. A messenger and a father. I am father to pigs and goats and chickens and many girl children."

"No boy children?"

"No boy children. We do not need boy children very often."

"The girl children are yours?"

"Yes and no. Mostly, I am father to the chickens."

"What does it mean, to be father to chickens?"

"When they hatch, someone must fetch food to cast before their feet. Who but their father would do this?"

"Are we going to see our friend, Sophy?"

"I have heard Sophy was your friend."

"Were you the one who brought her food when she was in the desert?"

"She told you that?"

"She told her followers someone had brought her food, someone who lived in a school bus."

"Perhaps it was I. I do things like that. Bring food. Bring help. Not long ago I brought help to someone you know. Helen, her name is."

"Helen! Helen Jagger?"

"I found her alone on a hillside, hiding under a tree like a rabbit. I took her to a safe place."

Carolyn merely stared. "How . . . how did you know she was there?"

He peered at her intently. "Didn't you ask someone to help her? I thought you did."

She bit her tongue until she could hold it no longer. "Where are we going?"

"To a place of sun-warmed stone. To the Sisterhood. To the family place of Sovawanea."

"Who is she, Father Josephus?"

"Don't you know?"

"She was just . . . Sophy. Our friend."

"Her people may not agree with me, but I think she is still your friend. You are wise to have such a friend."

"I'm not sure we're wise."

"It is hard to be wise in the body. Hard to be wise when one is hungry, or tired, or lusting. I know. I was young once, too. How the blood simmers, making a steam around the brain, a mist that fools the senses. How the words of passion crowd up in the throat. How the muscles twitch and dance when one is young."

"I'm afraid none of my friends and I are young."

"Oh, some of you are very young." He turned the bus slightly to the north, and she saw they were going downhill into a hidden valley. Now the light was pure gold. There were cottonwoods around them, which meant a stream, but she saw no stream. Then, in a moment, she did see a stream—bubbling water, fountains springing forth from the bare earth, filling rocky hollows from which they spilled to make a brook that flowed beside them, dancing silver skeins of water marking their way. The water was edged in grasses and soon passed into the shade of trees. All around them was bosque, riverine woodland, the green boughs hiding them from the sky. Carolyn fished in her pack for her map.

"This place is not on any map," chided the old man. "This is a place one must know before one goes there. One cannot arrive, one can only return."

"Then the ones following us can't find it?"

"That is true. They may find your car, but they will not find you."

"We should have brought the car."

"It would not go in. Only this vehicle goes in and out. It was created to go in and out."

She set her instant apprehension aside, forced herself to be calm. She was living in a story Luce might have read and told her about. "Some fairy-tale place?" she asked hesitantly. "Some . . . what? Magical door between the worlds? Some fold in space?"

He chuckled. "This is not a fairy tale. It is, perhaps, technology of an unfamiliar kind, one that allows a place to exist with an invisible wall around it. People who come to the wall walk around the place, without knowing there is a wall."

"Why here? Miles from anything?"

"It is easier to make the wall when few people approach it. In a city it would be very hard. The disjunction would be noted. Walls would bend inexplicably. Streets would not meet at corners. It could be done . . . has been done in old cities, I am told, where alleys wind and walls curve. There you could go through a door, turn a corner, turn another, wind here, wind there, and be suddenly elsewhere, all the disjunctions hidden by evasive corridors and delusive stairs. Here it is simpler. Who comes? A few cows. A man or two on horseback, hunting the cows. A pig hunting his dinner. A cougar hunting the pig. Who goes over? A few planes, very high. Once in a great while one like last night, a helicopter flying low and slow, looking for someone. What do they see? Mesquite and sand and yucca and more mesquite and more sand.

Who will notice that mesquite does not make a straight line? Who would expect it to?"

"But there are detectors," she said uncertainly. "Radar? Things like that?"

"The wall makes no trace on such devices."

"And you still say this is not fantasy?"

"No. Real people here sent for you."

"Sent for us?"

"Sent me for you. In my role as messenger, or as you say, postmaster. You are the post I am delivering."

"This place where we're going . . . has it always been here?"

He shook his head. "It has been here for a very long time. Not always. Nothing is always."

She went back toward her seat.

Faye raised her head as Carolyn sat down. "Learning things, schoolmate?"

"Many things," she said. "All of them like eating wind pudding."

"Yeah," she said, laying her head back again. "Sophy was always hard to get hold of."

The jouncing journey went on only briefly before the bus slowed and stopped at the edge of a glade, a streamside meadow, sheltered under giant cottonwoods with dark evergreens standing behind them. Carolyn had been over the map a dozen times. There was no stream upon it, only dotted blue lines to show where spring melt or summer cloudbursts cut knife-edged arroyos into the dry clay of the desert. There was no wooded place on the map. There was no town on the map, but here was a settlement beneath the trees, small houses, along with several larger structures.

"Lizard Rock," said the old man, pointing toward a vast, ramified outcropping that reared itself into the golden light beyond the nearest trees. He went to the side door, opened it, fetched a barrow from a few feet away, unloaded the chicken and pig feed into it, and trudged off with it along the stream.

Carolyn descended the steps to stand at their foot. The extreme quiet made her uneasy. It was some time before her roving eye saw a figure clad all in green standing in the door of a nearby house, one so robed and veiled as to be completely hidden, though from the attitude she could see the person was facing them, no doubt looking at them.

There was nothing threatening in that quiet watching, but it made Carolyn shift uncomfortably nonetheless. Behind her, Bettiann came down the steps and put her hand on Carolyn's shoulder, gripping it firmly. As though cued by this appearance, the veiled one left the house and approached them.

"This is friend Carolyn," the person said softly, in a warm and welcoming voice. "And with her are friends Bettiann and Agnes."

Agnes, so mentioned, stopped halfway out of the bus, frozen totteringly in place. Carolyn turned and reached out to her, afraid she would fall.

"I have seen your pictures," said the person. "I feel I have known you for many years. Come. Water has been made hot for the brewing of tea. Chairs have been placed upon the porch. We have been expecting you."

Afar, men's feet thundered down the pavement of streets, traversing the cities, attracting considerable notice from those men who did not march, who were not moved to march, who regarded all this with a shudder of primitive fear, as men might once have done at the approach of a great cave bear or mammoth, or even a tribe other than their own, a tribe bent on evil business, busy with something monstrous and fell.

"You know," whispered one bystander to his neighbor, "it reminds me of those old newsreels, the Nazis, goose-stepping down the street."

"It reminds me of the nature programs on TV," said the other. "Those ants, the ones in the jungle, the ones that eat everything!"

"Somebody ought to stop them."

"Why?" He shrugged, not without some apprehension. "I guess they gotta right to march if they want to."

Enough of them had that right to make the pavement tremble with an avalanche of purposeful feet, causing shivers of discomfort among the watchers. From windows and doors people looked out to see feet falling in unison, legs tramping, arms swinging, eyes straight ahead as the armies marched to the beat of the drum. Some had shaven heads and some had beards. Some had armbands and insignias, others had none. Some were tall and broad, their shirtsleeves rolled high to show tattoos and bulging arms. Others were slender ascetics with hollow cheeks and piercing, angry eyes. Of whatever type, they all marched to the same drums.

In one of those cities, on one of those streets, in the lamplit kitchen of a white clapboard house, far from the man and the fate she had escaped, Helen Jagger sat with others who had also needed a place of refuge.

Rebecca Rainford was telling them a story.

"So then," said Rebecca, raising her voice a little to be heard over the tramp of the feet on the pavement outside, "the men went where Elder Sister was sleeping, and several of them held her down, for she was very strong, while the one man found the medicine bag she had hidden their sex in . . ."

The sound of the marchers reached a crescendo, then passed, the pom, pom, pom of the drums diminishing into the night.

". . . and when each man's sex came out, a tiny piece of the medicine bag

stuck to it, and so they are stuck today to the tip of each man's sex, shaming him
for what he did to Elder Sister in the long ago, and some men even cut them off,
so as not to be reminded of their shame. . . ."

A questioning hush fell as Rebecca went on to the end of the story.

". . . and each time a woman is hurt, Elder Sister weaves a little on her
medicine bag, and in time it will be all woven again."

"Is that why the men are marching out there?" asked Helen, talking a deep
swallow of hot tea. "Because Elder Sister is weaving a new medicine bag?"

"Has just about woven, I think," said Rebecca, with a trembling laugh.
"Has just about woven."

Jessamine, Ophy, and Faye came out of the bus like sleepwalkers and were
shepherded with the others across the short grasses to the nearest house: a
brown wooden house with a wide-planked porch set about with chairs and
small tables. Ophy perched like a bird, alert and interested. Bettiann sat
demurely erect, ankles crossed, hands folded, as at a formal tea. Jessamine
sprawled, her mind busy cataloging what she saw. The voice that had greeted
them was as quiet as the surroundings, a charming female voice, much as she
remembered Sophy's voice had been.

"You're female," said Jessamine, ticking off a category.

"That is a truth," said the person in a voice that smiled. "I am Tess,
aTessuraea Pausiuane [ah-TAY-soo-rah-AY-ah pa-OO-see-oo-AH-nay], which
means, in our language, Pausi's daughter, the balanced one. It is a beautiful
name when spoken lovingly, but Tess will do admirably. My mother is
Pausiliafe Flomuinsuane [pah-OO-sil-ee-AH-fay flow-MOO-in-sue-AH-nay],
Flomuin's daughter, the long-sighted. She is called Pausi. She brings tea."

Pausi came onto the porch, robed and veiled in blue, bowed her head to
each of them, then seated herself. The person next out of the house, carrying
a tray set with cups, was in purple.

"This is my grandmother: Flomuin. We are Tess, Pausi, and Flo."

The robes they wore were like Japanese kimonos, with long, loose sleeves
that covered their hands. The veils covered even their eyes, though with a fine
net through which they could evidently see without trouble, for they did not
fumble or peer. Cups were distributed and tea was poured without their
hands coming into view. Carolyn fought a hysterical giggle that welled at the
back of her throat; Faye and Jessamine were relaxed but concentrated, one
seeking appearance, the other substance. Ophy seemed watchfully at ease,
while Bettiann was politely eager. Agnes, however, could as well have been
dreaming. She could have been at home, at the abbey, in meditation for all
the attention she paid the strangers. Though a visitor in their land, she had
shut them out.

Fragrant steam rose into Carolyn's nose, a pleasant scent in an unfamiliar context. She had smelled it before, but not as tea.

She gestured toward the bus. "The old man? He's not . . . not one of you."

Tess replied, "Padre Josephus is one of our connections with the outside world. He sees things through eyes unlike ours, tells us things he sees that we do not. We provide for him, he provides for us."

"Are you my grandma's sisters?" called Lolly from the bus door. "Are you?"

"Who was your grandmother?" called Tess.

"Her name was Immaculata Corazon."

"We are some of her sisters."

Lolly approached, rubbing the sleep from her eyes, stared at them as at a carnival show or a zoo exhibit. "What're you all covered up for?"

"When showing reverence or meeting strangers, we consider it appropriate. We are not blood sisters to your grandma. We are her foster sisters." She patted the low railing beside which she sat, drawing Lolly down to perch upon it.

"You adopted her grandmother?" grated Agnes in an accusative tone. "You took the child?"

"Only in a sense. When Josephus was only a young man, he found Immaculata lost or abandoned not far from here, a mere child, barely able to tell us her name. We raised her for a few years, and when she was old enough to need company of her own people, he took her out."

"How long have you been here?" Carolyn asked.

"Oh, some thousands of years."

"You, personally," cried Ophy. "You?"

Tess laughed, the laughter echoed by the others, a soft sound, like the windblown scuff of dried leaves across a stone. "No, la. I would feel bored, living so long! I speak of our people. Our ancestors. In earlier—much earlier—times, they were as your people are now, widespread across the world. When your people began to press upon us, long, long ago, we moved into remote enclaves. To us, numbers are not strength; wisdom is strength. What profiteth a race to be numerous and stupid, la? *Behold how great we are, saith the lemming!*" She laughed.

"Where did you live before?" Lolly asked.

"We lived for a time where is now Tibet, dressing ourselves in furs and walking the heights. We lived for a time where is now Ireland, where we lived in barrows among the hills and along the shore. Not long ago we lived where is now Mesa Verde and Hovenweep. All high places or far places. Your people came closer. They saw us, made stories about us, crowded us, named us: we are the Yeti, the Sidhe, the Kachinas. . . ."

"Devils," said Agnes.

"Aggie!" cried Ophy. "Please . . ."

"It is all right," said Tess. "Strangers have always been called devils. We understand the tendency. Agnes is overwrought. When she sees we mean no harm, perhaps she will think differently."

"You were saying?" said Carolyn stiffly, with a glare at Aggie.

"When your people pressed in upon our old places, we learned how to make the wall; then we came here and built it, for no place is really empty of your people anymore." She brought the cup up under her veil, to her lips, then brought it out again. "We regret each move. We become attached to our homes. This has been our home."

Carolyn fixed her eyes on Aggie and asked, "You're not . . . from somewhere else, then? You're not . . . supernatural? Extraterrestrial?"

"Supernatural? No. Is there any reason to think so?"

Carolyn kept her eyes on Aggie, who flushed. "The bus. The wall. The fact you're not on the map."

"As for the bus and the wall, they are only technical tricks. Once they are understood, they are no more wonderful than electricity or television. If you showed electricity to a tenth-century man, he would think you a devil. The bus is not actually a bus, of course, but as a bus it may travel almost anywhere, unremarked, and it is often useful to travel unremarked. The walls are there to keep us away from you, to keep us quiet and unseen. We are of this earth, not from some other place. We are, so to speak, native Americans. Some might say more native than the Indians, for we have been here longer than they. Before the last ice age made a bridge to Alaska, we had come to these continents. This is our home as it has become yours."

Aggie flushed. Her mouth worked. "You are . . . Sophy's people?"

"Yes."

"How many of you are there?" asked Ophy.

"Not many." Tess turned and spoke to her kinswomen in a quick, sibilant tongue, then turned back to the others. "This small village, and two others, other places."

"So few!"

"So few. We cannot be fewer and sustain our people. We cannot be many more and avoid discovery by your people, whom we have had great difficulty both avoiding and understanding. Sophy told us you do not understand yourselves?"

Carolyn laughed without humor. "I guess that's true."

"La. How difficult for you. How difficult for us! With us the inner nature accords with the outer expectation. The body follows the mind, and the mind seeks the soul, which it strives toward but has not yet won. With you it is otherwise. The mind follows the body in pursuit of the soul you have been told you already have. Because you cannot find it, you assume you have lost it somewhere in your past, and this keeps you from achieving it in your future."

"But we do have souls. . . ." cried Agnes.

"I know you are taught so," said Tess. She sipped again before continuing. "We are so few and you are so many, you have driven us into such tiny corners that whether you understood yourselves or not, we had to understand you. Our study of you has been grave and troublesome."

"Troublesome?" asked Jessamine.

"Yes. Since you were in the trees, your people have contended, one with the other, making battles and then making peace, and then battles, and then peace again. You have been proliferate and violent and have demanded dominion over all things. You have fought language against language, culture against culture, convulsion after convulsion. Still, even very early in your history, we saw some of you following the path intelligence must follow as it evolves, the path all thinking races follow: You were gradually learning ways that would lead to wisdom. Ways of respect for nature, ways of peace, ways of quiet cooperation.

"It was then that something happened we did not understand." She fell silent, sipped once more.

"What was it?" asked Faye.

"A persecution began. Here and there around the world, certain of your societies began the persecution of females. There had always been some violence between your sexes, there had always been misunderstanding and pain, as well as great joy, but this was a new thing, a considered thing: an orderly, prescribed persecution of females."

"But that's always happened," laughed Faye. "That's the way it's always been."

Tess shook her veiled head. "You think so, now, for you have no memories of its being otherwise, but some thousands of years ago there were female things and male things, female gods and male gods, respect toward each by each. Then rulers died for the good of their people rather than as now, when people die for the pleasure of their rulers. Though individual men and women may have had stress between them—as what people do not?—at one time there was no organized persecution.

"But such persecution began. First was disrespect of female persons, the violation of the female temples, and the denying of female gods. Then was the disrespect also of other men's gods and the teaching that only one god was true, and he male. Then was the teaching about the devil, also male, and to his jurisdiction were assigned all enemies, all strangers, just as Aggie has assigned us that role. One's own people were of God; other persons were of the devil; both were male. Then we saw the making of rules by old, powerful men to assure they would have many females to serve them or to bear their sons; from these occasions the habit ramified, and it was said to be the will of the male god. Women were enslaved, shut up in harems or cloisters, prostituted, raped, and this was said to be the will of the male god. Women's names were taken from them and they were named for their male owners. Women were considered possessions to be thrown away, burned, killed, battered, mutilated, and this, too, was said to be the will of the male god, and those who objected were said to belong to the devil. In every nation man might cry, 'Behold, we are godly and our women are kept pure, but those others are the great Satan and their women are whores.' "

She stood up and moved about restlessly, moved to action by her own words.

"This was not the pattern we had observed in the beginning. We found it troublesome and terrible. We began to listen to the voices of men, we paid attention to what they said and did, both subtle and overt. We watched the religions they invented, the scriptures they wrote down and claimed their male god had dictated. We listened to the disrespectful words they used for women, in all the various languages. When women longed for communion with the center of their own nature, when they reached for connection with the female principle, men sneered and spoke of the Goddess with contempt and told women to worship the Father God or die. When women turned toward their own ancient wisdom, men accused them of being witches, servants of the devil, and sent them to be burned.

"It seemed a strange and unprofitable thing to happen by chance, not in accordance with nature. After a time we realized it had not happened by chance. We realized it had been planned."

Aggie's eyes were very wide, and she stared at the robed figure in horror.

"You're saying sexism is being controlled by someone?" Faye raised her eyebrows. "Promulgated?"

"Does it surprise you? When racism is promulgated, someone is usually responsible. A death camp, an ethnic cleansing, a marching of skinheads does not happen by itself; there is always a leader, maybe several layers of them. When religious hatred takes place, someone causes it. An inquisition, a crusade, a reformation does not simply occur out of nothing; someone always kicks the first pebble down the cliff, or breaks the first rift in the dike. The persecution of women was also caused, planned, intended. How could we have thought otherwise? How can you?"

"I guess because we can't imagine how it could be done, or why," said Jessamine after a silence. "At least I can't."

"As to how, it was very simple. The planner, the persecutor, simply turned evolution around and defined human females in ape terms. As, for example, in matters relating to reproduction: Women would prefer to be healthy and have healthy children, so the wise woman would choose when to bear and when not to bear. The enemy of woman, however, does not care whether women and children are well and healthy. Your enemy makes men look at females as male apes look at them, as a source of fuck. He focuses all eyes on what is natural to the proliferate ape."

Jessamine murmured, "You're saying . . . chimps do not control their numbers? So . . ."

"So you were told not to control your reproduction because control is unnatural—which, of course, it is. Wise, but unnatural. All wisdom is unnatural. Microscopes are unnatural. Dialysis machines are unnatural. The internal-combustion engine is unnatural. Heart-lung machines are unnatural. Aspirin and antibiotics are unnatural. Thought is unnatural, or at least highly unusual, and many of your religions limit it as much as possible! Do not think, they say. Simply believe. But gracious me, in your world fucking is natural, everything does that, so your enemy defines it not as an animal trait to be dealt with but as a natural law that can't be interfered with."

"So if chimps have the natural capacity for violence . . ." Ophy offered.

"If chimps have that capacity, then the tendency of an ape to pick up a stick must be built into custom and religion, not as an animal trait to be overcome but as a divine right! Listen to your countrymen proclaim the right to bear arms. Look at the work of paranoid militias and fanatical terrorists. Listen to your national rifle group, listen to rapists and wife beaters and men in the sex trade. The mind behind the persecution of women simply takes man's chimp nature and reflects it back to him, putting the imprimatur of natural law on bestial behavior."

"That still doesn't tell us why."

"Why, for power! If you wish to lead men, you tell them that your power or religion or whatever will allow men to do just what they want to do. You want to rape women? Our God allows that. You want to kill homosexuals? Our God approves that. You want to force women to bear your children? Our God insists upon it, and upon your shooting anyone who would help her do otherwise! You want to have eight children? Or a dozen? Fine! Our God says that's just wonderful. And when the children die of hunger or neglect, when the very earth fails under the weight of humanity, why, that is God's will.

"Also, to control men, one must unify them around some goal or symbol, something to stir them into hot blood and battle. To control men, one must give them a cause and an enemy! Yes?"

"It always helps," said Carolyn.

"Of course. So if one wants to control men, one canonizes the ape nature of men. One makes one's cause the protection of apishness, or, as men would say, liberty! Let every ape be as apelike as he wants! Civil liberties means liberty for each ape to do as he pleases, and civility be hanged. As for the enemy, one provides men with the best enemy possible, an enemy so different it cannot be absorbed, so necessary it cannot be totally destroyed, and enough weaker than the alpha ape that she is easy to steal from, to disrespect, and to abuse."

"Woman?" breathed Jessamine.

"Woman. Yes. And since the abuse of woman as enemy (which is quite natural) can itself result in mindless procreation (which is also quite natural), it all fits together nicely. You are a man, you feel violence, which feeds your lust and anger—why, then, commit rape. You may do it violently or you may threaten or seduce. You may do it yourself, with your own organ, or you may do it at several removes, by making laws that allow rapists to walk freely. You wish to further violate the woman or women you have raped? Then insist she may not abort. You may do this by attacking a doctor outside a clinic or you may do it at several removes, by making it unlawful for abortions to be provided to any woman. You wish to continue violating her? Then persecute her if she does not care properly for the offspring that results from an act she did not want and a pregnancy she did not accept."

"You talkin' about me!" cried Lolly.

The veiled one stopped, stilled, then, after a pause, said gently, "Why not, child? Has not the race of man been your enemy since your birth?"

"Not all men!" cried Carolyn.

"Of course not! Most of you, male and female, are striving to understand yourselves and put purpose and meaning into your lives. All men are not woman's enemy, but it doesn't take all men to do great damage! It doesn't even take a majority! Wars are usually begun by a minority. Terrorism is always the fruit of a minority. A fanatic few are quite enough to do the enemy's bidding."

"Who?" begged Carolyn. "Who is this enemy if men are not?"

The veiled figure stood, moving with some agitation. "Ah, well, that is what we wanted to know! We looked first among the general run of men, of course, but we soon learned that most men were not involved. So we looked harder: We found individual men, sometimes even religious men, who blamed women for all the world's ills, but they weren't the cause. They died and their works died with them, yet the persecution went on. We found popes, like this last one, who dedicated their reigns to keeping women in their place, but even they died, and often the next pope was closer to heaven and undid what the earlier man had done.

"*We couldn't find who began it!* So we said to ourselves, la, if one desires to learn about slavery, one becomes a slave. If one would learn of persecution, one becomes the persecuted. If we want to know what is happening to women, we must send someone to live among women. So we sent Sovawanea aTesuawane to live among you. She was one of my twin daughters."

Silence. They had not expected this. They had not expected the finality of the words. *She was . . .*

"You sent your own daughter?" Bettiann asked wonderingly.

"We had to know, so we sent her. Innocent as any child, we sent her. Knowing nothing of the enemy, we sent her. She was ignorant of evil, as each of you is born ignorant of evil. But she had not spent long among you before her intelligence perceived what we knew was there. She did better than we; she traced the persecution to its source. She found the devil among you."

"Who?" Carolyn demanded. "Is it someone behind Webster and his Alliance?"

The figure before them shook her hooded head. "Not behind, friend Carolyn. Though Webster has taken a human name and a human face, he is not a person. He is a force, an unembodied hunger that settled upon this world millennia ago, to feed here, as a great boar might root up a garden to fill his belly. Among ourselves we call such creatures pain-eaters. The dumb pain of brutes does not appeal to their appetites, for they come to a world only when language and intelligence are evolving, to feed upon the pain of articulate grief and shattered dream, of frustrated fulfillment, of mutilated hope. They are the enemies of wise peace and thoughtful contentment; they manure the earth with ignorance and superstition, for in such fields pain is best grown. They are indeed devils."

"Satan?"

Tess shrugged, her robes quivering and settling. "Whatever name you care to give them. Satan. The Beast. The Serpent. I have read your scripture. You have a story of a snake in a garden, and your God says there shall be enmity always between that snake and womankind. Perhaps the writer of that scripture had seen this pain-eater as we do."

"But a real devil?" Jessamine asked skeptically.

"Do you believe in power?"

"Yes."

"Do you believe in evil?"

"I've seen it."

"Do you believe some other life-form might be both evil and powerful?"

"I don't disbelieve it."

"Then you don't disbelieve in devils. You are merely surprised to have encountered one. It is perhaps less surprising to learn that what this devil commands is said by many of your religions to be commanded by God. It is how he works. He hides himself in the dress of sanctity and sentimentality. He ignores the inevitability of drought to whisper of the sweetness of babies.

He ignores the reality of war to tell men they must prove their manhood. Then, when the babies are conceived in their millions, and born in their millions, and are mutilated or starved in their millions, he feasts upon their pain and the pain of their parents. Oh, he is very clever; he hides himself well, but Sophy found him."

"Found him," murmured Carolyn. "And what does he intend?"

"He is no husbandman. He is no farmer or pastor. He has no covenant with earth. He will break the world, glutting himself on one final banquet. One monstrous feeding frenzy, leaving only a remnant behind before he goes to graze upon another world. It is the way of such beings."

Silence. A long quiet, like a pool into which water seeps, the surface barely quivering over a measureless depth. Agnes drew breath, harshly.

"I can't accept this. I can't—"

"It is hard for you," said Tess in a kindly voice. "You have learned the world is otherwise. Drink your tea, friend Agnes. You have scarcely sipped it."

Obediently, Agnes dipped her lips toward her teacup. The person in blue brought a dish of little cakes and passed them around, an obviously ritual act, accompanied by bows and graceful embracing movements of the arms.

"So," said Tess when the cups were empty. "We have eaten and drunk together. This is our ceremony of hospitality. Having done the correct thing, we will now walk together. We want you to see how we live."

The other two robed figures bowed farewell as the DFC straggled after Tess, away from the porch, across the open road, past the animal pens, along the creek where the small houses stood, gradually taking in the curvilinear carvings on the house pillars and along the eaves, the way the dwellings emerged from the land, as though they had grown there. There were goats and sheep grazing in clearings and chickens wandering along the paths; there were people at work in a sunlit garden, all of them as swaddled and veiled as Tess.

The vast outcropping of rounded boulders loomed ahead of them, so glossy and lichen free that it might almost have been polished. Bettiann exclaimed, and they followed her pointing finger to see jeweled lizards dancing upon the stone, each raising a foot to cool it, then putting it down to raise another, coral tongues flopping out and up to wet unblinking moonstone eyes.

According to Carolyn's internal clock, it should have been midnight, or thereabouts, but here, though they could not see the sun, it seemed to be full day. They walked on, circling, more houses, more little gardens. When they returned to the stone, the lizards had been joined by a dozen of Tess's kindred, who were also dancing. One foot up, one foot down, hands swaying, head turning, veils and robes flowing, a mysterious gavotte, like a ritual.

"Dancing on the sunny stone, left foot, right foot," breathed Bettiann, seemingly content merely to watch.

"Come," said Tess, paying no attention to the dancers as she moved on toward the largest structure in the village. They went through a doorless opening in a curving wall that was tall but featureless and found themselves in a simple enclosure open to the sky. At the center stood a stone image, an erect figure, robed and veiled as Tess was, its draped right hand extended to hold a flaming cup. Scattered inside the enclosure were many rough natural stones, gently hollowed and smoothed on their tops, obviously intended for sitting. Following Tess's example, they sank down on various of these, entranced by the dancing flame.

"I have brought you here for Agnes's sake," said Tess. "Perhaps this will convince her who we are. This is our deity. We call her Sovanuan, Essence of Knowing. The name is akin to my daughter's name, Sovawanea, which is Essence of Seeking. Your people might call this goddess Wisdom, or Sophia, as she was once called, when your women had a right to a female goddess. Wisdom is mysterious and hard-won. We portray her as veiled, for we can never know what she looks like, and every veil lifted shows us others behind it. We veil ourselves when we come to revere her, to remind us that Sovanuan dwells within us also, and even there is veiled from our clear sight."

"You come to her with prayer?" asked Agnes in a faraway voice. "With rites of some kind?"

Tess shook her head. "No prayers. No rites. We eschew such formalities."

"Sophy talked about gates," Faye remarked. "Toll gates."

Tess nodded. "Formalities are gates, yes. Catechisms and rites and canons, all of these are gates. We believe that each of us has an inner and an outer path toward Sovanuan, each of us must find our own. This isn't a place of worship. We believe that nothing worthy of our worship would want our worship. This is merely a place of reverent attention."

"It is peaceful here," breathed Aggie, her voice breaking. "The sky seems very pure. The wind is hushed. At night, I suppose, you can look up at the stars."

Tess nodded in agreement. "We come here at night sometimes, when something troubles us, some problem we cannot think out. Now and again the Sovanuan within us raises a veil or lets her flame brighten, dispelling shadow, showing ways that were hidden, letting light in. If we are very fortunate, once in a great while we may see the aureoles and rainbow splendor of the Goddess Herself, and we come away dazzled."

"See what?" Agnes cried.

The veiled head turned, regarding her. "I said, if we are very fortunate, we may see the splendor of the Goddess, plumes of light, glories of radiance—"

"Could that . . . Was that . . . maybe what I saw?" Agnes choked.

"What did you see?" Tess asked gently.

"Splendor. Like fireworks. Facets like scales, and a glory like nothing I have ever seen. . . ."

"When, Aggie?" Ophy squeezed her shoulder. "When are you talking about?"

"There, in San Francisco. When Sophy took the vial." She swallowed, groping for words. "I saw a glory around her, an aureole of pure light. I heard music, instruments and voices, human voices but others as well, a chorus so huge and a harmony so ramified there was not room for it in this world. I felt the universe pulse around me, the walls of the room where I stood pushed out, each pulse an expansion, as though I were in some mighty lung that breathed in. There was a scent, a savor, so fragrant and delicious! All those years, every day spending hours in prayer, and I never felt . . . never anything like that, and then suddenly, there, with no warning. . . ." She put her hands to her face, shuddering with each breath, still murmuring, "I thought it might be a peacock devil, luring me as Sophy had always lured me, but then no warning, nothing, no word, and she was gone away. . . ."

Tess stepped forward, her pose tense and strained, one hand extended toward Aggie, becoming a twin to the carved figure that stood behind her. Ophy shook her head at the rest of them as though to say watch it, don't press it. She put her arms around Agnes.

Tess ignored the tacit warning. She said wonderingly, "If you were one of us, I would know what that means. But you are not one of us."

"What would it mean if I were?" Agnes cried from Ophy's sheltering arms. "What would you think?"

"We would know the Goddess spoke. We would know we were receiving guidance."

"Nothing spoke to me!" Agnes cried. "Or if it did, I couldn't understand it. As for guidance! I couldn't even think, much less be guided! And then later . . . later it all seemed impossible. I told myself I must have been seeing things. Hearing things. And Father Girard said it could have been satanic. . . ."

Tess shook her head, her veils shaking with an almost liquid agitation. She cried out, a shrill bird sound unlike her usual voice, a clarion warning. "No! Agnes McGann! There is a devil, but you would know him if you had seen him. You have seen the Goddess! If you have been given this gift, you must not refuse it. You must not make it less than it is! You must not believe this comes from evil! How can you?"

The cry broke the peace of the place, and they shifted uncomfortably, glancing at one another.

Tess spoke more quietly, shaking her veiled head. "Forgive me. I have no right to direct you; you are not of my people. Besides, we did not come here for disputation. We came so that you could see us, learn about us, so that you will understand."

A long silence threatened to stretch forever.

"Enough," breathed Tess. "Let us go back where we will be more comfortable."

They departed the enclosure, Ophy and Jessamine supporting Aggie, the others walking silently, leaving the veiled Goddess staring at her flaming cup. None of them noticed that Lolly stayed behind, her eyes fixed on Sovanuan's flame as though it held some secret she had long wanted to unravel.

19

THEY RETURNED TO THE HOUSE. A chilly wind had arisen, so they went across the porch into the large room behind it, where they found a few chairs of woven cane and comfortably cushioned bed-benches against the wall. Aggie dropped into one of the chairs and huddled there, Ophy protectively at her side, while the others sat or sprawled on the wide benches. Each of them was looking toward Carolyn, whom they seemed to have appointed their spokesman.

They were all thinking the same thing. They had been confused to the point of rebellion. They could tolerate no further delay or complications.

Carolyn became all too self-consciously diplomatic, made more uncomfortable by the sound of her own plaintive voice. "We appreciate your hospitality, Tess. We appreciate the trouble you've taken with us, but we haven't talked about what brought us here. Is Sophy here?"

A long silence. Tess murmured, "My daughter you called Sophy is departed."

"You mean dead?" Faye challenged.

Tess drew a deep breath. "Sophy is gone. She has been gone for some time."

Faye said, "She can't be! She talks to me! She dictates verses to Bettiann!"

"She walks around with me," said Ophy. "She's there with me in the hospital!"

"And with me in the nights, and in the pastures," said Carolyn. "She's been with all of us!"

Tess stood up, her form rigid and angular with surprise. "All of you?"

"All of us. We've seen her or heard her. Whatever she may be, she's not gone."

The veils shivered. "But she must have gone. Always my daughters lived in one another, your Sophy and my Sovawanea, like two bodies with one mind. But then Sophy was gone. Sovawanea could not reach her, could not hear her. . . ."

"That tells us nothing!" Agnes drew a breath so sharp it cut her like a knife, the blade sliding along her ribs, piercing her heart. "You tell us nothing! What are you? What was she?" She moaned, clutching her side.

Ophy bent over her. "Aggie. Aggie, dear. Come on. Sit up a little. Someone get me my bag. I left it on the porch. You're all right, Aggie."

"I'm not," cried Agnes. "Never."

"She loved your daughter," Bettiann told Tess very softly when she returned from the porch with Ophy's bag. "She could never . . . show it, because of her religion, you see."

"I know," said Tess. "We know. Sovawanea told us."

Agnes panted, "If Sophy is gone, then let me see her sister. Let me see Sovawanea! Let her tell me what she is!"

"Yes," said Carolyn. "Please. It's the only thing that will convince her. Do let us see her."

Tess spoke hesitantly. "She wants to see you. But she is somewhat . . . fearful. She became very fond of you, through Sophy. She doesn't want you to . . . reject her, not to be . . . surprised by her."

"Reject her!" cried Faye, outraged.

"Surprised at what!" demanded Jessamine.

"Surprised . . . at what we are." Tess's voice was tense as she turned and took a few steps away from them, as though separating herself. Her veiled arms were folded high across her chest, protectively.

"You see!" Aggie cried triumphantly. "I told you. . . ."

They shared confused glances, casting sidelong looks at Tess, who stared at Aggie, teetering back and forth, her indecision plain despite the veils. After a moment she made a painfully inhuman sound, something between a hiss and a scream, and put her hands to the fastening of her robes. She wrenched at the closure and let the robes fall to the floor around her feet.

Ophy gasped. Aggie made a strange choked noise. The others were silent, with no breath for speech.

Slowly, Tess pulled the veil from her face to stand before them naked-faced, naked-armed. They saw scaled skin, very fine scales, so fine as to be almost invisible on the face and throat; hair that was not so much fur as feathers, on the head and shoulders and down the backs of the arms; no ears, but a definite tympanum at each side of the head; eyes that were protuberant and individually mobile, lashless, with vertical slits; the mouth more muzzle-like than their own, but with mobile lips.

Faye focused on the hands. They were bonier than human hands, and the nails, claws, were triangular in cross section, stronger than human nails. The teeth were sharper, too. At least those in the front of the mouth were. She assured herself that at a small distance the figure would appear quite human. That was important, though she couldn't say why. It was important that the figure should appear human because . . . because Sophy, well . . . It was important that Sophy had been human. Wasn't it? Except for the narrower shoulders, Tess looked human. Under the loose shift, or in profile, Tess might appear quite inhuman, of course. Which was, for this moment at least, unthinkable.

Jessamine wondered, might they have tails? No good reason they should, but it did rather go with scales. There was a folded structure around the neck and back of the head, possibly erectile. . . .

"Exactly the kind of person one would extrapolate arising from a saurian ancestor rather than a primate one," she murmured, not realizing she was speaking aloud.

"Would you like me to take off my shoes and shift?" Tess asked, her voice noticeably less tense than before she had disrobed. "I will if you like."

Ophy looked up sharply, realizing that Tess had been really afraid of them. Of them!

"Only if you would not be disturbed by it," she said in her gentlest voice.

Tess dropped the shift, kicked off her soft shoes, actually more like foot socks, with soft soles, then turned slowly so they could see all sides, gradually relaxing as she preceived their interest. They were surprised, yes, but they were not angry, or fearful enough to become angry—except for Faye. She seemed more shocked than the others. And Aggie more dumbfounded.

They saw an incurved remnant of a tail, a stubby thing, rather graceless. The scales on Tess's back were individually larger and more ornamental than on the arms, making a definite though subtle pattern. The belly was even more finely scaled than the arms, almost silver in color. The shoulders were definitely narrower than human, the neck longer. No breasts. Not a mammal. No pouch. Not a marsupial. Nothing like a vulva. Whatever was down there was protected by the incurved tail. Now exposed, the feet were long-toed like a lizard's.

"No horns," giggled Aggie hysterically.

Ophy patted her shoulder. "May I?" she asked, holding out her hand toward Tess.

"Of course." Tess submitted to being touched lightly; stroked lightly. Her crest rose, broad at the sides and high behind, elegantly patterned. Jessamine thought of the frilled lizard of Australia. Faye thought of a portrait of Queen Elizabeth, with her extravagant ruff. Around her neck Tess wore a simple chain with a heavy pendant. She touched it now, stroking it, like one touching a talisman.

"What are you?" breathed Agnes from the depth of her private nightmare.

Tess shrugged, a weirdly human shrug from this inhuman form. "Not devils, friend Agnes. We are what we are. Another branch of the bush. Another twig on the evolutionary tangle. I am as earthly as you are. We are saurian, not mammalian. Not monkeylike, but lizard-bird-like, though we can't fly any more than you can still swing through the trees. Our lineage separated from the saurian-avian branch a long time before yours separated from the primates, so we've come a bit farther from our nearest kin."

"But you can talk!" cried Bettiann.

"So can parrots," Tess said softly.

"But you left no fossils," cried Jessamine. "No remnants of cities!"

"The fossils are there, you just haven't known they were us. And we never lived in cities." She lifted her hands, an age-old gesture, her eyes swiveling to light upon each of them. "Since men started swarming about, we've been careful to destroy what older traces were left and not to leave new ones."

Jessamine persisted. "And have I understood correctly, from the seeming absence of any males at all, that you're parthenogenic!"

"That's true."

"What does that mean?" demanded Agnes, eyes darting wildly.

"It means we have children without males. It means we are identical mothers and daughters, with a few males every tenth generation or so, to allow genetic variation."

They stared for a long time, wordlessly.

"Have you seen enough?"

Her voice was not offended, merely patient. Something about it reminded Faye strongly of Sophy. Sophy, who did not mind being painted or sculpted in the nude, so long as the work did not resemble herself. Not self-conscious, merely modest.

She asked, "Sophy . . . she is, was, one of you?"

"Her mind was, yes," said Tess, resuming the light shift that covered her body from shoulder to ankle but left her taloned feet bare. "Though it happens rarely among us, once in a great while a very large egg is laid, and twins come from it, each able to share what the other feels and knows. So

Sovawanea was twinned in the egg, each twin to know what the other knew and feel what the other felt. One twin kept her own body, but we grew a human body for Sophy."

"How?" breathed Jessamine.

"We borrowed some human people to get the cells we needed. We always returned the people, of course, with memories, if any, of quite some other creature than ourselves. It took us a long time to find the right way to do it, to make, as it were, a chimera . . . a mosaic, a human body with another's mind, but at last we succeeded in creating grace and beauty. We were too proud to let one of us go among you in an ugly form, but her perfection was a mistake. Pride is always error. She drew too much attention until you helped her become plain."

"Why?" cried Agnes. "Why would you do such a thing?"

"Because we needed to find the enemy! We could look from this place and see what was happening among you, but that wasn't enough. We could hear your voices, but that wasn't enough, either. If we were to find your enemy and ours, one of us had to be among you and feel it. One of us had to live it."

Carolyn whispered, "They were both Sovawanea?"

"Both of them, yes."

"And our friend, she . . . you think she died?"

Tess paused; her eyes swiveled. They could not read the expression on that unfamiliar face, but the voice seemed uncertain. "I don't know what to believe. You believe you have heard her, seen her. And what seems even stranger to me, Agnes has seen our Goddess, though she still half believes we are demons and is a sworn bride of your male God! How could that be? Such a thing is unkown!"

She shook her head, obviously baffled. "So what is true about Sophy? I don't know. You must ask Sovawanea."

"May we go to her?" Carolyn asked.

A moment's silence while she pondered. "Now that we are sure she will not be . . . endangered, she will come to you."

Tess picked up her robe and sandals and went away, down the dusty street. Across the road, in a paddock, old Josephus was currying a mule. Down the street three robed forms were hoeing a garden. As Tess passed, they looked up, nodded, then took off their robes, hung them across the fence, and went back to their work. They, too, wore simple ankle-length shifts. Their scales varied in color: soft green, ivory, gray.

"I wonder why they wear anything at all," Faye said in a dull voice. "They have no sexual parts to conceal."

"Perhaps as we do, for protection. Or for warmth," suggested Jessamine.

"But aren't they cold-blooded?" asked Bettiann. "Like snakes?"

"She is warmer than the air," said Ophy, staring at the hand that had stroked the scaled skin.

Carolyn said, "Like birds, Bettiann. And, as she said, egg laying."

Jessamine nodded. "Which would make fiddling around with fetal DNA much easier than when it's in a womb inside someone's body."

During all this Agnes had said nothing, had merely stared, paling, breathing more quickly, clasping her arm as though it hurt her. Seeing her distress, Ophy beckoned to Jessamine, and together they lifted Aggie onto one of the cushioned benches along the wall.

Ophy used her stethoscope, muttered instructions to the others to help Aggie lie down and put pillows under her feet. She rummaged among bottles in the bottom of her bag, coming up with a small pill that went under Aggie's tongue.

"What?" Carolyn asked, drawing her away to speak privately.

"Heart," said Ophy. "I think it's just an arrhythmia, but she's really stressed out by this."

"Can't accept it?"

Faye joined them, murmuring, "Can't or won't. She was in love with Sophy. She told us, there in Vermont."

Carolyn nodded thoughtfully. "Of course. She'd have thought of that as sinful, wouldn't she? She's probably long since confessed it and expiated it, but now she doesn't know what she was in love with, or how sinful it may have been. All the confessions and expiations are useless if Sophy wasn't even human. And if she was a demon, well . . . where does that put Aggie?"

They turned back to Aggie and were all closely huddled around her when the well-remembered voice said, "Let me see."

They turned, stood, looked, and looked away, then looked back even as they made room. It was Sophy. Not her face, form, eyes, features, nothing. Not her hair, breasts, hips, no. Not those sweet legs and lovely feet. No. But, still, Sophy. Her voice. Her hold upon them, whatever it had been, so strong still that it made them gasp. Sophy, in a simple white shift like the others.

Not Sophy, they told themselves. Sovawanea.

Sovawanea, who knelt beside Aggie and took her into her arms. "Aggie, love," she said, patting the woman's shoulder. "Aggie, my dear."

And Aggie wept, leaning upon that scaled breast, arm across that scaled shoulder, weeping as though her heart would break, while Sovawanea murmured over and over again: "It's all right, Aggie, dear, it's all right. I'm not some awful thing, dear, I'm not. It's all right. . . ."

Time passed. The room seemed chill. Carolyn built a fire in the tiled stove and shut the wide-flung casements against the cool. They found a kettle, heated water, and made tea, the six of them and this scaled stranger who was no stranger to any of them. For a time they dwelt in a timeless enchantment; the one they had lost was returned to them; they feared to say anything to break the spell.

It was Faye who did so. She could not look upon this unimagined form without the shape of her own Sophy invading the space between. Her Sophy, the sculptured form in her studio, all that loveliness, all that incomparable and incorruptible beauty, hung like a ghost in this alien air, a beauty that deserved more than the talk-around chitchat, the circuitous blather they were all uttering, like so many chickens in a poultry yard. They had come, after all, to find the person they loved, had loved, in one way or another. The words crowded her throat.

"I have to know about Sophy," she demanded of the familiar stranger. "Tell us about Sophy."

The scaled one was sitting beside Agnes, holding her hand. "I wish I could tell you."

"You must try . . . ," Faye insisted.

The scaled one squeezed Aggie's hand. "She was reared outside our village by Padre Josephus and his old wife, visited by our robed teachers, told appropriate stories, given appropriate ideas to make her proof against losing objectivity. At first she knew me only as a voice in her mind, a presence, a ghostly companion. I knew of her as my life's work, my reason for being. Arrangements were made to support her and keep her and educate her as you were educated, to learn of the world, to find the enemy.

"So when she was grown, she went out into the world and met you, the six of you. She learned about women from you." She breathed deeply, in very human distress. "She learned how very different you can be, one from the other: God loving, God rejecting, man loving, man rejecting, life loving, life rejecting. She learned of a world in which it is hard to be a woman, a world where women's worth is undervalued, where their achievements are belittled, where their good sense and humanity are denied. She lived as a woman in a world where some men rape women and excuse themselves by saying the woman asked for that treatment. She lived as a woman in a world where some men mutilate women, and beat them, and burn them, and are excused for doing so by male religious leaders who say that all this is proper and right. She lived in a world where these same religious leaders are shown respect by other nations in the name of expedience or cultural diversity. She lived as a woman in a world where women may not be angry or resentful or they are thought strident, where women may not fight back or they are considered militant, where any assertiveness makes them bitches, where, whether Judeo-Christian, Muslim, Hindu, or Buddhist, they are expected to be dutiful to their wombs, as Sophy herself defined it, in accordance with the Hail Mary Assumption.

"All this made sense for a primitive, sparsely populated people, prey to

disease and predators and war. But for an overpopulated, scientifically advanced people, it made no more sense to Sophy than it had to us. She
thought perhaps your persecution resulted from a conspiracy among males.
We had considered that and rejected it, but she in her turn explored that
possibility. She found that the males who would desire such a conspiracy are
too xenophobic to maintain one beyond the tribal level. She looked elsewhere, discarding this notion and that, as we had before her. Finally she did
what we had not done: She began tracing individual lines of influence from
each persecutor to the one who had influenced him, and from that one to the
next one higher, and from that one to the next one higher yet. She researched
each of these, learned about them, found out, so she said, what made them
tick.

"She traveled here and there, following stories of pain, and in each of
those places she traced the cause. When a crazed man shot women's doctors,
she found who had written the book or given the speech or television talk that
the crazed one listened to; then she sought the teacher of the one who wrote
the book or gave the speech or broadcast his venom; then the one who had
influenced that one. So she went from lonely psychopaths to crackpot groups
moved by preachers and commentators who were in turn moved by lords of
dominion. Always it led back to the Alliance. When a few years ago your *Wall
Street Journal* quoted the dean of an Islamic university as being in favor of
mutilating women, Sophy found he had been taught by an imam who had
been taught by a member of the Alliance.

"The Alliance was headed by a man named Webster. The enemy of
women was a creature named Webster."

She breathed deeply, staring over their heads.

"And then?" asked Aggie.

"Well, we are female, too. Your enemy is our enemy. If he knew of us, he
would not merely eat you and leave us in peace. Knowing that one has an
inexorable enemy is corrosive. It sickened Sophy, like a cancer." Sovawanea's
body trembled in an almost human shiver. "Add to that the fact that she had
always had great trouble coping with the feelings of her chimp-human body,
that lusting that drives you to ignoble ends, all that passion that commits you
to foolishness. Your chimp-human violence racked her. She couldn't cope
with the pain your chimp-human procreation causes, the millions of people
who can find no place or use in life, the hopeless people, too many to be cared
for and, thus, uncared for.

"She suffered. I felt her suffering. And I felt her resolution when, at last,
she determined to go into the lair of the beast and see for herself what he
planned for womankind."

After a long silence Carolyn breathed, "Where?"

"A place called the Redoubt."

"I've heard of it."

"I believe many have heard of it. To their pain."

"Have you been there?" Jessamine asked.

Sovawanea shrugged, that oddly human shrug. "I knew she had gone there. I could not read her thoughts while she was there, but when she disappeared, I thought she might have been captured by that enemy, so I went to the Redoubt seeking her. Then I saw the place."

Carolyn regarded her through slitted eyes. "How did you get there?"

"By our ways."

"Your ways. Like how?"

"Like the bus."

"Which isn't really a bus?"

"No." She frowned. "It isn't really a bus, but when you get on a thing that looks like a bus, you expect to move with the bus in the direction it is facing. When we use our ways to travel, mental alignment is a precursor to movement, and on a bus mental alignment is automatic."

"What are we talking about?" Jessamine demanded. "Telekinesis?"

Sovawanea shook her head. "No. Mentally assisted technology. A tiny device implanted in the head that amplifies certain wave patterns. The travel is technological, but it is thought controlled. Padre Josephus doesn't really drive the bus, though it amuses him to go through the motions. He merely *thinks* it where he wants it to go. And since you expect it to go in whatever direction it is pointed, your own thoughts do not interfere."

"So you went there. You saw the place," said Faye. "Can you take us there?"

Sovawanea clutched her hands together, half turned, gritted her teeth with an audible sound of agitation. "I could."

"Will you?"

"There is danger. Too much danger. The place is well guarded. With so many of us, we could be caught. If we are caught, we are as good as dead."

"But you went," said Carolyn. "Wasn't there danger for you?"

"I am only one. It is easier to hide one."

"Hide, how?"

"People see what they expect to see. It takes only a minor influence to bend space around oneself, to keep oneself unseen. . . ."

"Like the walls around this place that Padre Josephus spoke of," Carolyn said.

"Like that, yes."

"But you could hide us that way."

"No. Not all of us. I could only . . . make things hazy. It wouldn't be good enough."

"You understand that we have to see."

Sovawanea shook her head sadly. "I understand that you think you do. Isn't my word enough?"

"No," said Agnes. "It isn't. At this moment we could be talking to a demon who is seeking to undermine the word of the Church. My Church. Which is allied with Webster. Shall I take your word for it that the Alliance is evil? Or shall I keep in mind that we are fallible? That we may be wrong."

Carolyn said, "I agree. We have to know what is happening. And why."

Sovawanea teetered on her long, clawed toes. "If you are very good. Very . . . obedient. If you think only quiet thoughts, no matter what you see. . . ."

Carolyn stared around her at the others, and they at one another doubtfully. It was Jessamine who said firmly, "We must know. Mustn't we?"

After a long pause Sovawanea nodded. "I suppose you must. Sophy needed to see. You probably need to see, as well." She went to the stove and opened the door, disclosing the glowing coals within. "Come close around me. We must hold hands, so that we travel together."

She wore a chain and pendant like the one Tess wore. Now she took it from about her neck and set it on the floor in front of her. The pendant had a faceted stone set within it that spun and glittered in the firelight.

She said, "Look at the sparkle and try to think of nothing very much. When you feel yourself going, do not fight against it."

"Going?" whispered Ophy.

"This device does not look like a bus, so we must align ourselves in the direction of movement. Look at the light. Let it show you the way. . . ."

They looked as she directed, weary from too much happening, too little sleep, too much apprehension, finding it surprisingly easy not to think of anything much. Their eyes remained fixed on the glitter, unable to leave it. Sovawanea spoke, her voice murmuring in the sibilant, softly melodic tongue of her people. The glitter coalesced, became a glow that crept toward them, like water. The glow expanded in a plane, making a gleaming pool around them. Then the circle turned on its diameter, making a sphere, and within this bubble of light they were gathered up and moved. Through the substance of the light they could see the world flowing beneath them like a river, a liquid running, desert and mountains and rivers, cities alight, dark untenanted spaces sweeping by like dark water.

Carolyn looked from face to face, seeing variously apprehension or fear or wonder or eagerness. Aggie's face was expressionless; her eyes were tightly closed. She kept them closed as time went by, opening them only when their movement slowed, as the world halted beneath their feet.

They stood in a circle of ashen fire on a barren hillside where a throat of darkness gaped into the earth. All around them were mountains, dire and menacing under a lowering sky that spread a mat of filthy cloud upon the jagged horizon. These were badlands, volcanic lands, tortured and drear and black. In one direction a contorted road wound into a distant valley, marked along its length by guard posts and gates; in the opposite direction that road ended in a pair of heavy doors. The tunnel between the doors was guarded by a partially lowered portcullis, where a few visored, anonymous men moved restlessly in and out, like ants crawling through the teeth of a skull. On the portcullis were broad convex bosses graven with a symbol: a spider's web with a thunderbolt at its center.

"Look upon this place," said Sovawanea. "This is the Redoubt. This is the place of your enemy. Here your spider lairs."

"Where are we?" Carolyn murmured.

"Almost on the Canadian border. The builder of this place took some trouble to confuse its location. The Canadians think this is U.S. soil, the Americans think it is Canadian. As a result, neither bothers it. Look here at our feet, where we stand in this gray circle. We will step out of this circle, the circle will remain, and in order to return we must come to this circle once more. Hold the location in your mind so that you can find it."

Her whispering voice grew sharp. "Listen to me. Aggie, whether you trust me or not, you must listen. Here it is night. They do not expect us. Because they do not, and because we will dress ourselves in their clothing, they will not think of invaders, but you must do nothing to attract attention to yourself. They would hear us if we spoke, therefore do not speak. Listen. Look. Hear and see for yourself. I will do nothing to impede you. I will try to cover us, to veil us from their sight, but it will work only for a short time, only so long as we do not touch them, so long as we hold our emotions at bay. If you feel strongly, he who lairs here may feel that emotion and track upon it as a dog does a scent. *You must remain calm*, no matter what you see or hear."

She stepped out of the circle, and they followed her, walking slowly, carefully, hiding behind the nearest stones as the visored men came in or out of the entry. An interval came when no forms moved beneath the portcullis, and they followed Sovawanea's darting form as she slipped beneath the iron teeth. Inside was a long, broad corridor, almost a road leading into the mountain. To their left was a short corridor with doors opening along it. They skulked past the first few rooms where they heard men speaking inside, then slipped into one that was dark, silent, and empty. They saw it only in the light that came in from the corridor, a dressing room, clothing hanging on racks, showers at the rear, urinals and toilets to one side. The uniform included loose trousers, boots, a light long-sleeved tunic that fell to the knees, an ornamental breastplate, and a visored helmet. It took longer for Ophy and Carolyn to find trousers short enough not to drag on the floor than it did for the rest of them to get dressed.

"Anonymity is one of the tenets of the Alliance," murmured Sovawanea as she thrust her arms through the sleeves of the tunic. "All the men here are Webster's servants. It works to our benefit that he does not bother to distinguish among them." She cursed briefly in her own language at the boots as she stuffed them with pieces torn from one of the tunics. Her feet were too thin for the footwear to stay on otherwise.

They went back to the wider entry hall and turned left, into the mountain, walking quietly down the broad though ill-lit tunnel, passed by an occasional little cart that came spinning by in either direction. Scores of smaller tunnels opened out on either side. The one they walked along was long and straight, vanishing into nothing at its end. Carolyn was reminded of the endless concourses of some badly designed airports before they began to hear a distant reverberant clamor, voices echoing in a large room. They felt the effort of the walk. Partway, Sovawanea took the boots off and carried them, and Bettiann bit her lip to keep from groaning at the pain in her legs.

The clamor became louder, gradually differentiating itself into separate voices whose converse echoed in some great enclosure. The hallway expanded before them to reveal a domed space like some great old railway station, lofty, dust moted, and full of shadows. Here the mosaic floor was patterned with the spiderweb and the thunderbolt, and high on one vaulted wall, almost within the dome, another mosaic made a huge portrait of a man who held the world in his hand, like a ball. Behind him was the web once more, and a carved motto: Through Alliance, Power.

"Webster," whispered Carolyn, staring at the huge image. "Just as I saw him, forty years ago."

Here there was constant noise, an ebb and flow of movement and talk. Sovawanea thrust her feet into the boots once more and led the group out of the way of a group of men who came across the huge space, escorted by a docent who gestured and explained.

"What would you like to see next?" the docent demanded of his flock as they went past.

"Webster said we should see the vaults," one of the men replied in a heavily accented voice. "We need to see for ourselves whether the plan can be fulfilled."

The docent nodded. "The vaults are our proof of final victory over the enemy who has sapped our strength and weakened our natures; the vaults are the manifestation of our manhood and the assurance of our immortality as a people. The vaults are restricted to authorized personnel only, but visitors such as yourselves are allowed to observe them. Come."

"Follow them," whispered Sovawanea. "Though you are not 'authorized personnel,' this victory, this manifestation, this assurance is what you have come to see!"

Leaving a sizable gap between them and those they followed, they went into a side tunnel and then onto an escalator. The place reeked of oil and chemicals. There was no traffic on the way down and the lights were dimmed. They descended one level, then another, three, four, five levels. At the bottom they heard the voices of the men, which they followed into a side tunnel, keeping in the shadows. The corridor they were in ended in a pair of tall doors.

Carolyn caught herself yawning. Ophy stumbled.

"Careful," murmured Sovawanea, looking alertly about herself.

"Sleepy," murmured Carolyn. "Why?"

"There is an influence here, something in the air. Keep your minds on where you are and what we're doing."

The visitors had turned aside at the tall doors and had vanished through a lesser side door. Briefly the women could hear feet hammering on a metal stair. Sovawanea waited until the door had swung shut behind them, then led them to the tall doors, where she fingered a keypad. A small door within the larger one opened just enough to allow them through, one at a time. It remained open as they entered, like so many sleepwalkers. . . .

They had come into cavernous space grayed with distance and obscured with cold mist. . . .

Agnes thought she recognized the place. She had dreamed of this place! Here was the terrible wall, tall and gray and thick. Somewhere the last workmen were packing up their trucks and hosing down their tools, leaving a gray foam like a cancer on the green meadow. The wall was pockmarked with cells, each cell with a door, each door with a grate, and at each grate a sister, thin hands clutching the iron, hands reaching through the bars, hands silently begging for release.

Aggie shut her eyes, shivering, felt herself being driven, her hands tied behind her. What was it the person had said to her? "The cell at the end is for you, Reverend Mother. To close you in. To close all of you in, where you belong. . . ."

She remembered the sisters pleading with her as she went by, their eyes begging, their hands extended. In the next-to-last cell was Sister Honore, who opened her bloody mouth to show the Reverend Mother she had no tongue.

"They do not speak," she said aloud.

"They do not speak," someone said to Faye, who had dreamed this dusty aisle, this hazed interior, piled with sculptures on every side, all covered with fine gray dust. Women's forms lay all about her, some stocky, some slim, some close-capped, some with flowing hair, some with matronly breasts, some sylphlike, some swollen in pregnancy, all women. Faye turned in distress, breathing the dust, feeling the decay, crying out in complaint:

"They should be standing, on pedestals, high and beautiful where the sun can touch them. They should speak to the heart. Why are they silent? Why do they lie so still?"

"Why are they all lying so still?" Ophy repeated as she took a chart from the foot of a bed that stood in an endless line of beds in a great ward, huge as a stadium. All the beds held women. Some of the women were pregnant, the covers belled upward over the swollen forms. All of them were unconscious, all of them were tied to the beds, their hands bound to the railings, their feet tied to the iron footboards. "Why are they restrained? What is this writing? I can't read this writing! What is wrong with these women?"

"The doctor knows," said the person following her. "He will take care of them."

"But I'm a doctor. I want to take care of them!"

"No. You're a woman. They'd never let you be a doctor."

Ophy eluded clutching hands and went to the head of the bed to look down at the sleeping face. It was her own face.

Her own face, Bettiann saw, in the mirror. All these thousands of mirrors showing her own face, a thousand different Bettianns, but all Bettiann, nonetheless, the whole world reflecting herself, she here inescapably confronting herself, unable to avoid herself, like being caged up with herself. . . .

Caged up, thought Jessamine. Here all her animals were, caged up in little tiny cages. Lily, all the other females, caged in these tiny, inhumane cubicles, alone, deprived, unable to learn or to be complete. . . .

Carolyn, who saw more clearly than the others because her dream had been a different dream from theirs, heard someone saying her name very softly, over and over. "Carolyn!"

It was Sovawanea, her lips at Carolyn's ear. "Your friends are slipping away from us. *He* is here, somewhere, summoning you, confusing you. Your friends are lost in their own terrors, their own evil dreaming. They must awaken! They must see what is here!"

Carolyn reached out blindly to grasp an arm, which she pulled toward her until she found herself looking into Ophy's fearfully vacant face. She shook Ophy, hissing at her. "Ophy! Come out of it!" shaking her even harder until Ophy's eyes focused once more. Then she reached again, and again, finding another of them, thrusting the form at Ophy or Sovawanea, grabbing another to shake or slap until the woman woke once more.

"The wall," Agnes moaned.

"You are not seeing what's here!" Sovawanea whispered. "You are seeing what he wills for you through your own fears. Look again!"

Holding each to the other, they looked again. The images in their minds shivered and broke; the wall, the cells-cages-beds, the statues, the mirrors, all changed, shifted, becoming something else.

"Look at what they are," murmured Carolyn in a voice of despair. "You see what they are? Just like the prison. Where they were keeping Lolly. . . ."

On either side they rose, tier after tier of them, extending upward into the mist-filled space above, each pod a tiny cell, a tiny cage, a little bed. The bodies inside were still as sculptured forms behind the mirrored faceplates in which the women found their own images superimposed over the faces of the girls who slept there, the young girls, the thousands, ten thousands, hundred thousands of young girls. . . .

The meaning of it came slowly, a creeping dread, a swelling certainty, and they turned to one another in horrified and sickened perception.

"Don't feel," said Sovawanea, her voice trembling on the edge of a terrible sadness. "It is no different for them than it has always been for many women. They do not speak, they do not act. Whether they wish it or no, they will be used to make babies. That has always happened to many. In some times and places it has happened to most. Don't let yourself feel, or he will find you. He notices women who feel! He feeds upon their feelings. . . ."

She tugged them toward a stairs at one side of the great room, and they climbed upward. From below the place had seemed labyrinthine, but from above they could see it was laid out in an orderly grid, level upon level, aisle after aisle, an enormous storage cavern where black-clad warehousemen strode up and down behind wheeled carts, where lights glowed green and red, where chill air flowed in from ducts high on the wall to fall in layers of ghostly fog across the dark floors.

High in the vault to their left a vacant balcony festooned in gold and black gave upon an open arch. On the opposite wall, in a glass-fronted booth over the tall doors, the sightseers looked down and nodded approvingly as their guide gestured and explained.

Sovawanea said: "When I was here before, Webster stood on that balcony, gloating over this . . . greenhouse. Here in this place is the seed crop he will leave behind when he takes his last great feasting on terror and torture and moves on. Above us are the rooms and apartments of the men who will survive, and here are the wombs needed for reproduction. Perhaps in several millennia, when the world has been repopulated, Webster will return again."

"How long?" whispered Carolyn. "How long have they been building this?"

"It has been building for hundreds of years, starting with a great natural cavern, but they only began stocking it with females a few years past. Alliance members send their children to the Redoubt when they are only three or four. The boys attend the Institute. I saw where they keep the girls. They are not taught anything. They are merely fed, bathed, given exercise, raised so until puberty, at which time they are culled. The enemy does not want either

rebellion or thought bred into his followers, so any who show signs of independence or unusual intelligence are culled.

"Those selected for breeding are brought here to sleep their lives away.
There are over three hundred thousand pods in this chamber, all filled with
the female offspring of Alliance members. Here they will be bred and here
they will bear, here they will lactate, and here they will be disposed of when
their reproductive life is over. They feel nothing, they say nothing, they care
nothing. Even this is not good enough for some members of the Alliance, who
are now working on an advanced type of pod, a kind of dummy that will look
and feel like a woman, that will hold the reproductive organs of a real woman,
allowing the rest of the real women to be discarded."

As they went back down the stairs, they leaned out to look more closely
at the faces in the pods—empty faces, without experience, without expectation.

"No pain there," said Carolyn, echoing Josh. "No need for learning."

Jessamine murmured, "No need for equal pay, equal rights, equal anything."

Sovawanea added, "What Sophy called the Hail Mary Assumption is
here made manifest, Aggie. This is what she saw when she came here."

The men in the aisles beneath them muttered as they passed, pausing in
their work to talk among themselves, their voices rising in irritated and quarrelsome tones. Twos and threes of them followed the wheeled carts along the
aisles, some taking sleeping bodies away, some bringing sleeping bodies back.

Sovawanea murmured, "The Alliance members have been well satisfied
with their system, until now."

Carolyn said, "The workers seem dismayed about something, but I can't
make out the words."

"I can," Sovawanea said. "They are dismayed because Webster is angry
with them. They are unable to impregnate the sleepers. Inside the pods the
women's breasts have shrunk and their ovaries have become quiescent. The
epidemic has come to the Redoubt itself."

She led them back toward the door, and as they went, Carolyn read the
labels on the pods nearest them. Each bore a long code number, then the
words: genetic output of so-and-so. With a sense of horrid surprise she saw
Albert Crespin's name; then, in the next rank, that of Jake Jagger. . . .

"Ah," Carolyn cried, her eyes fixed on the small sleeper within, "here is
Helen's child!"

"Hush," whispered Sovawanea, grasping her painfully by the arm. "He'll
hear you!"

She looked up and they followed her gaze. A figure had come out onto
the festooned balcony, someone who stood tall and high-shouldered behind
the parapet, his head bent forward as he peered down toward them. At this

distance Carolyn could not see who it was, but the vulturine posture infuriated her. Here he was, to feast upon these, who might as well be dead! She felt her own anger growing. She warned herself, she tried to calm herself, but it was too late. If her surprise had not drawn his attention, her anger had. He seemed to see them, to be following the growth of her fury with his eyes. . . .

"Out quickly," whispered Sovawanea. "Withdraw. He feels our presence. He knows outsiders are here."

They walked swiftly in the directions they knew, the way they had come. From behind them an alarm sounded, a wailing shriek, as from a banshee throat. Men began to run. As they neared the door, Ophy tried to avoid one of them, stumbling and falling, her helmet rolling away. The man who had tripped her leaped to his feet, glaring around him, looking past Ophy, then back, curiously, then angrily.

"A woman loose in here," he howled at the top of his lungs. "Here, a woman loose!"

From around the huge room came answering shouts. The man who had cried the alarm grabbed for Sovawanea and drew back with a scream of astonishment, his arm slashed to the bone.

"Quickly," breathed Sovawanea, licking his blood from her fangs. "Out the door!"

They slipped through, and the door slid shut behind them in time for half a dozen men to crash into it from the inside.

"She bit me!" howled a voice from beyond the door.

"Shut up," said another voice, deeper, more authoritative. "That's a knife cut, you fool. Get that door open."

The tumult behind the door was echoed by another alarm, a blaring horn. They ran for the escalator, racing up the moving stairs, their hearts pounding, only to hear men's voices coming toward them down the opposite flight. Behind them a noise of pursuit gathered. They were cut off.

"Off, here," Sovawanea ordered, pulling them away at the top of the second flight and leading them in a headlong scramble down a narrow corridor.

They stopped at a corner while Sovawanea cautiously looked around it.

"Can't keep up," moaned Aggie from behind her. "Can't. Go on. You go on without me."

"No!" breathed Sovawanea. "We can't. You know too much about us, Agnes McGann." She took Aggie's arm, and with Jessamine on the other side, they managed a stumbling run down the left-hand way.

"Where are we?" breathed Carolyn.

"We can't go through the central hall," whispered Sovawanea. "Not that level. Too many there. We'll go this way, and hurry!"

She led them down a side corridor, one obviously little used. The sound of pursuit fell behind them. They came to a cluster of doors, small ones, of ordinary size. Sovawanea gave up her place at Aggie's side, letting Bettiann fill in as she fiddled with keypads, opening one of the doors to disclose a flight of narrow stairs.

They went up, stumbling, breathing hard, and then into a chain of small rooms equipped as living and sleeping rooms, now empty, awaiting tenants during the last days. Locking the door behind them, Sovawanea let them pause in one of these to catch their breaths. "I think we're one level below the main entry."

"Did they see us?" Carolyn panted. "How did they know?"

"I think that first man fell over Ophy," Sovawanea said. "He saw Ophy, but he didn't see the rest of our faces. His superior officer told him he had a knife cut. I'm grateful for that. I pray he didn't realize we weren't all alike. He already knows about you, but my people must remain hidden. We are too few to fight him." She cracked a door and peered out into a narrow and empty hall. "We can't delay long. The longer we stay inside here, the more likely he is to find us."

"I'm all right," breathed Aggie, clutching her side.

"No, you're not," said Ophy. "But there's nothing I can do about it here."

Sovawanea opened the door more widely and said, "Quickly, to our left, and up at the next stairs."

The stairs gave upon a side corridor, which meandered for some distance before making an abrupt turn to intersect the main corridor, debouching beside a depot where a row of empty carts was parked.

"Speed, or sneakiness?" Sovawanea asked them, her voice calm but her figure tense with apprehension.

"Speed," said Faye. "They may think we are on official business, but once they shut the main portal . . ."

Sovawanea gestured them into the nearest cart, and she herself got behind the controls. "They are simple devices," she muttered. "I have watched them being driven." One knobbed stick and a foot pedal seemed to control everything, and she sent the cart racing toward the entrance. Far behind them voices shouted questions without answers. A gate fell across the corridor some distance behind them, then another, close enough that they felt the shudder, and Sovawanea pushed the control knob to its highest position. "When we get out, think of something like grass or trees," she demanded. "I'll try to hide us. . . ."

They raced for the portcullis as it too began to drop, and they went under it like liquid sucked through a straw, slurped out through an impossibly narrow opening, crouching, feeling the vehicle shudder as the portcullis slammed down, hearing the scream of metal on metal. They left the cart stalled against tumbled stone and ran, gasping, panting, across the rough rocks to the pale circle of light that awaited them. Guards gathered at the portcullis, looking out at the cart, puzzled faces turning this way and that, seeking the person or persons who had driven it.

In the circle the women clustered, feeling rather than seeing the circle spin to enclose them, feeling the earth flow away around them, closing their eyes at the giddy swim of space, breathing, feeling breath slow, hearts slow, fear diminish, finally opening their eyes once more in the comfortable room, before the stove, where the fire burned warmly. The small device on the floor was now dull, its sparkle dimmed.

Sovawanea staggered. Carolyn reached out to her, steadied her. In a moment Sova leaned over, picked up the device, and put its chain around her neck. Her face was haggard and gray; her eyes were sunken. "At the end I was afraid they would track us by our fear. Our own emotions were masked, however, for the men there were also feeling anger and fear. The enemy could not locate us among all that hubbub. We moved too quickly for him to follow us, but he knows someone was there. Perhaps he does not know who. Perhaps he has not identified you yet."

"Were we really there?" begged Jessamine. "It wasn't some hypnotic trick or some virtual-reality thing?"

"We were really there," said Sovawanea, laughing shortly. "I would not be this weary if we had not been."

"Sophy actually went in there alone?" asked Carolyn. "As we did?"

"Not as we did, no. She really traveled there, as you might travel, in her flesh, in her own body, in real time. She went across those mountains, hiked there; she went in there alone, and somehow she came out again. I don't know how. Though I had felt everything else she had felt and experienced everything else she had done since we were born, I did not feel or experience that. Perhaps the Goddess protected her. I know of no other way she could have done it."

"But you knew about it," said Carolyn.

"I saw in Sophy's mind her memory of what she had seen, the way memories are seen, in fragments, in disorder. I saw no detail of how she got there, or got out, but I saw enough that it seemed to me Sophy had done what she had been sent to do, that her purpose had been achieved. She knew who and where the enemy was. I told Tess and the others. They decided there was no reason for her to stay among you any longer, no reason for her to risk her life.

"So I went to San Francisco to bring my sister home."

"Ah," whispered Agnes.

Sovawanea shrugged, that almost human shrug, a gesture of infinite regret. "She refused to come. I told her her job was finished, she had identified the enemy, but she said no, only the job we had given her was finished, there was another task she had set for herself. I pleaded with her, but she said she loved you and could not let you or your children go into that terrible future, to die in the feeding of that monster, or to live as his remnant will live, seed for a future harvest. She said she knew something could be done. There had to be a way. . . .

"I asked her, what way?

"She said she had faith in Sovanuan, she knew Sovanuan would answer her prayers. She knew the veils would lift. She would not let the enemy conquer womankind, for womankind had become her friends, especially you six. Though there were hundreds that she taught and helped, she cared most for you.

"In the end, when she would not come with me, I came away alone, leaving her there among you."

"There in San Francisco," Jessamine whispered. "You were in my house? You're what Patrick saw?"

"A carelessness on my part, but yes. I am what Patrick saw. If I had felt less tragic at leaving Sophy there, I would have thought it funny. He turned a very peculiar color, and I thought he might choke to death. His confusion did not trouble me greatly; I knew him through Sophy, and we knew what unworthiness had brought him to her room.

"So I came back here feeling anguished and horrid and angry at Sophy and angry at myself. I could not rest. Tess gave me a drug to make me sleep, which I did, for almost a day. When I woke, the anguish was gone and in its place was this great starburst of gladness and discovery! I felt Sophy in my mind as never before, larger than herself, like a tidal wave! The Goddess had answered her prayers."

"That's when I saw . . . whatever it was . . . ," whispered Agnes.

"Tess told me. Yes. That must have been when you saw."

"Was it real?" Aggie cried. "Was she real?"

Sovawanea reached out a hand and stroked her cheek. "As real as life, Aggie. Of course She's real. You have believed in a male god all your life. Why is it so hard to believe in a female one? Have they succeeded so well in making you feel that everything female is inferior?"

"They have," said Aggie. "Yes. They have. They laugh at the idea of female priests. They ridicule the idea of a female pope. They mock the idea of a goddess, belittling the very thought. All the Church is male, through and through."

"Male, and largely homosexual," said Sovawanea. "Whose only acceptable relationship with women is as mothers and sisters. It is not coincidental that those are the roles the Church assigns to women, mocking all others. Well, their mockery will not help them now. Sovanuan exists. She is immanent in all things, in all space and time and matter. She is Sophia, she is Wisdom."

"I can't believe," whispered Agnes.

Sovawanea took her hand. "When I was very young, I fretted over how few we were and how many the tribes of man. Tess sat with me in the temple and asked me why I thought intelligence develops, whether there is purpose there or not. She said if there were no purpose, then we might ignore our intelligence and behave like brutes, like brutes we might worship our taste receptors or our pleasure receptors or our reproductive organs instead of our minds; we might put food or pleasure or reproduction higher than wisdom, and we might assume our deity is more interested in our cooking, our sensuality, or our ovaries than our ideas. She told me this is what the religions of man teach their followers.

"But if there is purpose in intelligence, then we must acknowledge that purpose. We must strive toward it and believe in it. Sophia personifies it, and she lifted her veils so that your race might be saved. She did it because Sophy asked Her to."

They didn't say anything. They merely stared.

"Then what happened?" demanded Carolyn.

Sovawanea stared blindly at the wall. "You know what happened. Your meeting ended in San Francisco. You all went home. Days passed. Months passed. From our little village here, we looked out to see a great change beginning in humankind. Men were troubled by the change. Some of them became violent, but then, as the change continued, they grew calm. Women were less driven. Peace began to creep into your affairs, scarcely noticed, and before that change could be widely noticed, there were distractions. All across the world old women began their legerdemain, drawing attention away from what was really going on, making the eyes look elsewhere. We saw Sophy's hand in that. We looked and wondered what she was up to.

"It was at the same time that the devil's troops began marching, as had been long planned, and this, too, served to keep men's attention elsewhere. Through all that time I felt Sophy in my mind, floating softly, like a leaf on a stream, full of anticipation, warm and loving and utterly certain of something wonderful that was coming."

Aggie said in a dead voice, "She had decided to make us over."

Sovawanea sighed, a very human sigh. "Was it she who did that, Aggie? Or was it the Goddess? I believe the Goddess did it. I believe she showed Sophy how different you might be if you had branched from a slightly different place on the evolutionary bush. If you were less like the promiscuous chimpanzees and more like the monogamous gibbons, the enemy would lose his hold over you. If your natures changed, he could not control you any longer."

"So it's gibbons' decline and fall we're in the midst of," Agnes laughed, her voice cracking. "Gibbons' decline and fall. How funny! How funny!" And she went on laughing, seeming actually amused. "But even the gibbons have babies, Sovawanea. Even the gibbons have young. What good is our intelligence without children to teach? Where are our children? Where is our future? Ah?"

Sovawanea shook her head. "I don't know. I wasn't there when the Goddess came. I felt Her, but if She spoke, it was only to Sophy. Whatever comes, I remind you that Sophy loved you and would not have chosen to hurt you. If you can hold to nothing else, keep faith in her intentions."

Faye demanded, "So what *happened* to her?"

Sovawanea shook her head. A tiny tremor ran down her skin, from head to foot. "She had the ability to end, to stop. With all she had suffered, she had that right."

"She may have had the right, but I don't think she did," Carolyn said firmly. "We told Tess the same thing. Sophy woke me in the night a few days ago. She spoke to Faye in her studio, to Ophy at the hospital. . . ."

"Who did I see but Sophy?" asked Aggie. "Who was the young nun who moved away, always away . . ."

"Someone we think of as Sophy has been with us," Jessamine said firmly, her jaw set. "It wouldn't have happened if she was dead, so she can't be dead."

"But wouldn't I have known?" cried Sovawanea. "I felt everything she felt. Wouldn't I have known?"

"You didn't know when she went into the Redoubt. You didn't know when she saw the Goddess in the desert. Some things you didn't know," said Faye. "Perhaps she wasn't only your twin. Perhaps, at least in part, she was a separate person, on her own." Someone stronger, she thought, not saying it. Someone forged in hotter fires than these, made of stronger stuff. A hybrid strength, perhaps. Born of this brain in a human body.

Carolyn stood up. "Padre Josephus said we'd been followed here. He said there were men in a helicopter, looking for us. Webster's men. Was that Webster we saw at the Redoubt?"

Sovawanea answered, "That was he, scenting your feelings as a coyote scents a jackrabbit. He wants you. He wants the women who have threatened his plans. He has sent his minions after you in the helicopter, but they haven't found you or us because they know nothing about this kind of place."

"What do you know about him?" demanded Carolyn.

"I know only what Tess has already told you. His like are spawned out there somewhere, among the stars. They find worlds where intelligence is evolving and they come to those worlds as gods. As gods they demand the impossible, thereby causing sorrow and pain, feeding on that sorrow and pain until they have glutted themselves. Then they leave a remnant to reseed the pasture while they move on for a time to some other world. Sometimes they cause such sorrow, such pain, that evolution stops, that people turn back on themselves, becoming animals again."

"How do you know that?"

She shrugged. "We talked with people from another world. Long ago."

"Other worlds," gasped Aggie. "There are people on other worlds?"

"From time to time."

"Why haven't we . . ."

"You haven't looked. You started to, but your leaders believe such a search is unimportant because man is at the center of their universe. And, too, you have not had a peaceful thousand years in which to carry on a conversation. I will not say more about that. As to Webster, we know he inhabits a natural body that becomes immortal when he moves into it. We know he cannot leave that body unless it is utterly destroyed. We know that destroying the body does not kill him. If his body is destroyed, he merely moves on to another body, somewhere else."

"So killing his body wouldn't help, and killing him is impossible! So there was no Webster the elder. This creature is the same creature," said Carolyn. "Has always been the same . . ."

Brooding silence, the surface of their awareness quivering in little wavelets of consciousness. Everything had been said except the thing they most wanted to know, and no one knew the answer to that question. After a long time of quiet, Sovawanea rose and came to each of them, hugging, laying her hands on them.

"We must part now. We must return to our own lives. I wish I knew about Sophy, but I don't. We must move on without her."

"But we won't just let you go," cried Jessamine, taking Sovawanea's hand. "We'll come back to hammer on your gates, Sovawanea. We'll walk around yelling."

"Come all you like." She smiled sadly. "We won't be here. Whenever we disclose ourselves, as rarely we have done, we assume that discovery will follow. Our mutual enemy does not know about us, but perhaps you will be forced to tell him. We would be anathema to him, and we do not intend to be here if and when he comes looking."

"You couldn't fight him?" asked Faye.

"We don't know. Long ago, past memory or record, there may have been times that we did, but we have only old tales and tags, out of ancient times. Every brute has a bane, so our saying goes. In your language, we would say:

"To every brute a bane.
If both brute and bane are found,
And summoned onto holy ground,
brute may be slain.

"So it is said in legend. You have similar stories about vampires. Well, he is a kind of interstellar vampire."

"What is the bane for this brute?" interrupted Faye.

"I don't know. I know only that Sophy asked Sovanuan to help you find it."

"And will she help us?"

"Wisdom's face is always veiled. Who knows?"

She kissed them once more, putting her finely scaled lips to their cheeks, then departed, going out and away, leaving the DFC to sit silently staring after her.

"It is early morning out there," said Padre Josephus, appearing suddenly in the doorway. "As soon as you are ready, I will take you back to your car."

He turned and trudged away. Carolyn went after him, out into the road.

"That creature out there. He will find us," said Carolyn. It was something she couldn't say to the others, scarcely dared admit to herself.

Padre Josephus nodded. "True. But his kingdom is falling apart. He has fed well on the pain he causes women, but he depends for that pain on the hatred felt by his followers; and they do not hate as strongly now as they did a few months or even a few days ago. Still, you're right. He will find you, Carolyn. Sooner or later he will find you all."

"It sounds fairly hopeless," she murmured, wiping tears from the corners of her eyes.

He patted her arm. "I raised her from a baby, the one you call Sophy. I know her, better even than they do." He gestured toward the village. "Better even than her sister. Sophy is like the metal you heat and quench and heat and quench. She is strong. Out there, in the desert, she learned things even these don't know. In the pain of battle, you remember her. You call upon her." He raised the patting hand to her cheek, as though to comfort a child. "You call upon her."

She turned toward the others, who were just now coming out of the house. There was already someone standing by the door of the bus, and for a moment Carolyn couldn't think who it was. Then she remembered. Lolly. Of course. She'd completely forgotten about Lolly.

◆ ◆ ◆

At the airport, Webster had given Keepe, Martin, and Jagger their instructions and had then left them, to attend, so he said, to important business elsewhere.

A few miles south of Albuquerque, the three men had picked up the signal from Carolyn's borrowed vehicle and had followed it, not too closely, until the signal had stopped moving. It was dusk by then. They had circled under the darkening sky, using the light and looking for any sign of the women without seeing anything at all. When it was obvious that searching would do no good, they had landed and all three of them had simply sat in the machine, quite sleepless, motionless, waiting. Keepe was no less silent than Martin, and they both no less silent than Jagger, who might as well have been dead except for his shallow breathing and his restlessly twitching eyes.

When first light came, they rose as one organism might have done, summoned up like so many extra arms or legs, returned to life by the will of the one they followed. They took off into the pale dawn, and soon Martin located the area where Ophy had thrown the transmitter. He brought the chopper down, found the transmitter, picked it up, turned it off, and then joined Keepe in exploring the area around it. Jagger prowled like an automaton, but he perceived no more than the others. He was only a shell of a man, stretched around some small core of being in which ambition still burned sullenly, like a damped fire, the coals of himself flaring now and again into flames of denial: It couldn't be over. There had to be some way of retrieving the situation. If he found the women. If only he could find the women . . .

"There's nothing down here," murmured Keepe. He was still capable of feeling fear, and he felt it now. Webster wanted there to be something, and Webster should, at all costs, have what he wanted. "Nothing at all here, Martin."

"Martin, can you track them?" Jagger asked in a toneless voice.

Martin hid his surprise. This was the first thing Jagger had said since yesterday, and Martin had thought it unlikely he would ever speak again. He shook his head, avoiding Jagger's eyes. "I'm no tracker, Mr. Jagger. Sorry. I see only what you do. There was gusty wind last night and this morning. If they went up out of this gully into the wind, it probably wiped out their tracks. They took their stuff, so they plan to be away for a while."

"There's no town within walking distance? No resort, ranch, anything?"

"A ranch back east some miles. Nothing else I know of. Nothing on the maps and nothing we've seen from the air."

"Could they have gone underground? Caverns around here, aren't there?"

"Not that I know of, but I suppose it could be possible. This area isn't all that different from the Carlsbad area, and there are all kinds of caverns there."

These questions had been all Jagger was capable of. They had exhausted him. He had no sense of the presence of the women the way he had sometimes sensed the presence of people, his mother, his wife. Still, seven women could not just disappear into nothing. Eventually, they would emerge from whatever hole they had crawled into.

He approached the chopper, summoning the will to mumble, "Martin? Did they say when they were getting back?"

"She told her husband they'd be back today or call him today. She told him if they didn't get back or call today, he's to send somebody looking for them."

"Well, then," said Jagger, forcing his mind to work, his tongue to obey. "We'll go back there. They'll get back there today, or tonight, or they'll call and say where they are. And the three of us will be waiting for them. They can be questioned there as well as here."

Keepe whined, "Shouldn't we wait here? What if they come back past here with the other one? Or what if they come back past here without her, but they know where she is?"

"Besides, there'll be people at the woman's farm," said Martin, staring at Jagger's unblinking form, nothing of him moving except one tiny muscle near his left eye, which twitched again and again, like something trying desperately to get loose. "Three or four others besides the women."

Jake shrugged. So there would be others besides the women. Even if there were many, it wouldn't matter. Did anything matter?

He said, "They may not be back this way. We could sit here all day while they may be long gone. But we know they'll go back to Santa Fe. If they know where she is, we'll make them tell us."

"Are you going to let Webster know?" asked Keepe. It was totally essential that Webster know everything—every thought, every intention.

"Of course," said Jake. "Of course I'll let him know." After Jake had made Carolyn Crespin tell him everything he needed to know, and after Jake had found the other woman, and after . . . and Webster would congratulate Jake on a job well-done. And Webster would reinstate him as a candidate. And today would be a bad dream, forgotten, and everything would be as it had been before. . . .

Wordlessly, the three men got into the machine and lifted away to the north.

20

THE BUS ARRIVED AT THE Land Rover quite early on what Padre Josephus assured them was only Thursday morning, seemingly too short a time for so much to have happened. As Carolyn was about to leave the bus, she turned to Padre Josephus and asked:

"Helen. My friend. Where is she?"

"Better you don't know where she is. She is safe."

"Safe? Forever?"

He shook his head. "Safe for now. Who knows about forever?"

He lifted his hand in farewell, then drove away, the bus becoming a dwindling yellow dot upon the desert. Carolyn had half expected an ambush at the car, but no one was there. They loaded themselves and their belongings rather wearily. Carolyn made a wide loop into the desert and headed back the way they had come. Most of them slept, including Lolly, and Carolyn woke Jessamine to take over the driving when she felt herself dozing behind the wheel.

They reached Animas at about nine. Carolyn stopped to call Hal and tell him they would be home around six.

"What did you find, sweetheart?"

"Hal, you won't believe me when I tell you. I'm not even sure I do, and it's way too much to try to tell now."

"I'll have supper waiting. You sound tired, so you all drive carefully, now."

They did drive carefully, trading off, one napping while another drove. They stopped in Deming to buy gas and use the rest room.

"What are we going to say about what happened?" Ophy wanted to know as they climbed back into the car. "Are we going to tell?"

"I suppose we could tell some people," said Faye. "Sovawanea told us they're leaving."

"Tell only those we trust," muttered Carolyn. "But no one else. Or they'll lock us all up in the loony bin."

"And what do we do about Webster?" Bettiann asked.

Silence. None of them had the least idea.

When they stopped in Albuquerque, Carolyn phoned home once more, telling herself that something might be needed for supper: milk, perhaps, or vegetables. No one answered her bedroom phone. She tried the other number, and Stace answered, a Stace who sounded most unlike herself.

"I'm in Albuquerque, Stace. Should we pick up anything as we come through Santa Fe?" Carolyn asked, concentrating on Stace's voice, afraid to know what that voice wasn't saying.

"No, I can't think of anything." The words were mechanical, impersonal, and false. Totally false. Like a computer voice.

"Stace . . . ?"

"Yes." The word was laden with weariness and hopelessness.

Comprehension flooded up around Carolyn, an absolute cold-blooded certainty. "Didn't you want me to pick up some hairpins like Grandma's? You said you wanted some."

"That would be nice."

Carolyn swallowed deeply. All she could think of was the look Jagger had given her during the trial. That look of obdurate enmity and utter resolution. She swallowed painfully and made herself ask, "How's Luce's bionics project coming?"

"It's coming fine."

Carolyn went back to the car where all but Lolly were walking out the kinks. "Someone's at the farm. In the house, with Stace and Hal. Jagger, I imagine." The words hurt her throat.

"Stace said so?" Faye demanded.

"I offered to stop on the way and get her some hairpins like mine."

"So?"

"Mine are my grandmother's. Tortoiseshell. She knows what they are. She's quite critical of my using them, but she said fine, get her some."

"Is that all?" asked Ophy.

"That and saying Luce's bionics project was coming along fine. He doesn't have a bionics project."

"My God," breathed Jessamine.

"Bettiann, can you call your husband and have him send the plane to the airport here in Santa Fe—"

"It's already there, Carolyn."

"Then all of you get on it, including Lolly."

"Not me," said Faye. "My maquette is in the back of my van, and I've got a deadline."

"Not me," said Ophy, staring at Faye. "Unfinished business."

Carolyn cried frantically, "If you won't go home, you must stay away from the farm! It's important that you not be where you can be got at, don't you understand? It's important we limit the number of people who might be taken as hostages."

"Us?" Agnes laughed without humor. "Hostages? For what?"

"So they can find out what we know! We'll have to agree on a story, but the fewer people who tell it, the less likely we are to get tripped up."

Bettiann said, "We're not going to leave you alone, Carolyn."

"It's all right," said Carolyn.

"It's not all right," said Faye. "It's dangerous. We need to do something to guarantee they don't hurt you or take you away from there!"

"I'd been thinking about that," she said. "I've got an old friend I thought I'd call."

"Carolyn. An old friend. One person?"

"He . . . he knows other people."

"William could—"

"We don't have time for William to do anything! I don't want anyone else to know anything about this, can't you all understand that? We don't want other people brought into it. It isn't just me and Stace and Luce and Hal and you. It's the world! It's hundreds of thousands of young women sleeping their lives away in pods and all other women dead, gone, vanished! It's whatever Sophy managed to do to prevent that."

"You're sure she's prevented it?" Aggie asked almost angrily. "You're positive?"

"Of course I'm sure! Aren't you, Aggie? In your heart, don't you know that she has done something wonderful and miraculous? Nothing must interfere with whatever she's done, can't you see? He mustn't find out!"

They stared, white-faced, Aggie still angry, her eyes slitted.

"You don't still think she's a devil or something, do you?" Ophy asked. "Aggie, you don't."

"No," said Aggie grudgingly. "But I don't think she's an angel, either."

"Nobody ever said—"

"All right," cried Carolyn. "Now isn't the time."

Bettiann said, "All right, Carolyn. I just don't think you ought to have to carry this alone."

She said tiredly, "I won't carry it alone. Faye will carry her part, and so will Ophy and the rest of you. Even Aggie will snap out of it here in a little while and figure out that she's going to carry a part, no matter what Sophy was. We saw the place ourselves. We saw what Webster plans. Whatever Sophy was or wasn't, we know what he is!"

She went back to the phone to make a call, which turned into several calls. Bettiann and Faye took the opportunity to make a quick trip across the street to a convenient car-rental agency.

"She can go it alone all she likes," Faye muttered, "but I'm not going to leave it that way! There'll be a car waiting for us at the Eldorado Hotel in Santa Fe."

When Carolyn returned from the phone, they piled back into the car.

"Listen," she said. "We've got to have a story we can agree on."

"Story?" asked Aggie. "You mean a lie."

"I prefer to call it a cover story, Aggie. You don't have to tell it, of course. You can choose to remain silent. Or you can sic Webster on Sova's people. The rest of us may not be either that resolute or that . . . ungrateful."

"What story?" Ophy asked, putting her hand on Carolyn's shoulder.

Carolyn chewed her lip. "Okay. If someone asks. We didn't find Sophy. We did find an old man who knew her family, and he told us she died."

"What about the . . . *you know?*" asked Jessamine.

"There was no *you know*. Aggie misinterpreted what she saw in San Francisco. Sophy was really just . . . miming her comment on the whole business of genetic engineering. When you took that vial back to the lab, Jessamine, it was still sealed."

Jessamine demanded, "So what took us overnight? We were gone overnight."

"Damn."

Faye nodded. "We obviously don't want to tell Jagger or whomever about Tess and her people. So where were we?"

Carolyn scowled. "Right. Ah. The old man offered to take us to Sophy's grave. It wasn't far. So we hiked there and had a kind of vigil in her memory. Aggie said a prayer. We talked about our memories of her."

The rest nodded. Aggie asked, "What if he wants you to tell him where it is?"

Carolyn shook her head. "I don't know. The old man took us right around sundown. We just followed him up into the hills. We walked for over an hour. He showed us the grave. There was a boulder there, unshaped stone, with her name carved on it, spelled out. The stone was gray with lichens on it. We picked some wildflowers to put on her grave—let's see . . . some yellow ones—and by then it was too dark to come back, so we spent the night, then he led us back to the car early this morning."

They glanced at one another, then agreed.

"Let's get on the way," said Carolyn. "The timing should work out about right."

"Timing?"

"My helpers need some time to make arrangements and then get to the farm. They'll have to go from across town."

The others said nothing, merely stared at one another grimly. Lolly raised her head from her nest of coats and peered around herself, rather blearily. Carolyn realized for the first time that Lolly was a loose cannon. They couldn't depend on her. On the other hand, she hadn't really seen anything. . . .

"Are you feeling all right?" Ophy asked her.

"Sure," the girl said in a distant voice. "Sure. Why not?"

The road north was heavy in evening traffic. Carolyn pounded on the steering wheel and cursed silently. Why did people who worked in Santa Fe live in Albuquerque, and people who worked in Albuquerque live in Santa Fe? So many people making so many excruciating journeys. Clogging the arteries. Being . . . people!

"Where shall I drop you off?" she asked when they entered Santa Fe.

"The Eldorado," Faye replied with a significant glance at her coconspirators.

Carolyn dropped them at the Eldorado, with less fuss than she had expected. Even Lolly went off with them, without a backward glance. As for Carolyn herself, she couldn't remember ever being so tired or so frightened. What if the people she had called couldn't do what they thought they could?

What if she herself couldn't do what she thought she could? She imagined blood and torture, carnage and death. She saw Stace dying, Hal dying. She bit her tongue and was silent.

She checked the time and saw it was a little earlier than planned. She stopped at a fast-food place for a quick cup of coffee, something warm to thaw the frozen pit of her stomach, not noticing the other car that pulled in and then just sat there. All Carolyn was aware of was that her stomach hurt, that she was frantic.

"You're a coward," she told herself. "A poor, pathetic, cowardly old woman." A ewe sheep. Fatalistic as nature itself. Scared to death, but live or die, this lamb is mine!

Twenty minutes later she turned off the highway into the narrower road leading past her house. She thumbed the button that controlled the right-hand window.

"There's a truck," she murmured to herself. "Right where it's supposed to be."

It was a blocky, wide vehicle, with cardboard taped across the front door, hiding its designation. She had to pull around it, and as she did so, something came plopping through the window into the front seat: a two-way radio, already turned on.

The radio said, "We're in place."

She wasn't sure whose voice it was. "Thank you."

The gate was closed across the driveway. She leaned from the car window to use the key, fumbling with the lock with her left hand. The gate rolled to the side. . . .

Something buffeted her face, like a sudden gust of wind. There was a smell of sage and flowers, and an echo in the car, as though it had become a much larger vehicle.

"Sophy?" she whispered. Her eyes slid sideways. Nothing. Nothing there. Outside the car the trees bent in a flurry of leaves. It had been the wind, only the wind. She left the car window open, took a deep breath, and let the car trundle slowly down the drive, trying to look in all directions at once.

The dogs were in the pen—all the dogs, including Leonegro. She cleared her throat. "The dogs are in the pen," she said aloud to whoever was listening on the radio. "The dog dishes are in there. That means they were fed this morning, but Hal never picked up the dishes. He usually picks them up around nine, nine-thirty, when he lets the dogs out. Or Carlos does. There's no car in front of the old house. If Fidel and Arturo were home, their car would be there. They leave around eight in the morning. I called Hal around eight-thirty. I'd say whoever's here came soon after that and has been here since."

There was no reply from the radio. She didn't expect one. If the plan had been put into action, there were people waiting outside the back of Fidel and Arturo's house. Of course, Fidel and Arturo could be dead and their car disposed of. In which case the whole plan was down the toilet. Assume it wasn't. Assume Fidel and Arturo had gone this morning. Assume the plan would work.

She let the car slide to a stop in front of the house and shoved the radio under the seat. She got out and stretched, leaving the car door open. The dogs barked from the pen, then quieted when she went over and spoke to them at length, rumpling each one. A dusty old car came down the drive; the driver leaned out to wave at her. "Hi, Fidel," she croaked from a dry throat. She had to do better than that. She swallowed, moistened her mouth, said loudly, *"Buenas tardes,* Arturo."

It wasn't Fidel, of course. Or Arturo. Still, they drove to the house Fidel and Arturo occupied, parked, and got out of the car. They would go in the front; their cohorts would come in the back. If there was anyone in there . . .

Her head came up at the sound of crunching gravel. Another car came down the drive, this one driven by Faye. All of them were in it, six of them, even Lolly. All of them, coming like lambs to the slaughter. They pulled to a stop and got out, stretching. They chatted, they laughed, all but Aggie, who regarded Carolyn from deep-set, fatalistic eyes. So the DFC had rigged a sideshow of its own, trusting that Carolyn couldn't make a fuss. Not now. Not here. And Aggie had come along because she hadn't known what else to do. Or because she thought she was already damned and it didn't matter what she did.

Carolyn felt eyes watching her from the house. She felt stares from the kitchen window, but she took no notice as she went to Aggie and hugged her, pulling her close. "Thank you, love," she breathed before turning to the others.

"You damned idiots," she muttered at them. "You stupid, silly . . . ! Follow my lead, will you? And don't say anything unless I say it first."

She dropped her house keys at the base of the wall, went to the door, tried it, made a fuss, went through her purse, slow item by slow item.

At the old house the two men who had just arrived, each carrying a plump grocery sack, were letting themselves in the front door. She waited for a sound, a shot, a yell, counting to herself. A minute went by. Nothing. Which could mean there had been no one in the house but might mean a good many other things as well.

She went back to the kitchen door to hammer on it and shout, "Stace! Hal! I've lost my house keys somewhere. Let me in."

Footsteps inside. Not Stace's. Luce's.

He opened the door and stood aside. "Carolyn. You're later than we expected. Did you lose your keys?" His voice was tense, his eyes unfocused, as though he did not really see her.

"Looks like it. Probably left them at the gas station. I need a glass of water. I'm absolutely overdosed on coffee. . . ."

If he moved too quickly, he'd twang from the tension, she thought, watching him go almost on tiptoe. Stace was somewhere else. Probably being held accountable for his behavior.

He said in a falsely bright voice, "Well, it's the whole club. Did you find your friend Sophy?"

"No, we didn't," said Bettiann, all too smoothly. "Come on in, ladies, don't lollygag. You want some water, Aggie? Ophy? We didn't find her, Luce. We found an old fellow who knows the family. He told us Sophy died a couple of years ago."

"Oh. That's too bad."

Carolyn said, "None of us even knew she was sick. We all spent the trip back grieving over her and kicking ourselves. She should have come to us. Maybe we couldn't have done anything, but at least she didn't need to be alone!"

"Very interesting," said a voice.

Carolyn turned toward the doorway. "Who . . . ," she gasped, truly surprised. She'd gotten so firmly into her role that she'd actually forgotten for the moment. It was Jagger. Of course. She had known it would be. And someone else with him, the rumpled man who had been speaking to Jagger in the courtroom. And they had guns. Of course they did. Men like this always had guns. She had never noticed before how theropsian was Jagger's smile, how feral his eyes were as they fixed on her, ignoring the others as though they did not exist.

"Don't pretend you're surprised, Ms. Crespin. After that ridiculous farrago in court, surely you expected to see me. Did you think I'd let it go?" He glared in Lolly's direction. "And here's the little murderess herself. Well, courtrooms have one set of rules. Here we have another. We've been waiting for you, my friends and I. We came looking for you yesterday, as a matter of fact. In a helicopter."

From a dry mouth she said, "Looking for me? You mean, before? I heard a helicopter, but . . ."

"Come into the other room. Just you, not them. Keepe, make sure they stay put." His eyes swept across them, weighing and rejecting them. "Your daughter's in the den. And your spouse." His voice made a crude joke of the word.

The others stayed where they were, mere statues, standing, staring after Carolyn as she turned and followed Jagger, Luce at her side. Their faces held both fear and a sudden awareness. They had worked themselves up to being high on loyalty and only now realized what they were up against. Well. She had tried to tell them.

Stace was sitting white-faced and blind-eyed in a chair, with another man seated behind her, his handgun pointed in her direction. Hal was on the couch, blood on his forehead. Carolyn fastened her eyes on his chest, seeing slow movement there. Unconscious, then. Not dead. Luce fell into the chair next to Stace, like a dropped marionette.

She started toward Hal, but Jagger pushed her into a chair, and she sat. "I don't understand," she said. "What do you want with me?"

"In this house, a week or so ago, you said that one of your group had been responsible for this current emergency. This sexual matter."

She thought for a moment. "I can't imagine how you . . . well, Agnes did say that, yes. She got us all in a panic over it. It turned out to be a tempest in a teapot. We should have had better sense. . . ."

"In what way?"

"We shouldn't have gotten so hysterical over it—"

"I *mean*, madam, in what way did it turn out to be a tempest in a teapot?" His voice came like steam, a hot cloud obscuring everything but his fury.

Carolyn stared bemusedly at the other man, desperately trying to concentrate. The other one hadn't said anything. He hadn't done anything at all but just sit there, and only the arm holding the gun looked alive, quivering with tension, obviously ready to commit violence. This must be Martin, the man who had probably killed Swinter.

Struggling to get the words out, she said, "It was a tempest in a teapot, Mr. Jagger, because Sophy didn't do anything with the stuff. Aggie misinterpreted what she saw. Jessamine should have realized it as soon as Aggie said it, because the bottle hadn't been opened when she returned it to the lab."

"I don't believe you."

Carolyn shuddered inwardly. His voice was like a twisting knife blade. She let her mouth drop open, breathed in around the pain, made herself speak. "I can't help that, Jagger. Perhaps you'd be kind enough to tell me what the hell you're doing here. Never mind. I'll bet I know. The FBI put you up to this, didn't they? Vince Harmston mentioned something about the FBI, about Albert Crespin's little friends. You tell Albert that just because I told him almost forty years ago that I would not marry him is no reason to continue this stupid harassment! If you have something to charge me with, or my daughter or son-in-law, then do so, but please don't make these vague accusations and—"

"Mr. Jagger," said Martin. "If you want me to, I can make her tell us."

For the first time Carolyn noticed the bruises on Stace's face, the dark trickle of blood emerging from her hair. She felt the icy cold of her belly spread to her chest, her heart. Stubbornly, she opened her mouth to continue her complaint when a surprised shout came from the kitchen.

"Go see what Keepe wants," Jagger said to Martin, who got up and went without a word.

"It's probably my hired man," said Carolyn plaintively.

"It isn't. We sent him home this morning. As for the two who live in that other house, they'll never even know we're here."

"You have no right—"

He laughed. "Such a cliché. Rights! My rights. Your rights!" He breathed deeply. "The way I see it, I have the right to do whatever I can do. I suppose you have the right to try to stop me until you learn you can't. You're like all women. You have to be taught to obey."

"Mr. Jagger!" A strangled voice from the kitchen. "You'd better come here."

Jagger glared at Stace and Luce. "The two of you stay where you are. Don't move. If you move, I'll kill her, then him." He gestured toward Hal's recumbent form as he grasped Carolyn's shoulder and thrust her before him into the hallway.

She staggered toward the kitchen door, seeing trousered legs sprawled on the floor. It was Keepe, supine on the floor, face blank, eyes open. In one corner Lolly cowered, her hands over her face. Across the room, before the open door, Josh, Ophy, and Aggie held Martin facedown while Josh thrust at a straining shoulder with a hypodermic. Jagger pushed Carolyn to one side and raised the gun toward Josh. Out of nowhere Faye appeared behind him and grabbed his arm. He turned, throwing her away, only to be seized by Bettiann and Jessamine, who had also erupted from the pantry behind him. Josh disentangled himself from the struggle at the door and stumbled across the room, still bearing the hypodermic, which he applied to Jagger's neck. Jagger bellowed, throwing all three women away from him and raising the gun once more. Carolyn started toward him, but he sagged in that instant, glaring, then folded to the floor.

"I've got Teo's brothers outside," Josh panted to Carolyn. "You didn't tell me you were bringing a female army. I'll go get the truck."

He started for the door, leaving the women gasping for breath.

"You really got 'em," said Lolly, taking her hands from her face. "You really did."

"All three," murmured Faye. "Just like that."

"Stace is in there," Carolyn murmured, rubbing a wrenched shoulder. "And Hal. I've got to go to Hal. . . ."

She turned, thought she turned, at least formed the intention of turning to go to Hal, then lost that intention at the approach of something enormous that pressed her to her knees, smothering her. She heard Aggie cry out, heard Faye grunt as though she'd been hit in the stomach. She looked up. Josh had opened the kitchen door and stood with the knob still in his hand, facing out. His face was blue, his free hand paddled the air as he tried to breath. Outside on the doorstep stood . . . something. Someone. Dark as night, fiery, terrible, smiling with real amusement as he watched Josh dying.

Webster. Webster in a human body, but with his own guise gathered around him. A boiling cloud of darkness, a heaving mass of troubled storm shot through with sullen lightning. A mass, immovable and horrid, man-shaped, man-size, yet looming like a typhoon. His eyes swiveled and came to rest upon Carolyn.

"You," he muttered in a thunder voice. "You were in my house. You trespassed upon my house."

Josh gurgled. Carolyn couldn't move. Only her lips, her mouth . . .

"Sophy!" Carolyn cried from a well of despair. "Oh, Sophy!"

The word left her mouth like a bird, darting across the room to strike Bettiann like a visible thing, like a splash of clear water that coated her face, released her paralysis. Bettiann's mouth opened to echo the cry. "Sophy!" she called, turning to Aggie. "Sophy!"

The name struck Aggie over the heart, and she bent as though stabbed, then threw her head back to croak the name, which flew once more. Jessamine caught it with a lifted hand, raised her eyes, shook herself, grasped Ophy by one arm and cried like a gull. "Sophy!"

"Sophy!" echoed Ophy, crying the name to Faye, who opened her mouth and sang, her voice deep and velvet black, reaching into infinite distances, summoning, "Sophy. Help us, darling! Oh, we need you, Sophy."

Webster looked back at Josh, then turned again in their direction, his eyes at first arrogant, then wary, then suddenly surprised. The form that held him seemed to lose its balance. He went down on one knee, shook his head dazedly, then fell all at once.

Josh gasped for breath, his face gradually losing its cyanotic hue. "What? What happened?" Outside, in the driveway, men approached from the other house, carrying burdens. "How'd you do that?"

"Breathe, Josh," Carolyn commanded. "Just breathe."

"No time," he gargled. "No time. Are there more?" Josh stared down the corridor behind Carolyn.

"Only these three and . . . him, Josh."

He put his hands to his throat, shaking his head slightly. "I picked up your key all right, got that guy to the door and bushwhacked him, then we got the other one when he came in. Your friends went in the pantry place to grab Jagger from behind. Where'd that other one come from? My God, who is he? I couldn't breathe. That guy, he looked at me, and I felt my heart stop." He gasped for a moment more, his eyes flicking toward her and away in angry confusion. "Hypnotism, right? Or a kind of gas? Something like that?"

"Something like that, yes."

He took a deep breath. "Well, so long as he's out of it! We got to get them loaded."

She stepped into the kitchen like a person wading through deep water, laboriously, pantingly. She entered upon a space that was not what it appeared to be; her kitchen, yes, so the details of furnishing and equipment confirmed, but she realized that now the space did not end at the walls or the floor or the ceiling. The putative boundaries were only screens of seeming; the real walls were distant as stars. Even the tiled floor was permeable, herself and the others tenuously poised on a fragile crystalline lattice over an empty universe. Lying on the lattice were four bodies. Her mind labeled them— Keepe, Martin, Jagger, Webster—but she saw them as concretions of shadow, distance, and intent. Three were motionless clots of shadow. Webster was a pour of magma, the substance of him still quivering with heat, momentarily immobilized, but not yet bound. Around the room were presences, six of them, the women, glowing with shifting veils of color, half a dozen rainbow slices, waiting. And herself, likewise, waiting. From the window a jungle thrust its way toward the heavens, great trees breathing a subtle fragrance. Her herb garden. A whole world there, on the sill.

Teo's brothers came in, knelt, and started peeling the jackets off the unconscious men. Josh fished a metal case from his pocket, took out a hypodermic, jabbed it into a lax arm.

His voice came from the far edge of the universe. "The first shot immobilizes 'em so they don't thrash around when you give 'em the second one, 'cause the second one hurts 'em some. It takes both shots to get them ready for the pods." His words slipped through a veil as from an echo chamber, resonating with distance. He did not know he was poised in the midst of plunging space, lost among the stars. He thought he was in a kitchen, kneeling on a kitchen floor. He started on the next man while other hands went on peeling the clothes away.

Josh took out another case, bent over Webster's body, thrust down with his hypodermic. "Better do this, even though he's out. What did that to him? I didn't get nowhere near him with the needle. Well, this'll slow him down, and then the second one'll freeze his mind, make it stop thinking."

The four young men helping Josh were four dream images, haloed in prismed light, glittering, recognizable as men for all their dizzying splendor, though men permeated by the immaterial, the ineffable.

"You're Emilia's sons?" Carolyn asked, her voice coming as from somewhere else, a long time ago. Emilia had promised to send them, and here they were.

They nodded. One replied, "We got the cousins, too. Josh said maybe we need an army."

The voices were only human, but the effulgence shivered by the sound was more than that. Each word they spoke traced itself in a coruscation of violet light upon the substance that held them. Forces blossomed, energy became concrete, a presence moved upon them, something larger than the room it occupied.

Josh patted his pockets, started for the door. "I'll go get the truck. You get the clothes off them."

He went out and Teo's kinsmen finished stripping the lax bodies, piling the clothes to one side, suit coats, shirts, ties, trousers, socks, but, with a glance at the women, leaving the shorts on the bodies. The inane courtesy of it made her want to shout with immense laughter, but she could not. She was as incapable of laughter as she was of movement. Something possessed her, held her, cradled her, leaving only a tiny space around her. If it had not given her that tiny space, she would have been unable to stand, to breathe, to keep her own heart beating. If it had not allowed her that space, she would have been compressed into nothingness.

The truck came into the driveway, swerved, and backed toward the kitchen door. One of Emilia's sons opened the door, and through it Carolyn could see Josh raising the back of the truck to disclose the racks there: eight pods, racked two high, four against each wall.

Josh beckoned to Teo's brothers, who leaped up beside him. "Open the four bottom ones," he said. "I started the cycle before I left. They should be awake, or almost. Drag 'em out of there if they're not."

Two were awake. Two were not. One of the awake ones was Teo, though he looked like a dishrag. All four were lifted out and gently carried toward Fidel and Arturo's house.

"That's Teo," said Josh unnecessarily. "And some other guys didn't belong in there."

Aggie said, from the far side of the universe, "They don't have any clothes."

"Clothes in the grocery sacks the boys brought," he said. "The boys'll get 'em dressed."

Two of the young men came back to help Josh carry bodies to the truck, strip off the shorts, and lift them in. Naked and unconscious, they didn't look like devils. They looked like men. That was the trouble with devils, Carolyn thought. Too often they looked like men.

They took Keepe first, then Martin, and then Jagger, each more slowly, as though they waded through curdled space and time. When Jagger was carried out, both space and time solidified. The room closed behind him. No way out was left. Outside, all motion stopped, no leaf moved. Through the door they could see Josh standing frozen, one leg halfway into the truck, and beyond him a tree bent in the wind, unmoving, also frozen.

Inside the room a presence seethed in every direction, light shattered as the space that held them was first vacated, then stretched. A chill music fell upon the bubble they stood within, coming from cavernous elsewhere, immensity stretching unseen on every side, all sensation centered at the body lying on the floor:

Webster. Left all alone on the kitchen floor while they stared down at the images wavering and changing, flowing like water, becoming a mirror that showed to each her own icon. . . .

Bettiann saw her own face, her own body. Perfect. Her body was sylphlike, desirable, so lovely that it moved even her to passion. Heat bathed her, her lungs labored, panting. Here was what she really was! What she had always sought to be. Truly beautiful. Forever beautiful!

Carolyn saw herself as a perfect Crespin woman, surrounded by her children, poised, smiling gently, the perfect mother, the perfect wife. This was what she was, what she really was. She needn't have felt guilty anymore about letting the family down. She smiled up into Albert's face, happy in the knowledge she was exactly what the family wanted!

Aggie saw herself—pure, sexless, angelic, the white edges of her veil blown behind her like wings, the archbishop bending forward, putting his hand on her forehead, and saying, "You are a living rule, Reverend Mother. You have become a perfect nun. . . ."

Ophy was holding her baby, the other little ones tugging at her skirt, while her father beamed his approval. Oh, it felt so good to have given up being a doctor. Better by far to be a mother, a wife, to make her menfolk comfortable. Jessamine was preparing a Thanksgiving feast for her parents, and for Patrick, and for her son. Oh, it felt so good to have given up being a scientist. Better by far . . .

Faye felt a sexual lure like a hook set into her flesh, drawing her. Looking down into Webster's face, she saw an image of herself, saw the face change, become like her own, infinitely seductive, but male. Herself, but a self that would control her, take care of her. . . .

"You see," he whispered to them. "You see. Everything you really need is here. What woman needs and really wants. Not all that nonsense about freedom, or rights. No. Your true nature is here, right here. . . ."

They were all moving toward him when his eyes snapped open. They were red, like the smallest borehole of a volcano, a fiery hotness that ran from this room in this place, away to the center of the earth and from there into forever.

Awareness came into his eyes. His face moved. His lips curved into a dreadful smile. His hand reached out, summoning, pointing, directing, and they saw what he moved. . . .

Afar, in city after city, the marching men came upon their quarry at last. A great shout went up from a hundred thousand throats. The old women were silent, only waiting.

Afar, in city after city, men cried out their rage.

You, they cried. You witches, you sperm stealers who would put the goddess in place of the God I have built in my own image! You vessels of sin, you imperfect creation, you faulty, you foul, you impure. You broads, bimbos, bitches. You evil mothers, conniving sisters, you castrating wives who never bowed down to me as you should. You . . .

Webster sat up. Carolyn couldn't see him clearly. He was blurred. The air in front of him wavered, like heat waves rising from pavement. His glance swept around the kitchen, and, touched by that glance, the women seemed to stop breathing.

Carolyn felt a breath in her ear, felt an arm slide around her in a silken caress, embracing her, interposing itself, deflecting Webster's gaze. The searchlight glance swerved around her harmlessly through space that was somehow compressed. Light bent and split into prisms; positions shifted; people warped and elongated, as though seen through a wobbly lens, but she went on thinking, moving, sweating. She felt the drops running down her back, down her neck and cheeks from under her hair. For a moment she saw him clearly. He was the same man she had seen forty-one years ago. No matter this robe of cloud and storm, he was the same.

He got to his feet, raising his hand like a conductor. It almost could have held a baton.

Afar, in city after city, men howled their rage.

But afar, in city after city, "Hush," said the old women, as with one voice, making one great wave of sound that rushed and frothed across the sands of time and space: Hush, hush, hush.

"Hush," said Aggie, Bettiann, and Carolyn. "Hush," said Ophy, and Jessamine, and Faye.

"Hush," said another voice, full of laughter. Sophy's voice.

It was Lolly's body that moved, but it was Sophy who was there, the person well-known and loved, the sound, feeling, smell of her, the presence of her, dressed in her old, sloppy clothes, her hair pulled into an ugly bun, her hand reaching out to touch him. Carolyn wanted to cry out, Beware, Sophy. Get away. He'll destroy you, Sophy. This is your enemy, this is the one who had been seeking you. Oh, Sophy, Sophy, take care.

She could not make a sound. There wasn't room for the smallest movement, no room for lips to twitch or eyes to blink. All space not occupied by their bodies was filled with something besides Sophy, something vastly larger than she: a warmth like hearth fires, a flowing like a hot tide, like an endless river of sustaining blood, a flowing not around, but through, a permeation. . . .

Sophy's fingertips, Lolly's fingertips, gently stroked the lids of those fiery eyes; the heel of Sophy's hand reached up to press his mighty horned brow; but it was some other power than Sophy's that flowed through those fingers. Time stopped. The red eyes blinked, staring upward, awed perhaps, certainly surprised at what they saw, maybe even terrified, for Webster's dreadful mouth opened, and he said, "You."

"You," whispered the men in their myriads. "You . . ."

Only that one word. Every muscle of his body writhed beneath his skin, but he could not move, no more than Carolyn could. There was no room for him to move.

"You are dominion," said a voice that was not Sophy's voice, a voice Sophy's had only hinted at occasionally. A Gorgon's voice, a voice of adamant, a voice that was also the voice of millions, old women, old voices, wise with age and the androgyny of time, the Goddess's voice. "You are dominance. You are lust and terror. You are pain and persecution. From the beginning you have been our enemy. My daughters of all worlds and I, we have summoned you on this holy ground. Here brute and here bane, and here we stand, sisters, to claim this victory."

Carolyn was choking on her own breath, listening. There was something coming, like a volcano or a wind or a towering wave; something immaterial, monstrous, marvelous, a thunder of wings, a mountain of water, something formless from distances unimaginable. For a moment she was filled with ecstasy, a luminous presence, a wondrous in-habitation; for a moment she knew . . . oh, the things she knew that she had no words to describe. There were aureoles of light, enormous voices calling greetings across an eternity of time, a crying of choirs aloft, a name! A name cried out by every voice in the universe, by every creature who had a voice to cry.

And for an instant Carolyn saw them as they were, Sophia and him: she scaled with rainbows, shining with the light of the primal dawn; he as he was, the star swimmer, the feaster upon souls, the monster who takes the form of his prey, the shadow, the amorphous presence defined by what it consumes. They saw him for only a moment, a man-shaped hole in the fabric of being, black and sucking, grasping, eating, gulping. In the next moment he receded from before them. They felt him going inward, swiftly and more swiftly still, with a long, horrified whine, like a bullet shot from a gun into unfathomable chasms, the fabric of him stretching from outside to inside, from the eyes and brain of the body he occupied into the very substance of that body. They felt something break, a snapping, like one quick shock of earthquake with no following tremor but only a whispering sigh as of gravel falling or dust sifting, a filling in. His body remained, and he within it, but he was no longer connected to this time, this place, to any time, any place. He was a singularity, a tininess, spinning upon itself inside that body, caught there forever, immortal, unable to escape.

In city after city, the drums stopped beating. Men stumbled, then turned to one another, confused. They rubbed their foreheads fretfully, trying to remember why they were where they were, why in this company? Why at this time? Muttering, they wandered off in any direction, forgetting that they didn't know why they had come.

In the kitchen there was one moment more while the Goddess breathed them in and out. Then the marvelous inhabitant withdrew, pouring away as a tide pours from the beaches out into the sea, leaving behind only the memory of permeation, the anticipation of return. Still, Sophy was there, herself, looking into Carolyn's face, reaching out to her. *"I have not finished, Carolyn."*

"Oh, Sophy. We've missed you."

"And I you, love, all you loves. Listen. The bubble that holds us will not last. I must tell you now, quickly, before it breaks. See the lights, my friends. See them, here, in my hand."

She spread her hand. It seemed to them that she held on her palm a fragment of rainbow, a shard thrown by a prism, red, yellow, green, blue, and a violet so dark it was almost black.

"Look," Sophy said, turning to the others. "See."

All of them saw.

"Listen," said Sophy. *"Listen carefully.*

"These lights are given me by Sophia. We have done what we have done to save you; still, we have done it without your consent. We have shut a certain door, closed a certain gate, but life demands you must have the means to open that gate. Just as you were changed, so you may be changed again:

"You yourselves must choose the ground on which you will stand, never to decline or fall from that place. If you choose the ruby light, then in all future time only pairs mated for life will breed once in a decade. A woman may have one child or two. Rarely, three. Never more than that. Your numbers will fit themselves into the wholeness of life. There will be room for other life than yours and better perception than now. Do you understand?"

They nodded, all of them. It was the only motion in the universe.

"If you choose the topaz light, you will become like us, parthenogenetic, mothers and daughters, with a few males born only each eighth or ninth generation."

Carolyn swallowed deeply, thinking of Hal. And Luce. Ophy shook her head, rejecting; but Faye whispered, ah . . .

"There is an advantage to our way. Where men are many, they fall easy prey to creatures like Webster. And where there are only women, you need only half as many. Do you understand?"

They did. More than her words was being conveyed. They saw what she meant.

"If you choose the emerald light, all will be with you as it was before, except that no woman will ever conceive unless she chooses to conceive, unless she is ready in mind and body and heart and has chosen so over long and careful time. No pregnancy can be forced upon any woman. If this light is chosen, no woman would say, 'Be it done unto me.' Each woman would have to say, 'I want this for myself.' "

There was quiet. Outside the door Josh stood halfway into the truck. On the trees the leaves were still.

"If you choose the sapphire, you will return to your former nature except in one regard. Men and women will mature quickly, almost overnight, but not for thirty years. Some creatures take that long to mature; it is not a great change. Think of a long and lovely childhood, a long and lovely youth in which to learn and travel and work, learning of oneself and of the world, followed only then by a brief reproductive maturity. Think of a life with no adolescence, a life in which only the mature may bear. Do you understand?"

They nodded, understanding.

"And last, if you choose this lapis light, you will be as you were, your world will be as it has always been. Remember the stories you have told me of yourselves, remember the stories I have told you of others. Remind yourselves how your world has always been. Much was His fault, but as much was not."

They were silent. Sophy moved swiftly, to each of them, one at a time, giving a kiss, a caress, bending to touch her cheek to theirs. Good-bye to Carolyn and Faye, to Ophy and Jessamine, to Bettiann. And last to Agnes, holding her close, closer than she had ever held her when they had been girls together.

"Good-bye, Agnes. You see. I am not a devil."

"Don't go!" she cried.

"I have gone." Sophy smiled, an expression of such radiant joy that Agnes blinked before it. *"I have already gone."* And she gestured, the movement of her hand encompassing all that had happened, all that was being accomplished. *"Don't be afraid, Aggie. It's all right. It isn't a sin to be wise. . . ."*

Afar, in city after city, the old women went away, by ones and twos, invisible.

And Sophy was indeed gone, leaving Lolly slumped on the floor, quite limp, her chest rising and falling only a little. Carolyn's eyes squeezed shut. When she opened them a moment later, she stood in her own kitchen. Through tear-spangled light she saw once again a small, useful space ending at the walls. The herb garden sat quietly on the windowsill. Webster's body lay quietly, relaxed, eyes shut. Faye and Ophy were against the far wall, as was Jessamine. Bettiann was just inside the door. Aggie knelt beside Lolly, with her arms protectively around the girl. All of them gasped for breath, as though they had not breathed for a long time. Carolyn tried to tell herself she had imagined it. She was very tired, stressed—she had imagined it.

As she might have done, except for the five small vials that sat on the kitchen counter, fragments of rainbow, self-illumined, ruby and topaz, emerald and sapphire—and that one of livid light, lapis made effulgent to glow with a hard, aching heat, like a bruise. Carolyn picked them up, reading the label on each. "Choose. Decant into Sophia's chalice. All will be as you have chosen."

So. She hadn't imagined any of it. Even thinking so was a betrayal. She had imagined none of it. It was all real.

"What did she leave us?" Ophy asked.

Carolyn gave her the vials, and from her hand they went the round, returning to Carolyn, who put them into her jacket pocket.

Josh came in, seeing nothing unusual, unaware of any happening beyond what he had planned. Carolyn managed to remind him of the second shot for Webster, though she thought to herself it probably wasn't needed. Then the young men came to carry Webster outside while the women stumbled after them, watching while they loaded him into the last empty pod and closed the heavy lid upon him. Josh went from pod to pod, referring to a card he held in his left hand while he pushed buttons with his right, waiting, frowning intently until each little green light came on. When the last one shone, he nodded in satisfaction, then came down to close, lock, and seal the door. The boys went back into the kitchen, gathered up the scattered clothing, and departed.

Carolyn gargled hoarsely, astonished at the pain in her throat, as though she had gasped her way across a desert. "Ophy. My family's in the study. I think Hal's hurt." She looked at her watch, feeling guilty for the time that had passed, then confused that no time had passed. No time at all.

Ophy and Jessamine hurried off down the hall, followed by Faye. Aggie and Bettiann helped Lolly get up, then walked her into the adjacent dining room. Carolyn and Josh were left alone.

Carolyn asked, "You want some coffee, Josh?"

"I could sure use a drink."

"Better avoid that. We don't want an accident on your way down south."

"Right. Coffee, then. I'll have the drink later."

Ophy put her head in the door. "Stace and Luce had already called for an ambulance," she told Carolyn. "They say Hal was hit on the head. I don't think his condition is serious, but let's not take the chance. There's a wound on Stace's head that needs some stitches, too. I'll go with them to the hospital when the ambulance gets here."

She went back to the den. Carolyn thought of going with her, discarded the idea. Ophy would care for Hal better than Carolyn could. Ophy would look after Stace's cuts and bruises. She, Carolyn, had to stay there, see that all went as planned. She put the coffee on to brew, asking, "What do their pods say, Josh?"

"Fifty years, murder of a police officer. FAT."

"That isn't what Teo was in for."

"I faked up some New Mexico conviction forms, then some add-on-sentence forms from Montana and Florida and Kansas and Illinois. They're all in the files, out at the jail. I didn't do the FUD forms, though. With no federal forms, there can't be any federal audits, like." He seemed almost euphoric, totally relaxed.

"How do you feel?" she asked curiously.

"I feel . . . like I could fly. First time I've really felt good about those pods, you know."

"And where do they go now?"

"Down to the Waste Impoundment Pilot Program." He savored each syllable lovingly. "Down to WIPP. Underground. Way back in the salt caves. With the rest of the waste."

She dug out a thermos, poured the freshly brewed coffee, added milk and sugar. "I suppose the pods could stay there forever."

"No reason why not."

If Webster's body was immortal, if he couldn't leave it so long as it was alive, certainly no reason why not.

"Long trip, Josh. Thank you."

"Thank you." He grinned. "First time I've felt useful in ages."

The truck pulled out of the drive only a few minutes before the ambulance arrived. When it left, Ophy and Jessamine followed it, Ophy in her own rental car, followed by Jessamine, returning the one they'd picked up at the hotel.

Stace came into the kitchen, Luce's arm around her.

"What did you do with those men?"

Carolyn equivocated. "They've gone. They realized we didn't know anything about anything. Really stupid."

"I know Jagger, but who were the others?"

Carolyn bit her lip. "Remember, I told you about cousin Albert? They were some of his FBI cronies."

"I don't believe this! Mom, they were awful. That Jagger! He put some kind of stranglehold on Daddy, and Daddy just fell down like he'd been shot. And they hit me!"

"Some men do things like that, don't they? Especially men with a little power. Be thankful you've got a nice one like Luce." Luce, who was giving her a very percipient look. Luce, who didn't believe the men had gone peacefully away. Luce, who might have to be encouraged to forget about the whole thing. Cross that bridge when she came to it. "Luce, would you take Stace to the hospital to get stitched up, and so she can be there with her dad? I'll get there as quickly as I can."

From the dining room came Lolly's fretful voice. "I fell down," she whined. "Why did I fall down?"

Aggie and Bettiann murmured wordlessly, soothingly.

Stace and Luce departed, Stace still muttering. Carolyn went into the dining room.

"Aggie, maybe Lolly would like to lie down or clean up. She can go back to the big bedroom. There are fresh towels in the bathroom cabinet."

"I'll take care of Lolly." Aggie pulled the girl to her feet and led her away. A silence fell. A hole in the fabric of happening; a momentary emptiness.

Carolyn went to wash her face. The first touch of water on her cheeks brought a flood of tears. Sophy had been there. Sophy herself. Whatever she was, she wasn't dead. She'd been with them all the time. She'd protected them, taken care of them. Somehow, if Padre Josephus was to be believed, she had protected Helen, too, and cared for her. Then she'd gone back into . . . into that personage, that great assemblage, the Goddess. They had all seen Sophy. They had all seen the Goddess, too. No doubt. No question. No gates in the way. No guide, no conveyance. No rites needed. Just her, there, disclosing herself.

The hasty plan she and Josh had devised . . . well, it had worked out all right against Jagger, Keepe, and Martin. Nothing she or Josh could have devised would have worked on Webster. She'd known that, at some level, ever since the beginning. Once Webster got a foothold, no placating word would help. No amount of subservience. No exaggerated obedience. No tactic for female survival would ever have worked with Webster. Nothing could have defeated him except the one who had defeated him.

What was it Sovawanea had said? One must announce the battle. One must find the bane, then summon bane and beast onto holy ground. Her own homely kitchen? Which Sophy had made holy ground seven years ago in that ceremony they had so enjoyed, with the feathers, and the drums, and the planting of the herbs. In that more innocent time.

And why was she crying?

She told herself to stop it. There was something that had to be taken care of, quickly, before she forgot it. She found a small box, got out the tape, dug out some tissues for padding. She fished the vials out of her jacket pocket—red, yellow, green, blue, violet—and packed them safely away.

She hadn't figured out the allusion to Sophia's chalice yet. The Goddess Sophia and her flaming cup had probably gone away with Sovawanea and Tess and all the aunts and grandmas and great-grandmas. Still, the answer would no doubt become obvious, once she had a little time to think. Did she remember which vial was which? She told them over in her head. Mated pairs. Women and daughters. Individual decision. Long youth. Or things as they had always been. Yes. She remembered. She jotted them down on a card and put the card in with the vials, sealing the packet with tape.

Who would make the choice?

No one, just now. There was no strength left to do anything just now. Carefully, she put the sealed box at the very back of a drawer in her medicine cabinet.

She heard Faye's voice outside, dried her face, and went out to the kitchen, where Faye and Bettiann and Aggie had assembled.

Faye was shaking her head. "Did I really see Sophy . . . ?"

"We all did," said Aggie in a wondering voice. "We all did." She sounded stronger, suddenly resolute. "We really did! I feel such a fool. Why on earth have I been behaving like this? I've acted like—"

"You've been you, Aggie." Bettiann hugged her.

"Well, I'm tired of being me if being me actually let me forget . . . forget that Sophy was my friend. All those years that I knew her, knew what she was like, and I actually believed she might have been evil. What kind of a life am I living that would let me believe that?"

She went away, biting her lip, tears in her eyes, with Bettiann close behind.

Stace phoned from the hospital. She had been stitched up. Hal was all right, sleeping comfortably. They'd keep him at the hospital until after they'd done some tests tomorrow. No need for Carolyn to come in.

What next?

Set out some leftovers for whoever might be hungry, including Lolly, of course, who was only Lolly again, very pale and stretched looking, yet with a shadow of beauty on her face she had not had before. She poured Faye and Aggie and Bettiann each a small drink, delivered them, then poured one for herself. There was no sign of Carlos, so she went down the hill to feed the sheep, to put the ewes and half-grown lambs in the barn. To stand in the starlit darkness, thanking the presence that brooded there that all Carolyn's loved ones were still alive and would also be able to stand in the starlight.

The black-and-white lamb nudged her, begging grain. She knelt, offering a handful. The lamb wandered away, but the touch of soft lips in her palm went on. She found herself crying again. That's all right, she murmured, half to herself, half to the invisible, the ineluctable, the immanent. That's all right, dear. I know you're here.

EPILOGUE

HIGH ON THE TOWERING WAVE the figure of Fecundity soared, arms raised, reaching for the heights of ecstasy. Down from her fertile loins the children plunged, like dolphins, like fish, into the quieter pool and from there onto the sculptured shore.

Watching from the left was Hal–Noah–Dionysus–St. Francis–Silenus, with the fox in his arms and the eagle on his shoulder. At his feet a bear caught a fish, geese flapped in the pool; from behind him a great cat watched from a cave. Across the pool stood a gardener with a sheaf of grain, knelt a shepherdess with a lamb in her lap, crouched a dryad crowned in oak leaves.

The fountain held the hurry and rush of rivers, the placidity of pools, the slow seep of hidden springs—perhaps, so the speech makers had hinted, the very waters of life itself. Center front stood Sophy, Sophia, the figure of Wisdom, her figure now chastely robed, but her beautiful face looking out over the multitude, her hand extended to carry the awful weight of a goblet of clear glass from which water dripped slowly onto the outstretched hands of the children below.

The hoopla was over. The fountain had been dedicated, the speeches had been made. "In this time of great uncertainty . . . to express our hope for the future . . . to beg wisdom for our leaders . . . waters of life . . ." And so on.

Faye had been honored as the sculptress. It was she who had named the work: A *Tribute to Sophia.* The consortium had accepted it, and even Herr Straub, recently a much less opinionated Herr Straub, had signified himself satisfied. Now Faye was with the others, having a quiet lunch at the hotel, and only Carolyn remained in the plaza, among the passersby and lookers-on, sitting on the granite rim of the circling pool with one hand trailing into the chill water, the other clutching one of Sophy's vials, now empty, wrapped in a wadded tissue in her pocket.

"We want you to do it," Jessamine had told her months before, during a brief and unique "special meeting" of the DFC. "The five of us voted on it. We've all written briefs for you, what we think about it. But we don't think a committee decision is a good idea. It has to be someone who's been happily married, someone who's had children. Someone who's seen . . . both sides."

"Though not all sides," Faye had commented with a snort.

"But don't you want to know . . . ?"

"We don't want to know," said Ophy.

"We trust you," said Aggie.

Bettiann had giggled, her eyes wet, "Let it come as a surprise." When Bettiann showed up at the dedication, William had been with her. That had come as a surprise.

And so Carolyn had risen this morning very early, slipping out of the bed without disturbing Hal and dressing quietly before coming down into the street, past the polyglot scatter of cleaners and sweepers who were readying the avenues for the coming day, then down the broad stairs that brought her into the echoing vacancy of the plaza, where her footsteps clacked intrusively on the patterned stones. All had been silence here. She had located the fountain by its dark silhouette against the eastern sky. She had stepped out of her shoes, leaving them beside the granite curb while she waded ankle deep through chill water, across the encircling pool. Sophia's crystal chalice was held out almost level with Carolyn's eyes. She'd thought a prayer might be appropriate, but after considering a few half-forgotten phrases learned in childhood, she rejected them in favor of something both simpler and more heartfelt:

Please, let this be right.

The contents of the vial made only a small puddle in the chalice. She had brought only the one vial with her, afraid that if she allowed herself a choice, last-minute worries would confuse the decision made with so much thought, so much troubled concentration.

Oh, please, Sophia. Let this be right.

Later in the morning, properly dressed and combed, she had returned with the others to witness the dedication. By then the plaza was alive with motion and sound, with the flap of banners and flutter of wings as hundreds of white doves were released into the soft airs. Through a tube hidden in

Sophia's bronze sleeve, water flowed into the chalice, filling it until it over-flowed. The first drops sounded clearly in the silence; then the pumps started and the huge wave flowed and the plaza was filled with water sounds as all the surfaces sparkled wetly under the morning sun. At the back of the fountain the pool emptied into a long, lovely water stair that tumbled from lily pool to lily pool between sloping paths, down the long hill to a park below, and thence under bridges and around gardens into some hidden course that led to a river, and thence to the sea. By the time all the speeches were over, it was too late to wonder if she had been right. Sophia's chalice had been emptied into the pool, and the pool into the river many times over. Too much water under the bridges for second thoughts, she told herself solemnly. Right or not, it was done.

Still, she had stayed behind, as though waiting for a sign, while Hal and the others went off to lunch, seemingly untroubled by whatever choice had been made. Of course, they hadn't known she was going to do it here, this morning. Maybe they thought she would do it some other time. Or had done it, long ago, while the fountain was being tested, before it was installed.

She didn't feel like joining the others, not just yet. She was weary of happening! So much, so terribly much had happened. The terrors of that journey from Lizard Rock. The windup of Lolly's trial, which had turned out to be a complete anticlimax. Jagger was replaced by a novice prosecutor, and Rombauer was replaced by Judge Frieze. The perjured jurors were named as alternates and then removed from the jury: a jury, which, in due time, had brought in a verdict of not guilty with recommendations for counseling, that all-purpose—though often quite useless—contemporary ameliorative. Today's snake oil.

Lolly was in the care of Agnes McGann, who was still Reverend Mother. She had carried Lolly off to be rebuilt, retrained, refurbished. Not as a dem-onstration project. More as the tail end of the former order of things. Aggie had decided she was tired of gates but was darned if she was going to give up a life that meant a lot to so many women.

Faye had seemingly had a remission, though she told Carolyn she thought it had been something mightily curative in Tess's tea. And Jessamine had a new companion, her co-worker, Val. Ophy and Simon had not changed, no more than Carolyn and Hal or Stace and Luce.

Helen was home, and she had her children with her. Her daughter Emily was like a three-year-old: infantile, uneducated, illiterate. Her son had been taught what all the boys at the Redoubt had been taught. It would take all Helen's strength to undo what the Alliance had done to them, had taught them, but without reinforcement of those teachings, in time they would forget. One prayed.

As for the Alliance, according to Mike Winter, it had melted away.

There were stories and even film clips of a vast marching in the cities, a great demonstration building for days, getting larger and larger, like some huge storm gathering. And then, at the end, it had come apart, tattered like a wind-torn cloud into tiny rags and shreds. The driving force that had welded it and wielded it had vanished. The misogyny that had driven it had ended. The men who had taken part in it could answer no questions about it. They disliked being reminded of it and could not even remember why they had been there.

And now, now it was done.

And what would she say if they asked her?

Perhaps she would say, as Sovawanea might have said: Perhaps I chose, or perhaps Sophia chose for me.

If Sophia had done so, she wasn't telling. There was no sign, no omen, no nothing. With one last look into Sophy's well-remembered face, she rose and walked off across the plaza toward the stairs. A waste receptacle stood beside the steps. She stopped beside it, gathering the contents of her pocket into a single wad, which she dropped into the basket, vial and all. Now all evidence of her act was gone. There was a finality in the gesture that had been missing this morning.

She stopped, motionless, listening. There was a sound, as of a door opening, far off. A vast silence. Then the door closed, leaving an echo from childhood, as of a child's voice calling in the summer dusk . . .

". . . ninety-nine, one hundred. Ready or not, here it comes."